Also by Tom Holt

ONLY HUMAN
WISH YOU WERE HERE
OPEN SESAME
PAINT YOUR DRAGON
MY HERO
DJINN RUMMY
ODDS AND GODS
FAUST AMONG EQUALS
GRAILBLAZERS
HERE COMES THE SUN
OVERTIME
YE GODS!
FLYING DUTCH
WHO'S AFRAID OF BEOWULF?
EXPECTING SOMEONE TALLER

I, MARGARET

LUCIA TRIUMPHANT
LUCIA IN WARTIME

THE WALLED ORCHARD

Tom Holt

WARNER BOOKS

A *Warner* Book

Goatsong first published in Great Britain by Macmillan 1989
The Walled Orchard first published in Great Britain by Macmillan 1990

This edition published by Warner Books 1997
Reprinted 1998, 1999

Goatsong copyright © Tom Holt 1989
The Walled Orchard copyright © Tom Holt 1990

The moral right of the author has been asserted.

A CIP catalogue record for this book
is available from the British Library.

ISBN 0 7515 2138 8

Typeset by Solidus (Bristol) Limited
Printed and bound in Great Britain by
Mackays of Chatham PLC, Chatham, Kent

Warner Books
A Division of
Little, Brown and Company (UK)
Brettenham House
Lancaster Place
London WC2E 7EN

For James and Hilary Hale,
Theo Zinn and Dennis Moylan

With thanks

CONTENTS

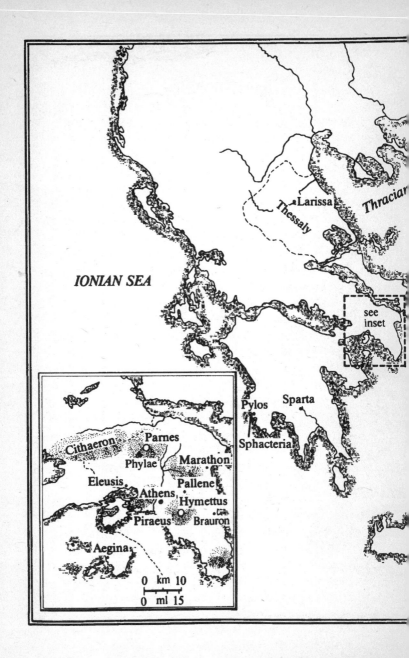

IONIAN SEA

Larissa

Thessaly

Thracian

see inset

Sparta

Pylos

Sphacteria

Cithaeron Parnes

Phylae Marathon

Eleusis Pallene

Athens

Hymettus

Piraeus Brauron

Aegina

0 km 10

0 ml 15

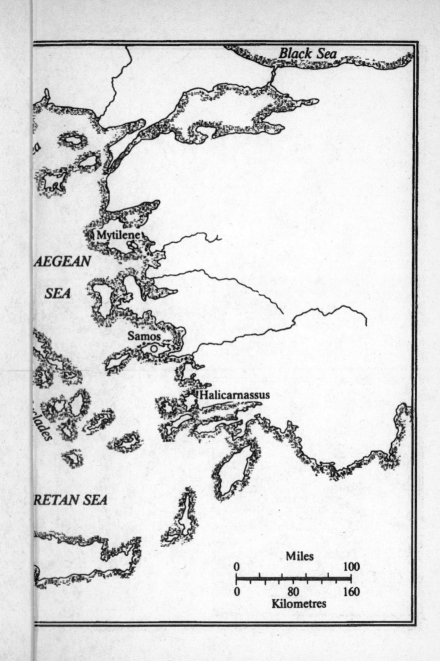

Black Sea

AEGEAN

SEA

Mytilene

Samos

Halicarnassus

CRETAN SEA

Miles
0   100
0   80   160
Kilometres

PART ONE

GOATSONG

PART ONE

GOATSONG

CHAPTER ONE

Athens is a large city situated in the middle part of the country we call Greece. To the north lies Thebes, Corinth is due west, and Sparta some way to the south. The City is surrounded by the region known as Attica, a miserable rocky district where very little can be persuaded to grow. That is all I have to say, for the moment, about the City of Athens.

Well, almost. The first really memorable cockfight I ever saw took place in the City of Athens, outside the Propylaea, where the little path that leads up from the right joins the main stairway. It was a quite unbearably hot day, the sort of day you get when your early barley is wilting for lack of rain and your grapes are turning into raisins on the stalk, and I can't have been more than nine years old. I have no idea what we were doing in the City at that time of year, but I remember that my father had had to come in to see to some business or other and had taken me with him. This was supposed to be a treat, and in the normal course of events it would have been; but what with the heat and the crowds of people I was as sullen as only a nine-year-old male child can be, and if Zeus himself had chosen that moment to come down to earth in a fiery four-horse chariot, I doubt if I would have taken very much notice. But this cockfight was something else.

Of course we had cockfights in our village, and I didn't think much of them, although I imagine that I was every bit as bloodthirsty as most normal small boys of that age. What this cockfight had that all the others had lacked was atmosphere.

From what I could gather, the challenger, a huge, brightly coloured bird with the magnificent name of Euryalus the Foesmiter, was taking on the southern Attica area champion, a rather tattered-looking creature called Ajax Bloodfoot, and the best part of a hundred drachmas was riding on the outcome. Although I knew little of such matters, I soon guessed that the Foesmiter was expected to make extremely short work of Bloodfoot, who was coming towards the end of his useful life as a fighting-cock and was widely regarded by the better informed spectators as little better than a self-propelled kebab. Had anyone asked my opinion I would undoubtedly have sided with the majority view, since Bloodfoot was considerably smaller than Foesmiter and something drastic had recently happened to his left wing. The Master of Ceremonies – a short man with a neck like a log – announced the two combatants in a loud and glorious voice, such as one imagines Homer must have had, and recited their various pedigrees, contests and victories. From this catalogue of ancient valour what emerged most clearly was that Bloodfoot's most notable achievements had all taken place well over two years ago, whereas Foesmiter was nicely at the peak of his form, having practically disembowelled a creature called Orestes the Driver of the Spoil only a fortnight ago, and had been living on a diet of ground wheat and lugworms ever since. Then the log-necked man announced that this was the last opportunity for staking money on the contest, and withdrew to the edge of the chalk circle.

At that time, my most prized possession was a single obol. It was the first piece of coined money I had ever possessed, and it was not a beautiful object at that. Some time before it had come into my possession, a previous owner had been extremely sceptical about the nature of the metal it was made of, and had taken a chisel and cut no less than four deep slices in it, three across the owl on the tail side, and one, extremely blasphemously, along the line of Athena's nose on the obverse. Be that as it may, I loved that obol, for I had traded for it three good-quality hare skins and a broken sickle-blade I had found in the bed of a small stream. When the Master of Ceremonies made his announcement about wagers I can remember saying to myself that I was far too young to start gambling, and that if my father ever found out he would quite rightly skin me alive. But then I seemed to hear the little obol crying out from its resting-place under my tongue – we used to carry our small change in our mouths in those days, before they started issuing those silver-plated coppers which make you ill if you swallow them – and it was saying that it was feeling terribly lonely, and here was a unique opportunity for me to acquire some other little obols for it to play with. There was no risk involved, said the obol; all I had to do was wager on Foesmiter at three to one, and I would have quite a little nest of owls rattling up against my teeth when I went home that evening.

So, when the mob of eager gamblers had subsided enough for me to squeeze my way to the front, I picked the obol out of my mouth, dried it carefully on the sleeve of my tunic, and wagered it solemnly on Euryalus the Foesmiter. Then the trainers each slipped their respective charges a small lump of garlic, which makes them fierce, and thrust them into the circle.

It took Ajax Bloodfoot about thirty seconds to dispose of the challenger. I think that what did it was the mindless ferocity of his onslaught. There was none of that careful walking round the ring and clucking that I was used to back home in Pallene; Bloodfoot simply stuck out his head, made a sound like tearing linen, and jumped on his opponent's neck. His entire strategy seemed to consist of getting his claws round the other bird's throat and pecking his head off, and this is a most unorthodox way for a cock to fight. A properly brought up, well-educated bird will fight with his spurs, as a heavy infantryman uses his spear; he disdains the other weapons that Nature has armed him with, just as an infantryman prefers not to use his sword unless he absolutely must. The orthodox fighting-cock is therefore at a loss when a small but agile enemy attaches itself to his neck and refuses to let go. I had scarcely got back to the shelter of the edge of the crowd when the Master of Ceremonies was standing in the middle of the chalk circle holding up a rather disordered bundle of feathers, lately known as Euryalus the Foesmiter, and declaring that the champion had retained his title at odds of seven to one. The crowd then seemed to melt away, and I was left standing there with nothing but the grandeur of the Propylaea to look at, and no obol. In the end I walked away and found my father, and explained that I had swallowed my obol. He sympathised and said that it would work its way through my system in a day or so, and be none the worse for its experience. This worried me tremendously, since obviously it wouldn't and then he would guess that I had gambled it away and be seriously annoyed with me. Luckily, however, he forgot all about it, and I was able to earn a replacement obol by scaring crows by the time I had to account to him.

In many respects I feel a certain identity of experience with both of those birds; for throughout my life I have found that things which one would naturally expect to be easy have proved very difficult for me, while I have successfully survived trials and ordeals that have finished off much taller and more splendidly plumaged men than myself. If I stretch the analogy to its absolute limits, I can also claim that the cockfight is a nice epitome of the story of Athens during my time; Athens, of course, being

Euryalus the Foesmiter. Unless your memory is as bad as mine has become over the last few years, you will remember that the Foesmiter had led up to his last encounter with a string of victories over extremely impressive opponents, and that it was the final battle, against an opponent that he was universally fancied to sweep aside, that finally did for him. Add to that his great size and the magnificence of his feathers and crest, and there you have Athens as it was in my childhood, just two years before the outbreak of the Great Peloponnesian War.

Dexitheus the bookseller, who has paid me good money to write this, would far rather that I started off in the correct manner with something like 'These are the Histories of Eupolis of Pallene, written down so that the glorious deeds of men shall never wholly be forgotten,' and then went on to narrate the genesis of the Gods, the birth of the Divine Athena and her founding of the City, the childhood and heroic deeds of Theseus and the second foundation of Athens, the reforms of Solon, the tyranny of Pisistratus, and the part played by the Athenians in the Great War against the Persians.

Here is where Dexitheus and I part company. Dexitheus believes that a book describing itself as a History should have plenty of history in it. I maintain that my readers will either be Athenians and know all that sort of thing already, or else they will be barbarians and outlanders who know nothing at all about our City, and that any prologue capable of putting them in a position where they can hope to understand everything I am about to say would be likely to be twice as long as the book itself and not particularly entertaining. I therefore propose to plunge straight into my story and let my readers sort things out for themselves as they go along. I believe that they will soon get the hang of it, and if Dexitheus doesn't like it, he can find someone else to write something to go on all that Egyptian paper he bought so cheaply last summer and has had on his hands ever since.

That still leaves me with the problem of where to start my story. You see, what I intend to do is to tell the story of my life, from my birth in the village of Pallene, thirty-eight years after the battle of Salamis, down to the present day. Nobody has ever been sufficiently egotistical to do anything like that before, and I must admit that the prospect alarms me rather. So I am tempted to skip over the events of my early life and concentrate on the period I can best remember, which nicely coincides with all the most fascinating parts of the history of Athens. But if I do this, and you know nothing about Athens beyond what I have just told you and what you have read on the necks of wine jars, you will soon be quite lost and very upset at parting with a solid silver drachma for such an obscure book; whereas if I start at the beginning and work my way doggedly through to the end, my readers will have lost patience by the time I describe cutting my first tooth and will be following Dexitheus round the Market Square loudly asking for their money back.

All I can do, then, is give you my word as an Athenian and a servant of the Muses that once this book gets nicely under way it will be extremely entertaining, moving and informative, and ask you to bear with me while I deal with all the tiresome material that has to be seen to first. Imagine, if you will, that you are at the Theatre on the first day of the Great Dionysia, and that you have walked in all the way from Marathon or Eleusis on a hot day to see the latest play by that celebrated Comic poet Eupolis of Pallene. First, you must sit through three apparently interminable Tragedies on such mundane and hackneyed themes as the Fall of Troy, the Revenge of Orestes, or the Seven Against Thebes. But you are prepared to make this sacrifice of your time and patience, since you know perfectly well that a Eupolis Comedy is worth waiting for, and when the Chorus come trooping on in their marvellous costumes singing their opening number you will enjoy yourself all the more because of the dreary stuff that you have endured before.

It has just occurred to me that some of you, being young and ignorant, may not have heard of Eupolis of Pallene, the great Comic dramatist. You may never have heard my name before. You may never even have heard of the Great Dionysia, or been to a play in your life. I don't really know what to say to you if that really is the case, except that the Great Dionysia is one of the two annual dramatic festivals we have at Athens, when for three successive days new plays are presented and the best example of Comedy and Tragedy is awarded a prize by the panel of judges, and that in my youth I frequently won the prize for Best Comedy, although most certainly not frequently enough. In fact, before we go any further, I think we should deal with this question once and for all, and then at last I can get on with telling the story. There are a great many things in this book which would conceivably need explaining, and I am certainly not going to explain them all. That would be insufferably tedious. If, therefore, I refer to something which you do not understand or have not heard of, I advise you to keep quiet and use your intelligence to try and work out from the context what is going on, as I have had to do all my life. Pretend that this is not a book at all, but some enthralling conversation you are eavesdropping on in the Baths or the Fish Market.

And now, at last, I shall start my narrative, and soon you will be so completely enthralled by my powers of story-telling that all these problems I have been agonising over will melt away like bad dreams on market-day.

Athens, as it was in my childhood. Now I cannot imagine that you don't know at least something about the great days of the City, between the Persian Wars and the war with Sparta. 'They were giants in those days,' as that buffoon Teleclides says in one of his plays, for it was the time when the plays of Aeschylus were still recent enough to be remembered, and Sophocles was at the height of his powers, and a young man called Euripides had just started to make an impact; when Pericles was laying the foundation-stone of a new temple every other month, and the tribute-money from the Great Athenian Empire was rolling in like a flooded river.

That, at least, is how it seems in retrospect. Now, I was born and bred in Attica, and the City of Athens was always there in the background; but I had little to do with it in those days when the great men you all know so much about were carving their names on the walls of history. My early boyhood was not spent in the company of great men; in fact, it was spent mainly in the company of goats. My father was reasonably well off, and a fair percentage of his wealth consisted of a flock of hardy but troublesome goats which needed looking after. Goatherding is not difficult, but neither is it particularly stimulating and pleasant. Accordingly, as soon as I was old enough to be out on my own, I was appointed Chief Goatherd and turned out on to the sides of Hymettus.

Although I disliked goats (and still do), I preferred goatherding to education and soon became as proficient at the business as it is possible for a small boy to be. At Pallene we were between two mountain ranges, so that pasture was available at no great distance from home, and since the beasts themselves were generally docile I was able to devote most of my time spent on goatherd-duty to what was, even then, my greatest passion and preoccupation; the composition of iambic verse.

At first I composed Tragedy, since Tragedy, and in particular the works of the celebrated Aeschylus, was what was mostly recited at home and in the village. Most people had at least a few passages of the great man's plays by heart, and one old man, who made his living mostly by paying visits and staying to dinner, claimed to know all the seventy-four plays. He had been (so he said) a member of the State Acting Corps; and he certainly had a fine reciting voice, which I used to carry in my head when deciding whether a line would sound well when spoken.

But I soon gave up Tragedy; the long streams of polysyllabic compounds and arcane kennings that make up the high Tragic style seemed to me both difficult and ridiculous. As soon as I saw my first Comic play – it made such an impression on me that I cannot now remember who wrote it or what it was about – I decided to compose only Comedies; and, with one exception which I shall tell you about in due course, I have kept that vow all my life. The Comic style, after all, is closely based on the patterns of speech of ordinary people, so that the greatest compliment you can pay a Comic poet is to say that you didn't realise that his characters were speaking verse at all. In fact, I maintain that Comedy is far harder to write than Tragedy (nobody believes me, of course) since Tragedy has a language all of its own which is expressly designed for writing plays in, whereas ordinary speech was never meant to be chivvied into an iambic line and neatly broken up with caesuras. Fortunately, I was born with the knack, and my mother used to say that I spoke in verse virtually from the cradle. Coming from my mother, that was not a compliment; she came from a minor political family and had been brought up to despise satirists.

From the age of nine onwards, then, I took to warbling childish *parabases* and *stichomythiae* to the goats and the thorn trees. I had not as yet learned the art of writing on wax tablets or Egyptian paper, and so I carried the lines, once finished, in my head. I still do this even now, and only write a play out when it is finished. After all, actors have to learn their parts, and if the author cannot remember the play, how can the actors be expected to?

By the time I was eleven, I had started composing

choral lyrics, which in fact I have always found easier than iambic dialogue, and soon I had completed my first Comedy, of which I was absurdly proud. It was called *The Goats* after its Chorus and first audience, and it was awarded first prize in the Pan-Hymettic Festival by the old white billygoat whom I had elected as chairman of the twelve judges. Since my play was the only entry that year, I don't suppose he had much choice in the matter, and shortly afterwards he butted me very painfully when I was trying to pleat his forelock, which gave me an early and invaluable lesson in the fickleness of audiences.

The Chorus, dressed as goats, represented the People of Athens, and their goatherd was the glorious Pericles, the great statesman who led Athens at the time. No Comedy worth the name was complete without a vitriolic and obscene attack on Pericles, and *The Goats* was no exception. One day, the goatherd is pasturing his flock on the fat uplands of the empire when a band of Spartan bandits waylays him and steals from him the cheeses he has himself stolen from his master the Treasury. I am rather better at allegory now, I am pleased to say; at the time, I thought this the height of subtlety.

Enraged at this cowardly attack, Pericles resolves to declare war on Sparta and build a wall of trireme ships all round the empire to keep the Spartans out and the goats in. There was a nice scene in the Goat Assembly, where Pericles proposes the motion; his speech, the *agon* of the play, was a parody of all I could remember of a speech by the great man that almost everyone in Pallene had learned by heart, while the counter-speech by Tragosophus ('Wise Goat') was a close imitation of the reply by one of his opponents. There was also a good Chorus scene where the Potidaean goat tries to break through the wall to escape, and is sacrificed and eaten by Pericles and the other goats (that was for my father, of course). To this day I could quote you the Prologue speech, the first I ever composed ('This goatherd now;

he's quite another thing/We think he means to make himself our King'); but I have acquired a certain reputation as a Comic poet, and it is not quite worthy of me.

Then came the outbreak of the Great War against Sparta, and my idyllic life of poetry and goatherding was interrupted every year by the annual invasion by the Spartans, which involved two unpleasantnesses; going to school to learn oratory and the poetry of Homer, and having to live in the City while the Spartans were about. On the whole, I thought Homer more of a nuisance than the Spartans, because inside the City there were men who had recently been in a Chorus and so could recite the latest Comedies. Since there was nothing for men to do in the City between Assemblies and trials, with most of the population cooped up inside the walls for months at a time, everyone had time to spare for a small boy who said he was going to be a Comic poet as soon as he was old enough to be given a Chorus. The only condition was that I should give Pericles a hard time in my first Comedy; little did they know that I had already done this.

The leading Comic poet of the time was the celebrated Cratinus, whom I was privileged to meet when I was twelve years old. There are few people in this world who truly merit the epithet Disgusting, but Cratinus was one of them. He was a little, stooped man with a leering smile, and his hands never stopped shaking, even when he was relatively sober. There was always vomit on his gown somewhere, and his interest in small boys was not that of a teacher. Nevertheless, he was always an honoured guest, at least for the early part of the evening, and in spite of his unfortunate personal habits, such as wiping his fingers on his neighbour's hair when he sneezed, I never met anyone (apart from other Comic poets) who really disliked him. He was a born politician, and he loathed and despised Pericles with every ounce of his small, frail, unpleasant body. It was therefore quite easy to win his undying friendship, and my mother's uncle Philodemus, who knew him quite well, instructed me in the art when I said that I would like to meet him.

To endear yourself to Cratinus, all you had to do was this. As soon as the conversation turned to politics, you had to look troubled, as if you were on the point of making some dreadful confession. 'I know it's very foolish of me,' you would say, 'and I know he's made this country what it is today, but in my heart of hearts I think Pericles is wrong about . . .' (Here insert the leading issue of the day.) 'I can't tell you why,' you would continue, looking sheepish and if possible mumbling slightly, 'it's just a feeling I have.'

This was Cratinus' cue. He would break in and start explaining, very forcibly and with many gestures, exactly what was wrong with Pericles' latest policy. During the exposition, you would frown and nod reluctantly, as if you were being forced, against your will, to accept some great truth. Cratinus would then believe that he and he alone had converted you to the right way of thinking, and you would be his friend and political ally for life.

After several rehearsals I was judged to be word perfect, so a drinking party was arranged and a cheap second-hand dinner-service was bought from the market, in case Cratinus started throwing things when he got drunk. It was my job to be Ganymede and pour the wine, and my uncle invited a couple of old friends with strong stomachs to be the other guests. As usual, Cratinus was unanimously appointed King of the Feast (which means he had the right to choose the drinking-songs and topics of conversation and declare who should sing or speak first), and the food was quickly and messily eaten. Then I was brought forward to play my scene, which I did perfectly.

Cratinus swallowed the bait like a tunny-fish, and started waving his hands about furiously. If only, he exclaimed, spilling his wine over my uncle's gown and tilting the neck of the jar I was carrying over his cup, all in the same movement, the voters of Athens had the common sense of this clear-thinking brat!

'You'd think,' he said, quivering with indignation, 'that if the idiots award first prize to a play entirely devoted to obscene and scurrilous attacks on a man, then they don't like him. It stands to reason, surely. Not in this miserable city it doesn't. Every year I put him on the stage and those imbeciles in the audience wet themselves laughing at his expense. Then they go home, change into something clean, and troop off and elect him for another term. I don't understand it; it's almost as if having the piss taken out of him makes the bastard more popular.'

'Maybe it does,' said my uncle. 'Maybe all you're doing is giving them an outlet for their natural frustration. If they didn't have that, maybe they wouldn't vote for him so much.'

'And anyway,' said one of the other guests, a neighbour of my uncle's called Anaxander, 'so long as you win your prize you don't care, surely?'

Cratinus nearly choked. 'What the hell do you take me for?' he snapped. 'I wouldn't give you a dead frog for all the prizes ever awarded. What do you think I want out of life, for God's sake?'

'Come off it,' said Anaxander cheerfully. 'All this crusading stuff is just for the audiences. Everyone knows that as soon as the Chorus have left the stage, the poet and the politicians go off and get drunk with each other, which is why we have all those pools of curiously coloured vomit in the streets the day after the Festivals. I bet you fifty drachmas that if Pericles died tomorrow you wouldn't know what to do with yourself. He's your meal-ticket and you're his pet jackal.'

Cratinus went as purple as the wine and started to growl, so that I was quite frightened; but my uncle just smiled.

'That's just the sort of crap I expect from a voter,' said

Cratinus at last, when he had finally managed to control his fury. 'I'll bet you fifty drachmas you voted for the little sod at the last election. Well, didn't you?'

'As a matter of fact,' said Anaxander, 'I did. What of it?'

Cratinus leaned over and spat into Anaxander's cup. 'Now we're even,' he said. 'You foul my cup, I foul yours.'

Anaxander didn't think this was terribly funny, and my uncle started to frown.

Just then, it occurred to me that I might be able to save the situation, so I cleared my throat timidly and said, 'But isn't what Anaxander said right, up to a point? Isn't winning the prize, or at least writing a good play, what it's all about? Just because the audience don't get the point, that doesn't make the play any less good.'

Cratinus turned on me and scowled. 'The boy isn't quite so sensible after all,' he said. 'If I wanted to write good plays, I'd be a Tragedian, and then perhaps I wouldn't get thrown out of quite so many polite parties. If all I wanted to do was write good iambics I wouldn't fool about with Comedy, which is mostly hard work; I'd write Oedipuses and Sevens against Thebes and all that kind of crap, and then I'd win all the prizes in the world, and nobody would have the faintest idea what I was on about, and neither would I. You listen to me, and I'll tell you something. If ever you want to be a Comic poet – God forbid you should, it's a really rotten life, I'm telling you – find yourself someone to hate, and hate them as much as you possibly can. For me it's easy, I've got Pericles and I actually do hate him. That's why I do Comedy better than anyone else. But you're young, you probably don't hate anyone enough to want to eat their guts warm off a meat-hook. In which case, you'll have to imagine you hate him. Picture him in your mind's eye killing your father, raping your mother, pissing down your well, smashing your vine-props. When you cut your little toe, say "That's Pericles' fault"; if it rains during harvest, say "Pericles has made it rain again." Everything that goes wrong in your life, I want you to pin it on this enemy of yours. That way you'll get a sort of lump in your intestines like a slowly forming turd which you've just got to squeeze out, somehow or other, and then you'll start writing Comedy. At first, you'll just write hours and hours of vulgar abuse, like "Pericles has got balls like a camel", but then you'll realise that that doesn't do any good. You'll find that if you want to hurt you've got to write well, so that when the audience laugh they're siding with you and against him. Now I'm still not good enough to be able to make them do that, but it's too late now. One of these days I'll have his nuts, and then I can retire and grow beans.'

'You'll never manage that,' said my uncle. 'Or don't you know anything about Athenians?'

'I've been a Comic poet for fifteen years,' Cratinus replied. 'I know more about Athenians than any man living.'

'No you don't,' said my uncle. 'All you know about is making Athenians laugh, which is a trade, like mending buckets. You obviously don't know what makes them work, or you wouldn't still be trying to put a message across in the Theatre. If you knew the first thing about your fellow citizens, you'd have realised by now that what they love above all things is the pleasure of words. The Persians love gold, the Spartans love bravery, the Scythians love wine and the Athenians love clever speaking. The fact of the matter is that an Athenian would far rather listen to a description of a banquet in the great king's palace than eat a nice bean stew, and he much prefers voting to annex the silver mines of Thasos to harvesting his own winter barley.' He paused, took a long gulp of wine, and continued. 'Why do you think we invented the Theatre, for God's sake? Come to that, why do you think we have a democracy? It's not because a democracy makes for better government; quite the opposite, as you well know. It's because in a democracy, if you want to have your own way, you've got to make the best speech, and then all the farmers and the sausage-merchants and the men who work in the dockyards go away from Assembly in the morning with their heads full of the most glorious drivel and think they own the world. That's how your beloved Pericles got to be Zeus' favourite nephew; by clever speaking. And it's the likes of you that keep him there, because just as soon as the fumes of all that oratory have worn off and the voters start wanting to see some public expenditure accounts, along you come with your incredibly funny plays and your brilliant speeches, and soon they're all soaked to the skin in words again.'

'Hold on a moment,' interrupted Cratinus. 'I write cleverer speeches than anyone in Athens. If they always do what the best speaker says, why aren't Pericles' nuts roasting on a spit on my hearth this very moment?'

'Because it's just the Theatre,' said my uncle, 'and so they don't take any notice; they've worked off their anger against Pericles by having you make a monkey out of him, and the next time he stands up in Assembly and proposes an expedition to conquer the moon, they stand there and gobble up his golden phrases like spilt figs. The Theatre is the place for making fun of Generals and Assembly is the place for voting for them. I'd have thought you'd have worked that one out ages ago.'

'So you're anti-democracy as well as pro-Pericles,' said Cratinus irritably. 'Don't bother asking me here again.'

My uncle laughed. 'What makes you think I'm anti-democracy?' he said. 'Just because my nephew here is an idiot doesn't mean I don't love him, and just because my city does a lot of very stupid things doesn't mean I want to overthrow the constitution. I love the democracy and I hate tyranny. Which is why I get irritated with people who don't understand the nature of democracy, and people who abuse it.'

'If we're going to start discussing democracy,' said Anaxander, yawning ostentatiously, 'I'm going home. I've got vines to prune in the morning.'

'You stay where you are and shut up,' said my uncle. 'You're just as bad as the rest of them really. Just now you provoked a quarrel with Cratinus just to see if he'd say something funny when he got angry, and then when he spat in your cup you didn't like it at all. That's typically Athenian. We all like a nice juicy crisis because it makes for such entertaining public speaking, so we all vote to annex this city or make that treaty, and when some smart-arse politician makes a good speech we feel so proud of ourselves that our little tummies swell up as tight as wineskins. Then when the crisis turns into a war and our vines get burnt we want to kill someone important, and we execute the first politician who catches our eye – probably the only one who really wants what's best for the City and is trying to clear up the mess. And then the whole circus starts up all over again, with factions and political trials and more and more and more speeches, and in the meantime we've sent five thousand infantry to some god-forsaken rock in the middle of the sea to fight a load of savages we've never even heard of. Now all this comes from us Athenians being the cleverest and most intelligent race on earth, and loving the pleasures of the mind more than the pleasures of the body. That's why Cratinus here is our most popular playwright, why Pericles is our most popular politician, why Athens is the greatest city in the world, and why one of these days we're all going to meet with a nasty end.'

'The hell with you,' said Cratinus, after a long pause. 'When I go out to dinner, I expect to do all the talking.'

'Exactly,' said my uncle. 'That's why I asked you. But then you got all incoherent, so like a good host I provided the entertainment myself. Where's that boy with the wine? I've got a throat like stone-mason's sand after all that pontificating.'

Anaxander emptied his cup out on to the floor and held it out to me to be refilled. 'If I'd wanted to hear you speaking,' he said, 'I wouldn't have come half-way across the City on a wet night. I propose that we don't give Cratinus anything more to drink until he's given us a speech from his latest play.'

'Steady on,' said my uncle. 'You'll give him a heart attack.'

'You can keep your lousy wine,' said Cratinus. 'After everything you've said about me, it'll take more than this goat's piss of yours to get me to do any reciting.'

'I've got a jar of quite palatable Rhodian out the back there,' replied my uncle. 'Now I know it would be wasted on you, but I'm such a typical Athenian that a really good speech might induce me to part with some of it.'

Cratinus grinned, displaying his few remaining teeth. 'Listen to this,' he said.

Which is how I came to be one of the first four people ever to hear the great speech from *The Lions* in which Pericles' descent, conception and birth is described in loving and exquisite detail. It is quite the most revolting thing that Cratinus ever wrote, and will be remembered when everything I have written is long forgotten. Cratinus said later that he wrote the whole thing at a sitting while the barber was lancing a particularly objectionable and inconveniently situated boil. Of course we all fell about with laughter, stuffing cushions into our mouths to stop ourselves choking, while the great man sat there with a face as straight as a spear-handle, timing each line to absolute perfection, and when he had finished he got his Rhodian wine and shortly afterwards passed out. But my uncle was right, of course; if anything, it made me feel fonder of Pericles than I ever had before, if only because he had afforded me such glorious entertainment. To this day I believe that Comedy has very little effect on the part of the human brain that makes political decisions – God only knows what does.

It was not long after that dinner party that Pericles died in the Great Plague, and sure enough, Cratinus was inconsolable for months afterwards. He felt that Pericles had tricked him yet again, slipping quietly out of the world before he had had a chance to savage him properly. He had to tear up the Comedy he had been writing, which he swore was the best thing he had ever done, and immediately started on a new one, in which Pericles is brought up before the Judges of the Dead and condemned to the most frightful punishments, in most of which horse manure plays a prominent part. But he gave it up before it was finished and wrote a miserable little farce about Heracles and Alcestis instead. He dashed it off in a few days just before the deadline for entries for the competition, and to his unutterable disgust it won first prize at that year's Lenaea.

CHAPTER TWO

And now I think it is about time for me to justify the boast I made at the beginning of this book, when I claimed that in my lifetime I have seen all the most remarkable events in our city's history, and tell you about my experience of the Great Plague. After all, that's something you're bound to be interested in, even if you can't be doing with Politics or the Theatre; so we might as well make the most of it. It is, with one exception, the most interesting of the events which has shaped my life, and so I can get on and describe it without having to be clever and witty to retain your attention. This will be a great relief to me.

Mind you, it doesn't necessarily follow that because an event is of great historical importance it will have any significant effect on the lives of the people who were there at the time. I remember there was one very old man in our village when I was a boy who had been in the City when the Persians came. Now you would imagine that seeing the City burnt to the ground and the temples of the Gods levelled with the dust would profoundly affect a young man's character and development; but this was not so at all in this man's case. He was a tomb-robber by vocation, and he had only gone back to the City after the general evacuation to see if many people had left any articles of value behind in their hurry to escape, and when he found that the place was swarming with weird-looking savages with red faces and gold-plated armour, he very sensibly hid in a charcoal heap until they had gone past. When the burning started, he slipped out and escaped through a gap in the Wall with a sack full of small gold and silver statuettes he had found in a house in the Ceramicus, which later provided him with the capital to set up in business as a part-time blacksmith. The great event in his life, which entirely changed his perceptions of the world and the behaviour of mankind, was when the owner of these small gold and silver statuettes caught up with him and had him thrown in the prison.

The Great Plague, then, came early in the war and lasted for two or perhaps three years. I must be honest and confess that my memories of that period are all inclined to run into each other, so that I tend to look back on the plague as happening in the space of about a week; but then, I was young and it's remarkable how quickly you get used to things when you're that age. Recently I heard an account of the war by a very learned and scholarly gentleman – he had been a general at one time, and got himself exiled because of a terrible blunder; whereupon he retired to some safe little town in neutral territory and started writing this monumental *History of the War*, so that when everyone's memories were getting as bad as mine is now he could read them his book and show them that everyone else had been at least as incompetent as he was and probably more so – and he claimed that Pericles died of the plague in the third year of the war, which surprised me very much. But I suppose I prefer to remember the years before the plague to those immediately after it, and so I have made that time seem longer than it actually was. Now I come to consider it, I'm probably not cut out to be a Historian.

Of course, everyone you meet in Athens claims that he had the plague and survived it; somehow it's regarded as a mark of great moral and spiritual merit, as if you have been tried and acquitted by the Gods. Even the little general who wrote the book says he had the plague, and to be fair to him his account of the symptoms is at least recognisable. Mind you, he also gives you the impression that he was there on the spot when all the famous and significant speeches were being made, and since some of these took place simultaneously in opposite corners of Greece, I doubt very much whether he was sitting there with his wax tablets on his knees taking down every word as it cleared the speaker's teeth. I do know for a fact that I did have the plague, and that only the intervention of the Gods saved my life.

The plague arrived in Athens on a grain boat, and was soon making its presence felt in the Corn-Chandlers' Quarter. At first nobody took much notice, since most corn-chandlers are resident foreigners and one more or less makes no great difference to anyone. But soon it began infecting citizens, and then we all realised that we had a major problem on our hands.

My own experience of the plague was this. I had been on a visit to my aunt Nausimache, and there was gossip going around the City that she was having an affair with a rich corn-chandler called Zeuxis, who came from somewhere near Mytilene. In fact, if you have a copy of Cratinus' *Ants* (I don't; I lent it to someone years ago, like a fool) I think you'll find there's a reference to that affair in it. Anyway, the plague was one of those diseases which you can catch from other people, and my guess is that she caught it from Zeuxis and I caught it from her; I distinctly remember her giving me an auntly kiss when we arrived, and wiping it off with the back of my hand when she wasn't looking.

A day or so after this visit, I started getting these quite unbearable pains in the front and sides of my head, as if some idiot had knocked over a brazier inside my brains and they had caught fire. Then my eyes started to itch, just as though I had been peeling onions, and something horrible happened to the inside of my mouth. Even I could tell that my breath smelt like rotten meat, and my tongue was swollen and tender.

My grandfather, who I had gone to live with after my father died – I think I was about twelve at the time – took one look at me, diagnosed plague, and had me locked up in the stable with the goats and donkeys. The last thing he needed, I remember him saying as he put up the bar on the door, was a house full of plague, and if that was the Gods' way of rewarding him for taking in orphans he was going to have to think very seriously about his theological position. Luckily we had a Libyan housemaid at the time, and she had got it into her head that her black skin would protect her from the disease. She reckoned that if she fed me and looked after me and I got well again, my grandfather would be so pleased that he would set her free and let her marry his understeward, and so she brought me out the scraps from the table and a jug of fresh water every day.

So there I was once again, entirely surrounded by goats, and the disease went into its next stage. For about a day I could not stop sneezing and coughing, and I vomited up bile of every imaginable colour; there was one peculiar shade of yellow that I have never seen since, except in some rather expensive Persian tapestries that someone was selling in the market. Then my skin broke out in little blisters which itched unendurably; but I think some God whispered in my ear not to scratch, and I managed not to, somehow. The worst part of it was the thirst, which I simply cannot describe, and here I think my grandfather's treatment of me saved my life. You see, I had only a few cupfuls of water each day, and sometimes nothing at all when the maid forgot or couldn't get away, whereas I have heard since that the people who were able to drink as much as they liked invariably died. In fact, my belief is that once the God saved me from the disease itself, this lack of water stopped me from catching the murderous diarrhoea which killed more people than the plague did, and which inevitably follows the disease itself, like a stray dog following a sausage-maker. After all, what with no food and no water, there was nothing inside me to come out, and so my body was spared the convulsions of the diarrhoea and I survived.

I fully appreciate that I must have been an unlovely companion while the disease was on me, but from that day to this I have not been able to forgive the attitude of the goats and donkeys towards me, which was little short of downright offensive. Did they come and bleat reassuringly over me, and soothe my fevered brow with their tongues, like they are supposed to do in the old stories? Did they hell. They all backed away into the far corner of the stable and didn't even come across to eat the leaves and bean-helm in their mangers, and the hungrier they got, the more they seemed to blame me. This made me feel absolutely dejected, as you can imagine, and for a while I felt like giving the whole thing up.

On the seventh day of my sickness the maid stopped bringing food and water and I resigned myself to death, which was not a concept I had given much thought to previously. I remember thinking that it would be nice not to have to go to school any more, but that it would be rather a shame that no one would ever see one of my Comedies. However, I consoled myself with the thought of meeting my father again beside the waters of the Styx, always assuming that I could recognise him after so many years. Then I started worrying about how on earth I was going to pay the fare, since Charon the Ferryman takes nobody across the river unless he pays his obol. Then I remembered hearing somewhere (I think it was in a Comedy) that Charon had finally retired and that an Athenian had bought his pitch, increasing the fare (naturally enough) to two obols, but letting Athenians across for free. This comforted me greatly, since I had been greatly distressed at the thought of spending the rest of time on the wrong side of the river with all the murderers and parricides and people who hadn't been buried properly, and so I settled back to die in peace.

Now I hadn't slept at all since the disease started, and I think I must have fallen asleep then, for I swear I saw Dionysus himself standing over me, leaning on his vine-wood staff and wearing a Comic mask and boots, with the floppy leather phallus which all the actors wear in the Comedies dangling from his groin. He seemed very big and fierce and jolly, but I wasn't frightened by him, or particularly surprised to see him there at all.

'Cheer up, Eupolis of Pallene,' he said, and the whole stable seemed to shake, like those caves down south that are supposed to vibrate to the pitch of your voice. 'Pull yourself together and stop snivelling; you'll have to put up with far worse things than this before you see the last of me – in the front row of the Theatre when they hiss that clever Chorus of yours, and in the walled orchard, of course. But remember, you owe me some prizes which you must pay, and I've hand-reared you from a puppy to write me a Comedy or two. If you die now and leave me to make do with that idiot Aristomenes, I'll never forgive you.'

I wanted to promise but I couldn't speak; so I nodded, and kept on nodding, and then I was definitely asleep, because I remember waking up. And when I did wake up, I knew that I was going to live; just as you can feel when you walk into a house whether anyone lives there or not. I know that I just lay there for a very long time, filled with a joy that kept me warm and made me forget how hungry and uncomfortable I was; not because I had escaped death and was clear of the pain of the disease, but because I had seen the God of Comedy and been promised success. It had been well worth the disease, I reckoned, to get that promise.

After a long, long time I remembered that I was starving hungry, and I thought it was time to do something about it. I started shouting at the top of my little voice that I was well again and wanted to be let out, but nobody came; so I assumed that nobody believed me, which was reasonable enough. So, as soon as I felt confident that I had my strength back, I examined the door of the stable, which was barred on the outside and wouldn't budge. Now, after surviving the plague and being promised a Chorus by the God, a little thing like a stable door wasn't going to get in my way, and so I sat down on the manger and thought hard. Unfortunately, probably because the war kept interrupting my education, I had never been taught how to get out of locked stables – unless you count that bit in the *Odyssey* where Odysseus escapes from the Cyclops' cave, which I had been made to learn by heart. But I say that doesn't count, because the circumstances of that case were quite unique and highly unlikely to recur. Just as I was starting to feel baffled, I caught sight of my uncle's old black donkey, and I had an idea.

As soon as I was cured, the animals (who were just as hungry as I was) had resumed eating and drinking, and had finished off all their fodder. They were now getting extremely restive, and I saw how that could be turned to my advantage. You see, this old black donkey of my uncle's, which he kept for hauling olives and ploughing in the season, had the sort of temper you only usually come across in bath-attendants and the commanders of naval vessels, and hunger had not made him any sweeter natured. I'll swear that donkey hated everything and everybody in the world; but what he hated most of all, with the possible exception of other male donkeys and hard work, was being prodded in the ribs with a sharp stick. I happened to have a sharp stick handy – it had been in with the fodder in the mangers – and so I wrestled him over until his hind legs were almost touching the door of the barn. Then I took my stick and gave the donkey the most terrific poke and sure enough he lashed out with his powerful legs and gave the door a tremendous kick. I waited until he had settled down again and prodded him once more, and once again; and that was about as much as the stable door could take. The bar snapped, and at once I shooed the donkey away and threw myself at the door. It gave way, and out I rolled into the blinding sunlight of the yard. As I picked myself up, I saw that the little finger of my left hand had snapped clean off, just like a dead twig, although I hadn't felt a thing. I picked the finger up and stared at it – it had shrivelled away into a little white stick and it smelt quite disgusting – and I tried to fit it back on, but of course it wouldn't stay. Eventually I gave up and threw it away, and a crow who had been busy with something behind the muck-heap fluttered over and took a very tentative peck at it. Apparently, the loss of fingers and toes and even whole hands and feet was quite common among people who had survived the plague, but of course I didn't know that at the time and it startled me considerably.

Well, there I was, safe and sound, and I wanted to see the expressions on everybody's faces when I walked in and told them I was well again. Being a horrible child in many ways I thought I would give them a surprise, so I crept over to the back door and tiptoed in to the inner room, where I expected my grandfather would be sleeping after his midday meal. But he wasn't there; instead I saw my mother, sitting bolt upright in her chair in front of her spinning-wheel, as dead as Agamemnon. I could see from the state of her and the horrible expression on her face that she had died of the plague; typically she had stayed at her household duties to the last, so that Hermes would be able to report to the Judges of the Dead that she had died as a woman should. That was my mother all over.

I found our Syrian houseboy doubled up in the corner of the inner room – he had taken off his sandal and bitten clean through the thongs – while the Libyan maid was lying in the storeroom. The pain had clearly been too much for her to bear, poor creature, and she had cut her own throat with the fine ivory-handled razor my mother used for shaving her legs and armpits. However, I could find no sign of my grandfather anywhere in the house, and I began to hope that he had somehow survived, and maybe even gone to get help. But I found him, too, a little way down the street, which was utterly quiet and deserted, the way an Athenian street never is. He was in one of those big stone troughs set up to catch rainwater in the dictator Pisistratus' time, and I guess that he found the thirst so unendurable that he had jumped in and drowned. It was a sad way for such a man to die, for he had been at the battle of Plataea, when the Athenians and the Spartans had defeated King Xerxes' army and killed his great general Mardonius.

It was a most peculiar feeling to come out of that stable and find that all my family and household had died without letting me know. While I had been ill, I had assumed that I was the only person in the whole of Athens to be afflicted, and that if and when I ever got out of there the world outside would be roughly the same as it had been when I went in. As I stood there looking at my grandfather floating in the rain-trough, I must confess that I felt little or no grief or sadness, and ever since then I have never been able to take the Choruses in the Tragedies very seriously. You know what I mean; the Messenger bustles on with the news of the great disaster, and at once the Chorus start moaning and singing *Aiai* and *Hottotoi*, and all those other things that people are supposed to say when they're upset but never do; and then twenty lines or so later they've pulled themselves together again and are saying that the Gods are just. Whereas, in my experience at any rate, I find that bad news takes at least a day to sink in properly, and it's only after people have stopped sympathising and are saying what a callous brute I am that I start going to pieces. Well, there you are; I felt no great urge to lament or tear my hair, only a sensation which I can best describe as a Godlike detachment, as the Gods must feel when they look down and see mortal men. After all, I had survived and everyone else in the whole world hadn't; this created a division between them and me as wide as that which separates the immortal Gods from mortal men. I couldn't feel any sorrow, or even any involvement, just as a human being can never feel involved when he pours boiling water on an ants' nest and so wipes out a city which in their terms might be as great as Athens or Troy. Perhaps, after all, I was too young to have feelings, or I was stunned by the sheer scale of the disaster. But I don't think so; I felt the same way when I was a grown man in the walled orchard, and that was just as great a disaster, or maybe even greater.

So there I was, standing by the rain-trough and thinking these deep thoughts, when I saw a man in armour hurrying up the street with his cloak round his face to keep the bad air out. I was just thinking that this was pretty foolish, since there is no special magic in a cloak that can counteract the effects of plague and death, and that was just another example of the folly of these puny mortals, when the man caught sight of me and nearly jumped out of his skin. Of course, I said to myself, he's frightened at seeing a God: I must reassure him; so I called out, 'Don't be afraid, I won't hurt you.'

'The hell with you,' said the man. 'You've got the plague, haven't you?'

'No,' I replied, 'I had it for a while but the God cured me. You're quite safe, I won't infect you.'

He didn't look at all convinced, so I started describing the symptoms and how I had recovered, and then he wasn't so frightened. It turned out that a fellow soldier of his had had the plague and survived, and so he knew I was telling the truth. He came over and sat down on the edge of the trough, with his cloak still up around his ears; but I could see his face. He was about twenty-two, with a long thin nose and sandy hair just starting to recede from his temples.

'What's your name?' I asked him.

'Callicrates,' he replied. 'I'm looking for the house of a man called Euthydemus son of Euxis, of Pallene.'

'The house is down there,' I said, 'just before you get to the corner; but if you're looking for Euthydemus himself, you'll find him right behind you.' For of course Euthydemus was my grandfather's name and Euxis was his father, and our village and deme was Pallene.

Callicrates looked round but could see nobody; then he caught sight of the body floating in the trough and started violently.

'For God's sake,' he said, 'what do you want to go playing tricks like that for? You nearly gave me a fit.'

'Honestly,' I said solemnly, 'that's Euthydemus there. I should know, because I'm his grandson, Eupolis. All the rest of us who were in the house are dead, except me. The God cured me, like I said.'

Callicrates stared at me, as if I had just told him that Babylon had fallen. 'Is that true?' he said, after a moment.

'Of course it's true,' I said. 'If you don't believe me, you can go and have a look for yourself, but I wouldn't advise it. They all had the plague, you see.'

He was silent for a very long time, staring at the knots on the thongs of his sandals as if he expected them to burst into flower. Then he turned his head and looked at me gravely.

'Eupolis,' he said, 'I am your cousin, the son of your mother's elder brother Philodemus. My father and I have been away at the war and we've only just come home. As soon as they told us about the plague my father went off to see if our house was all right, and he sent me to look for his sister.'

'I'm afraid she's dead,' I said gently, for I could tell that the shock of seeing my grandfather had unnerved him and I wanted to spare him any further pain; he was only a mortal and might be upset. 'But she died at her spinning-wheel and I'm sure the Ferryman will take her over for free, since she was Athenian on both sides. Have you got any water in your bottle? I'm really thirsty and I don't want to drink the water in the trough.'

He handed me the bottle and I'm afraid I drank it all, without thinking where we would get any more. But Callicrates didn't say anything, although I expect he was thirsty too. Then he opened his knapsack and handed me a piece of wheat bread, white and still quite soft, as good as cake.

Callicrates smiled when he saw how much I was enjoying it, and he said that where he had been they ate wheat bread as a matter of course and imported all their wine from Judaea.

I hope I haven't given you the impression that Callicrates was a coward, because he wasn't. He had made up his mind to go into the house, which not many men would have done, and the only reason he did it was for my sake. You see, he knew that if there was a lawsuit about property someone would have to give evidence about how everyone had died, and I was too young to take the oath. So he screwed his face even more tightly into his cloak, took a deep breath, and plunged in. He wouldn't let me come with him, and I was secretly relieved, since I no longer felt that the people in the house had anything to do with me. He was gone about five minutes and then came back, shivering all over as if he had been out in the snow in nothing but a tunic.

'Right,' he said, 'I've seen everything I need to see. Let's go to my father's house.'

That sounded like an excellent suggestion, since I

liked Philodemus; you may remember that he was the one who arranged for me to meet Cratinus, and he knew a lot of people and was always quoting from plays. He was a small, jolly man and I thought it would be more fun living with him than with my grandfather, who had never really liked me very much.

'Callicrates,' I said, 'did you really have to go in there?'

'Yes,' he said, 'like I told you.'

'There won't really be a lawsuit, will there?' I said. 'I thought that was only when people did something wrong, like stealing.'

He grinned, and the cloak fell off his face. 'Don't you believe it,' he said. And he was right, too, as it turned out. There was the most almighty lawsuit, and if he hadn't gone into the house we would have lost, because of some legal presumption or other.

Whatever else I may forget, such as my name and where I live, I shall always remember that walk through the City. Everywhere we went, the streets were either totally deserted or frantic with activity; and where there were people, they all seemed to have bodies with them. There were bodies in handcarts, or on the backs of mules, or slung over men's shoulders like sacks, so that it looked for all the world like the grapes being brought down for the vintage. Some were taking them to be properly burnt (there was no space to bury anyone, not even the smallest child) but they had to hurry, because if anyone saw a pyre burning and no one watching he would pitch the body he was carrying on to it and go away as quickly as he could. Others were actually digging shallow trenches in the streets to bury their dead; in fact there was a lot of trouble about it later on, when people started scraping up these trenches to recover the coins that the relatives had left in the corpses' mouths for the Ferryman, and the whole plague nearly started all over again. Then there were many people who dumped dead bodies in the water-tanks and cisterns, partly because they reckoned that water would wash away the infection but mostly because by that stage they couldn't care less; and only a complete idiot left the door of his stable open, or even his house; because if he did he would be sure to find two or three corpses there when he came home, neatly stacked like faggots of wood. Really, it was like watching a gang of thieves desperately getting rid of stolen property when the Constables arrive.

Naturally I wanted to stop and watch, since I felt that if ever I wanted to try my hand at a Tragedy or a Poem this would make the most wonderful set piece; the plague in the Greek camp at Troy, for instance, or the pestilence at Thebes at the start of an Oedipus. But Callicrates just wanted to get away as quickly as he possibly could, and he virtually pulled my arms out of their sockets in his haste to get home.

'For God's sake, stop dawdling, can't you?' he said several times. 'You may be immune, but I'm not.'

And so I had to let all those marvellous details go to waste and scamper along at his heels, like a dog who can smell hares in the corn but has to keep up with his master. Eventually we reached Philodemus' house, which was mercifully clear of infection, and I was just able to eat a huge bowl of porridge with sausage sliced up in it and drink a cup of wine and honey before falling fast asleep.

Apparently I slept for the best part of a day and a night, and while I was asleep Philodemus and Callicrates took out the cart, fetched the bodies out of my grandfather's house, and cremated them honourably. Of course my grandfather himself was saturated with water from the trough and wouldn't burn, so they had to dry him in the sun like goat's meat for a journey; but they didn't tell me that until several years later. They performed all the proper rites, however, mixing the ashes with honey and wine and milk and burying them in an urn with all the right invocations, and I'm very grateful for that, since properly speaking it was my job. When they got back, both Philodemus and Callicrates washed themselves very thoroughly and even burnt the clothes they had been wearing when they handled the bodies; Philodemus had got it into his head that the plague was somehow directly connected with all the dirt and squalor that went with having the whole of Attica cooped up inside the City walls. But Philodemus always did have a thing about cleanliness, even to the extent of having all the household refuse put into jars and dumped in the next street.

So I came to live with Philodemus and Callicrates, which I suppose was the greatest benefit I derived from the plague. I say the greatest, since of course with so many of our family dead I was the heir to a considerable amount of property. It's true what they say, after all; men die, but land goes on for ever, and in those days people were only just starting to realise that land could be bought and sold. As a result of the heavy mortality among my kinsmen (most of whom, I confess, I had never even heard of) I stood to inherit a considerable holding.

Of course, there were endless lawsuits. About the only human activity not interrupted by the plague was litigation; indeed, with so many deaths the probate Courts were almost as busy as the political and treason Courts, and the litigants themselves never seemed to fall ill. Some of them were survivors like myself, laying claim to family estates, but even the others seemed to stay clear of the disease, at least while their case was being heard. Cratinus said that all the hot air and garlic fumes released in Court kept away the infection, and that Hades was in no hurry to crowd his nice orderly palace with noisy Athenian litigants, all shouting and calling each other names; he preferred to take quiet, honest men who would be a credit to his establishment. Cratinus, incidentally, went everywhere throughout the City visiting sick friends, helping them to laugh their way through the final agonising stages of the disease, and then burying them when even his jokes could keep them alive no longer. He claimed that his preservation was due to the prophylactic effects of cheap wine, but I prefer to think that Dionysus was looking after him too.

Philodemus conducted all my lawsuits for me, and although we lost some things we should have kept – I particularly regret five acres of vines down in the plains near Eleusis – I ended up with a personal estate of no less than sixty acres. Over half this land was hill-country and so no use for anything except scenic effect – although the land had been in our family since Theseus was a boy, apparently none of my ancestors had ever got around to removing the stones from the ground – and so my estate was in fact not nearly so impressive as it sounds; but it was easily enough to elevate me into the Cavalry class, 'and with a little bit over in case of bad harvests', as Philodemus put it. He was, for an Athenian, an almost divinely honest man, and apart from a few fields in Phyle and my grandfather's stake in the silver mines he handed all my property over to me when I was old enough to take charge of it, with a written account and record of the expenses of maintenance and repair to justify his use of the income. Yet he was no more than comfortably off himself, and paid for my keep while I was in his house entirely from his own resources, as if I had been his own son, so I never had the heart to sue him for the return of the stake in the mines.

The plague did not abate for two years, and learned men (like that little general) say that it killed one man in three. It spread from the City to our men in the army and the fleet, but somehow we never managed to pass it on to the Spartans; and it nearly brought the war to a premature end. But after a while the people in the City became resigned to it – it is quite remarkable what city dwellers will put up with, so long as they feel that everyone else is having just as horrible a time as they are – and carried on their lives as best they could. They redesigned the economy of the City slightly to accommodate their changed patterns of living, so that more people got out of agriculture altogether and started to specialise in the urban industries, like sitting on juries, metalwork and burglary. In fact, quite a substantial number of men caught the plague from breaking into infected houses, which caused considerable amusement to their neighbours.

One thing I must mention is the prophecy, because it was the one great topic of discussion wherever people still met to talk. As soon as the plague became widespread, someone or other dug up an ancient oracle, which had actually been carved on stone in the time of the celebrated Solon. It went: '*The Spartans come bringing war, and hateful Death in the vanguard.*'

Most people took this as a reference to the plague, since in Solon's time the word Death was commonly used as a synonym for plague, particularly in poetry; but some grammarians and learned teachers disputed the reading for sound philological reasons which have slipped my memory, and amended the line as follows: '*The Spartans come bringing war, and hateful Dearth in the vanguard.*'

This, they said, meant that there would soon be a famine, compared to which the plague would be about as serious as a bad cold; and of course this caused great anxiety and panic-buying of food. Those who accepted the original reading replied by saying that the learned scholars were all in the pay of the corn-dealers, who were the ones who had started the plague by catching it themselves in the first place, and that something ought to be done about what was plainly a conspiracy. The City was soon divided into two rival camps, the Dearth-men and the Death-men (we were Death-men, I remember, except for a cousin of mine called Isocles who had a share in a grain ship) and these two factions took to going round the streets after dark burning each other's houses. This went on for a long time and ended up with a full-scale riot in the Market Square, during which several silversmiths' stalls and a butcher's shop were looted.

CHAPTER THREE

Not so long ago I went to the Theatre – I think it was the second day of the Lenaea – after staying up late the night before with some friends. I was so tired that I fell asleep towards the end of the first of the three Tragedies and only woke up half-way through the second. I believe the first one was a play about Oedipus, and the second was some nonsense about Odysseus; I can't remember terribly well, to be honest with you. Anyway, when I woke up, to start with I thought we were still in the Oedipus play (it didn't seem to matter terribly much – it was that sort of play) and when I realised that it wasn't I was totally unable to work out what was going on. Eventually I came to the conclusion that it was something to do with Perseus and the Gorgon, and it was on that basis that I followed it through to the final exit of the Chorus. In fact it was several weeks before someone happened to mention what the second play that day had been about, and at first I didn't believe him.

Bearing this unfortunate experience in mind, I feel that I ought at this stage in my story to clarify exactly what is going on, just in case any of my readers has got it into his head that this book of mine is set in the middle of the Persian Wars or the dictatorship of Pisistratus. You see, I cannot in all conscience assume that you know the background to this story, even if you are an Athenian; after all, it is a well-known fact that we Athenians are not particularly good at history, and the only way we can be sure when something happened or who did what two or three generations ago is by asking a foreigner. I suppose this is because we Athenians make all the history in Greece, and just as you generally find that a weaver's own cloak is threadbare and worn and a potter's house is full of chipped and unglazed crockery, so we Athenians are most disdainful of our own principal export and take no great interest in it.

Now, of course, I am faced with the problem of where to start. For example, I would be perfectly happy to take you right back to the Heroic past, when the Gods walked undisguised among men and Athena competed with Poseidon as to who should be Athens' patron deity. After all, that sort of thing is extremely easy to do – I could fill a whole roll with it and never have to stop and think once – but I suspect that you would lose interest fairly quickly and start worrying about getting your winter barley in or manuring your vines. On balance, I think the best place for me to start would be just after the end of the Great Patriotic War, when all the Greeks were united against the Persian invaders and the world was a very different place.

Even before the war we Athenians had not been able to grow enough food in Attica to feed ourselves, and when the Persians broke into Attica, destroyed the City and dug up or burned all our vines and olive trees, we were all in a rather desperate situation. As you well know, it takes five years at the very least for a vine to become sufficiently established to yield harvestable grapes, while an olive tree can easily take twenty years or more to come to maturity. The Athenian economy was based on the export of wine and oil, in return for imported grain; our only other exportable commodity was silver, and the silver mines were all owned by the State and leased out to rich men, so there was no way that that source of income could be used to feed the people.

The one thing we did have was warships. You see, shortly before the Persians invaded, a man called Themistocles was put in charge of our long-running feud with the island of Aegina, and he had used the revenues from the silver mines to build and fit out the biggest and best fleet of warships in the whole of Greece. It was this fleet that we used to evacuate the City when the Persians came, and to defeat the Persians conclusively at the battle of Salamis.

The important thing to bear in mind about a warship is that it takes a considerable number of people to man it and make it work, and all these people have to be paid or they will get out of the warship and go away. In fact, a warship (or fleet of warships) is probably the most efficient way of providing gainful employment for men with no particular skills that has yet been devised by the human brain, and Themistocles realised this. On the one hand, he had a city full of people unable to make a living off their land, and on the other hand he had a harbour crammed with redundant battleships which had recently proved themselves capable of making mincemeat out of the most powerful navy in the world.

At the time, Athens was still part of the Anti-Persian League, the confederacy of Greek cities hastily formed to resist the invaders. By all accounts it was a wonderful thing while it lasted, for it was the first time in the history of the world when the Greeks had not all been at war with each other. Having driven the Great King out of Greece, the League was obviously redundant, and there was no reason why it should not be dissolved so that everyone could go back to cutting each other's throats, as their fathers and grandfathers had done. But for some reason the League continued to exist.

Now the best theory I have heard is that most of the cities of Greece were in roughly the same situation as

Athens; their economies were in ruins because of the war, and nobody wanted to go home and face the mess. They greatly preferred drawing regular pay for fighting the Persians, and if the Persians had all gone back to Persia the only thing to be done was to follow them there. So they did; and for a while they had a perfectly splendid time sacking cities and looting treasuries. But then some of the Greeks, particularly those who lived on the islands in the Aegean and on the coast of Asia Minor, thought that it was high time they went home and started farming again, on the principle that sooner or later the supply of Persians would run out and they might as well get back to work before the soil had got completely out of hand.

By this stage, Themistocles had had his Great Idea, and so the Athenians pretended to be terribly upset at this defection by their allies, and spoke very eloquently at League meetings about avenging the fallen heroes and the desecrated temples of Athens. The islanders were profoundly embarrassed and didn't know what to say; and then the Athenians, with a great show of relenting and making concessions, said that they quite understood, and as a special favour they, the Athenians, would carry on the Great Crusade on behalf of all the Greeks, until the Persian menace had been wiped off the face of the earth and the anger of the Gods had been fully appeased. All the islanders had to do was contribute a small sum of money each year towards general expenses, as a gesture of solidarity; we would provide the ships and the men, and the loot would be shared out equally at the end of each campaigning season.

Naturally enough the islanders thought this was eminently reasonable; either the Athenians would wipe out the Persians or the Persians would wipe out the Athenians, and either way the world would be rid of a nuisance. So they swore a great many oaths and undertook to pay a small contribution each year into the League treasury. The hat was taken round, and the

Athenians used the money to build more ships and fill them with Athenian crews, until nearly every adult Athenian who disliked the idea of hard work was adequately provided for. Shortly afterwards, however, when the islanders began to notice that the Athenians hadn't been near the Persians for some considerable time and the Great Crusade seemed to have lapsed, they stopped paying the small contribution and declared that the matter was closed.

The next thing that happened was that the Athenian navy turned up under the walls of their cities looking extremely hostile and demanding to know what had become of that year's gesture of solidarity. When the islanders tried to explain that the war was over, the Athenians were greatly amused and replied that on the contrary, unless the Tribute (as the small contribution was now called) was paid at once, plus the incidental expenses of besieging the island and a substantial Loyalty Premium, the war would begin immediately. Now an island, being entirely surrounded by water, is particularly vulnerable to overwhelming seapower, and the islanders realised that there was nothing for it but to pay or be killed. So they paid, and with the money so obtained the Athenians built more warships and hired yet more oarsmen.

Thus was formed the Great Athenian Empire, previously known as the Anti-Persian League, and for a while it seemed as if there was nothing that anyone could do about it. The Athenians were able to buy all the imported grain they needed, and there were no political difficulties since the City was a democracy and enough of the citizens were on the payroll to constitute a majority. In addition, the professional oarsmen mostly lived in or near the City, while those Athenians who had wanted nothing to do with the idea and were struggling to get their land back into cultivation tended to live out in the villages of Attica and were usually far too busy tilling the soil to spare a whole day every few weeks to attend Assembly. When there was no serious rowing to be done, the oarsmen were able to get on with the work of reclaiming and planting out their own land, which was not too difficult with their navy pay to tide them over while the vines and olives matured, and in this way the Athenian democracy took on its unique and unmistakable form. Power lay with the poorest and most numerous section of the population, who naturally enough voted for the system that provided for them. Anyone who wanted to succeed in politics had to make friends with the oarsmen and buy their favour with appropriate measures, entertain them with clever speeches, or both. Short of giving away free wheat on the steps of the Propylaea, the scope for buying favour was limited to a few well-tried and unsubtle methods which anyone could use, and so making and listening to political speeches became the national pastime and obsession of the Athenian people. The oarsmen had plenty of leisure when there was no naval action in hand, since most of them by definition had only small holdings of land to work (if they had more than a few acres they would qualify for the Heavy Infantry or Cavalry class, who are far too grand to live off the proceeds of State piracy) and there is no better way known to man of spending an idle afternoon than sitting in Assembly with a jar of dried figs listening to clever speeches and then voting to annex a few more cities.

This new style of politics called for a new breed of politicians. There was no longer much point in striving for the high offices of State now that the real power lay with Assembly. But in theory at least, any Athenian citizen was allowed to address Assembly and propose a measure, and it soon became obvious that the way to get on in politics was to make speeches and propose measures, as often and as loudly as possible. It was also open to any Athenian citizen to prosecute any other

Athenian citizen in the lawcourts, and Athens has a great wealth of un-Athenian Activities legislation specifically designed to be useful to politicians. By this time we Athenians had already developed our wonderful judicial system, whereby all trials are heard by mass juries of several hundred citizens; all that remained to perfect the system was the introduction of a living wage for jury service. Thus was created the Athenian professional juryman, who gets up before dawn to stand in line for a place on the jury. If he gets there early enough he is assured of entertainment of the very highest quality from the speechmakers plus a day's wages at the end of the performance. This way of life is particularly attractive to older and less active men who can neither dig nor row, and they are extremely careful to convict anyone who threatens to destroy their livelihood by proposing political reforms. On the other hand, they are always grateful to people who do a lot of prosecuting, since for every prosecution there has to be a jury, and these people are very rarely convicted of anything, even if they are genuinely guilty.

And that, more or less, is how Athens came to have the most pure and perfect democracy the world has ever seen, in which every man had a right to be heard, the law was open to all, and nobody need go hungry if he was not too proud to play his part in the oppression of his fellow Greeks and the judicial murder of inconvenient statesmen. The by-products of the system included the perfection of oratory and a universal love among all classes of society of the spoken word in its most delicate and refined forms. No wonder we are a nation of aesthetes.

The only problem was Sparta. Ever since Zeus, whose sense of humour is not particularly attractive to us mortals, put Athens and Sparta on the same strip of land, there has been war between the two cities. Asking Athens and Sparta to live together without fighting is like expecting night to marry day, or winter to form an offensive and defensive alliance with summer. Having unquestionably the best land army in the world, the Spartans generally had the best of these wars; but since the population of Sparta was small and spent most of its time reminding its own empire in the south of Greece about the merits of absolute loyalty, it had never been able to take any lasting measures against Athens, such as burning it to the ground and sowing salt on the ashes.

Sparta had been the nominal leader of the League during the war, but as soon as it became clear that the Persians could only be defeated at sea the real leadership passed to Athens, and since the Spartans were busy with violent internal politics as soon as the war ended, there was nothing they could do to stop us building our empire in the way I have just described. As soon as they were clear of their local problems, however, they began to get seriously worried, for it was obvious that as soon as the Athenian Empire was strong enough, it would use every ounce of its new strength to stamp Sparta flat, liberate the subject races, and remove the one serious obstacle to Athenian supremacy in Greece. So, with a degree of hypocrisy remarkable even for them, the Spartans set themselves up as the champions of the oppressed and enslaved and demanded that we stop extorting tribute from our allies and disband the fleet.

And that is how Athens came to be at war with Sparta, eleven years after I was born. One of the first Athenians to be killed was my father, who went with the expeditionary force to Potidaea. By that stage, Themistocles had proved beyond question that he was the wisest and cleverest man in the whole of Athens, and had paid the inevitable penalty. As I recall, he escaped with his life and immediately went to the court of the Great King of Persia, who gave him a city to govern, and if he had managed to conceal his cleverness a little better he might have lived to be an old man. But he contrived to avoid being killed, for he took his own life by drinking bull's blood, stylish to the very end. A number of marginally less clever Athenians took his place in turn, in particular the glorious but profoundly stupid Cimon, who actually believed that the purpose of the League was to fight the Persians, until the celebrated Pericles came to power, just as the Spartan situation was beginning to come to a head.

In fact, it was this same Pericles who gave me my first set of armour. You see, in those days it was the law that when a man's father was killed on active service, the State provided his son with a suit of armour absolutely free, which is a very generous gesture in view of the price of bronze, if not exactly tactful. There is a touching little ceremony, and the General for the year makes a speech before handing each bewildered infant his breastplate, shield and helmet. Now in those days the General was elected, and Pericles' power depended on his being elected General every year – it was the one great office of State that still retained even vestiges of actual power – so it was natural enough that he should make as much as possible of this great speech of his, in front of the whole population of the City. Since I was already a budding dramatist I was extremely excited about the coming performance and looked forward to it with the greatest possible anticipation. For I would be placed right up close to the Great Man, in an ideal position to make mental notes of all his mannerisms and personal peculiarities, all of which I would lovingly reproduce in dramatic form.

You remember I told you about that little general who wrote that incredibly dull and pompous history of the war, the one who thought he'd had the plague? Well, I came across a copy of the first part of his book the other day; I had bought some cheese and someone had used the immortal work to wrap it in, which shows the degree of aesthetic judgement our Attic cheesemongers have.

Before putting it on the fire I looked up a few things in it, and to my amazement I found that the little general had included the speech Pericles made that day. In fact, he had made a great fuss of it, using it as a convenient place to stuff in all the things he thought Pericles would have said if he had been half as clever as the little general, and by the time he'd finished with it the speech bore no relation at all to what I remembered Pericles saying; and I think I ought to know, since I was actually there, in the front row, studying the whole thing with the greatest possible care for the reasons I have just given you. But then again, my memory is not what it was. Still, I feel I ought to put down just a little bit of what I remember Pericles saying, just to set the record straight; and then if anyone else who was actually there reads it, he can either confirm that I am right or go around telling his friends that Eupolis of Pallene is a silly old fool, which may be the truth.

I remember that we all walked out to the public cemetery, which actually lies outside the walls of the City, and that it was a remarkably warm day for the time of year. Now I had been dressed up in my smartest clothes and had some sort of foul sweet-smelling oil daubed all over my hair, and I was feeling distinctly uncomfortable – the oil on my head seemed to be frying my brains – and the whole thing seemed entirely unlike the way a funeral should be. On the one hand there were plenty of women howling away and gouging their cheeks with their nails until they bled, the way women do at funerals; but the men seemed to regard the whole thing as a party of some sort, for a lot of them had brought little flasks of wine and jars of olives and figs, and were chattering away as if it were market-day. There were sausage-sellers hovering around the edges of the crowd, and the very sight of them made me feel hungry (I love sausages) but of course I wasn't allowed to have one since I was supposed to be mourning my dead. As it happens, I didn't feel particularly grief-stricken, since I couldn't associate all this fuss and performance with my father's death, and the thought that his body was in one of the big cypresswood trunks trundling along on the carriers' carts seemed distinctly improbable. Still, I think I would have been able to make a reasonable job of looking solemn if it hadn't been for the flies. The smelly stuff on my hair seemed to have drawn out every fly in Greece, and I defy anyone to look serious and dignified if he can't see where he's going for a thick cloud of flies. I tried my best, but in the end I had to start swatting at them, and that was it as far as I was concerned.

It's a strange feeling being part of a huge crowd of moving people, and I don't suppose I had ever seen so many human beings congregated together in one place before. It wasn't the same as the Theatre, where the people don't all arrive at once. It was as if the whole world was crowded into one small space, with some of them feeling miserable and others feeling happy, and most of them feeling slightly bored and wishing they were doing something else, just as you'd expect. As we came near the cemetery it occurred to me that I was going to have to step out in front of all these people to collect a suit of armour, and I knew in my liver that I was bound to make a fool of myself – drop the helmet or send the shield rolling off on its rim into the crowd like a hoop – and for a while I was paralysed with fear in the way that only a small and self-conscious child can be.

At last it was time for Pericles to make his speech, and the crowd divided to let him through. It was the first time I had seen him close to, and it was rather a shock. I had been expecting a tall, important-looking man with plenty of presence and bearing, and sure enough that was what I saw. I followed this figure with my eyes, dazzled by the dignity of the man; he was wearing a suit of burnished bronze armour that shone like gold and his back was as straight as a column. Trotting along beside him was a chubby little fellow with a strange-shaped head and rather thin legs, who I took to be his secretary, since he was carrying a scroll of paper. These two made their way to the side of the coffins, and the glorious fellow stopped. I held my breath, waiting for him to start speaking, but he just stood there, while the little chubby man climbed up on to the small wooden stage and cleared his throat, rather like a sheep in the early morning. Everyone immediately stopped wailing and chattering, and I realised that the man who I had taken to be the secretary was Pericles himself.

Once he started to speak, of course, there was no mistaking him, and when I began listening to that rich, elegant voice the man himself seemed to grow a head taller and lose about a stone in weight in front of my very eyes. It's extraordinary the difference a person's voice makes to the way you perceive him. I remember when I was in the army in Sicily there was a huge man with a head of hair like a lion's mane, but with the silliest little voice you've ever heard in your life. Before I heard him speak, I had always taken care to be near him in the line, since he looked like a useful person to be near in the event of fighting. As soon as he opened his mouth I revised this opinion and kept well clear of him, since it is well known that freaks tend to come to a bad end.

Where was I? Oh yes. Pericles cleared his throat and began to speak, and for the first few minutes everyone was spellbound. But after a while, I began to feel strangely uncomfortable with this wonderful speech. He was speaking tremendously well, even I could tell that; but he didn't actually seem to be saying anything. The words just sort of bubbled out of him, like one of those beautiful little springs you see in the mountains after the rain, which then soak away without leaving any trace of moisture behind. I particularly remember this bit, which doesn't appear anywhere in the little general's version. See what you make of it.

'Men of Athens,' said Pericles, 'when we say that these glorious heroes died for liberty, what exactly do we mean by liberty? Is it the liberty of the individual, to do what he pleases when he pleases? Can this be the sort of liberty for which brave men would selflessly lay down their lives? Is that rather not a form of lawlessness and self-indulgence? No, surely we mean the liberty of our great and imperishable City, which will still be here, in one form or another, when we are all long since dead and buried. For no man can be free while his fellow citizen is in chains, and no one man can claim to live in a free city when his brother Athenian is not every bit as free as he is. It is precisely this, men of Athens, which these comrades of ours shed their priceless blood for, and that same liberty shall be their memorial when all the temples of the Gods have fallen into dust and the statues of famous men are buried by the sands of Time.'

I wanted to interrupt at this point, for the celebrated Pericles had just said that the City would always be here, and now he was saying that the temples would one day fall down and the statues in the Market Square would get covered up with sand. In short, I was feeling terribly confused and I didn't think much of a public speaker who allowed his audience to lose the thread of what he was saying. But everyone else in the audience was standing there with his mouth open, as if this was some message from the Gods, and I remember thinking how stupid I must be to have missed the point of it all.

Then the great speech came to a splendid but largely obscure end, and it was time for the presentation of the armour. We children were formed up in an orderly queue, with me somewhere towards the end, and a large cart full of trussed-up breastplates, shields, helmets and leg-guards was backed carefully into the space by the rostrum. A couple of men let down the tail-gate and started unloading suits of armour and reading off the names, and the recipients walked forwards, were embraced by Pericles (who seemed to have shrunk back into a chubby little fellow once again) and clanked off into the crowd to be fussed over by their mothers. After what seemed like years I heard my name, and so I took a deep breath, prayed to Dionysus for luck, and plodded across to the rostrum. By this stage the two men who were unloading the armour were feeling tired and thirsty, and they bundled the great mass of metalwork into my arms and virtually shoved me at Pericles, who tried to embrace me and nearly lacerated his arm on the sharp rim of the brand-new shield. Without altering the expression of dignified grandeur on his face he whispered, 'Watch out, you clumsy little toad, you nearly had my arm off,' then he dragged me towards him, gave me a token squeeze, and pushed me away. I was so intent on keeping hold of all that armour that I bumped into the next child on his way up to the rostrum and knocked him clean off his feet. After a journey that seemed longer than all the wanderings of Odysseus put together I found my way back to my place in the crowd, breathed a deep sigh of relief, and let go of the armour. Of course it all fell to the ground with the most almighty clang, and everyone in the crowd seemed to turn round and stare at me. I hated that suit of armour from that day forward, and it didn't bring me a great deal of good luck, as you will see in due course.

Well, a year or so later Pericles was dead, as I have told you. I suppose as a Historian I should consider myself lucky to have met such an important and significant man, but I don't. I think it would have been much better if my father hadn't been killed and I had never received a suit of public armour. My excuse for this deplorable attitude is that although I am a Historian now, I wasn't one at the time – in fact, I'm not sure that the writing of History had been invented then – and so my impression of the whole business was formed without the benefit of the Historian's instinct. As for Pericles himself, I have managed in a quite extraordinary way not to let my meeting with him influence the vaguely superhuman image of him that I have to this day. The dumpy little man with the funny head, I argue, can't have been the glorious leader who led the City in the days before the war, and neither can he have been the spectacular monster of depravity that springs to mind whenever I hear one of my contemporaries singing a passage from a play by Cratinus after a good night out. Those two beings had, and still have, a life of their own, and it's enough to make you believe in all that nonsense you hear these days from the men who hang around talking in the Gymnasium about the Immortality of the Soul and the Existence of the Essential Forms.

In fact, all this remembering the past has got me confused, and I find it difficult sometimes to come to terms with the fact that I was there in those days and mixed up in all those great events which are now thought worthy of being recorded. There's a bit in the *Odyssey* that's quite like this strange sensation. Odysseus has been shipwrecked on some benighted island miles from anywhere, with all his ships lost and his men drowned, and nobody has the faintest idea who he is. But he's sitting there in the King's hall, eating his porridge and minding his own business, and the minstrel starts singing a tale of ancient valour, all about the legendary hero Odysseus and the fall of Troy. For a moment our hero thinks of standing up and saying 'That's me', but he doesn't bother; after all, it's a hero they're singing about and not him at all, and he never did the wonderful deeds that are being attributed to him.

Come now, Eupolis, return to your story while you are still within a long bowshot of coherence. Pericles' policy for fighting the Great War was nothing if not simple; he reckoned that since any major land battle between Athens and Sparta would be bound to result in a decisive Spartan victory, it would be a shrewd move on his part to delete major land battles from his programme of events. Instead, he crowded the population of Attica into the City whenever so much as the toe of a Spartan sandal crossed the border, and sent out the fleet to cause legitimised mayhem up and down the coast of the Spartan possessions in the Pelopennese. The Spartan army came bounding into Attica like a dog after a cat, only to find that the cat climbed up a tree and refused to come down to fight. So the Spartans amused themselves as best they could by chopping down our newly matured olive trees and rooting up our vines like a lot of wild pigs, and then went home again, having achieved nothing that a really good thunderstorm couldn't have done twice as thoroughly in half the time. With the tribute-money pouring in and the grain ships jostling each other for space in the Piraeus we were none the worst off for the annual burning of our crops – indeed, some of the people who think that agriculture is a science and not a lottery declared that the annual destructions prevented us from overworking the soil as we have been doing for generations and would result in bumper harvests once the war was over. Now this was an exaggeration, needless to say, and it stands to reason that the plague would have been far less serious had the City not been crammed to bursting-point with human beings. But by and large the policy of Pericles would have worked if we had had the patience to persevere with it, and if Pericles had survived.

Which is much the same as saying that we could grow far more to the acre if only it rained more often. One of the hallmarks of an Athenian is his impatience and his restlessness, and when you coop all the Athenians in the world up inside a walled city, this characteristic becomes more marked than ever. Another thing that happens is that all these Athenians will go to Assembly and vote for things just to pass the time. For the first time in history, the ideal on which our democracy is based was being put into action; all the citizens of Athens did go to Assembly and listen to the speeches, and of course the result was absolute chaos. Simple-minded straightforward men from the back end of Attica suddenly found out how their State was being run, and of course they wanted to play too. Even Pericles couldn't have kept control of fifty-odd thousand thinking Athenians for very long.

By God, though, it made the City an interesting place to live in (though decidedly squalid), having all those people hanging around with nothing at all to do except talk. It may just be the exaggeration of childhood memory, but I'll swear the City hummed just like a beehive, so that wherever you went you weren't far from the sound of human voices. With no work to do and not much money to spend, the only available pleasure was the pleasure of words. If ever there was a time and a place to be an aspiring Comic poet, that was it; because, with a few minor exceptions, the one topic of conversation was politics and the war, which of course is what all Comedy has to be about.

When the Spartans had had enough of smashing up our crops and went away again, and the fleet came back from doing roughly similar things in Messenia and Laconia, we all trooped off home to see what had been burnt or chopped down this year and plant out our winter barley. It's an extraordinary thing, but we always did plough and plant out vine-cuttings, in the hope that there would be no invasion next year. I think it goes to show that none of us ever dreamed that we could possibly lose the war, and that the worst that could happen is that we would all meet up in the City next year to continue our conversations and discussions. But in those days, we Athenians knew that there was nothing that we could not achieve and no limit to our realisable ambitions; not only were we bound to conquer all the nations of the earth sooner or later, but we were all on the point of pinning down the answers to every question that anyone could ask, and that anything could be solved or explained if you thought and talked about it for long enough. In short, there was always something to be busy with and something new and wonderful to look forward to, and the fact that in the meantime we all had to get on with the business of scratching a living from the same little scraps of land that our fathers had worked themselves to death over before us tended to be overlooked in the general excitement. I remember once an exile from the court of some Scythian chieftain came to Athens at a time when the City was full of people – and this was many years before the war, on just an ordinary market-day – and he couldn't believe all the things that he heard people saying. He heard them talking about how once the Persians had been dealt with we would be able to get on with conquering Egypt, and how it should be perfectly easy to work out whether the Soul survived the moment of death by making comparisons with things like fire and the attunement of musical instruments, and finally he could restrain himself no longer and burst out laughing in the middle of the Market Square. Of course his hosts were terribly embarrassed and didn't know where to look, and the barbarian at once apologised for his extraordinary behaviour.

'I'm sorry,' he said, 'but I just can't help laughing. You Athenians are all so incredibly perverse.'

'Why?' said his hosts, puzzled. 'What do you find so peculiar about us?'

'Well,' said the Scythian, 'here you all are busily dividing up the world between you and neatly explaining the heavens and making excuses for the immortal Gods, and yet you still empty your chamber-pots on to each other's heads first thing in the morning. So while you're walking about with your heads in the air and your undying Souls are flying through the ether, your feet are up to their ankles in someone else's shit, and all it takes is a shower of rain to make this glorious city of yours utterly intolerable. In my country we may have no intention whatever of annexing the valley next to ours, and none of us has the faintest idea about whether rain is caused by the action of the sun on the ocean or not, but at least we carry all our excrement to a place outside the camp and dump it there where it isn't a nuisance to anybody.'

I used to know what the Athenians replied; I expect it was very brilliant, because the whole point of the story is to show that we are superior to all other races on earth. But there's a sequel to the story which verges on relevance, and since I feel in the mood for telling stories you will have to bear with me a little longer.

This same Scythian, while he was in Athens, had an affair with the wife of a citizen. Her name was Myrrhine, and her husband was a man called Euergetes; he was a very upright, pious sort of man and probably quite unbearable at home, so it's not too hard to forgive his wife for seeking a little fleeting entertainment.

Anyway, one day the Scythian came to call, confident that Euergetes would be out at Assembly until well into the afternoon. He brought a little jar of expensive Syrian perfume with him as a present, and had just got his cloak and tunic off and was struggling with the laces of his sandals when Euergetes pushed open the front door and walked in. Assembly had been cancelled because of a bad omen – something to do with a polecat giving birth under the altar in the Temple of Hephaestus – and he had hurried home to make propitiatory sacrifices.

He was rather startled to see a large, naked stranger standing in his house, and probably expressed himself rather forcefully. But the Scythian was a quick-witted man and had heard all about Euergetes' piety from Myrrhine. So he drew himself up to his full height (these Scythians are often quite tall, and this one was taller than most by all accounts), scowled hideously and shouted, 'How dare you come bursting in like this?'

Euergetes was puzzled, and for a moment he wondered whether he had come to the right house. But the next moment he saw his wife standing beside the stranger and trying to do up her brooch, and so he knew he was right.

'I like that,' he said. 'Just who do you think you are, God Almighty?'

The Scythian was just scrabbling about in the back of his mind for something to say when these words of his antagonist provided the necessary inspiration. 'Yes,' he replied.

Euergetes blinked. 'What was that?' he said.

'Are you blind as well as impious?' said the Scythian. 'Can't you see that I am Zeus?'

It took Euergetes a moment to come to terms with this, but as soon as his mind had managed to choke the concept down he believed it implicitly. After all, in the legends Zeus is always slipping in between some human's sheets, with such results as Sarpedon, Perseus and the glorious Heracles. To a naïve and trusting man like Euergetes it must have seemed far more probable that his lifetime of piety was being rewarded by a visit from the Great Adulterer than that his wife could possibly think so little of him as to have taken a lover. He hesitated for about a seventy-fifth of a second and fell on his knees in a stupor of religious awe.

Now Myrrhine was a sensible girl and she knew that this fortunate state couldn't last. After all, if the God was a God he would now perform some miracle, such as filling the room with flowers or making a spring rise from the floor, and he certainly wouldn't put on his tunic and cloak and just walk out into the street. Then she happened to notice the little jar of perfume. While her husband was busily praying to the Scythian, she crept up behind him and hit him on the head with the jar as hard as she could. Of course Euergetes went out like a lamp in a gale, and the Scythian flung his clothes on and fled. A few minutes later, Euergetes came round and sat up, holding his head and moaning. There was blood, mixed with expensive Syrian perfume, all over his face and he was distinctly disorientated.

'What happened?' he asked.

'You idiot,' said his wife, 'you got struck by lightning.'

'Did I?' asked Euergetes. Then he remembered. 'Was the God really here, then?'

'He was,' said Myrrhine. 'And you insulted him, so he hit you with a thunderbolt. I was terrified.'

Euergetes drew in a deep breath and of course he smelt the perfume. 'What's that funny smell?' he said.

'A God has been in our house and you ask me that,' replied Myrrhine.

At once Euergetes staggered off to make preparations for a sacrifice, and to his dying day he swore that he had seen the God. And when, nine months later, his wife bore a son, there was no prouder man in the whole of Athens. He named the boy Diogenes (which means 'Son of Zeus') and had a mural of Leda and the Swan painted on the wall of the inner room, with Leda looking just like Myrrhine. Unfortunately the blow on his head did some sort of lasting damage and he died not long afterwards, but that was probably no bad thing; for his son turned out most unZeuslike, and the family fortunes declined from that moment on, so that Diogenes' children had been reduced to rowing in the fleet and sitting on juries by the time that I made the acquaintance of one of them. Nevertheless, parts of the commemorative shrine that Euergetes built on his land just outside Pallene can still be seen to this day; indeed, it was quite a well-known landmark when I was a boy. But the roof blew off in a storm a few years ago and then people started taking the stones to build walls and barns with, and all that's left now is the sacred enclosure and the altar itself.

CHAPTER FOUR

There are some people, I know, who can't enjoy a poem or a story unless they're told what the hero looks like. I suppose this is due to some deficiency in their imaginative powers that I ought really not to encourage; but I can sympathise, since I was exactly the same when I was a boy and attending that miserable little establishment, the School of Stratocles.

The professed purpose of this organisation was to teach the sons of gentlemen to recite Homer – in my day, it was universally believed that the only skill a young man needed to acquire before he was launched into the world was the ability to recite the *Iliad* and *Odyssey* off by heart, like one of those rather sad-looking old men who make their living that way on the edges of fairs – and for all my aspirations to being a literary man and an aesthete I couldn't be doing with it. For a start I don't like Homer (I know this is like saying that I don't like sunlight, but I can't help that) and at that age my patience with things I didn't hold with was far shorter than it is now. However, the schoolmasters at the School of Stratocles were all bigger than me (I think it was probably the only qualification Stratocles looked for when buying staff at the slave-market) and so I was compelled to find some way of tricking my mind into accepting the endless passages of galumphing hexameters that I had to commit to memory each day. I eventually hit on the idea of identifying each of the protagonists in the epics with someone I knew; I could thus picture a familiar figure doing and saying the absurd things they got up to in the Heroic age, and my task became marginally easier.

For instance, Achilles, who I have always heartily despised, became Menesicrates the sausage-seller, a strikingly handsome man with a violent temper who sold rather gristly sausages outside the Archon's Court. Agamemnon, being boastful, cruel, cowardly and stupid, merged seamlessly with Stratocles himself, while Agamemnon's fatuous brother Menelaus will now always remind me of the young slave Lysicles, who was one of my teachers. The school's clerk Typhon suited the part of the slimy and scheming Odysseus perfectly – that's Odysseus in the *Iliad*, of course; Odysseus in the *Odyssey* is a different proposition, and I must confess that I rather liked him. So he came more and more to look like my father, which inevitably made me Odysseus' son, the handsome but intellectually negligible Prince Telemachus, who waits for his glorious sire to return from the war. As for Hector – well, I reckon that all the small boys of Attica had the same picture of Hector in those days: a man in early middle age, but looking rather younger, with a careworn face forced into an encouraging smile and a strangely shaped head that Homer somehow forgets to mention; in other words, Pericles. In fact, this Hector-Pericles even survived my friendship with Cratinus and my meeting with the man himself, and has lasted to this day.

All this gratuitous reminiscence is simply an excuse for putting off for a little longer the unpleasant task of describing myself. I have justified this omission thus far in my story on the grounds that there would be no point in describing what I looked like as a boy – all children under the age of ten are exactly identical, and don't let anyone ever tell you otherwise – besides which, the plague altered my appearance drastically.

The loss of a finger wasn't the only scar that I was left with. Something unpleasant and permanent happened to the muscles in the left side of my face; I think they must have withered, or at least stopped developing. Ever since, I have gone around with a permanent grin on my face, which is appropriate for a Comic poet but profoundly irritating to everyone I have ever met. My hair, which was formerly thick and very curly, started falling out in handfuls like a punctured cushion, so that by the time I reached thirteen I was as bald as marble. Also, I never grew to full stature, so that now I am a full head shorter than most men. My arms, chest and shoulders never filled out or became round and attractive, and I look much weaker and feebler than I actually am. In fact, I can do a full day's work as well as the next man, even if I do have arms like a girl; but I have never been what you might call handsome, and so I never had the swarm of admirers that most boys acquire when they are on the verge of maturity. Nobody gave me little presents of apples or pears on my way home from school or ogled me at the baths, and no vases with '*Eupolis is beautiful*' painted on them ever came my way. Nor, for that matter, did anyone ever sing songs outside my window at night or scratch obscene compliments on our doorposts – except once, and that, I do believe, was my dear cousin Callicrates, who didn't want me to feel utterly left out.

Now the invariable rule is that all Athenians are beautiful, and only beautiful people can be good or well born or clever or anything at all. This is why we call the upper classes, the Cavalry and the Heavy Infantry, 'the beautiful and good', while the oarsmen and landless classes are described as 'the ugly men' and 'the snub-noses'. There is, of course, a degree of logic behind this, since in order to be good-looking you have to be healthy and have plenty to eat, while unsightly complaints such as rickets and eczema are largely caused by malnutrition.

Since I was palpably not beautiful, it stood to reason that for all my acres I must have the soul of a slave, and not many people were prepared to waste time on me. But I soon learned that human beings can be induced to disregard even ugliness if they can be made to laugh. Naturally, you will never have so many true friends as you would if you looked right, but it's better than nothing, and I made the best of the talent that Dionysus had given me. I soon came to realise that when two people meet together they will sooner or later start criticising a third; and if a fourth joins them who can make himself unbearably amusing at the absent party's expense, they will accept him into their fellowship, if only temporarily, and may even invite him to a relevant dinner party.

After the plague had subsided, there was a remarkable feeling of euphoria in Athens, and indeed the whole of Attica. If the war was not going well for us, it was not going particularly badly, and although the Spartans continued to visit us once a year, we had come to tolerate them as just another of the hazards of agriculture. For my part, I hardly thought about them at all; I had wonderful things to see and do.

It seemed as if there was no limit to my domains, or to the number of men and women who called me master (at least to my face). I expect that if I had been born to it I wouldn't have taken very much notice; I'd have been far too busy eating my heart out with envy whenever I saw anyone who had two more acres or a better plough. It's a curious thing, but I've always found that the wealthier a man becomes, the more obsessed he is with the idea of wealth, until he gets to thinking that nobody but he should be allowed to own anything at all. Then of course he goes into politics, and ends up crawling on his belly to the oarsmen in Assembly, licking their sandal-straps and pretending to take an interest in food distribution and rural poverty. I suppose it's Zeus' way of keeping the extremely fortunate under control.

One such man, indeed, was Pericles' successor as Leader of Athens; a man called Cleon. Oddly enough, I can justify including a few words about him at this point since this Cleon's wealth was in part derived from a tanner's yard which should by rights have belonged to me. I won't bore you with the details; my grandfather had taken a share in it many years before, and had promptly forgotten all about it, and when my grandfather died my uncle Philodemus briefly considered going to law to get the share back for me. But, quite understandably, he didn't bother, since at the time Cleon was not the sort of man you took to law for any reason whatsoever, unless you wanted an excuse for travelling the world for the next ten years.

It was Cleon's father who owned the other share in the tanner's yard, and despite (or because of) his partner's lack of interest in the business it did tremendously well. At the time there was a great demand for quality leather for making shields and other military necessities, and since Cleon's father didn't fool about with the running of the thing but left it to a competent manager the yard got its fair share of business. But when his father handed over the yard to him as part of his marriage settlement, Cleon took a great interest in the leather industry – he was the sort of person who just can't leave well alone – and had soon made it twice or three times as profitable as it had been before, so that it represented the most valuable part of his possessions and the stench of tanning could be smelt from the Propylaea to the Pnyx.

Now had he stuck to tanning and the management of his land, I doubt whether Cleon would have had a single enemy in the world, apart from the people who happened to live next to the yard. He was a quiet, sensitive man by nature, who liked nothing more than a couch in a friendly house, a cup or two of good wine, and a few friends to join him in singing the Harmodius. But he had this restless streak in him that drove him to try and improve things; he couldn't bear the sight of inefficiency, muddle or wasted opportunities. In addition, the Gods had cursed him with a very loud voice and an innate ability with words, and at some stage some idiot must have told him that if he could run a tanner's yard so well he could probably run Athens. So Cleon goes ahead and takes up politics; and since he has this terrible need to make a success of everything he does (typically Athenian, you see) he sets about politics as he set about the leather trade, by cutting out the middleman and selling direct to the mass market. He doesn't waste his time standing for election to any of the great offices of State, as Pericles had done; he simply stands up and speaks (or shouts) his mind at Assembly. Now it turns out that his mind is perpetually filled with new and more exciting ways of enriching the voters, or else defending them by way of prosecutions in the Courts from the largely undefined but extremely threatening and dangerous activities of his rival politicians. As a result, he quickly becomes the most powerful man in Athens.

Shame on me for a sentimental, soft-hearted old democrat, but I find it hard to be savage about Cleon, for he was a much-maligned man. I'm not saying that he was a good man, or even a well-meaning one; on the contrary, he was a self-centred megalomaniac who did untold damage to Athens. But the same can be said for all the great statesmen in our long and glorious history, so that after a while one takes it for granted. Cleon at least brought a touch of style to an otherwise sordid and unedifying spectacle, and if he hadn't done it someone less entertaining undoubtedly would. What I cannot forgive Cleon for was more of a crime against the God than against the City; he prosecuted a Comic poet.

When I say Comic poet I mean Aristophanes, the most talentless man ever to be granted a Chorus by an overindulgent nation; and Cleon was undoubtedly provoked beyond endurance. I don't mean by what Aristophanes said about him in the Theatre; he could appreciate a joke, even a bad and endlessly reiterated joke about the size and appearance of his reproductive organs, as well as the next man. Indeed, I watched him in the audience during a play of Aristophanes' which was entirely devoted to personal attacks on him, and I believe he enjoyed it much more than I did. No, what aggravated Cleon so much was what Aristophanes said about him behind his back, at parties and sacrifices and in the Market Square. For some reason which I have never been able to understand, people believe things that Aristophanes tells them, although anyone who knows him half as well as I do wouldn't believe him if he told them they had two ears.

Nevertheless, the fact remains that Cleon prosecuted Aristophanes the poet on a charge of slandering the City in the presence of foreigners. This is a terrible crime to be accused of, although nobody has yet got around to defining it, and Aristophanes was duly tried and convicted. He escaped with his life but was very heavily fined, and from that day onwards not only Aristophanes but every other Comic poet in Athens marked Cleon down as a prime target. Not only did they attack him (which was only to be expected and therefore quite innocuous); they also refrained from attacking his enemies, which is a rather more serious matter. You see, nobody had ever before thought of challenging the Comic poet's right to say exactly what he wanted about who he wanted, from the Generals and the Gods down to the street-corner birdseller who sells him a diseased hoopoe and refuses to give him his money back when it dies. It is a matter of principle, and although I would be hard put to it to name a Comic poet who wouldn't spend the next week celebrating if he heard that one of his fellow poets had just been sentenced to death, a threat to the freedom of the poet is a threat to all poets. It was just like the Persian invasions, in fact; we all stopped fighting each other and united against a common enemy.

Naturally, Cleon never tried anything so stupid ever again, and next year it was business as usual. The only difference was that whereas before his conviction Aristophanes was just another hack Comic poet, for ever afterwards he was the man Cleon tried to muzzle, and accordingly anything by Aristophanes had to be good. This is the only explanation, apart from a total lack of taste and discrimination on the part of the Athenian public, for Aristophanes' brilliant record of winning prizes in the Festivals.

Now, about Aristophanes. He's seven or eight years older than me, and he started young. His first play, *The Banqueters*, was put on years before he was legally old enough to be given a Chorus, and so he had to go through the charade of pretending that his uncle had written it; although as soon as the Chorus had been allotted he wasted no time in setting the record straight. But by then it was too late to stop him having his Chorus, since the Committee on Plays and Warships had already appointed him a producer, and in those days nobody would even have considered trying to back out of their duty to finance a Chorus. It was a splendid system, all told; the Committee assessed the means of all the citizens and drew up a list of those wealthy enough to equip a trireme warship for the fleet and to pay the production expenses of a play. Rich men were actually proud to be appointed (it was a sure way of letting the whole world know how rich they were) and by and large the system worked. It was a good way of doing these things, and considerably better than the way we do it now.

I suppose that if I had met Aristophanes in the Market Square or at some literary gathering I might conceivably have got on well with him, and the whole course of my life would have been different. But I first set eyes on him among the goats above Pallene, although then, of course, I hadn't the faintest idea who he was. I was eight at the time, so he must have been about fifteen or sixteen, and probably writing his first play. His father had a strip of maybe two and a half acres in our part of Pallene; most of their land was over in the south-east of Attica, and they had various properties on Aegina. Anyway, Aristophanes occasionally had to tear himself away from the City to do a little half-hearted agriculture, and to relieve the tedium of this he would play tricks on his neighbours.

One day, then, I was on Hymettus with my goats, sheltering from the sun under a stunted little fig tree, which was all that was left of some desperate individual's attempt to farm in that miserable region. In fact, there's a story attached to that attempt, and since it's a Pisistratus story I think I'm justified in putting it in here under the general heading of Athenian history. Pisistratus, as you know, was the dictator of Athens well over a hundred years ago; he was the first man to coin silver money, and he used State revenues to set up many poor landless people in small farms. In his day, every cultivable acre was pioneered and reclaimed, and he carried on his programme of subsidy long after there was nothing left but bare rock. He has a bad reputation these days because he ruled without the People and imposed taxes on citizens; but I have taken the trouble to find out about him over the years and my belief is that without him Athens would now be a little village surrounded by a wooden fence.

Be that entirely as it may, one day Pisistratus came up to this steading on Hymettus, and saw the crazy fool who was trying to turn it into a farm. He was ploughing, but all he succeeded in doing was turning over a few of the smaller boulders. Pisistratus was impressed, for this was a man after his own heart, and so he strolled over and started talking with the man.

'That looks like hard work,' said the dictator, amiably.

'Yes,' said the man, 'it is.'

'So you're taking advantage of this new scheme, are you?' said Pisistratus encouragingly. 'What sort of thing do you grow up here?'

'Blisters, mostly,' said the man, 'together with a little pain and suffering, of which that bastard Pisistratus takes five per cent. Well, all I can say is that he's welcome to it.'

As soon as he got back to Athens, Pisistratus abated the tax on the pioneers, and that was the beginning of his downfall. In order to cover the shortfall, he increased the tax on everyone else to ten per cent, and everyone who mattered was so livid with him that he met with nothing but obstruction and bad feeling until the day he died.

It was on this historic spot, then, that I met Aristophanes the son of Philip for the first time. I was lying on my back with my eyes closed, thinking how nice it would be if only I didn't have to herd goats, when I was woken by a sharp kick on my collar-bone. I woke up and reached for my staff, and there was this tall man standing over me.

'Right then,' he said, 'on your feet.' He had a City voice, high-pitched and sharp, and I took against him at once. 'Who's your father and what's his deme?'

'Euchorus,' I replied, rubbing my collar-bone, 'of Pallene. Who wants to know?'

'Shut up,' replied the stranger. 'I'm charging Euchorus of Pallene with goat-rustling.'

Now I started to feel suspicious of the stranger, since I knew my father would never do a thing like that. He knew every animal he owned by sight and had names for them all, and even when someone else's stray got into his flock he would go out of his way to try and find out who it belonged to, and if he couldn't he would sacrifice it to the Gods and hold a party for the neighbours.

'Are you sure about that?' I said. 'Name your witnesses.'

This shook him, I think, since he hadn't expected a child to be so well up on criminal procedure. Not that I was, of course; it just so happened that the words were a catch-phrase in our family, and I think they must have slipped out without my thinking. Anyway, the stranger looked around, as if seeking inspiration, and he happened to catch sight of the old white billy-goat, who was destined one day to be my chairman of judges.

'For a start,' he said, 'I hereby cite as chief witness for the prosecution Goat son of Goat, of the steading of Pisistratus. That goat there, which belongs to me.'

'No, you're wrong,' I said. 'It belongs to my father.'

'Be quiet, you little heathen,' said the stranger, 'or I'll have you for receiving.' Then he seemed to be torn by some inner conflict, which made him want to relent. 'Tell you what I'll do,' he said. 'I don't want to go to all the trouble of a lawsuit; they can drag on for days and they cause bad feeling between neighbours. I'll just take back what's mine and you can tell your father what a narrow escape he's had. How does that sound?'

'I think that's really nice and Athenian of you,' I said humbly. 'And since he's your goat you'll know all about his habits.'

'Habits?' said the stranger. 'Yes, of course I do. I reared this goat from a kid, and I've rescued it from wolves more than once with my own hands.'

So he advanced on that old white goat, shooing it with his hands and the hem of his cloak. Now I knew he would do that, just as surely as I knew that that was one thing our old white billy couldn't abide; after all, it was a Goat King and had rights. It lowered its head, made a noise like a disappointed audience, and charged straight at the stranger, butting him in the pit of his stomach and knocking him over. He fell awkwardly, bumped his head on a stone, and swore. The goat gave him a look of pure contempt, nodded his beard like a councillor, and trotted off to join his flock.

'To the charge of goat-rustling,' said the stranger, dabbing the blood elegantly from the side of his head with the hem of his cloak, 'I shall add a charge of witch-craft tending to cause a breach of the peace. Your father, who has evidently been to Persia and is almost certainly a collaborator, has cast a Babylonian spell on my poor goat and turned him into a savage, man-slaying monster. It is my sacred duty as a Greek to kill that goat and appease the anger of the Gods.' He rose painfully to his feet, wrapped his cloak around his left arm and drew his sword with his right. As he did so I saw that he was wearing a little Hecate charm round his neck to ward off evil spirits, and that told me that he was superstitious. That was all I needed to know.

'You're clever as well as brave, stranger,' I said. 'Not many people would have noticed that. What gave it away? Was it the split hoof on the offside front leg?'

The stranger paused for a moment, and his hand may instinctively have moved towards that charm I was telling you about just now.

'Split hoof,' he repeated.

'It's not a Median spell, though,' I continued brightly. 'I think it's Thessalian, or something like that. It's been really dreadful, ever since Father came back from Thessaly. None of the neighbours will talk to us any more, and I think they've put a dead cat down our well.'

'Your father's been to Thessaly, has he?' said the stranger.

'Oh yes,' I said, trying to sound miserable. 'That's where he brought that *thing* back from. It's really horrible, making those awful noises all night. And we haven't had a fresh drop of milk in the house since it came.'

'What thing?' said the stranger.

'That goat over there,' I said, pointing to a big black goat with a twisted horn, which had raised its head and was staring at the stranger, the way goats do sometimes.

'Eurymenes in our village says it's a witch and they tried to burn it the other day, but it wouldn't burn, even when they poured pitch all over it. Then it went trotting through their houses setting all the hangings alight. They were going to take Father to Court but they were too frightened.' I stopped and gazed at the stranger as if he were a Hero come to deliver us. 'Will you really prosecute my father for witchcraft?' I said. 'We'd be ever so grateful.'

'Of course,' said the stranger, backing away, with his eyes fixed on the black goat. 'In fact, I'll go straight to the Archon this very day.'

Then he turned round and walked away terribly quickly. I managed to keep myself from laughing until he was out of sight, and told my father the whole story as soon as I got home. Of course he thought I was making the whole thing up and made me learn fifty lines of Hesiod as a punishment.

Well, that was the first time I met Aristophanes. The second time was over seven years later; but I recognised him at once and he recognised me.

My cousin Callicrates and I were returning from a quiet dinner party with some boring friends of his, where we had drunk very abstemiously and discussed the nature of Justice. It was as dark as a bag in the streets, and Callicrates and I had our hands on our sword-hilts all the way. We were nearly home and safe when we rounded a corner and saw the one sight that the traveller by night fears above all others: a Serenade.

Perhaps you have never been to Athens, and the young men in your city are rather better behaved; so I will tell you what a Serenade involves. A group of young men, probably Cavalry class, meet at a party which they find uninspiring. So they appropriate what's left of the wine and the better-looking of the flute-girls, light torches and set off to find a better party. In their search for the Perfect Party they spare no pains and leave no flat stone unturned; they surge out into the Market Square and run in and out of the Painted Cloister, then they throw up outside the Cloister of the Herms, cross the Square, and work their devastating way uphill from house to house like a Spartan army, to the sound of flutes and singing. There are, of course, the inevitable casualties by the way; some of them fall over and go to sleep, and others who find themselves passing under their girlfriends' windows stop to sing a Locked-Out song until they get the slops in their faces. Generally, however, they stick closely together, like heavy infantry in enemy territory, for while the Serenade itself is vaguely sacred to Aphrodite and Dionysus, any straggler can be picked up by the Constables or charged with assault by a citizen. The general objective of most Serenades is to capture the Acropolis and overthrow the Democracy; but since in the history of the City no Serenade has ever managed to stay together long enough to get much further than the Mint, little substantial political change has ever come out of one of these affairs.

This particular Serenade was a truly terrifying spectacle. There were at least forty young men, armed with swords and torches, wreathed in myrtle and singing the Harmodius. The ten or so girls with them looked scared out of their wits, and I noticed that one of them was a free-born girl, whom they had presumably confiscated from one of the houses they had visited.

It was round her neck that Aristophanes was hanging, and he was clearly one of the leaders of this Serenade. He was yelling at the top of his voice – I think he was shouting orders, like a taxiarch – and his companions replied by cheering loudly and occasionally being sick. Callicrates and I stood very still and pretended to be doorposts, but they noticed us and stopped in their tracks.

'Line halt!' called out Aristophanes. 'Spartans to your left front. No prisoners.'

Callicrates, who had been on Serenades himself when he was younger, knew better than to run, for they would have been sure to chase after us and beat us up or kill us if they caught us. Instead he stood his ground and said nothing, in the hope that they would go away. This usually works, but not always; and this was one such occasion.

'Look, gentlemen,' said Aristophanes, 'there's a Spartan over there who isn't afraid of us. What'll we do to him?'

His co-Serenaders made several excellent suggestions, and I could tell that Callicrates was beginning to get worried. Now I am not a brave man, as you will discover in due course, but I was too young to understand the real danger I was in, and besides, fear brings out the cleverness in me like nothing else. Also, some malicious God was urging me to rescue the poor free-born girl that Aristophanes was holding, since if he got her to himself for any length of time later on, her chances of a good or even reasonable marriage would be gone for good. Remember, I was then at an age where girls have that sort of effect, although now I regard them as an intolerable nuisance.

Anyway, I filled my lungs with air and called out, 'Are you so drunk that you don't recognise the Goatherd of Hymettus, from the Steading of Pisistratus?'

Then I raised the torch I was carrying so that he could see my face. Of course, there was no guarantee that he would recognise me after so many years, not to mention the effects of the plague; on the other hand, I was so ugly, particularly by torchlight, that recollection on his part might not be necessary to achieve the desired effect. But he recognised me all right, and nearly dropped his torch.

'Have you still got that little Hecate?' I asked. 'Because if you have, you'll need it. Remember the Thessalian spell, and the goat who broke your head, and my father who learned magic?'

Here I raised the torch over Callicrates' head, and he, although he hadn't the faintest idea what I was on about, did his best to look sorcerer-like and evil. Aristophanes turned his head to spit in his cloak for luck, and that gave the girl the chance she needed. She bit Aristophanes' hand, he let go, and she ran over to us and hid behind Callicrates' shoulder. At the time I took that rather hard, since it was me who saved her.

'Tell you what I'll do,' I went on. 'I can't be bothered to put a spell on you, seeing as how it's late and tomorrow is the Feast of All Witches. I'll just take this goat of yours, in full and final settlement, and you can tell yourself what a narrow escape you've had.'

Aristophanes may have been terribly superstitious, but he wasn't a complete fool and he realised that he'd been had. His companions seemed to tumble to it as well, although of course they didn't know the joke, and they started sniggering. At any rate, their interest in killing us seemed to have evaporated, and I imagine they were starting to feel thirsty again. They started jeering at Aristophanes, who gave me a scowl that would curdle mustard. Then a thought seemed to strike him and he suddenly smiled warmly.

'I think that's very good and Athenian of you,' he called back, 'and since she's your goat, of course, you'll know all about her habits. You can keep her, mate, and welcome. Her name is Phaedra, daughter of Theocrates, and she lives just behind the Fountain House.'

At this, all the Serenaders burst out laughing, though I couldn't imagine why, and the procession moved on, singing the Leipsydrion at the tops of their voices, leaving me, Callicrates and the girl standing there feeling greatly relieved.

We recognised Phaedra's house from the way its door had been kicked in, and restored her to her parents, who had given her up for lost. In fact they were in floods of tears and were kneeling by the hearth pouring ashes on their heads when we walked in, and when they learned from Phaedra herself that she had been rescued before anything drastic had happened to her they were beside themselves with joy. Callicrates nobly ascribed the entire rescue to my quick thinking and they hugged me and washed my feet in perfumed water, which made me feel like Hercules restoring Alcestis from the dead.

'Don't mention it, please,' I kept saying, 'it was the least I could do, really it was.' But of course I wasn't looking at them but at the girl, who was blushing and glancing at me from under her eyelashes in the way girls do – I think they must learn the trick from their mothers at an early age. She was, on close inspection, rather a pretty girl, and I expect you can guess what was going on inside my idiotic little soul.

'It's positively the last time that man comes into our house,' the girl's mother was saying, 'and I don't care how much money he's got, or who his rich friends may be. And he's married already, so if he'd . . . why, we'd *never* have got Phaedra off our—'

At which her husband kicked her under the table and offered us some wine and honey in a loud voice. I should have taken notice of that 'never', but I was far too preoccupied to notice.

'Our Phaedra is the best girl in the whole of Attica,' said Theocrates. 'She's got all the accomplishments, she can cook and she can sing, she even knows her Hesiod, don't you, pet?' He scowled at her till she nodded, and then gave me a long, meaningful look that nearly took the top of my head off; the sort of look that fathers usually only give young bachelors just before they get down to working out dowry figures. 'And there's ten acres down by the coast with her. Oh yes, the young man who gets our little girl will be very lucky indeed.'

I remember once I was out shopping and I saw this really handsome horse in the market. I stood there for a while and I couldn't see anything at all wrong with it, and so I walked over and asked the dealer how much. Instead of answering my question he started off into a long and noisy encomium of the animal's virtues, half-way through which the horse arched its neck across and bit me painfully on the arm for no apparent reason. In other words, when a salesman starts praising wares that look good enough without further description, put your hands over your ears and walk away. I didn't know that, then. I think Callicrates did, because he started getting restive, but it was my moment, and I guess he hadn't the heart to interfere. He just suggested that it was time we were getting along, and of course I ignored him. For Phaedra had brought the wine and honey, with grated cheese on it, and when I took the cup my fingers brushed against hers and seemed to burn as if I had inadvertently leaned on a hot tripod.

'So who exactly was our noble assailant?' Callicrates was saying. 'Eupolis seemed to know him but he won't let me in on the secret.'

Theocrates spat ostentatiously into the fire and replied, 'That was Aristophanes son of Philip of Cydathene, the Comic poet. First thing in the morning, I'm going to see the Archon about a kidnapping suit.'

For a moment, I forgot even about Phaedra. 'Aristophanes?' I squeaked. '*The* Aristophanes, who brought on a Chorus of our allies dressed as Babylonian slaves and turning a treadmill?'

Theocrates sniffed disdainfully. 'That's an old gimmick,' he said. 'Cratinus did it in *The Sardines*, only you're too young to remember.'

Then, of course, we started talking Comedy, and after that Tragedy, until it was dawn and time to go home. I remember walking through the streets in the pale red light and thinking that I must have died and been born again as a God, the way the Pythagoreans say, since how else could I account for the fact that I had met the great Aristophanes and overcome him in battle, recited the *parabasis* of the play I was composing (which had seemed to amuse old Theocrates greatly) and above all, been given permission to call again whenever I liked, all in the space of one brief night? The last point could mean only one thing; that, if suitable terms could be worked out between our two families, I could become Phaedra's suitor, since we were both the right age and unpromised and our families were compatible. It was only when I got home and climbed into bed that Aristophanes' words about her habits flashed momentarily across my mind, and before I could consider them I was fast asleep.

Although many people have competed for the honour over the years, I still maintain that I am my own worst enemy.

CHAPTER FIVE

This book is rather like a cousin of mine called Amyclaeus, who has a truly appalling sense of direction. He's bad enough in the country, but if you put him in the City he has no more idea of where he is than a blind man. To make matters worse, he himself firmly believes that he's a born navigator and is always insisting that he knows a little short cut here or a back way there, which of course he doesn't. But, because the Gods look after fools, he has this uncanny knack of eventually ending up where he meant to go, even though he has no right to end up there at all.

It's the same with me and writing prose. I start off meaning to tell you a story, and then I get sidetracked with something that interests me, and I go wandering off all over the place; yet here we are, nicely on schedule, at the point where I have just met Phaedra and am just starting off on the long process of getting betrothed to her. In fact, we are here rather ahead of time; so, while we are waiting for the main stream of my narrative to catch up with us, I shall tell you about my first meeting with the Spartans.

As I was about to tell you before I started on about Cleon, I had inherited rather a lot of land as a result of the plague, and as soon as I came to understand what this actually meant, nothing would satisfy me but to go and inspect all this property myself. Philodemus and Callicrates approved of this notion by and large, since it's right and proper that a man should take an interest in his possessions and not just leave them to a steward or a slave to look after, and so we set off for a tour.

Nowadays, of course, what with the amalgamation of holdings and the buying and selling of land for commercial motives, things are very different; in my day, virtually the only way land changed hands was by inheritance, and so most people with more than two or three acres to their names had little snippets of land here and there all over Attica, and I was no exception. Quite apart from my father's lands in Pallene and Phyle (which were good properties, if a touch on the mountainous side), I had bits and pieces all over Attica, from Prasiae to Eleutherae and Oropus. Admittedly, none of these parcels of land was large, and with some of them you couldn't put down a cloth to spread out a picnic without trespassing on the land of at least two neighbours, but that was more or less beside the point as far as I was concerned.

Well, my uncle and my cousin humoured me as far as Eleutherae, but their patience was worn down almost to the lettering, as the saying goes, and I can't say I blame them; I must have been a quite insufferable companion, with my perpetual boasting and self-preening. For I would insist on examining every last inch, and it was getting on towards the time of year when sensible people were moving back towards the City. We had seen virtually everything there was to see except for a tiny patch of land on the very slopes of Cithaeron – half an acre if that – which had been thrown in as a makeweight in a marriage-settlement about four generations back, and where there had been a few stringy old olive trees the last time anybody had bothered to look.

We were staying at an inn at Eleutherae, and reports

were already coming in of the approach of the Spartan army on their annual holiday. As soon as Philodemus heard about this, he paid the bill and gave orders for our mules to be loaded up.

'We aren't leaving yet, are we?' I asked. 'We haven't seen the property on Cithaeron.'

'Don't be a fool,' said Philodemus, 'you heard what the shepherds said. The Spartans will be up here soon.'

'I don't care,' I said. 'I'm going to see my land.'

'Eupolis,' said Philodemus patiently, 'one of the great things about land as opposed to Spartans is that it stays put. There's a good chance that it'll still be there in the summer when the Spartans have all gone home. If you insist we can come back then. Now, we are going home.'

'You can if you like,' I said. 'I'm going to look at my land.'

'Eupolis,' replied Philodemus, not so patiently, 'you can do what you like. Callicrates and I are going home while we still can. If you want to stay here and get killed, that's a matter between you and your soul.'

What with seeing all that land I had become exceptionally arrogant, and I replied to the effect that neither I nor my soul were going to be kept from taking possession of what was ours by a load of Spartan garlic-eaters. Then Callicrates tried to reason with me – he always had more patience with idiots than his father – and that just made me more stubborn than ever, since when he explained it I could see I was in the wrong. Then Philodemus flew into a temper and stormed out. Callicrates stayed where he was.

'Aren't you going too?' I said grandly.

'Don't make things worse,' said Callicrates angrily. 'I can't leave you here on your own, there's no knowing what stupid things you might do.'

'You suit yourself then,' I said. 'First thing in the morning, we're going to take a look at my property.'

And we did. Callicrates said that if we were going to do this stupid thing, we might as well do it in the least stupid way possible, so he woke me up about two hours before dawn, bundled me into my sandals and hat, and led the way off up the mountain.

I don't know if you've ever been to Cithaeron, but if you haven't I can assure you that you haven't missed anything. It is an indescribably miserable place, even when dawn breaks over it, and the thought that he was risking his life just to give an idiot a guided tour of half an acre of it did little to improve Callicrates' temper. He wasn't talking to me and I was damned if I was talking to him, so we stomped along in silence like an old married couple who have quarrelled on the way to market. After what seemed like a hundred years of difficult walking we came to a rocky outcrop with three tree stumps on it, and Callicrates stopped in his tracks, flung his arms wide and said, 'This is it.'

'Is it?' I said.

'Yes,' replied Callicrates.

'How do you know?' I replied. 'It looks just the same as everything else.'

'I recognise that mortgage-stone over there,' said Callicrates, pointing to a lump of rock sticking out of the earth. 'It's one of the few they never got around to pulling up in Solon's time. It's the only interesting thing on the whole of Cithaeron, and I came up here when I was a boy to see it. Can we go now?'

'Hold on,' I said. 'I want to have a look at this ancient monument of yours.'

'Oh all right then,' said Callicrates. 'But for God's sake hurry. You realise anyone for miles around can see us up here.'

I wandered over and had a look at the stone. It was nothing but a pillar of rock with some very old writing on it which said something like '*Mnesarchides to Polemarchus; one sixth*'.

'Satisfied?' Callicrates asked. 'Or do you want to take measurements?'

Of course I wasn't the slightest bit interested in a slab of old rock, but just to irritate Callicrates I made a great show of examining the thing minutely, as if I was carried away by the historical significance of it. While I was doing this, I noticed the smoke.

The first thing that struck me about this smoke was that it wasn't like chimney smoke at all; it was coming up in a big cloud, and it was black. I had seen smoke like that once before, when our neighbour's barn caught fire when I was a boy.

'Callicrates,' I said, 'come and look at this.'

'Don't fool around, Eupolis,' said Callicrates. 'I've had just about enough of you for one day.'

'There's smoke coming from over there,' I said. 'What do you think it could be?'

Callicrates followed where I was pointing and his mouth dropped open. 'There's a little farm over there,' he said, 'I went there once. One of those little places. Belongs to a man called Thrasydemus.'

We looked at each other for a moment. For my part, I admit I was terrified, the way I had never been before in my whole life. Far away in the distance, I could hear the sound of flutes, and everyone knows that the Spartans march to war to flute music. Either that, or it was the God Pan; and I would be hard put to it to say which I would least like to encounter.

'Let's go home,' I said. 'I don't like it here any more.'

Callicrates nodded. 'That's right,' he said, 'you go home, quickly. Keep your head down and don't show yourself above the skyline if you can help it. Head for the village; you'll be safe there until midday at least if I know the Spartans.'

'What are you going to do?' I said, feeling quite weak with fear. 'I'm not going back on my own.'

'Don't be stupid,' said Callicrates. 'Just so long as

you take care you'll be all right.'

'Stuff that,' I said, 'I'm coming with you.'

Callicrates thought for a moment and then nodded. 'Maybe that would be best,' he said. 'That way I can at least keep an eye on you. But I've got to take a look at that farm over there.'

'Why?' I said. 'You can't fight a Spartan army on your own.'

'Of course not,' said Callicrates irritably. 'But there may be people down there who need help.'

'Oh, for God's sake,' I shouted, 'what about me? I want to go home.'

Callicrates was angry now. 'Go ahead,' he said, 'I'm not stopping you. You got us into this, so you might as well clear out now before you cause any more disaster.'

We both knew that I wasn't going anywhere on my own by this point, since I was far too scared and Callicrates was far too conscientious. So I nodded wretchedly and followed on.

The nearer we came, the more obvious it became that the fire was coming from a house of some description. I think we had both been hoping that it was just a field of barley or a rick; but it was definitely the sort of smoke that comes off burning thatch. Eventually we came to the edge of a sharp ridge, and Callicrates stooped down to avoid making himself visible to anyone watching below. I did the same and we peeped over.

Down below us was one of those small farms that used to be scattered about the remoter areas of Attica then, before they were finally abandoned after the war. It consisted of a long, thatched house and a storage tower, all enclosed by a little courtyard. From where we were, we could see that the whole place was on fire, and that in the courtyard there were a lot of men in red cloaks, apparently enjoying the spectacle.

'Do you think they got away?' I whispered.

'I hope so,' replied Callicrates. 'But if we didn't notice

them coming out on the hill, I don't suppose they did down here. This place wasn't built as a lookout station, it was built as a farm.'

Then I saw two of the red cloaks coming out of an outhouse that hadn't been set alight yet, and they were bundling along an old woman and an old man. They made these two kneel down beside the brick wall of the well. A third red cloak walked up and seemed to inspect them; then he reached for an axe that was lying beside a pile of logs ready for splitting. He pulled out one of the logs and the red cloaks put the old woman's neck across the log. The old man didn't want to watch, but the red cloaks made him. The third red cloak threw his cloak over his shoulder so that it wouldn't get in the way, and cut the old woman's head off; it took him three or four strokes. Then the red cloaks threw her body and head down the well, and dragged the old man up. He didn't seem to struggle as much as the old woman had done. The third red cloak managed rather better this time; he had the head off the old man in two strokes and a bit. I was glad we weren't closer.

Then they threw his body down the well too, and set light to the outhouse. As soon as it started to burn, a little old grey dog dashed out and they killed that too. Just then a small child came running out – I suppose he had been hiding in there hoping to escape notice – and at first they didn't see him. I held my breath, but then one of the red cloaks must have caught sight of him out of the corner of his eye, because he pointed and two or three of the others went off after him like dogs after a hare. They caught up with him as he was trying to scramble over the courtyard wall – it was just too high for him to get over – and brought him back. The third red cloak had lifted his axe up again, but then he seemed to change his mind, and he pointed to the burning outhouse. The red cloaks who had caught the child lifted him off the ground by the arms, the way parents do when they're walking a child round the market, and pitched him in through the window. I heard a very small, faint scream.

Then the red cloaks had a good look round to make sure they hadn't missed anything, and formed up into a column. The third red cloak went along the column counting them to make sure they were all there, and he stopped at one point and relieved one of them of a chicken he was trying to hide behind his shield. He hit the offender behind the head with the flat of his sword and threw the chicken into the fire, and then they moved off, marching extremely quickly. There were three boys playing flutes marching along beside them. I shall remember that tune till the day I die; in fact, I sometimes find myself whistling it when I'm not thinking.

We watched until they were out of sight over the brow of the slope, and then went scrambling down the hillside as quickly as we could go. But we had to take a long way round even then, because the hillside overlooking the farm where we had been watching was more cliff than hill, and by the time we got there the thatch was almost burnt away and there was nothing left but bare rafters, like the branches of an oak in winter.

Callicrates wound his cloak round his face to keep out the smoke and went into the house; I didn't try to stop him. He came out again a moment later coughing dreadfully, and shortly after that there was a crashing sound as the house started to fall in. He shook his head to signify that there was nothing he could have done anyway.

Round the back of the house, by the cowshed, we found the farmer Thrasydemus. He had tried to defend himself with a pruning-hook. There were four deep holes in his chest and he was quite obviously dead. We couldn't find any trace of his wife or any other of the children; they must have been in the house, or perhaps they hadn't been there at the time, although somehow we couldn't bring ourselves to believe that. But when I was looking at the farmer's dead body, I saw something shining under a small fig tree and went to investigate. It was a small jar full of silver money, which someone had smashed. I wondered why the Spartans hadn't taken it; then I remembered that they don't use silver for money, they use iron bars like roasting-spits, so of course it wouldn't have been any use to them. Probably one of the Spartans had found it and the captain had made him throw it away, just like the chicken. The Spartans are very honourable and don't hold with looting.

'Right,' said Callicrates, 'there's nothing we can do here. We might as well get back to the village and make sure they know what's going on.'

I was delighted to leave the place, and we walked very quickly away. Obviously we couldn't go back by the road, since that would be courting disaster, so we picked our way along just under the line of the hill, where we could see but, with luck, not be seen. After about half an hour, we cut across the top of the mountain, following a little goat-track that Callicrates remembered, which he reckoned would bring us down a few hundred yards from the village itself. That way, we ought to outrun the Spartans comfortably and maybe in time to raise the alarm, if it hadn't been raised already. As we walked we saw another column of smoke coming up from a sheltered little combe below us, but this time we didn't try and interfere.

'Callicrates,' I said as we hurried along. 'Do the Spartans always do things like that? I haven't heard any stories about it.'

'Only the last year or so,' Callicrates said, 'ever since we started doing that sort of thing in Messenia when we go raiding there.'

I was horrified. 'You mean we started it,' I said. 'We're in the wrong.'

'What do you mean, in the wrong?' Callicrates replied. 'It's a war, things like that happen. And they only happen when people are stupid enough to hang around when the enemy are approaching.'

I couldn't believe what I was hearing. 'Are you trying to say it was their fault they got killed?' I asked.

Callicrates stopped walking and looked at me. 'Don't you understand anything?' he said. 'It's nobody's fault. It's just the way things are. Why does everything have to be somebody's fault all the time?'

I wanted to argue but suddenly I couldn't think of anything to say – a most unusual state for an Athenian to be in, whatever the circumstances. Then Callicrates started walking again, faster than ever, and his legs were much longer than mine.

That walk seemed to go on for a very long time. The closer we got to the village, the more scared I became, and I made myself dizzy staring at the horizon looking for more columns of smoke. But we didn't see any and Callicrates seemed to cheer up, hoping that we had managed to steal a march on the Spartans.

'I reckon that what we saw back there was just a raiding party,' he said. 'If they're going to have a go at the village they'll concentrate their forces and surround the place. They don't want any more trouble than they can help – I expect they're as fed up with it all as we are, and they certainly won't want to risk getting themselves killed by taking on a populated place without proper forces. All they're really interested in is doing as much damage to crops and livestock as they can; they'll want to give the bigger places plenty of time to evacuate.'

'It didn't look that way back there,' I said, but more out of general argumentativeness than for any other reason. I wanted nothing more than to find the village undisturbed; even the prospect of getting the better of Callicrates in an argument (which was something I had never managed to do) was not particularly inviting at that moment.

We were getting down on to much more level ground now, among the vineyards and olive groves, and we couldn't see any sign that the Spartans had been through before us. Callicrates told me that he had done much the same sort of thing in his military service, and that after a while it turns into a very boring sort of a job, with no one displaying any sort of enthusiasm for it or wanting to find ways of doing it better or quicker. I didn't ask him if he had killed any farmers himself; I didn't really want to know.

Callicrates had a splendid natural sense of direction, and we came out more or less exactly where he had said we would, on the top of the ridge above the village. We looked down and to our immense delight saw a column of mules, ox-carts and men with parcels on their shoulders streaming out of the place as fast as they could go. The Spartans hadn't arrived yet, and this was the village evacuating itself, in a proper and organised fashion, according to the proper custom of war.

I was just about to go plunging down the hill to join up with this column when Callicrates put his hand on my shoulder and pulled me down. I couldn't understand what he was doing and struggled, but he clapped a hand over my mouth and pointed. Just behind the village there was a cloud of dust.

'Sit still,' he said. 'Perhaps it's nothing, but we'd better just stay here for a moment.'

I pulled his hand away. 'Don't be stupid,' I said. 'If they haven't seen it, we've got to warn them.'

'Shut up and stay here,' Callicrates said furiously. 'Do what you're told, just this once.'

So I crouched down beside him in the shade of a boulder, while the cloud of dust came nearer. The people in the column had seen it too, and they didn't like the look of it any more than I had. Some of them dumped their loads in the roadway and started running, along the road or up the hill. Others turned back towards the village; others just stood where they were.

The cloud of dust suddenly turned into a column of horsemen, riding very fast. I couldn't see the colour of their cloaks, but they had helmets that flashed in the sun and they carried two javelins each. They didn't look anything like any of the cavalry units that I had seen in Athens; they were far too businesslike and organised. Under different circumstances, it would have been a pleasure to watch them.

Callicrates pulled me further behind the rock, and then we peeped out. The cavalry had caught up with what was left of the column, and they were throwing javelins. It was rather like a high-class boar-hunt, such as you get in the hills when a lot of rich young men go out for a day's sport – except that there weren't any dogs or nets, and the quarry were rather less inspiring in their resistance than the average wild boar. When the cavalry-men had thrown their spears they drew their sabres and closed in, and since I had had quite enough of that sort of entertainment for one day, I didn't bother watching too much after that. I had this strange feeling that I was at the Theatre – probably because I was sitting a long way back and watching what was going on – and that some taste-less God was laying all this on for my benefit. I wanted to stand up and tell him that I was a Comedian not a Tragedian and so all this was wasted on me; and besides, it was against all the conventions of the Theatre to have the actual killing on stage. Besides, I wanted to say, I've seen this play before not two hours ago and I didn't reckon much to it then.

I don't suppose it lasted more than ten minutes. I remember Callicrates saying, 'It's all right, they've gone now,' and me thinking that that was exactly what my father used to say when my cousins from Thria came to visit and I used to hide in the stables because the woman had a hare lip and frightened me, and then looking out and seeing the mess.

Mess is the only word to describe it. I don't know if you've ever been in the City the morning after the Festival of Pitchers and wandered down to the Market

Square; but it was just like that, I promise you – exactly that same sort of sorry-looking, depressing mess that comes of people trying to enjoy themselves just a little bit too much. Except that instead of smashed wine jars and abandoned sandals and little pools of vomit at the feet of the statues of the Heroes of Athenian History, there were dead bodies and shattered carts and puddles of blood; and even they were the same colour as spilt wine, until you looked closely at them. The way I account for it is that the human soul can't really cope with strange and horrible things, and so it tries to pretend that what it's seeing is something everyday and normal; I guess that's why similes work so well in poems. If I tell you that the roadway was littered with severed arms and legs you can't really picture that in your mind since, unless you've seen a few battlefields, your soul doesn't know what that looks like and probably doesn't want to imagine it. But if I say that there were arms and legs scattered about like bits of driftwood on the beach after there's been a storm at sea, you'll be able to identify with that; and, if you know your Homer, you'll be able to say exactly which passage from *The Cypria* I've just lifted that simile from. But there we are.

Callicrates and I wandered down the hill – there didn't seem to be much point in hurrying – and did our best to make ourselves useful, but there was nothing much we could do. The other villagers who had had the wit to run away when they saw the cavalry coming had crept back and were seeing to such of their relatives and friends who weren't completely past helping and sprinkling dust on those who were, and Callicrates and I just got in the way for most of the time. I remember we saw one man lying on his side, and he didn't look partic-ularly dead; but when we lifted him up to see if he was still alive, his head rolled right back and dangled from his neck by a strip of skin, and the expression on his face was frankly ludicrous, so we scooped a little dust over him and walked away quickly, the way you do when you're shopping in the Market Square and you accidentally bump into one of these neatly piled pyramids of melons or oranges and knock them over.

Just as we were despairing of being able to do any good, we found an old man who apparently didn't have any family, because he was just squatting there all over blood and nobody was taking any notice of him. Anyway, he was calling out for water in a horribly wheezy voice, and so I sprinted off and found a helmet which one of the cavalrymen had dropped, and I filled it with water from a stream that ran down the hill and brought it back, feeling like the God of Healing. The old man grabbed it from me and poured its contents into his face; but none of us, not even he, had noticed that he had a great big hole in his throat from a sabre-cut, and of course most of the water just poured out of this on to the ground. A moment later the man made a sort of rattling noise, like someone gargling with salt water when they've just had a tooth pulled, and rolled over and died, so that was a complete waste of time. Now I come to think of it, that was the first time I ever saw anyone die when I was close enough to see the expression on their face.

And then there was a little girl – she couldn't have been more than eight or nine – who had had an arm cut off at the shoulder, and what with the fear and the pain she had wet herself, and this seemed to be causing her more unhappiness than her injury. She wasn't weeping or screaming, just grizzling like any other small child, and her mother had finished doing the best she could to stop the bleeding and was trying to change her wet clothes, and was swearing at her for not keeping still. Really, it made me want to burst out laughing to see them, but maybe I was just getting hysterical. Now perhaps you're thinking that that sounds a little strange coming from someone who had seen Athens in the plague, but I assure you that it was all very different. You see, there had been no blood and no wounds in the plague, just a lot of dead bodies, and besides I was very much younger then. But it was like the plague in one respect, because however unhappy and sick it all made me feel I nevertheless couldn't help noticing the little details, not because they were heartrending or disgusting but because they were interesting, as being curious specimens of human behaviour.

I'd better stop talking like this before you start getting the idea that I'm some sort of ghoul, like that terrible fellow Chaerophon the scientist who goes around watching people having their gallstones cut out. Please don't think I was enjoying any of this; I was absolutely terrified, since I was firmly convinced that the Spartan infantry were going to arrive at any minute and finish off the job. I think Callicrates had much the same idea, for all his good intentions about helping the wounded, because he kept looking over his shoulder in a worried sort of a way. But for all my fear, I don't think it ever seriously entered my head that anything was going to happen to me; I was rather more interested in not witnessing yet another massacre. I seemed to have the idea that I wasn't really part of what was going on, as if I was a tourist from one of the islands, or a God who could make himself invisible.

I think we were both nerving ourselves to get out of there when I felt this incredibly sharp pain in my foot and found that I had stepped on a broken sabre-blade and lacerated my right heel. I communicated this fact to Callicrates, who sagged as if someone had just melted his spine with a candle.

'You *idiot*,' he said miserably, 'what the hell did you want to go and do that for?'

I explained that it wasn't intentional, and that I must have lost my sandal somewhere; I felt terribly guilty for some reason and very conscious of having picked quite the wrong moment. Callicrates cut a strip off his cloak and bandaged my foot as best he could; but for all the inventiveness of mankind, there is no known way of bandaging a heel effectively, because it's such a difficult shape and so there's nothing to tie the bandage to. So we glanced round to see that nobody was looking, and tugged a right sandal off the body of a dead man lying close by, and tied that firmly to my foot with the strip of cloak. It was better than nothing, but it was profoundly uncomfortable.

'That settles it,' said Callicrates, as if he was secretly glad of the excuse, 'we'd better get going.'

'Where?' I asked, like a fool. 'We're surely not going to try and get back to Athens.'

'Well, we aren't going to Sparta,' Callicrates snapped, 'and we'd better not stay here. Look around and see if you can find something to use as a walking stick.'

I found a javelin – I won't mention where – and Callicrates chopped the head off with his sword. With this to lean on, I was able to hobble along reasonably well, but I won't pretend that I was relishing the prospect of a ten-hour hike back to the City across the mountains. Callicrates could see that I was worried and even offered to carry me on his back – he would have done it, too, if I'd let him – but that was obviously a stupid idea. What we needed was a horse or a mule or something like that.

'You're off your head,' said Callicrates when I suggested it. 'I'm not wasting time combing through the village looking for our mules. And anyway, Philodemus may have taken them back to the City with him.'

'All right then,' I said, 'we'll buy one.'

Callicrates blinked. 'In the middle of a massacre you want to stop and buy a mule.'

'Yes,' I replied.

'Oh, for God's sake.' Callicrates scratched the back of his head, and I could see he was lost for words. 'Have you got any money on you?' he asked after a while.

I turned out my purse into my hand. 'Yes,' I said. 'Thirty-two drachmas.'

'You won't get much of a mule for thirty-two drachmas.'

I didn't bother to reply to that. Instead I hoisted myself up on the javelin-shaft and hobbled over to where I could see an old woman standing beside a cart. The cart itself had been smashed – the axle was broken – but there were two mules standing beside it with their harness still on. I looked them over for a while and then said, 'How much for the little grey one.'

'You what?' said the old woman.

'I want to buy the grey mule,' I said. 'How much are you asking?'

The old woman frowned. 'I don't know,' she said. 'I'll have to ask my husband.'

Then she seemed to remember something, and she looked down at the cart. What had broken it was being turned over by the cavalry, and under a big clay jar, obviously crushed to death, was an old man's body.

'Well,' said the old woman, pulling herself together, 'it's no good asking him, is it? How much are you offering?'

'Twenty-eight drachmas,' I replied.

'Thirty,' she said.

'Done with you,' I answered, and tipped the eight coins into her hand.

'Hold it,' she said, 'you've given me too much. There's thirty-two here.'

I was busily stripping the harness off the mule. 'Oh,' I said. 'I haven't got anything smaller, I'm afraid.'

She frowned. 'I might have some change,' she said, and she opened her mouth and picked out two half-drachmas and an obol. 'That's still five obols short,' she said.

'Never mind,' I said, 'that'll do.' I pulled the harness clear and tried to get up on the mule's back, but I couldn't make it. Instinctively, I stood on the cart as a mounting-block and there was a sort of creaking noise where the running-board was resting on the dead man's head. I didn't look to see the expression on the woman's face; I just kicked the mule with my good foot and trotted it over to where Callicrates was standing.

'Ready?' I said.

'Yes,' he replied. 'I reckon if we go back the way we came we can go overland to Thria and then on to the City from there without crossing too many roads.'

That sounded eminently sensible to me, and so off we went. We made good time, what with me riding along like a gentleman and Callicrates striding along beside me, and it was comforting to see Parnes away in the distance on our right. After about two hours and a bit we were in country that I knew reasonably well; in fact, we weren't far from a bit of land that we had been looking at only a day or so before, which belonged to me.

'Callicrates,' I said, 'why don't we go to the house at Phyle instead of making for Athens? We'd be safe there.'

'Why?' said Callicrates.

I thought. 'I don't know why,' I said. 'Except the Spartans have been raiding for all these years and they've never burnt it yet.'

'They've never attacked Eleutherae yet,' Callicrates replied. 'Haven't you had enough of visiting your estates for the time being?'

'My foot is hurting and I want to go to Phyle,' I replied.

So we went to Phyle, getting there just before nightfall. They were all most surprised to see us, but not half as surprised as we were to see them. They had no idea the Spartans had arrived; they were just considering packing up to go.

'So they've come early this year, have they?' said the steward. He made the Spartans sound like the frost or locusts.

'I think we ought to move on tonight,' Callicrates replied. 'I don't imagine the Spartans will be too active in the dark.'

Of course, I protested like anything, but I don't think my views on matters were being taken too seriously by that stage. The steward hurried off to see to the last of the packing, while Callicrates eased the dead man's sandal off my foot and put on a new bandage.

Well, there's nothing to tell about our journey back to the City, except that it seemed very long and unpleasant and that as soon as we got home I tumbled on to a couch by the hearth and went straight to sleep, leaving Callicrates to take the news of the massacre at Eleutherae to the Council. My foot healed up quickly enough, since it was a clean wound and I was young, and a week or so later I was virtually back to normal and playing at being a landlord again. I didn't even have nightmares, which was a great relief to me, as I need my sleep; but I remember that I got rid of that mule as quickly as I could. In fact, I got forty-five drachmas three obols for it in the Market Square, and I felt dreadful about making a profit on the deal. It wasn't even a particularly good mule; but the man who bought it from me seemed happy enough. He was probably an idiot too.

It was at about this time that I composed the bulk of what was to be my first Comedy, although it wasn't presented for some time, as you'll hear in due course. In fact, between composing it and presenting it to the Archon I changed most of the jokes and completely rethought two of the characters, since the political situation changed and even I couldn't salvage material that was so hopelessly out of date. Nothing, except possibly fish, goes stale so quickly as topical jokes, and if I hadn't lost all my hair as a result of the plague I'd probably have torn it all out in exasperation at seeing my funniest jokes floating hopelessly out of my reach just because some fool of a politician fails to get re-elected.

You see, I can't abide wasting good material, and this is a serious handicap for a Comedian. I think the root of the trouble lies in the way I started off as a Comic dramatist, composing things on Hymettus among the goats. What I did then was to work up little set pieces and then fit them together to make up a play; which is rather like trying to build one pot from the smashed fragments of six different pots. I know I shouldn't do it. A proper poet starts off with an idea or a theme and creates characters and situations to illustrate and dramatise his idea. But if you're a bodger like me, you start with some clever little scene, like a fight between two pastrycooks or a Big Speech, or even just a single very funny joke, and you make up a story to go round it. Mind you, I'm not the only one who does it this way; and at least I don't repeat myself endlessly, like Aristophanes does.

The idea for this first play of mine was a single joke, and as it happens the joke was cut out as being no longer topical long before the play was produced and I can't remember it any more (which shows that it can't have been all that funny). Once I had the Joke, I knew who two of the characters in the play had to be, and after that it just seemed to flow. The next thing I had to think of was a new and startlingly funny costume for the Chorus; if you can do that, then you stand a chance of winning the prize however dreadful the dialogue is. And there's nothing quite like that tension you get in the Theatre when the audience all lean forward in their seats to catch the first glimpse of the Chorus as it makes its entry. I've heard it said that it's physically impossible for ten thousand people to be absolutely quiet all at the same time, and I suppose that's right; but the audience in the Theatre come pretty close to dead silence in that crucial moment. And then they either burst out into furious applause or they start muttering, and one way or another the tension is broken.

Well, my Chorus was original, if nothing else, since they were all dressed as trireme warships. So as not to give this away, I called the play simply *The General* – I don't hold with the school of thought that says that you ought to whet their appetites by calling the play *The Four-Toed Camels* or *The Two-Headed Satyrs*, because all that happens then is that the audience expects too much and will be disappointed when they see what the costume designer has actually managed to come up with.

I started off with a good safe opening scene; two slaves sitting outside their master's house at sunrise, listening to some peculiar and unexplained noise going on inside. This is scarcely original but it's the best way to start a play off unless you're going for a really high-powered opening, since it doesn't commit you to anything and it doesn't let the audience know too much about what's going to happen next. Anyway, the slaves sit there exchanging wisecracks about the domestic problems of prominent statesmen, and meanwhile the noises get louder and more inexplicable. The trick with this, of course, is to know exactly how long you can keep it up without the audience seeing that you're just doing it to be clever (which is fatal). At last one of the slaves catches sight of the audience out of the corner of his eye and condescends to let them in on the secret.

Their master, he says (like countless Comic slaves before him), is a lunatic. A complete and utter lunatic. What sort of a lunatic? Well, he's got this idea for ending the war at a stroke and providing for the People for ever, not to mention making himself General for life. He's going to take the fleet and sail up Olympus, to make the Gods into allies. Since the Athenian fleet has never been defeated, and an oracle has just said that it never will be, even the Gods themselves won't be able to stop him. Then he'll confiscate Zeus' thunderbolt, flatten Sparta, wipe out the Great King, and set himself up as King of Heaven with all the citizens of Athens as his new Pantheon. There is then a short digression about which prominent public figures of the time will replace which Gods, which was probably very funny in its day but which wouldn't mean a thing to you and doesn't mean much more to me, after all these years.

The only problem, the slave continues, is that Olympus is quite some way inland. That worried his master for a bit, but he's found a way round it. He's going to fit little wheels to each of the ships, like the platform in the Theatre, so that they can be propelled along the ground.

This doesn't explain the funny noises off-stage, of course, because they aren't hammering and wheel-fitting noises at all. Oh well, says the slave, we thought you'd be able to work that one out for yourselves, since you're Athenians and so damned clever about everything. You can't? Honest? Well, then, you'd better see for yourselves.

Then the stage-hands wheel out the platform with the interior set on it, to show what's going on inside the house. There we see the hero – originally Pericles; eventually, after many changes, Cleon – being sliced up like bacon by two sorcerers armed with whopping great knives. The sorcerers are in fact the City's two leading teachers of public speaking – I can't remember their names any more, I'm afraid – and they're chopping Cleon up and boiling him in a tanning solution, just as Medea chopped up Aegeus and boiled him to make him young again. But the purpose of this experiment is not to make Cleon young but to transform him from a reasonably honest man into a politician capable of getting his motion passed by Assembly. You can imagine what this scene was like, with the two sorcerers flinging in little turns of phrase and figures of speech like herbs and potions, until Cleon is well and truly tanned.

When they've finished and said the magic words *Three Obols a Day for Life*, out jumps Cleon, in the most grotesque portrait-mask you've ever seen, and indicts the two sorcerers for conspiracy to overthrow the democracy by helping him to succeed in justifying the conquest of Heaven. Then he stomps off to the Pnyx, and we have the big debate scene, with his speech. And still the Chorus haven't come on – the voters in Assembly haven't said a thing, since they're just the stage-hands without masks on. Then, as soon as his bill is passed, Cleon claps his hands and out comes the fleet, complete with little wheels, hats shaped like battering-rams and little banks of oars instead of sleeves.

The upshot of all this is that the fleet goes off to Olympus and besieges the Gods, just as we besieged the people of Samos, until they surrender and are sold as slaves to the Savages. Zeus, for instance, is sold to an Egyptian who wants him to make rain, and Aphrodite is bought by a Syrian pimp, while the celebrated poet Euripides turns up to buy some of the strange metaphysical concepts he keeps putting into his Tragedies, only of course they don't exist anywhere outside his needled brain. Eventually he buys Hermes, since as God of Thieves and the Dead he'll be able to help Euripides steal even more ideas from his predecessors on the Tragic stage. The play ends with Cleon taking his place on Zeus' throne, while the fleet is wheeled off to be broken up and sold to the Spartans (in whose pocket Cleon has been all along) for firewood.

From all that, you can see that it was a dialogue-play rather than a chorus-play, and that's my personal preference. But I was particularly pleased with the Address to the Audience, when the Chorus-leader takes off his mask and comes to the front of the stage and addresses the audience as if he were the author. In it, I begged the citizens of Athens not to allow the campaigns in Sicily (which, as you've already guessed, was what the play was all about) to get out of hand; they were simply State piracy, I said; and although there's nothing wrong with that *per se*, it was plain stupidity to embark on any ambitious scheme of that sort when we hadn't dealt with the Spartans on a permanent basis. There would be plenty of time for conquering the universe when Sparta was a heap of rubble, I said; in the meantime, we should get on with the job in hand. I reminded everyone of the great disaster in the days of the celebrated Cimon, when we sent our whole army and fleet off gallivanting round Egypt when we should have been consolidating our gains against the Persians in Ionia, and most of them were wiped out in the marshes. If that happened now, I said, we would inevitably lose the war and the empire, and the Spartans would pull down the Long Walls and leave us an open city.

When I showed the play to Cratinus (for I was still young and naïve) he was quite sullen and bad-tempered, which meant that he thought it was good. Never believe what they say about truly great poets always being ready to encourage talented young newcomers; in my experience, the better a poet is the more paranoid he is about competitors. Anyway, I pressed him for a comment of some sort, and he finally admitted that it might conceivably stand a chance of coming second, in a bad year, if everyone else presented farces.

'Only for God's sake,' he said, 'fix that *parabasis*. That Sicilian stuff is a load of crap. When you advise against something, make it something that's likely to be proposed, or you're wasting your time. Nobody in their right mind would ever seriously consider trying to conquer Sicily.'

I think the Gods must hate sensible people.

CHAPTER SIX

Do you remember Diogenes the offspring of Zeus, who was the son of the Scythian who had an affair with Myrrhine, wife of the pious Euergetes? Well, his eldest son was named Diogenides (*'son* of the offspring of Zeus') who was born on the same day of the same year as me. Everyone knew the true story of his parentage, of course, and so he acquired the nickname of Little Zeus.

I met this remarkable person when I first harvested my own olives at Phyle; he was one of the itinerant day-labourers who came looking for work. You may be surprised that the scion of such a noble line should be reduced to being another man's employee, which is the worst degradation (barring actual slavery) that a human being can endure; think of what Achilles says in the *Iliad*, when he renounces glory —

> I'd rather be alive and a farm labourer,
> Working for a poor man with only a few acres,
> Than be King and Kaiser of the glorious Dead.

But Little Zeus had been the victim of one of those family disasters that can ruin the noblest of houses. His father had had seven children, all sons, and none of them had died in childhood.

Diogenes had done his best to reduce this formidable total. He had brought them up to love boar-hunting and horse-racing and other aristocratic but dangerous sports; but they had all proved naturally talented, and all survived. He set them, while still young, to watch the sheep on wolf-infested hillsides; but they killed all the wolves with their slingshots and became heroes. Finally, during the plague, he moved house to the middle of the Ceramicus; but the only member of his family to die was Diogenes himself.

The result was that his thirty acres of vines, which produced enough wealth to keep him in the Cavalry class, was split up into seven plots of just over four acres, one for each son. This would have been bad enough, but since the Spartans chose that year to devastate Archarnae, the seven heirs of the Offspring of Zeus each inherited nothing but vine-stalks and smashed trellises.

The brothers paid for Diogenes' funeral by selling his Infantry armour, registered for service as oarsmen, and set out to make the best living they could. The other six stayed in the City and were soon regular jurymen, loyal members of what we used to call the Order of the Three Obols; but Little Zeus (who was, by the way, the tallest and biggest man I ever met) felt that such a life was too demeaning for a descendant of a family who had been in Athens before Theseus was ever born, and became a hired hand, hoping to save enough money to buy vine-shoots when the war was over and replant his four acres.

He told me this tragic story as we harvested the olives – me up in the tree knocking them down with a stick, and Little Zeus underneath catching them in a basket – and I am not ashamed to say that I wept (with laugher, naturally). However, since his four acres shared a short boundary with some land held by my mother's uncle Philodemus, he was effectively a neighbour, and since I was young and full of my new Cavalry status, I decided to help him.

Descending from the olive tree like Prometheus the Saviour from heaven, I said, 'Your troubles are at an end, Little Zeus. I will buy your four acres as a present for my uncle, and with the money you can set up as a trader or a craftsman, which is a better life than day-labouring.'

But Little Zeus shook his head vigorously. 'I wouldn't dream of it,' he said. 'That land is our land. We've lived there since before the Dorians came, and my forefathers are buried there. Do you want their Furies to haunt me?'

I was rather taken aback by this. 'All right then,' I said, 'I'll enter into a bond of hectemorage with you, and plant out your land for you in return for a sixth of your produce until you've paid off the debt.'

Again he shook his head, and spat into his gown to avert evil. 'My great-great-great-great-uncle was related by marriage to the sons of Solon, who tore up the mortgage-stones,' he replied. 'Do you think he would rest easy in his grave if one of his seed became a hectemore?' He lifted the basket of olives on to his shoulder with all the resignation of Niobe, and carried it over to where the donkey was tethered.

'Tell you what I'll do, then,' I said, struggling to keep a straight face, 'I'll plant out your four acres for you as a gift between neighbours, in memory of your immortal ancestor Solon.'

'He wasn't actually an ancestor, just a relative by marriage,' Little Zeus started to say; then he dropped the basket of olives. 'You'll do what?'

'And if,' I continued blithely, 'when your vines are yielding fifteen jars to the furrow, you would care to share your good fortune with a neighbour, I'm sure the great Solon would approve, from whichever mansion he shares in the Isles of the Blessed with Harmodius and Cleisthenes the Liberator.'

'As it happens,' said Little Zeus, 'I am indirectly descended from the glorious Cleisthenes.' And he told me all about it as he shovelled the spilt olives back into the basket.

From that day onwards, I found it hard to turn round without finding Little Zeus there, all six and a half feet of him, watching me intently like a dog at feeding-time. He was forever warning me to take care lest I slip when the street was muddy, and warning me of the approach of fast-moving wagons; and if he thought the water I was about to drink was in any way tainted, he would snatch the cup from my hand, pour the water out, and sprint off to refill it from the nearest reliable well. At first I put this down to natural gratitude and was deeply touched. It was only later that I realised that he was determined not to let any harm come to me until his four acres were safely planted and producing. Twice he was nearly arrested and brought to trial for striking citizens, because they dared come near me when Little Zeus thought they might have the plague; and when I went to visit Phaedra once, he killed her father's dog because he imagined it was about to bite me.

Apart from this obsession, however, and his total lack of a sense of humour, Little Zeus had many sterling qualities. He was totally fearless – which is under-standable given his immense size – and a tireless worker, once he had got it into his head that he was not so much a hired hand but a sort of dispossessed prince at the court of a royal benefactor who would one day restore him to his possessions. As befitted a man in this Homeric position, he strove to act as a hero should, 'always being the best' as the poet says, and excelling all around him in whatever the task of the moment happened to be. He would stay at the plough when the rest of us had long since given up and collapsed under a handy fig tree; and when he stood guard over the vines with a slingshot, not a single bird dared show the tip of its beak for miles around. He swung his mattock as if he were Ajax and the clods of earth were Trojan warriors, so that the rest of us were showered with flying stones and fragments of root; and when the harvest or the vintage was carried in, he would bear almost his own weight in produce, all the way from the barns to the City, watching me every step of the way like a hawk to make sure I didn't slip or fall on the mountain-tracks.

In the City, too, his zeal to please and excel was unabatable. Whenever there was wine or company he would sing the Harmodius until the roof shook; he had a fine voice but rather too much of it. As befitted a gentleman, he knew all the aristocratic poets – Theognis and Archilochus and every word ever written by Pindar – which was a great help to me when I needed a quotation for parody in a play. His greatest aesthetic accomplishment, however, was his ability to give a one-man performance of Aeschylus' *Persians*; his great-grandfather, needless to say, had been in the same rank of the phalanx as the great poet at Marathon, so the play was virtually family property. First he would be the Chorus of Persian nobles – with occasional interpolations such as 'This is the authentic mourning posture of the Persian aristocracy; my great-grandfather saw them in the battle, you know' – and then he would be each of the actors, turning round to indicate a change of speakers during the dialogues and raising his voice to a squeak for the female roles, until his audience had to stuff their gowns into their mouths to keep themselves from laughing. Once my dear Callicrates was too slow and a snigger eluded him, at which Little Zeus stopped in mid-verse and looked round to see who had cracked a joke.

By and large, then, Little Zeus was an asset to me as I started to go about in Cavalry society. For I had outgrown, in a very short time, the Infantry friends of Callicrates and Philodemus, and I wanted to get to know the men I was insulting in my Comedy: the politicians like Cleon and Hyperbolus, and their henchmen Theorus and Cleonymus; the Tragic poets Agathon and

Euripides, and the wicked and corrupt scientists, men like Socrates and Chaerophon, who was reputed to be a vampire.

Of course I knew all these people by sight and had greeted them by name in the Fish Market or the Propylaea, but that was not the same thing as drinking out of the same cup or joining them in the songs. It is essential for a Comic poet when he brings on a real person that he should be able to reproduce exactly the way that person speaks, and teach his actor precisely how each man makes his characteristic gestures. There is no substitute for close observation in this respect; anyone can make Cleon shout or Alcibiades talk with a lisp, but what makes the audience laugh is the way Cleon always brushes away the dust with his hand before he sits down, and Alcibiades' habit of sneezing elegantly over his shoulder.

I remember as if it was yesterday the first really prestigious party I went to. It was given by Aristophanes to celebrate his victory with *The Acharnians* – a truly awful play and well worth avoiding if you ever come across a revival of it in one of those theatres-cum-cattle-pens in the outlying parts of Attica where they still occasionally produce old plays for people who can't get to the City – and I was in two minds whether to go or not, bearing in mind my previous encounters with that gentleman. However, a houseboy had appeared at our front door that morning, bidding Eupolis of Pallene to bring food and himself to the house of Aristophanes son of Philip at nightfall, and I could not resist the invitation, especially when I heard who else the boy had been told to summon.

'I've already called on Theorus, and he's coming,' he said, 'and Socrates the scientist, who's promised to come, and next I'm going to call on Euripides the poet, who's bound to come after what my master made him say in the play; and Cleisthenes the Pervert will probably accept, because he likes being put in plays and wants to be in the next one.'

'Why me?' I asked, and added, pouring out a cup of wine, 'Go on, you can tell me.'

'My master said invite you so I did,' said the boy, draining the cup quickly. 'And now I've got to get on. Good health!'

So that evening, with Callicrates and Little Zeus as my supporters, I set off for Aristophanes' house, carrying with me two fine sea bass in a rich cream sauce, a basket of wheat bread and twelve roast thrushes which Little Zeus had snared the day before. I had not the faintest idea what to expect, and my heart was beating like a drum.

You could hear the singing half-way down the street.

> 'We call upon our local Muse,
> Our wonderfuel goddess Coal;
> The radiant heat thy chips produce
> Shines in the embers of our soul . . .'

Which was the Invocation from *The Acharnians*, of course, and the loud and rather tuneless voice leading it was unmistakably that of the poet himself, as I had heard him singing the Harmodius in the Serenade. One day, I thought, they'll be singing something of mine to celebrate a victory, with Little Zeus bawling out the words so loud they'll hear them in Corinth. I set my jaw as firmly as I could, and hammered on the door with my stick.

'You heat the pan,' they sang, 'that fries the fish,

> That turns the sprats a golden brown,
> (Golden BROWN!)
> Come, Anthracite, and grant a wish,
> To all who love Acharnae town!'

Pathetic, I murmured under my breath, and the house-boy opened the door.

'You're late,' he said, shouting to make himself heard, 'so they've started without you. Don't you know how to behave in good society?'

This scarcely encouraged me, but Callicrates grinned, and we made our way through to join the party.

Let me first describe the house. It was most sumptuously furnished, with hangings on the walls that had obviously been liberated from the Theatre; I recognised the front of Chremylus' house from *The Banqueters*, and the treadmill from *The Babylonians*. The floor was newly strewn, there were couches *and* chairs for everyone – never had I seen so many chairs together in one place – and the mixing-bowl for the wine was not earthenware but bronze. All the storage jars were painted, the flitch of bacon hung over the hearth by a brass chain, and the clothes chest was richly carved cedarwood, almost certainly imported. Up in the rafters I could see Aristophanes' shield; the rim was embossed with figures, and on its face, where usually there is a painted Gorgon to strike terror into the enemy, was a grotesque portrait of Cleon, his jaws open in the middle of a thundering tirade. The shield was also totally unmarked, which showed how much soldiering the fearless young poet had actually done. The rest of his armour was draped over an old-fashioned statue of Hermes in the corner of the room, with a sword-belt hanging from its upraised phallus, and three Victor's Wreaths encircling its brows under the (virtually unworn) helmet.

If the house made Philodemus' establishment look like a hovel, the company was enough to make me feel as if I had lived my life among grooms and fishmongers. Not only had all the guests that I had been told about turned up; there was also Philonides, the best Chorus-trainer in Athens, and Moschus the flute-player (specially hired, would you believe, just to entertain the guests), and, reclining next to the host and looking thoroughly bored, the most notorious man in Athens, Alcibiades.

Imagine what effect this had on me, already petrified and hardly able to speak. But my soul inside me told me to be strong, as if I were facing a squadron of cavalry or a ravenous bear, and I stepped forward, presenting the food I had brought with a modest smile. Cleisthenes the Pervert must have heard the words 'roast thrush', for without turning his head he leaned back, grabbed one of the birds from the tray, popped it into his mouth, crunched it up, and spat out the bones, and never once interrupted the highly dramatic story he was telling. Obviously the art of being a gentleman didn't just consist of being able to recite Archilochus.

Aristophanes rose languidly to his feet and embraced me, whispering in my ear as he did so, 'Say one word about that damned goat and I'll kill you.' Then he banged on the table with a jug for silence and introduced me, declaring, 'This is Eupolis son of Euchorus of Pallene', which seemed to be all he could find to say about me.

There was a mortifying silence, as all the guests looked at me. I did my best to smile, and Alcibiades sniggered.

'And this is Euripides the poet,' Aristophanes went on, 'and Theorus the politician, and here we have Socrates son of Cleverness,' naming each guest to me in turn as if I were an idiot or a foreigner, who had never been in the City before and thought the Acropolis was a public granary. Not for the first or the last time, I could cheerfully have murdered Aristophanes.

I took my place on the end couch and hid behind my neighbour, Theorus, whom I knew very slightly. He had been made to look a fool in *The Acharnians*, and was ever so faintly resentful, so I decided he might be an ally. As he passed the cup to me, therefore, I whispered to him, 'Noble Theorus, why in God's name have I been invited to this? All these exotic people . . . I've never been in company like this in all my life.'

Theorus laughed; he was a fat man, and seemed to tremble all over. 'In a way it's a compliment,' he said, taking back the cup and spilling wine over his gown. 'Our host has heard of you.'

'Me?' I said, astonished.

'What do you expect,' Theorus yawned, 'if you go about reciting your choruses and dialogue to anyone who'll listen? The son of Philip has heard most of your *General* from one source or another, and I believe you have him worried. So for God's sake, whatever you do; get drunk, smash up the tables, set fire to Socrates' beard, anything you like; but don't go reciting any speeches, or you'll find that when your *General* is brought on, the audience will have heard that speech before, only slightly modified.'

I was stunned. 'You think he'd steal it?' I said.

'If you're lucky, yes,' said Theorus, 'and then let it be known that you stole it from him at this very party, abusing his hospitality like a Theban. If you're unlucky, of course, he'll write a parody of it. Then you'll get laughs all right, but not the sort you want. I think he's already nobbled your joke about the eels.'

I was uncertain whether to be furiously angry or deeply flattered, but my soul within me advised being flattered, so I laughed. It was obviously the right thing to do, for Theorus drew a little closer to me and went on:

'If you want to get your own back on the son of Philip, see if you can't find some excuse to tell the story about the goats on Hymettus, which we're all simply dying to hear.' Then a thought seemed to strike him, and he said quickly, 'No, don't do that. Just tell me now, quietly.'

I told him, and he laughed again, and by then all the food was finished. Little Zeus and Callicrates (who was pretending to be my servant so that he could stay and watch the party) rescued my plates and trays, and the flute-girls came out and started playing. The party was about to begin.

I don't know if you go to that sort of party very often; if you do, you'll know what the talk is like before the wine starts to take hold. At first, it's all very aristocratic stuff – 'When I was on an embassy to Mytilene', and 'The largest boar we ever bagged when I hunted in Crete', or 'That was the year Alexicacus won the chariot-race at Delphi; I shall never forget.' This was where Theorus and Cleisthenes the Pervert were in their element, although of course Alcibiades had the last word on everything. Then Aristophanes made a sign to the houseboy to increase the ratio of wine to water in the mixing-bowl, and after a while everyone was talking frantically about the Gods and the nature of Justice. Socrates the scientist and Euripides started a private two-handed battle here, and gradually everyone else stopped talking and listened. As for me, I had both my ears open, since this was the sort of thing I so urgently needed for my play. For a while, the issue hung in the balance, for Euripides was able to speak very quickly. Eventually, however, he began to tire, and Socrates managed to seize the reins.

'I take your point, Euripides,' he said, unfairly taking advantage of his opponent's fit of coughing, 'but I'm still not sure what you mean by *attending to*.'

'Well . . .'

'I presume,' Socrates continued blithely, 'that you don't mean attending to the Gods in the way we use the word . . . Well, to take an example at random, we say that not everyone knows how to attend to horses, but only the horse-trainer. Correct?'

'Well, yes, but . . .'

'Because horse-training is attending to horses?'

'Yes, but . . .'

'And in the same way, not everyone knows how to tend dogs . . .'

'Quite, but . . .'

'But only,' Socrates went on, raising his voice ever so slightly, 'the dog-trainer?'

'Absolutely, yes, But . . .'

'And cattle-farming is attending to cattle?'

'Undoubtedly. But . . .'

'Then piety must be attending to the Gods, mustn't it, Euripides? Is that what you're getting at?'

'Well . . .'

Socrates grinned and went on, 'Yes, of course. But isn't the effect of attendance always the same?'

A pause, for Euripides has lost his train of thought entirely. 'Yes,' he says lamely. 'But . . .'

'What I mean is, it's for the good of the thing attended to, so that, to use your example, horses are benefited by horse-training.'

'Actually, it was your . . .'

'And so (I presume) are dogs by dog-training, and cattle by cattle-farming, and so on.'

'But . . .'

'Or do you think,' said Socrates, narrowing his formidable brows, 'that attendance aims to hurt the thing attended?'

'Obviously not,' replied Euripides. 'But . . .'

'It aims at the benefit of it?'

'Yes, yes, of course. What . . .'

'Then if piety is *attending on* the Gods, as you said, is it a benefit to the Gods?' A little gesture here; a shrug of the shoulders and a raising of one eyebrow. 'Does it help them in some way to become better Gods, or somehow more Godlike?'

'No, of course not. But . . .'

'I didn't think you meant that, Euripides,' replied Socrates, sitting back in his couch. 'Now, what were you saying?'

Of course, by this stage Euripides had entirely forgotten what he had been trying to say, and just sat there with his mouth open. Before he could marshal his thoughts, Socrates started off again, and soon had him tied up in little knots over the meaning of the word 'service', until Aristophanes restored order by banging on the table again.

Then the mix of wine and water was strengthened again, and we began to talk about Poetry. Especially Comic Poetry, with particular regard to the excellence of *The Acharnians*. This went on for quite some time, as you can imagine, what with Euripides trying to be ever so polite about the extended personal attack on him in the play, and Philonides the Chorus-trainer telling a long and pointless anecdote about a Chorus-member who always kicked left when he should have kicked right. All this talk – even the boring anecdote – was extremely exciting for me, and I think Aristophanes must have noticed how enthralled I was, for he sent his boy over to me with the wine, and said, 'Friend Eupolis here is going to be a Comic poet.' He didn't add 'when he grows up', but he certainly implied it. 'I think we should hear a little of this *Colonel* of his, don't you?'

Theorus dug me in the ribs with his elbow, and I had an inspiration.

'Surely not,' I replied, mumbling slightly. 'I'd be ashamed to repeat my rubbish under the roof of a master. Can't we have the big speech from *The Acharnians* instead? I know that by heart.'

'Later perhaps,' Aristophanes said. 'But now we'd like something by the immortal Eupolis. Wouldn't we?'

'Well, if you insist,' I replied modestly. 'Let me see,' I mused, 'I could give you the Goatherds' dialogue from *The Steading of Pisistratus*.'

Aristophanes turned bright red. 'Not a dialogue scene,' he said. 'They're so hard for one speaker to do properly. Let's have something from this *Brigadier* of yours.'

'There's a good scene at the end,' I replied. 'A drunken party, with a Thessalian witch in it.'

Some of the others had got an idea what was going on by now. 'That sounds good,' they said. 'Let's have the Thessalian witch.'

'Dreadfully *passé*, those witch scenes,' Aristophanes muttered, 'don't you think? What about your *parabasis*? That would be worth hearing, wouldn't it?'

It was a nasty moment, but I kept my head. You may remember that I told you that my mother used to say that I spoke verse before I spoke prose. Well, when really pushed, I can extemporise verse – not very good verse, granted, but verse that scans. I took a deep breath, cleared my throat, and began to recite anapaests.

It took several lines before Aristophanes realised what I was doing, and then, of course, it was too late to stop me. The theme of this extempore *parabasis* of mine was that hardy perennial, scurrilous abuse of one's rival competitors. I started off with the hackneyed attack on Cratinus – his drinking and repellent habits and so on – then did a couple of lines on Pherecrates before launching into my main target Aristophanes, basing myself on his own attacks on Cleon for the more virulent compound epithets.

Not only (I said) does the son of Philip steal goats; he also lifts jokes and scenes and whole choruses from better and cleverer poets, which he overhears in wine shops and the public baths and copies down in the little pocket tablet he carries inside the sleeve of his gown. Of course he writes so quickly that he often gets a word wrong here or there, and since he's too thick to understand really clever writing, he doesn't notice the mistakes and reproduces them in the text he gives up to the Committee. His motive for this wholesale plagiarism is not, as you might suppose, envy; rather, it's partly to eke out his own bald and unimaginative texts, and partly because he doesn't have much time for writing, what with all his little trips to Sparta to tell his friend Brasidas about our naval tactics – what, didn't you know about that? Why else do you suppose he's always urging the City to accept the peace offers from Sparta, when it's obvious that they're woefully inadequate. You ask for proof? Well, you know how the Spartans don't use coins for money like normal people, but instead use great big iron bars, like spits. If you'd ever been to Aristophanes' house, you'd see a brand new iron spit in his hearth, with '*Made in Sparta*' stamped on it in Doric letters.

At which, everyone's eyes turn to the hearth, and see a beautiful iron spit inscribed in Doric letters ('*Made in Plataea*', actually, but I was the only person close enough to read it), and a great shout of laughter goes up from the company. Euripides in particular seems highly amused.

'Encore!' he shouts. 'And *now* let's have the Thessalian witch.'

'No, really,' I said, holding up my hand for silence, 'off with the flute-players and on with the actors, as I believe you poets say. Let's have the big speech from *The Acharnians*, like you promised.'

Of course, the big speech from *The Acharnians* is a plea for peace with Sparta, saying that the outbreak of the war was as much our fault as theirs – which was exactly why I'd made him promise to recite it. In short, I did to him what Theorus said he intended to do to me, and although the audience laughed at his great speech, they laughed for quite the wrong reason.

After that, we sang Harmodius and played riddles, and Moschus played the Orthian; but I was too exhausted to take much of a part in the proceedings. I ended up sitting next to Philonides the Chorus-trainer; and while Theorus (who by now was completely drunk) was singing a Hymn to Dionysus, he leant over to me and said, 'When you're old enough to bring on your *General*, you'll need a Chorus-trainer.'

'Certainly,' I replied.

'I like to see a play as soon as it's written, so that I can start blocking out the moves. My house is near the Temple of Hephaestus – anyone round there will point it out to you.'

I thanked him as best I could, but he grinned and

turned away. In those days, for a Chorus-trainer like Philonides to approach a poet was almost unheard of; rather like a captain of a warship asking the crew's advice on when to start rowing.

Not wishing to push my luck, I left the party shortly afterwards. This, of course, was a mistake – you should never leave a party until either all your enemies have gone or everyone is too drunk to be dangerous. I later heard that after I had left my name was linked with a number of very unsavoury characters. For some reason, when someone spreads a rumour at a party, people always believe him; and one of the guests who heard that rumour was Alcibiades . . .

But I was so full of myself for days afterwards that there was no living with me, and even Philodemus and my dear Callicrates began to regard me as insufferable. I naturally put this down to jealousy; but it started me thinking that when quite soon I came of age, I would be leaving Philodemus' house and becoming a householder in my own right. In which case, obviously, I would need a wife.

I had been visiting Phaedra and her family ever since the night of the Serenade, so that my intentions by now were plainly obvious. Her family seemed to welcome the idea of me as a son-in-law, which I put down to my wealth and, I fear, my wit and magnetic personality. In fact, they seemed quite happy to do without some of the required stages of courtship and get straight on to a betrothal.

But Philodemus, who was conducting the negotiations for me, seemed unwilling to press on so quickly, and insisted on formal discussions about the dowry, even though they seemed quite happy to pay what we asked. I found this infuriating, and we quarrelled about it.

'But don't you see, you young idiot?' he told me. 'If they're so keen to offload the girl on you, there must be some reason . . .'

'Offload?' I replied angrily. 'What do you mean offload? She's beautiful and accomplished, they're offering ten acres . . .'

'Exactly,' said my uncle. 'And still, at nearly sixteen, the girl is unpromised. What's your explanation?'

'Simple,' I replied, trying desperately to think of one. 'She was promised to a man who suddenly lost all his wealth or was killed in the war.'

'Don't you think they'd have mentioned something like that?' he persisted.

'Since the subject has never come up,' I replied grandly, 'no.'

'If the subject has never come up,' said my uncle despairingly, 'all that proves is that you're a bigger idiot than I thought.'

I decided to attack. 'All right, then,' I said, 'what do you think the reason is? Like I said, she's beautiful and accomplished, and the dowry is marvellous, and I'm absolutely sure she doesn't have any deformities or diseases. That doesn't leave much, does it?'

Philodemus shook his head. 'I don't know either,' he said, 'and neither does anyone else. But all the people I know are Infantry; they don't mix in Cavalry circles. And Callicrates says he thinks his army friends know something but won't say.'

'You've been asking?' I said furiously.

'Of course I have,' said Philodemus. 'It's my duty to ask, or why do you think marriages are arranged this way? It's so that young idiots like you with stars instead of eyes don't end up marrying girls with Thracian grandmothers or only one leg.'

I decided to be reasonable. 'Look,' I said, 'I know you're doing what you think is for the best and I appreciate it, really I do. But there's nothing wrong with Phaedra. I swear there isn't.'

'Then why,' said Philodemus, 'don't you ask some of your new Cavalry friends we hear so much about in this house, and see if they know anything?'

This made me very angry. 'So that's what it's all about, is it?' I shouted. 'You think I should be marrying some Infantry girl with red hands and a few goats on Parnes. Got someone in mind, have you, with a nice little commission in it for yourself from her grateful father?'

For a moment I thought Philodemus was going to hit me, and I backed away. He turned bright red in the face and grabbed his walking-stick; then with a visible effort he calmed down and became as cold as ice.

'If that's the way you feel,' he said, 'I shall conclude the negotiations on the terms as offered, and then you can go to the crows for all I care. And I hope your damned Phaedra turns out to have two club feet and leprosy.'

I tried to apologise but he was offended, so I made my excuses and left. As I walked up to the Market Square I thought over what he had said, and it occurred to me that the only person I knew who seemed to know something about Phaedra was Aristophanes. Hadn't he said something about her 'habits' on the night of the Serenade? But how could I go and ask him for help, when I had made him look a fool in front of his guests? True, I had only been paying him back in advance, so to speak, for what he was going to do to me; but I doubted whether he would see it in that light. And then a horrible thought struck me. What if Theorus, who had a grudge against him, had lied to me about Aristophanes' motive in inviting me? What if he had invited me so that I could meet Philonides the Chorus-trainer and all those other important people? My blood seemed to freeze in my veins. Supposing the great Comic poet had been extending the hand of friendship, as one craftsman to another, and I had repaid him by wrecking his Victory celebrations? The more I thought about it, the more convinced I became that Theorus had been lying – he was not, after all, the sort of man you would believe if he told you your name – and that I had made the most terrible mistake.

As I wandered through the anchovy stalls, feeling as if I had just murdered my host, who should I bump into but Aristophanes himself? He was arguing heatedly with a fishmonger about an eel he had bought the day before, and which he swore blind was off. The fishmonger was adamant that a real Copaic eel, smuggled through enemy lines at the risk of the courier's life, was bound to smell a bit hooky, that that was what gave them their flavour, and a proper gentleman would know Copaic eel when he tasted it. Aristophanes replied that he knew perfectly well what Copaic eels tasted like, that he had eaten them in the company of the richest men in Athens, and that a proper Copaic eel doesn't make you throw up like Mount Aetna half an hour later. The fishmonger, who obviously never went to the Theatre and so didn't know the risk he was taking, replied that even the best-behaved Copaic eel is likely to get a bit frisky when a man of dubious citizenship like Aristophanes son of Philip gobbled it up like a starving dog, instead of chewing it like a gentleman, and then washed it down with half a jar of unmixed wine.

Aristophanes gave up the unequal struggle and retired to a neighbouring stall to buy a crab. I came up behind him and tapped him on the shoulder. He jumped.

'What in God's name did you do that for?' he snapped. 'I nearly swallowed my change.'

I apologised, feeling that I had not begun this vital interview in the best possible way. Aristophanes fished an obol out of his mouth, paid for the crab and started to walk away.

'Please, Aristophanes,' I said humbly, 'I want to apologise for spoiling your party.'

'So I should think,' he said cautiously. 'That's the last time I try to help a young poet.'

'Someone told me a dreadful lie about you,' I

explained, 'and I got so drunk that I believed it.'

'You didn't seem very drunk when you were spewing up those anapaests,' he said. 'Honestly, I didn't know where to look. And can you think of a worse omen than that for a Victory party? I'll be lucky if I get a Chorus at all next year.'

I had forgotten how superstitious he was, and I blushed. 'I really am sorry,' I mumbled. 'It really was a stupid thing to do.'

'Never mind,' he said, forcing himself to smile. 'After all what could be a better omen than to be mentioned in a *parabasis*? Means I'm bound to get a Chorus, or why am I being mentioned at all? Forget it, Eupolis. Set it off against that confounded goat.'

He slapped me, hard, on the back and I smiled. 'I'm glad we've got that sorted out, then,' I said, 'because I want your advice.'

'Certainly,' he said warmly. 'Got a scene you're having trouble with?'

'No, it's not that.'

'Oh.' He looked disappointed, and I saw that he really was taking an interest in my career.

'No, it's about my marriage. You remember that girl you . . .'

'At the Serenade?'

'Yes.'

'Phaedra. Nice girl. What about her?'

'That's what I wanted to ask you, actually. I've been wondering why a girl like that, with everything going for her, is still unpromised.'

A smile crossed Aristophanes' face, and he put an arm around my shoulders. 'I thought you might wonder that,' he said.

'Do you know something then?'

'As it happens, I know the whole story. Buy me a drink and I'll tell you all about it.'

We went across to a wine shop and I bought a jar of

the finest Pramnian. We exchanged healths, and he told me the story. It was just as I had guessed. Phaedra had indeed been promised, and to a truly marvellous man called Amyntas. I had heard of him, vaguely.

'Wasn't he killed in the war?' I asked.

'It was a tragedy,' said Aristophanes sadly. 'Friend of mine, actually. Died defending a wounded comrade. Phaedra was heartbroken.'

'I can imagine,' I said.

'Of course, the family hadn't announced a formal betrothal – there was some problem with the dowry; apparently Amyntas' family were asking seven acres, when the girl would be a bargain without any dowry at all. What are they offering you, by the way?'

'Ten acres,' I said. Aristophanes whistled, and went on:

'I imagine they haven't mentioned it because of the bargain they had to strike with Phaedra after she heard the news. Apparently she was so upset that she was all for running away and becoming a priestess of Demeter. They only stopped her by promising never to mention his name again. You know what girls are like.'

'Of course, I see,' I said. 'Well, thank you, you've taken a great weight off my mind.'

'If I were you,' said Aristophanes, drinking off the rest of the wine and wiping his chin daintily, 'I'd get the betrothal all sealed and concluded as quickly as possible, before she starts thinking about her lost love and changes her mind. You may have noticed that her parents are a bit anxious to get her married off; you can see their point, can't you?'

'Absolutely. Thank you.'

'Not at all, not at all,' said Aristophanes. 'After all, considering how I insulted the poor girl that night, the least I can do is make sure she gets a suitable husband.'

'And what you said about her habits. . . .?'

'I forgot to mention that,' said Aristophanes. 'She's a

lovely child, but she's a terror for accidentally knocking over vases. It's the only thing that can be said against her, so far as I know. Is that the time? I've got to rush.'

I thanked him again, and set off for home to make my peace with Philodemus. Not only, I reflected, had I found out the truth about my beloved Phaedra; I had also made a good and worthwhile friend.

CHAPTER SEVEN

In Tragedy, of course, there is a convention that the action – the battles and the murders and so on – always happens off-stage. Orestes drags Clytemnestra off into the wings and we hear horrible screams, while the Chorus turn to face the audience and make their breathtakingly profound comments, like 'All is not well within the house'; then the playwright treats us to five minutes of metrical lamentation and the proceedings are adjourned. When I was young I always felt cheated by this squeamishness, and I remember one year slipping out of my seat (I think it was an Agamemnon of some description) and sprinting round to the wings to see if I could see the King getting his skull split. I found a little tear in the painted backcloth and looked through, but all I saw was the actor frantically pulling his mask and gown off to change into the Messenger costume.

So now I am tempted to follow the Tragic convention, and let my wedding take place behind the curtain. Flutes. The torchlight procession winds its way round the orchestra and in through the left-hand door, the door closes, all is not well within the house. But there; any fool can be a Tragedian. It takes courage to compose Comedy.

Actually, I remember very little of the wedding itself.

It was a mild evening, not too warm, and I had the sort of headache that makes everything else seem entirely irrelevant. It was obvious from the start that the whole thing was going to be a complete and utter disaster, but that was only to be expected, considering that I had seen my name posted in the Market Square that morning on the Three Days' Rations list.

'Where are we going?' I asked the man standing next to me.

'Samos,' he said, 'just for a change.' He spat out a mouthful of chickpeas. 'You ever been there?'

I said no, I hadn't.

'Samos,' he said gravely, 'is the armpit of the Aegean. The goats are all gristle and the people pee in the wells. The west coast is all right if you're not prone to catching fever, but we're probably going to be over on the east. This time of year, of course, it's worse than usual . . .'

'I'm getting married this evening.'

He scowled at me, and spat into the fold of his tunic. 'Get away from me,' he said. 'I don't want anything to do with you if you're unlucky.'

That, I think, is when my headache started. I spent the rest of the morning cleaning my armour, which had gone green up in the rafters, and putting a new plume in my helmet. Little Zeus tried to help, but his contribution consisted of putting his foot through my shield. I sent him out to get it mended, and poured myself a large cup of neat wine, which was a mistake.

'Cheer up,' Callicrates said, as we tried to force the plume into the socket. 'After all, you've got your wedding to look forward to, don't forget.'

My hand slipped and came down hard on the sharp bronze of the socket, splashing blood on to the white horsehair. 'I'm not likely to forget,' I replied. 'Have you seen my sword-belt anywhere?'

'Borrow mine,' he said, 'it's about your size. It's just a tax-collecting expedition, apparently. I was talking to a man who'd heard the debate. You'll be back in a month or so, I expect.'

I shrugged. 'I couldn't care less,' I said.

'The important thing to remember about Samos,' he went on, 'is not to eat the sausages. A friend of mine – you know, Porphyrion who has that dog with the stunted tail – he was in Samos a year or so ago when there was that trouble, and he says they don't boil the blood properly before pouring it into the skins. Otherwise it's not a bad place, except that the women throw stones a lot.'

'Why?'

'They don't like Athenians, I guess. Has anyone been across to tell Phaedra?'

'No,' I replied. 'Will you go?'

He shrugged his shoulders. 'If you want,' he said. 'I promised to take the cooks around some time this morning.'

I had forgotten about the cooks. We had hired five of them for the wedding, but one had gone down with dysentery. It made me wonder about the other four.

In the afternoon, I went to the baths and had my hair cut and scented. The barber talked about nothing but the war, and how it was not going well, and how someone had seen a really horrible omen.

'What I heard,' he shouted over his shoulder, 'was that when the watch were handing over the keys last night, this great big snake appeared out of nowhere – thick as your wrist and a sort of olive green was what they told me – and curled all round the key. Now if you ask me . . .'

'Bollocks,' said a man at the back of the shop. 'Now if the key had curled all round the snake, that would be an omen.'

The barber ignored him. 'The key's obviously this lot they're sending off to Samos. Stands to reason.'

'Why's that?'

'Don't show your ignorance,' said the barber, picking a spot of verdigris off the blade of his razor. 'The top man in Samos these days is called Draco – "The Snake" – right? This Draco's going to surround our boys and squash them flat.'

'There's an oracle about that,' said someone else. 'The snake is going to bite the feet of the owl, and the wedding-torches will light a hundred funerals.'

'What wedding-torches?' said the barber. 'I think they just put in any old thing to make it scan.'

When I got home, the torch-bearers were having a fight with the flute-girls and Little Zeus was back with my shield. It had a great big plate of new bronze riveted over the tear, which was apparently the best they could do at such short notice.

'It's all for the best, if you ask me,' he said cryptically. 'Do you want your sword sharpening, or can I get on with my packing?'

'Where are you going?' I asked.

'With you, of course. Shield-bearer. You're entitled to a shield-bearer, being Cavalry class. I asked about it down at the smithy.'

For a split second I was touched; then I remembered the five acres. 'Get the rations packed,' I said wearily, 'and put in plenty of cheese.'

About an hour before sunset I started to shiver, and I drank another cupful of neat wine. I had discovered that my left greave was too tight, and in trying to open it up I buckled the clips. While I was wrestling with it, Philodemus came in and asked me if I had made a will.

Not long after, I heard the flutes in the street; they were bringing in the bride. Suddenly I felt a sort of blind terror. They were singing the wedding-hymn, but for some reason it sounded flat and mournful, and I remember hoping that they would pass on to the next house.

Callicrates put his head round the door. 'For God's sake,' he said, 'aren't you ready yet? I'd better tell them to slow down. Get your garland on, will you? And try to look interested.'

I pulled on my new sandals, fumbling with the straps. There were little Cyclopes forging thunderbolts in my head, and I felt sick. The thought of dancing made my blood run cold. I could hear Philodemus arguing with the women in the inner room, something about some idiot sprinkling the wrong flower-petals on the marriage-bed, and whose brilliant idea was it to put out the coverlet with Pentheus and the Bacchae on it? I stood up and splashed cold water on my face. 'Get that fool of a nephew of mine out here this instant,' Philodemus was shouting. 'I wish to God I'd stayed in bed this morning.'

The smell of burning resin from the torches made my stomach lurch, and I wanted to hit somebody, but there is a time and a place for everything. I made my way to the front door and jammed a smile on to my face. It didn't fit. I think my teeth were in the way.

> 'With just such a song hymenaean
> Aforetime the Destinies led
> The Master of Thrones empyrean
> The King of the Gods, to the bed
> Of Hera, his beautiful bride . . .'

I had made a point of asking them not to sing that particular wedding-ode; but perhaps it was the only one they knew. Something with a bit of a *tune* to it, they must have said to themselves, something that everyone can join in . . .

> 'And Love, with his pinions of gold,
> Came driving, all blooming and spruce,
> As groomsman and squire, to behold
> The wedding of Hera and Zeus . . .'

Which, as any child will tell you, has never exactly been a success, what with Zeus turning himself into swans and showers of gold, and Hera sending plagues of sores down on all her husband's favourite cities. I adjusted my garland; but I felt more like a sacrifice than a bridegroom. Who gives this lamb to be slaughtered? And why, in God's name, was I feeling like this?

Then I saw Phaedra being led along by her father, and she looked like that painting of Galatea by Scythines in the Temple of Hephaestus, on the left as you go in. You know how she's just turning her head to look at Pygmalion, who's standing there with his mouth open, obviously feeling a complete fool; and her head is just slightly tilted, as if she's just noticed him, but she knows who he is; and she's just about to say something, and you stand there for minutes at a time in case she opens her lips. I've been in love with that painting as long as I can remember, and that was how Phaedra looked; and my head was hurting so badly I could hardly stand up straight. Perhaps it was the way she seemed so still, with all the wedding-guests lolloping about around her; or perhaps it was the glow of the torches, which seemed to make an unofficial sunset, with her as the setting sun. Certainly she looked very young indeed in the torchlight, but not a bit nervous, wrapped up like a parcel in all her wedding finery; and I thought of the old story of how the dictator Pisistratus got back into Athens after his exile by dressing up a woman as Athena, with gold dust sprinkled in her hair, and sending her in front of him in a golden chariot, so that all the City guards threw away their spears and fell flat on their faces, thinking that the Lady was bringing Pisistratus home.

The flutes stopped, and I stepped forward, feeling rather as I used to feel when it was my turn to recite at school and I couldn't remember beyond the third line. I reached out and made a grab for her hand. I think I got about three fingers. Her father was saying his lines, and I smiled idiotically. I couldn't remember mine to save my life. In fact, I believe we would all be there still if Callicrates hadn't whispered them in my ear.

Phaedra raised her head and looked into my eyes. Her face seemed as bright as the sun, and I suddenly felt much better. I drew her towards me into the house. She stumbled.

'Oh my God,' someone said, 'she's touched the threshold.' That is, of course, the worst possible omen.

'Shut up,' hissed someone else. 'For God's sake, somebody, sneeze.'

'It's a bit late for that, isn't it?' said the first voice. There was a trumpeting noise, which I took to be somebody feigning a sneeze.

'Oh well,' said Phaedra's father, 'it can't be helped now, I suppose.'

'Now,' she said archly, 'we're alone at last.'

The thong of my left sandal had resolved itself into an impenetrable knot, and the little miners inside my head had found a new lode. I mumbled something like 'How nice', and sat down on the floor. Things were not going well. My armour, spear and three days' rations were propped up against the wall, all ready for the morning, and I knew that two or three of the Thracian housemaid's children were listening at the door, for I had heard them sniggering about a quarter of an hour ago. Phaedra, apparently, had gone deaf.

'How's your poor head?' she cooed. 'Does it hurt awfully?'

'No,' I said sullenly. The sandal-thong broke, and I kicked it away.

'Would you mind putting something over *that*,' she pointed to the pile of armour with the helmet perched on top of it. 'It looks like somebody watching us.'

She had a point. I looped my cloak over it, and sat down on the bed.

'Shall I put the light out?' she whispered. I nodded and pulled my tunic off over my head. She licked her fingers and there was a tiny hiss as she pinched out the lamp. For some reason, I felt utterly miserable. 'Come on,' she said.

I crawled in beside her. She smelt, very faintly, of sweat.

'My cousin Archestratus went to Samos once,' she said.

'Oh yes?'

'He got bitten by something. They had to cut his foot off in the end.'

I took a deep breath and moved my arm, with the general idea of putting it round her shoulders. 'Ouch,' she said.

'Sorry.'

'That was my ear.'

I moved my arm and put it down on the pillow. 'Now you're pulling my hair,' she said. 'You really know how to get a girl in the mood, don't you?'

'Perhaps we'd better light the lamp,' I suggested.

'No,' she said firmly. 'Better not.'

'All right.'

'There are rose-petals all over this bed,' she said after a while.

'That's traditional, isn't it?'

She sniffed. 'It might be in your family,' she said. 'Can't you brush them out or something?'

'I'll light the lamp.'

'Please yourself.'

I always have been a fool with flints and tinder, and by the time I had the lamp going I could sense a distinct atmosphere of hostility in the room. 'Now,' I said, 'let's see about these rose-petals.'

'Forget it,' she said, and she threw her arms around me, like a swimmer nerving himself to dive into cold water. I had my mouth open at the time, and I felt her chin connect with my teeth. She unravelled herself and said, 'God, you're so clumsy. What do you think you're doing?'

'I'm sorry,' I mumbled. My lip hurt where she had banged it against my lower teeth, and when she kissed me, I winced. 'That does it,' she said, and she folded her arms across her breast.

'Don't be like that,' I said; but for some reason I felt rather relieved, just as I used to feel when the schoolmaster said, 'You obviously don't know it, do you? Sit down and let's hear from someone who does.' There was something not exactly inviting about Phaedra, just then.

'I've met some cack-handed people in my time,' she went on, 'but you're just about the worst, do you know that? This is supposed to be the happiest day of my life, you realise. That's a joke.'

'I'm sorry.'

'You're pathetic.' She blew her breath out through her teeth. 'And for God's sake shut your mouth. You look like a dead tuna.'

'Oh.'

She closed her eyes. 'And what did you think you were playing at, dragging me through the door like that? Anyone with any sense would have realised I was bound to catch my feet on the threshold, especially in those ridiculous sandals they made me wear. And now I'll have everybody saying I'm unlucky, and the maids blaming me if the milk goes sour.'

'I don't believe in all that stuff,' I said soothingly.

'I do,' she replied sharply. 'I suppose you don't believe in the Gods, either.'

'Yes I do.'

'That's not what I heard,' she muttered. 'I heard that you go around with that Euripides, who thinks that the Gods are all states of mind or something, and Helen of Troy was spirited away to Egypt before the Trojan War. Absolute rubbish.'

I felt I had missed something somewhere. 'What's Helen of Troy got to do with anything?' I asked.

'Do you believe in the Gods or don't you?'

'Of course I believe in the Gods. Phaedra, this is our wedding-night.'

'You've realised that, have you? Oh *good*.'

I put my hand on her shoulder. She removed it with her finger and thumb, as if it was a spider. 'And what sort of man,' she went on, 'gets called up for military service on his wedding-day? When they told me I couldn't believe it. I thought they were being funny, honestly I did.'

'That's not my fault, is it?' I said. I felt as if I was arguing with five different people at once, all about different things.

'Well let's just get one thing straight, shall we?' she said. 'There'll be none of that nonsense till you get back, and that's final.'

'What?'

'You heard me. If you think you're going to get me pregnant and then wander off and get yourself killed fooling about in Samos, and leave me to bring up your horrible little child on my own—'

'Phaedra—'

'I am a free-born Athenian woman, not a breeding heifer. Have you made a will?'

'What did you say?'

'Deaf as well as feckless,' she confided to the pillow. 'I said, have you made a will?'

'No.'

'Well, don't you think you should?'

I blinked. 'What, now?'

'For God's sake,' she snapped, 'you're going off to war in the morning. Have you no sense of responsibility?'

I took a deep breath, closed my mouth firmly, and tried to draw her towards me. 'No,' she said, 'not till you—'

I think that must have been the last straw for the housemaid's children, for there was a shriek of childish laughter, and Phaedra's face went bright red. She hopped out of bed, grabbed the chamber-pot, opened the door and let fly. Unfortunately there was nothing in it.

'Go away!' she shouted – I hadn't realised how loud her voice was – and slammed the door. 'You buffoon,' she said.

'What have I done?'

'How could I marry someone so unlucky?' She flopped back into bed and pulled the coverlet over herself, right up to her chin. 'You realise this'll be all over Athens in the morning?'

I shook my head feebly. 'Phaedra—'

'What makes it worse,' she said, 'is those stupid plays of yours.'

'What?'

'You'll never live it down,' she sighed, 'once Aristophanes and those other idiots hear about it. And people will point to me in the street, and say—'

'Shut up, will you?' My head was just about to split. I could feel it pulling apart, like a log full of wedges.

'Don't you talk to me like that,' she yapped, 'or you can sleep on the floor.'

'I might just do that anyway,' I replied.

'Good.' She made a snuffling noise which was presumably meant to be weeping, but I suddenly realised I couldn't be bothered. I leaned over her, pinched out the lamp, and banged my head down hard on the pillow.

'Now what are you doing?' she said.

'Going to sleep,' I said through the pillow. 'You can do what you like.'

She said quite a lot after that, and I found it strangely soothing, for I actually fell into a sort of a doze. When I came round from it, my headache had gone completely and she was fast asleep, with her nose pressed against the back of my neck. Very gingerly, so as not to wake her, I turned and looked down at her.

One of my father's neighbours used to tell the story of

the creation of woman; how the Good Gods moulded woman's body out of clay, making it more lovely than anything else in the world, and left it to dry in the sun, and how while they were away, the Bad Gods came and put woman's soul into it, so that mortal men should never know quiet and happiness. I will never forget how beautiful Phaedra looked just then. A strand of hair had fallen over one of her eyes, and I stroked it back over her forehead; then I tried to kiss her, but her lips were half-buried in the pillow, and I only managed to make contact with the corner of her mouth. I slid a finger down under her chin to lift her face, but she woke up, said, 'Get off,' and rolled over on to her other side.

'No,' I said. 'Come back here.'

'Go to hell,' she yawned. 'You snore, too. I hope the Samians get you.'

'What's that supposed to mean?'

'It means that, right now, given a choice between you and no husband at all . . .'

'Look . . .'

She wriggled away on to the edge of the bed. 'Given a choice . . .' she repeated; then she was suddenly quiet. My soul was whispering something to me, and then everything seemed to fall into place, like a wheel fitting on to an axle before the pin is driven home.

'So that's what's wrong with you,' I said.

'Look who's talking.'

I sat up and rubbed my eyes. 'Seriously, though,' I said.

'What is it now?'

'Whenever I asked people about you,' I said, 'I always got the impression that there was something I ought to know, but I could never find out what it was.'

She made a despairing face, as if I were a troublesome child who could not be bribed, not even with a slice of honeycomb. 'Go to sleep,' she said wearily.

'But I never thought . . .' At that moment, I hated the

sound of my own voice, high and infantile in the dark and nothing to do with me, 'I honestly never thought it could be as simple as . . .'

'As what?'

'As a really filthy temper,' I said, driving the words through the gate of my teeth like unwilling sheep. 'That's what it is, isn't it? Do you throw things as well, or do you just shout?'

'I have not got a filthy temper,' she shouted. Just for a moment, I sensed that I had the advantage, and I was glad.

'And that's what everybody else knew, and I didn't,' I continued, raising my voice and not caring what it sounded like. 'That's what your father managed to keep from me. That's what Aristophanes meant when he said . . .'

'That's absolutely typical, isn't it,' she hissed. 'It's all right for men to yell and throw things about, oh yes. They're allowed to be as loud-mouthed and disgusting as they like, especially when they're going about in packs like dogs. I suppose when you come home in the middle of the night with vomit all down your cloak and some pretty boy you've picked up in the Shoemakers' Quarter—'

'I might have known,' I went on, leading my picked troops out against the enemy cavalry. 'It's like the fish-monger's, just like that—'

'And you start howling the place down and upsetting all the jars, and wanting fried whitebait and cream sauce double quick, and why hasn't this floor been swept—'

'Anybody's got any rotten fish to sell, it's all right, lads, here comes Eupolis, we can sell it to him. Eupolis will buy anything, everyone knows that—'

'What are you talking about?'

'You know perfectly well,' I said furiously. 'And you knew all along, didn't you?'

She snorted, just like a horse. 'For God's sake,

Eupolis,' she said, 'exactly what is it you want out of life? You didn't expect me to sidle up to you and say, "You'd better not marry me, I throw plates", did you? And even you couldn't have been so utterly stupid as to think we agreed to the match because we *liked* you.' She shook her head vigorously. 'I mean, look at you. I've seen better-looking men in the silver mines.'

I stared at her open-mouthed. Just then, I could have strangled her.

'That's it,' I said. 'First thing in the morning, you go back to your father.'

She stared at me with such hatred that I was sure I could feel the skin on my face starting to peel. 'You wouldn't dare,' she said.

'And if you think you're getting back a lead obol of your dowry,' I went on, 'you're more stupid than you look, because I know the law and—'

Then she jumped at me. I put my arm up to cover my eyes, but that wasn't what she had in mind. She went for my mouth with her tongue like a thrush with a snail, and by the time I realised what she was doing it was far too late to do anything about it, although I tried my best. My mouth was full of blood from where she had bitten into my upper lip, and I felt sick.

'Right,' she said, pulling herself off me, 'now try and divorce me.' She pulled the coverlet towards her with a jerk. 'And if you do, I'll make sure that every Comic poet in Athens hears the full story. In fact, I might just do that anyway, because you make me want to throw up. And another thing; that's the first and last time, so far as I'm concerned. You're pathetic, do you understand?'

Just then, I was in no mood to argue. I was thinking, this must be how Agamemnon felt, when his wife split his head with an axe as he lay back in his bath, and the water turned royal purple all round him. I felt bad luck buzzing round me like flies in summer; you can't catch them and they climb all over you, into your ears and down under your tunic. I crawled out to the extreme edge of the bed and sucked the blood from my cut lip.

But then again, said my soul inside me, think how lucky you are, Eupolis of the deme of Pallene, to have dog-headed Comedy as your most intimate companion. There will be laughter in this before your nails next need cutting – not for you perhaps, but for others certainly. When they have tired of Heracles and the pot of soup, when the capture of the Cercopes is met with stony silence, and even Cleon and the thirty talents cannot move them, someone will say, 'Come on Eupolis, let's have the story of your wedding-night, and don't forget the bit about . . .' Remember, whatever happens to you, they can only hurt your body; but your mind is the mind of a Comic poet, and everything ridiculous, grotesque or absurd is more valuable to you than coined silver. Pull yourself together, my soul shouted inside me, it's time to pull off Agamemnon's mask and put on the Messenger's.

'Well, say something,' said Phaedra. 'Or are you dumb too?'

I smiled, lay back on the pillow and closed my eyes.

'Alas, dear wife,' I said, more to myself than to her, 'I fear that all is not well within the house. And the hell with you, too.'

CHAPTER EIGHT

For most of the first day out of Piraeus, I slept peacefully; but after that I felt horribly sick. Not all Athenians are more at home on ships than on dry land, whatever we try and make you believe in the Comedies, and the thought that I was on my way to a distinctly unfriendly part of the Athenian empire did little to settle my stomach.

To get from Athens to Samos on a troop-ship, you have to cross a lot of open water; first, Euboea to Andros and Tenos, then straight across to Icaria (where they threw stones at us when we went to get water) and eventually to Samos, which is unquestionably the most miserable place I have ever been in my life.

True, parts of it are quite remarkably rich and fertile – much more so than anything we have in Attica – and a large proportion of the rest of it is perfectly good for vines. But the generosity of Zeus has done nothing to sweeten the people, who have a generally bad attitude towards the rest of the world, and Athens in particular. The key to understanding Samos is their hatred of their neighbours the Milesians, which has lasted ever since time began. You may think you hate your neighbour (that is, after all, the natural condition of mankind) but you occasionally think of something else; whether the vines will get blight again this year, and is the King of Persia going to invade Bactria? Not so the Samians and the Milesians. It was fear of the Milesians, not the Persians, that made the Samians join the Athenian alliance in the first place, and when we sided with the Milesians over some local squabble at the beginning of the war, they broke away from the empire and sent for ambassadors from Sparta. As a result, Pericles had to go over and sort them out, which he managed only after a long and bloody siege. Since then, they have not liked us at all; but fortunately, they have the Milesians to keep them busy. I am told that a Samian's idea of a good time is to invite his friends and neighbours round, open a jar or two of wine (Samian wine tastes like tanning-fluid, incidentally) and stick knives in a woollen cloak, since wool is the principal export of Miletus.

Our job in Samos was to get in the taxes, and nobody knew whether this was going to be easy or not. According to our taxiarch, it would be like picking apples off a low tree; all Samians are fat, on account of their eating too much ewes-milk cheese, and since the democrats and the oligarchs are perpetually at each other's throats about the latest plan for a surprise attack on Miletus, one side is bound to betray the other, open the gates of the city, and cut the General's throat as he sleeps. On the other hand, a couple of men who had been to Samos with Pericles told a very different story. According to them, incessant war with Miletus has made the entire citizen body as hard as shield-leather, and once they get inside their city walls, nothing short of actual starvation will get them out again. Also, they are very good at defending fortified towns and cities (the Milesians again), and have an unpleasant habit of pouring boiling lead on the heads of anyone who comes close enough to make it worth their while. The Samians have plenty of lead, the veterans added, which they get from the Carians in exchange for olive-curd and decorated pottery.

In fact, we didn't see a single Samian during the whole of our first week on the island. Instead, we built a wall. Nobody knew what it was for, where it was supposed to come from or go to, how high it should be, or which side of it we were eventually to defend. It started in the middle of a vineyard, and finally petered out on the gentle slopes of a hill, either for sound strategic reasons or because we ran out of stones. Speculation as to its purpose and exactly why both ends had been left open kept us reasonably well entertained for the first two days, and after that it rained; by all accounts, for the first time in that particular month since the days of the dictator Polycrates. I had done a little gentle wall-building once or twice before, but there seemed to be a general feeling among our taxiarchs that this wall, although inexplicable, was going to be needed very soon: and when a large section of it fell down during our third night in Samos, redoubled efforts were called for, and my attitude towards soldiering took a turn for the worse.

Eventually, however, the job was finished, and no sooner was the last stone triumphantly in position than our unit got orders to fill our water-skins and march up into the mountains, which in Samos are very high and crawling with political dissidents (which is Samian for bandits) to collect the taxes from the outlying villages. We waved goodbye to our wall, which we never saw again, and set off to die for our country, should the need to do so arise.

When we did meet some Samians, they didn't try and kill us; they were only about twelve years old, and small for their age. Instead they tried to sell us local pottery and the company of their sisters, who were (they assured us) very nice girls. We marched on until we came to a large village, I think it was called Astypylaea, where we were due to collect the first payment of taxes.

Astypylaea was just like any other substantial hill village, with a sprawl of houses, a small thatched temple and a market square marked off with weather-beaten boundary stones; it could have been anywhere up the mountain from Pallene, or out towards the back of Phyle. There were rather more sheep and rather fewer goats than we're used to in Attica, and some of the people had a rather unGreek look to them, which my companions attributed to interbreeding with the Persians when Samos was part of the Persian satrapy of Ionia. But if they weren't exactly friendly they didn't throw stones, and there was no shield-wall in the main street as some of us had been expecting. Instead, there was an old man who we took to be the village spokesman, and a couple of bored-looking boys of about fifteen holding some very thin sheep on short reins. These, it appeared, were a gift to their beloved Athenian guests, hand-chosen by Polychresus himself to grace our tables when we dined together. Our taxiarch indicated dignified thanks and made tactful enquiries about the tax money.

At this the old man looked truly sad, as if we had reminded him of something he had been trying to forget about.

'To our lasting shame, Athenian brothers,' he said, 'we no longer have the tribute-money. I say "no longer"; had you been here this time yesterday, there would have been no problem. But,' he bowed his head, 'honoured friends, these mountains are wild and lawless. Up there,' and he waved his stick vaguely at the encircling rocks, 'live a band of fierce and wicked men, oligarchs who were made outlaws when they tried to seize the temple of Hera by night two years ago. This morning, my house was broken into and the tribute – ten minas of fine silver, just as you commanded – was stolen. My boy Cleagenes here,' he said, and shoved one of the boys, who was staring at his sandal-straps, 'tried to resist them, and look what they did to him!' The old man pointed vigorously at a minute cut just above the boy's left eye. 'We are poor men,' he went on. 'All our silver went to make up that ten minas.

We have nothing more to give you. So if you want the tribute, you must go and get it from those thieves and bandits.' He shook his fist at a different sector of the horizon, and leaned heavily on his staff.

Several of my companions made rude noises, but our taxiarch, who was new to this sort of work, ordered us to be quiet and assured the old man that we would have the silver back by nightfall if he would provide us with a guide.

'The best in Astypylaea,' said the old man, 'my boy Demetrius here' – he gave the other boy a shove – 'he knows the hills like a mountain goat, and is entirely without fear. You may follow him to the ends of the earth.'

Somehow we soldiers had the feeling that the ends of the earth would probably be a reasonable guess in the circumstances, but we had been ordered to keep quiet, so we said nothing. The taxiarch called out, 'Be ready to march in five minutes,' and went into one of the houses to be briefed on the bandits. I sent Little Zeus off to get fresh water and some bread, if there was any to be had, and sat down on a mounting-block to rest my feet. My head was sodden wet under my helmet, and I wanted to be left alone.

'This is going to be interesting,' said a voice beside me. I looked round and saw Artemidorus, one of the men who had been in Samos before. He was a demesman of mine and we had met at festivals, although I could remember very little about him.

'So how do you like soldiering, young Eupolis?' he said cheerfully. 'A bit different from prancing round the Market with Cleon and Alcibiades, isn't it?'

I made some feeble joke or other and he laughed loudly. 'That's good,' he said when he had managed to regain control of himself. 'Man with a sense of humour's always welcome in the wars. You'll find that out before you're much older, I reckon.'

'Why's that?' I asked. Artemidorus chuckled.

'You could put it in one of your plays,' he said, and a thought struck him. 'Are we all going to be in your next play, then? That'd be good, wouldn't it?'

'Marvellous,' I said. 'Do you know what's going on?'

He grinned. 'Like I told you, I've been here before, I know these sheep-shaggers like Homer. What's happening is, they've got these bandits up in the hills they want shifting, and they're too chicken to do it themselves. Also they don't want to pay any taxes, which is fair enough if you ask me. I'm a democrat, I don't hold with taxes, except for the empire of course, because when it comes down to it they're foreigners, they're used to it. Anyway, they put up this load of old cock about bandits, we go up into the hills and either we get lost and die of exposure, or the bandits get us, which saves them paying any taxes, or else we get the bandits, which suits the villagers, and they still don't pay any taxes, because they say the bandits have got it stashed somewhere and they don't know where. So we give up and go away, and everyone is happy.'

I stared at him. 'For God's sake, man,' I said, 'why don't you tell the taxiarch? We could get killed up there.'

Artemidorus shook his head. 'Son,' he said, 'you'll learn this about the army. You don't go telling things to the officers because one, they don't believe you; two, it gets you noticed; three, if it isn't here it's somewhere else.'

'What's that supposed to mean?' I asked.

'It means that we're here, and there's nothing we can do about it, so we might as well get on with it. When you're in the army you don't try and change things; you wait till you get home and you vote to have the General executed. That's democracy. Don't knock it.'

'But this is stupid,' I burst out. 'Are you sure about this? I mean, it's not just some rumour, like the women in Andros having three breasts, because Epinices saw one washing in the river, and ...'

Artemidorus smiled, displaying his remaining teeth. 'It's true all right,' he said, 'solid silver all the way through, you could cut it with a chisel. For God's sake, my brother Callides told me. Are you calling him a liar, or what?'

'No, no,' I reassured him. 'Look, can't we jut *suggest* it to the taxiarch?'

'Forget it,' Artemidorus said, and just then Little Zeus came back with the water-bottles and a huge black loaf, which he said had cost him a quarter-stater. We smashed the loaf up with a stone (it was hard and brittle, like pumice), soaked it in water, and ate it. By the time we had finished, the taxiarch was back and yelling orders.

It was a long way up the mountain, even with Little Zeus carrying my shield and pack for me, and the sun was unbearably hot. Even our guide seemed to be feeling the strain, for he kept stopping and looking round for no apparent reason. By midday we were high above the cultivable zones, and there were only a few emaciated sheep to be seen, scattered about like little white thorn trees. The taxiarch had set off at a parade-ground pace, singing some military chorus to set the tempo; but that had soon given way to a festival hymn, which was replaced in turn by a sort of dirge, all about the death of Theseus. Nobody knew the words, and his voice eventually dwindled away into a sort of semi-private hum.

Then the rocks started coming down on us. The first one bounced just in front of our guide, who decided that it was probably time he went home. The taxiarch tried to grab him, but a couple of small rocks hit him on the backplate and he fell over. Someone yelled something, but none of us could understand him – we had our helmets on, and of course you can't hear a thing inside a helmet, something that your average taxiarch (or general, for that matter) finds hard to remember. But I saw Artemidorus kneel down and put his shield over his head, and so I snatched my shield from Little Zeus and did the same. Something banged on the shield, like a gatecrasher at a party, and I remember thinking, 'Oh God, I bet it's hit that new bronze patch'; then I felt a sharp blow on my head, and my helmet-plume, which Callicrates and I had spent so long wrestling into place, was lying on the ground beside me. I let go of my spear to pick it up, and of course the spear rolled away down the side of the mountain. I stayed where I was; but Little Zeus, who had been trying to fit his enormous body under a small ledge of rock, jumped up and dashed after it, like a three-year-old dog chasing a hare. I almost expected him to bring it back in his mouth.

Someone shoved me from behind, and I saw that we were moving on. The taxiarch was on his feet again, dusting off his cloak, and no one seemed to be seriously hurt. I fell in beside Artemidorus, and pushed my helmet up on to the back of my head. He did the same, and we were able to talk.

'What was all that about?' I asked nervously.

'Could be the bandits,'he said gravely, as if he were Miltiades himself, sizing up an enemy formation, 'or it could just have been a couple of startled sheep or something, I don't know. I don't think the taxiarch's too happy.'

I wiped the sweat out of my eyes, and my arm felt very weak. 'What are we going to do now?' I asked. 'I mean, are we going on, or what?'

'We're going on, of course,' said Artemidorus. 'You wait till you've been in a couple of real battles. First time I was in a battle, we saw some horsemen coming up – great big cloud of dust, we were terrified. I pissed all down my legs and never knew it. Turned out to be our own men, actually. When we got to see the enemy we were all so knackered with marching up and down in the heat that we weren't frightened at all, just glad to get it over with. This sort of thing is just routine.'

As we marched on I began to feel unbearably tired – my legs were weak, and I had to lean heavily on Little Zeus' shoulder. Apparently, that was normal too, because of the sudden shock, but that didn't make it any easier. I asked Artemidorus if there was likely to be any more trouble; he drew on his vast military experience and replied, No, probably not.

We had come round the side of a spur into a narrow defile, with the main bulk of the mountain on our right and a sort of rampart of bare rock to the left. I had known just such a place on Parnes when I was a boy, and had often lain there under a bent old fig tree, imagining that I was an Athenian general and a Spartan army had been foolish enough to march straight into this naturally perfect mantrap. The final deployment I had decided on, after a year or so of intermittent speculation, was to put my heavy infantry at both ends (like Leonidas at Thermopylae) and my light infantry on the heights on either side, shooting and throwing javelins.

Perhaps I should have been a general. I was just about to tell the story to Little Zeus when I felt a tap on my shield, like the first drop of rain on a roof. There were other taps up and down the line, and we started looking round. Then someone went down on his knee, lifting his shield in front of his face, and we realised what was going on; we were being shot at by slingers, positioned on the side of the mountain. This time, I wasn't nearly so startled; in fact, it was almost a pleasant relief after the tension of the past couple of hours. What I wasn't prepared for was sling-bolts coming from the other side of the defile. I braced myself as best I could, tucking my head into the hollow of my shield. But nothing came, although I could hear sling-bolts pattering down on either side of me.

'Put your helmet down, you idiot,' someone hissed in my ear, and I remembered that it was still perched on the back of my head. I put up my hand, and something smacked against my forearm. I swore, calling on all the Gods I could think of; then it occurred to me that the blow had not been particularly fierce; I could still move my fingers and everything.

Hold on a moment, said my soul inside me, they're out of range.

I thought about it for a moment, then looked up to my left. Sure enough, I could make out a figure against the skyline; a boy, maybe thirteen years old, loading his slingshot. He was at least sixty yards away, much too far away to do any serious damage, especially to a man in armour. I suddenly felt extremely foolish; an Athenian heavy-armed infantryman, the terror of the Greek world, cowering under his shield against the blood-chilling but entirely ineffectual onslaught of a thirteen-year-old goatherd.

My fellow soldiers were slowly coming to the same conclusion; one man in particular. I can't remember his name, but I think he was a shipwright by trade, and certainly not used to being made a fool of. He got up, laid his shield down carefully beside him, and turned to face the foe, for all the world like Ajax in the *Iliad*.

'All right,' he shouted up the mountainside, 'pack it in.'

There was no immediate effect; but after a while the pattering started to die away, and the Athenian expeditionary force resumed its formidable order. It was then that we noticed the enemy infantry, leaning on their spears at the mouth of the defile.

When I say spears, I am exaggerating slightly. Most of them had sharpened vine-props, and some of them had nothing at all. There were four men sharing a suit of armour between them – one had the helmet, another had the breastplate, and the other two had one greave each; the rest of them had nothing but home-made wicker shields and tunics, and their feet were bare.

The taxiarch let out a great shout, and we charged,

shouting *Io Paian!* at the tops of our voices. The Samians threw their spears and bolted, scrambling away over the rocks like sheep. Their volley fell well short, and we drew up, breathless but happy, our honour totally restored, to find that two of the Samians were still there. Just two, no more.

I heard the story later. One man, who was the son of an Infantry farmer, had slipped and twisted his ankle, and his lover had stayed with him to defend him to the death if need be. As a result he was extremely excitable, and he also had one of the few genuine spears in the whole band. I can picture him now, jabbing his spear in the general direction of a taxiarch and calling on some obscure local Hero.

Nothing would have happened if the taxiarch hadn't still believed in the existence of the tax money. As it was, he wanted a prisoner to interrogate, and he sent two men forward to grab the Samians. The man with the twisted ankle made a remarkable recovery and rolled off down the hill as fast as he could; but our two men were on to the other one and he couldn't follow. Instead, he ducked out of their way and ran forward, apparently straight at me. Then Little Zeus, perceiving a mortal threat to his five acres, jumped out and slashed wildly at him with his sword, smashing his wicker shield into pieces and taking a lump out of his arm. That was another mistake. The poor Samian turned and stabbed with his spear at Little Zeus, who of course had no shield to protect himself with. He jerked back out of the way, tripped over his feet, and came down heavily on his backside. The Samian raised his spear over his head – and I stabbed him.

I couldn't believe that I had done it. There was this human body on the end of my spear, looking at me with such utter astonishment that I wanted to smile, and then turning carefully round, like a man who has stepped in something nasty in the street, and looking at the spear-blade sticking out of his side. For a moment I thought he was going to strike at me; then I realised that he had forgotten about everything else except the extraordinary fact of there being a spear right through him. I don't think it was hurting him. He just hadn't expected this at all.

'You *bastard*,' I heard myself saying. 'Really, I'm sorry.'

I think he was going to laugh; then he suddenly collapsed, as if he had noticed he was late for his own death. His weight jerked the spear out of my hands, and his body sagged on to the ground. And there was blood too – so much of it, creeping along the weave of his tunic like the waves on the shore, except not pulling back. I broke a jar of honey once, and stood there watching it oozing out into the dust on the storeroom floor, visibly spoiling in front of my eyes, going expensively to waste. Yes, there was blood all right, and how dark it looks when there's a lot of it. It was a fascinating sight for someone who has learned his Homer, line by painful line, and yes, that sort of blood is black, not red, just as it says in the *Iliad*, and a dead man does fall with a thud, and he does look rather like a felled tree, with his arms spread out like branches. He also looks rather like a man who has fallen over; he has short black hair and long, thin legs and a mole on his neck, and you wonder why he doesn't get up.

Then Little Zeus started praising me in a great voice and thanking me for saving his life, and pledging his eternal allegiance, and that of his children and his great-grandchildren to me and my House for ever, and I turned and kicked him on the shins. And the taxiarch said, 'What the hell was all that about?' and Artemidorus was muttering about having the whole of Samos after us now, and what in God's name did I think I was playing at? And someone pulled the spear out of his body and wiped it on the grass and gave it back to me, and said, 'That's one up to us,' and there seemed to be a lot more noise besides. And for some time they stood there discussing whether we should take him down to the village or leave him up there for the kites and the crows, until they finally agreed on throwing some dust on his face as a form of burial and telling the villagers where his body was in case anyone wanted it.

So we didn't get any tax-money in Astypylaea. From there we went to another village – I can't remember its name – where they tried to play exactly the same trick, except that they claimed that the money had been stolen not by local bandits but Milesian pirates.

The taxiarch listened to the tale, which was well told, and withdrew as before into the village headman's house. Outside in the street we could only hear a few thumps and some squealing, but when they came out again, the headman was rubbing his ears and the taxiarch was grinning. We got five minas in the end, which was three less than the assessment but all the silver we could find.

After that, we met with a different sort of obstruction as we toured round Samos. Instead of ostentatious courtesy and stringy but complimentary goats for our evening meal, we were greeted with barred doors and showers of stones and potsherds whenever we entered a village. It was obvious that the Samians were expecting us, for when we broke into their houses we found that everything of value had been removed. Our taxiarch (who was growing up fast) realised that there was no hope of keeping our movements a secret or arriving unexpectedly at any place; so he thought of another and a better way.

At the next village we came to, he sent us out to secure the headman, whom we found hiding under an over-turned barley jar in his house, and sat this gentleman down on a mounting-block in the Market Square. He then explained to him, slowly and loudly, that he was fed up with traipsing through this god-forsaken island in search of what was obviously enchanted silver; he was going to stay right here in this village until it was time to go home, eating and drinking as much as he pleased and letting his men do the same. To pass the time, he added, he would set his men to building a little shrine, as a memento of our stay. As soon as it was completed, he added, he would personally dedicate this shrine to the Luck of Miletus, in memory of a little-known Milesian Hero who had been killed here when some princes of Miletus sacked the village ten or so generations ago. But since he was not an ostentatious man, he would not name himself as founder on the foundation-stone; instead, he would inscribe it with the names of all the villages he had visited, and send a herald to the main cities of Samos inviting all pious men to come and worship there. He stood up, as if his discourse was finished; then he turned round and added, in a nicely matter-of-fact way, that if by some miracle the tribute-money was suddenly to arrive from the villages he would be so busy checking it and drawing up accounts that he would have no time for his pious undertaking, and the other Samians would probably never know of their fellow citizens' religious zeal.

The next morning, we awoke from a sleep curiously untroubled by stray dogs, mysterious falls of rocks and sudden inexplicable noises (which we had come to accept as a way of life in Samos) and set out to quarry stones for the shrine. But when we arrived in the Market Square, we found a small group of harassed-looking Samians holding donkeys on short reins; and on the donkeys' backs were jars overflowing with coined silver. We tipped them out on to blankets and started to count, and the mixture of denominations alone was a feast of entertainment. There were Athenian Owls and Aeginetan Turtles, Horses from Corinth and Carthage, Lions of Leontini and Arethusae from Syracuse; there were Ajaxes from Locris Opuntia, which few of us had seen before, and some very pretty coins with doves on them that nobody could identify. There were even Persian sigloi, stamped with the King dressed as an archer, which must have dated back to before the wars, when Samos was still part of the empire. In fact, it seemed to us that some people had been digging very deep into ancient reserves to find us all this silver; in some cases, a little too deeply, for we found when we made up the final account that we had just over twelve staters a man more than the required sum. But by then, of course, all the silver was so thoroughly mixed up that there was no way of telling which villages had paid too much; and since it would undoubtedly cause bad feeling among neighbours if we tried to sort the matter out, we decided to forget all about it and accept the surplus as a sort of anonymous gift.

The taxiarch put all the money back into the jars and sealed each one with a leaden seal. Then he sent for the headman, who this time came a little more willingly, and sat him down as before in the Market Square. By now quite a crowd of Samians had gathered to see the money, and the taxiarch drew us up in front of the jars before he started to speak.

He started by confessing that up till now he had held a very poor view of Samian loyalty to Athens. He had somehow got it into his head, he said, that the Samians didn't want to pay their contribution to the cost of fighting the Great War of Freedom; that – perish the thought! – the honest men of Samos had forgotten who had freed them from the Persian yoke and given back to them their ancient freedom and privileges. But it was time, he continued, to revise that view. He had learned, from this truthful old man their headman, that leading citizens from all the villages had walked all night along treacherous mountain roads, undoubtedly shadowed all the way by the terrible outlaws and bandits of whom he himself had personal experience, just to be able to pay their taxes. Such behaviour, he said, cried out to be acknowledged; it shone like a beacon in a treacherous and ungrateful world.

He smiled and bowed slightly to the headman, who shifted about in his chair. Yesterday (continued the taxiarch) he had discussed with his friend the headman his plans to build a little shrine to a local Hero. For a while he had been afraid that counting up the tax-money would leave no time for building the shrine; but since everything had been paid so promptly, and since so many able-bodied men were now gathered in the market-place, he could see no reason why the shrine should not be built after all. There would be no time now, he regretted, to send a herald to the Cities, but that could doubtless be done later, after he had gone.

This was our cue to draw our swords and look fierce. For some reason the Samians worked very hard all day and late into the night, by the light of torches which we held for them. It was a pretty little shrine when it was finished, with a sloping roof of tiles, which the headman felt compelled to provide by stripping his own roof, and a charming painting of the Milesians sacking the village, done by a local painter. We held a proper formal service of dedication, with hymns and a little procession, and sacrificed two white kids, also the property of the headman, to the music of flutes and harps. There was dancing too, and a modest amount of wine; and we Athenians enjoyed ourselves tremendously, although the Samians seemed to feel the gravity of the occasion rather more than we did.

I would like to think that the little shrine was still there, high up in the wild country of Samos. But as we marched away over the mountains we saw a plume of smoke rising from the Market Square; and when we stopped and looked carefully, we saw that the shrine was on fire. I can only suppose that some over-zealous worshipper banked the altar fire up too high, and that the sacred flame set light to the rafters.

CHAPTER NINE

When I was a boy I had something wrong with my eyes – nothing serious; my sight is perfect even now – and my father, who had a horror of illness, used to take me to the house of a horrible old woman who lived in the next village. She professed to cure all illnesses by a combination of prayers to some of the less reputable Goddesses and fierce herbal poultices; though I believe to this day that such cures as she achieved were effected by fear of the remedy. Each time we came away, my father poorer by a four-drachma piece and me with my eyes so red and painful that I could scarcely see the sun, he would slap me cheerfully on the shoulder and say, 'Well, that wasn't so bad, was it?' And I would reply, 'No, it wasn't,' and say a prayer under my breath that I would go blind and so be saved another course of treatment.

But my first taste of soldiering wasn't so bad after all, and I was almost sorry that it was over. I had my arms and armour intact, and a rather tatty crown of laurel leaves presented to me by the taxiarch for saving the life of a fellow citizen, which in spite of certain reservations I wore prominently as I strolled through the Market Square back to my house; and of course nine or ten bosom friends with whom I had sworn oaths of undying friendship, as one does in the army, and most of whom I never managed to get around to seeing ever again. The only one I kept up with at all was Artemidorus, the veteran. Since he was a neighbour I saw rather more of him than I would have wished. He had guessed (correctly) that his wealthy young comrade-in-arms was a good touch for the use of a plough or a jar or two of seedcorn, and it came as something of a blow to him to find out that I was already married, for he had a spare daughter. It came as something of a blow to me, as well, for I had not given Phaedra much thought while I was in Samos.

I had just arrived outside Philodemus' door and was about to go in when a Libyan slave-boy whom I had never seen before dashed up and tugged at my cloak.

'Get off,' I said, for people were watching. 'What do you want?'

'My mistress says you're to come home with me,' he said urgently. I stared at him.

'Get lost,' I whispered, 'I'm a respectable married man.'

'Are you Eupolis of Pallene?' asked the boy. I said yes, I was, if it was any of his business. He started to tug at my cloak again, and I was afraid he would break the brooch.

'Then you're to come home with me *now*,' the boy said loudly. 'My mistress says so.'

'Look,' I snapped, 'who in God's name are you and what do you want? I'm just back from Samos and I want—'

'I'm your slave Doron,' said the boy. 'You'd better come.'

I shouldered my shield and followed right across the City until we came to the rather grand houses near the old Fish Market; that was where Aristophanes lived, and many other rich, fashionable young men. We stopped outside the door of a large, imposing house, which I remembered as the home of one Execestiades, who had been executed for treason just before my wedding.

'What are we doing here?' I asked.

'You live here,' the boy replied. 'Hurry up.'

I couldn't make head or tail of that, so I spat into my cloak for luck (since I was going into an unlucky house) and followed him.

It was a big, bleak place with a high ceiling, and somebody had been doing a lot of very expensive decorating. There was a silver mixing-bowl on the table, with embossed silver and gold cups all round it; there were Persian tapestries all over the place, and Bactrian rugs on the floor. The couches had bronze legs, and beside the hearth there was a tall, gilded statue of Agamemnon being killed by Clytemnestra on his return from Troy which, I calculated, must have cost the owner as much money as I got from my estate in Phylae in a whole year. In front of the fire two expensive Spartan hounds were sleeping, and there were two bird cages and a baby monkey hanging from the rafters. It looked like the house of an extremely wealthy widow.

The door of the inner room opened, and there was Phaedra, dressed in a saffron gown. 'So you're back, are you?' she said.

'What in God's name is going on?' I demanded.

'Don't stand on that carpet in your muddy sandals,' Phaedra said. 'It cost you twelve drachmas, and you were lucky to get it for that.'

I stepped off the carpet on to the floor. 'Whose house is this, Phaedra?' I asked. 'And what the hell are you doing here? You should be at my uncle's.'

'It's your house, you ungrateful oaf,' she said irritably, 'or it will be after you've got yourself down to the Archon's office and paid for it. Your infernal uncle wouldn't release any of the money in your strongbox.'

'You bought this from the Public Confiscator?' I gasped.

'No,' she said, 'you did. I'm not allowed to buy real property, remember.'

If I hadn't been so astonished, I don't know what I'd have done. As it was, I stood there, with my laurel crown (for saving the life of a fellow citizen) hanging lopsidedly from the side of my head, and tried to find a few appropriate words. While I was searching, Phaedra continued.

'Well, I couldn't go on living in your uncle's house – I mean, the man is unbearable, he keeps ordering me about as if I were a servant or something. And I don't like that goody-goody cousin of yours, Callicrates. I don't think we'll see any more of them from now on. And it's a good house – expensive, of course, but you can just about afford it, if you're careful for a year or so. Of course you'll be short of ready money for a while; you might have to mortgage some of your vineyards in Pallene, but that shouldn't be a problem. I'm sure my father will take them on, if no one else will.'

'You bought confiscated property in my name? Have you any idea what people are going to say about me?'

'Yes,' said Phaedra, and she smiled.

I wonder now why it took me so long to work it out. Phaedra knew as well as I did that buying up the confiscated property of a man who had been executed was not only ill-omened in the extreme but regarded by all decent men as little better than grave-robbing, and that was why she had done it – to make me look as bad as possible. She also knew that there was now no way that I could get out of it, for she must have used my personal seal to make the contract with the Public Confiscator. If I repudiated a document under my seal, I would for ever after have difficulty buying anything in Athens bigger than a single whitebait.

'It's lucky you came back today,' said Phaedra. 'It's the last date for payment, and the interest rate is quite high, I believe.'

I knew that I was beaten. 'All right, you bitch,' I said, 'how much has this cost me?'

'One talent,' she said, and she giggled.

I sat down on a couch and put my head in my hands. Then another thought struck me.

'And what,' I asked, 'is all this junk?' I waved my arm at all the couches and silverware. 'Where did all this come from?'

'If we're going to entertain my family and my father's friends,' she said sweetly, 'we can't have the place looking like a barn, now can we? But you needn't worry,' she continued, 'they wouldn't give me credit, so all the furniture and so forth is already paid for. I sold my ten acres.'

'You what?'

'My dowry, my ten acres.' She giggled again; she was enjoying herself. 'It hadn't been made over to you formally when you left, if you remember, so my father was able to give a receipt. Of course, we couldn't get anything like the full value for it – who's buying vineyards these days? – but there was just about enough, together with the loose cash you hadn't sealed up before you left. Hadn't you better get across to your uncle's for that talent?'

'Who told you I had a talent?' I yelled at her, but she simply turned and walked out into the inner room. I dared not follow her there, for fear of seeing what wonders of the silversmith's trade she had furnished it with. So I kicked the Libyan boy, took off my armour, and set off for my uncle's house.

Just for fun, I tried fighting the Public Confiscator; the contract was not quite perfectly drawn – I think one of the Gods had been left out of the Invocation Clause – but the lawyers I consulted told me to forget it; no jury would have any sympathy with a man who bought confiscated property and then tried to cheat the State by backing out of a sealed contract.

My uncle solved my immediate financial difficulties by taking a ten-year lease of some of my land in Phylae, which was contributing nothing at the moment and was unlikely to be anything but a burden for the foreseeable future. But he paid me a premium assessed on pre-war yields, which was much the same as giving me the money; in fact, for a long time afterwards he referred to it as my wedding-present. He was able to be so generous because my grandfather's stake in the silver mines, which he had kept back when he transferred the rest of my property, was paying handsomely, thanks to the war. He also lent me enough to buy a share in an oar-blade workshop owned by some friends of his, which turned out to be one of the best investments I ever made.

Now that my new house was paid for, I tried to make the best I could of living there; but I hated the place. For a start, I couldn't help feeling that the previous owner's bad luck was everywhere, and although I sacrificed several times to his ghost, and sprinkled everything in sight with chickens' blood (which did not please Phaedra), the thought of being alone in the house was never agreeable.

Then, of course, many of the people who had known Execestiades refused to set foot in the house, for he had been a popular man and, by all accounts, a good and honest politician. As if to compensate me for the loss of so much good society, Phaedra took to filling the house with her relations and her brothers' friends, none of whom I could stand. On the other hand, I would have preferred to eat and drink with a household of Thessalians rather than spend an evening alone with Phaedra.

You can imagine what my life at home was like when I tell you that I never managed to get around to shouting at Phaedra properly for buying the house in the first place; she always pre-empted me. As soon as I set my foot over the threshold she would be at me with some new catalogue of complaints, so that I was forever on the defensive over some minor domestic trivia. I have always detested arguments and bad temper – I get a headache, and I can't seem to get my words out properly – so I soon took to making tactical withdrawals (like the Athenian generals at Marathon), usually into the storeroom or even the stables, where it was warm and quiet except for the breathing of the horses. I got very little sleep – I think Phaedra slept a lot during the day so as to be able to sit up complaining at night – and of course I had no hope at all of composing any Comedy in my own house. The only course open to me was to be at home as little as possible, which was of course what Phaedra wanted.

So I spent most of my time in the Market Square or at my uncle's, or visiting friends, and the joy of being out of the house added an extra glow to all my occupations. I was making useful friends at this time, and knew most of the leading citizens. It is a strange thing, but people who are gossiped about tend to seek the company of other notorious men, and since the story of my domestic arrangements had long since become a source of lasting delight all over Athens, I never lacked for company or confidences. Once you have got used to being a laughing-stock it is quite a useful attribute, if your skin is reasonably thick. People are not afraid of you, and that tends to break down barriers.

Whenever possible, of course, I went out to the country, especially to Pallene, where Phaedra would not go. There was always something to do on the land, and the work kept me healthy. Because it was pointless trying to replant vines and olives with the threat of Spartan invasions, we concentrated on growing what we could manage to grow in the available time. Many of the crops we tried were rarely grown in Attica (flax and hemp, for example, and some rare varieties of beans and pulses), and I was proud of some of our successes and not too distressed by our failures. In particular I found that beans and lupins were a vastly underrated crop. Because Attica is so dry, and manure of all kinds is worth its weight in gold, most Attic farmers grow beans as green fertiliser; that is to say, they grow them on fallow land and plough them back unharvested before they come to maturity. But I found that you can harvest beans off the fallow without noticeably damaging the soil; the mere act of growing them seems to do the ground a great deal of good. Also, where the Spartans had burnt standing corn, the earth was much lighter and more productive, and I remembered something in one of the old poems – Hesiod, I think it was, or someone like him – that led me to believe that our forefathers deliberately burned off the stalks and helm of some crops to enrich the land. As for water, I managed to organise my neighbours into diverting some of the mountain streams, which never fail even in summer, so that they flowed down through our terraces and so could be used to irrigate. Most people thought we were mad, until we began carting in the produce; then they started lawsuits for illegal conversion of water. I also insisted that all over my estates we ploughed at least five times throughout the year, to work in the frost and the dew. It was hard work and expensive, too – hardly a day seemed to go by when I wasn't down at the smithy ordering a new ploughshare – but the results were little short of spectacular, and I could hardly wait for the return of peace, and the chance to start growing barley again.

And there was hunting, too – the Spartan invasions meant that Attica was alive with hares and deer, and wild boar and even bears were starting to come back – and fowling, and fishing, of course, which had become a very important part of many people's lives since the start of the war. My dislike of the sea meant that I took little direct part in that, but I spent money on fishing-boats and even a small coaster, so that I could take surplus produce round the coast to sell in other parts of Attica instead of having to drag it by land all the way to the City and out again. In short, as you may already have guessed, I enjoyed myself tremendously in the country, and did no harm to anyone.

And, above all, I got back to my play. I found manual labour extremely conducive to composition, and since I carried the entire text of *The General* about with me in my head, I could work on it wherever I happened to be. I'm sure that several of my seasonal workers, if they are still alive, could even now recite you the big speeches from that play, for they heard them often enough, and, being sensible men, were always careful to laugh in all the right places. Sometimes we performed a few scenes for my neighbours, when it was too hot to work and we drifted together under the shade of the nearest trees. Naturally I took the lead, and Little Zeus was my one-man Chorus; the rest of the parts were shared out among the slaves and free hands. I don't suppose I shall ever have a more appreciative audience than those farmers of Pallene and Phrearrhos, who were pleased enough for an excuse to lie still after a hard morning's work, and who hadn't had to sit through three Tragedies before the Comedy. Nevertheless, it was worth watching to see exactly what did make them laugh and what slipped by unnoticed, how far a joke could be drawn before it became boring, and just how long a scene should be.

I suppose I was putting off for as long as possible the horrible day when there was nothing more I could do to it without spoiling it entirely, and I would have to take it to the Archon, like a tenant farmer taking his year's produce to be measured and divided. I dreaded the thought of not getting a Chorus. After all, there were already more Comic poets than Choruses, and new ones coming forward almost every day, as far as I could see. I was starting to bristle with hatred whenever I heard an established poet's name, and often found myself praying that one or other of them would be killed in the war or struck down by the plague. But when I fell to contemplating my *General*, which was something I did far too often for a modest man, I could honestly see no flaw or imperfection in it, from the first joke to the exit of the

Chorus. But at other times, after a long struggle with an unwieldy scene, I doubted if anyone, however sick his mind might be, could ever be made to laugh by such dreary nonsense; there was nothing which had not been done a hundred times better a hundred times before. To be brief; there were days when I loved it and days when I hated it, but my play was never far from my mind. It was the one thing I really had to look forward to, yet it was a terrible shadow hanging over me. If it succeeded – would that I could die in that moment! – and if it failed, then I might as well throw myself off the tower in the Potters' Quarter and be done with it all.

To make matters worse, Philonides the Chorus-trainer had not forgotten about me. You may remember that he expressed an interest, that night at Aristophanes' party. Well, I had expected to hear no more from him, but that was not the case at all. In fact, it became quite embarrassing, for I seemed to meet him everywhere – not just in the City, but even in the country, for he had land at Phrearrhos not far from mine, and I always seemed to be running into him on the road home at night – and each time we met he would ask, 'Have you anything for me yet?' and each time I would say, 'Well, nearly; but there's still a few things I must iron out . . .' But instead of putting him off, this seemed to make him all the more eager, and in the end he took to calling at my house in the City, where Phaedra made him as welcome as a beggar with the plague.

I can understand Phaedra's reluctance to have any acquaintance of mine in the house, for she was filling in the long hours of our marriage quite as effectively as I was, if half the rumours I heard were true. Of course, a husband always believes rumours about his wife, and they're very seldom true; but there were so many of them and they all sounded so probable that even the most sceptical juror would have found it difficult not to be convinced.

To start with, I was overjoyed at the thought that I might be able to divorce Phaedra for adultery and be rid of her for good. I remember joking about it, at home in Pallene or at Philodemus' house; we drank toasts to my liberator as if he were a new Solon come to free the serfs, and adapted the words of the Harmodius. But somehow I could never get around to doing anything about it, even though Philodemus and Callicrates offered to fight the case for me.

'For God's sake, boy,' Philodemus would say, 'it's like a gift from Olympus, and you just sit there and do nothing. If it's losing the dowry you're worried about, I've spoken to half the lawyers in Athens, and—'

But I would shake my head and change the subject, and after a while they stopped bothering, looking on me as mad and already lost; or perhaps they were waiting until Phaedra got pregnant and I was forced to take action. I couldn't understand it myself; I only knew that it was something to be done next week, or next month, or after the figs had been harvested.

The day came when, to my inseparable joy and sorrow, *The General* was finished and, try as I might, I could think of no reason why I should not take it down to the Archon. It was as near perfect as it would ever be, I had the backing of several influential people including Philonides himself, and I was old enough to take out a Chorus in my own name. By the way, I realise that I have omitted to describe my coming-of-age celebrations and setting-down in the phratry lists. When I started writing this History I intended to give a full account of it, so that generations yet unborn should know what such a ceremony was like in the heyday of the Athenian power. But to be honest with you, it's such a tedious business that I can't be bothered; so if you wish to read about it, I recommend that you dig out one of the metrical accounts by one of the old lyric poets.

Anyway, I trudged unhappily over to my uncle's house with a big knapsack full of Egyptian paper, commandeered his secretary, and dictated the whole thing at a sitting; then I made the poor boy read it all back to me and corrected the mistakes, and told him to write out five fair copies, while I stood over him just to make sure he was doing it properly. I live in terror of having my words distorted by incompetent copyists. One lapse in attention can ruin a whole roll, in my opinion, and they hate the sight of me at the copying workshops when I come down to see how they are getting on.

When the rolls were finished, cut, dried and folded and properly polished with pumice, I packed them up in little bronze cylinders which I had had specially made in Pallene, with 'The General of *Eupolis son of Euchorus of the deme of Pallene*' and the first line of the play neatly inscribed on the outside, and set off for the Archon's house. My dear Callicrates could see how nervous I was and offered to come with me, but I refused. I wanted to go alone, without even Little Zeus. I felt like Theseus going into the Labyrinth.

It was nearly dark, and I was terrified in case I ran into robbers who would steal the rolls for their bronze covers; but apparently there was a big funeral over on the other side of the City that night, and so the streets were deserted and safe. I arrived at the Archon's door and knocked loudly, to raise my spirits.

A housemaid opened the door and asked who was making such a noise at this time of night. I gave my name and said that I wanted to see the Archon.

'Is it important?' she said. 'He's got visitors. They're singing the Harmodius.'

The thought of going away and coming back the next day was more than I could bear. 'Yes,' I said, 'it's very important, you'd better let me in.'

As I stepped into the house I immediately thought better of it. What, after all, could be more likely to inspire the fury of the Archon than bursting in on him when he was drinking with a few friends? It would be a miracle if he even accepted the rolls. I looked despairingly around the room. To my horror, I saw that the guests, who were all staring at me, included some of the men I had most savagely and obscenely attacked in the play. There, for example, was Hyperbolus, and beside him Cleonymus the Vulture, and Cleon himself, who I knew to speak to and who was smiling at me in a friendly and welcoming way. I stammered out my business, thrust the rolls at the Archon (for some reason I cannot remember his name, although every other detail of that scene is etched on my mind as clearly as my name was inscribed on those confounded roll-covers) and prepared to make my escape.

'So this is your famous *General*, son of Euchorus,' said the Archon drowsily – he had reached that stage of relaxation that is easy to confuse with drunkenness. 'Lie down and have a cup with us. We've all heard about this marvellous play of yours, haven't we?'

His guests murmured that they certainly had, and I started to sweat. It was, I decided, that defile in Samos all over again, except that this time the enemy were well within range.

'Let's have a few lines,' said Cleonymus, wiping oyster sauce from his chin. 'I feel like some poetry.'

'The hell with that,' said Cleon. 'It's early yet, and we have the author here. Let's have the whole thing. You're not busy tonight, are you, Eupolis?'

I started to explain all about this party I had promised to go to. In fact, I was late already.

'Well then,' someone said, 'if you're late already, you'd better not go at all. Dreadful manners to arrive late. Stay here and let's hear your play. Isn't there a scene with an old woman and a pot of lentils?'

I cursed my mother under my breath for ever having given birth to me, sat down on a couch and gulped down the cup of strong wine which somebody passed to me. Then I fumbled the roll out of its cover (whatever possessed me to order those stupid bronze cylinders in the first place?) and drew it open across my knee. Of course, I didn't look at it since I knew the play by heart already, and Cleonymus told me later that I had it upside down.

The opening scene went down very well, and Cleon in particular laughed at the old joke about the size of his private parts – which must have been a politician's instinct, for it was a very unfunny joke and only put in because such a joke was now virtually obligatory in the opening scene of a Comedy. The entry of the Chorus too was rapturously received. It all seemed so horrible, for any moment now the really unforgivable personal attacks would come along, and they would probably cut my ears off with their meat-knives. I couldn't bear to look; instead, I crouched down over the roll and tried to give the play the best reading I could. My favourite lines, which I had nursed since they were little more than a patter of sounds in my head, rattled off my tongue like olives falling out of a punctured basket, and I wished that I had never composed them.

The Cleonymus scene came and went, and the scene where Hyperbolus sells his grandmother to the stone quarry foreman in return for a pound of salt and two cloves of garlic, and still they were laughing. I was just about to start on the Cleon scene when the man himself laid his hand on my arm and asked, 'Am I in this?'

Cleon, the only man in history to have prosecuted a Comic poet. 'Yes,' I said, staring at the writing on the roll.

'Have you got a spare copy?' Cleon asked. I handed him one, and he found the place. Then he motioned to me to continue. Suddenly I heard his voice – he was reading his own part, and roaring with laughter as he did so.

'This is quite good,' he kept saying. 'Do I really talk like this?'

'Yes,' Cleonymus said. 'Get on with it, will you? I'm enjoying this after the beating I took just now.'

Somehow I struggled on to the end, and when I had finished, they clapped me on the back until I thought my spine would snap.

'Eupolis of Pallene,' said the Archon gravely, 'do I take it that you are petitioning me for a Chorus at the City Dionysia?'

'Yes,' I replied. It was not the most graceful speech in the world, but I felt too drained to say anything else.

'Then I shall read and consider your play,' he replied, taking the roll from me. 'Of course, it would be most improper of me—'

'*Most* improper,' said Cleon. 'Don't be so damned pompous.'

'Most improper of me to make any comment,' the Archon continued, 'but if you know of a suitable Chorus-trainer, it might be worth your while giving him a copy now. They like to have time to work out the dances, you know.'

'Actually,' I said, 'Philonides the Chorus-master . . .'

'Oh well then, you're all right,' said the Archon. 'If he's behind you, I don't know why you bothered bringing it to me.' A wicked sort of grin passed over his face. 'Who shall we nominate to finance your play, Eupolis son of Euchorus, of the deme of Pallene? Cleon here is rich enough; do you fancy it, Cleon?'

Cleon laughed. 'It'd be the kiss of death to it if I did. Who else gets a hard time, Eupolis? What about Nicias son of Niceratus?'

The Archon made a very peculiar noise and spilt his wine down his chest. 'You're evil, Cleon,' he said. 'I'll summon him first thing in the morning.'

'Nicias,' explained Hyperbolus, who was the only man present (except me, of course) with a straight face, 'is a good man but he has no sense of humour. None whatsoever.'

Then someone demanded an encore, and this time not only Cleon but Hyperbolus (who would have made a superb actor) and Cleonymus took their own parts, and the Archon was the Chorus-leader, and we went through virtually the whole play all over again. Two of my beautifully prepared rolls were ruined by having wine spilt all over them but by this stage I couldn't care less; and I don't think I'll tell you what we did with those elegant bronze covers.

So, about four hours before dawn, I bade the Archon and his guests goodnight and took my leave of them. I was far more drunk than I had ever been in my life before, and I had no real idea of where I was going. I dropped the torch they had given me and it went out, so I blundered along in the dark, and soon fell over. By now I had no idea where I was, and I didn't really care. My *General* was going to be produced – my Chorus was as good as dressed and trained, and I could almost hear the rumble of those little wooden wheels as the trireme-costumes trundled across the orchestra of the Theatre of Dionysus. I levered myself up out of the puddle into which I had fallen, and continued on my random way.

What happened next is still fairly vague; someone stepped out in front of me and hit me over the head with a stick or a club or something, while somebody behind me jerked my cloak off my shoulders and pulled my purse out of my belt. I fell heavily on my shoulder and lay still, trying not to breathe.

'You've done it now, Orestes,' said the man behind me, and the blood turned to ice in my veins. The man standing over me had been, ever since I could remember, the most feared robber in Athens. 'You've killed him, you realise.'

'Not hard enough for that,' laughed Orestes. 'Come on, move.'

I waited until their footsteps had faded away, and then I tried to move, but I couldn't. My soul inside me wailed,

'This is what comes of your pride, Eupolis, you fool. You're paralysed. They'll have to carry you to the Theatre on a chair.' I could feel tears running down my cheeks and nose, but I couldn't move my hand to wipe them away.

I don't know how long I lay there, sobbing miserably to myself; but some old men on their way to be first in the jury queue tripped over me and saw the blood on my head. They asked me what had happened, and I croaked out the single word, 'Orestes'.

'Don't talk soft, son,' said one of the old men, 'he was hung five years ago.'

That somehow seemed to add the finishing touch to my misery; to have been crippled for life by the great Orestes would have been something to boast about, in the long years of utter stillness that lay ahead of me.

'I can't move,' I gasped. 'Do you understand me, I can't . . .'

'I'm not surprised,' said the old man, 'You're lying on your cloak. That's why your arm's trapped.'

'He's not hurt at all,' said another old man. 'Have you smelt his breath?'

They started laughing and walked on. As soon as they had gone, I made another attempt at moving and was soon standing upright rubbing my head. It was nearly light now, and I recognised the district I had wandered into. Phaedra's house – my house – was just around the corner. I picked up my stick, which had broken under me, and crept slowly to my front door.

There was light under it, and the sound of voices singing inside, but I had no strength to be angry. I just beat on the door with the crook of my stick and leaned heavily against the frame.

'If that's Mnesarchus come back again,' I heard Phaedra call out, 'tell him to go away until he's sobered up. That tapestry cost twenty drachmas.'

The door was opened a crack, and I threw my whole

weight against it. 'You paid twenty drachmas for a tapestry, you stupid cow?' I yelled, and fell forward into the room.

There was a sort of shriek, and Phaedra hurriedly wrapped a tablecloth around herself. The men weren't so quick.

'What the hell do you think you're doing, coming home in that state?' Phaedra said, but her heart wasn't in it. Still, I had to admire her for the effort.

My soul within me reminded me that my sword hung over the door, and I pulled it down and waved it ferociously. 'On your feet,' I snapped, 'all of you.'

There were three men with Phaedra, all undressed and obviously drunk. Two of them I had never seen before, but the third one I had known for a long time.

'You two get out,' I said to the strangers, 'now, before I change my mind. But you,' and I pointed to Aristophanes son of Philip, of the deme of Cholleidae, with the point of my sword, 'stay right where you are.'

The two strangers ran out into the night without even trying to collect their cloaks. Aristophanes tried to hide behind Phaedra, but she stepped aside.

'Thank God you came, Eupolis,' she sobbed. 'He was just about to—'

'I could see that,' I said, and my soul sang within me. 'Go into the inner room and stay there. Don't you dare come out,' I added sternly, 'whatever you may hear.'

Of course, I didn't really intend to kill Aristophanes; for a start, he's much bigger and stronger than me, and if I'd tried to attack him I would probably not be writing this now. But I was enjoying myself too much not to play the scene for all it was worth, and perhaps I played it a little bit too well. Anyway, as soon as I said these words, Phaedra picked up a dish of mushrooms in garlic and cream cheese and threw it at me. I ducked, and Aristophanes dashed past me out of the house. I picked myself slowly up off the floor and felt the edge of my sword.

'That only leaves you, Phaedra,' I started to say, but before I could finish I got a fit of the giggles and let the sword fall to the ground with a clang. 'Now look what you've made me do,' I quoted.

'Oh, very funny,' Phaedra said, and went into the inner room, slamming the door behind her. I picked up my sword and put it carefully back on the wall; then I followed her.

'There's garlic and mushrooms all over your statue of Clytemnestra,' I said. 'Help me off with my sandals, there's a good girl.'

She gave me a look of pure mustard, then undid the sandal-thongs and threw them into the corner of the room. 'You smell like a wine-press,' she said. 'Have you been fighting?'

'I got robbed,' I replied, 'but they're going to give me a Chorus.'

'There's blood on your forehead,' she said. 'I'll get some water.'

'Don't bother,' I said. 'Did you really pay twenty drachmas for a tapestry?'

She blushed. 'It was a bargain,' she muttered. 'Genuine Sidonian. There's only two or three in the whole of Athens.'

'Crap,' I replied. 'They make them in Corinth by the thousand and the Aeginetans ship them over here as ballast. Twenty drachmas!'

Then she tried to kiss me, but I pushed her away. 'Not until I've made my will,' I said. Her scowl wavered, very slightly.

'I didn't expect you home,' she said. 'If I had, I'd have been waiting for you. With an axe, like Clytemnestra.'

'Are you pleased I've got my Chorus?' I asked, peeling my sodden tunic off over my head.

'So long as it makes you happy,' she said, pouring water into a cup and handing it to me, 'and provided it keeps you out of the house. I trust you're going to wash before you get into bed. I may be a slut, but I'm a clean slut.'

'You're the cleanest slut in all Athens,' I yawned. 'But I'm too tired to wash right now. Besides, it deprives the skin of all those natural oils that make for a healthy complexion.'

'You're no better than a pig,' she said. 'Do you ever wash when you're in the country?'

'Never.'

She let down her hair over her shoulders, like new wine pouring into an ivory bowl. 'You looked a complete idiot standing there in the doorway waving that sword,' she said. 'Honestly, I was ashamed of you, in front of those people. It'll be all round the City in the morning.'

'It's the morning already,' I said, 'and I've got to go and see Philonides the Chorus-trainer first thing.'

'Well then,' she said, letting the tablecloth fall around her ankles. 'You'd better get some sleep.'

'Why bother?' I replied. 'It's too late now.'

CHAPTER TEN

Now I suppose you will get the idea that that was a reconciliation, and that henceforth all was well within the house. Not so. I don't think we hated each other any less; but I believe we started to enjoy fighting. For a start, we were no longer afraid of each other, and our marriage developed into a sort of running Contest Scene, which is, of course, the heart of any good Comedy. Certainly, I found myself spending more and more time at the house, though that was at least partially because I needed to be in that part of the City, to work with Philonides on the play. Phaedra and I fought all the time, day and night; and yet it was a strange sort of conflict. In fact, it reminded me of those two Spartan hounds of hers, who were always at each other's throats; blood and broken crockery and no end of noise. But when one of them was run over by a cart in the street, the other one refused to eat and died soon afterwards, leaving me thirty drachmas worse off. I don't understand what people see in dogs.

Nicias son of Niceratus was formally appointed as my producer, and I worked out the costings for the production and took them over to him. He was virtually a neighbour, and he lived in one of the best houses in the whole of Athens. His wealth came mostly from the mines, which made some people look down on him, but there was nothing of the silver-king about Nicias. He didn't smell of money, like so many people who make their own fortune; in fact, he didn't smell of anything much. Of all the men I have met in my life, I can think of few that I have admired more and liked less; for Nicias was without question the most boring man in Athens.

He was the sort of man who thinks everything through, slowly, sensibly, carefully, and does nothing until he has satisfied himself that it is prudent (and morally right) to do this particular thing in this particular way. You could see him going through a sort of checklist in his mind, and he was a terror for long, thoughtful silences. Of course, he was a martyr to kidney trouble, but he never let his illness get in the way of his responsibilities (everything in his life was a Responsibility); and although he was obviously in a great deal of pain, he never mentioned it unless he felt it his duty to confess that he would not be capable of doing such and such properly, because of his infirmity. He regarded the production of Comedy (which he could not begin to understand, and found generally distasteful) as a religious as well as a civic duty, and since he firmly believed that he held the bulk of his personal wealth as a trustee for the Athenian people – I am convinced that he enjoyed paying taxes, in so far as he ever enjoyed anything – he was determined that no expense should be spared, and that my Chorus should be equipped and trained to the highest possible standard. But then his prudence and sensibleness came into play; there must be no stinting or false economy, but there must be no waste. Waste is an affront to the Gods, who provide for us. Waste is morally wrong.

The result was that my triremes had genuine Tyrian purple cloaks; but when the cloaks were made, he sent a slave round to gather up all the offcuts and sell them in the market. The Chorus was rehearsed over and over again, on full pay; but his instructions were that anyone who was late was to be fined one obol, and the accumulated fines used to pay for a sacrifice to Dionysus on the eve of the play. As for the actors; the rules said that they were to be paid by the hour, and so every rehearsal was timed with a water-clock, which was stopped as soon as the rehearsal was finished, and the water left in the clock was carefully measured to work out what each man was owed, down to the last obol.

This was insufferable enough, and caused more bad feeling among the company than the usual miserliness and late payment would have done. But Nicias held that his responsibility to the production did not end with regular disbursements of silver. Although he hated speaking in public, he felt it was his duty to make regular speeches of encouragement (with the water-clock running, of course). These speeches never lasted more than a few minutes, and he had a good, polished turn of phrase; but I have never been so bored in all my life.

I can picture him to this day, standing by the altar in the middle of the stage, leaning on a stick, since making speeches always made him feel ill. He would clear his throat, wait for silence, and then tell us how we should always strive to do our best for our City, since between Athens and ourselves there was a perfect harmony of interest. In helping Athens, he would say (over and over again) we were acting both altruistically and selfishly – which, of course, is morally right; a man must do what is good but must also always do what is prudent, so long as he observes that Godlike balance of moderation in both. And he would always end by saying that it is men who make up a city, not walls and houses and temples, and that without good men, all the silver and triremes in the world are nothing but trouble and sorrow. He would then turn quietly away and walk painfully home, leaving us, thoroughly depressed, to try and rehearse a Comedy.

A marked contrast to Nicias' homilies were the

addresses of Philonides, which the company dreaded even more. I have heard Sicilian gang-masters, and the foremen in the stone quarries and the silver mines, but even they do not speak to slaves in the way that Philonides spoke to the free citizens of Athens who made up my Chorus. The actors had all worked with him before, but that did not stop them bursting into tears at times and even running out of the Theatre; but when I begged him to stop for fear of jeopardising the whole production, he didn't seem to hear me. During those rehearsals, everything about the play – not least the words themselves – seemed to fill him with unbearable physical pain. Yet when I went to see him at his house after a particularly agonising day in the Theatre, he would smile and pour me wine, and assure me that it was the best play ever written, and that it would be a crime against Dionysus to alter a single word, and how was my lentil crop coming on in Phrearrhos now that I had taken to using seaweed as fertiliser?

During our rehearsals, the doors to the Theatre were firmly barred and slaves with wooden clubs were stationed outside to make sure that nobody got in. But some people did manage to slip past, pretending that they were messengers from Nicias come to count the oil-lamps, or even guests of the author. It was generally known, too, that the other playwrights had their spies in the Chorus, while there was nothing that anyone could do to stop the actors selling whole speeches. I firmly believe they did it more out of hatred of Philonides than for the money; but whatever the reason, I became aware that my rivals, and Aristophanes in particular, were taking a considerable interest in the production.

All playwrights do their best to sabotage the work of their rivals. It is a mark of respect, if you choose to see it in that way, and I do it myself. Even the great Aeschylus used to try and get his rivals' actors drunk on the day of the performance, and everyone knows the story of how

Euripides kidnapped the actor Gnatho when he was waiting for his cue in Agathon's *Perseus*, and how Gnatho escaped by wriggling through a hole in the floorboards of Euripides' house, and ran back through the streets in his Tragedy boots, and entered on his cue as if nothing had happened. But somehow, during the rehearsals for *The General*, I had got it into my head that nothing like that would ever happen to me. Of course, Philonides dealt with most of the attempts to disrupt the play, and retaliated with all his characteristic ferocity. It was Philonides who ordered the attack on the poet Phrynichus, which left him with a broken collar-bone; while he nearly killed one of our actors with his own hands for trying to set light to the costumes. But he didn't tell me any of this, of course, and what I heard from other people I dismissed as silly rumours.

But I really should have begun to suspect something was up when Phaedra seemed to undergo a sort of transformation. At first, it was nothing more than a smile instead of a glare when I went home in the evenings, and I was probably too preoccupied to notice. But then the statue of Clytemnestra disappeared, and in its place was a fat leather purse full of coined silver; she knew how I hated it, she told me, and Philander's wife had liked it so much. The pet monkey had a mysterious accident at about the same time, and Phaedra began to talk quite seriously about coming to Pallene with me, since, deep down, she felt more at home in the country. She also definitely confirmed that making my will could wait for as long as I liked.

Being young and foolish, I rationalised all this as being just another aspect of my good luck, which appeared for the moment to be unstoppable. Also, Phaedra was shrewd and careful, or perhaps the strain was too much for her; anyway, we continued to have spectacular battles over nothing in particular, only rather less frequently. For my part, I was beginning to feel, at the back of my mind, that it would be no bad thing if they stopped altogether. It was becoming steadily harder for me to work up a good froth of hatred towards her, and in my soul I was afraid that our contests in future might be a little one-sided.

Then she started asking me about how the play was going. This really did shock me, for if she had ever mentioned it before, she spat the name out as if it were a bad olive. At first, it was only a casual, slightly scornful enquiry, just as you might ask a small child how its pet worm was doing, or if it had made any more of those little frogs out of mud and pomegranate-rind. But then she wanted to hear about the costumes for the Chorus (if my Chorus could have purple, why the hell couldn't she?), and was it true that I was saying horrible things about Cleon, who was the only honest man in Athens? From there it was only a short step to asking me to recite some of the speeches; and although she pretended to fall asleep, I could see that her eyes were ever so slightly open, and following me about the room as I went through the moves. In the end, I promised to take her to next week's rehearsal, and she said that would be nice, since she had just been sent a copy of the *Thebaid* by her father and when else was she going to find time to read it, with all the housework she had to do?

As we walked home from the Theatre, I asked her what she had thought of it. She wrinkled her nose, as if she could smell rancid oil.

'What's it supposed to be about?' she asked.

I ignored her. 'What did you think of the Chorus costumes?' I asked.

'I was going to talk to you about that,' she said. 'I thought you said they were meant to be triremes. Or is that another Chorus which comes on later?'

I smiled affectionately. 'I think it's Semonides,' I said, 'who says – I think it's in his *Malignity of Women* – that there's no greater gift a man can have than a stupid wife.

Did you like their little wheels? That was a stroke of genius, if you ask me.'

'How long will it be before they can stand up without them?' Phaedra replied. 'Once you've taken those off, they might look quite realistic.'

I stopped and kissed her. 'You've been eating parsley again,' I said. 'If you want to drink in the afternoons, you go right ahead. I can smell it through the parsley, so you needn't bother in future.'

'I wouldn't drink that wine from Pallene if I was dying of thirst in Egypt,' Phaedra said, and she breathed heavily into my face as she kissed me back. 'No wonder people don't come to our house any more. I heard that Amyntas was ill for a week the last time he came to see me.'

'So you're still seeing Amyntas, are you, even though he stole your Phoenician mirror with the ivory handle?' I shook my head sadly. 'And after it cost you so much to get it back from his boyfriend. You're such a bad judge of people, Phaedra, I don't know what's to become of you.'

'Actually,' she said, 'I haven't seen Amyntas for weeks, or anyone else for that matter. Can we go home now?' She yawned. 'I had a good sleep during your play, but I'm still quite tired.'

'It's drinking in the afternoons that does it,' I replied. 'If you're a good girl, I'll show you where I keep the proper wine.'

'Under the figs in the storeroom, and most of it's turned to vinegar,' she said drowsily. 'One of these days I'll get my brother to show you how to seal a jar properly.'

I have just been reading over what I have written, and I notice to my horror that I have been so carried away with my own story that I have said nothing at all about what had been happening in the war. If I were a conscientious man, instead of being naturally frivolous, I would tear the roll across and start all over again. But if I am to be honest for once, I must confess that I remember that part of the war no better than any other Athenian; as a nation we have remarkably poor memories for things that have happened in our own lifetime. We are rather better at the deeds of our fathers and grandfathers; but since we get our information about those times from men who were equally negligent and forgetful in their own day, it stands to reason that if any part of our historical tradition is accurate, this can only be by pure chance, or because we have asked men from other cities what they can remember.

But you have been counting through the years on your fingers, and are sitting there like men at Assembly waiting for the good news about whitebait prices, in the hope that I will say something about Mitylene and Pylos. So I had better say something about that, or you will despair of me and my History, and sell my book to the men who scrape down paper to be used again. Very well, then.

Actually, I did go to Assembly when they debated Mytilene; the first day, that is, not the second, when they changed their minds. I hadn't meant to go; in fact I was standing in the Market Square haggling with a man for a bundle of sheepskins, which I wanted to use as blankets in Pallene. I was so busy trying to save myself a few obols that I didn't see that the constables were coming through the Market Square with the rope dipped in red paint, which is how they used to drive people with nothing to do up to Assembly in my day. The fleece-seller suddenly ducked behind his bales, and when I looked round there was the red rope, heading straight for me. I just managed to get up to the Pnyx before they caught up with me, and so avoided the chant of 'Redleg!' which always greets the last arrivals.

It was there that I heard Cleon speak in public for the first time, and you can imagine the impression it made on me. He was a truly awe-inspiring figure when he had worked himself up into a fury, and although I felt it my duty as a Comic poet to hate him, I found it very difficult.

You probably know more about the Mitylenean crisis than I do, but the basic situation was this. Our subjects in Mitylene, the largest city in Lesbos, had rebelled, and after a lot of trouble we broke the rebellion and regained control of the city. The motion before Assembly, therefore, was what we should do with the Mityleneans, and most of us, at least before Cleon started to speak, would have given the same answer; kill or exile the ringleaders, double the taxes, and leave a garrison. But Cleon, typically, had a much better idea. He wanted to turn an episode which did not, broadly speaking, do us much credit into an opportunity for 'clear thinking and radical action', to use a favourite phrase of his. He wanted us to put to death every adult male in Mitylene, regardless of any plea or excuse. That way, he argued, he would demonstrate not only how dangerous it was to play games with the Athenians, but also how totally unlike other cities we were.

'Who else in the whole of Greece,' he said, in that wonderful, horrible voice of his, 'would dare to contemplate such a dreadful act, the destruction of an entire people? Never mind who else could do it – although there are very few who could; who else *would* do such a thing? Who would dare?'

Here he paused, and looked around slowly, as if daring someone to interrupt him. 'But you would, Men of Athens, if you have courage to match your position. And why? Because you are a democracy, the only true democracy in the history of the world. For a democracy which is a true democracy can do anything it pleases, and no constraint of expediency or morality can restrain it. Because the People have no permanent identity, because they are immortal and are influenced by no factor other than their own benefit, the only limit to what they can do is the physical limit of what they can get away with, what they can actually start and complete without inter-ruption or being bodily prevented by others. It is this that gives us Athenians the ability, and the right, to be the servants of none and the masters of others.

'But, I hear some of you muttering, just because we, alone of all men, can put the Mityleneans to death, surely that doesn't mean that we must? On the contrary, Men of Athens. Because we have this unique power, we must exercise it; we must be ruthless in exercising it, or else it will float away from us, like a dream on waking. Otherwise we will create for ourselves mental restraints more deadly than physical ones; we will begin to say, "We *dare* not do this", not, "We *cannot* do this", which would be like binding ourselves in chains because no other man is able to bind us.

'No; if it seems true to us that the best way to preserve our empire in the future is to set it such a terrifying example that no man would ever dare to rebel again, we have no real option other than to set that example, and show the world that Athens will stop at nothing to get what it wants. For you all know the rest. If we lose our subject-states, then we lose our whole way of life, which is that of the landlords of Greece. At present, no man in any of our cities can plough his land or promise his daughter in marriage or buy flour in the market, except by the consent of Athens. I do not mean that we authorise all these things, or that each man must receive a licence written in wax before he does anything; but he knows that he is the property of Athens, just as your chattels are the property of each one of you.

'Supposing Nicias or Callias the son of Hipponicus, who each has hundreds of slaves, had one slave in particular who not only ran away but incited his fellows to do the same, and cut their master's throat into the bargain. Nicias and Callias are honest, pious men; but would they hesitate to have that slave whipped and tortured to death? Of course not. They are rich enough to bear the loss, and if they did not do so, they would be positively encouraging their other slaves to run away too, and asking to be murdered themselves. And you, fellow Athenians, you have more slaves than anyone else. You can afford the loss, but you cannot afford to give treason a precedent. So if you value your empire and your democracy and your very lives, vote for my proposal. But if you do not, and if you are prepared to hand over your true and only wealth to the Spartans and the Corinthians, then vote against it.'

Of course, we all voted for him, and cheered him until our throats were dry, and went home to tell anyone unlucky enough not to have been present what a feast of oratory and good sense they had missed. But we are Athenians, and so the next day when someone demanded that we reconsider the resolution, we did, and overruled it, too. The general view seemed to be that since we had voted both for and against the motion, we must have got it right either the first or the second time, which was very clever of us.

So Cleon didn't get his way over Mitylene. But this defeat did him no harm at all, no more than all the attacks in the Comedies. The real test of his abilities came much later, at about the time I married Phaedra and went to Samos.

It all started when Demosthenes, a brilliant, dashing and quite remarkably lucky general of ours, made rather a mess of an important and fairly straightforward campaign in Aetolia. He was far too frightened to come home, since he would have been exiled or put to death, and so he hung around in Naupactus waiting for his luck to change. And change it did. Before he knew quite what was happening, he had won a notable victory in Messenia and was able to come home safely.

But Demosthenes never knew when to leave well alone, and so he persuaded the Athenians to give him forty first-class warships, to use at his absolute discretion in and around the Peloponnese. For he had seen a place on the Messenian coast called Pylos; once the home of the fabulous King Nestor, but now a god-forsaken place with nothing much to it except a certain shape, which Demosthenes but no one else could see. His fellow generals told him not to be so damned stupid and come and join them in a little recreational crop-burning; but Demosthenes would not be diverted from his arcane purpose. Since he could not openly dissent from the opinion of his fellow generals, he sat down in Pylos and read Homer, and his colleagues washed their hands of him and got on with the war. But Demosthenes' soldiers, either from boredom or because they had had the idea planted in their heads, set about fortifying Pylos with whatever materials came to hand.

King Agis of Sparta, on his way home from burning the best crop of early beans I have ever managed to produce, heard about what was going on at Pylos, and nearly had a stroke. Apparently, he too had seen that natural shape at Pylos, and had been meaning to do something about it for some time. Perhaps my early beans got in his way; certainly he recognised that once a force of determined men got dug in at Pylos, there was nothing on earth that could get them out. He marched as fast as he could, hoping to take Demosthenes by surprise.

Lying next to Pylos is a wooded and uninhabited island called Sphacteria, on to which Agis transferred the flower of the Spartan army, with some idea of using it as a base for attacking Demosthenes without having to risk a sea-battle. The main point about Sphacteria is that there is no water on the island; but this seemed irrelevant, since the Spartans did not intend to stay there for more than a day or so.

Just then, a large Athenian fleet, which Demosthenes had sent for, arrived unexpectedly, and there was a messy battle between the Athenians and Agis's forces on the mainland, both by land and sea. Despite the efforts of a certain Spartan captain called Brasidas, the Athenians won, and the Spartans drew out feeling hard done by. Except, of course, for their best troops, who were cooped up on Sphacteria with no ships and no water.

Demosthenes realised that his position, although it looked good for the moment, was untenable. Unless he thought of something quickly, the Spartans would overcome their profound respect for him and come back, and even his luck was unlikely to hold out much longer. There was no way of knowing how long the reserves of water on Sphacteria would last, and even though he had swept the sea clear of Peloponnesian warships, it would be impossible to stop small fishing-boats slipping out by night and supplying the Spartans on the island.

So he made a deal, which under the circumstances was the best he could do. In return for being allowed to send food and water in to Sphacteria, the Spartans were to hand over all the ships they had in the area as securities (to be returned if the truce was observed) and keep well away while they sent an embassy to Athens to discuss peace terms. The Spartans sent their embassy, which Cleon, who was then under considerable pressure from the moderate faction, sent away again. Accordingly, Demosthenes stopped the food shipments, but claimed some minor infringement of the truce and refused to return the ships. The Spartans attacked at once by land, and Demosthenes, despite reinforcements from Athens, didn't know what to do next. He could see no hope of taking Sphacteria by storm, and if he let the men on the island die of hunger and thirst, he would lose his hostages and with them the best opportunity Athens had yet had of ending the war. In addition, he was running short of food and water himself, in spite of now having seventy first-class warships to fetch and carry for him, and since the Spartans were managing to get some supplies through to Sphacteria, it looked as if the whole thing could still end in disaster. So he sent a full account of his position to Athens and asked for any sensible suggestions.

Cleon, who had turned away the Spartan ambassadors, was now in deep trouble, and all he could think of was to accuse Demosthenes' messengers of lying. It was therefore proposed – I think as a joke – that he be sent out to have a look for himself, and the proposal was overwhelmingly accepted. But Cleon kept his nerve and counter-proposed that Nicias son of Niceratus, who was one of the generals that year, should be sent out with reinforcements to help Demosthenes.

Nicias, being Nicias, stood there like a thoughtful sheep and said that although it was a great honour to be chosen for such an important mission, his infirmity was such that he could not accept it. At this, Cleon tried to be rather too clever. He said that Nicias was nothing special, and neither was Demosthenes, whom everyone was calling the best thing since fried whitebait. Any fool, he said, could have those Spartans off that island and back in Athens in a couple of days. Why, even he could do it . . .

Nicias, who had been sitting there fretting about failing to do his duty in his city's hour of need, suddenly brightened up and said that that was a wonderful idea, and everyone started agreeing with him and cheering at the tops of their voices. Cleon, who knew about as much about the arts of war as I do about sponge-diving, went a ghastly shade of white and started to talk very fast. But nobody would listen to him; the more he gabbled, the more they cheered, until he realised that there was no way out.

So he stood up and held up his hand for silence, and everyone stopped laughing and shouting, to hear what this clever man would say next. Cleon started by saying that he was moved and honoured by his fellow citizens' confidence in him, which was a generous reward for the few small services he had done the Athenians, but which he could not help feeling was misplaced. He had never held a military command before, and although nothing would please him more than to go, he felt he could not risk the lives of his fellow Athenians in this venture. Instead, he said, raising his voice so as to be heard above the groundswell of rude noises coming from his beloved fellow citizens, he would take with him only the few allied heavy infantry who were stationed in Athens, and a force of light infantry and archers, also allies. Then he took a deep breath and shut his eyes, and promised that if he wasn't back, mission accomplished, within twenty days, they could duck him in one of his own tanning-vats and cut him up for sandals. The Athenians roared with laughter and cheered so loudly that they could be heard all over the City; for even if Cleon couldn't hope to deliver, it had been great fun listening to him, and there would be more fun still, first when he made his excuses, and later at his trial.

Twenty days later, he was back; and with him were the Spartans from the island, including one hundred and twenty Spartiate noblemen, in chains. There was a different sort of cheering after that, and although Aristophanes' next play, which was entirely devoted to the most vicious attacks on Cleon, won first prize, that was little more than an Athenian way of telling him how much they loved him, just as they had loved Pericles and Themistocles before him.

In fact, it wasn't fool's luck, as everyone said afterwards. Because Cleon wasn't a soldier, he didn't think like a soldier. He saw that heavy infantry, the heart and soul of any Greek army, are never much more than a liability, and since the object of the exercise was to take as many Spartan heavy infantrymen alive as possible, he couldn't use Athenian heavy troops against them. So he used his brains instead. First he set fire to the woods which cover Sphacteria – Demosthenes had been too clever to think of anything so simple – and when the Spartans came dashing out, like hares out of barley when it's being cut, he harried them with his light infantry and archers until, out of a mixture of exhaustion and frustration at not being able to come to grips with their tormentors, they threw down their shields and surrendered quietly. It was all totally new and barbaric, but it worked, with minimal losses to them and virtually none to us.

That, then, was Cleon, perhaps the most typically Athenian of the City's leaders during my lifetime. It's wrong to think of him as being in the same class as Themistocles or even Pericles, since those men left Athens stronger than they had found her. But in a way they can be compared; for each one of them taught the world new tricks. It was my duty as a Comic poet to hate Cleon, and I did my best. But I met him many times and could not help liking the man.

I once saw a crowd of people down at Piraeus watching a hawk killing a dove. The foreigners wanted the dove to escape, since it was weaker and more beautiful; but the Athenians were cheering on the hawk. Then, when the hawk had killed the dove and was pulling its head off with its talons, a man stepped forward with a sling-shot and the Athenians started betting on whether he could kill the hawk, since the range was quite long and a hawk is a tough sort of a bird. The slinger had bet three obols on himself, so he put forth all his skill and a moment later the hawk was lying on its back, stone dead, with a great chunk of dove-meat still in its beak. The cheering that greeted the shot reminded me of the cheering that greeted Cleon's return from Pylos, and also the announcement of his death at Amphipolis, rather bravely in battle, against the invincible Spartan general Brasidas, a month or so after my play was performed. He had been trying to repeat his previous stunning success, but this time he had overreached himself, and the defeat at Amphipolis cancelled out everything that he had achieved at Pylos.

I believe Aristophanes went into deep mourning for his death, just as Cratinus had done for Pericles. But unlike Cratinus he continued attacking him in his Comedies for years afterwards, and I remember sitting through a particularly dreary play of his, all about Dionysus going down to Hell to bring back a poet or some such nonsense, and a foreigner sitting next to me asking, 'Who is this Cleon he keeps going on about?' I closed my eyes for a moment, and wondered how I could possibly explain; about Pylos, and the informers, and the Brotherhood of the Three Obols.

'Search me,' I replied. 'Never heard of him.'

CHAPTER ELEVEN

Phaedra took to coming to rehearsals with me regularly. So as not to scandalise the company, who were all very superstitious, she dressed up in a boy's going-to-school clothes and sat there with her tablets on her lap, while I told everyone who asked that she was a cousin up from the country.

A week before the Festival, someone took a hammer to the little statue of Hermes outside my house, and pushed a cock with its head and spurs cut off under my door. This didn't worry me at all; I replaced the old Hermes with a new one by a leading sculptor, and we had the cock, stewed in wine, for dinner. I was rather more concerned by the rumours going round that Phrynichus, who had the third Chorus that year, had got hold of one of the big speeches in the Contest Scene, and had adapted it to fit into his play. If his play was called on before mine, they told me, he was going to use that speech instead of his own, so that mine would be jeered off the stage. I consulted Philonides, who said that it had been done before, and so sat down, with a headache and three rolls of scrubbed Egyptian paper, to try and compose a substitute speech. Eventually I got one written, and gave it to the actor to learn. If Phrynichus tried it on, I would be ready for him.

The Tragedies that year included Agathon's *Electra*, Euripides' *Teucer*, and something by Melanthius – there was a scene in it where the hero went off-stage and came back transformed by a God into a pig, with a dainty little pig's mask and trotters, which got a bigger laugh than anything in any of the Comedies, but I can't remember anything else about it. The Comedies were mine, Phrynichus' *Garlic-Eaters*, and Aristophanes' *Veterans of Marathon*. He had two plays that year, for he got a Chorus for his *Wasps* at the Lenaea, which did depressingly well.

Phrynichus was called on the first day. I was told the result of the ballot just before dawn, and sent Doron over to tell Philonides. Of course, I still had no idea whether I would be called on the second or the third day, and I sat through that day's Tragedies in a fever of impatience. For some reason I kept wishing I had Phaedra with me (she was sitting with the other women, of course, on the other side of the Theatre) and at one stage I absent-mindedly reached out for the hand of the man sitting next to me. Luckily he was too wrapped up in the play to notice, since he wasn't my type at all. As Aegisthus or Diomedes or whoever it was droned his way through his cosmic passion, it suddenly struck me that my feelings for Phaedra had undergone an unhealthy change. Instead of wishing she had never been born, I realised, I could feel a sort of smile wriggling on to my face whenever I thought of her, and a warm sensation all over my body. This was only when she wasn't there, of course; it took only a few minutes in her company for all the old, familiar feelings of exasperation and fury to come flooding back. But that was an overstatement too. I felt that we were like two ageing boxers who work in one of those travelling fairs that sometimes pass through the country districts. Every day of their lives, they have to fight each other and put on a show of pain and violence, but if you watch closely they don't hit each other at all; and when the people have all gone, the older one, who isn't married, takes his tunic round to the younger one's tent so that his wife can darn it for him.

Yet all we seemed to have in common, apart from bad luck in having been married to each other, was an unending battle. You know how young husbands and wives are always stretching their minds to think up little treats and surprises for each other – a pretty, old-fashioned grasshopper brooch, or a new way of preparing anchovies; well, we seemed to spend just as much time and effort thinking up new snubs and insults and ways of inflicting annoyance, but never anything that hurt too much. If I heard a fishmonger make some particularly unflattering comment on the appearance of one of his women customers, I would say it over and over to myself under my breath as I walked home, for fear of forgetting it; and whenever a book arrived for me from the copyists, Phaedra would always go through it first and put a little charcoal mark beside any passage concerning Clytemnestra or Medea, or any other heroines who killed or injured their husbands. At night, we rarely did anything but sleep, and when we climbed into bed together we would lie on our sides, each grimly facing the wall on either side. But by the morning it often happened that we had turned to face each other, and usually she was lying on my arm, so that I was woken up by the numbness in it. Then we would start to bicker, still half asleep, until one of us jumped out in a rage and went to wash. And on those few occasions when one of us had the itch, the other never refused, but preferred to make nasty remarks or pretend to be asleep until the clumsy process was over. I was fairly certain that Phaedra had stopped seeing other men (although she denied it vehemently), while I could never see any point in chasing after flute-girls and housemaids, who never wash and are forever pestering you for money.

All this passed through my mind as I sat there, and I

quite forgot about the hardness of the seat (I had forgotten to bring a cushion) or the dreariness of the play, or even my fear of Phrynichus. In fact, by the time I came round, the King (or whoever it was) had been killed, or blinded, or turned into whatever he was turned into, and the Chorus were into their second round of lamentation. I dismissed all thoughts of Phaedra from my mind, and started surveying the audience.

It's probably my imagination, but I believe that I can tell just by looking at them whether an enemy line is going to stand or run, or whether an audience is likely to be friendly or not. With audiences, you can work out a great deal beforehand. If it's been a bad year or the enemy have burnt their crops, they will be anxious to be pleased, and will roar with laughter at anything that resembles a joke. But if the vintage has gone off well, or news has just come in of a naval victory, they'll sit there like a jury at the trial of a politician, just waiting for some little flaw or slip. If the play is good they show no mercy to the actors, and if the acting is good, it stands to reason that the play is weak and the costumes were cobbled together at the last minute out of old cloaks and sail-cloth. It's the other way round with Tragedy, of course. People like nothing better than blood and death when they've been gorging themselves on freshly made cheese and new wine; but if there's been a food shortage, or the list of casualties has been read out, the prancing and howling of actors will irritate them beyond measure. This is why, when the fleet sails, the Tragedians go down to Piraeus and offer sacrifices for its safe return, while the Comic poets say a silent prayer to Poseidon for a violent thunderstorm.

But this year had been neither bad nor good; there had been as many victories as defeats in the war (or so we assured ourselves) and if the Spartans had burnt most of the barley, they had missed more than usual. So a great deal would depend on the plays, Comedies and

Tragedies, that came on before mine. If an audience falls in love with the first Comedy in the Festival, they don't give the others a fair chance. But if not, then they tend to give the benefit of the doubt to the play which is called on last. If the Tragedies have bored them, they enjoy the Comedies more; but if they are still talking about the Tragedies when the Comedy is called on, they're quite capable of chatting away throughout the opening scene and then blaming the author for not explaining the situation properly.

Of course, the reaction of the audience is not what really matters. What every playwright has nightmares about is the twelve judges. It's a remarkable effect. A play can be booed off the stage, and the actors barely escape with their lives. But if it's subsequently awarded the prize, then by the next day everyone is quoting it as they work in the fields, and declaring it the funniest thing ever, while the play that comes third is universally ridiculed, even if while the Chorus was on stage the audience was choking with laughter and yelling for reprises. And then, of course, there are always those people – I tend to find myself standing behind them in queues – who always disagree with the judges, praising the play that came third and saying that if the prizewinner gets a Chorus next year they'll stay at home and make vineprops.

That year I couldn't recognise any of the judges – in those days they really were chosen by lot from the electoral roll – which I considered on balance to be the best thing. A friend among the judges can be a blessing, but it can also be a disadvantage, while an enemy is always disastrous. I remember staring long and hard at them, trying to prise open their ribs with my eyes so that I could see the shape of their souls, but the more I stared, the less I could see. There was a very old man who kept whispering to his neighbour; I could almost hear him saying, 'When I was a boy, of course, we had Aeschylus and Phrynichus – that's Phrynichus the Tragic poet, of course, not this young man who writes the Comedies.' And the man next to him would nod absently, but he never took his eyes off the stage, and instead of wriggling about in his seat he sat absolutely still, with his hands neatly folded in his lap. He would probably vote for the play with the fewest metrical errors, and I squirmed as I thought of the three fluffed caesuras in *The General*. Another one had his eyes closed, and I was filled with fury; if he dared fall asleep when my Chorus was on stage I would get a sling and knock his eyes out for him. But when the strophe ended, he moved his head and nodded, and I realised that he was paying strict attention. That's the judge for you, my soul said smugly within me; he won't be swayed by smart costumes or clever masks. It's the words he's interested in. Then his head fell on one side, and I could see that he really was asleep after all.

By the time the herald called out 'Phrynichus, bring out your Chorus!' I was drenched in sweat and my heart was pounding like the drum on a trireme when the drummer is setting the pace for the attack. I clamped my teeth together, for I was determined not to laugh, and sat up straight in my seat, praying that Philonides had bribed the Chorus or put sand in the leading actor's mask. Yet when the first big joke came, I felt this strange feeling in my chest and something seemed to well up inside me, as if I had eaten beans and drunk new wine, and I heard myself laughing. A feeling of terror came over me, as I realised that the play actually was funny, and when the audience laughed it was like the sound of hooves making the earth shake, when the enemy cavalry is coming towards you and there is nowhere to run.

Then my soul spoke quietly within me, telling me that there was nothing more that I could do, at least until the play was over and I could go straight over to Philonides' house and fix those fluffed caesuras and the joke about the sprats. I pressed my feet hard on the stone and pushed myself back in my seat, and soon I was enjoying the play. It was a good play, too, all about a man who wins the war by drawing the sun down into a jar so that the Spartan army loses its way in the dark and marches off a cliff, and there was a hilarious scene with Apollo trying to charm the lid off the jar by reciting passages from Sophocles.

I enjoyed it so much, in fact, that I forgot all about everything else, and clapped as loudly as anyone when the Chorus lined up for the anapaests. Phrynichus' addresses to the audience were always the best part of his plays, and he had an uncanny knack of guessing, at the time he wrote the play, what would be most topical when the Festival came round.

He started off by praising the army and the fleet, and comparing them to the men of Marathon and Salamis; then there was a rather witty invocation to Lady Garlic; then he went into one of his favourite themes, the poets.

First, inevitably, Cratinus, who by now had entered into his final illness; Phrynichus had great fun with that, saying how while Dionysus and Aphrodite were quarrelling like two wild dogs over his miserable carcase, Hermes, as God of Thieves, was sneaking up behind them to secure for himself the greatest stealer of other men's jokes the world had ever seen. Then we were given some marvellous stuff about Ameipsias throwing away his shield at the battle of Delium and having to be rescued by Socrates, who he had made mincemeat of in one of his plays. I was grinning like an idiot by this stage, in eager anticipation of what the poet would have to say about Aristophanes. What I and several thousand others heard was this.

As if it wasn't bad enough (Phrynichus' Chorus-leader said) having these stray polecats jumping up on Dionysus' altar to gobble down the offerings left there by Thespis, there was now a new poet in Athens; a cripple with a perpetual grin and nothing between his legs but a nasty rash. (It's true I sometimes have a rash there in hot weather; God knows how Phrynichus found out about it.) We hear that his play, which you will soon be able to judge for yourselves, has some pretty bits in it. They aren't his own, of course; Aristophanes gave them to him in exchange for his life, when he caught that bald-headed son of a goat up to the hilts in that pretty young wife of his.

It's a strange feeling being insulted in a play, and hearing the people hooting with laughter. The man on one side of me was stuffing his cloak into his mouth and snorting, while my neighbour on the other side had a smile which would have stretched right round the coast from Piraeus to Anaphlystos. I would gladly have castrated Phrynichus just then; but I felt a strange sort of glow, almost like pride, and I wanted to turn to my neighbours and say, 'That's me he's talking about.' And when I've spoken to men I've made jokes about, they say roughly the same thing, and attribute the feeling to the power of the God Dionysus himself. Later, of course, I became hardened to remarks about me in plays, until I only noticed them when they weren't there.

I met Phaedra outside the gate and we walked home together.

'If you really *were* a man,' she said, 'you'd kill that Phrynichus for me.'

I shrugged. 'Why?' I asked. 'Because he agrees with you?'

'I don't care a damn what he says about you.'

'He said you were pretty.'

'I didn't say he wasn't telling the truth,' she replied quickly. 'But how I'm going to hold my head up in public again after that, I just don't know.'

I put my arm around her waist. 'Never mind,' I said. 'He didn't steal my speech, that's the main thing.'

'How did he know about that rash of yours?' she went on.

'You must have talked about it in your sleep.'

'Now all the women will refuse to sit next to me,' she went on, as if I hadn't spoken, 'in case they catch it from me. It's not catching, is it?'

'I expect so. I hope I don't get called on tomorrow. They may not tell me until the morning, of course, and then I'll have to go round the wine shops flushing out the actors. I'll enjoy that,' I pre-empted her.

'Eupolis.' She had stopped in her tracks and was biting her lower lip.

'There's something I've got to tell you.'

'Who's the father, do you know?'

Suddenly she got very angry. 'Why must you always be making *jokes*?' she shouted. 'I'm really sick of it, do you hear? All the time. I just don't think it's funny any more.' She pulled her hand out of mine and turned away. I suddenly felt very foolish, although God only knows why, and I stood there on one leg waiting for her to say something.

'I mean,' she went on, with her back still to me, 'if you hadn't been such a complete waste of time ever since our wedding-day I wouldn't have done it in the first place.'

'Done what?'

'So if anyone's to blame,' she said, rounding on me and scowling, 'you are, you utterly stupid man.' She spat neatly between her feet. 'You pushed me just too far, that's all.'

'What have you done?'

'Go to hell,' she snapped, and started to walk quickly away. I ran after her and grabbed her by the wrists. 'Let go of me,' she said, and pulled her hands free. 'You see,' she sneered, 'you can't even bully me properly.'

'I asked you a question,' I said. 'What have you done?'

'It was all Aristophanes' idea,' she said, 'while I was still seeing him. Do you know,' she went on, 'he's almost as big a washout as you are? Anyway, he wanted me to find some way of wrecking this play of yours. I told him not to bother, it was bound to fail of its own accord; but he's stupid, just like you, and he wanted to make sure. And that's why I started being so nice to you—'

'When? I must have missed it.'

'For God's sake, Eupolis.' She was tight-lipped with fury, and I decided to leave well alone. 'I let you take me to your stupid rehearsals, and you kept on about your stupid costumes for your stupid Chorus. So I listened carefully to what they said about where they stored them.'

'They're over at Philonides' house,' I said. 'He keeps them in his inner room in a locked chest.'

'I know,' she replied. 'I heard him saying so. So I told Aristophanes, and tomorrow morning, before dawn, he's going round there with his actors and he's going to dig through the wall of the house and steal them.'

It was like being hit by that footpad all over again. I felt my legs go weak, and I couldn't think. 'For God's sake, woman,' I groaned, 'why didn't you just kill me instead? That's a horrible thing to do.'

Then I felt her head under my chin and her arms around me. 'But you deserved it,' she sobbed. 'You deserved it so much. I knew it would hurt you more than anything in the whole world, because you're so stupid.'

The feel of her so close to me was like fire, and my soul filled my arms and my legs with strength.

'How do you know it'll be tomorrow?' I asked her. 'For all he knew, I could have been called on first.'

She shook her head. 'He fixed the ballot,' she said. 'He bribed someone, he didn't tell me who. He wanted you on tomorrow and himself last, to be sure of beating Phrynichus. Eupolis, I—'

'We'll discuss that later,' I said. 'Go home and mix plenty of strong wine. I've got to find Philonides.'

So, when rosy-fingered dawn was spreading across the eastern sky, I was hiding behind a large jar in Philonides' inner room, feeling that mixture of fear and righteous anger that Theseus must have felt when he strode through the Labyrinth in search of the Minotaur.

Philonides himself was crouched uncomfortably behind the costume chest, and positioned at strategic points all round the room were our four actors, Little Zeus, three large slaves from Philonides' household, and a man who had been passing in the street when we arrived, who we pressed into service as an independent witness. Apart from the witness, we were all wearing our helmets and breastplates, and we had heavy olive clubs hastily cut from vine-props.

'Of course,' said Little Zeus (one of whose ancestors had been a famous general), 'the whole thing could be a clever trick.'

'I don't know about clever,' Philonides said. 'Dirty, maybe.'

'No, you don't understand,' said Little Zeus earnestly. 'It could be a false message, a diversion, like Themistocles at Salamis. Aristophanes might want us to be here, while he does something else on the other side of the City. He could be poisoning our Chorus-leader at this very moment.'

Philonides told him to be quiet, but I started to worry, and I picked all the bark off the handle of my club with my fingernails without realising it. The effects of the strong wine we had all drunk at my house were beginning to evaporate, as was the righteous anger. The residue was mostly fear, combined with a feeling that I shouldn't really be there. I had wanted to send someone for Callicrates and Philodemus, but there hadn't been time. And I was sure someone had followed Philonides and me back to my house after I found him.

'Perhaps he isn't coming,' said one of the actors. 'We've been here for hours now, and I'm dying for a pee. Are we getting paid for this?'

'You'll get the back of my hand if you don't shut up,' said Philonides.

'And will you all stop jabbering like a lot of birds? This is supposed to be an ambush.'

At least worrying about the attack kept me from worrying too much about my play, though I had suddenly remembered that we had never got around to fixing the fluffed caesuras. Still, I felt, this would probably not be a good time for a major rewrite, even though we had all the actors with us.

Then I saw Philonides lift his head suddenly, and I heard the sound of a crowbar clinking on the bricks of the wall. Philonides put up his hand and placed a pot carefully over the lamp. In the total darkness, the sound of the crowbar seemed to fill the room, and I started to think of all the battles in tight places that I could remember; Thermopylae, and Pylos, of course. The more I thought, the more uneasy I felt, for in every such engagement that I could call to mind, the attackers had eventually prevailed. We had no idea how many men Aristophanes had brought; he might have his whole Chorus out there, with swords and damp leaves to make smoke. We were well off for heavy infantry, but where were our slingers and archers? And we had forgotten to bar the door; Aristophanes could not expect the house to be empty – what if he were to send a detachment of his forces round to the front of the house, to take us from both sides, as Xerxes had done at Thermopylae? And although we were armed with clubs, they had heavy iron crowbars, and none of us had thought to bring our shields. If only Callicrates was here! If only Callicrates was here, and I was somewhere else.

Then my soul within me told me to be quiet and fight well when the moment came, and I gripped the handle of my club so tight that I pinched the skin inside my signet-ring, which seemed to hurt as much as a sabre-cut. The sound of crowbars was growing louder with every heart-beat, and I was sure I could hear voices, many voices. Not only his Chorus, I said to my soul, but all his household slaves as well, and probably some cooks or other ruffians hired in the Market Square. I felt trapped, like a grasshopper in a jar. Demosthenes himself would have trouble getting out of this mess.

There was a sound of rubble falling on our side of the wall, and a shaft of early morning light came into the room, very faint but enough to dazzle me for a moment. My mouth was dry, and every muscle in my body seemed to ache. More hammering; whole bricks were coming through into the room, and I remember thinking that whoever had built Philonides' house had made a pretty poor job of it. The hammering stopped, and with it my heart.

'Boss,' whispered a voice from the wall, 'I can get my head through the hole now.'

'Get on with it, you idiot.' Unmistakably Aristophanes. 'We haven't got all night.'

'Boss,' whispered the voice again, 'what if there's somebody in there? I mean—'

'Philonides is at Eupolis' house,' Aristophanes said, 'my man saw him go in, they're probably making last-minute changes. And he always sends his wife to the country for the Festival. Can we get on now, please?'

That seemed to satisfy the voice, for the hammering started up again, and more bricks came tumbling in, until I could see a man-sized patch of blue light where there had been only darkness before. I promised a firstling lamb each to Dionysus and Ares the Driver of the Spoil, and waited. There was silence, then a rustling noise, and the blue light was blotted out by moving shapes.

Then Philonides lifted the pot off the lamp and shouted *Io Paian!* at the top of his voice, and there was Aristophanes, frozen like a statue in the lamplight. In his hands were a crowbar and a lump-hammer, and his tunic was gathered over his shoulder like a stone-mason. With him were four men, similarly dressed and equipped. The head of a sixth man, which was poking through the hole in the wall, was hurriedly withdrawn and not seen again.

I aimed a terrific blow at the man nearest to me, but I missed and decimated a terracotta figure of Europa riding the bull, which, Philonides told me later, had belonged to his grandfather. But Little Zeus made straight for Aristophanes and grabbed him round the waist like a wrestler, lifting him up so high that his head banged noisily against the rafters. Meanwhile, Philonides and his men were laying about them with their clubs, shouting ferociously and occasionally making contact. The actual fighting was over disappointingly quickly, and by the time I had picked my club up off the floor, there was no one left for me to hit with it.

Philonides and his men had dumped their four captives on the floor and were tying them securely with scarves and rushes, while Little Zeus manhandled Aristophanes round to face me. Now during our interminable vigil I had prepared a little speech, in case such an opportunity arose. 'Aristophanes son of Philip,' I intended to say, 'what you have done here tonight is a crime not only against the laws of Athens but against our Patron God Dionysus himself. To sabotage one of His plays is no better an act for a free man and a citizen than burning His temple or robbing His priests. But Dionysus is a merciful God, and so I shall leave your punishment in His hands. You may go free, son of Philip, on the following conditions. First, that you make good all the damage you have done here, and lodge a bronze statue of Dionysus the Bringer of Joy in the shrine of Philonides' choice. Second, that you cease to trouble the God with your ill-made plays and henceforth live quietly on your Aeginetan estates without causing annoyance to anyone. What do you have to say?'

It was probably just as well that I did not deliver this address, or my name would have become a byword for pomposity, wherever two Athenians met together. As it was, I had got as far as 'Arist—' when Aristophanes, slipping out of Little Zeus' clutches, made a dash for the hole in the wall and escaped, bumping into me as he went. I tried to catch hold of his tunic but lost my footing in a puddle of lamp-oil, slipped, and sat down painfully on a pair of sandals.

'Pathetic,' grunted Philonides. 'Couldn't catch a fever in the marshes. Right, let's have a look at them.'

He grabbed each of the captives by the beard and stared fiercely at them for a moment. 'Now listen to me,' he said. 'Fun is fun but I can't be doing with nonsense, so when you next work with me, you'd better be very careful. All right, Aristobulus, untie them. I said untie them, you idiot; those scarves cost money.'

'Are those Aristophanes' actors?' I protested. 'We could lock them up, and then—'

Philondes told me to be quiet, and threw each one of the prisoners out with his own hands. 'They'd have done as much for me, I expect,' he said, and sat down on the costume chest.

'But, Philonides—' I protested.

'Now listen, you,' Philonides replied angrily, grabbing me by the arm, 'I have to work with these people, right? And with Aristophanes, come to that. So that's an end of it, right?'

I nodded and he let me go. I went and stood in the corner of the room, feeling rather upset. But Philonides stood up and started to survey the damage to his property.

'Since you let the son of Philip get away,' he said, 'I'm holding you liable for all this damage.' He turned to the witness, who was looking thoroughly confused. 'Have you got that? Eupolis son of Euchorus, of the deme of Pallene. And if I find out which one of you clowns smashed up my best chair, I'll pull his head off.'

There was far too much for us all still to do for any of us to feel tired or elated; there were costumes to be assembled, masks to be lined, and (I'm sorry to say) lines to be learned. By the time the messenger arrived, sent on from my house, to tell me that I was to be called on that day, the Chorus had already assembled and was making one last desperate attempt to come to grips with the major dance routine. Philonides seemed to have put all the events of the early morning behind him, as if such things happened every day, and was frantically chasing after bits of wool and leather strapping for the masks, on which it appeared that the success of our entire enterprise now depended. He seemed to have no use for me whatsoever and finally ordered me to get out from under his feet; he was a busy man, he said, and greatly though he valued my friendship and society, this was neither the time nor the place for amateurs. So I withdrew in a huff, like Achilles, and went home to dump my breastplate and helmet and change my clothes.

The streets seemed to be full of people, some with cushions under their arms, others carrying their children on their shoulders, all apparently making for the Theatre. I thought I heard my name mentioned once or twice, and that made me feel as if I was the King of the Athenians on his coronation-day, or a politician about to be tried for high treason, depending on the tone of voice of the person I was listening to at the time.

Phaedra was looking out of the open door as I came up the street.

'Well?' she demanded, as I pushed past her into the house. 'What happened? Did you get them?'

'More or less,' I replied, slinging my armour under a couch. 'Like a fool, I let Aristophanes get away, but Philonides got the rest of them and sorted them out once and for all. I don't think we'll have any more trouble.'

'Good,' said Phaedra, and she put her arms round my neck.

'Not now,' I said. 'Is there anything to eat in this house?'

She unhooked herself. 'I'll make you some porridge, if you like,' she said. 'You'll need something—'

'There isn't time,' I replied, 'I'll get a sausage or something at the Theatre. What I need now is some clean clothes. These are full of brick-dust.' I poured some water into a bowl and washed my face, which felt as if all the silt of a Nile flood had accumulated on it, and dried my hands on one of the twenty-drachma Persian tapestries. While I was doing so, Phaedra came back in with some clean clothes; but instead of throwing them at me, she pretended not to notice what I was doing and said, 'Here you are.'

I took off my old tunic and she gave me the new one. 'I haven't seen this before,' I said.

'I know,' she replied. 'And do try not to get it too filthy, because it took me weeks to make it and you know how much I hate weaving.'

I stared at it, as if it had been the tunic of Nessus. 'You made it?' I asked stupidly. 'For me?'

'No, for the bath-attendant, but he didn't like the colour. Don't sound so amazed, you ungrateful pig.'

'Bet it doesn't fit,' I said, shoving my head through the collar. It fitted perfectly, and smelt faintly and surprisingly of roses. 'Thought not,' I went on. 'Tight under the arms.'

'Good,' she said. 'So I don't suppose you'll want the cloak.'

'Far be it from me to give offence,' I said. 'I can always take it off when I get outside.'

She came close to me to fasten the brooch round my neck, and I kissed her without thinking. I was starting to lose count of the number of times I had kissed her. 'How's that?' she asked.

'It'll do,' I said.

She had fastened the brooch, but she didn't move away. 'And when do I get shouted at?' she said softly.

'What for?' I asked.

'Oh, for telling Aristophanes about those stupid costumes.' She closed her eyes and raised her head towards me.

'Later,' I said, 'when I've got a minute.'

'You've had your chance,' she said. 'Now, rather more important, when are you finally going to get around to thanking me? For saving the play at the last minute, like a Goddess on the flying machine?' She stood on tiptoe until her lips were very close to mine, and I kissed her again.

'Call that thanks?' she said. 'You didn't even open your mouth.'

'I did,' I replied, 'and that's all the thanks you deserve. Now will you please stop climbing up me and let me get on?'

She pulled a face and let go of me. 'Go on,' she said, 'get out and stay out. I can't stand the sight of you.'

'Good,' I said. 'So you won't be coming to the Theatre, then?'

'What, and miss you getting booed off the stage? I wouldn't miss that for all the perfume in Corinth.'

I picked up my walking-stick and looked at my reflection in a polished bronze jar; an idiot, I told myself, but a talented idiot. Then I saw Phaedra's face over my shoulder, and turned round. She pressed her nose against my chest and said, 'Eupolis.'

'Now what?'

'Good luck,' she whispered. 'I know they'll hate it, but I hope they don't throw stones at you. I'm sick and tired of you coming to bed all over blood.'

'Luck?' I said. 'Who needs it?' I swirled my cloak round on my shoulders like a cavalry captain at the Panathenaea, and darted a sudden kiss at her, but I missed her lips and connected with her nose instead. She called me a clumsy idiot and giggled.

'When you see me next,' I said, posing in the doorway like a statue, 'I shall be the greatest poet in all Athens, and then you'll be sorry.'

'I'm not exactly ecstatic now,' she said, smiling.

'I shall return,' I continued, 'like King Leonidas himself; with my harp, or on it.' I strode magnificently out of the door, pretended to trip on my cloak, waved, and walked away.

'Do I get a choice?' Phaedra called after me.

As I bounced down the street, I pressed the collar of the tunic against my cheek, and I felt as Achilles must have felt, when he first went out to fight in the armour that the Fire God himself had made for him. Or perhaps I felt more like Hector, setting out on that day when Zeus promised him success so long as the daylight lasted. For although my body was on fire wherever the tunic and cloak touched it, and my heart as well, my soul inside me was still as cold as ice.

The Theatre was filling up when I got there, and after I had bought a sausage and a small loaf from one of the sausage-sellers, I sat down on the end of one of the middle rows and looked about me. There is no sound like the Theatre just before the start of the first play; like a hive of angry bees when they smell the first wisps of smoke from the beekeeper's bellows. Away on the very back rows a drunk was singing a country song, something about the swallow bringing back the good times, and when he had finished, there was a ripple of applause and some cheering. The audience were in a good mood, and I lifted my head and thanked all the Gods.

Someone walking across the stage waved to me, and I saw that it was Phrynichus, who I knew only by sight; a big man with a black beard, and his left arm in bandages. I waved back, just in case anyone was watching, for I didn't want to be talked about as a man who bears grudges. Then I looked around for an omen; but no birds flew overhead, neither on the left nor on the right, and since the sun was sharp I gave up and ate my sausage, which tasted horrible. I decided to save the bread for after the first Tragedy.

I saw Callicrates and Little Zeus and my uncle Philodemus coming down the stairs towards me, but I signalled to them to go away since I wanted to sit among strangers. Philodemus seemed offended, but Callicrates said something to him and he nodded, and they sat down where they were. I could hear Little Zeus saying something in his loud, flat voice, but I couldn't make out the words. I hoped he was praying for me.

Then I saw a bald head with a nasty-looking cut on it walking past a row or so beneath me, and I couldn't resist calling out. Aristophanes stopped and sent on his friends to reserve him a place, and looked up at me, grinning like an ape.

'Hello,' he shouted, 'and how's the cripple with the nasty rash this morning?'

'Couldn't be better,' I replied. 'And how is our two-obol Odysseus getting on, after his bungled shot at stealing the Palladium?'

He broadened his smile until I thought his face would crack. 'This is a very historic occasion,' he said. 'The very last time Eupolis ever leads out his Chorus.'

Just then, I couldn't think of a good reply (I thought of plenty later) and so I threw a nut at him instead. He walked on, laughing at his own joke and waving to somebody important in the front row. I scowled, and it occurred to me that Dolon would have been a neater comparison than Odysseus, but my soul told me to forget it, and I shifted up to make room for a fat man in a leather hat.

I soon found out a great deal about my neighbour, for he told me himself. He was a stranger in town, he said, here on business, but he had brought his wife with him to see the show, and she was sitting over there with the other women, but she had a cushion, so that was all right, and her name was Deianeira, by the way, and he was Pericleidas son of Bellerophon, and his home town was Catana, which was in Sicily but an ally of Athens of course, and very proud of it, too, and he was in the dry-fish business, which was why he was here in Athens, since back home folks were always telling him how Athens was the biggest market outside Persia for dried fish, especially now, with the war and all, although for some reason the Athenians just now seemed to get most of their dried fish requirements from Pontus, which was very strange and hard to believe, since he couldn't think why the Athenians should want to pay two obols a quart over the odds for an inferior product instead of buying from honest-to-God Greeks, especially since there were such strong ties of loyalty and affection between Catana and Athens, which were very important to a man like him, who was just mad about the Theatre, which was really the reason he was over in Athens this time of year, when the best time for dried fish was really later on around the time of the Lenaea, but of course foreigners weren't allowed to go to the Lenaea, which of course he could understand, what with it being a very special and meaningful religious occasion here in Athens, but which was a pity nevertheless for a man who was just wild about the Theatre, like all Sicilians were, although there is no domestic Theatre in Sicily, because most of the cities in Sicily were Dorian foundations, not Ionian, and the Dorians worship Dionysus in a different way, although it didn't actually seem to make the slightest bit of difference to the wine yields, because if old Dionysus got it into His head to make it a bad year then that was that, or so he reckoned, and what did I think?

'My name is Eupolis,' I replied. 'Welcome to Athens.'

Then the herald called on the first Tragedy, and Pericleidas quietened down a bit, once he understood that I knew the story of Oedipus quite well already. I don't remember anything else about that Tragedy, or the others after it, except that I wanted them to go on for as long as possible, provided that they did it quickly. And then the herald called out, 'Eupolis, bring on your

Chorus,' and I put my hands in front of my eyes and took them away again quickly for fear of missing anything, and Pericleidas leaned across and whispered, 'Is that you?'

'Yes,' I said.

'Well,' he said, 'isn't that just wonderful?' and he slapped his knees with the palms of his hands for pure joy.

And the actors said their lines and the Chorus danced, and Aristobulus got the Cleon scene right for the very first time, and not one member of the Chorus forgot to do his rowing motions during the Hymn to Poseidon, and when it was all over and the Chorus had danced out again, Pericleidas leaned across to me and whispered, 'Well anyway, *I* liked it.'

For once, I seemed to have no trouble getting out of the Theatre, for the other people seemed to melt away in front of me, as if they were ghosts. But I could hear them chatting away, as Theatre audiences do, and they were all saying, 'Never mind, we've got the Aristophanes to look forward to tomorrow. Now he really does know how to write a Comedy.' And instead of crowding round me as I passed by them, the sausage-sellers stood aloof and let me go by, as the gate-keepers shrink back from lepers.

Philonides tried to cheer me up, but I could see that he was furious at having backed a loser and made a fool of himself, while the Chorus were pulling off their costumes and flinging them back into the costume chest as if they were afraid of catching something from them. So I made my excuses and left, and strolled back into the Theatre, which was now quite empty, with only the slaves sweeping up the rubbish ready for the next day. I sat myself down under the big statue of Dionysus and burst into tears.

As I sat there, I heard a voice above me, and I knew that it was coming from the statue.

'Pretty bad, Eupolis,' it said, 'but there's worse to

come. No, don't look round; you'll see me soon enough, in the walled orchard, as I promised you. It was a bad play, son of Euchorus. Show me something better next time, if ever you get a Chorus again.'

I listened, but there was no more, and I got to my feet and set off home. The streets were as quiet and empty as they had been that day when I escaped from the stable during the plague, and the only living creature I saw was a dog, who followed me for some time until I threw a stone at it.

Phaedra was waiting for me when I got home, with a cup of wine with herbs and cheese. She tried to put her arms round me, but I pushed her away and sat down by the fire. I needed warmth. Phaedra came and knelt beside me, offering me the wine. I pushed it away, and the cup fell out of her hands and broke on the floor.

'Please don't be upset,' she said. 'It was a good play, really.'

'No it *wasn't*,' I shouted. 'It was the worst play ever written.'

'All right then,' she said, and her voice seemed to come from a long way off, 'you may be right, I don't know. But even if it was, you'll learn from it, and you won't make the same mistakes again. And next year . . .'

Her voice was irritating me, like the buzzing of a fly, and I turned my head away. Had Aristophanes started celebrating already, I wondered, now that the prize was as good as his? Lord Dionysus, I prayed, if you love me and are my patron, let Phrynichus win, not Aristophanes.

'Look,' she said, 'it's not the end of the world, I promise you. Really, you are a good poet, I mean it. Just because this time—'

Suddenly I felt hot, and I pulled at the cloak round my neck so hard that the cloth tore all around the brooch. I wrenched it loose and threw it on the ground.

'Can't you just shut up, for God's sake?' I shouted. 'Why don't you just go away and leave me alone?'

She made a grab for my hand, but I pulled it away. After a moment, she got up from where she had been kneeling, said, 'The hell with you, then,' and went into the inner room, slamming the door behind her.

I didn't go to the Theatre next morning, but in the evening Callicrates came by and said that Phrynichus had won, with Aristophanes coming second, by unanimous vote of the twelve judges. By then I was feeling all stupid and Spartan, and I said something idiotic about thanking the Gods that Athens had two playwrights better even than me. Callicrates very sensibly didn't reply, and he got up to go.

'By the way,' he said, 'we got a message from Phaedra this morning. She says to tell you she isn't coming back till you apologise. I don't know what she's done this time, but if I can help in any way . . .'

I frowned, feeling as if I were drunk. 'Coming back?' I said. 'I didn't even know she had gone.'

'She's at her father's house,' he said, 'she's been there all day. Do you mean to say you hadn't even noticed?'

I started to laugh, and Callicrates, who had been very patient with me, finally lost his temper. He told me to stop acting like a child, and slammed the door behind him. I called after him, but he didn't come back; it was hard to make him angry, but, like everything else he did, he did it well. I sat down by the fire, which had gone out long since, and listened hard to my soul; but nothing came.

The next morning I had two visitors. One was a messenger from Phrynichus, inviting me, as is usual, to his Victory party. I can't remember what I threw at him, but whatever it was I missed. The second was Phaedra's father, dragging Phaedra along behind him like an unwilling dog.

'She's your problem now,' he said, pushing her at me like a man returning rotten fish to a fishmonger. 'I've got guests staying, I don't need her banging about the house. A man should be able to keep his own wife under control.'

He had scratch-marks on his left cheek, just like a set I had seen in my mirror one time. 'I'm sorry,' I said, 'it won't happen again.'

'It better hadn't, that's all,' he said. 'And let me make this clear, young man; I'm not having her giving birth in my house, and that's final. You can clear up your own mess yourself.'

He stormed off, shutting the door quickly behind him, as if he was afraid Phaedra would slip out after him. She stood there looking at me for a long time.

'Did you hear that?' she said.

'I'm not deaf,' I replied. 'Is it true?'

'Yes, it's true,' she snapped. 'I only wish it wasn't.'

'Well,' I said, 'I don't know what you expect me to do about it, since I'm obviously not the father.'

'Of course you're the father,' she shouted. 'And look at me, will you?'

I turned my back on her. 'I'm not the father and I'm not going to accept it. You can do what you like.'

'Fine,' she said. 'I'll leave it out on the hillside for the wolves. Is that what you want?'

'I couldn't care less,' I said, and I closed my eyes and breathed in deeply. 'How long have you known?' I asked.

'Oh, about a week or so,' she said wearily. 'I was going to tell you when you won your stupid prize with your stupid, stupid play. I thought you'd be in a good mood. But trust you to make a mess of that.'

'So that's what it's all been about, you devious bitch,' I said, suddenly feeling angry. 'All this—'

'All this what?'

'That,' I said, and I kicked the cloak she had made me across the room. 'You really wasted your time making that.'

'Did I?' She was standing quite still and looking at me, and I couldn't meet her eyes.

'Yes,' I said firmly. 'Look, it's obvious it's never going to work, so I think it would be best if we just kept out of each other's way from now on, just as we did when we started. Don't worry, I'll accept the child. Just don't expect me to have anything to do with it, that's all.'

'That's what you want, is it?'

'I think that would be best for both of us,' I said. 'Don't you?'

'Yes,' she said, 'That suits me fine.'

I stood up and took off the tunic she had made, and put on the one that was covered in brick-dust. It seemed to hurt me wherever it touched my skin.

'I'll send you money,' I said, 'as soon as I get to Pallene. If you don't mind, I'll set off now. I've got everything I need there.'

I walked out without looking back, and rode straight to Pallene without stopping. They were surprised to see me, and as usual asked if my wife was with me. I told them no, not this time, and was there any hot food, because I was starving after my ride. The next day I sent a reliable man and his wife to the city, to give Phaedra the money I had promised her and to stay in the house if she was afraid of being there on her own; also, if she wanted anything, to send a messenger to me, or Callicrates if it was important. She sent the man and his wife back, saying she would get in some of her father's people, if that was all right. I did not reply.

Shortly afterwards, as I have already told you, Cleon was killed at Amphipolis and the Spartans sent an embassy offering peace. There were last-minute hitches and tantrums from both sides, but in the end Nicias son of Niceratus took charge of the negotiations and brought back peace for fifty years, by land and sea, not long after Aristophanes won the first prize at the City Dionysia for his play *Peace*. The war was over at last.

CHAPTER TWELVE

When the Peace was concluded, I was twenty-one years old, a member of the Cavalry class – however hard I tried I could never squeeze more than four hundred and sixty measures of produce, wet and dry, out of my estates, and for reasons best known to himself, Solon set the limit for the upper class at five hundred measures – and shortly to be a father. I could reasonably expect to live for another thirty years, or even longer; my family regularly survives into the sixties, and I had a grand-uncle who made it to eighty-four, to the extreme disgust of his children. It was not as uncommon then as you would suppose for a man to live apart from his wife, if he could afford it, and, apart from gossip, I heard nothing from or about Phaedra. I sent her money regularly, but spent most of my time in Pallene.

There was so much to do there that I had little time to think of anything else. You may have noticed from what I have written that I have always been interested in the life and times of the dictator Pisistratus – I can say such things now, of course, even in public – and whenever I met someone who had a story about him, I would make sure I heard it. From all these stories I was able to confirm my belief that in his time, the Athenians cultivated far more of Attica than they do now, thanks to subsidies and support from the Dictator. I felt that I was in a position to undertake a Pisistratean programme of my own, using the resources of my more productive land to support the recovery of the desert areas. So I bought and hired labour, and set about taking in land on the mountainsides, wherever there was enough topsoil to dirty my fingertip.

It was, looking back, an absurd idea; but I was young and looking for something to do, now that I had turned my back on Comedy. We hacked terraces where even goats hesitated to go, scraping the soil into baskets and lowering it with ropes down to the new working. We built dams like the walls of Babylon just to persuade little trickles of water to drip the right way, but the only moisture that regularly got through to the ground was our sweat. I can't bear to think how much money and food I wasted trying to chip a few acres out of the side of Parnes and Hymettus, but once I had committed myself to it, I was determined not to turn back. In the end it was all done, the vines and olives were planted, and we were able to sit back and watch them wither away and die. Out of twelve acres of terraces that we festooned round the mountainsides, only four are still working today.

While I was about my fool's errand, Phaedra had her baby, and after all that trouble it was only a girl. Phaedra named it Cleopatra – 'Daddy's pride and joy'; her sense of humour was just as bad as ever – and gave it to one of her father's women to nurse. I didn't go and see it, of course, for I was still maintaining privately that it wasn't mine. But Callicrates went, taking with him a little box of gold and lapis jewellery, which he bought with his own money. His own wife was barren, and he had refused to divorce her. When he next came to see me, he made a point of telling me how like me little Cleopatra looked, but I didn't want to know, so I said that he was probably right – bald, with an idiot grin and a nasty rash. He never mentioned her after that.

It was only after Cleon's death that I discovered that he had been using his influence to keep me off the army lists. I was completely astonished, since I could think of no reason why he should want to help me. I had wondered why I had only been called on once, of course, but I had put it down to luck. But Cleonymus the Vulture, who told me about it when I met him by chance one day in Pallene, said, No, on the contrary, Cleon had liked me, he said, and besides, I was the only poet in Athens he had any chance of getting on his side.

'That was when you still were a poet, of course,' he said, warming his huge hands in front of my fire, 'before that nasty experience of yours.'

I laughed; that was quite easy now. 'Then he made a mistake, didn't he?' I said cheerfully. 'Nobody's right all the time.'

'I don't know so much,' Cleonymus said. 'Now, personally, I think all Comic poets are the scum of the earth, and the sooner you're all sent down the silver mines the better. But Cleon was different. He liked Comedy – said it was worth thousands of votes to him to be made fun of, because it stopped people seeing him as a threat. More fool them, of course.'

'But he prosecuted Aristophanes,' I replied. 'I'd have thought you'd have approved.'

'Murder, yes,' I said, pouring him more wine, 'prosecution, no. It was a terrible thing to do. Impious.'

'Well,' gurgled Cleonymus through the wine, 'everyone makes mistakes. It wasn't the jokes about him that Cleon minded, anyway. That son of Philip is mixed up with some very unsavoury people. You know, long hair and fleece-lined riding-boots and elocution lessons and little trips to Sparta when no one's looking.'

'Your Great Conspiracy again? I thought that was strictly for the Assembly.'

'Oh it is, it is,' said Cleonymus sadly. 'But we're getting away from the point. Cleon thought you were a good poet, Eupolis, and it was his trade to know such things. Now you may have made an unsightly mess all over the Theatre, and I may be old and a nasty piece of work, all told. But I care about the democracy, young man, just like Cleon did; if it wasn't for scumbags like him and me, you'd be taking your orders from a King, not sticking your hand up in Assembly.' He put his cup down and leaned forward, until I felt he was going to roll on me and crush me, like a sow.

'You owe us,' he said, 'just as much as if we had mortgage-stones all over those new fields of yours. I don't want you to forget it.'

'Get out of my house,' I said timidly. Cleonymus smiled.

'I've been thrown out of better places than this,' he replied cheerfully, and lolled back in his chair. 'I'm not threatening you,' he went on. 'If I was, you'd know it, believe me. What I'm actually doing is encouraging you. Start writing again, that's all I want, and perhaps your friends might see that you get another Chorus.'

'Thanks,' I said, 'but I'm through with all that.'

'Oh well, what a pity. Never mind.' Cleonymus stood up. 'Don't bother letting me know when you change your mind. By the way,' he added, 'you were right about one thing.'

'What?'

'Cleon making a mistake about you. He thought you'd have brains enough to see that he gave you your *General*, that night when you called to see the Archon. I thought that, too. Pity.'

He rolled out, got on his horse, and rode away towards the City, leaving me feeling as if he'd just blown his nose on my head.

After that, it came as no real surprise when, about a month later, I was summoned to the Prytaneum. As I rode I speculated as to what it was likely to be; some sort of punishment for my ingratitude, I supposed. By the time I got to the gates, I had decided that it was probably my turn to pay for the fitting-out of a warship, or (more probably) a Chorus. As I passed the Theatre, I prayed to Dionysus not to let them make me pay for the latest Aristophanes.

I sat on the steps for an hour or so waiting for the Council to call me, and while I was sitting there a man passed by whom I knew from somewhere. I smiled at him, trying to remember his name.

'Hello, Eupolis,' he said brightly, 'how are your new terraces doing?'

'Could be worse,' I replied. The face was definitely familiar – long and thin, with a big nose, and the beard shaved close to the chin. In his middle to late thirties, to judge by the grey hairs. 'Not worth the effort, of course, but then, what is?'

He laughed. 'Quite right,' he said. 'Are they sending you somewhere, then?'

'Your guess is as good as mine,' I replied. 'That, or a trireme, or hemlock, of course.'

He grinned. 'I wouldn't worry,' he said, 'we only execute generals now. Good luck, whatever it is.' He waved and ran gracefully down the steps. As soon as I heard him mention generals, I realised that I had been speaking to the glorious Demosthenes, Cleon's partner at Pylos. I was amazed that he should even recognise me, let alone know about my terraces, for we had never talked to each other before as far as I could remember, and even I wouldn't have forgotten meeting Demosthenes.

Then they called me in, and the palms of my hands started to sweat. For some reason I had got it into my head that I would be called in front of the full Council, and have to stand there while they fired questions at me from all over the chamber; so I was greatly relieved and not at all disappointed when I was shown into a little annexe about the size of a poor man's storeroom. A man

I knew, a neighbour of mine from Phrearrhos, was sitting there, and I assumed that he was waiting too.

'Hello, Mnesarchides,' I said. 'Have you been summoned as well?'

'Don't talk soft,' he replied, 'I'm on the Council. Don't you ever listen to what people tell you?'

Now that he came to mention it, I remembered hearing that his name had come up for the year. I smiled broadly and offered my commiserations. He thanked me.

'Well, young Eupolis,' he said, in that voice which even quite sensible people use when they get lumbered with a public office they don't want, 'I'm delighted to have to inform you that you have been selected to accompany our forthcoming mission to Thessaly.'

'What mission to Thessaly? I thought that was all over now.'

'Events have transpired,' said Mnesarchides, 'that necessitate high-level discussions between ourselves and the present regime.'

'I see.' I could feel his disapproval, but I somehow couldn't force myself to take Mnesarchides in his new role as Councillor seriously; the last time I had spoken to him we had discussed how best to rot manure, and very boring he was too. 'So what do you want me to do?'

'You will accompany Theorus and Strato to Larissa, and report back your findings to the Assembly and to me personally.'

'Personally?'

'That's right.' He nodded decisively, and continued, 'You will receive a drachma a day as compensation, to be paid on your return, and of course should some unfortunate event occur, you will be entitled to a public burial, and your children will receive their first set of armour free of charge from public funds.'

'That's nice,' I said. 'So when do we leave?'

'First,' said Mnesarchides, frowning, 'I must brief you on the purpose of your mission.'

'That would help,' I agreed.

'You will interview the princes Alexander and Jason,' said Mnesarchides, 'about their attitude to sending cavalry assistance should any unforeseen situation arise within the next year. You are authorised to offer five obols per man per day, plus a premium of two talents.'

'Five obols?' I said. 'That's a bit much, isn't it, for a rabble of Thessalian horse-thieves?'

'That is the maximum the Council has authorised,' said Mnesarchides defensively. 'Naturally, we hope that you will be able to come to a more advantageous arrangement.'

'Are you expecting any unforeseen situations, then?'

'We have to provide for every contingency,' said Mnesarchides. 'You leave in three days from Piraeus on the *Salaminia*. You will sail as far as the mouth of the River Tempe, where the princes will meet you with horses and escort you to Larissa.'

'How many cavalry do we want?' I asked.

'Don't specify a number,' he said. 'As yet, our exact requirements are uncertain.'

'Unforeseen?'

'Precisely.'

'But more than a hundred, say?'

'In excess of a hundred, certainly. We can safely authorise in excess of five hundred.'

There was a long silence. 'How are your lentils coming on, Mnesarchides?' I asked.

'Champion,' he replied. 'Good luck.'

I had met Theorus at Aristophanes' party, if you remember, and several times since, and since he had a great reputation for knowing what was going on, I asked him why I had been chosen for the mission.

'Easy,' he said. We were standing on the deck of the *Salaminia*, looking back at Athens disappearing behind us. 'Ask me something difficult.' He yawned, for he was used to sea travel.

'Go on, then,' I said. 'Then I can go and lie down.'

'Well,' said Theorus, 'you're a poet, aren't you? And all these Thessalians and Thracians and Macedonians and wogs like that, they're obsessed with the Theatre. Not that they do anything themselves, of course, because none of them can read or write; but they know all the latest plays by heart, because they send for Athenians to come and recite them, and they're always spouting speeches at you, in those horrible voices, which is very funny because they don't understand a word they're saying. When I was at the court of old man Sitalces, we made up a great chunk of the biggest rubbish you ever heard and swore blind it was from an unfinished masterpiece by Aeschylus. They're probably still reciting it to this day, poor fools. It's all part of them pretending to be Greeks, I suppose,' Theorus said sadly, 'but it'll never work. I mean, most of them look like Greeks, and if you try really hard you can make them talk quite like Greeks, but basically they're animals, like all foreigners.'

'Hang on,' I said, 'you mean I'm on this mission because I had a play produced?'

'Why else?' he said. 'And since all the Tragedians they're likely to have heard of are either too old or – well, you know, not quite sound – and Phrynichus refused to go and Amyntas is ill and Aristophanes is busy with his next and Plato's got toothache, that just left you.'

'You think they've heard of me?'

'I sincerely hope so. We sent them up a couple of copies of that thing of yours that came third a while back – and someone to read it to them, of course – so they'll probably all know it by heart by now.'

I thanked him and went to be sick. It was hard to associate Cleonymus the Vulture and Theorus with my neighbour Mnesarchides in a conspiracy against me, but I have always found sea travel conducive to paranoia, and by the time we arrived in Thessaly I was thoroughly miserable.

The valley of the Tempe is one of the loveliest places I have ever been to. It's where they come to gather the laurel for the crowns they give to the winners in the Pythian games, and no matter where you live, you're likely to find scenery that will appeal to you. There are spectacular rocks and mountains, woodlands quite unlike anything we have in Attica, and good, well-ordered fertile country beside the river. On your left is Mount Ossa, rising almost vertically from the plain; while on your right is Olympus itself. So enchanted was I with the place that I almost expected to see Zeus and Hera standing on the hillside waving to me.

What we did find was a squadron of cavalry, sent by the princes to meet us. Like any good merchants, they had set out their best wares to tempt the buyer, and I must confess that I was impressed by those Thessalians. They were tall men, with big broad-brimmed leather hats and two spears each, sitting so easily on their horses that I was irresistibly reminded of Centaurs; not the grotesque monsters in the carvings, but the Centaurs that you see in some vase-paintings, young and dashing, superhuman rather than subhuman. They said very little, and their faces were strange, too, for many of them were clean-shaven, despite their age, and most of them had bright blue eyes and long, straight hair. I should think Achilles probably looked like that, since he was from Phthia; but I've never liked Achilles, and I liked those Thessalians.

It was hard getting many words out of them as we rode to Larissa; they certainly weren't interested in the Theatre, or in anything much except sheep and Thessalian politics. The latter, I gathered, consisted almost entirely of assassinations among the ruling families. One of our escort told me a bit about what was going on, but I soon lost track, since most Thessalian chieftains seem to have the same names, and when I heard my instructor say, 'And after that, Perdiccas son of

Scopadas killed Perdiccas son of Perdiccas, which left Scopadas the son of Thettalus at the mercy of Perdiccas son of Cersebleptes,' I gave up and started counting birds instead. But there was something reliable and straightforward about the Thessalians which made up for their shortcomings as conversationalists, and they had that slow dignity which you often get with unintelligent people. They were the sort of men who don't mind if you say nothing at all for half an hour, and there aren't many like that in Attica.

When we reached Larissa I took it for a village at first. It had walls, and gates, and was really quite large, and the people in the streets, particularly the women, were all well (if curiously) dressed. But it had that small-town feel about it that some people like and others don't. Theorus plainly didn't – he's one of those people who feel uncomfortable if they can't reach out their hands and touch marble – but I admit that I did; if I was ever exiled, I thought, I could find worse places to live than this. Naturally, Strato, the third member of the party, was visibly drooling, but he'd been doing that ever since we'd met up with our escort. I don't think he got very far with any of them.

I expected our hosts the princes to be like their cavalrymen; but they weren't, not at all. When we reached the palace – a large, rectangular building, like an oversized trireme-shed – they came out to meet us, two very fat men in their late twenties. I had expected them to be older, but then I remembered what my friend the cavalryman had been telling me about Thessalian politics, and realised that not many chieftains live much longer than twenty-nine.

There's nothing like meeting foreigners to make you think hard about your own people. Alexander and Jason were dressed in what would have been the height of fashion in Athens among, say, Alcibiades' circle about eight months ago, except that Alcibiades and his friends would never have worn so much heavy gold jewellery. For a start, they couldn't have afforded it, and even if they had managed to get together as much gold as Jason had hanging round his chins, they'd have used it to bribe a jury with instead of having it made into a massive great necklace. When he spoke, Jason used Attic Greek, except that he didn't quite understand where he should change T to S, and his voice was almost but not quite a City voice. Theorus shuddered when he heard him, and I don't think even Strato fancied him much. Alexander wasn't much better; his Attic was almost perfect, but he kept putting on a lisp – more mimicry of Alcibiades, I suppose – and it was rather disconcerting when he forgot to do it. Also, Strato lisps naturally, and I think Alexander thought he was trying to be funny.

The princes, although they were extremely talkative, seemed reluctant to discuss such tiresome matters as cavalrymen and money, although Theorus, who was now sulking and generally behaving very badly, kept trying to drag the conversation round. But Alexander was clearly not going to be cheated of his ration of spoken Attic; and when Theorus asked him bluntly when we were going to start talking business, he waved his hand in a very affected way and said that tomorrow, or the next day, we might have some preliminary discussions. Meanwhile, he said, he had such a nice surprise for us, and we weren't to spoil it by talking about silly old cavalrymen. That seemed to be the last straw as far as Theorus was concerned. He put his feet up on his couch and pretended to go to sleep.

After what seemed like a very long time, we were able to escape, on the pretext of changing our clothes, and we were led off down a long corridor that formed part of the wall of the town. After what seemed like a day's march, we were each shown into a house-sized room crowded with heavily carved furniture and silverware. I put on my best tunic and cloak, looked at my face in a big bronze mixing-bowl (what it was doing there I could not imagine), and knocked on Strato's door to find out what was going to happen next.

'What do you think the surprise will be?' I asked.

'Something dire,' he replied. 'Belly-dancers, human sacrifice, gladiatorial display, poetry reading, you can never tell with these people. Sometimes it's like being at a really boring party, sometimes it's like something out of the adventures of Odysseus. Whatever it is, keep a straight face and smile a lot.'

The main hall of the palace was how I'd always imagined a palace to be, with long tables and benches, just like in Homer, and a fireplace running the length of the room. The roof was high and black with smoke, and they were roasting pigs and deer on spits; I'd never seen so much meat before in my life. The benches were filled with huge, fierce-looking men wearing coarse woollen clothes and enormous quantities of gold jewellery, and they were making an extraordinary amount of noise. Most of them looked like Greeks, but there were men wearing trousers like Persians, or Phrygian felt caps and tiaras, and some of them had breastplates on, for reasons best known to themselves. It all seemed very strange and intimidating to me, but my two companions merely found it distasteful, and muttered that there must be easier ways to earn a living, such as digging coal.

As guests of honour we sat with the princes, and were soon being overwhelmed with food. Among the beautiful and good of Thessaly the belief seems to be that if it moves, it can also be eaten, and if it doesn't, it can't, for the only vegetable I could see was leeks, boiled into a sort of mush and slopped out of a huge silver cauldron. We got wine to drink – lovely stuff from Rhodes and Chios, served neat in hollowed-out buffalo horns – but the Thessalians seemed to prefer a sort of sticky black stuff which they apparently make from rotten honey. No one offered us any, which was a great relief. If this was the lovely surprise, I thought as I started on my third helping of roast venison, it could be worse. But it seemed a terrible waste somehow, and I wished I could find some way of hiding some of the roast meat inside my tunic and taking it back to Athens with me.

Eventually the stripped ribcages were cleared away, and the entertainment began. I think the Thessalian nobles seated below us were dreading it almost as much as we were – in Thessaly, I am told, they like to while away the evenings by grabbing hold of the smallest person present, tying him to a pillar, and throwing bones at him. Anyway, Prince Jason called for silence by hammering on the table with his goblet, and the roar of voices dwindled away like water out of a punctured skin.

'Men of Thessaly,' shouted Jason – and I was amused to see that he used his proper voice for addressing his peers – 'today we feast three honoured guests from Athens in Attica.' Loud cheering and much banging of tables. 'They come to seek our aid in their war against the Spartans of Laconia. They, who are invincible by sea and excellent above all men for their armoured infantry, beseech us as friends to send them cavalry. What is your opinion?'

More cheering, banging on tables, waving of arms, throwing of bones. While all this was going on, I leaned over to Theorus and asked what Jason meant by our war with the Spartans. Hadn't they heard about the Peace?

'Don't be an idiot,' he whispered back. 'The princes know all right, but obviously they haven't told this lot. I don't think most of them would understand the meaning of the word, and those that do probably don't hold with it.'

'I thank you, men of Thessaly,' said Jason. 'Now, to celebrate the presence amongst us of three such noble guests, I command you all to assemble in the Field of Zeus tomorrow three hours after sunrise. That is all.'

He sat down; muted cheering, no banging of tables. 'Savages,' muttered Jason under his breath, and picked up a roast rabbit that everyone else had overlooked. 'You can't imagine, my dears,' he said through a mouthful of rabbit, 'what a trial it can be living among these barbarians. How I long to see Athens again – the Market Square, the Necropolis . . .'

Alexander giggled. 'You mean the Acropolis, silly.'

'Just my little joke,' Jason replied irritably. 'You're the silly, for not spotting it. And of course,' he said, turning his head and looking straight at me, 'the Theatre. You can have no idea how I long for the Theatre.'

Strato kicked my ankle under the table. 'You're interested in plays, then?' I asked.

'I live for the Drama,' replied Jason, and to emphasise his sincerity he stopped eating for a moment. 'Which is why today is the happiest day of my life. To have, under my roof, the great Eupolis, greatest poet of his age – well, if I died tonight it would be like the answer to a prayer.'

To judge by the way Alexander was looking at him, his prayers could easily have been answered. I took a long pull at my wine, and thanked him for his kind words. Jason stood up and bowed, and then sat down again, and started firing questions at me – did Euripides really not believe in the Gods, and was Moschus as brilliant as everyone seemed to think, and what was Theognis going to do next, and could we expect anything more from Sophocles, and what was Agathon *really* like, and was Phrynichus (who Jason had obviously got confused with the old Tragedian of the same name) ever going to give us an *Oedipus*? I replied as best I could, but for the most part I had to make it up as I went along; for Theorus and Strato really did know all these people, and were bound to tell them what I had said as soon as we got home.

'And now,' said Alexander, after Jason had choked on a mouthful of roast pork and so fallen silent for a moment, 'do tell us all about the Comedy, which is what we're really interested in. I mean, the Tragedy is all very well, in its way, but . . .'

So I had to go through the same procedure all over again with Ameipsias and Plato and Cratinus and

Aristomenes and Aristophanes – I didn't mention Phrynichus, so as not to upset Jason – until my voice was hoarse and my head was dizzy with nodding. By the time the princes were drunk enough to be carried away, I had had enough of the Theatre to last me a lifetime. But they lasted long enough to demand a précis of the plot of my own next play, and I had to improvise furiously.

I slept well that night, despite having the feeling that I had got myself locked into the treasury of a temple, and when we were summoned next day I felt relatively restored, which was just as well.

The Thessalians don't eat much during the day, but as Athenians we were expected to be starving hungry as soon as we opened our eyes; so there was roast venison and boiled beef to be got through before we could proceed to the surprise at the Field of Zeus. Theorus managed to get hold of one of the skin-and-bone dogs that are everywhere in Thessaly, and we fed most of the food to it, but it couldn't eat it all.

The Field of Zeus is about an hour's ride north of Larissa, and it has a spectacular view of Olympus. To get there, however, we rode through what our escort told us was typical Thessaly: rocky, bleak and miserable, and populated by starving people who are effectively the slaves of the ruling families. Just as I had never seen such wealth as I saw in Larissa, I have never seen poverty like that of these Penestae, who are of the same race as their masters, and theoretically citizens. They would run up to us as we rode past begging for food (I don't think they knew about money), and the cavalrymen would knock them aside with the flats of their sabres. The cavalryman next to me said that there was quite an art to it and offered to teach me if we ran into any more of them, but I said I had a pulled muscle in my shoulder.

The first thing we saw when we arrived was a sort of horseshoe-shaped earthwork. Whatever it was, it wasn't quite finished, because there were men scurrying about with baskets of earth on their shoulders and other men, on horseback, shouting at them and hitting them with olive branches. Then Alexander and Jason rode up, on enormous white stallions, and welcomed us to the Theatre.

I nearly fell off my horse.

'Next year,' said Jason, 'we shall line it with stone, and then it will be just like the Theatre of Dionysus.'

I doubted that somehow, but I remembered that I was here to further the interests of Athens, and said on the contrary, it would be better. 'In fact,' I went on, 'I wish that I could put on a play here. 'It's so . . .' I couldn't think of anything to say, so I waved my hand in the air instead.

Then Jason giggled, sounding just like one of the conduits at Nine Fountains when it gets blocked with leaves, and I felt a terrible sense of foreboding.

'Then your wish is about to be fulfilled,' Jason said. 'If you would care to take your seat, we'll see what we can do.'

I got slowly off my horse and followed him down into his earthwork – I refuse, even now, to call that overgrown sump a Theatre. Alexander was already sitting there, in a great big carved oak throne. He was obviously livid that the Theatre wasn't ready yet, and there was a man on his knees in front of him, who I took to be the overseer of the work.

'This miserable dog,' growled Alexander in his own Thessalian voice, 'has betrayed his trust. He swore by the head of Poseidon that all would be ready, and he has broken his oath. Very well, then; his blood shall—'

'No, don't do that,' said Theorus suavely. 'It's terribly unlucky, you know. Isn't it, Eupolis?'

'Terribly,' I said.

Alexander shrugged his shoulders and became all Athenian again. 'But it's so terribly naughty of him,' he whined. 'He knew we were expecting honoured guests, and just look at it.'

'It's perfect,' I assured him. 'Don't change a thing.'

'Well, if you think it's right, it must be right,' chirped Jason. 'So why don't we all sit down and let the revels commence?'

The Thessalian lords who had been at the feast last night were filing in and saluting the princes; they looked as miserable as I felt. Finally Alexander called for silence and warbled out, 'Eupolis, bring on your Chorus!'

I once saw a play by Cratinus which was a burlesque on the blinding of Oedipus, and although I enjoyed it, I wondered what Oedipus himself would have made of having his Tragic sorrow made into a Comic travesty. By the end of the opening scene of my *General*, as performed by members of the flower of Thessalian youth, I knew the answer; he would have loved it. To start with, I didn't know where to look; I was so embarrassed, especially with Theorus and Strato sitting there looking like a couple of owls, that I would gladly have cut my own throat if I could have borrowed a razor. But when the actors started forgetting their lines and I had to prompt them, I actually started to enjoy myself. It helped that the entire company, Chorus as well as actors, hadn't the faintest idea what any of it meant, and so recited their parts with a sort of Tragic profundity. They had tried their best to make trireme costumes out of old goatskins and the staves of buckets, but the people wearing them had no idea what they were meant to be, and apparently nobody had thought it wise to tell them; so they must have assumed that they were some sort of sacred vestments, and moved accordingly. As the play went on, I could see exactly what was wrong with it; why the dialogue was so flat, and why the Choruses had failed so utterly. There was, quite simply, too much of everything; twenty years of wanting to be a Comic poet jammed into one little play. That was why the jokes had flown over everyone's heads; like Xerxes' arrows, they had blotted out the sun. As for the choruses, they were far too complicated for anyone short of Athena herself to follow at first hearing. Written down, of course, and read slowly at leisure, it quite probably seemed to coruscate with wit. On stage, it was a meaningless torrent of words.

So, when the Chorus had floated gracefully off, there was real feeling in my voice when I thanked the princes.

'It was marvellous, really,' I said. 'You don't know how much pleasure that gave me.'

Jason seemed rather taken aback – I think he had prepared a little speech of apology – but Alexander beamed, and said that it was an honour. I replied that no, it was an honour for *me*, and I think we'd be there yet if Jason hadn't got bored and suggested we eat something.

I had a Thessalian appetite for my food, but my mind was full of Comedy again; it was as if some God had inspired me, and all I wanted to do was sit down somewhere quiet and start composing. It didn't matter that I had no plot or theme or characters – mere details. What mattered was that the cloud of the *General* had been lifted from my shoulders. And then, as if a second God had joined the first, I remembered what Cleonymus had said when I spoke to him in Pallene; he could get me a Chorus, and then everything would be all right.

Don't ask me to remember how much we paid for the cavalry in the end – it was something like four obols a day and one talent, and we got past the Assembly on our return without too much trouble. The next thing I can remember is sitting under my fig tree at Pallene, with half an opening scene in my head searching frantically for a name, and someone in the fields above the house calling out the name of my steward, who was called Maricas. Not long after, I took three rolls of Egyptian paper to the Archon, and was granted a Chorus.

Maricas won first prize at the City Dionysia in the year that Ameipsias came second with his *Wineskins*. Aristophanes won third prize with *The Two Brothers*.

CHAPTER THIRTEEN

I hadn't expected to win first prize with *Maricas*, and so I hadn't thought of a suitable place to hold my Victory party. The true horror of my situation only dawned on me at the Cast party, immediately after the performance (I had been called on last), and for a while I sat with my head in my hands, trying to think of some way out of the mess. As I saw it, I had three options: not to hold a Victory party at all (which was unthinkable, like fighting a battle and not raising a trophy afterwards, or growing corn and not harvesting it); to hold it at Phaedra's house; or to find somewhere else. I had just decided to beg the backer – a cumin-seed-splitting, parsimonious old fool called Antimachus – for the loan of his pottery warehouse in Piraeus, when a messenger came looking for me. It was Phaedra's slave Doron.

'My mistress asks me to tell you that she's visiting her father in the country,' he said, 'and so the house will be empty for three days. She asks you not to let your friends be sick on the couches.'

At the time, I raised my hands in thanksgiving to Dionysus and started issuing invitations immediately; but as I was being carried home to Philodemus' house, my soul pointed out to me that this was a generous gesture from someone whom I had not treated well.

Mind you, I think that I had drunk so much wine that some of it must have seeped through into my soul, for it was being unusually sentimental that night.

After a few hours' sleep I was up and busy, sending all Philodemus' household, Callicrates, and even Philodemus himself out into the City with invitations, which were on no account to be refused. My own role in this Xerxian campaign was quartermaster, and I filled my purse with handfuls of money and set off for the market. The sunlight hit me like a hammer as soon as I set foot outside, but I persevered manfully and bought up every drop of wine in Athens, together with a good stock of food, mostly fish, in case people should forget to bring any of their own. Then I descended on Phaedra's house, with a train of porters behind me that seriously disrupted the movement in the streets, and got to work.

Phaedra's house, which I had not seen for some time, was a splendid setting for a party with all its expensive and ostentatious fittings. There were more couches and chairs than in Aristophanes' house, and enough mixing-bowls to mix the Aegean with Ocean. Phaedra had removed every feminine object from the place, and the floor was scrupulously clean and dry. But outside the back door, I found a cache of empty wine jars, all ready for the jar-collector, and I wondered how on earth she had managed to empty so many.

Needless to say, I hadn't expected the prize guests – what you might call the collector's items – to turn up, for I had invited men who I had never even met. But they came. Everyone came, from Cleonymus and Theorus down to my nearest neighbours at Pallene; even Cratinus came, although he was very ill indeed and had to leave early. Only Socrates son of Sophroniscus didn't come, at which I was secretly relieved, for he never seems to get drunk and monopolises the conversation. Oh no, it wasn't one of those cosy little parties where seven or eight close friends sit in a semicircle and talk about the

Meaning of Truth, which is how people celebrate victories nowadays. It was a good old Athenian thrash. The formal drinking-rules I had devised, the subtle order of courses and succession of toasts and libations, were abandoned like the shields of an infantry-line when the cavalry attacks it from behind. I have heard many times how Atlantis was overwhelmed by the sea, but I could never visualise it properly until that night.

It was touch and go at times, but I stuck it out to the last drop. About an hour before dawn, the only people still capable of speech were me, Callicrates, Philodemus, Euripides and Cleonymus, and we were talking about the Soul; we had decided that it couldn't possibly live in the liver, where everyone thinks it lives, but that it couldn't live in the chest, since that's where the heart lives and the two never seem to agree. That left the head (which is absurd), the groin or the feet, and I can't remember what we finally decided.

The next morning I left the slaves to scrub the floor and make good the damage, and rode off to Pallene. Cleonymus rode part of the way with me, and I screwed up my courage to thank him. He made a noise that was something between a laugh and a sneer, and changed the subject. Of all the men that I have ever liked, I think he was the most repulsive, with the exception of my dear Cratinus.

I spent my first few days at Pallene going round my rapidly crumbling new terraces, to remind myself that I was not successful in everything, and then settled down to work. The old Tragedian Phrynichus, who wrote his best plays in Themistocles' time and was once prosecuted and fined because his *Sack of Miletus* depressed everyone so much, used to say that when a playwright sat down to watch his Chorus being led out, he should already have his next opening speech perfect in his mind; and I have always tried to follow this advice. When a play is presented and the actors run out to speak the first words, you know that that is the first and last time that that play will ever be heard. It's like raising a son who is the pride of your heart to run in one race at the Games; even if he wins, you know that you'll never see him again. So I have always had another play in my mind, and as soon as I hand my words over to the actors I do my best to forget them utterly. Likewise, I am always striving to do better, as if my last play were my own most deadly rival.

I had rivals enough as it was. My next play, *The Man With Two Left Hands*, came second, well beaten by Hermippus and only narrowly beating Ameipsias, at a Lenaea for which Aristophanes, Phrynichus and Cratinus had not contributed anything. My *Vines* and *Cities* were only saved from third place by the brilliance of the costumes – I paid the vase-painter Phrygus to do them, out of my own pocket – and Aristophanes narrowly beat my *Corinthians* at the Dionysia when Aristomenes' *Heracles* was booed off the stage. I had resigned myself to a future of second prizes when I won, quite unexpectedly, with *The Flatterers*. After that, I seemed to lose that sense of urgency which had been driving me to compete as often as possible. Although I was never without a play in my head, I found that I could bring myself to wait for a while, instead of forcing myself to complete it in time for the next Festival. I have had a good run, all in all; I have led out seventeen Choruses and won seven first prizes, and only once come third. As for my reputation with posterity, I no longer worry about it. The other day, for example, I came across a book of Aristophanes' plays, with the copyist's scribble all down the margins and on the back of the roll, in which some fool had written that Aristophanes' *The Acharnians* beat a play called *The New Moons*, which was there ascribed to me. I have never written a play of that name, and if the copyist had had the sense to ask someone who knows me, he would have found out that I was far too young to have been given a

Chorus that year; as you may remember, *The Acharnians* was the play for which Aristophanes gave the party I went to. But I couldn't be bothered to look up the copyist and make him correct the mistake, even though this *New Moons* of mine was supposed to have come third. Twenty years ago, of course, I would have cut his head off for saying such things about me.

It wasn't long after *The Flatterers*, at a time when I was as near content as I have ever been, that I heard that my daughter Cleopatra had died, quite suddenly, from drinking bad water. By the time the news reached me the funeral had already been held, since I was staying with a friend at Araphen, and nobody knew where I was. My host commiserated with me and sent away the guests he had invited, but I must confess that my principal feeling was relief. I suppose that sounds very heartless, especially nowadays, but I had never so much as set eyes on the child, and somehow, given the circumstances of her birth and that stupid, insulting name that Phaedra had given her, she seemed to represent the division between us. You know the story of the Hero Meleager; how when he was born the Goddess prophesied that he would live only as long as it took a certain log on the fire to burn, and how Meleager's mother grabbed up the log and kept it safe, until one day many years later, she flung it on the fire in a fury and so brought about her son's death. Well, it had somehow got into my mind that as long as Cleopatra was alive, I could not bring myself to see Phaedra again, even though I had long since come to accept that Cleopatra was my child. Now she had died, as suddenly and inexplicably as Meleager. I felt no guilt for her death; but it seemed to me that there was a purpose to it. If I was one of those people who believe in what they say at the Mysteries, I would no doubt explain it all as the innocent child sacrificed for the good of the People; but I could never be doing with that sort of thing.

So I took my leave of my host at Araphen and rode to

the City, only to find that Phaedra wasn't there. The doorkeeper at the house said that she had gone to stay with her uncle, out near Eleusis, and wouldn't be back for a month. I thought of going to Eleusis after her, but I had business in the City which couldn't be put off, and so I decided to wait until she got back. I moved into the house, and asked the servants how Phaedra had been getting on.

They were reluctant to talk to me at first, but when I had convinced them that I wanted a reconciliation between us, it was hard to make them stop. Their mistress had been terribly unhappy, they said; she had stayed in the house, spinning her wool and weaving cloaks and tunics for me in the hope that one day I would come back. She hadn't touched a drop of wine – wouldn't have it in the house – and had been to see all my plays. I was deeply touched by this, until I found the remains of several broken wine jars on the ash-heap, which made me suspicious. So I asked the servants to show me the clothes Phaedra had made for me; there must be several chests full of them by now. They looked mustard at me and admitted that they had been exaggerating slightly, about both the clothes and the wine. But they swore by Styx that there had been no men in the house at all, and offered to be tortured if I didn't believe them.

Then a messenger arrived from Eleusis to say that Phaedra wouldn't be back for another couple of weeks at least. He was rather surprised to find me there, and didn't want to say any more, but a four-drachma piece did wonders for his sense of loyalty, and he told me what had happened.

Phaedra had gone with her aunt and some other women to make some offering or other at one of those little country shrines; it was more an excuse for a picnic than a religious occasion. They had made their offering and eaten the rest of the food, and the groom was just harnessing the donkeys to the cart when one of them was stung by a fly and went out of control. Phaedra, who had been putting the picnic things in the cart, had been kicked in the face, and her jaw had been broken. They had done what they could – the eminent doctor Eryximachus had been staying near by, and they had sent for him to set the fracture – but the bone had been too badly damaged for much to be possible. Phaedra, said the messenger, would never look the same. She would have a sort of permanent smile; just like that, he said, pointing to me without thinking, only on the other side of her face . . .

I burst out into uncontrollable laughter, until everyone was quite angry with me, but I just couldn't help myself. The thought that my beautiful Phaedra would henceforth be as repulsive as her husband – a matching pair, in fact, except that presumably she still had some hair – was a sort of pure delight, such as you feel when you recognise the intervention of a God. It was not that wonderful feeling you get deep inside you when you hear of the misfortunes of an enemy; there was nothing vindictive about it at all. When I had control of myself again, I told the messenger to go back to Eleusis as quickly as he could and tell Phaedra that I was on my way, and that if he said anything at all about my reaction to his news, I would make sure he spent the rest of his life in the silver mines. First thing next morning, I set out for Eleusis with Little Zeus riding with me, since it would be just like my luck to run into bandits at such a time if I went on my own, and I was determined to go straight there. But my soul made me stop off at Callicrates' house to pick up the gold and cyanus necklace which I had been given as a parting gift by the princes in Thessaly. It was the most valuable single object I owned at that time.

I once bought a tripod from a Syrian; it was a wonderful thing, with bronze lion-heads all over it and inlays of lapis and glass. It was far too expensive, and when a man offered to buy it from me, I sold it to him gladly, since I had been worrying about spending so much money ever since. But almost as soon as I had delivered it, I regretted what I had done, and finally I went to the man who had bought it and begged him to sell it back to me. He was a shrewd man, and asked rather more for it than he had given me, but I paid what he asked and took the tripod back with me. When I got it home, I saw that one of the little bronze lion-heads had been broken off and most of the lapis had been dug out with a small knife, probably to be used for earrings. But I didn't feel that the damage spoiled my precious tripod; it made me value it all the more, and I never had it repaired.

It was nearly dark when I reached Eleusis, and Phaedra's uncle, who was called Parmenides, was standing by the door.

'I don't know what you want here,' he said. 'I'd have thought you'd done enough damage without coming to gloat.'

Parmenides was shorter than me, and I wasn't afraid of him. 'Does this look like gloating?' I said, waving the Thessalian necklace under his nose. 'Where is she? I want to see her.'

'She's told me not to say where she is,' said Parmenides firmly, as if his house was as big as the Labyrinth. In fact it was quite small, and I could see over his shoulder into the main room. She wasn't there, so she had to be in the inner room or upstairs.

'Don't worry,' I said, 'I'll find her. I'll just have to break down all the doors, that's all. Right, Little Zeus, you'd better start looking round for something you can use as a hammer.'

Little Zeus' face lit up, for he dearly loved smashing things; I think he thought it was rather aristocratic. He pushed past Parmenides and picked up a big bronze lampstand.

'She's in the inner room,' said Parmenides, 'and if you

break anything I'm calling a witness.'

I thanked him and strode like the avenging Odysseus to the inner door. As I put my hand on it I heard the bar go up.

'Let's see that lampstand,' I shouted, but before Little Zeus had a chance to move, Parmenides was standing beside me hammering on the door with his fists.

'Phaedra,' he shouted, 'this is your uncle. Open this door immediately. I won't have violence in my house.'

That didn't have much effect, and Little Zeus stepped forward, with his Heracles face on and the lampstand in both hands, but I pushed him back. He shrugged and put the lampstand back exactly where it had been, for he was a most meticulous man.

'For the last time, Phaedra,' Parmenides was saying, 'will you open this door, or do I send for the carpenter?' I left him to it, and crept out through the door. I went round to the back of the house and sure enough, there was a nice big window. The shutters were drawn but not barred, and I gingerly pulled them open, so as not to make a noise. Then I climbed in.

Phaedra was leaning against the door, obviously preparing to resist the onslaught of the lampstand to the last drop of blood. She hadn't heard me come in so, treading as carefully as if I were walking on ice, I made my way over to a chair beside the bed and lowered myself into it.

'Hello, Phaedra,' I said.

She jumped about a man's stride in the air, whirled round and stared at me. 'You left the window open,' I went on. 'Leonidas wouldn't have done that, and neither would Demosthenes. You're slipping.'

I got up, went to the window, and closed and barred the shutters. I didn't want any interruptions.

'Go on, then,' she said, and her voice was slow and painful. 'Have a good look.' She thrust her face at me, as if she were a soldier on parade presenting his shield for inspection.

I needed no invitation. It looked much worse than it really was, because of the bruises, but I could see that it was the sort of disfigurement that could ruin somebody's life, especially in Athens, where we are obsessed with beauty. But I'm proud to say that I didn't shudder, or spit in my cloak for luck. Instead, I stood up and turned my own face to her.

'They say husband and wife get to look like each other in time,' I said. 'I'm sorry it had to happen to you.' Then I pulled the necklace out from under my belt and fastened it round her neck, and I kissed her.

'Idiot,' she said. 'What do you mean by it, creeping up on me like that?'

I put my arms round her. 'You've put on weight,' I lied.

'No I haven't,' she replied. 'And take your hands off me.'

'Does it hurt?' I asked.

'Yes,' she said, 'and that last play of yours was the worst yet. I was so ashamed that I didn't go out for days.'

'What did you do all that time,' I asked, 'stay in and catch up on your drinking?'

'Who says I can afford wine, on the pittance you send me?' She tried to smile, but it hurt her too much. 'Is it very horrible?' she asked.

'No.'

'Liar.'

'You look like Medusa,' I said. 'Both before and after she was transformed.'

Even she could think of no answer to that, so she looked down at the necklace and stroked it. It was the first thing I had ever given her.

'Where did you get this piece of junk from?' she said. 'If you expect me to appear in public wearing it, you're very much mistaken.'

'The hell with you,' I said.

'And how dare you be so rude to my uncle?'

'The hell with him too.'

'And now I expect I'll have to put up with you under my feet all day long,' she whispered, 'not to mention your disgusting friends.'

'It'll be just as bad for me,' I said, 'coming home and finding your lovers hiding under the—'

It was the wrong thing to say. 'That's not really likely, is it?' she said, pulling away from me. 'Not unless I take to sleeping with blind men.'

'I'm sorry, Phaedra, I didn't think.'

She tried to laugh. 'What's up, Eupolis,' she said, 'lost your sparkle? Or are you so big in the Theatre now that you can't spare a clever insult for your poor, ugly wife? Don't say you're running out of jokes at last.'

'You know me, Phaedra,' I said, 'Eupolis the song-and-dance man. Always good for a laugh, young Eupolis, especially if you kick him hard enough.'

She sat down on the bed and took off the necklace. I think she was going to throw it on the floor, but she just sat there with it in her hands, as if it was a dead bird. 'Just what do you want from me?' she said.

'I don't know,' I replied.

'Well it can't be much, can it?' she said. 'Look at me, will you? I'm an ugly woman with a dead child, and nobody can bear to have me in the house. I can frighten the thieves away for you, but not much else.'

'You're all I deserve,' I said, sitting down beside her. I wanted to take hold of her hand, but I was afraid to. 'Listen to me for a moment, will you? You know the story of how, when the Gods made the first man, he was so happy and content that they were afraid he wouldn't need them any more, so they went away and made the first woman? Well, I think the Gods made us marry each other so that we'd each have someone else to hate instead of ourselves. They even gave us both crooked faces, to make sure we never go off with anyone else. That's why I think—'

'Oh do shut up,' said Phaedra, 'you're giving me a headache with all your whining.' She gave me a look that I'll never forget; contempt and pity and something else, too, which made her look more lovely than ever before. 'You never know when to stop talking, do you?'

'Will you have me back then?' I asked.

'I don't remember throwing you out in the first place,' she said. 'It was you who went prancing off to Pallene and digging holes in the mountains rather than sleep with your wife. It was you who wouldn't touch me on our wedding-night. It was you, I seem to remember, who wouldn't even come to see your own child.' She shook her head and sighed. 'Oh, Eupolis, why are you such a complete fool?'

'Because your father couldn't get you a proper husband,' I said. 'Don't you remember?'

'Come here,' she said softly. 'No, not like that, with my uncle listening at the door and my face all full of splinters. Just come here.'

The next day, we drove back to the City in Parmenides' cart, and we quarrelled all the way.

CHAPTER FOURTEEN

My son Eutychides ('son of a lucky man' – Phaedra's idea) was born just over nine months later, in the year when Alcibiades was elected General for the second time. He was a small, sickly child, although he hadn't inherited his parents' idiotic grins, and nobody expected him to survive longer than a week. But he did, and as soon as he looked big enough to last we got him the best nurse money could buy.

Naturally, Phaedra and I quarrelled bitterly over him from the day he was born. I was all for having him brought up in the country, among the goats and the olive trees, as I had been, away from the fads and trends of the City; that way, I said, if later on he wanted to live in Athens and take part in City life, it would be his own choice. But a man who has been brought up in the City is never really at home in the country, I said. He hasn't learned to use his eyes and ears, and he never values his neighbours properly. But Phaedra said that I could do what I liked, but her son was going to be brought up a Cavalryman, with a proper education in polite society, so that he would one day be a General. We compromised; she was to have her own way, and in return, she wouldn't shout at me about it. In fact his upbringing was quite different, as you will see.

Now on the one hand we were still theoretically at peace with Sparta; on the other hand we seemed to be at war with everyone else. But it was the sort of war that seemed to do nobody much harm – that is to say, it stayed well outside Attica, so that we were able to farm in peace, while there was plenty of employment for anyone who needed it, particularly for the fleet. There were still the annual State funeral celebrations for the heavy infantrymen who had been killed on active service, and every year I lost another fifteen or twenty men who I had come to consider friends. On the other hand, I inherited another twelve acres, being the nearest surviving heir to some dead cousin or other, which brought me perilously close to the five hundred measure mark at one stage. Most of my wealth comes from plague or war, yet it was all honestly acquired. Perhaps that is why I have never striven after money and property as so many other men do; I have simply continued to live, and the Gods have crowned me with flowers. Yet because I was not born rich, I have never felt the need to become richer still. My attempt to improve the yield of my land was more instinct than anything else. After all, it is not as if I were a Corinthian or lived in Persia, or needed money for a political career; there is not very much that I want that money can buy.

At long last, Athens had put the effects of the plague behind her. The tribute-money from the empire was coming in promptly every year – and each time I went down to read the Tribute lists, I thought of that little shrine in Samos – while our own produce in Attica, though still below pre-war levels, was like an unexpected bonus after all the years of war. Wise men say that the earth needed a good long rest after years of being driven too hard by a population too large for it to sustain, and that the Spartans had provided her with it. Men were talking about returns of fifty gallons of wine an acre in some parts of the country, which had not been heard of since the days of the dictator Pisistratus, and as soon as the new vines, which we were putting in every day to replace the ones cut down by the Spartans, started yielding, we all expected to be as rich as kings. But none of us expected to see the olive trees yield much in our lifetime; it takes nearly a generation for a tree to be of any use in Attica.

That reminds me; to celebrate the birth of my son and to get rid of the man generally, I fulfilled my oath to Little Zeus and planted out his land in the best vines. I had been meaning to get around to it ever since the war ended, but there had been a lawsuit about them – I wrote Little Zeus some good speeches, the first time I ever tried my hand at such work – and that had dragged on for some time, and then I was busy with a play. Then two of Little Zeus' brothers were killed at sea, and neither of them had children, so there were more lawsuits. Eventually it was all cleared up, and Little Zeus was master of nine and a bit acres of good but empty land. I planted out the whole lot, for which the man was embarrassingly grateful, lent him enough money to tide him over until his first vintage, made him promise to come to me if he needed help, and wished him good luck. When I next passed by his holding, I was amazed at the transformation. What had been a useless little drip of a stream coming off the side of the mountain had been hacked into a model irrigation channel, with branches off it right across the estate. Every vine was nicely propped and expertly pruned, and every inch of ground between the trenches had been ploughed for barley. There was not a stone to be seen anywhere, and from behind an ambitious-looking half-built wall I heard an unmistakably loud voice reciting the Entry of the Chorus from Aeschylus' *Persians*. I called out, and Little Zeus, looking bigger than over, came running over.

'Well,' I said, 'I don't think I've ever seen a better vineyard.'

He nodded enthusiastically. 'I know,' he said, 'it's the best in Attica. And there's more.' He pointed away over towards the mountainside. 'I've taken in another acre, waste land that nobody was using.'

I stared. 'But that's all bare rock,' I said.

'You did it,' he said. 'Everything here I learned from what you did in Pallene and Phrearrhos. Whenever I felt myself getting discouraged, or I couldn't think what to do, I said to myself, What would Eupolis have done? And then it all became clear in my mind.'

I didn't know whether to laugh or cry. 'But you've achieved more here than I could ever have done,' I said. 'I mean, it's extraordinary. Where did you get the men from?'

'Oh no,' he replied, 'I did it all myself. I didn't want to spend more of that money you lent me than I had to, because it'll be at least a year after my first vintage before I can pay you back, and—'

The thought of him half-killing himself up the mountain just to pay back what I thought he had understood was a gift was almost more than I could bear. 'For God's sake,' I said, 'don't worry about it.'

He smiled beatifically, as if he had seen a God. 'That's just like you,' he said, 'but it's a debt of honour. Now, if you've got a moment, I'd like your opinion on these trellises. Should they be a finger higher, do you think, or are they too high already?'

I almost expected to find a little shrine of the Blessed Eupolis somewhere about the place, and I was glad to get away.

Little Zeus wasn't the only man working hard at that time, and with the return of prosperity, men started to think hard thoughts about Sparta. The general opinion was that we as a city, and Nicias in particular, had more or less let them name their own terms. It went deeper than that, of course; deep down, everyone was convinced that Athens would never be safe until Sparta was a heap of rubble and her people were exterminated. But if we were actually to destroy Sparta, so the argument ran, we needed to double or even treble our strength, in terms of ships, money and above all, manpower. We needed to enlarge the empire, and that must be our next priority. There was little room for expansion in the east, although some people spoke grandly of casting the Great King of Persia from his throne and stamping Sparta flat under the heels of Egyptian and Median levies. But that was foolish talk; the King was much too powerful, and besides, what we needed was Greeks. So men's eyes began to turn west, to the Greek cities of Italy and Sicily, and even further. People started to remember the stories they had heard from their fathers; about the man called Colaeus who was blown off course sailing west, and came back with his ship loaded with silver, or the Golden Islands on the edge of the world, which are so far over that the sun sets in the east. There were more sensible stories, too, about the wealth of the west; not just corn, although the whole region is incomparably fertile and nothing is grown but wheat, but also metals and timber, hides and wool, gold, silver, amber and precious stones – everything that the east has to offer, but guarded only by a few fat Greeks and sub-human savages. From Italy, men were saying, we could conquer the land round Massilia, where it rains so often that men dig ditches not to gain water but to get rid of it; and we could go south, to Carthage and Cyrene, and down into the hot country where there are people blacker even than the Libyans. The Pillars of Heracles were not the end of the world, as our fathers had taught us; the Phoenicians had gone beyond them, and found tin and copper, and huge animals with thick hides suitable for making shields. There was no limit to the opportunities that awaited us, just as soon as we had secured ourselves a base.

It occurred to me that if we could take over so many

distant lands without exerting ourselves too much, it was curious to say the least that we had so much trouble in dealing with a little city not two hundred miles away, where they use iron spits instead of money. What appealed to me was the argument I heard from Cleonymus and his friends. They asked who among the Peloponnesian Alliance had the most warships? Corinth, of course. And wasn't it true that Corinthian ships carried most of the corn imported into the Peloponnese? True indeed. And where did the Corinthians get the corn that they supplied to their allies? Wasn't it from the golden plains of Sicily, and most particularly from their allies the Syracusans? And didn't we have allies in Sicily already, good, trustworthy places with plenty of money, who lived in fear of Syracusan aggression? What better pretext would we need for interfering in Sicily than coming to the aid of our own cities there? But there was more; these cities had actually offered to pay for the war out of their bottomless reserves of coined silver. The war would not cost Athens an obol; yet if we were successful (and how could we fail?) not only would we seize the immeasurable wealth of Sicily for ourselves, but we would also cut off Corinth, and through her the Peloponnese, from their main source of imported food. Corinth would be ruined and would have to defect to us, the Peloponnesians would lose their food supplies and their fleet, both together, and with absolute control of the sea and the Isthmus of Corinth in our possession, we could simply starve them to death.

It was not, they went on, as if Sicily was an unknown land to us, for we had fought wars there only a few years ago. True, we had not been successful, but neither had we failed; and the forces we had sent out then were small and poorly equipped, and fools had led them, men like Laches. Some people said that Syracuse was a great city, strong and well armed; but they were living in the past, in the time of the Persian Wars. Then, it was true, the power of the cities of Sicily had been equal to that of all the other Greeks put together, when the dictators Hiero and Gelo had been in control. But they had worn themselves out in wars with the Carthaginians, and the dictators had been deposed and replaced in Syracuse by a ramshackle democracy, who were constantly fighting with the aristocrats for control of the city. With two sides to play off against each other, in the way which we Athenians know better than any other nation in the world, it was highly probable that we could gain control of Syracuse, which was effectively control of Sicily, without having to fight a single battle.

These arguments were put forward at a time when the urge to be doing something was at its height. Without them, I believe the fever would have broken – there would have been some scandal or crisis, and everyone would have forgotten all about the world to the west of Piraeus – but by giving a realistic shape to their hitherto quite nebulous ideas, the propounders of the Sicilian project were able to harness the dreams of the Athenians, just as Aeolus once tied up the Four Winds in a sack.

There were people who opposed the idea, of course, but most of those were lovers of words who oppose things just to provoke an interesting debate. They were not short of arguments, of course; no Athenian ever is. Some of them recalled the Great Armada to Egypt, just after the Persian Wars. That was when we sent the best part of our army and our fleet to help Inaros and Amyrtaeus, the Kings in the Marshes, against the Persians. The motives were almost exactly identical, except that the enemy then was Persia. By seizing Egypt, it was argued then, not only would we become masters of the richest country in the world, and add the mighty Egyptian fleet to our own, but we would also cut off the Persians from their principal source of food. Then, with Egypt as a base, we proposed to overrun the east and take the Great King's sceptre from his hands, with which to crush our real enemies the Spartans into dust. What happened was that the Armada, both land and sea forces, was wiped out in the biggest disaster ever to befall the Athenians.

But that was different, came the reply. Then, we had taken on the whole of the Persian empire; now, we proposed to deal with one or two cities. Then, we had been fighting a land-locked country, and our fleet had not been much use to us; now, we were sailing against an island. Then, our only allies had been two bandit chieftains and our enemy the best-organised system of government the world has ever seen; now, we had rich and substantial allies in the country we proposed to invade, and our opponents were in a state of virtual civil war. Then, the Persians had the manpower of all Asia to call upon; now, the Sicilians could not hope to receive any assistance from our enemies, since everybody knew that the Spartans never went to war outside Greece. In fact, the superficial resemblances between the Egyptian disaster and the Sicilian project served only to highlight our wonderful prospects of success.

And so on, day after day, wherever two Athenians met together. For we Athenians love to have something to look forward to, and something to discuss; and since everyone enjoyed talking about Sicily so much, they fell in love with the project itself. I have said that we had all been working hard since the end of the war to get our fields and vineyards productive again; well, that was part of it too. Athenians love working hard in short bursts, but the prospect of working hard at the same thing for the rest of their lives fills them with gloom and misery, and they start to consider themselves little better than the slaves of their own land. On the other hand, they had done most of what they could usefully do already – the vines and olives and figs were planted, and it would be years before they could enjoy the fruits of that work. What they wanted now was some new project, preferably with unlimited scope; something which they could hand on, unfinished, to their grandchildren.

Above all, I believe, it was the complete safety of the enterprise that thrilled them so much. For even if we lost the war, what harm could possibly come of it? After all, the Syracusans were hardly likely to leap aboard their ships and come after us; and even if they did, we always had the City walls to keep us safe. There was no power on earth capable of storming the City, and so long as we had the fleet, no siege could starve us out. As to the cost of the war, hadn't we been assured that Egesta and Catana and all those other fat, wealthy Sicilian allies would pay for the whole thing? Hadn't our men been to those cities and been entertained in private houses there, and seen that every vessel, from the mixing-bowl to the chamber-pot, was made of solid silver? Hadn't they been shown the floors of the temple treasuries, knee-deep in four-drachma pieces?

Now the trouble with being a Comic poet is that you see everything in terms of individual people; if you don't like an idea, you look for some person, some notable public face, to attack. And then you don't attack his policies or his public work – that would make terribly dreary poetry. No, you go for him personally, and in particular his sex life, for it seems to be a generally held belief that what a man does in bed is a perfect paradigm of all his other activities. Now it so happened that the man behind the Sicilian project did all sorts of funny things in bed with all sorts of peculiar people, and so I started to feel instinctively suspicious.

The whole thing, you see, had been Alcibiades' idea. The best Alcibiades story I know, as it happens, has nothing to do with his sexual activities; if I find time, I shall tell you some stories about those later. No, this story originated as a Pericles joke, and I got it from Cratinus, so you may feel quite free to laugh if you so wish.

When Alcibiades was about twelve or thirteen, his lover was no less a man than Pericles himself; and it was about the time of the Euboean crisis. Now Pericles, as you know, was faced with the problem of presenting his annual accounts, as General, to Assembly; there was a truly staggering sum for which Pericles could find no explanation which he could give to the Athenians without ending up on the wrong side of half a pint of the best hemlock. At the time, then, he was terribly worried about this, and even talked about it in his sleep.

Now Alcibiades has always liked to get his full six hours, or even more if possible, and he found this extremely upsetting. So one night, as Pericles was lying there muttering, 'I must find some way of giving my accounts, I must find some way of giving my accounts,' Alcibiades shook him by the shoulder and woke him up.

'You're looking at this from the wrong angle,' he said. 'What you've got to find is some way of *not* giving your accounts.'

Pericles said something memorable, like 'Shut up and go to sleep,' but when he woke up he had the most marvellous idea. He simply put the whole sum down under 'necessary expenditure', and provoked a major international crisis to divert attention. In that way, Pericles escaped not only with his life but unimpeached, and was able to lead us through the first part of the war.

That story is typical of Alcibiades; first, that he should see that the way to deal with an insoluble problem is not to try and smash it open but to walk round it and leave it alone; second, that he should exercise his brilliance not for the good of the City but so that he could get his full quota of sleep; third, that he should be in bed with the leading man of the day. I confess that I have never liked Alcibiades, and the reason I dislike him is the reason everyone else adores him; because he's the best-looking man in Athens. I tend to resent good-looking people. The Athenians, as I have said before, believe that the beautiful are good and that only the good are beautiful.

Alcibiades must have thanked the Gods that the only person prepared to make a real stand against him was Nicias son of Niceratus, because even his best friend (if he had one) could not pretend that Nicias was a thing of beauty, particularly when his kidneys were giving him trouble. I think Nicias started off as much in favour of the idea as everyone else; but then he saw a few inconsistencies in the project as outlined, and felt it his duty to point these out. Now everyone listened when Nicias spoke, even though it was generally agreed that he was the most boring and depressing speaker in Athens; I think they listened because they reckoned that something that tasted so horrible must be doing them good, like medicine. Whatever the reason, Nicias spoke and they listened, and Alcibiades started to worry. You know how the Athenians are, being a democracy; the more they love a man, the more they want to see him destroyed. Alcibiades had no wish to meet with the same treatment that they had handed out to Themistocles, Pericles and Cleon. He also knew about Nicias' obsession with duty. If Nicias was somehow bounced into joining him as co-leader of the Sicilian project, with some nonentity as third partner so that Nicias would always be outvoted, that would put an end to all opposition; with Nicias on the team – thorough, meticulous, conscientious, screamingly dull old Nicias – even the most timid and cautious people could not help feeling absolutely safe.

So Nicias was appointed a second General; and he panicked. The only way he could think of to discourage the Athenians was to rely on his reputation and give them a grossly inflated estimate of the resources that the project would need if it were to be absolutely safe, in the hope of scaring the people off. So he prepared an enormous schedule, and read it out. The project would need scores of ships, he said, virtually every ship we had, and most of the male population of Athens would be needed, either as soldiers or sailors. And you couldn't expect these heroes to go forth and conquer for the usual rates of pay; you'd have to give them a whole drachma a day, at least until the Sicilians started paying their share. Then there would be supplies and materiel; so many hundred thousand arrows and throwing-spears and sling-bolts, so many pairs of sandals and cloaks (thick, military) and cloaks (lightweight, military) and helmet-plumes and spear-covers and rowlock-pads and coils of rope and jars of sardines (fresh) and jars of sardines (dried); all of them at market price or above, because of the urgency, so there would have to be property taxes to raise the money. In short, he said, Athens would need to prepare the greatest army and navy ever assembled outside Persia; she would have to put forth almost her entire strength.

He finished his speech, in the confident expectation of silence broken only by discontented grumbling. What he got was a roar of approval and an almost unanimous vote in favour. I remember the expression on his face as if it were yesterday, like a man struck by lightning in the evening of a cool summer day. What he hadn't reckoned with was the almost unnatural gregariousness of us Athenians; when something nice is happening, we don't want to be left out, and for weeks people had been tortured by fears that they would be left behind. Now Nicias had said that there would be room for everybody. Everybody was going to go to Sicily!

Except me. I found out later that the person drawing up the enlistment roll was an unimportant little man who I had made some passing remark about in a Comedy. This had so enraged him – he wasn't used to it, I suppose – that he decided out of spite to leave me off the roll.

I remember how furious I was when the roll was read out, and how I stumped back home, kicking a stone in front of me all the way. I was nasty to Phaedra, refused to eat any food, and went to bed while it was still light.

I lay in bed for hours, unable to get to sleep, and mused on the unfairness of life. About the only person I knew who wasn't going was Aristophanes son of Philip, and the only reason he wasn't going was because he was a coward and had bribed someone at the draft board. And now, I supposed, people would think that I had done the same. Only a few days before, I had been to see Little Zeus, and he had been anxiously going over his property to see if he could manage to squeeze another cupful or so of produce out of it to bring him up to Heavy Infantry status, so that he could go to Sicily too – for if he went to Sicily, he said, he could probably make enough in pay and plunder to pay me back what he owed me. Knowing him, he had probably managed it, so he would be there. So would everybody in the world, except me and Aristophanes.

But Callicrates wasn't going, said my soul. He was slightly too old for military service, and had refused to lie about his age, saying that a man who strove too hard to get mixed up in a war probably had something wrong with his brain. The more I thought about it, the more I was comforted, in a way, for most of the people I valued most were too old to fight. This set me worrying in a different direction (why did I only make friends with old people, and what would become of me when they died?), and between the two conflicting streams of anxiety I fell asleep.

I was woken up by the most appalling noise. Phaedra woke up too, and threw her arms around me out of pure terror, and as soon as I realised it was her and not the heavily armed Syracusan cavalryman I had been having a nightmare about, I felt rather brave and told her not to worry, I would protect her.

'Marvellous,' she said. 'What from?'

'Whatever made the noise,' I said.

'Idiot,' she said, unwinding herself from me, 'go back to sleep.'

There was another terrible crash, right outside our front door, and a lot of confused shouting. My first instinct was to hide under the bed, but that would have been the sort of behaviour one would expect from a man who *wasn't* going to Sicily. Besides, I didn't want to appear a coward in front of Phaedra, or life would be intolerable for the next week or two. So I pulled on a cloak, found my sword, and poked my head out of the front door.

The first thing I saw was my little statue of Hermes, with its head and phallus smashed off, lying on its side. I am not a brave man, but I had paid good money for that statue after its predecessor was wrecked, and I wanted a word with the person responsible. I looked up and down the street, but there was no one in sight; just moonlight, a few stray dogs and a little pool of fresh vomit. Just like any other night in the violet-crowned City of the Muses.

A sensible man would have cursed freely and gone back to bed. Instead, I looped my cloak round my arm, gripped my sword firmly, and set off in pursuit. For I could hear smashing-noises just round the corner; the assassin had not got far. Walking quietly, on the sides of my feet, I crept round and saw a gang of very drunk-looking young men dismembering the statue outside the house of one Philopsephus, a grain merchant.

There were rather a lot of them, and some of them were quite big, and drunks can be terribly violent. I decided that Callicrates was right; only a fool would strive too hard to get mixed up in a battle. I started to retire, but unfortunately I had left it rather late for that. One of the jolly stone-masons had seen me, and was yelling to his friends.

How do drunk people manage to run so fast, I wonder? Before I could cover the few yards to my door they were on to me, and I brandished my sword at them as if I were Achilles himself. One of them made a rude noise and took it away from me, and another one grabbed my arms from behind.

'I said no witnesses,' said a voice behind me, slurring its words somewhat. 'We'll have to cut his throat, whoever he is.'

'Good idea,' said the man who had taken my sword. He was a tall man with a bald head, and I recognised his voice.

'That would be typical, Aristophanes son of Philip,' I said, 'using a drunken drawl as an excuse to murder your chief rival.'

'Oh, for God's sake,' said Aristophanes, 'it's not you again, is it?' He peered at me and made a sort of whining noise, like a dog after a titbit. 'Gentlemen,' he protested to his friends, 'this is too much. Every time I have a little bit of fun in this city, this little creep pops up and gets under my feet. It's getting beyond a joke, it really is. Please take him away and cut his head off.'

'Who is he, then?' asked the man behind me.

'My name is Eupolis,' I said, 'and as a poet I am under the direct protection of the God Dionysus. Anyone who so much as nicks my skin will be condemned to drink nothing but water for the rest of his life.'

Someone giggled, and soon they were all roaring with laughter, the way drunks do – all except Aristophanes, who was begging them to kill me. It would be such fun, he pleaded; they could cut off my head and put it in a bag, and use it for turning people into stone.

'And now,' I said confidently, 'if I may have my sword back, I will leave you to your work, which I can see is of considerable public importance.'

'That's right,' someone said. 'Got to stop the fleet sailing. Can't have Alcithingides prancing round Sicily nibbling all the cheese off the cities. Going to burn the fleet soon as we've finished here.'

'What a splendid idea,' I said. 'Then no one can go.' I prised my sword out of the hand of the man holding it (I recognised him too; in fact I knew most of them now I could see them clearly – all people who weren't going to

Sicily, which probably explained why they had been having a party) and walked quickly away without looking round. The sound of breaking marble indicated that they had resumed their work. I shut the front door behind me, and put up the bar.

'Well?' Phaedra called out. 'Who did you kill? You were gone a long time.'

'They'd gone by the time I got there,' I replied. 'You were worried, weren't you?'

'No I wasn't,' said Phaedra. 'Who cares a damn what happens to you?'

I tossed my sword into a corner. My little brush with danger had taken most of the sting out of not going to Sicily, and my own moderate cleverness in getting out of the danger had left me feeling rather cheerful.

'Come here and say that,' I said.

The next day, nobody was feeling very cheerful. You must understand how superstitious people were then, before Philosophy became so fashionable, and how everyone was terribly edgy because of the sailing of the fleet. So when they woke up and found that someone had been smashing up statues of the Gods (apparently the jolly stone-masons had made a clean sweep of most of the little Hermeses in the City), they were appalled and took it as an omen. Hermes, they said, was the God of Escorts – He goes with us when our souls travel across the Styx, and watches over all embassies and perilous journeys – and now all His statues were only fit for the lime-kilns; the God was angry with us. I think the main reason for the panic was that nobody knew who had done it, because everyone (except me) had been asleep; either they were sailing the next day with the fleet and had had an early night, or they had been to good-luck parties and were sleeping it off. So it was anybody's guess who was responsible, and under such circumstances, anybody tends to guess at hidden conspiracies. By dawn, the general view was that the anti-democratic faction, whoever they were, had done the deed in order to bring disaster on the fleet and then, by some undefined means, seize control of the State. It was all very worrying.

Put together three or four worried Athenians, and they will immediately demand that the General be impeached. The General at this time, of course, was Alcibiades; and thanks to the inscrutable processes of the democratic mind, it was assumed, without question, that since the expedition was Alcibiades' idea and had been conceived and organised by him, he must have sabotaged it. After all, people said, Alcibiades is always going to parties and getting drunk, and people who get drunk smash up statues. Therefore it followed, as night follows day, that Alcibiades, single-handed or with accomplices, smashed up the statues.

Now I knew for a fact that he hadn't, but even I am not so stupid as to open my mouth at such a time, and so I kept quiet. After all, I had no great love for the man, and given his career to date it was inevitable that he was going to be put to death sooner or later, so why not now? Besides, I am an Athenian and so must always find someone to blame for my misfortunes; and I think that deep inside my soul, I was blaming Alcibiades – if he hadn't organised it, there would be no fleet for me not to sail with. It was the wrong thing to do, of course, but I was amply punished for it later.

So the Athenians were in a difficult position. Unless they impeached Alcibiades, they couldn't execute him for blasphemy; but if they did that, there would be no Sicilian project and everybody would have to go back to work. There was a frenzied debate about it in the Assembly which amused me very much, with everybody calling everybody else a monarchist and accusing each other of betraying naval secrets to the Persians, and finally they reached an Athenian compromise. Alcibiades would lead the fleet to conquest and glory in Sicily, and they would try him for blasphemy on his return. This would give his enemies plenty of time to buy the requisite witnesses, and everybody would have two treats to look forward to instead of one.

Do I sound as if I hate my city and this monster we used to call democracy? I don't. I suppose I felt for Athens in those days the same tortuous jumble of emotions as I felt for Phaedra; even when she behaved most terribly, she fascinated me utterly, and I would not have had a different city, or a different wife, for all the wealth of King Gyges. All my life I have loved the Festivals, where three Tragedies are followed by one Comedy, and the horror and the humour get mixed up in your mind until you can barely tell them apart. Now I am a worshipper of Comedy: I believe in it absolutely, as being the purpose of the world and of mankind, and I believe that Zeus thinks as I do, which is the only possible explanation I can think of for most things that happen, and so I winnow out the Comedy and let the wind blow everything else away. Now tell me, where else in all the kingdoms of the earth could Zeus and I find a richer Comedy than in Athens, where men used to conduct their affairs in the way I have described to you? And of all the little Comedies of Athens, what could be better than the Comedy of bad-faced Eupolis and his bad-faced wife?

Dexitheus the bookseller, who is a man of taste and discrimination, tells me that I should stop here. He thinks that this first part of my life makes a complete story in itself, dealing as it does with Athens before its downfall. He feels that in what I have written so far I have so perfectly blended Tragedy and Comedy that to add any more would be a display of sacrilegious ingratitude towards the Muses who have so clearly inspired me up till now, and that the next part of my story, which deals with what actually happened when we got to Sicily, would therefore be best published under separate cover. Now I have known Dexitheus since before the holes in his ears healed up and everybody thought he was just another ex-slave on the make, and so I can honestly say that the fact that he can make two drachmas by selling two short books but only one and a half by selling one long one has not influenced his advice to me on this matter in any respect, and I am bound to say that on the whole I agree with him.

I shall therefore leave you at this point and catch up on my sleep, which I have been neglecting lately. If you want to find out what happened in the end, and what became of the greatest expedition ever mounted and the most perfect democracy the world has ever seen, I recommend that you buy at least three copies of this book, and advise all your friends and relatives to do the same; that way, Dexitheus may feel justified in asking me (and the Muses, of course) to exert ourselves just one more time.

One last thing. I was talking to a man of my age yesterday night, and he assured me that the fighting-cock killed by Ajax Bloodfoot wasn't called Euryalus the Foesmiter at all. He is positive that I've confused the bird I saw (which, according to him, was called The Mighty Hercules) with the bird that eventually did for Ajax Bloodfoot about three months later. He may well be right, at that; so, since this is meant to be a work of history, I record his opinion on the matter as well as my own and leave the final choice to generations yet unborn.

PART TWO

THE WALLED ORCHARD

CHAPTER ONE

We Athenians despise optimists, but we occasionally perpetrate unintentional optimism in the sacred name of shrewdness. For example: Dexitheus the bookseller commissioned me to write the history of my times for three hundred drachmas, at a time when History seemed to be the coming thing and paper was cheap. I settled down to my task and was happily scribbling away when he came to me and suggested that, since my life had clearly been so fascinating and packed with incident, it would be a good idea to publish my history in two volumes. Being somewhat oversceptical as a result of this long and fascinating life of mine, I assumed that he wanted to sell two volumes at a drachma each rather than one long one at one drachma three obols, and agreed. After all, it suited me fine, since I anticipated that Dexitheus would be left with a lot of copies of my first volume on his hands and would abandon the idea of a second, and that I would therefore get three hundred drachmas for half the work.

Well, nothing definite has been said about the matter, but I believe Dexitheus still has plenty of Volume One taking up space in his barn at Cholleidae and getting nibbled by mice; but he has just come bounding back asking me how far I've got with Volume Two, and making vague breach-of-contract noises when he hears that I haven't actually started yet. What his clever little soul is saying to him is that if enough people buy Volume Two, they'll want to buy Volume One to catch up on the first part of the story, and then he'll have some space in his barns again to put his winter barley in once it's cut.

Personally, I think Dexitheus' reasoning is somewhat flawed, but far be it from me to argue with a man as depressingly litigious as Dexitheus of Cholleidae. I only mention this sordid little detail as an illustration of the Athenian character, and in particular my fellow citizens' obsession with cleverness.

You will understand the relevance of this if you've just finished reading Volume One, and recall that I broke my narrative at the point at which the great Sicilian Expedition was about to set sail. But I don't suppose you have, so in order to do my duty by Dexitheus and the Muse of History, I will now give a very brief epitome of what is contained in the first roll. Once you have read this, you will immediately want to read it, and so before I begin I must just tell you that Dexitheus' stall in the Market Square is just to the left of the shield-maker's stands as you come in from the Acropolis past the Mint. Say Eupolis sent you.

I, Eupolis of Pallene, the Comic playwright, was born thirty-eight years after the defeat of the Persian fleet at Salamis, and eleven years before the outbreak of the Great Peloponnesian War between Athens and Sparta. I lived through the plague which killed the celebrated Pericles, catching the disease myself but being cured of it by the God Dionysus, and in my twentieth year I presented my first Comic play at the Dramatic Festivals, which came third out of three. I was not put off, and eventually won first prize with *Maricas*, which is undoubtedly the best Comic play ever written. By this stage I was married to one Phaedra daughter of Theocrates, whose temper was so filthy she made

Medusa look like a kitten. At first we didn't get on terribly well, but shortly before the start of this volume she had had her very beautiful face kicked in by a mule, leaving her looking as well as sounding like Medusa, after which her behaviour towards me became rather less ferocious.

While all this was going on, Athens had been getting further and further into the Great Peloponnesian War; and, after the short, brilliant and disastrous career of the celebrated Cleon, had fallen under the spell of the celebrated Alcibiades. This Alcibiades had hit on the idea of conquering the fabulously rich island of Sicily as a means of replenishing our depleted exchequer, and had so filled the heads of his fellow Athenians with his idea that everyone, even I, wanted to be part of it. A great expedition was organised, and a huge army was raised, in which every man in Athens except me and a few people with only one leg seemed to be enlisted. I was livid at not being allowed to go, but on balance this didn't seem to worry our leaders terribly much. Then, the night before the fleet was due to sail, a group of drunks (including my rival Comic poet and evil spirit Aristophanes son of Philip) smashed up all the little statues of Hermes in the City, causing a wave of superstitious hysteria. I was about the only eye-witness to this, by the way. For some reason which defies logical analysis, the Athenian people decided that Alcibiades was behind the sacrilege; but, not wanting to be deprived of their treat, voted that Alcibiades should continue to lead the Sicilian Expedition, subject to his coming back to Athens after it was all over to be impartially tried and executed for blasphemy.

If that is not a complete summary of Volume One it will do to be going on with, and I think you have a general idea of who everyone is. Various other points to note, such as the fact that Aristophanes and I had been generally getting in each other's way and on each other's nerves since childhood, and that Aristophanes had an affair with my wife before her face got kicked in, will no doubt emerge from context, and you will guess without my having to tell you that the Callicrates who occasionally crops up was the son of my uncle Philodemus (who looked after me since I was orphaned by the plague as a boy) and general guardian angel, and that the curious person named Little Zeus was a hanger-on I acquired in the course of my boyhood as a result of a rash promise to plant out his tiny and unproductive holding of three acres in vines for him as soon as the War was over. I certainly won't insult your deductive powers and general knowledge of Athenian history by telling you who Nicias and Demosthenes are, or how I came to be quite comfortably off and a member of the cavalry class by virtue of inheriting land from relatives who died in the plague. Now then, about Alcibiades.

CHAPTER TWO

Alcibiades was not a fool. He jumped ship as soon as he could and hurried off to Sparta, where they were very pleased to see him. The Athenians consoled themselves for his loss by holding his trial *in absentia*, which was almost as much fun as if he had been there. They didn't get to hear him speak, of course, which was sad, but on the other hand they were able to find him guilty (which might have been tricky had he been present) and so prove conclusively that it was indeed he who mutilated the statues.

The fleet carried on, with Nicias now the overall commander, and at home we waited anxiously for the news of the fall of Syracuse. But weeks passed, and no news came, and so we forgot about Sicily and started grumbling about how empty the City was these days, and how difficult it was to get together enough people for a dinner-party. The weeks turned into months, and still no news, until everyone in the Market Square was convinced that Nicias had finished in Sicily and moved on to the Golden Isles or the Islands of Perpetual Rain.

The money that our loyal Sicilian allies promised us didn't arrive, either, and we soon found out why. You remember that Alcibiades' messengers had been entertained in private houses where everything was made of silver; well, the Sicilians had been clever there. A week or so before the messengers arrived, they had been all round the cities requisitioning every silver object they could find, and every single piece of coined money, and they had put on a special show for their Athenian guests. Then, when the messengers moved on to the next city, the silver preceded them, and the Sicilians prayed that the Athenians wouldn't wonder why the silverware in Egesta looked so very like the silverware in Catana. As for public treasuries, they had covered the floor with figs and stones, and spread the coined money very thinly over the top, except for the areas near the doors.

After we had got over our initial fury at being outwitted by the Sicilians, we decided to put the whole thing down to colonial high spirits and forget about it; after all, the treasury of Athena in the Acropolis was full of coined silver, and it wasn't as if we were spending the money; rather, we were investing it, and a few hundred talents was a cheap price to pay for mastery of the world and the destruction of Sparta. But that, together with the Alcibiades business and the lack of reports of glorious successes, set people worrying about the project in a way that they had not worried before. But nobody, not even the most paranoid of us, thought for a moment that the expedition should be recalled; only that someone somewhere ought to be punished for something at some time. This was so close to our normal state of mind that we soon stopped discussing it. Then a letter arrived from Nicias which was quite different from his earlier, utterly uninformative despatches.

There is an art to writing military despatches, I suppose; my favourite is one supposed to have been sent by a Spartan officer later on in the War, which went something like, 'Ships all sunk. General dead. Soldiers starving. Haven't the faintest idea what to do next. Advise.' Nicias' letter was longer than that, but not much more cheerful.

According to his letter, he had spent the time since his arrival in Sicily building walls. I knew from my own experiences in Samos how much the military mind loves a good wall, especially if it goes nowhere and gets under the feet of the infantry. It gives a man a sense of achievement to be able to point to a wall and say, 'I built that'; and since (according to Nicias' letter) there was nothing else he could hope to achieve in Sicily, I could understand why he had occupied his time in that particular way.

The truth behind Nicias' letter was that he was in a hopeless mess. Because he had been his usual cautious, painstaking self, he had given the Syracusans plenty of time to sort out their internal problems (they killed a few people, I believe, which seemed to solve everything) and they had presented a united and resolute front to the invading army. They also had promises of help from our enemies in Greece, and the Spartans were sending them a general. The worst thing about it all was that there were rather more Syracusans than we had been led to believe, and they were by no means incompetent when it came to the arts of land and sea warfare. Nicias' only intelligent colleague, a brave and fairly honest man called Lamachus, had been killed, and the General could see no way of achieving his mission without substantial divine intervention – a plague, say, or a large-scale earthquake. Obviously the sensible thing was to call it a day and go home; but if he tried that, he would be in court on a capital charge before he had time to take off his helmet. His only chance of being around to taste the next vintage was if he was actually recalled; then at least he could say (at his trial) that he had been just about to trample the towers of Syracuse level with the mud when the *Paralia* had drawn up on the beach with his marching orders.

So, being Nicias, he tried the tactic he had used the first time, and which had gone so disastrously wrong. He begged to inform the people that, in order to do the job he had been sent out to do, he needed twice as many ships and twice as many men, and every four-drachma piece in Attica and the Empire, plus a colleague or two to help him with the command, plus could he please come home now, because his kidney trouble made it impossible to do his job properly? He realised that if the forces he had requested were sent to him, Athens would be emptied of men, almost entirely without any form of shipping larger than a lobster-boat, and bankrupt; but if Athens wanted Sicily, that was what it would take.

Oh my beloved city. You listened to the letter of Nicias, you made a few speeches, you coined a few clever phrases, and you sent Nicias everything he had asked for, except his recall. I think it was only then that I realised the true extent of your power and your wealth and your resources of ships and men, and your imperishable stupidity. To have mounted an expedition like the first fleet would be beyond any city or confederation of cities today; but to raise and man a fleet bigger even than that, and to send it out on the strength of a single letter from an idiot – that was an act of such magnificent folly that no man can ever blame you fot it. It surpasses even the lunacy of the Persians. And to wage this war thoroughly, to the death, to the last drop of blood, you called on the brilliant Demosthenes, your ablest general, and sent Eupolis son of Euchorus, of the deme of Pallene – and five thousand or so others – to help him do it.

'For God's sake, woman, stop fussing,' I said to Phaedra as I prepared to set out for Piraeus, 'and don't worry, please. We'll be back before you know we've gone.'

'You keep saying don't worry,' she said, packing my ration-bag tightly into my shield, 'and I'm not worrying at all. If anyone's worried, it's you. Now are you sure you've got everything?'

'Of course I've got everything.'

'Spare blankets?'

'Yes.'

'Clean tunic?'

'Yes.'

'Needle and thread?'

'Yes.'

'Spare helmet liner?'

'Oh hell, no. I knew I'd forgotten something.'

She grinned triumphantly. 'I've packed it in with your food. It'll smell of cheese rather a lot, but you won't mind that.'

'You bitch,' I said, 'you did it on purpose.'

I looked out of the door. The sky was growing pink, it would soon be dawn.

'Hector didn't call his wife a bitch when he went out to fight,' said Phaedra.

'But Andromache was a sweet, loving and good wife,' I replied, 'and you're a bitch.'

'That would account for it,' she said.

I frowned. 'Don't you want to have the last word, Phaedra?' I said. 'That's unlike you.'

She smiled. 'I'll have it when you come home,' she said. 'I'll pass the time by thinking of nasty things to say to you when you come back. Oh, Eupolis, you do look silly in your armour.'

'I feel silly,' I said, shaking my head to make my plume nod. 'Whoever first thought of putting bits of horsehair on top of helmets has a lot to answer for. Be good.'

'I will,' she said, 'then I can be bad when you get home. You will come home, won't you?'

'Now I say "Yes" and you say "Pity"?'

'That's right.' She kissed me, and pulled my helmet down over my face. 'Now get on, or you'll be late, and I'd be ashamed if my husband was the only man in Athens to miss the boat.'

Then she pushed me out of the door and slammed it, and I walked away as quickly as I could, without turning my head.

On my way to Piraeus I bumped into Callicrates –
literally, since my helmet had fallen down over my eyes,
and I couldn't see where I was going. For a moment I
didn't recognise the man in armour on the hem of whose
cloak I had just trodden; but as soon as he cursed me for
being a clumsy idiot I recognised his voice.

'Callicrates!' I said. 'What are you doing dressed like
that?'

'Is that Eupolis under that chamber-pot?' He lifted
the helmet up. 'I was just coming to find you. I thought
we could go down to Piraeus together.'

I stared at him. 'Are you coming to Sicily too?' I asked.

'That's right,' he said. 'Late addition to the list this
morning. They wanted to make up the numbers.'

I was so delighted I hardly knew what to say. 'Why,
that's marvellous!' I cried. 'I'm so pleased.'

Callicrates frowned at me, just as he used to when I
was young and did something stupid. 'Why?' he said.
'What harm have I ever done you?'

'But don't you want to go, Callicrates?' I said,
mystified. But he only shook his head, so that the plume
on his helmet nodded.

The nearer we came to the docks, the more crowded
the streets became; and I have never seen such a curious
spectacle. It was like a cross between a pageant and a
funeral. There were dancers and flute-players and
women handing out garlands, and next to them wives
and mothers dressed in mourning, wailing and shrieking
as their men tried to prise their fingers off the hems of
their cloaks. There were sausage-sellers, and jobbing
poets, and painters with trestle tables offering to do a
five-minute portrait of the departing hero on a wine-jar
or oil-flask for a drachma, and next to them old women
from the country selling charms to avert evil; and spear-
polishers and crest-makers and while-you-wait shield
menders, and fortune-tellers and sprat-sellers (in case
anyone had forgotten to bring his rations); and creditors

waiting for their debtors, and moneylenders, and men offering to take short leases on land, and landlords wanting their rent, and merchants buying options on shares of loot, and old soldiers promising to tell you everything there is to know about Sicily for an obol. And, directly underneath the most magnificent plume you ever saw in your life, Aristophanes son of Philip, giving last-minute instructions to his Chorus-trainer about the two plays that he had committed to him in case he wasn't back in time to see to them himself.

Callicrates and I avoided him as best we could – he was in a different regiment sailing on a different ship – and took our places in the line for our names to be pricked down. As I stood there, I saw a head towering over all the others. It was topped by a battered green helmet that had probably last seen action when Themistocles was General, and it was reciting a passage from the *Seven Against Thebes* to a somewhat restless audience.

I asked Callicrates to keep my place for me, and went to see. Sure enough, there was Little Zeus, in fine voice and a suit of armour that was far too small for him. As soon as he saw me he broke off in mid-strophe and called out my name in a voice that must have shaken the trees on Parnes.

'What are you doing here?' I asked. 'I thought you went with the first fleet.'

'The idiots,' he said passionately, 'the wretched, miserable fools at the Polemarch's office, wouldn't let me go. They said my armour wasn't good enough, would you believe.'

'Well,' I said, 'it's not exactly pristine, is it?'

'This is my new armour,' he said coldly. 'It cost me twenty drachmas and a yearling goat, every last coin I had. A complete waste of money, I may say – there was nothing at all wrong with my old armour, nothing at all. The helmet belonged to my great-great-grandfather, who wore it before the Persians came.'

I couldn't think what to say to that. Luckily, I didn't have an opportunity to say anything.

'But I look upon it as an investment,' Little Zeus continued. 'At last, I promise you, I'll be able to pay off my debt to you. On my word of honour.'

'I do wish you'd forget about that—' I started to say.

And you're really coming too?' he continued. 'You're sailing with us?'

'Yes,' I replied.

'That's the best news I've heard all month,' said Little Zeus. 'Now I know everything will be all right. And we're in the same regiment, of course; why didn't I think of that before? It'll be just like that time in Samos, when you killed the enemy champion and saved my life.'

People were looking round and pointing, and I could feel my face burning with embarrassment. 'Keep your voice down,' I muttered, but it was too late.

'What's that you said?' asked one of the men next to us. 'Is this bloke some sort of hero then?'

'Was that Pericles' campaign in Samos?' asked another.

'Who is he, anyway?' said a third. 'Hey, Crito, come over here. There's a man here killed a general in Samos and saved the entire fleet.'

I made an attempt to slip away, but it was too late. Little Zeus was answering questions from all sides, confirming that I was indeed a hero, and that they were all lucky men to be in the same regiment. It was several weeks before I was able to live it down.

In case any of you have ignored my earlier excellent advice and haven't yet secured a copy of the first half of these memoirs of mine (Dexitheus informs me, by the way, that he still can't see the floor of his barn for copies of it, but that the mice seem to enjoy it tremendously, which is one of the nicest things anyone has ever said about anything I've written), I should make it plain that I didn't actually kill a general in Samos. I did kill a Samian of sorts, in circumstances that would have been very funny but for the blood and loss of life, and anybody with the sensitivity of one of those thick-skinned Egyptian animals, who live in rivers and whose name escapes me for the moment, would have taken particular care to see that the subject was never mentioned in my presence again. But that was Little Zeus for you.

We boarded the ships, and stowed our equipment as best we could, and waved and shouted to the people on the quayside; and then we were off. We were going to Sicily.

Except that we went the long way round. First, we had to meet up with Demosthenes, who was chasing round Laconia with the Operational Fleet; and, Demosthenes being Demosthenes, he couldn't resist a few little diversions on the way.

The idea was that we should raise a few troops here and there, on the principle that you can never have enough men, so we scooped up some Argives, who didn't really want to come but didn't like to refuse; then, since we happened to be passing Laconia, we stopped off and spent a pleasant few days chopping down olive trees, rooting up vines, and generally getting our own back for what the Spartans had been doing to us since we were all children. It's a strange feeling for a farmer to destroy vines and trees. At first, you don't enjoy it at all, but after a while you get into the spirit of the thing and it becomes immensely entertaining. I got the feeling that I was venting my fury not only on the Spartans but also on the recalcitrant, perverse and incomprehensible Spirit of Nature, which torments anyone who lives by growing things. 'Take that,' I found myself saying as I put an axe to a fig tree, 'that'll teach you to get blight and leaf-rot for no readily apparent reason.'

While we were there, we also fortified a little isthmus as a safe haven for runaway helots, and then sailed on towards Corcyra, stopping on the way to sink a Corinthian ship at Pheia and take on more heavy infantry at Zacynthus and Cephallenia, while Demosthenes went off collecting light infantry in Acarnania. Do I sound, by the way, as if I know where all these places are? That would be misleading. The fact that I have been somewhere does not necessarily mean that I know where it is, or anything about it at all. The truth is that we Athenians are not great geographers, although we claim to be. In Assembly, we listen gravely to the Great Men discussing the strategic value of Caulonia, or the implications of the situation at Syme for the route to Cnidus, and we vote for whoever speaks best; we haven't the faintest idea where Syme is, any of us, but not one of us would admit this for a second.

After Corcyra, then, we went to the Iapygian Promontory, the Choerades (which, I am reliably informed, are islands quite close to the Iapygian Promontory), and Metapontum, which is somewhere in Italy. On the way we gathered a great host of outlandish-looking people, including a number of Italian Savages, before dropping in at Thuria (I have not the faintest idea where Thuria is). There, or somewhere quite like it, we landed and had a parade, marched about for a while until the locals politely asked us to go away, and then sailed on to a place called Petra. At every place we stopped we took on yet more reinforcements, until nobody could quite remember who we had with us, let alone why. But in the end I think we had about seventy-three ships, seven or eight thousand heavy infantry (Athenian and foreign) and goodness knows how many light-armed troops, savages as well as Greeks, when we sailed up to Nicias' camp outside Syracuse one fine morning. We were feeling supremely confident after our journey, which had been more like a holiday than an expedition, and we felt that not even the gods could stop us now.

The shore was lined with men waiting to greet us. We

saw the flash of their shields long before we made land, and immediately started waving and shouting. Some of the men on the deck with me were looking out for friends and relatives, others were searching for the piles of loot and captured weapons which we all expected to see; everyone else was looking out for the smoke of the cooking-fires. Because we had taken on more troops than we had expected in Italy and all those other places, the supplies of food had started to wear a little bit thin; and although we were by no means hungry, none of us would have refused a large meal by that stage. And what we had seen of Sicily from the sea – one enormous wheatfield, trimmed at the edges with vineyards and topped off with the olive groves that go right the way up the few mountains they have on the island – was enough to make anyone salivate, let alone men like us who scratched about in the dust on the side of the mountains of Attica. The general consensus was that we would be greeted with tureens of pea soup, followed by roast mutton with mountains of white bread, huge square chunks of cheese and heaped dishes of beans, washed down with neat wine and milk. A considerable minority wanted to add roast thrush, tunny and eels, but the rest of us were not convinced, despite their eloquence.

But when at last we were close enough to see the men on the shore, we started to worry. They didn't look like a conquering army somehow; more like a crowd of slaves just coming out from a shift in a big workshop, or down the silver mines. Only a few ran out to meet us; the rest just stood and watched, without moving, as if we were a vaguely interesting spectacle but nothing to do with them; and those that did come seemed to be shouting something about food, and which ships were carrying it, and did we need any help unloading it? So instead of jumping out into the sea and wading or swimming ashore, we waited until the ships had stopped moving and the taxiarchs told us to disembark.

I recognised a face among the men standing on the beach – Callippus, a man from Pallene from whom I had once bought a diseased goat – and as soon as I had answered to my name I slipped out of line to talk to him. I greeted him cheerfully and asked him how things were.

'Terrible,' he said, without any visible emotion – he seemed totally uninterested in any of what was going on – 'particularly after the sea-battle yesterday.'

'What sea-battle?'

'I forgot, you won't have heard,' he said. 'The Syracusans heard you were coming and attacked us, twice. The first time they didn't get very far, but yesterday they hammered us. For God's sake,' he suddenly shouted, 'they don't fight *fair*.'

I stared at him. 'What do you mean?' I asked.

'You won't believe this,' he said, lowering his voice. 'The Syracusans kept us fooling around all day, sending their ships out and then drawing them back, until our men had got thoroughly bored and gone back to base for their dinner. Then they come roaring out, this time for real, and our men rush away from the cooking-fires on to the ships, starving hungry – the Syracusans timed it beautifully – and try to get into some sort of order. There's a god-awful mess, and while the ships are fighting each other in the proper way, they send out hundreds of little boats full of javelin-throwers and archers and shoot up the crews of our ships, while we just flounder about like beached whales and can't do a thing about it. They sank seven ships and damaged I don't know how many more. It was total chaos. Did you ever hear the like, Eupolis? You just can't fight these people, on land or sea. They don't say put and they don't fight *properly*; they just shoot at you and run away.'

'Don't worry,' I said soothingly. 'We're here now. Demosthenes won't take any of that stuff, you'll see.'

'Sod Demosthenes,' said Callippus, 'what can he do? These men are savages. They don't fight like we do.

They're really vicious, I tell you; they aren't interested in winning battles, they're interested in killing people without getting killed themselves. It's inhuman.'

'Demosthenes will make them fight,' I said. Callippus laughed sourly and shook his head.

'Did you bring any food on those ships?' he asked. 'We're starving to death here.'

'You can't be,' I replied. 'For God's sake, you're the besiegers.'

'Tell them that,' he said, waving his hand in the direction of Syracuse. To be honest with you, I hadn't really looked at the city – that sounds very strange, but I hadn't. I looked now; it was just a city, with walls and a gate. 'Do you know they hold regular markets in there? With merchants and fishmongers and sausage-sellers and everything? We're down to a couple of pints of flour a day out here. They throw their crusts over the wall for us, and we actually go and pick them up.'

I felt as if whatever I was standing on had suddenly given way. 'You're exaggerating,' I said. 'It can't be as bad as all that.'

'It's going to get worse,' said Callippus, grinning unpleasantly, 'with you lot to feed as well. I take it you haven't brought any food.'

'We thought . . . for God's sake, this is the richest country in the world. Where's all that wheat and cheese?'

'Good question,' replied Callippus. 'But Nicias has managed to get the whole of Sicily against us, somehow or other.'

'Can't you bring anything in by sea?' I asked.

'Of course,' said Callippus impatiently. 'We get things from Catana and Naxos, just enough to keep us from starving. No more.'

'But this is terrible,' I said.

'Yes.' He grinned again and walked away, like a man going to a funeral. I went back to our ship and told my friends what I had heard. They had been told the same, many times over. Meanwhile, Nicias' men had got bored with us and had mostly wandered away, making us feel like fools.

I remember one time someone got up a rumour – completely untrue – that the King of Somewhere Else had sent the Athenians a present of a million bushels of wheat, and it was being handed out to all adult male citizens in the Market Square. Of course, I jammed my feet into my sandals and sprinted off as fast as I could; and sure enough, there were crowds of people milling around with big jars on their shoulders. The only thing that was missing was the wheat, which (like the King of Somewhere Else) did not exist. Even when the point sank in, we stayed there for some time – the general feeling was that the Archons ought to open up the granaries to compensate us for our disappointment. Anyway, that was what it was like, that day we landed in Sicily.

So there you are, commander of a huge and useless army; your men are demoralised and have nothing to eat, the enemy is in a strong defensive position with no incentive to come out and fight, and has just beaten you at sea. What do you do? Attack, of course.

Demosthenes had seen that the only way to break into the city of Syracuse was by going over the slopes of Epipolae, which is a large rocky hill, roughly triangular, on the other side of the city from the sea. It wouldn't be easy; but we would either take the city or prove that the job was impossible – and either way, we would all soon be going home.

So, after a miserably hungry night, we set off early next morning to damage such olive trees and vines as Nicias' men had overlooked, down by the river Anapus; apart from a few bored-looking light infantry, we saw no enemy soldiers and had a pleasant enough time – we even caught a couple of skinny-looking goats, which we converted into an approximation of food. I was particularly struck by Little Zeus' attitude to the laying waste of crops, bearing in mind his Herculean efforts to squeeze a living out of the hide of Mother Demeter. After the first hour or so, he seemed to go absolutely berserk; he had got hold of a big double-headed axe from somewhere, and he fell upon a small plantation of fig trees like mad Ajax killing Agamemnon's sheep. So strenuous were his efforts that he quite wore himself out – and he broke the axe, missing the trunk of a tree with the head and so striking the shaft against the wood and smashing it in two. When I asked him what had got into him, he confessed that he hated fig trees; he always had, and he always would.

What with the goats, and smashing things up, and stretching our legs after all that time on board ship, we all came to the conclusion that fighting under Demosthenes was much better than work. In fact, the only man who didn't seem to be enjoying himself was Callicrates, who was always far too sane and well balanced a person to come to any good end in this life.

While we were busily occupied in this manner, Demosthenes had been attacking the outlying fortifications of the Syracusan position with battering-rams, without any success at all. Most people are terrified of battering-rams; the noise of them, and the way they make the ground shake, and the fact that, being tree-trunks, they cannot be killed. But the Syracusans were quite blasé about it all; they threw burning torches on to the hide canopies that protect the men operating the ram from arrows, and then shot the men down as they ran away. It was all rather humiliating; and when Demosthenes sent some heavy infantry forward to try and recover the rams before they were burnt to ashes, they shot arrows at them too, until the weight of arrowheads in their shields made them too heavy to carry, and they had to withdraw. A few men were killed; but they were Zacynthians and Corcyreans, so nobody was unduly upset about it.

In fact, Demosthenes had only done these things – ravaging the countryside and making his attack on the outer defences – to satisfy himself that they were point-less, and to make the Syracusans think that he was as unimaginative as Nicias. What he really had in mind was something utterly Athenian in its daring, novelty, and sheer ambition. He had made up his mind, as soon as he first set eyes on Epipolae and learned that the Syracusans had three large camps up there, to attack the position by night. After all, nobody had ever done such a thing before, so it would be totally unexpected. In the dark, the Syracusans' local knowledge would be useless; and, above all, so would their arrows, javelins and slingshots, about which he had heard so much. Once we were inside the wall, the enemy would be utterly terrified, not know-ing where we were or what we were up to, just as the defenders had been at Troy when the Greeks came out of the Wooden Horse. We would keep in touch with each other by shouting secret passwords, and this would terrify the Syracusans even more.

When we were told of this, we didn't know what to think; but the sheer cleverness of it all so caught our imaginations that we could scarcely wait until nightfall. Although most of us were exhausted from all the work we had done during the day, we couldn't sit still to rest, for we were all too excited. One thing was certain; this was quite unlike any other campaign anyone had ever been on before. No marching all day with a heavy sack on one's back, or building endless walls for no very good reason, or tramping up and down outside impregnable walls wishing one was somewhere else. There was a feeling of being involved in something very special and important, and everyone was talking, very quietly and intensely, to everyone else – not just their neighbours and friends and relatives, but people from the other side of Attica whom they had never met, or even to the foreigners. We all suddenly felt that Demosthenes was a friend of ours, someone we knew personally – and still our leader, of course; in charge and somehow incapable of failure. It was like being a child again, and being in one of those gangs of herd-boys who elect a king and execute daring raids on other people's orchards; there was that same thrill of taking part in something daring and exciting, with a strong dash of danger about it but no real fear of death or injury. It's hard to imagine grown men feeling that way. Perhaps it was because the whole City seemed to be there; it felt more like a festival or a holiday than a military expedition, with so many of one's friends and neighbours present. There were plenty of strangers, of course, but you felt that you were bound to know someone who knew them. As it started to get dark, we lit our camp-fires and moved around like an army going to bed, and as we did so we kept running across people we knew, friends and distant cousins and the like; I met five or six men who had been in choruses of mine, and many neighbours, and (needless to say) Aristophanes son of Philip. He was creeping furtively round the back of a tent with what looked like a baby in his arms, and when I called out his name he jumped high in the air.

'For God's sake,' he hissed, as he recognised me, 'what did you want to do that for?'

'What have you got there, Aristophanes?' I demanded. 'You're acting very strangely.'

'Since when have you added informing to your list of accomplishments?' he muttered. 'Go and play with the Syracusans, there's a good boy.'

It suddenly occurred to me that Aristophanes' baby might be a wineskin. 'Let me guess what you've got under your cloak,' I said loudly.

'If you must know,' he said, 'it's a dead play. One of yours, by the look of it. You know, stunted, off-colour, never expected it to last as long as it has. I'm going to give it a decent burial, if there are any compost-heaps in Sicily.'

'Give me a cupful and you can bury it in peace,' I offered.

'Vampire,' replied Aristophanes. I held out my cup and he filled it.

'Where did you get this from?' I asked.

'Sicily,' he replied. 'Haven't you got anything better to do?'

I drank the wine and left him to it. Then Demosthenes himself came hurrying by, in his red cloak and gilded armour, and I stepped aside to let him pass. He turned his head as he went past and said, 'Hello, Eupolis,' just as he had that day in Athens, when I went to see the Council. Before I could reply he had passed on, and I stood watching him in the light of the camp-fires; a man always busy, always doing something, always striving to be the best, as a true hero should. 'Where the hell are those stone-masons?' I heard him shouting. 'And has anybody seen the Chief Carpenter? Come on, I haven't got all night.' Other men came running up to him, and their cloaked backs hid him from me. Then someone called my name from inside one of the tents. I put my head round.

'I thought I recognised you,' said Nicias. 'It's a long time since we met.'

I didn't know what to say. Ever since we arrived in Sicily, Nicias had been a sort of bad joke that nobody could resist repeating, me least of all. It was very strange to see him, joint General of this mighty enterprise. He looked very ill, and he wasn't wearing his armour. He was sitting on a little cedarwood stool with a pile of wax tablets on his lap, obviously working out some tiny discrepancy in the lists of supplies that nobody but he would have worried about.

'Good evening, General,' I said. 'Aren't you coming?' I must have made it sound like a party, for he shook his head and said he hadn't been invited.

'I'm to stay here with the reserve and look after the camp,' he said, and to my amazement there was bitterness in his voice. 'It's just as well,' he went on. 'I would only be in the way. Demosthenes would be sure to consult me on points of tactics, and what could I say to him?'

I was in much the same dilemma, and so I kept silent and fiddled with the buckle of my sword-belt.

'It won't work,' he said at last. 'Demosthenes is a fool.'

That was more than I could stand. 'You should know,' I blurted out – for I was an Athenian and a voter, and I could say what I liked. 'It's just as well you're not coming,' I went on. 'Much better to let Demosthenes save your skin for you.'

He wasn't angry or even offended. 'Is that what your chorus will say when you get home?' he asked. 'That Nicias let the bull out of the pen, and Demosthenes had to get it back for him? Shall I tell you something, young man?'

'If you like, General,' I said insolently.

'The Athenians elected a fool,' said Nicias slowly, 'for a fool's errand, and the fool made a mess of it, for he could do nothing else. Then the Athenians elected a clever man for the fool's errand, and he will be a greater fool than the experienced fool, since he does not know the work. They should have left the fool to fall over and break his neck.'

I began to feel very uncomfortable. There was obviously something very wrong with Nicias, to start him off talking like a drunken oracle, and I didn't want to know. I backed away and hurried off, feeling as if I had just seen a ghost. Soon after I ran into Callicrates and Little Zeus, and we filled in the rest of the time until the first watch, which was when we were due to set off, by looking for Aristophanes' wineskin. We found it in the end, as it happened, stuffed under a thorn bush, but by then it was too late to do much about it; so we emptied it out and filled it with water, and put it back exactly where we had found it.

CHAPTER THREE

Oddly enough, I rarely have nightmares about Epipolae now. Shortly after my return I used to have them all the time, but they faded after a year or so and were replaced with a composite nightmare that dealt with a wide variety of issues. While they lasted, however, they were extraordinarily vivid, and were some of the few dreams that I have ever been able to remember after I have woken up. This is highly relevant to the account I am about to give of that adventure; for after all these years I cannot reliably distinguish between my actual recollections of the geography of the battle and the slightly amended and amplified version in the nightmare. So if one of you knows the place well and objects that I have put in a sheep-fold where no sheep-fold has ever stood, or littered an otherwise bare escarpment with gratuitous and wholly unfounded olive trees, I must ask you to keep your erudition to yourself. My Epipolae bears the same relationship to the real Epipolae as, say, Homer's Achilles bears to the real man, whoever he was. The loss in accuracy is more than adequately compensated for by the author's exquisite handling of the theme, and all alterations are strictly necessary for legitimate literary purposes.

Shortly after the first watch we received the order to

move out, and we dragged our way up the steep sides of Euryalus, trying to make as little noise as possible. The sound of a large and excited army making as little noise as possible is quite deafening on a quiet evening, particularly if you are terrified, as we all were, and the prospects of getting such an enormous gathering of people past the enemy without being noticed seemed poor, to say the least. But I suppose we must have managed it somehow; certainly I saw no sign of any Syracusan forces. Mind you, I had enough trouble seeing my own feet, despite the relatively bright moonlight, so I am hardly qualified to pontificate on this point. Every time that I, personally, trod on something that made a noise or dislodged a loose stone, I expected to hear the roar of enemy voices all around me, but it was not so. Whether I would have been able to hear an anemy attack above the noise of several thousand Athenians trying to be quiet is another matter entirely.

We didn't so much attack the Syracusan fort that was our primary objective as trip over it. In fact, we went past it twice looking for it and had to turn back, and the man next to me, a part-time carpenter from the north of Attica, was muttering something under his breath about sending someone down into Syracuse and asking the way when suddenly there it was, a vaguely circular pile of heaped-up stones like an overgrown goat-pen, outlined against the dark blue sky.

I had been expecting something slightly grander – the taxiarch had talked about 'forts', and I had conceived a picture of a miniature Persepolis, with castellated walls and gateways flanked by carved lions – and the sight of this ramshackle structure cheered me considerably. Anyway, I think Demosthenes was so delighted at finding the wretched thing, after all that frantic searching, that he abandoned his siegecraft (he was, as you will remember, the expert on assaulting fortified positions), yelled out something like 'Right, let's *get* the bastards!' and went scampering off in the general direction of the wall. We followed him as best we could; and since it appeared that it was now permitted to make a noise, we started screaming and whooping like a Chorus of Furies.

I can well imagine how those Syracusans must have felt. They were almost certainly asleep; and you know what it's like when you're woken up unexpectedly and asked to take some frightfully important decision. Your mind refuses to operate; you stand there trying to collate certain preliminary facts, like who you are and what is going on. Then, as soon as a coherent scheme of action forms in your brain, you follow it, however inappropriate it may be. The Syracusans' reaction, as it happens, was perfectly logical; they ran like hell. Unfortunately for them, they ran straight into a detachment of our forces under the general Eurymedon which had got separated and come up on the other side of the fort, apparently still trying to find it.

From what I have heard since, it seems that the Syracusans assumed that the mob of soldiers milling about below them were reinforcements of their own from the city, and so ran to meet them. The Athenians, for their part, took the men coming towards them to be Athenians sent out to find them – certainly they had no idea that they were Syracusans, the results of their searches for the fort having led them to believe that the species were extinct in those parts. So each unit trotted eagerly across to the other and asked it what was going on; and I am told that they had been chatting away for some time before one of the Syracusans noticed that the man he was talking to spoke with a funny accent and stuck a spear clean through him.

After that there was a disorganised sort of a fight, in which matters were not helped by the fact that by this stage nobody knew who anyone else was; then most of the Syracusans slipped away and ran down to the main Syracusan camps to wake up their colleagues. As soon as the taxiarchs managed to part the Athenian and Corcyrean contingents, who were beating hell out of each other under the impression that the other was the enemy, the detachment hurried up to the fort to see if there were any Syracusans left in it. Regrettably, Demosthenes had in the meantime got to the fort, discovered the way in (after several exasperated circuits), found it unoccupied and occupied it. Thus when the victorious Athenians came dashing up and found it full of human beings they quite naturally assumed that the position was still being vigorously defended and attacked it with arrows and javelins. Since we Athenians are not terribly handy with such weapons little actual harm was done, and the mess was quickly sorted out by the general Menander, who was about the only person on our side who could cope with the darkness. He was a great sportsman in peacetime, and his favourite occupation was long-netting hares at night, which trains a man for this sort of work.

My part in all this was fairly straightforward; I simply followed the man in front of me as if I was Eurydice being rescued from the Underworld by Orpheus, found myself inside the fort just as Eurymedon's men came charging up at us, and sat down under the wall with my shield held over my head until somebody told me that it was safe to come out. Since several javelins and a large rock had come sailing over my part of the wall in the last few minutes I needed quite a deal of persuasion, which eventually the taxiarch administered with the toe of his boot.

Demosthenes had by now realised that night-fighting was rather different from day-fighting, and held a quick conference with his officers. It was no good (he said) just blundering about and hoping to identify the enemy by their Dorian accents. Not only was this method both time-consuming and unsoldierly, it was also unreliable, since many of our allies spoke in the Dorian dialect, while many of the Syracusans' allies spoke Ionian like us.

What we needed, Demosthenes said, was a password, and the password would be *Victory!*, unless anyone had a better suggestion. The officers agreed that *Victory!* would do to be going on with and set off to tell the men. There was a great deal of sniggering from the soldiers, which did not bode well for the rest of the operation, and we re-formed into files and set off to attack the Syracusan camps. By this time I had located Little Zeus and Callicrates, and we practised saying the password until we were word perfect.

I think Demosthenes' idea had been to come down on the Syracusan camps without any warning and massacre them in their beds. This would have been a good idea had it worked, but unfortunately it required the presence of the Syracusans in their camps to be one-hundred-per-cent successful, and by this time the Syracusans had left their camps and come out to find us. In this they were not entirely successful. For our part, we had no trouble at all in finding the first Syracusan camp, and we charged it, in perfect formation and with remarkable cohesion, only to find there was nobody there. Of course, I had had many similar experiences of dropping in unexpectedly on empty houses after dinner-parties, and was not unduly distressed; I knew perfectly well that we would all meet up later on at someone else's place. But Demosthenes seemed rather put out, and so we stayed where we were.

I gather that the Syracusans eventually got tired of looking for us, accused the survivors from the fort of making the whole thing up, and went home to bed. By this time, Demosthenes had resolved to go out and have another shot at finding the enemy, and the two armies bumped into each other a short way from the camp. We charged – what we charged I am not quite sure – and met with surprisingly little resistance. It transpired that we had missed the enemy completely, and as we were coming back the Syracusans charged us. Unluckily for them, they didn't know the password, and so we were able to identify the mass of heavily armed men running towards us and throwing javelins as the enemy and beat them off. Of course when I say 'we', I am speaking collectively; the celebrated Eupolis was wedged in the middle of a file and only vaguely aware of what was going on. For a short while I was very frightened, for I could hear the screams of men being hurt and I had never heard that sort of sound before. Apart from my experience in Samos (which was entirely different) I knew nothing about what it was like in a grown-up battle, and I suddenly realised that a great many people were in danger of serious injury. I was reminded of the time when I had seen a nasty accident in the street – some men were knocking down a house and some bricks fell on to a group of men walking underneath; one of them was hit on the head and screamed quite horribly until they took him away, and it unnerved me for days afterwards. I found my first experience of an infantry action similarly distressing, and when the enemy had gone away I found that I was shaking all over. I particularly remember seeing a man who had had his hand cut off – accidentally, by one of our own men, which can't have made it any more pleasant for him – and being struck by the unreality of it all. He looked so strange without a hand on the end of his arm where a hand should be, and he was shouting and sobbing quite terribly, saying that this couldn't be happening to him, since he had a farm to work and nobody to help him. I felt a sort of impulse to say that he should be used to running the place single-handed by now; I'm glad I didn't say it, but somehow it was very difficult not to. I suppose my terror was turning into jokes inside my head, which is what usually happens to me when I get frightened. Of course, the Spartans are great ones for this sort of humour (although they are rather better at it than me), and everyone says that it proves how brave they are, that they can crack jokes in the midst of suffering and death. I think it proves exactly the opposite; but I may well be wrong on this point.

Well, as soon as the Syracusans had gone away – they had got considerably the worst of the encounter – we pulled ourselves together and went plunging off after them. There was a great shouting of orders from our officers, and for all I knew these may have been very good, sensible and constructive orders; but I couldn't hear a word of them through the padding of my helmet, and neither, I suspect, could anybody else. Nor could we see any signals or even the other parts of the army, let alone the enemy; so we did the logical thing and followed the men in front of us. As a result, I suppose, the front of our lines was pushed forward and stumbled onwards in no particular direction, and soon the detachment I was with began to have a horrible feeling that nobody knew where we were or what precisely we were supposed to be doing. We blundered on, yelling out the password at the tops of our voices; and I guess that the Syracusans must have worked out the significance of the word *Victory!* bellowed loudly and with no great conviction by the all-conquering Athenian army, because they started shouting it too, from all sides. As soon as we heard it, we were delighted and moved off in that direction to meet up with our men, only to find small but ferocious groups of the enemy rushing down on our flanks and rear and making our lives distinctly uncomfortable. Thereafter we took the shouting of the password as conclusive proof of the shouter's hostile intent, and charged immediately. The result of this was some extremely bitter fighting between the Athenians and the Athenians, which the Athenians eventually won.

They tell me that it was the enemy's Theban allies who turned the battle, standing up to a powerful Athenian force and driving them back. If this is so, all credit to the Thebans, who are by and large a race of homicidal maniacs and quite capable of heroic action. Personally, I don't believe there was any need for valour on the part of the enemy; their contribution to our defeat was, it seems, largely peripheral. As well as the password and the impossibility of hearing orders, there was the incredible mix-up over the Victory Song. As you know, whenever an army wins an action (and quite often when it doesn't) it sings the Victory Song, and all Greek nations use more or less the same words and tune; but Dorian-speaking nations such as Syracuse naturally sing in Dorian, and Ionian-speaking nations like Athens in Ionian. Now our Argive and Corcyrean allies were Dorian speakers, and quite early on they pulped a contingent of the Syracusans' Siceliot allies – this was by no means difficult, as the Siceliots are a timid people – and lost no time in striking up the old, familiar melody. The Athenians behind them (of whom I was one) heard the sound of delighted, bloodthirsty Dorian singing, naturally assumed that the Syracusans had won a crushing victory over the men in front, and immediately formed themselves into a posture of belligerent terror. The Corcyreans, having disposed of all resistance in front of them, quite properly fell back on their own lines, and were greeted with an Athenian charge of considerable force – that was us, all resolving to die like men – accompanied by the Victory Song in Ionian combined with frequent reiterations of the password. The Victory Song confused our stout-hearted allies at first; but as soon as they heard the password they knew that the men coming towards them must be enemies, and retaliated with all their remaining strength. To add to all this, as soon as the taxiarchs had managed to part the two sides and formed them up to march onwards, one bright spark of an officer contrived to march his company off the edge of a cliff, with fatal results for most of his men.

As soon as the news of that percolated through, most of the Athenians came to the conclusion that the expedition was no longer a good idea and that the sensible thing would be to go back to the Athenian camp as quickly as possible. Unfortunately, this proved to be rather more difficult than anyone imagined. To start with, nobody had the faintest idea where they were, and few people were willing to go blundering about in the middle of a battle asking the way home. There was also the small matter of the Syracusan army, which had been in just as much of a mess as we were, but which had somehow gathered itself together and was now busily engaged in killing Athenians. I believe that by this stage the Syracusans had chosen a password of their own, but had intelligently decided not to go about shouting it at the top of their voices. As a result, the only Athenians to hear it didn't live long enough to communicate it to their fellows, and the Syracusans were able to distinguish between friend and enemy, to a certain extent at least.

The unit I was with was one of the first to start moving out, and by immense good fortune we set off in roughly the right direction. We tramped along at a great rate, firmly ignoring any human voices from any direction, and eventually found ourselves on the path that we had originally come up. Unfortunately, there was a solid line of men blocking it, and although in the moonlight it was impossible to make out anything beyond silhouettes, it stood to reason that any contingent blocking the only escape route from the battlefield was quite likely to be Syracusan.

By now, our taxiarch in charge of our unit (a man from the east coast called Philo) had gone completely to pieces and refused to have anything more to do with the exercise of command in the Athenian army. This suited the majority of us, who had not been unduly impressed with his achievements so far, and we held a sort of impromptu Assembly, at which various opinions were voiced. Two main parties quickly evolved; those in favour of attacking, and those who supported the idea of trying to get round the side of the enemy line without being noticed. The pro-attack lobby pointed out that there *was* no way to get round the enemy, since they straddled the narrow strip between two steep and rocky slopes, and anyone trying to go round would almost certainly fall to his death. The opposing faction, to whom I devoutly belonged, replied that the Syracusans were mighty warriors and invulnerable and would certainly kill us all if we attacked and, further or in the alternative, these people would probably turn out not to be Syracusans at all but Athenians, as had been the case all night, and that it was a terrible thing to kill one's fellow citizens. Much to my regret, the pro-attack lobby won the day, and we lumbered off at a slow charge to break through the enemy line.

In the event we went through the Syracusan line like a stick through soft clay and made a pretty horrible mess of those fools who tried to stop us. As I'm sure you know, fighting in those days was more a matter of pushing and shoving than skilful manipulation of weapons offensive and defensive, and besides outnumbering the Syracusans we were so frantic with fear and general unhappiness that nothing much short of a mountain could have stopped us. Most of the enemy broke and ran before we got to them, and those that didn't were simply rolled into the ground and trampled to death. In fact, I can remember treading on a man myself – I hope he was Syracusan, though of course many of our men went down too, tripping over or being shoved, and they were killed just as surely. The man I trod on had lost his helmet, and I looked down just before I got to him, to see his face staring up in terror at me. There was no way that I could avoid him without risking being pushed down myself by the great mass of men behind me, so I looked away and pressed on. As my foot landed on his face I heard a loud crack, even through my helmet, which I think must have been his nose. I think he screamed too, though it may have been someone else.

I was nice and snug in the middle of the formation, and although I had been separated from Callicrates, Little Zeus was beside me, as he had been all evening. He had been taking the whole thing in his enormous stride, apparently only upset because he had not hitherto had a chance of saving his benefactor's life and so paying off at least part of the great debt he felt he owed me. It should have been reassuring to me to have such a large and strongly built companion, but it wasn't, somehow. We had reached the path that led down from Epipolae, which was confoundedly narrow, and were starting to feel relatively secure when the formation seemed to bump into something and tried to stop. This was, of course, impossible; we had picked up a fairly considerable momentum by now, and the threat of being trampled made any movement other than trotting forward extremely hazardous. What had happened was that we had run into the back of another Athenian unit; but of course we weren't to know that, especially in the middle and rear of the column, where you can't see a thing except the back of the neck of the man in front of you. We all assumed that the front of the column had been charged by the enemy, and started pushing with all our strength. It was about then that the real and actual enemy, who had re-formed behind us after we had pushed through them, and of course knew all about the narrowness of the way down, came thundering up behind us and started carving up the rear of the column. There was absolutely nothing that any of the Athenians could do about this, particularly the ones being carved up; we were all wedged tightly together, with no hope of turning round or using our shields or weapons. Instead we instinctively pushed forward against whatever was in front of us, while the impetus of the enemy attack behind us hit us like a hammer striking a piece of metal on an anvil. The man in front of me lost control of his spear, and I was jolted forward on to the butt-spike of it with such force that the spike went clean through my breastplate. I had no idea whether or not it had also gone clean through me, and no real way of finding out, since I couldn't move my arms. What I did know was that if anyone else pushed me from behind I would undoubtedly be spitted like a thrush, and this would do me no good at all. Since the only part of me which I could move was my head, I used it to bang on the head of the man in front of me to get his attention, and tried to explain the damage his spear was doing; but of course I couldn't make him hear me. Just in time the idiot must have realised that his spear sticking out like that was a public nuisance and pulled it free; a moment later, I felt a terrific thump between my shoulder-blades and was hurtled forward, so that my nose ended up buried in the hair of the plume of the man in front.

I lost my footing and went down, instinctively trying to roll up into a ball and feeling that this was my just punishment for trampling on that man's face. But the whole column had by now come to a dead halt, and apart from some fool standing on my ankle I came to no harm. The men in our rear had finally realised that they were being attacked by Syracusans and were desperately struggling to turn round. Most of them managed it at last, but only by ditching their shields and spears (which would have been useless anyway in that terrible crush), and managed to keep the enemy off them by grabbing hold of the shafts of their spears and pushing them aside. Fortunately, there was no room to draw a sword, let alone use one for its ordained purpose; and, anyway, by now the Syracusans' progress was halted by the mound of dead or near-dead bodies that had been built up by their enthusiastic efforts. The whole extended column – two Athenian units and one detachment of Syracusans – had come to a standstill, with no realistic prospect of ever getting disentangled. To add to the confusion, another force of Athenians trying to get away from the battle had come up behind the Syracusans, and was happily demolishing them just as they had demolished us.

What had been holding everybody up was another Syracusan force, quite a small one, which had earlier been sent to block the path. Into this the Athenian unit in front of ours had run, and up till now they had been unable to shift the enemy in front of them, because of a similar build-up of dead and wounded men to the one which was now guarding the rear of my unit. Eventually, however, this dam had been burst by the sheer weight of people pressing down on it, and the Syracusan unit must either have broken and run or been pushed out of the way down the slope. Whatever it was that happened, the column started to move. The result was, of course, total and utter chaos, with everyone scrambling over each other in their hurry to get down to the level ground. I had just managed to lever myself back on to my feet when I was knocked over by someone hurrying past. I grabbed at Little Zeus to break my fall; luckily he was quite stable on his feet and was able to drag me on with him until I could get back into my stride. I dropped my spear, of course, but at that moment I could conceive of no more useless item of equipment in the entire world, and was heartily glad to be rid of it. I did, however, cling on to my shield, which I felt might well come in useful at some later stage in the proceedings.

What happened then I do not know. Part of the column in front of us came to a sudden halt – I think the path got narrower a little further down and this had caused a bottleneck – while the rest of us kept moving. As a result, Little Zeus and I were stranded and unable to move, while men from the ranks behind us came surging past us down the hill. I was uncomfortably aware that the enemy weren't that far behind, but there was nothing I could do without risking being trodden into the mountainside, so I stayed where I was. After a while I saw my first close-up view of the Syracusan enemy *en masse*, and it did little to cheer me up. It was possible to tell them from the Athenians this time from the way in which the Athenians of our unit were hitting them and they were hitting back. I drew my sword and tried to turn towards them, and I confess that fighting was the last thing in my mind at that moment.

Then a man – an Athenian rushing down the path – tripped and collided with me, nearly knocking me over again. He grabbed hold of me to steady himself, and his helmet fell off. It was Aristophanes, the son of Philip. I cannot pretend that I was pleased to see him, since he had knocked most of the breath out of me and the Syracusans were nearly on top of us now, being driven down on to us by the Athenians above them. I tried to push him aside but he wouldn't let go of the rim of my breastplate, which is what he had grabbed hold of, and we wrestled there for a moment; me trying to fend him off with my shield, and him refusing to be fended. He had both hands on me – he had discarded his shield and spear – and apparently saw me as a sort of altar at which he could take refuge. Just then, the Syracusans started washing round us, and one of them aimed a blow with his sword at Aristophanes' bald and unprotected head.

I often wish, for the sake of the development of the Athenian Comic drama if for no other reason, that I had minded my own business at that point. If the Syracusan had killed Aristophanes, Aristophanes would of necessity have let go of me, and I could have joined in the escape with no further interruptions. But, like a fool, I put up my sword to parry the blow, and the weight of it jarred every muscle in my body. Atistophanes saw what was going on and let out a loud shriek, which seemed to do something to the Syracusan; I don't think he would have bothered us any further if my fellow poet had kept his mouth shut. As it was, the Syracusan took another mighty swish, this time at me, and succeeded in cutting the plume and plume-holder clean off my helmet. I tried to hit back but couldn't reach him. Then Aristophanes compounded his many felonies by letting go of me and running for his life. I lost my balance and lurched forward, received a dreadful glancing bump from the rim of the shield of another fugitive, and saw my Syracusan letting loose a third blow at me which I was in no position to parry. I felt it glance off the side of my helmet, shaking the brains up inside my head until they must have started to froth. The Syracusan realised that I was still alive and must have come to the conclusion that I was immortal, for he made no further attempt to do me violence and I was able to put my shield between his sword and my merrily vibrating head. As far as we were both concerned, the encounter was at an end.

That was when Little Zeus decided to intervene. He had had troubles of his own to contend with, I think, and had only just become aware of the risk to his beloved Eupolis. Anyway, here at last was his chance to save my life, and the mere fact that I was no longer in any sort of danger wasn't going to stop him doing it. He jumped on the Syracusan with a roar like a lion and lunged at him with his spear. The Syracusan tried to get out of the way but wasn't quick enough, and the spearpoint went through his forehead and out the other side, splashing a fair quantity of his brains over me. Little Zeus jerked his spear free, waved it jubilantly in the air, and set up a shout of triumph that must have been audible on the other side of Sicily. In his excitement he quite failed to notice the other Syracusan standing immediately behind him, at least until he stabbed him in the throat. Little Zeus fell silent in mid-yell – I think his windpipe was severed – and collapsed in a heap. The Syracusan left his spear in the wound and was swept away down the path before I could even think of trying to attack him.

I stood there for a moment, with another man's blood and brains all over my face, wondering what on earth was going on. I felt completely numb and detached, as if I was invisible, like one of those gods in Homer who goes unseen through the throng of battle. Everyone knows that he and his friends and the people he knows will die sooner or later, and after a while the thought recedes to the back of your mind, being a problem that must be faced when the time comes. But you feel that you at least have a right to some notice of such an event, to give you time to prepare your mind for it. Now during the course of that night it had frequently occurred to me that I myself might get killed; but the thought that someone else, Little Zeus or Callicrates or any of my other friends, might get killed had not occurred to me at all, and the sheer surprise of the thing left me totally bewildered. I honestly have no idea of how I got down off Epipolae that night. I don't think I had any trouble with the enemy; I'm sure I would remember something like that. I think I just stood there for a while, then walked away down the path. My brain wasn't functioning at all. I can't claim to have been shocked with grief; I'm not sure I was particularly horrified, although I was by no means used to such spectacles. I simply do not remember what I felt; it's as though the contents of my mind had been wiped away, as marks are wiped off a marble floor with a wet cloth.

Eventually, I suppose, I got back to our camp. I remember arriving there, and I think there were people with me. Anyway, Callicrates was standing by the gate, with a deep cut over his left eye but very much alive. I remember being pleased to see he was still alive, but only moderately; nothing seemed to matter very much just then. It was exactly the feeling I had had during the plague, when I came out of the house and found everybody was dead; it must have been seeing Callicrates standing there that reminded me of it, I suppose. It was almost as if all the time between the plague and this moment had been some sort of dream from which I had just woken up, and that I was on my own again, set irremediably apart from everyone else by the mere fact that I had survived.

Callicrates had come running up to meet me – he was limping, I remember, and it looked as if running was painful to him; I wished he wouldn't do it – and hugged me fiercely. I didn't hug back; I just stood and stared at him.

'Eupolis!' he said. 'Are you all right?'

This seemed a very strange question to me, given that I was so obviously immortal. 'Of course I am,' I replied. 'Why shouldn't I be?'

'You're covered in blood,' he said.

'Oh, it's not mine,' I replied. 'Somebody that Little Zeus killed. That reminds me, Little Zeus is dead. He'll never enjoy his five acres now, poor sod.'

Callicrates stared at me. 'Are you serious?' he said.

'Of course I am,' I replied.

'You said it like you were telling a joke,' Callicrates said.

'He's dead all right,' I told him. 'Saw it with my own eyes.'

For a moment I thought Callicrates was going to be very angry with me – for being so callous, I suppose – and then I imagine he must have understood how I was feeling, though how he could understand it I don't know. Anyway, neither of us said very much after that; except that I noticed that it was a rather pretty sunrise, and quoted the recurring line in Homer about Dawn, the rosy-fingered, which I detest and which always jars on me when I hear it. I washed my face and hands very carefully, as if it was something else besides dried blood I was washing away, and used a stone to beat out the jagged edge in the middle of my breastplate where the butt-spike had gone through it, so that it wouldn't cut me. Of course, the spike hadn't gone through to my skin at all; how could it? I was immortal after all. I went out to draw my rations and heard that some other friends of mine had been killed too, but the news meant nothing to me; it was like hearing that they had had a moderately good crop of silphium in Libya this year or something equally remote and meaningless.

The rest of the army trickled back in during the course of the morning; our losses had been heavy, since many of our men had gone off in the wrong direction and been ridden down by the enemy cavalry as soon as it was light enough for the cavalry to come out. I remember hearing that one very small allied contingent from a non-Greek city somewhere in the far south of Sicily had been completely wiped out except for a single man, and that for days afterwards he wandered round the camp looking completely lost, since there was no one left alive who could speak his language. I knew how he felt.

CHAPTER FOUR

The next day, heralds from the Syracusans came to announce a truce for collecting our dead without hindrance, according to the custom. They also thanked us for the vast amount of armour and weaponry which we had donated to the Syracusan war effort when we ran away; if we had any more, they said, they would be delighted to receive it, for although they now had more than enough for their own needs, including the construction of the appropriate trophies, they could always sell any surplus to their allies the Spartans.

I think the disaster at Epipolae must have turned Nicias' brain for a while. For Demosthenes, who was no fool, saw that we no longer had any hope at all of capturing Syracuse, and that the best possible thing for us to do would be to go home while we still could. The Syracusans were clearly feeling quite unbearably cocky after their victory, and would probably make some attempt to fight us at sea, where we still had a theoretical superiority. But Nicias would have none of it; he said that he wasn't going home without orders from Athens, since he would undoubtedly be tried and executed as soon as he set foot in the City and he was too old and too tired to defect to Sparta. Besides, he had reliable information from Syracuse that the oligarchic faction there (which was still quite strong) was seriously alarmed at the Democrats' ascendancy after the victory, and would be prepared to help us in any way we wanted. How Nicias had heard this, given that it was only a matter of hours since the battle, nobody knew; but he was adamant that he wasn't leading his army back, although Demosthenes could do what he liked. The two of them argued away for hours, with their junior colleagues Menander and Eurymedon contributing such helpful comments as 'There are good arguments on both sides' and 'Don't ask me, you deal with it.'

So we stayed where we were, and whiled away the time by collecting and burying our dead. That was a miserable business, as you can imagine, but for some reason it distressed me far less than it did my fellow soldiers. I did keep well away from the spot where Little Zeus was killed, but otherwise I just got on with the job, which was very hard work, as anyone who has done it will testify. But I do remember that instead of the rather splendid and dignified ceremony which the Athenians generally use when burying their fallen comrades, we simply dug a series of big round pits like granaries and pitched the bodies in; and that we hadn't dug them deep enough, and that in the end we were so sick of the thing that we couldn't be bothered to dig an extra pit to accommodate the left-over bodies, so we just crammed them in as best we could and covered them over with cairns of stones to keep the dogs off. A lot of people, Callicrates among them, weren't at all happy about doing it that way, but for my part I couldn't have cared less.

I didn't even have the heart to kick Aristophanes' head in for him when I saw him the next day, although properly speaking it was my duty to do so. Needless to say, he had got deeply involved in the Impeach-the-Generals Campaign, which was preparing the prosecution and condemnation of Nicias, Demosthenes, Menander and Eurymedon for when we got home. There is invariably such a campaign whenever an Athenian army takes the field; it frequently starts before the first battle has been fought, and in extreme cases has appointed its chairman and governing body before the troop-ships have left Piraeus. Anyway, Aristophanes was in his element, going over the proposed list of charges with some experienced political litigants and polishing up his speech for the prosecution; they had drawn lots for it and he had only got Eurymedon, which must have been a disappointment to him. I rather fancy he had set his heart on prosecuting Nicias or Demosthenes, both of whom he had, in his time, fearlessly championed in the Theatre. Anyway, Aristophanes had the nerve to deny that he had so much as seen me in the battle, let alone been saved from death by my intervention.

Several days passed, and I think Demosthenes managed to talk Nicias round, saying that whatever happened to them their first duty was to the men under their command, whose safety must come first. That was the sort of talk to give Nicias, and soon there was a healthy rumour going round that we would soon be on our way home. As you can imagine, there was general rejoicing at that. The entire army had had enough of Sicily and even the Great Peloponnesian War itself; I think the reaction was so strong because of the tremendous feelings of hope and expectation with which we had all set out, and which had now turned into abject despair. Men started talking about the enemy again (no one had mentioned them since the battle) and a few fire-eaters were already talking about teaching the bastards a lesson next time. As the rumours grew more and more substantial, and only the hardened pessimists refused to believe them, the camp started to come back to life and be recognisably Athenian once again. Assured that they would soon be safe at home, men started saying that it was a shameful thing to be running away like this, and that what they should really do was stay and give it another go – preferably by daylight, and unquestionably at sea, where there had never been the remotest threat to our supremacy. So eloquently did they express this view (being Athenian) that some people were actually convinced by it, and said as much to Nicias. That set him off again; was it his duty to make one last attempt to salvage the pride and good name of his city? Could he be a party to such a monumental act of cowardice? Had the ships' captains made their weekly rations returns? And so on.

But I assume we would have gone, had it not been for the eclipse. That was a stroke of bad luck, I think. Because, as I have told you, quite a few idiots had talked themselves into thinking that we ought to stay and fight at sea, the eclipse was widely taken to be a sign from the Goddess that we were being dishonourable in giving up the fight after one reverse. The longer it went on, the more people started to mutter, and Nicias (who was very superstitious) was quite unnerved.

Now I have my own theory about eclipses, which is as follows. Obviously they are signs from the Gods; I don't have anything to do with the blasphemous fools like Socrates who say that they are natural and meaningless. But my argument is that there is only one sun, and that when there is an eclipse, the sun must be blacked out all over the world. It is therefore highly presumptuous and arrogant of any individual person, group or nation to hold that this particular eclipse is a sign to them as against anyone else. For all we know, the eclipse might be a sign from Hera to the Ethiopians, or Poseidon warning the Odomantians of an impending earthquake. In addition, it is only reasonable to expect that when the Gods choose to warn us they will use several different methods at the same time; an eclipse and a flight of birds, and possibly a prodigy and a malformed sacrificial victim as well, simply in order to let the recipients of the message know that it is intended for them. Otherwise the system would break down completely; people who have nothing to fear would immediately break off whatever they happen to be doing at the time (which cannot be the will of the Gods) while the intended recipients of the warning would take no notice, having learned from experience that the majority of eclipses never have any special significance for them at all. Unless the Gods so arrange things that all the nations of the earth get into trouble and need warning at exactly the same time, I think my explanation is the only rational one.

Be that as it may. The Athenians took this particular eclipse as a positive order from Athena herself not to abandon the expedition, and so the expedition was not abandoned. Nor was it prosecuted with anything remotely resembling enthusiasm, mind you; it just lay dormant for a while as Nicias and Demosthenes went back into emergency session to work out between them, in addition to their more immediate difficulties, the purposes of the immortal Gods.

For their part, the Syracusans had no doubt whatsoever about the significance of the eclipse. It told them, in no uncertain terms, that unless they got a move on and finished off the Athenians while they had them on their knees, they were going to be in severe trouble before too long. It is not inconceivable that this interpretation was the right one. The Syracusans bustled about with their ships, deliberately practising the various standard naval manoeuvres in full view of our forces. Opinions on the quality of the sea-power of our enemy differed in the Athenian camp. Some of us, myself included, believed that they were demonstrating a high degree of skill and expertise which ought finally to dissuade us from any further involvement with them, especially by sea. Those of us who knew or professed to know anything about naval warfare were of the opinion that the Syracusans knew as much about the science of fighting at sea, both theoretical and practical, as various domestic animals of their acquaintance. As might have been expected with a gathering of Athenians, a suitably ingenious compromise was reached between the exponents of both interpretations; namely that the Syracusans were indeed a formidable enemy at sea as well as on land, and that the inept display they had mounted for our benefit was designed to lull us into a false sense of superiority which would provoke us into a disastrous battle.

After a few days of training, they attempted a minor amphibious assault on part of our line, and succeeded in running off many of our small number of cavalry horses. Encouraged by this, they followed it up with a full-scale attack by land and sea. When the order came for our men on land to form up I pushed my way into the front rank, since I was keen to test my immortality theory, which had become something of an obsession with me since the night-battle. I can honestly say that once it was clear that there was going to be a battle, all fear left me; I seemed to feel a sort of morbid calm, and as we marched out towards the enemy I suddenly understood why. They couldn't kill me; I was dead already. I had been dead for days, ever since Epipolae. Arguably I had been dead ever since the plague, except that at the time I had been too young to understand, and had never stopped moving long enough for rigor mortis to set in properly. I said as much to Callicrates, who looked at me most strangely and asked about the blow on the head I had received from the Syracusan whom Little Zeus had killed, so I could see that he could not understand.

The naval part of the battle was an utter disaster for our side, its only redeeming feature being the death, through his own incredible ineptitude, of our general Eurymedon. The defeat was not really mitigated by the fact that our land forces won a comparative victory (in which I, incidentally, played no part at all, since my section of the line was not engaged), in that we managed to prevent the Syracusans from burning those of our ships which they had not contrived to sink, and which had run for the cover of the shore.

It was this defeat, I think, that finally broke the spirit of our army. An Athenian believes in his navy as men believe in gods; and it was as if some ill-natured person – Socrates, say, or Diagoras the Melian – had just conclusively and irrefutably proved that the Gods do not exist. After the battle was over, everyone in the camp seemed utterly dejected. There was no panic or hysteria, just a total acceptance of the defeat. It was far worse than it had been after Epipolae; then, there had been fear and anger and considerable pain, but people had at least been busy, what with burying the dead and plotting against the Generals and looking after the wounded and having bad dreams at night. Now, nobody seemed interested in any form of activity. The dead bodies of our men bobbed up and down in the water of the harbour, but nobody could be bothered to take a boat out and pick them up. Nobody muttered about Nicias or Demosthenes. The wounded men were left to look after themselves, and many of them died – did I mention that our camp was in a fever-trap? – and nobody had any dreams at all, not even dreams of home. I tried to explain to everyone that this was in fact perfectly natural, since they were now all dead too. But such was the general apathy that nobody could be bothered to argue; and when Athenians refuse an argument, you can be sure that something is wrong.

A day or so after this, I was eating my meal (a pint of barley porridge and four olives) in solitary silence when someone came running into the middle of the camp waving his arms and shouting. Several people asked him mildly to stop, since they were trying to sleep, but this only seemed to encourage him. Finally, someone thought to ask him what the matter was, and he replied that the Syracusans were blocking the entrance to the harbour.

It took about half a minute for the significance of this to sink in; then there was the most extraordinary display of panic that I have ever been fortunate enough to witness. I expect you've seen an ants' nest when the woman of the house pours boiling water into it; well, that's the nearest thing I can think of to the Athenian camp at that moment. I was utterly fascinated by the sight, and I remember thinking that all the dead people had suddenly come back to life; which was rather pointless, because if the Syracusans blocked the harbour they would all be dead again very soon. Now I come to think of it, I didn't panic at all; I sat there speculating what a good Chorus scene this would make – like that scene in the *Agamemnon* where the Chorus suddenly loses its unified voice and collapses into a group of gibbering individuals. No one had ever done it in a Comedy; it would be hell on earth to rehearse, of course, but the effect would be spectacular. Then I remembered that I wouldn't be going home to Athens after all, and there would be no more plays, if the Syracusans succeeded in blocking the harbour. It seemed a pity, but not much more.

Apart from myself, the only person who didn't seem to be panicking was a small, round man who was sitting in front of a fire eating a very thin sausage. His tranquillity and the sausage seemed to draw me to him, and I walked over to his fire and sat down on my helmet beside him. He looked at me and returned to his meal, and neither of us said anything for a while.

'You don't seem worried,' I said at last.

'I'm not,' he replied with his mouth full.

'Everyone else is.'

'You're not.'

'Yes, but I'm dead.'

'Well, there you are, then. Your worries are over.'

He sounded like a man from the hill country, and I asked him where he lived. 'Here,' he said.

'No, but before that,' I asked.

'Can't remember,' he replied. 'Been here so long,' he

paused to swallow a lump of gristle, 'that I just can't recollect.'

'How long have you been here?'

'A very long time.'

'Tasty is it, that sausage?'

'Be even better with a dab of honey. You got any honey?'

'No.'

He had very big hands and forearms, and I guessed that he had once been a smith. He had that way of talking to you without looking at you that is unique to the trade. 'So you're not worried, then,' I said.

'No.'

'Why not?'

'Nothing's going to happen,' he replied.

'What makes you think that?' I said. 'The enemy are blocking up the harbour. That means they aren't going to let us escape. They mean to wipe us out to the last man.'

'They won't manage that,' he said.

'Don't be too sure.'

'They never manage to kill everyone,' he said. 'There's always one or two that get away. There was two men escaped from Thermopylae, so the story goes.'

'And you reckon you'll be one of the survivors.'

'That's right.'

'Why you?'

'Why not?'

Why not indeed? 'Trade you a bit of that sausage for an onion.'

'Don't like onions. Never did. Only thing that grew where I used to live.'

'Before you came here?'

'That's it.'

I leaned forward and pitched a small log on to the fire. All around us, the Athenian army was winding itself up into a thick knot of terror.

'I used to write plays,' I said. 'For the Festivals.'

'Comic or tragic?'

'Comic.'

He looked at me again, chewing vigorously. 'I used to like the Comedies,' he said. 'Never went much on the Tragedies. Couldn't see any point in making up sad stories. Gets you down, that sort of thing. Me, I always look on the bright side.'

'I can see that.'

'The one I used to like best of all,' he said, 'was that Eupolis. He was funny, he was. I liked him.'

'Really?'

'He's dead now, of course.'

'Of course.' I smiled. The smith went on eating his sausage. 'Are you dead too?' I asked.

'Don't talk soft,' he replied. 'Do I look like I'm dead?'

'I just wondered.'

'There's nothing in this world,' he went on, 'that can kill me.'

'Really?'

'Nothing at all.'

'I feel like that sometimes.'

'I don't feel, son,' he asserted firmly, 'I know.'

'That must be a comfort to you.'

He broke off a very small piece of sausage and offered it to me. 'You want to know why I know?'

'If you like.' I popped the sausage into my mouth and chewed. It was obviously home-made, probably out of cormorant.

'When I was a boy,' said the smith, 'my whole family got drowned in a ship. Not me, I swam ashore. Odd, that, 'cos I can't swim. So I get myself apprenticed to a smith, only he gets killed by robbers, and his wife and his sons too. Not me. I hid behind the anvil till they went away. So there I am a blacksmith, with a forge of my own and a little bit of land to scratch away in, and I've just got married and had a family when along comes the plague and kills the lot of them, except me. Well, this is a bit of a facer, but I'm not one to complain, I get on with my business, and now I've got a bit more land that came from my wife and I'm really quite comfortable, except my neighbours won't have anything to do with me. They say I'm unlucky, which is a bit of a joke. I must be the luckiest person in the whole world by now.

'And then I get called up to do my bit in the war, and they put me on a ship, and this ship sinks and I'm the only survivor. I get ashore and fall in with some of our lads, and what happens but the whole lot of them get killed by the enemy – don't ask me which enemy, mind, 'cos I've forgotten. Anyway, there I am in the middle of nowhere wondering what old Death's got against me, when I get picked up by the enemy and taken along to the slave market, where I get sold to a Phoenician and bundled on board his ship. But I had no worries. I knew that ship was going to hit a rock and sink, and I'd be the only survivor; and I was right, too. Laugh? I nearly wet myself. Anyhow, I got back to Athens all right and carried on with my trade, and I've done all right for myself, got myself into the heavy-infantry class and everything. Then when old Demosthenes gets his fleet together he sends out for all the smiths he can get, and they pick me up, though I'm way over the age limit, and here I am. I'm telling you, son, I didn't want to come on this. I really don't fancy being the only survivor out of this lot.'

He made a vast encircling gesture, taking in the whole enormous camp. I shuddered slightly. I could see his point.

'You came the same time as I did,' I said. 'I thought you said you'd been here a long time.'

'It feels a long time, son. Nice talking to you.'

He got up, stretched his arms, and walked slowly away. I spat out the taste of the sausage into the fire and sat quietly for a while thinking of nothing much; then, for the first time since I remember – that is, since I got off the ship – I started to compose verse in my head. It was good, too, I realised, and I closed my eyes, so that the words would take in my mind and not blow away. I find that my mind is like a threshing-floor. Unless I close the doors of my eyes, the wind carries off the grain and the chaff together.

I found that I was turning the old smith's story into a protagonist's speech, for a play called *The Long Sufferer* or something like that. The plot would come later, or maybe there wouldn't be the usual sort of plot, all politics and the usual jokes. That didn't matter so much; it could just be a play about this extraordinary lucky-and-unlucky man, and how he saw the world, how it was unbelievably cruel to everyone else and unbelievably kind to him. I sat there and built that speech like you would build a wall, first one layer, then another one on top of it; or a pile of apples which has been heaped up too much, and the slave keeps on putting on more and more, so that you stand there waiting for it to collapse, but it doesn't. It was a good speech, as funny as anything I had ever done, and as I heaped misfortune on to misfortune for this extra-ordinary character of mine, I forgot completely where I was or what was happening.

Then a taxiarch was standing over me and shouting something, and he wouldn't go away, so I picked up my helmet and my shield and went where he told me to go, still hammering out the words of my speech, like the slaves at the mint hammering coins and tossing them into jars. I joined a long queue of men leading to a ship, and I got the impression that the army was being embarked for a big sea-battle, to fight as marines. But just as I was coming to the head of the queue they shouted out that there was no more room; so I sat down on my helmet again and got back to work. I was left in peace for a while, then someone else pushed me into another line of men. I lifted my head after a while and looked out over the harbour, as I groped in my mind for an article of clothing that scanned long-long-short, and saw our fleet moving out from the shore. All the ships were riding very low in the water, and every inch of them was crammed with soldiers. I commanded my mind to hold the speech and started to count the ships, for I had never seen so big a fleet in all my life. There were a hundred and ten.

Nicias appeared from somewhere and started to make a speech to us. He explained briefly what was happening; he had embarked as many men as possible on the ships, and they would try and break down the barrier the Syracusans had put across the mouth of the harbour. If they succeeded they would disembark and the ships would come back for us, and we would all go to Catana. If they failed, we would have to go to Catana on foot.

Then he started talking about honour and our city and freedom and so on, and my mind was just about to wander back to my speech when someone yelled out that the Syracusans were setting sail, and we all craned our necks to see what was going on. Out by the mouth of the harbour we could see the enemy fleet, and there seemed to be a depressingly large number of them, fanning out like the fingers of a hand.

'Oh, for God's sake,' someone shouted, 'they're sailing straight into them.'

He was right. Our ships just went ploughing on, while the Syracusans opened up to receive them. I think Demosthenes (who was commanding) reckoned he could split the enemy in two, break the barrier, and get out into the open sea, where he would be able to turn. The enemy would follow, and he would turn quicker than they expected and be on to them before they could form. It was a typically daring Demosthenean plan, but it was obvious that it wasn't going to work. The Syracusans were too strong to brush aside like that, and our fleet had started to move too late. The enemy ships closed round us like fingers round a stone, crushing our ships closer together. It was brilliant work on their part. At least forty of our ships were trapped in the middle of a huge block, utterly useless, while all the enemy ships were spread out like a net; their ninety ships were engaging only seventy of ours, and ours were jammed and unable to move. They were the rocks and the Syracusans were the waves. In that enclosed space, of course, all our superior skills and seamanship were useless; the Athenians are open-sea fighters and need masses of space to execute their dazzling turns and sail-throughs. But in the harbour it was solid demolition work, like a land-battle on sea. Now I assume Demosthenes had foreseen this, which is why he crammed the larger part of his land forces on to the ships; but of course that was useless too, since the bulk of his forces were trapped on the ships in the middle and could do nothing. But what was worst of all was the way the Syracusans were fighting this land-on-sea battle. The normal way these affairs go is for the opposing ships to grapple on to each other and board each other for an infantry fight. But the Syracusans had rigged up rawhide shields over their ships so that our grappling-hooks would simply slide off; they drew their ships up alongside ours, just far enough apart so that our soldiers couldn't jump aboard their ships, and let loose volley after volley after volley of arrows, javelins and stones. There was absolutely nothing our men could do; there was nowhere for them to take cover since they were all packed tightly on to the ships like horses in a horse-transport. They stood there and the Syracusans shot them, clearing our ships one by one.

'Somebody stop them, for God's sake,' shouted a man near me. 'That's not fighting, it's just killing.'

For a while I couldn't understand; then it started to make sense. It was basically the tactic Cleon had used at Pylos, when his light infantry with their slings and bows had conquered the invincible Spartan heavy infantry, who had no bows and so could not shoot back. I started to laugh, for it struck me as unbearably comic that our own cleverness should be used against us in this way, until somebody got very angry with me and threatened to kill me if I didn't stop laughing. I tried to explain the joke to him, but he couldn't grasp the point. Meanwhile, Demosthenes and his squadron had managed to break a hole in the ring of enemy ships and was running for the shore as fast as possible. The Athenian ships in the centre followed him as best they could, pouring out of the gap he had made like water out of a punctured skin; but the Syracusan reserves were waiting for them and hit them as they came out, and there was a quite awful mess until the Syracusan ring was broken somewhere else and ships started pouring out of there too. Because there was so little room for manoeuvre, particularly with empty or sinking ships all over the place, neither side was able to do anything much; there was just a horribly confused jam. It reminded me irresistibly of a net that has just been drawn up and landed in the bottom of a boat; and the ships were all the fish, heaped on top of each other and thrashing and wriggling furiously.

It seemed to go on like that for hours and hours. I don't know what you would call it; it certainly wasn't a sea-battle. The ships didn't ram each other, they collided, and you could hear the oars being broken off, like the branches of a falling tree; and you could hear the screams of the oarsmen as the handles of their oars were driven back and through their bodies, or they were crushed against the side of the other ship. And then one of our ships would break free and make a dash for the shore, with half its oars broken, perhaps, or a great hole in its side; and our men on the shore would cheer it on so desperately that you imagined that if that one ship got away we would all be saved. And sometimes it made it to the shore, and sometimes a Syracusan ship would catch up with it and rake it with arrows, shooting the oarsmen dead at their oars, so that our ships would suddenly lose speed and come to a pathetic halt or drift round in a circle, struggling like a bird with a broken wing. And some of our ships managed to outrun their pursuers, broken oars and all, and dash across to where they thought they could see a force of Athenian infantry on the shore who would protect them; and they would flop up on to the beach like so many tunny-fish, only to discover that the men they had seen were Syracusans and not Athenians. When they discovered that, they didn't even bother to fight, but simply allowed themselves to be cut down where they stood. And whenever one of our ships was lost, all the men round me would shriek and yell and throw themselves on the ground as if they were completely mad.

Eventually the Syracusans withdrew. I heard afterwards that they had run out of arrows and felt they could achieve nothing more. Our ships were able to limp back to the shore, and every single one of them had dead men on its decks. But just as the battle was dying away, we saw a Syracusan ship being driven towards us by two Athenians; it had somehow got separated from the others and allowed our two to get behind it. The encounter between these ships was a remarkable sight, considering the wretched state they were all three of them in; it was like a fight I once saw between three decrepit old men, who hardly had enough life between them to keep from falling over; yet they were lashing out wildly at each other with their sticks and dealing their puny blows as if they were the Achaeans at Troy. As the ships drew nearer to us, the men around me fell silent, watching the attempts of the Syracusan to break away from its pursuers. For my part, I must confess, I wanted them to succeed, for I could make out the expressions on the Syracusans' faces as they came close in to the shore trying to turn, and they looked so pitiful that I could see no earthly point in their being killed, now that everything had been so conclusively decided. But for once that day the Athenians prevailed, and the enemy ship, after several desperate attempts to turn, ran aground on the beach and was unable to move. As soon as it came to rest, the men around me let out the most ferocious whoop of pure pleasure that you could possibly imagine and splashed out into the shallow water. In a matter of minutes they had turned every man aboard that ship, living and dead, into so many cuts of butchers' meat; including a couple of our Corcyrean allies, whom the Syracusans had fished out of the water earlier on. I distinctly heard these men yelling out who they were, but nobody took any notice, and I was reminded of a bad day in the Assembly or the Law Courts, when the voters get an idea into their heads and refuse to listen to the opposing view.

Just one more thing. A few hours after the battle I went down to the shore to pick up some driftwood for a fire, and I saw the body of a man floating peacefully in the water a few yards out. The shape of the body looked familiar, and my curiosity was aroused, so I waded out and had a look. It was the lucky-and-unlucky blacksmith. There was an arrow wound in his forehead and the fish had already started on him, but it was unmistakably him; and it might just have been the relaxation of the muscles in death, but I would swear he was smiling. As I walked back to the camp with my driftwood I tried to remember the speech I had been composing just before the battle started, but it had completely slipped my mind.

CHAPTER FIVE

A week or so ago, just before I started scratching this narrative down on wax – wax isn't what it was, by the way; in my young days, it never used to crumble or flake the way it seems to now, and you could melt it down and use it over and over again – I found I couldn't remember some detail or other and decided that I had better check it; so I walked up into the Market Square to Dexitheus' stall, to see if he had any copies of a book I had heard about which dealt with the matters I was concerned with. I found the book I was after and persuaded Dexitheus to let me have a look at it for nothing – you will remember that Dexitheus is the lucky entrepreneur who has secured the right to copy this great work of mine; and I persuaded him that it was in his own interests that all the facts in it should be accurate – and then partly since I had nothing else to do that morning and partly to irritate Dexitheus, I stood for a while browsing through some of the other books he had there, including one about this Sicilian expedition I am currently describing. As I stood there reading it to myself, a little old man (I would say he was about my age, or maybe a year or so younger, but bent up with arthritis) obviously overheard the words I was saying from the book and came up to me.

'What was that you said?' he asked me.

'It wasn't me,' I replied, 'it was this book. It's by . . .' I turned back to the head of the roll '. . . Pheidon of Lepcis, whoever he is.'

'What was it you just read, then?'

I looked back over the page. 'He says that in the great battle in the harbour between the Athenians and the Syracusans, the Athenians lost fifty ships, either sunk in the fighting or rendered useless, and the Syracusans forty. And he says that his authority for this is Sicanus, the Syracusan commander, who counted the wrecks himself and was regarded by both friend and foe as a truthful man.'

'Well I'm buggered,' said the old man. 'Did we really sink forty of the bastards' ships? It didn't seem like it at the time.'

'Were you there too, then?' I asked. And then, quite suddenly, I recognised him and was able to call him by his name: Jason son of Alexides of Cholleidae. Then I introduced myself.

'You owe me seven drachmas,' he replied.

The first and last time I had seen him was on the evening after that battle. He was sitting in front of an evil-smelling fire fuelled mostly by discarded helmet-plumes (which seemed to be rather significant in the circumstances) playing knuckle-bones against himself. To cheer myself up I asked if he wanted a game. He asked if I had any money and I said yes, some, so he proposed stakes of two obols a point. Those were quite high stakes in those days, but since I could see little point in dying rich I accepted and we started to play. Of course he won every point and took off me every last obol that I had, plus the seven drachmas alluded to above. When he found that I couldn't pay the whole amount he was most upset and called me all sorts of uncouth names, and started demanding that I put down my sword and armour as security for the debt. At this point I left rather hurriedly. But he followed me all round the camp, whining on about his seven miserable drachmas, until Callicrates and some of his friends came up and chased him away.

I mention this incident for three reasons: first, because it makes a moderately light-hearted opening for a rather miserable part of my story; second, in the hope that one day Jason son of Alexides will hear this being read and feel thoroughly ashamed of himself; thirdly as a comment on the profound bad taste of the Fates, who allowed men like me and this poisonous Jason to get out of Sicily alive but struck down so many good men there.

To return to my story. After the battle in the harbour the only question that remained was how, if at all, we would be able to get away. Although honest general Sicanus may have been aware that the Syracusans had lost forty of their ninety ships, no one on our side knew that, and when Demosthenes suggested to the crews of our ships that they might like to consider having another go at a break-out the following morning he barely escaped with his life. So it was decided that we should burn our remaining ships and march off over land to Catana, which at the moment represented a sort of earthly paradise to every man in our army. In fact our ships never did get burnt; the man whose job it was thought it was someone else's job, and they were left neatly lined up on the sand for the Syracusans, who thus ended the war, as they had started it, with exactly ninety warships.

The next problem was when we should leave. Demosthenes was for setting off straight away. Defeat had not addled Demosthenes' brains to the same extent as it had those of his colleagues, and he could see that if we set off immediately, not only would the enemy not have time to send out units to cut the roads, but our soldiers would not have an opportunity to burden themselves with all the useless junk that any army, given the chance, insists on taking with it, to the great detriment of its average marching speed. But Nicias flatly refused to budge without first taking full inventories of our supplies and making detailed calculations as to what we would need to get us to Catana without having to rely on finding food by the way. Demosthenes realised that, in his present near-hysterical state, the only thing that would calm Nicias down was a good five-hour burst of heavy book-keeping, and let him have his way. This was a disastrous mistake, of course; but I believe that Demosthenes had a genuine though misguided affection for Nicias, who was suffering the torments of the damned immediately after the battle, and could not bear to overrule him in anything.

So it wasn't until three days after the battle that we finally left that horrible, fever-stricken slaughterhouse of a camp, and there wasn't a single man in the army (except me) who wasn't heartbroken to leave it. For a start, most men were leaving wounded friends there – there was no possibility of taking our wounded with us – and those few who weren't were leaving friends and relatives unburied. Then there was the natural and instinctive fear of leaving a place that was apparently safe and going out into a world that was quite definitely hostile, which was made infinitely worse by the fact that we were leaving our ships behind. An Athenian soldier regards his ships as a small child regards his mother; so long as they are there he cannot truly lose hope, but once he loses sight of them he starts to panic and lose his wits.

Now I come to think of it, there was one particular ship in that fleet which had assumed an almost divine aura; it was obviously quite old, to judge by its design and the way it had been built, and the legend quickly grew up in the camp that it was one of the ships that the celebrated Themistocles had built all those years ago, just before the Great Persian War, and that it had seen service at the immortal victory of Salamis, when it had sunk the ship of one of the Persian admirals. Although this was obviously ludicrous most of us believed it, and by some strange chance it was virtually the only one of our ships not to suffer damage or casualties in either of the sea-battles; in fact, it had sunk a Syracusan ship by ramming in the second battle, and was one of the last of our vessels to retire from the fighting. As a result, we believed in this ship as if it was our patron God, and the thought of leaving it was the last straw for some of our people. In the end, we put the most seriously wounded men into it before we left; and oddly enough most of them survived and got back to Athens, since both the ship and its contents were bought by a rich Syracusan slave-trader who was secretly pro-Athenian. He sent doctors to look after the men, and when the war was over and the State had no further use for the ship, he had it dragged inland to his estate and set up on a platform outside his house, with a carved pillar next to it setting out its remarkable history. There it stayed for a good ten years, until a slave accidentally set light to it and damaged it beyond repair; whereupon it was broken up and the serviceable timbers used to build a cheese warehouse.

The army (I use the term loosely) that trailed away from the camp was over forty thousand strong; larger than the Greek army that defeated a million Persians at Plataea during the Great War. A large part of our force was made up of allies, of course, but it seemed to me that the entire male population of Athens, or all that was left of it, was present in that army, and I was reminded of nothing so much as the end of the final day of the Festival when all the plays have been dreadfully bad.

I marched with Callicrates and his two closest friends, Myronides (who was a distant cousin of ours) and Cyon, who had been in a Chorus of mine. For an hour or so we marched on in silence. Now I come to think of it, nobody had said anything much for days; there had been none of those busy conversations or animated discussions that are a sure sign of the presence of more than one Athenian, ever since the night-battle on Epipolae. The whole camp had been quite unnaturally quiet. But Cyon, Callicrates' friend, was one of those almost irritatingly cheerful people who cannot be miserable for long, and after a while he started humming one of the chorus-songs from the play of mine he had been in, and after a while I joined in too, since the song was one of which I was particularly proud. It was all about Demosthenes, as it happens, and a rather sordid business deal he had got mixed up in many years ago – something about a ship-load of seasoned timber from somewhere in the north that he had an interest in – and parts of it now seemed strangely topical; something about Demosthenes being reluctant to abandon his beautiful ship riding on the wine-dark water of the harbour. Anyway, the men around us took up the tune, as marching men will do, and when we came to the end we started at the beginning again. As we sang, we quickened our step to keep in time with the music, and soon we were striding purposefully along roaring out this song of mine about the petty dishonesty of our great general, who was marching boldly at the head of the column, as he always did. I guess the Syracusan outriders who had been following us ever since we left the camp must have thought we had all finally gone quite mad.

But this euphoria didn't last long, and when the song died away we were soon trudging along in silence once more. It wasn't a cheerful sight, that column, and matters were not helped by Nicias son of Niceratus. Noting the despondency of his soldiers, he took it upon himself to hobble up and down the line cheering us along and saying a few words of hope and encouragement in his inimitably grave and pompous style. This was, of course, profoundly embarrassing to every man in the army. For a start, his illness had got much worse since the battle and he now moved very painfully (which many men found quite remarkably funny); furthermore, I don't imagine there were that many men there who would willingly have given an obol to save Nicias' life, after the mess he had got us all into. But he was still our general; and so not many men yelled at him or threw stones as he passed. They simply looked the other way, and spoke loudly to their neighbours to drown out what he was saying, until Demosthenes came rushing down from the head of the column to protect his friend from self-induced humiliation. As soon as they saw Demosthenes, the soldiers started cheering, which only made matters worse for poor old Nicias. For my part I was sorry for him; he was an idiot, and would probably prove the death of all of us, but he had been my producer for *The General* (another disaster, I remembered) and so I felt a degree of loyalty to him. Unfortunately, I couldn't help bursting out laughing when he shambled up to our part of the line and launched into one of his tirades, since he repeated, almost word for word, that celebrated rigmarole of his about men, not walls and ships, making up a city with which he had reduced our rehearsals to a state closely resembling death. My laughter set off the men around me (who didn't know the joke but who desperately wanted to laugh at something) and poor Nicias shot me such a look of pure hatred that I wished the ground would swallow me up. Then he gave up trying to encourage the troops and was helped back to the head of the column. Every man has his evil spirit – some person who always seems to be involved, actively or passively, in his worst misfortunes. Aristophanes has always been mine, and I think that I may have played the same role for Nicias.

I can't remember when we first saw the enemy. As I think I said earlier, there had been Syracusan horsemen watching us ever since we left the camp, and the number seemed to grow all the time, though nobody could say that he had seen them come. But I remember looking up and thinking, There's a lot of them now, where did they all come from? and I think Demosthenes must have had the same idea, because he reorganised our line of march with the baggage-train and the more inadequate parts of our army in the middle and the rest of us forming a sort of hollow square around them. It was a highly intelligent arrangement, now I come to reflect on it, except that we should never have taken so much stuff with us in the first place. It wasn't food we were carrying with us; for all Nicias' fussing over wax tablets, there simply wasn't very much food in our possession. What was slowing us up was such things as supplies of arrows and sling bolts for the archers and slingers (we had no significant force of either), shovels, trowels, adzes and similar tools neces-sary for building walls and other operations connected with siegecraft, chains for binding prisoners-of-war, and other essentials such as plunder (not a large item) and the personal possessions of the dead (a very large item).

I do remember, however, that it was two days after we left the camp that the Syracusans first attacked. We were all heartily sick of marching by now; we were hungry and tired and our feet hurt, and many men were sick with fever and dysentery (marching in the company of men with dysentery is not to be recommended as a pastime). I was fortunate enough to stay relatively healthy, but I'm afraid that I showed far less fortitude and courage than many men who were genuinely sick, until I was shamed into pulling myself together by Cyon. He had the fever quite badly but never complained; and once, when I had been whining for several hours about how thirsty I was, he left the line and ran over to the river, which was on our right for a large part of our march, and brought me back water in his helmet. I drank it all and handed the helmet back to him, and then Callicrates started shouting at me and calling me all the names he could think of. Cyon told him to leave me alone, but Callicrates had clearly had enough of me and wanted to say his piece. Of course, when I realised how selfish I had been I tried to apologise, but Cyon wouldn't listen.

That was just before we reached the river Anapus, where the Syracusans were waiting for us. At first we were very frightened, but as we looked around we could see no heavy infantry drawn up in line of battle, only mobs of light infantry and a few cavalry. At once we began to feel better, since every Greek knows that light infantry, being composed of men from the lower orders of society, is rather less dangerous to a force of heavy infantry than a mild shower of rain. We pressed on and waited for the enemy to run away, as we knew they would.

They didn't. They stood their ground until they were within range of us, and loosed off a volley of spears and arrows. Now one expects such things in battle, but the unwritten rule is that the shooting of arrows and throwing of spears is primarily for the benefit of the thrower or shooter, to make him feel better and not quite so left out of the general fun. They are not meant to be serious contributions to the blood-letting, for the very good reason that a stray arrow can kill a brave man just as easily as it can kill a coward, and that sort of indiscriminate slaughter is downright immoral. The invariable practice therefore, ever since the Great Lelantine War between Chalcis and Eretria in which men first fought on foot instead of from chariots, has been for the light infantry to do their stuff in as cursory a manner as possible. There is generally no actual punishment for hitting someone, but it is regarded as the worst possible sort of clumsiness and makes the perpetrator feel particularly stupid.

After about the third volley, it dawned on us that the enemy were not doing it right. They were shooting and drawing back in relays, and inflicting quite serious losses on our heavy infantry. Demosthenes quickly decided to send out sorties to chase them away, but when he did so they would shoot and retire, not running for their lives as they should have done but pulling back just fast enough to keep clear of our men, so as to draw them forward until their line became disorganised and they were left unprotected by the shields of their neighbours. Then they would dart forward, loose off another volley and repeat the process all over again. Our sorties were very severely handled in this fashion, and Demosthenes called them off. But the only result of this was to encourage the Syracusans, who came in ever closer, until some of our men lost their tempers and broke ranks to go charging off at them; and those men did not come back.

I can't begin to describe the feeling of cold terror that this inspired in us. We had never heard of anything like this, for we could see no way to defend ourselves. It is one thing to accept and come to terms with the fact that you are probably going to die; it is another thing to have demonstrated to you well in advance the manner in which you are going to be killed, particularly if that manner is both new and humiliating and there is nothing at all you can do about it. I think some of us had been relying on a heroic death in battle to make up for the ignominy of being caught up in the worst military cock-up in the history of the City of Athens, and the sight of those Sicilian peasants darting backwards and forwards with bows in their hands like a lot of deer-hunters was more than they could stand. Our men started shouting and cursing at the Syracusans, and throwing things at them. At first they threw stones – they generally missed – and then swords and sandals and helmets and anything they had, which set the enemy laughing. This made matters worse, and there were a number of suicidal charges by individuals and small groups.

Then, almost as a sort of blessed release, we saw enemy heavy infantrymen forming a line on the other side of the river. I don't think any army has ever been so pleased to see the enemy in the history of warfare. There were tears of joy on Demosthenes' face as he ordered us to charge, and we went through that river and through the enemy line like an arrow through a rabbit. Unfortunately, not many of the enemy stayed to meet us, but those we managed to get hold of were chopped up so fine you could have made sausages out of them. But afterwards the light infantry came back, and stayed with us every step of our way until nightfall.

Although we were all exhausted, very few of us slept that night. We started off very early the next morning, I suppose in the hope that we might outrun the enemy; but they were with us again by mid-morning, and their attacks were exactly like those of the previous day. In the end we were forced back to the place we had camped the night before. The food had run out now, and the enemy cavalry made it impossible for us to go out and look for any. The next day we set off even earlier, and reached the blocked pass where we had been turned back the day before. There were heavy infantry waiting for us there, and we ran at them with a will; but the Syracusans had lined either side of the pass with vast numbers of archers and javelin-men who were able to shoot at us from above at short range without our being able to do anything to them, and I was reminded of that time on Samos when a handful of herd-boys with slings had briefly neutralised our column. We gave up trying to force the pass, and fell back over the dead bodies of our own men, both that day's and the previous day's losses. Then, just to add to the misery of it all, it started to rain very heavily, and through the rain we could just make out the Syracusans building a wall at the other end of the pass.

'This is fun,' said Cyon next to me. 'The buggers can't be doing with all this walking about, they're penning us in to murder us.'

But Demosthenes wasn't standing for that. He led the attack himself and threw down the wall, and we went desolately back to our campsite for the second time. The next day we set off in a different direction through open country, but this didn't help matters very much. They still came at us ('For God's sake,' Callicrates kept saying, 'they've got to run out of arrows soon. There isn't that much bronze in the whole world!') and there seemed to be more of them every day. I think that the Syracusans had their heavy infantrymen at it now, throwing and shooting side by side with the serfs and peasants, which was a striking tribute to the levelling power of patriotism but no fun at all for us. We struggled on like idiots for the rest of that day and camped where we could.

But Demosthenes wasn't finished yet. In the middle of the night the order came round to light as many camp-fires as we had fuel for, leave everything except our weapons, and move. Callicrates, I remember, suddenly became very cheerful as we discovered that we were now marching in a different direction; no longer towards Camarina but straight for Catana, which, as I seemed to remember, had been our intention in the first place.

'The only reason they've been chasing us,' he said, over and over again, 'is that they've been afraid we were just pulling out to re-form and would come back again. Now it's obvious that we're going home, they'll leave us in peace. They're civilised people, they don't want to kill us just for the hell of it. What earthly good will forty thousand dead Athenians do them?'

Put like that it sounded very reasonable, and I felt greatly relieved. Needless to say, this march by night was not a pleasant experience, bearing in mind what had happened the last time we went out after dark in this war. But Demosthenes had got things sorted out, and had rigged up a simple but efficient system of communications based on runners to keep the army together. Unfortunately, Nicias refused to co-operate – God knows why – with the result that his part of the army got separated from Demosthenes' force and went wandering off on its own. I heard afterwards that Nicias had got it into his head that if he separated from Demosthenes and made a run for it, he might get to Catana while the Syracusans were busy butchering Demosthenes' force; and it's certainly true that Nicias' men got quite some way ahead of us. But I refuse to believe that Nicias would deliberately have done such a thing, and I prefer to think that it was simply confusion and ineptitude.

Be that as it may; the army was now split into two parts, which made us that bit more vulnerable. We thought we would move more quickly without the rubbish we had been carting with us before; but now we had a large number of wounded men with us – the arrow attacks wounded many times more men than they killed, and since the wounded men invariably died sooner or later it made relatively little difference, except that the presence of so many dying men did little to improve our morale – and we refused to leave them behind. Many men attributed our present misfortunes to abandoning our wounded at Syracuse, and they were determined not to make the same mistake twice. So we didn't move significantly faster.

When it became light and there was no sign of the enemy, there was such a feeling of jubilation in the army that you would have thought we were safely home in Attica. We soon reached the sea, and the sight of it cheered us up still further. We may not have had any ships, but we were still Athenians, and the sight of all that blue water somehow made us feel nearer home. We joined a main road, and gradually our speed increased. The general opinion was that Demosthenes would head down this until he came to a river called Cacy-something (I'm hopeless at place names more than two syllables long); he would then turn up country in the hope of meeting up with the savages who were on our side. Apparently they had plenty of cavalry and light infantry, and they hated the Syracusans, and would see them off in next to no time.

The sheer exhilaration of not being chased or shot at made many of us act as if we were drunk; we had had the Syracusans on our backs for four days, and the effect was cumulative. Now that we couldn't see them any more we started singing and scampering along, speculating as to what they were up to and whether they were missing us. We wished we could see the expression on the faces of their mighty generals Hermocrates and Gylippus the Spartan, when they came out to play and saw nothing but an empty camp; and no way of knowing which way we had gone. Being Syracusans, we reckoned, they would immediately accuse Gylippus of letting us escape on purpose (they did, as it happens) and cut his head off (they didn't). We imagined what they were saying to each other right now; for example:

Gylippus: Well, you had them last.
Hermocrates: I'm sure I had them a minute ago. Hell, I'm always losing things; bits of string, old oil-jars, battles . . .
Gylippus: Where did you have them last? Have you looked in your other pocket? I'm sure I gave them to you to look after.
Hermocrates: We could ask Sicanus, he may have seen them. Hey, Sicanus . . .

We came to the crossing of the river Whatsitsname and found that there had been a battle. The Syracusans had built a wall across the road at this point, and obviously Nicias' men had been through it, since it was smashed down and the ground all around it was littered with bodies. There was no way of knowing whether they were dead Syracusans or dead Athenians, but we naturally assumed they were Syracusans. We started cheering and yelling and waving our spears in the air as if we had just won the victory ourselves, and suddenly it seemed to us that we might get away after all. Nicias had left some men behind, and they said that he had pressed on towards the river Erineus, which was a little way further on; he had been talking with some friendly natives, who had assured him that it would be better to turn in there, since that would be a better way into the mountains. The thought that there were friendly natives to give such advice was marvellously reassuring, and we set off towards the Erineus.

We were marching more slowly now, as if the urgency had gone out of it, and we realised we were extremely hungry. And sure enough we came across a large farm with five full barns, and nobody at home except a crazy old woman, whom the family had presumably left for us to kill. Since it was nearly time for the main meal of the day, we stopped and sat down to eat. I remember the buzz of conversation that rose from the army, for the first time in many days; it was like a hive of bees excited by the warmth of the sun after a long period of rain. Someone found where the farmer had buried his wine-jars and we helped ourselves. It was almost like one of those picnics City people love to take up into the country round Phylae.

And then we saw them behind us, the Syracusan cavalry. I will never forget how quiet it suddenly became, as everyone, nearly twenty thousand men, stopped talking and eating and just stared at them. It was so quiet that I could hear a hoopoe calling in the far distance, and the wind sighing in the trees. I don't know why, but I knew that this was where it would end. I tipped out the rest of my cup of wine and dusted myself off.

I think Demosthenes was as shocked as the rest of us; but he quickly pulled himself together and tried to form us up for battle, for he intended to fight here and have done with it. But as he paced up and down shouting his orders in that reassuring, slightly harassed voice of his nobody moved; they couldn't be bothered, there was no point. We did finally get up and shuffle morosely into formation, more to please him than with any intention of making a fight of it; but by then the Syracusans had brought on their Chorus, so to speak, all ready for the big number. There seemed to be more of them than ever, an endless line of men, a sort of grey and brown shape.

Demosthenes had noticed a large walled orchard beside the farmhouse, and he reckoned that the walls would provide good cover against the enemy arrows. I don't know how he planned to get out of it, but perhaps he wasn't thinking that far ahead. He led us off and the Syracusans made no effort to stop us; they simply marched parallel to us, watching us as a dog watches a mouse. They waited until we were all safely inside. Then they attacked.

I don't know if you've ever been caught out in a really severe shower of rain, when the water comes hurtling down so hard that it hurts your face when it lands on it, and you take shelter under a tree or a rock, which covers half of you but leaves the other half to get completely soaked. Well, that's what it was like behind this wall, with the Syracusan arrows and slingbolts coming down on us for hour after hour. Not that it was a downpour, after the first few volleys; more a sort of drizzle, since they had given up wasting their arrows on the walls and trees and were only shooting at such targets as presented themselves. Unfortunately Demosthenes had made a slight miscalculation, as to both the size of the orchard and the height of the walls. As a result of this slip (a mistake anyone could have made) we were crammed together so tightly that we could barely move, and the walls were just that little bit too low to offer full protection. Therefore the Syracusans had plenty of targets throughout the day, although they frequently wasted time and arrows shooting men who were already dead. We put our shields up, of course; but quickly they became so riddled with holes as to be useless; and besides, we were too tired and miserable to bear the weight of them.

I had managed to stay close to Callicrates and his

friends, and we were huddled together in the same place, right under the wall itself. Being small, I was able to get rather more of my body behind cover than most people; but Callicrates was rather exposed, since he had made room for me. Once I saw an arrow bounce off his helmet and I was terribly frightened for him, but he swore loudly and I knew he was all right.

As the day wore on we all started to suffer agony from cramp, since it was scarcely possible to move; and even if our movements had not been so hindered by the conditions I don't suppose anyone would have dared to shift from where they were. After we had been there about three hours, I nudged Callicrates with my elbow.

'Callicrates,' I said, 'I want to ask you something.'

'Well?'

'You remember when you first found me, after the plague?'

'Yes.'

'What were you thinking, then?'

He twisted his head and stared at me. 'What a peculiar question,' he said. 'I don't really know, to be honest with you. If you remember, I was just back from my tour of duty with the army in Messenia. Philodemus sent me out to find out what had happened to your family, and I found all of them dead except you. I suppose I was feeling pretty shocked; the City was a really horrible sight, in the plague.'

'As bad as this?'

I heard him laugh faintly. 'I don't know. This is rather nastier for me, but it's all men dead and dying here; back then, what really got to me was the women and children. I think you're brought up to accept that men might die before their time, but women and children are supposed to be protected from that sort of thing. I think the plague was worse, because it was so arbitrary and meaningless. This may be a defeat for us, but it's a victory for them. Someone's getting some good out of this. But the plague . . .'

'I think this is worse,' I said. 'Maybe because I'm old enough to understand now, and I was only a child then.'

Callicrates sighed. 'I never thought I'd have any trouble deciding what was the worst thing I'd ever seen in my life. It's a terrible thing having a choice.'

I laughed faintly. 'I don't know,' I said. 'I mean, it all just seemed to happen. One moment we'd just arrived, and we were going to eat up Sicily and then press on to Carthage and the Tin Islands. Then we lost a battle, and the worst that could possibly happen was that we'd have to go home without taking Syracuse this year. And then there was the sea-battle, and everyone was depressed because we would have to walk to Catana, but there was never any doubt that we'd all get there safely. And now look at us. What happened?'

Callicrates thought for a while, then he said, 'We're lucky men, you and I. We've been present at the moment when the world changed.'

'What's that supposed to mean?'

'Think,' he said gently. 'Out there is an army made up of small men, three-acres-or-less men, or men without any land at all. And in here is an army of ten-acres-or-more men, big men. And the little men out there have beaten the big men; well, that may have happened before, though it's not supposed to. But if you think, the Spartans have been beaten by their helots once or twice; that's not the unique thing here. What's new, what's going to change the world, is that once they've beaten us they don't let us go.' He paused to wipe the sweat out of his eyes; it was getting terribly hot. Then he went on, 'They're going to destroy this army, whatever it takes. I've been thinking about it, since we got cooped up in here, and I can't think of a single instance where it's happened before.'

I couldn't quite follow his line of argument, but I didn't say anything. It was just nice to hear him talking, in that explaining voice that made him sound so intelligent and authoritative. It was like the old days, when I was a boy and he would explain politics to me.

'That's the real point about all this,' he went on. 'Those men don't want to win a battle and set up a trophy and be big heroes. They want to kill us, and they want to do it as efficiently as possible. They know they'll never be heroes; they haven't got enough money to be heroes, they can't afford the armour. But they've got hate. I never knew one nation hate another like that. There won't ever be a peace between Athens and Syracuse, like there's peace between Athens and Sparta every so often, and they join forces to thump the Persians, and the Athenian envoys come back from Sparta and say they're not bad fellows actually, they get drunk just like us and they sing quite well, for foreigners. No, we made a mistake coming here. After this, fighting wars just won't be safe any more. And when that happens, God only knows what'll become of Athens.'

'But didn't we hate the Melians when we killed all of them?' I said. 'And what about the Mityleneans? We voted to wipe them out, only we thought better of it the next day.'

Callicrates didn't answer. I nudged him, and he didn't move. I looked at him, and there was an arrow right through his windpipe. I nudged him again, and his head fell forward on to his chest. It's extraordinary how floppy a dead body becomes. I remember thinking how funny it was; just like a rag doll, which you shake up and down and the arms and legs just flop about. And it was so very strange that I hadn't even heard the arrow hit him. I wondered how that could be, and I wanted to ask him, since he was in an explaining mood. Callicrates always knew the answer to everything.

Since I no longer had anyone to talk to, I nestled down behind my shield and tried not to think for a while. I could hear that damned hoopoe again – obviously that bird wasn't afraid of anything. Perhaps it was asking us to go away and leave it in peace, in that peremptory way animals have. We used to have a cat who would yowl at you when you walked into a room, as if you had no right to be there. It used to aggravate me beyond measure, that cat. And if I could hear the hoopoe, how come I hadn't heard the arrow that killed Callicrates? That was just typical, I thought, I always miss the big event, the moment when they light the sacred flame, or the longest javelin-cast ever at the Lady's Games. I've got up at crack of dawn and trudged all the way into the City to see it, and stood about in queues for hours to get a seat, and then when the moment comes I'm looking the other way or unsealing my wine-jar or something, and the first I know about it is the big shout.

I can't remember how long I was there for after that. My mind seemed particularly clear and sharp, but there was nothing to think about. Then the man on the other side of me turned and looked at me, and I recognised his face.

'Hello, Eupolis,' he said, and I felt as if my whole skin was on fire. 'I told you I would meet you here.'

'So you did,' I replied. 'I had forgotten.'

'You've had other things on your mind,' said the God Dionysus, and he smiled. 'Well, this is supposed to be our last meeting. I expect you're glad to see me.'

'I don't know,' I replied. 'So this is the walled orchard, is it? I've wondered about it a lot, over the years.'

'Is it how you pictured it?' asked the God. Once again his voice seemed to come from all round me. It echoed inside the bronze shell of my helmet, and I could hardly hear myself think.

'No,' I confessed. 'But you didn't explain, did you? You just said the walled orchard, and left it like that. And I've been in plenty of other walled orchards since then, in Attica and places. I've even got one on my estate at Phylae.'

'This is the walled orchard,' said the God, 'where the

old Chorus dances off and the new one comes on. It's a pretty Comedy I've given you to produce, though your Chorus,' and he made a sweeping gesture with his arm, 'look as if they don't want to dance any more. I think it's time they left the stage. They've done their best, I suppose, but they didn't understand the words they were saying. What can you do with a Chorus like that?'

I felt a tiny spurt of anger, despite the presence of the God. 'They danced as well as they could,' I replied. 'Perhaps it's really the poet's fault, for giving them such difficult lines. If the Chorus can't understand them, what will the audience make of them?'

Dionysus laughed, and I thought my head would split. His laughter rolled out over the tops of the trees like thunder, and echoed in the mountains above us. 'Now then,' he said. 'What you must do is this. I don't want my best poet getting killed here in Sicily, so I want you to hop over this wall and run for your life. Catana is over there,' and he pointed. 'Find Pericleidas the fish-merchant; he lives in a big house next to my shrine by the little gate, he'll look after you. I think we may meet again after all, Eupolis son of Euchorus of Pallene. Look for me in a house by the Propylaea, the day after anchovies sell for three drachmas a quart in the Market Square. And remember, look after my favourite poet. I don't want him getting hurt, understood?'

And then he turned back into the man who had been there before, who was also dead; I could see an arrow sticking through his ear. He must have been killed while I was talking to the God.

I took a pinch of dust between my fingers and dropped it over Callicrates' head by way of burial; I didn't have a coin to press into his hand for the ferryman, since I had gambled away all my money with the odious Jason. Then I picked up my shield and made sure my sandals were tied tightly, since I didn't want to trip up, and climbed over the low wall.

My legs were so stiff after being cramped up all day that first I could scarcely hobble. But when the first arrow hit me, bouncing off the side of my helmet and giving me the fright of my life, I found I could suddenly run quite freely. Actually, I wasn't in the least afraid of being killed, but I reckoned it would be disrespectful to the God to put his clemency to the test by standing there like a straw target while the Syracusans bounced arrows and slingbolts off me.

There was a wide gap in the Syracusan line not too far away from the wall (they had been coming closer and closer all day) and I ran straight for it. Several things hit me as I ran but none of them slowed me down, and I kept well in behind my shield. As I sprinted through the gap I heard a horse coming up behind me, and I remember wondering how Dionysus was going to get me out of this. When the sound was so close that I guessed the horseman was almost on top of me, I turned, dropped down on one knee (just as they tell you to) and put my shield up to cover me. It was a manoeuvre I could never get right on the parade-ground, but just for once I had no trouble at all with it.

The horseman was there all right. He pulled his horse's head round to come up beside me on my right, where my shield wouldn't cover me, but the stupid animal stumbled over something and he lost his balance for a moment. I could see his left armpit and ribs were unprotected, for he was pulling hard on his reins to control the horse, and I stood up and prodded at him hard with my spear. The spearhead went in as far as the socket, just as if there was already a hole there for it to go into, and as he slid off the horse's back I let go of the shaft. As easy as that.

There was no point walking when I could ride, especially since there were other horsemen approaching; so I grabbed the horse's reins and tried to get up on his back. But it was a big horse and I am not tall, and he kept moving about; in the end I had to jettison my shield. This is supposed to be a great dishonour to a man, but just then I couldn't care less. I had finally made up my mind to abandon the horse and keep on running when I managed to get the upper half of my body over his back and scramble into position.

I should have been in a great hurry just then, what with the enemy cavalry closing in round me and everything; but I took a moment to look at the face of the man I had killed. There was a look of such complete and utter disgust on his face that I couldn't help laughing. 'Oh, for God's sake,' he seemed to be saying, 'there has to be some mistake here.' I knew how the poor sod felt; it was truly rotten luck on his part. But how was he to know he was up against the God of Comic drama? I spat on his face for luck – I was feeling a bit full of myself, understandably enough – and pulled the horse round.

I gave him a ferocious kick and he broke into a trot, which wasn't nearly good enough, so I kicked him again and called him by several epithets that Comic poets usually reserve for rival dramatists. These seemed to do the trick, and he burst into a nice easy gallop. He was a good horse, now I come to think of it, though at the time I had no very great opinion of him.

There were at least two Syracusan horsemen after me, but I wasn't greatly bothered. 'Come on, Eupolis,' I remember saying to myself, 'you aren't taking this thing seriously enough.' But my soul refused to listen; after all, what was there to be afraid of? I was totally detached, no longer human.

The horse seemed to know where he was going, and after what seemed to me a grossly inadequate chase my pursuers reined in and turned back. I galloped on for a while, then slowed down to a gentle canter. When I looked round, I could no longer see the farmhouse, or even the tops of the olive trees in the walled orchard. There was nobody except me on the Elorine road, and it was drawing on towards evening on the sixth day since the battle in the harbour.

I drew up to let the horse drink from a little stream, and I found my mind was still sharp and clear. I had a good idea of where Catana was; to get there I would have to go in from the coast and round the mountains near Acrae; I daren't cross them, since Syracuse lay just below them, at the other end of the Anapus river. After that I would have to pass Leontini on my right and cross the Simaethus, before making my way through the flat plains to Catana. Going that way, the distance could not be less than a hundred miles, and all the great cities I would have to pass on the way were allies of Syracuse. My other option was to try and join up with Nicias' men, who were presumably not that far ahead of me up the road. But my soul wasn't interested in that idea. Anywhere where there were substantial numbers of Athenians in this country was not likely to be safe.

The best thing, then, was to make for Catana. I looked up to my right at the mountains, and thanked Dionysus that I had been brought up in the hill country at home. A man can live off the land quite easily in the hills, if he knows how, and can make himself difficult to find. In the plains you can't help being noticed – which is why the plainsmen are so sociable, I suppose, while hill people tend to be more withdrawn and suspicious. I took off my helmet and breastplate and dumped them under a fig tree. They were battered and dented, and I wasn't sorry to be rid of them. I was tempted to get rid of my sword as well, but it had been in the family for many years and I would need something for cutting wood and sharpening sticks. I wrapped my cloak round it so that it wouldn't be too obvious, and tried to remember how you do a Dorian accent. That was another stroke of luck; I had written many Comic Dorians in the past, Spartans and Megarians and the like, and since I'm a bit obsessive about getting my dialects right I had taken trouble to listen to as many Dorians as possible, and practised speaking Dorian at home, which used to aggravate Phaedra no end. I couldn't pass for a Syracusan, of course, or any other sort of Sicilian; but I could probably get by as a Corinthian, and I knew the names of the streets in Corinth from the stories my grandfather used to tell us about his visit there on a diplomatic mission.

This pleasant and reassuring train of thought was suddenly interrupted by the sight in front of me of a man in infantry armour, with his helmet down over his face, running towards me as fast as his legs would carry him. Behind him was a mob of herd-boys, yelling and screaming and waving sticks and stones. One or two of them had swords as well, which they had presumably picked up from dead Athenians somewhere. The running man was plainly an Athenian, and the herd-boys were after his blood. It was rather comic in a way, since the eldest boy couldn't have been much more than twelve years old; but there were at least ten of them, and there was no doubt in my mind that if and when they caught the soldier they could and would kill him. I felt a tremendous lack of enthusiasm about getting involved, but in the end I kicked the horse and rode forward.

'Hey,' I called out in my Corinthian voice, 'what's going on here?'

The Athenian stopped and turned, and the boys stopped too. 'He's an Athenian,' said the tallest boy after a moment, 'and we're going to cut off his head.'

'You can if you like,' I said, as casually as I could manage. 'Bit of a waste, though.'

'Waste?' said the tallest boy.

'Use your brains, son,' I replied. 'They're worth good money, Athenians.'

The child frowned; this had not occurred to him. 'Are they?'

'Forty or fifty staters, easy,' I said. 'You won't get anything like the full price, mind, because this island'll be swarming with Athenians for sale in a day or two. But forty staters is forty staters. It's up to you.'

'Will you buy him?' asked the child hopefully.

'I would if I had forty staters,' I said. 'Only I haven't.'

'I'll take thirty,' said the child decisively.

'I haven't got thirty staters, either,' I said. 'I haven't got so much as a half-stater' – I nearly said obol, but I remembered just in time – 'for the ferry. All I've got with me is this horse.'

'All right,' said the child. 'I'll take the horse.'

At this his colleagues started to protest vehemently, but he shut them up by clouting them with the flat of his sword. 'Well?' he repeated.

'Go to hell,' I said. 'This horse is worth twenty Athenians. And anyway, who said I was interested in buying Athenians? How would I get him home, for a start?'

'We'll tie him up for you,' suggested a smaller child.

'Then how would I transport him, without the horse? Talk sense.'

The tall child thought for a moment, and the other children gazed at him in confident expectation. 'Twenty staters,' he said, 'and that's my final offer.'

'Tell you what I'll do,' I said wearily. 'His armour's worth fifteen on its own. You take that, and I'll give you this ring and bracelet for the meat on the hoof. There's ten staters weight of fine silver in them, not to mention the workmanship.'

'All right then,' said the boy sullenly. 'You lot, get his armour off.'

The other children obeyed this order with relish. They were none too gentle about it either. For my part I pulled off the ring and bracelet. They had been a present from Callicrates. I leaned over and handed them to the child.

'You won't die poor, will you?' he said nastily.

'No, but you might,' I replied. 'You were going to cut his head off, remember?'

They tied a long strip of rawhide round the Athenian's hands and neck and handed it to me. I took it and wrapped it round my wrist, and kicked the horse.

'Which way are you going?' said the boy.

'Acrae,' I said.

'Straight up from here's the best way,' replied the boy, 'and turn left up that cleft in the mountains. That'll take you straight there over the top.'

'I know,' I replied. 'Come on, you,' I snapped at the Athenian, 'or you'll feel my boot up your arse.'

'What are you doing in Acrae?' the boy called after me.

'Wouldn't you like to know?' I shouted back, and rode off away from the road towards the mountains.

As soon as the children were out of sight I jumped off the horse and started to untie the rawhide. It was the first time I'd seen the face of the man whose life I'd saved. I recognised him.

'You're a total arsehole, Eupolis, you know that, don't you?' he said savagely. 'Why didn't you just give them the fucking horse?'

I should have guessed when I saw the bald head emerge from under the helmet. I should have guessed when the God told me to look after 'his favourite comic poet' rather than to look after myself. I should have known he didn't mean me.

It was Aristophanes the son of Philip.

CHAPTER SIX

'Admit it,' Aristophanes said. 'You're lost.'

'If I'm lost,' I replied, 'which I'm not, it would be because I did as you suggested and turned right at the top of the hill instead of left, as those children said I should.'

'If you had turned left,' replied the son of Philip, as if talking to an idiot, 'we would now be in Acrae. We do not want to go to Acrae. They would kill us if we went to Acrae. We want to go the other way. Therefore it was necessary for us to turn right, to avoid going to sodding Acrae.'

'Perhaps,' I conceded, 'what you say is true, although I would be prepared to point out the basic fallacies in your argument if I wasn't so bloody thirsty. But let us assume that you are right. That still doesn't mean we're lost.'

'I think it's my turn to ride the horse now.'

'You don't get a turn. I bought you, remember. I was robbed.'

It was the morning of the second day since the walled orchard, and I had had more of Aristophanes than I could take. One thing was certain. He wasn't going to ride my horse. I would hamstring the animal first.

Aristophanes had been with Nicias' men, and shortly after the armies split up he had got lost in the darkness.

He had finally managed to make his way on the Elorine road, but had slightly misjudged which direction he should take. He had therefore been walking back towards Syracuse for quite some time when he met up with the murderous children. When I asked him how grateful he was to me for saving him from them, he looked extremely surprised and asked me what I meant. Surely I hadn't imagined that he was frightened of a bunch of kids? I pointed out that he was running away from them. Had he been playing a game with them, I wondered? He gave me a scornful look, and said that since they were obviously intent on starting a fight, and since he, having at least some vestiges of decency about him, could hardly start beating up twelve-year-old children, however vicious they might be, the only course open to him was to retreat. Then I had shown up and started interfering. He couldn't do anything then, of course, for fear of blowing my cover as a stage Corinthian. In fact, if anybody had saved anybody's life, he had saved mine. For a while I was at a loss for a reply to this, but then I thought of one. I told him he couldn't ride the horse. I might be under orders from the God to look after this scumbag, but I was damned if I was going to get blisters in the process.

To do him credit, Aristophanes took this very well; and apart from trying to pull me down from the saddle every now and then, he had accepted the situation like a man. Luckily, I had woken up before he did that morning, and was up and mounted before he had opened his eyes. What he had taken an objection to was my very sensible idea that we should continue in the character of master and slave. He couldn't do a Dorian accent to save his life – I auditioned him very carefully, and he was utterly hopeless – and so we desperately needed some reason why a Corinthian should be taking an Athenian towards Catana. The only possible explanation was that he was my slave and that I was taking him to Leontini to sell him at the market there, where there wouldn't be such a glut of Athenian prisoners and I might be able to get a respectable price. And if we were going to play master and slave, it stood to reason that the master would ride the horse and the slave would walk. Aristophanes couldn't think of a (sensible) objection to this, but he continually complained about having to have the rawhide round his neck. It was degrading, he said, and it was giving him a sore throat. Also, he objected, what if I got carried away with my role and actually did sell him as a slave in Leontini? He wouldn't put it past me, and I had to confess that the thought had crossed my mind. I was triumphantly vindicated, however, when we were stopped by a detachment of Syracusan cavalry, although the son of Philip couldn't see it.

'They didn't ask us what we were doing or anything,' he said. 'They just wanted to know if we'd seen any Athenians.'

'There you are,' I replied. 'We were so convincing they didn't feel the need to ask.'

'When I get home I'm going to prosecute you for enslaving an Athenian citizen.'

'When you get home you're going to pay me forty staters.'

'You thieving sod,' he said. 'You only paid ten.'

'I've got to take my profit, haven't I?'

'You're only making the jokes because you're riding the horse,' he said.

By sticking to the slopes of the mountains and keeping the peaks on our right, I knew that we couldn't go far wrong. You may legitimately ask how I came to be such an expert on the geography of south-eastern Sicily; well, I had managed to get a look at a map after the sea-battle. It was a big thing, engraved on a bronze plate and bearing the name of the celebrated geographer Histiaeus, and I found it on the shore, all wet. I imagine it had been in one of the Syracusan ships which got sunk, since I knew perfectly well that no one in our army had such a thing. Eventually Callicrates insisted that it should be handed over to the Generals, but not before we had memorised its contents. Thanks to that map, I was fairly confident that I knew where to head for, and if my estimate of the distance was anything near right, I reckoned that it shouldn't take us more than a week, barring mishaps. All in all, I was reasonably happy about that side of the problem. What worried me was getting there. We had no food and no water, no money and nothing to trade except Aristophanes' cloak and my sword; neither of which we could sell without arousing suspicion.

'We could see the horse,' Aristophanes suggested.

'No, we couldn't,' I replied firmly. I had become very fond of that horse. 'If things get really bad we might eat him, but otherwise we'll keep him. Understood?'

'No.'

'Besides,' I went on, 'the last thing we want to do is go into any form of town, village or settlement. That would just be asking for trouble.'

'You're enjoying this, aren't you?'

It was a startling accusation to have to face, and I didn't reply. But there was a degree of truth in it, at that. After the utter helplessness of the sea-battle and the march, it was exhilarating to be one's own master again, to be free. It was almost a pleasure to be daring and take risks, just so long as the risks remained reasonably theoretical.

'There's always plenty to eat in the hills,' I said, 'if you keep your eyes open. We shouldn't have any trouble.'

'Such as what?'

'Berries,' I replied airily. Last night we had eaten the bread out of the dead cavalryman's saddlebag. There wasn't any more. 'Wild figs. Wild olives. That sort of thing.'

'Correct me if I'm wrong,' Aristophanes said, 'but don't figs and olives and berries generally grow on trees?'

'Yes indeed.'

'And can you see any trees? Anywhere?'

'Strictly speaking, no. But we're a bit high up here.'

'So why don't we go a little further down?'

'Because,' I said, 'it's nice and even up here and I can ride the horse. Also it's likely to be cultivated land further down, and that means there'll be people.'

'In other words, we're going to starve.'

'Be patient,' I said. 'There are also rabbits, hares, deer and wildfowl up in the hills. We aren't going to starve.'

Aristophanes expressed grave doubts about this, but I persuaded him that I was right by pulling quite sharply on the rawhide, nearly choking him.

'Sorry,' I said, 'accident.'

As the day wore on, however, and I started to feel steadily hungrier, I began to wonder if my confidence was well located. We had found several wild olive trees by this time, but there were no olives on them, this apparently being the off year. We found a hive of bees, and we finally succeeded in breaking it open (after being stung rather too often for our liking) but although there was plenty of wax in it there was no honey. We also saw a hare, but the hare saw us first.

'All right,' I said, 'what do you suggest?'

'I suggest we go down the hill,' Aristophanes said.

I considered this. 'Let's compromise,' I said. 'Let's go down the hill later.'

'How much later?'

'This evening, when it gets dark. It might be a bit easier then.'

That evening, we went down the hill. It wasn't a pleasant feeling, coming off our nice empty hillside, where there had been nothing to see except a few goats, into fields and terraces which seemed full to overflowing with chatty farmers. Actually, I don't suppose we saw more than three people, and only one of them spoke to us. He asked us the way to Acrae. But it was still nerve-racking; and when we saw a village up in front of us, I felt decidedly uncomfortable and wanted to turn back. As for Aristophanes, he was plainly terrified. He was sweating profusely and at every sound he would jerk his head round and stare wildly. I think it was the sight of his obvious terror that made me decide to press on.

I cannot for the life of me remember the name of that village; which is strange, because I can picture it in my mind so vividly that you would think I had lived there for thirty years. It had what I suppose might loosely be described as a street, lined with a number of impressively built but dilapidated houses, and at the head of the street was a little brick and thatch shrine. Aristophanes had completely lost control by now, and was quite insistent that we should go and take sanctuary in this shrine. I was not in favour of this proposal. To begin with, I doubted very much whether sanctuary would work in this armpit of the earth, since it is not exactly reliable in places like Athens and Sparta. But even if it did, I could see no prospect of us ever getting out of the shrine once we had gone into it, and I had no great wish to spend the rest of my life, which might be quite long given the history of longevity in our family, in a thatched hut in Sicily. I suggested that we go to the smithy instead, to see if we could get a cup of water and sell the horse.

'Sell the horse?' Aristophanes gasped.

'Oh, so you're not deaf after all. I thought you didn't have holes in your ears?'

Now you don't realise it, but that was a remarkably witty thing to say, since in those days slaves used to have their ears pierced as a way of marking them out from free men. Well, I thought it was funny. Aristophanes didn't; he just told me to keep my voice down. But he was obviously pleased that we were going to sell the horse.

There were about six men at the smithy, and the usual cluster of boys and youths who love the sight of other people working, and they all turned and stared at us as we walked diffidently into the firelight. There was a quite harrowing silence for what can only have been a minute or so (but which seemed longer) during which time I tied the horse's bridle to a tethering-post. Then I tried to make conversation. Unfortunately, somebody had secretly built a mud wall across my throat which stopped the words getting out, and for a while all I could do was gurgle. Finally, I forced myself to say something like, 'Good evening, friends, my name is Eupolidas of Corinth, I'm a merchant passing through on my way to Leontini and I'm taking this Athenian slave with me to sell in the market there, only I dropped my purse with all my money in it somewhere in the hills and so I've got to sell my horse.'

There was another long, long silence, during which the blacksmith laid down his hammer and wiped his hands thoroughly on his tunic.

'Going to Leontini, are you?'

'That's right.'

'Wouldn't do that if I were you.'

'Oh?' I tried to look unconcerned. On reflection, I don't think I made a tremendously good job of it.

'No.'

'Why not?'

'They don't like Athenians there.'

'You mean I wouldn't get a good price for my Athenian slave?'

'I mean you wouldn't get a lead stater for your Athenian head.'

That was what I thought he had meant. At this point I should have drawn my sword with a flourish and done something brave, but instead I just melted, like a hunk of cheese left negligently in front of the fire.

'Not in Leontini you wouldn't,' the smith went on. 'Out here we couldn't give a toss.'

I stared at him as if he had just grown an extra ear. 'Oh,' I said, or something equally brilliant.

'Nothing to do with us,' said a large man sitting on a

three-legged stool beside the hearth. 'I mean, anyone can see *you're* not dangerous.'

Now you might be affronted by that, but just then I thought that was the nicest thing anyone had ever said about me. I relaxed slightly.

'Mind you,' went on the smith, 'we could probably get a price of sorts for the two of you. Not a lot, of course, but something. Well, for him, anyway.' He pointed at Aristophanes with a pair of tongs. I pointed out, in a voice robbed of conviction by extreme terror, that there would be little point to this, since the market would soon be flooded with much higher quality Athenian slaves, and that he might well find himself stuck with us, eating our heads off at his expense and virtually unsaleable. He gave me a funny look, as if a cut of meat on his plate had just sat up and told him there was too much vinegar in the marinade, and stroked his chin thoughtfully. There was another silence, and I was starting to get nervous again when a little bald man poked me in the ribs with his stick and said, 'So you're Athenian, are you?'

'Yes,' I said.

'Right,' said the old man. 'Entertain us.'

He stretched out the word *entertain* as if it was a piece of dough for a honey-cake and for the life of me I couldn't understand what he meant by it, although some horrible alternatives went through my mind. But the other Sicilians seemed to approve of this idea, and the smith, who was clearly the nearest thing that village had to a First Citizen, told the cluster of boys to run and fetch their parents.

'I know you Athenians think we're just a lot of animals and Cyclopses,' the smith said, 'but we're not. We like the finer things in life, when we can get them. Tell you what we'll do; you give us a good show and we'll give you ...' He considered for a moment. 'We'll give you five staters each and a jar of wheat-flour and maybe a few onions. And we'll let you keep your horse. But if we don't like you, we'll sell you to the bosses at the stone quarries. They aren't fussy about the quality of their labour, since it mostly ups and dies on them after a week or so. We'll get maybe thirty staters a head. So are you gonna give us a show or not?'

I still couldn't see what he was driving at. 'What sort of a show?' I asked. The Sicilians laughed.

'We don't care, do we, lads?' said the smith. 'Just so long as it's Euripides.'

Then, suddenly, as if the sun had just risen, I remembered that fat Sicilian who had sat next to me in the Theatre at the performance of *The General*, my first (and worst) play. He had said that the Sicilians were obsessed with drama, and although I had assumed he was exaggerating, as all idiots do, perhaps I had been wrong.

'Euripides?'

'Yeah, of course Euripides. Who else is there worth a dead pig?'

'You wouldn't rather have some Comedy?' I said. 'I know plenty of Eupolis.'

'Never heard of him,' said the large man. 'Aristophanes, yes, I've heard of him. But not who you just said.'

Aristophanes stepped forward; he hadn't opened his mouth up till then.

'It so happens,' he said grandly, 'that I am Aristophanes the poet.'

'You?'

'Me.'

'Well,' said the large man, 'I think your plays stink. Especially the way you bad-mouth Euripides. Euripides is an artist.'

'As it happens,' I said quickly, 'I know Euripides quite well. I think he's our greatest living playwright, and I would be delighted to recite a few lines from his very latest play.'

This was a stupid thing to say, since I knew nothing by Euripides at all, except a few of the really silly bits that every Comic playwright has to know for the purposes of parody. But I knew for a fact that Aristophanes can't keep a speech in his mind for five minutes (unless it's one of his own), so I resolved to try my luck as a Tragic poet, for the first time in my life. As you know, I can improvise verse, and Tragic parody is easier than Comic verse, if anything; if you get into difficulties you just lament, or invoke the Gods, or say that dying is good, but not being born in the first place really beats cock-fighting. These sentiments generally come in ready-to-use units, and while you're getting those past the gate of your teeth your mind is concocting the next few lines.

'What play woud that be?' asked the smith.

'*Thersites*,' I said. 'You'll love it, it's a honey.'

'Never heard of it,' said the bald man. 'When was it on?'

'Last Lenaea,' I replied desperately. 'That's why, I suppose. Best thing he's ever done.'

Aristophanes stared at me but I kept myself from meeting his eyes and tried to herd together a few suitable Euripidean clichés. The smithy was full of people now, and there were others hurrying out into the street. When I reckoned that there was no space for any more I gave a signal for silence and stood up.

'Ladies and Gentlemen,' I said, 'I would like to perform for you now—'

'Speak up, will you?' shouted someone from the back.

'Ladies and Gentlemen,' I yelled, 'I would like to perform for you now the debate between Odysseus and Thersites from Euripides' *Thersites*, as it was recently performed in the Theatre of Dionysus in Athens.'

I took a deep breath and plunged in. I was horribly aware that I was composing for my life – I had heard rumours about the stone quarries of Syracuse, and I didn't want to find out whether they were true or not – and that I was by no means qualified to impersonate the celebrated Euripides. To get a little divine assistance, which I felt badly in need of, I started off with a full-blooded invocation by Odysseus to Lord Dionysus. This was difficult; in Comedy you have to be rude about Dionysus, but in Tragedy you have to be terribly polite about all the Gods. Also, I had somehow to stop myself drifting absent-mindedly into Tragic parody. Even a Comedy caesura would give me away, or a misplaced spondee (which you never get in a Tragic line); yet these metrical devices were second nature to me, and I tended to use them without thinking.

I didn't dare look at the audience. If I was laying an egg, the first I wanted to know about it was the blacksmith putting the fetters round my ankles. I just pressed remorselessly on, trying to act the lines as well as say them (I was supposed to be acting another man's work, remember), and kept my eyes rolling and my head moving, like the really hammy actors do in the Theatre. I guessed the Syracusans would like that.

The theme of my debate was Mercy versus Expediency. Odysseus wants to kill a group of Trojan prisoners, to terrify the Trojans. Thersites objects; it may be a really good idea, tactically and politically, to chop one's fellow man now and again, but it's not the sort of thing that pleases the Gods. Since the Gods order our affairs and are quick to punish the wrongdoer, surely Mercy is the true expediency? To which Odysseus replied that by stealing Helen the Trojans have made themselves into the enemies of the Gods, so ripping open a few Trojans would surely not offend them. Thersites then embarks on that old Euripidean nonsense about Helen not being stolen at all; in fact she was spirited away to Egypt, and a replica shaped out of cloud accompanied Paris to Troy. The Gods have punished the Trojans already, making them suffer the horrors of war for the sake of a handful of vapour; and they are punishing the Greeks in the same way for being so warlike as to launch the biggest armada ever seen on the pretext of recapturing Helen but really to carve out an empire for themselves. Well, now both Greeks and Trojans have had a rough time of it, and surely the killing ought to stop.

Well, as you can see this was all blatantly topical stuff, directly designed to speak to the hearts and minds of my audience; then the horrible thought struck me that this *Thersites* of Euripides was supposed to have been written at a time when the Sicilian campaign was no more than a warped little notion at the back of Alcibiades' mind. I changed tack quickly, and started giving Odysseus some clever things to say, all about the integrity of the Gods (dramatic irony) and the nature of Truth. Finally, after several false starts, I managed to find a convincing way to round the thing off, and drew the debate to a close. My mouth was as dry as paper, and I was trembling like a bad case of fever.

Now all authors love applause; there's nothing like it in the whole world. It's a strange thing, the effect it has on you. You can be a dyed-in-the-wool oligarch like that fool Pisander and regard the People as utter scum; or you can be aloof and intellectual – Agathon, say, or Theognis – and pronounce that the man in the street has no culture whatever and is entirely incapable of understanding the brilliance of your work; but the only approbation or praise you value is that of all the oarsmen and sausage-merchants and bath-attendants and carpenters and stone-masons and itinerant harvesters and olive-pickers packed on to the benches in the Theatre. You don't know – or care – what it was they liked; it could have been the costumes, for all you know, or the way the actors delivered their lines (not at one of my plays, probably). But that applause is the thing; that's better than all the compliments in the world from the young men at the baths or the old men at parties. You wouldn't reckon much to your average fishmonger or barber or caged-bird-seller as a dramatic critic; but when his hands join in clapping or he laughs at your joke about the eels, which you've been up all night fiddling with and still don't think is right, then you value his opinion above that of Cratinus himself. And what all this is leading up to is that those swinish Sicilian peasants applauded – how they applauded! – and I can't think I ever tasted anything so sweet. They jumped up and down, and they whistled, and they shouted, and I forgot entirely about the stone quarries and just flowed. Which was odd, considering that Tragedy is not my thing at all and that my performance was not even particularly good Tragedy, now I come to think of it.

The smith belted his anvil a couple of times with a lump-hammer to restore order, and silence fell over the smithy.

'Not bad,' said the smith. 'Now let's have some Euripides, or it's the stone quarries for you.'

I never met a more perceptive man in my life. I could see from his face that he wasn't bluffable; and I couldn't think of any way out of it. So I said, 'I don't know any Euripides. Sorry.'

Aristophanes let out a sort of wailing noise and buried his head in his hands. 'You cretin,' he said. 'You had to be clever, didn't you?'

'All right,' I said, 'you give them some Euripides, if you're so damned smart.' Just then, I thought of Little Zeus, and his *Persians* and his other extracts from The Poets. If anyone could have saved us here it would have been him. That depressed me even more, but I couldn't help smiling, as I always did when I thought of that dear idiot.

'What are you grinning at?' said the smith. He gave me an idea. I straightened my back and resolved to make one last effort.

'You,' I said.

'Me?'

'Yes, you,' I replied, 'the whole lot of you. You don't know you're born. Here you have, delivered into your hands by an overgenerous God, the two greatest Comic dramatists Athens has ever known . . .'

'Who are you then?' asked the little old man.

'I,' I said, 'am Eupolis. Now you haven't heard of me, I know, but that can only be because you've got enough wax in your ears to make candles for the whole of Sicily. I can see it from here, actually. Don't you *ever* wash?'

That got a good laugh, and I could see I was in with a chance. I took another deep breath and went on.

'You have here,' I said, 'not only the immoral – sorry immortal – Aristophanes but the even more immortal (and immoral) Eupolis, whose name will be remembered in Athens when the works of Euripides and Aeschylus – and, of course, Aristophanes – have long since been scraped over to make paper for a fishmonger's accounts. You have these two giants of Comedy at your disposal; you may command them to be as funny as humanly possible, or you'll send them to the stone mines. And what do you want them to do? You want them to recite you Tragedy. Gentlemen – I use the term loosely – would you try and squeeze oil out of grapes? Would you milk a stallion? Let us make you laugh.'

There was a cheer you could have heard in Naxos, and I let it run for a moment. Then I held up my hand for silence.

'Well, blacksmith?' I asked. 'What about it?'

'Go ahead,' he said equably. 'Make me laugh.'

'No problem,' I said, and cleared my throat. Unfortunately, that was when my mind went completely blank. I couldn't have scanned an anapaest to save my life. You may judge of my desperation from the fact that I grabbed Aristophanes by the cloak and pulled him on to his feet.

Now Aristophanes is very much a wax-and-stylus dramatist; he thinks by writing, and he's hopeless at improvisation. But I think he realised that this was absolutely our last chance, because he started straight into a dialogue scene. I recognised it as a bit out of his *Two Blind Men*, which is in my opinion the biggest load of tripe ever foisted on a long-suffering audience. Still, words were being said, and my mind slowly started to work. When it came to what I judged was my cue, I was able to nip in with a couple of lines with a joke in them, followed by a rough paraphrase of what I vaguely remembered the character in the play saying. I must have got it completely wrong, because Aristophanes gave me a startled look and for one dreadful moment I thought he was going to dry up; but he threw me back another joke that more or less scanned, and I could see he was improvising too. I had another two or three lines ready and we started to gather a little momentum. There was a slight problem, of course, since each of us wanted the other to be the straight-man; and there was a sort of wrestling-match for the feed which I eventually won.

I can quote you every line from that dialogue, word for word. It was between Aeschylus and Euripides, about which of them was the better poet. They go through all the old chestnuts about each other's works, and then they fight it out on points of metre and prosody. This was to both our advantages, since when we felt ourselves drying up we could quote a snippet or two of the original plays, which gave us a chance to think up the next joke. It tickled the audience, too, since it made them feel immensely erudite, and they followed all the technical stuff like schoolboys – which shows that they really did know their Tragedy, at that. The finale, like the rest of it, was my idea; Aeschylus would have it that Euripides' iambics are so lazily composed that you could fit any old phrase, like 'lost his oil-bottle', into them at any point. Euripides is furious, and starts firing off his best-known quotable lines, the sort of lines that people fire at you in support of the thesis that they don't write 'em like that any more. I was Euripides and Aristophanes was Aeschylus, so all he had to do was fit in 'lost his oil-bottle' at the appropriate point. My job was to find immortal lines from Euripides that could be subjected to this indignity, and this was not easy, since the charge of sloppy versifying was – is – totally unfounded. Still, I managed it somehow, and we got the biggest laugh that can ever have been heard in Sicily outside of a human sacrifice.

Does that sound familiar, by the way? If it doesn't, it certainly should. That scene, word for word, was reproduced by my dear friend Aristophanes son of Philip as his own unaided and original work in his most successful play *The Frogs*, together with a garbled recollection of our (mostly my) wisecracks on the subject of who should ride the horse, which he served up, boiled and hashed, as his opening scene between Dionysus and Xanthias. Our wonderful Greek language has many synonyms for the phrase 'thieving bastard', but none of them seems quite adequate to describe the depths to which that man is capable of sinking, so I shall leave the facts with you and allow you to find your own form of words.

When the laughter had died away and those incapacitated by it had been led away to be calmed down with hot wine and cold water, I turned to the smith and said, 'Well?'

He thought for a minute and then said, 'Me, I'd rather have had some Euripides, but I guess that'll do.' Why does everyone want to be a comedian?

We must have made a hit, because there was actual competition among those Sicilian peasants – who wouldn't normally give you the dandruff from their collars – as to who would give us a bed for the night, a decent meal, fodder for the horse, food for the journey, and even – incredibly – money. Aristophanes got extremely drunk and made quite a nuisance of himself with our host's daughter, so we were very nearly killed after all; but I was too exhausted to do more than eat and smile gratefully, and then sleep. I was certainly too tired to be frightened any more, stone quarries or no stone quarries.

Just before I went to sleep my host came to see me. After spelling out in graphic detail what he would do to both of us if Aristophanes laid another finger on his daughter, he told me that a neighbour of his had just come in from the Elorine road, and had passed a certain farm with a large orchard. He had stopped to ask what was going on there, and he was told that there had been a great battle between the Athenians and the Syracusans. Not that it had been much of a battle, he had been told. Nearly twenty thousand Athenians had gone into the orchard, but only six thousand had come out on their feet; and all of those were now in chains, together with their general Demosthenes, waiting to be marched on to the slate quarries, where Demosthenes would be beheaded and the rest would be kept until they were sold or died. They had taken all the money from these men, and it had filled four shields. Then the army had moved on to deal in the same way with the other Athenian army, under the celebrated Nicias.

I thought of Jason of Cholleidae, and wondered if he was still alive. If so, he hadn't managed to keep my money after all. Then I thought of what Callicrates had been saying, just before he died.

'Why did they stop shooting and take prisoners?' I asked. 'Did the man say?'

'They ran out of arrows,' replied my host. 'Otherwise they'd have killed them all. Sleep well.'

CHAPTER SEVEN

The next morning, fairly early, we set off again. Aristophanes said that, since he had a hangover and was in great pain, he should ride the horse, but I persuaded him that this would not be a good idea by kicking him in the head, which seemed to satisfy him, because he didn't raise the subject again for at least an hour.

Our host had advised me that the best way to keep out of sight would be to ride along the side of the mountains about half-way up (which is what we had been doing up till then); that way we wouldn't come across the farmers in the fields or the shepherds up on the top, and so long as we stayed well away from the Acrae side we should be more or less safe. Considering Aristophanes' conduct with regard to this man's daughter I was in two minds as to whether we should take his advice, but I couldn't think of an alternative, so we did. He said we should make Catana in three days, or less if we got a move on and didn't get lost. We had been given more than enough food to last three days, and just over twelve staters in small coin; mostly Syracusan Arethusas, which are acceptable all over Sicily. Somehow this good fortune worried me; apart from our brief brush with the stone-quarrying industry, things were going rather too easily.

This fear was starting to get to me by midday, and so preoccupied was I with it that I communicated it to Aristophanes. I should have known better.

'It's all right for you,' he said. 'You're riding the horse.'

I said something vulgar regarding the horse, and went back to my worrying. Perhaps anxiety has prophylactic powers, I don't know; but we managed to cover quite a few miles that day without running into any sort of trouble. We found a little hollow in the side of the mountain to stay the night in, and while Aristophanes was taking his sandals off and giving me a detailed description of the condition of his feet, I unpacked the saddle-bags, tethered the horse and went to sleep.

I knew as soon as I woke up that something was wrong.

'Aristophanes,' I said, 'where's the horse?'

'I don't know,' said the son of Philip. 'He'll be long gone by now. You might find him, I suppose, but I very much doubt it. He'll probably have gone off down the hill to the village. I think he liked it there.'

I frowned. 'And how do you think he managed that, bearing in mind that I tied him securely to that tree-foot last night?'

'Easy,' replied Aristophanes. 'I untied him, about an hour before dawn.'

'Why?'

Aristophanes shrugged. 'Because I was going to take the horse and ride on ahead. I'm sick of walking. But I tripped over something in the dark and he got away. I was going to tell you, so that we could go after him, but you looked so peaceful sleeping there that I didn't want to wake you up.'

'Well, that's bloody marvellous,' I said. 'Now neither of us can ride the bloody horse.'

'That's what I call democracy in action,' said Aristophanes. 'If I can't have him, neither should you.' I threw a stone at him, but I missed.

We no longer had the horse to bicker about, so we bickered about who should carry what. You will already know what we said if you have ever seen or read *The Frogs*, since Aristophanes filched that too; so I won't bother to repeat it.

We had been walking for maybe three hours when Aristophanes started to complain that he was feeling feverish. I assumed that this was just another variation on the luggage theme and ignored him; but so persistent was he that I had a look at him, and saw that he was showing alarming symptoms of fever. This was the last thing we needed, and I confess that I lost my temper and started shouting at him, although not even Aristophanes would deliberately catch fever just to spite me (or not in Sicily, at any rate). He asked me several times what I intended to do about it, and I replied, truthfully, that there was absolutely nothing I could do except keep well away from him to avoid catching it myself. He seemed greatly offended by this, so to make it up to him I let him tell me the plot of the play he had left behind in the hands of a producer, with instructions to update the topical bits should they become outdated by the time the play came on. It was, he kept insisting, his masterpiece (every play he writes is his masterpiece, according to him), but it sounded pathetic to me – all about a city in the sky and blockading the Gods. But I didn't tell him so, since the fever was getting worse by the hour, and he was starting to ramble in his speech. He went on talking, however, losing his place and going back to the beginning over and over again, until I could cheerfully have brained him with a rock to shut him up. In the end there was nothing for it but to stop and let him rest.

When he was lucid again, I gave him a cup of water (we had very little left, and we hadn't passed a spring or pool for a long time). He drank it quickly, spilling quite a lot. I gave him some more.

'Aristophanes,' I said, 'I expect you'll suggest to me

sooner or later that since you obviously can't make it to Catana and there's no point in us both dying in this miserable place, I ought to abandon you and try and get through on my own.'

'Get stuffed,' he replied. 'You let me die, I'll kill you.'

'I thought you'd say that,' I replied, 'it's a quote from one of your plays. In that case, we've got a choice. I don't know the first thing about what to do when a man gets fever. We can either try and press on and get you to Catana while you're still curable, or we can wait here and hope the fever breaks. What do you think?'

'I think you're a complete bastard,' said Aristophanes with conviction. 'Just get me safely to Catana, will you?'

'So you want to carry on, do you?'

'No,' he replied firmly. 'Get me off this god-forsaken hillside and under cover. If I die, my heirs will sue you for every obol you've got.'

Shortly afterwards he went off his head again, and I could see he was clearly in a very bad way. There was a funny side to it, of course; both of us had survived the Athenian camp, where men were going down with fever wherever you looked, only to get caught with it out on the clean, healthy hillside.

I suddenly got it into my head that it was going to rain, and that could be disastrous. So I draped the food-sacks round Aristophanes' neck and hoisted him on to my back – he was so heavy I could scarcely walk – and set off in the hope of finding some sort of cover. It was nearly dark when I saw a little stone building with light coming from it, surrounded by some of the scrubbiest looking vines you ever saw. I wobbled over to it as quickly as I could and kicked the door hard.

'Go away,' said an old man's voice from inside.

'Open this bloody door, or I'll kick it in,' I said ingratiatingly, and after a while the door opened a crack and a long, pointed nose appeared.

'What do you want?' said the nose.

'This man is dying of fever,' I said. 'I claim the sanctuary of your hearth, in the name of Zeus, God of guests and hospitality.'

'We haven't got a hearth,' replied the nose, 'just a tripod and a hole in the roof. What do you think we are, millionaires?'

That was a tricky one, since Apollo is the God associated with tripods, and Apollo couldn't care less about guests and hospitality. However, I snatched my mind away from the theological niceties of the thing just in time to put my foot in the door.

'I'm a desperate Athenian warrior escaping from a battle,' I said. 'If you don't let me in, I'll chop down all your vines.'

The nose said something unpleasant and opened the door. Now that I could see the rest of him, he turned out to be an extremely old man, once very tall but now bent almost double with age and rheumatism. I felt awful about forcing my way in on him so violently; but this remorse soon departed, for he was a singularly nasty old man.

'There's no food,' he said quickly. 'All my food is *buried*,' he spat the word out triumphantly, as if he had foreseen my coming with the help of some mysterious divinatory art. 'You'll have to kill me first.'

'I've got some food,' I replied. 'All I need is somewhere where my friend can rest until the fever breaks. I'll pay you,' I added brilliantly.

'Pay me?' His little round eyes lit up. 'Silver money?'

'Genuine silver money.'

'Let's see it.'

'Can I put my friend down first?'

He nodded irritably, as if making a great concession. I shifted Aristophanes on to a pile of goatskins on the floor and straightened my back. Sheer bliss.

'Let me see the money,' said the old man.

I took out the linen purse I had been given in the

village, turned my back and took out a Syracusan two-stater piece. It was not too badly worn and had no holes or banker's cuts on it; a persuasive coin. I showed it to the old man. He stared at it.

'So that's what they look like,' he said in wonder. 'I'll be seventy-three come the vintage, and I've never seen one of them before.'

I waited for a moment, to give him a chance to fall under its spell, and then said, 'If my friend gets well, you can have it. For your very own.'

That seemed to have a remarkable effect on the old man. He started moving round the house at a terrific speed, tipping out the contents of jars and poking up the fire on the little tripod until it roared. He was mixing something up in a little pottery mortar, and as he did so he sang a song in a language I could not understand. Then I realised he was not a Greek at all but a Sicel, one of the savages who lived in Sicily before the Greeks came. I have had little to do with non-Greeks in my life (apart from Orientals and Scythians, and you quickly get used to them) and he fascinated me from that moment onwards.

At last he seemed satisfied that his concoction was ready. As a finishing touch, he grabbed hold of the she-goat that was standing peacefully in the corner of the room and squeezed a little drop of milk out of her udders into the mortar; then he put it on the grid on top of the tripod to warm through. 'We'll have your friend up and about again in no time,' he panted (for he had exhausted himself with all that running about). 'Just let me see that coin again.'

'Later,' I said. He scowled horribly, and took the mortar off the tripod. Bending low over Aristophanes, he started smearing the stuff all over his face. Luckily, the son of Philip was barely conscious and didn't seem to notice.

'Give him a few hours, he'll be good as new,' said the old man.

'That's not saying much.'

'You what?'

'Forget it.'

The old man frowned, then shook his head. 'I know everything there is to know about fever,' he said proudly. 'Get it myself every year. Nothing to it.'

'That's good to know,' I said. 'Now then, I'm going to need a horse or a donkey or something.' I jingled the coins in the purse. 'Can you help me at all?'

The old man seemed to undergo an inner torment. He seemed to hear the voices of the little coins, imploring him to obtain them and look after them; but of course he had no donkey, and no way of getting one. He gave me such a pitiful look that I regretted raising the subject. Then a smile started to spread over his face, originating somewhere behind his ears and drawing his lips apart, revealing a startling absence of teeth.

'Sure thing,' he said. 'You wait right here.'

He scampered out of the house and disappeared, leaving me feeling highly perplexed. After a while I sat down beside Aristophanes and looked at him carefully. There was sweat pouring out of him, and he was starting to shift restlessly and moan. I wanted to pour water on him to cool him down, or at any rate do something, but I didn't like to interfere. Whatever the stuff was that the old man had cooked up, it seemed to be having an effect.

I must have fallen asleep – I was exhausted myself by then – because the next thing I remember is the old man shaking me violently. At first I couldn't remember what was going on and I was greatly alarmed.

'I got you a mule,' he said. 'Come and look.'

I dragged myself to my feet and followed him out of the house. Tethered to a dead fig tree was the most wretched-looking animal I have ever seen outside a silver mine. You could see at a glance that it still had all its ribs, but apart from that there was little to recommend it.

'This is my neighbour's mule,' said the old man

proudly. 'I just bought him. You can have him for four staters.'

I burst out laughing – not as a negotiating ploy but out of pure hilarity. The old man scowled and said all right, two staters. Still sniggering helplessly, I excavated two staters from the purse and gave them to him. When he felt the coins in his hands, he looked like Prometheus receiving fire from heaven.

'Hang on,' I said. 'If you haven't got any money, how could you buy a mule?'

'We don't buy and sell with money up here,' he replied scornfully. 'Money's for keeping. I gave him two hoes and a bushel of figs.'

'You were robbed.'

'That's a good mule,' he whined defensively. 'He'll keep on going all day, and doesn't need much feeding. I've known him since he was foaled, poor brute.'

'You'd better come and look at my friend,' I said. 'He's not well.'

The old man sniggered, and for a moment I felt terribly suspicious. But when we went back into the house, Aristophanes was sleeping peacefully.

'That old poultice never fails. Even works on Greeks,' he added, full of wonder. 'I always thought there'd be more malice in a Greek than it could draw out, so I put in more of everything.'

'He'll be all right, then?'

'Soon enough,' said the old man proudly. 'Mind, if you hadn't brought him to me when you did, reckon he'd have died on you.'

I nodded gravely and gave him the four-stater Arethusa. He took it like a mother receiving her baby from the midwife, sat down on a jar by the tripod and played with it for a while, rubbing grease from his hair on to it to make it shine.

I suppose I should have been sleepy, but I wasn't; and the old man showed no signs of being tired. For a crippled man, in fact, he was unbelievably active. When he had gazed his fill on the profile of our Lady Arethusa, he turned to me and said, 'So you're a soldier-boy, are you?'

'Sort of.' It was many years since anyone had called me a boy.

'Athenian, you say?'

'That's right.'

'That's in Greece, isn't it?'

'Yes.'

He shrugged, as if to say that it was too late to do anything about that now. 'So who're we fighting, then?'

'Us.'

'You what?'

'You're fighting us. The Syracusans against the Athenians.'

He looked at me as if I was mad. 'The Athenians against the Syracusans?'

'Yes. I'd have thought you'd have known.'

'We don't get news here,' he said, and his voice suggested that he didn't hold with news. 'Why?'

'Why what?'

'Why are the Athenians fighting the Syracusans?'

'They felt like it.'

That seemed to satisfy him, for he went back to studying his coin. I was feeling hungry, so I opened the food-sack and poured out some flour into my bowl. 'Have you got any water?' I said, looking pointedly at the three-quarters-full pitcher on the floor.

'No,' he replied.

'If you give me some water I'll give you some flour.'

He picked a wooden bowl off the floor and handed me the pitcher. I gave him some flour.

'What about him?' I said, nodding towards Aristophanes.

'In the morning.' The old man was mixing up his porridge. 'Have you got any honey?'

'No, but I've got an onion.'

'An onion!' Was there no end, his expression suggested, to this man's wealth of strange and delightful luxuries? I cut the onion in half with a small knife that was lying on the floor, and threw half to him. He caught it and bit into it as if it was an apple. 'I used to grow onions till maybe three years ago, but then the seed died.'

'Why didn't you get some more?'

'All the seed died in the neighbourhood,' he replied. 'Maybe they've got some over to Acrae, but I haven't been there in forty years.'

'They've got some at the village a day or so back from here.'

'The hell with it,' said the old man. 'So the Athenians are fighting the Syracusans?'

'That's it.'

'Foolishness, if you ask me. I was a soldier once,' he said, as if he had suddenly remembered after a long time. 'But we were fighting the Carthaginians. That was a long time ago. When I was eight years old.'

'Wasn't that young to be a soldier?'

'We were men earlier then. That was when there were kings in Sicily, in old Hiero's time, or was it Gelo, I forget. That was when the Persians were fighting the Greeks,' he said, as if revealing some great secret. 'But we were fighting the Carthaginians. That was a long time ago,' he added.

'It must have been,' I said.

'It was a big battle,' he said. 'Don't rightly know how we came to have any part of it. I was a slinger, and two of my brothers with me, and my father and my two elder brothers, they were archers. Good ones, too. We went out – oh, must have been two weeks from here, with that old king Hiero or Gelo, and you never saw anything like those Carthaginians. They were strange people, all black-skinned some of them, like olives. We won, too, but my father and my brothers, they got themselves killed and I got my back all messed up, when a chariot ran over me, and that was my fill of the wars right enough. But those Carthaginians – well, I wouldn't have missed seeing them. Did you ever hear of that war?'

'That was the Battle of Himera,' I replied.

'Himera,' he repeated. 'I never knew that before. Himera, you say?'

'That's right.'

'Well I'm damned. I never knew it had a name.' He shrugged again. 'Never too old to learn, hey?' Then he nodded forward and fell asleep. I took another look at Aristophanes and then lay down beside him and closed my eyes.

When I woke up next morning, the old man was exactly where he had been the night before, and I realised that he had died in the night. I found a mattock under a pile of rags and dug a grave outside the door – it was terribly stony ground, and I blistered my hands. Then I laid his body in it and put the four-stater piece in his hand, for the ferryman; it was just as well, I thought, that I had come along when I did, or he would have been stranded on the wrong side of the river for ever. Then I closed up the grave and sprinkled a little flour on it. It was the first time I had ever conducted a burial all on my own, but I think I got it right. After I had done everything I could think of, I went into the house and let the she-goat out.

Aristophanes was sitting up and yawning. 'What's going on?' he said sleepily. I turned on him angrily.

'Now look what you've done,' I said. 'You're nothing but bad luck.'

'The hell with you,' he said. 'I'm starving. Where are we?'

I told him. 'That's a stroke of luck,' he said.

'What do you mean, a stroke of luck?'

'Well,' Aristophanes explained patiently, 'all we have to do is find where he buried his food, and we'll have plenty to get us to Catana.'

Just then, I could have killed Aristophanes. 'Get out of my sight,' I shouted. He stared at me, and went outside. A moment later he came back in again.

'What the hell's happened to the horse?' he said.

'You turned him loose,' I replied, 'remember?'

'No. Why should I want to do a thing like that?' Then he seemed to notice something. 'Eupolis,' he said, 'what's all this muck all over my face?'

'You threw up,' I said. 'You'd better wash.'

'Where's the water, then?'

'There isn't any.' I gathered up the food-sack and went out to see to the mule.

Oh God, that mule. You know what the Pythagoreans say about the souls of the dead returning to this world in the bodies of animals; well, that mule must have housed the spirit of someone who didn't like Comic dramatists – some Athenian politician, say, or an oversensitive Tragedian – because it took against the two of us from the very first moment. This was very strange, since it was obvious from one look at the animal that we were the first human beings ever to go out of our way to supply it with such commodities as food and water. But perhaps it was a diehard Syracusan patriot; at any rate, we got no co-operation from it whatsoever. In particular I remember its charming habit of stopping dead in its tracks for no discernible reason and making the most extraordinary noise I have ever heard outside a play by Carcinus. It was also lazy, vicious and lecherous, and had it not been a reincarnated politician, I could have sworn it was the embodiment of one of Aristophanes' protagonists – Philocleon, maybe, or Strepsiades.

But Aristophanes was blissfully happy just because he was riding and I wasn't, which at least took one problem off my mind. He was still weak and not much use for anything, but at least he didn't look as if he would die at any moment (which was how I managed to tell him from the mule). Now that he was riding at leisure, like a gentleman, he started up an unending stream of conversation, which I was unable to take much part in owing to fairly continuous shortness of breath. He told me what was wrong with Athens, the conduct of the War, the Attic Comic drama, my plays, my marriage, the state of the mountain tracks in Sicily, the mule, the weather, my personality, his intestines, the Athenian commanders in Sicily, the Syracusan commanders in Sicily, Sicily itself, the Gods and the food, with frequent cross-references and recapitulations. By the time we reached the river Terias (which was as far as we could go in the mountains before crossing into the plain) I knew his opinion on every conceivable subject as well as or better than he did himself. I can honestly say that, with the exception of the second book of the *Odyssey*, which they made me learn when I was a boy, I have never learned anything less useful or with more suffering.

We differed in opinion as to how we should tackle the final leg of the journey to Catana. My view was that we should get down to the coast as quickly as we could, then press on and have done with it. There was, I argued, a reasonable chance that anyone we met once we crossed the river Symaethus would be either friendly or indifferent, probably indifferent, and that our one main problem would be to get past Leontini in one piece. Aristophanes, on the other hand, was not worried about Leontini, but doubted very much whether our food and the mule would last us as far as Catana. He therefore wanted to go into Leontini, sell the mule, buy another mule and more food, and stroll onwards to Catana without undue haste. All the Sicilians we had met so far had been helpful and friendly, he said, and since we had money there was no point in starving ourselves and making ourselves ill just for the sake of excessive caution.

I flatly refused to go into Leontini, and Aristophanes refused, equally flatly, to make a dash for the coast. The only possible compromise was to make a stroll for the coast, and that, needless to say, was what we decided to do.

I am not saying that that was the silliest decision ever reached. For example, you may remember that Theseus decided that it would be perfectly feasible to abduct the Queen of Hell, and Icarus saw no reason why he should not fly just that little bit higher and thus enliven his flight to Greece with a better view of northern Crete. I still maintain that it was the silliest decision in living memory, and will need sworn evidence from at least two reputable witnesses before I change my opinion.

We spent our last night on the mountain bickering, and set off early the next day across the plain. It was impossibly hot that day, and the mule had probably remembered something nasty Aristophanes had said about its foreign policy in its previous existence, for it stopped and started as often as a sacred procession in a thunderstorm. We were soon in open country, following what was clearly a main road, and the passers-by (who we met far too frequently for my liking) all seemed to stop and stare at us as we made our irregular way towards the little village on the horizon. I cannot say what most aroused their suspicion, but the fact that we were shouting at our mule in the Ionian dialect must have made them curious, to say the least. Whatever the main reason was, they must have felt sufficiently uneasy to mention us to the cavalry captain at the village, who was out patrolling for stray Athenians making their way to Catana.

We didn't know that, of course, when we made our way past a little grove of trees, arguing with each other about what to do next. Our minds were taken off the problem by the sudden appearance of three men in armour blocking our way.

My first reaction was to scream with terror and run. But one of the men dashed forward and grabbed the bridle of the mule, and said, 'Please God, are you Athenians?' He said it in Ionian.

'Yes,' said my moronic comrade, 'Aristophanes son of Philip at your service. Are you Athenians too?'

I took another look at the three men. They were dirty, ragged and starving. It was a fair bet that they were Athenians. Their spokesman thanked the Gods volubly, and begged us to tell them where Catana was, and whether we had any food.

'Catana is over there,' said the son of Philip, 'and we have plenty of food for all.'

I tried to object to this last statement, but Aristophanes would have none of it, and very shortly we had all retired into the grove and eaten the last few husks out of the grain-bag.

Our three compatriots were Nicias' men, and they had had a rough time of it. After they had devoured everything there was to eat except the mule (to which, as far as I was concerned, they were welcome) they told us their story. Nicias and his command were either dead or captured; they had been caught by the Syracusans and harried down to a river. Because, by that time, the whole army was out of its mind with thirst, the men had thrown down their weapons and crowded into the river to drink, and the Syracusans had shot them while they drank. But the Athenians went on drinking, although the water by now was fouled with blood, and fought each other for possession of it. When the Syracusans had emptied their quivers they charged, killed as many as their stomachs would allow, and took the few survivors prisoner. But fifteen neighbours from Eleusis had managed to fight their way out. Of that number, these three had made it thus far. The other twelve were giving the crows of south-eastern Sicily a rather inadequate meal – inadequate since ten of them had died of starvation. The remaining five had been on the point of giving up themselves when they found a goat wandering on the hillside. After spending their last reserves of energy cornering this goat, they killed and ate it; but the local goatherds saw them and ran down to the village nearby, where a cavalry patrol was resting after a large meal. The cavalrymen came thundering up the hill and killed two of the Athenians, who had eaten too much on empty stomachs and were unable to move; but the three had fought back and driven the cavalrymen off with rocks and their bare hands, and run for their lives. They now had no idea where they were and were desperately hungry again, and they were sure that the cavalry were after them, and would be upon them in the next few hours. So they thanked us tearfully for our food and our companionship, but urged us to get away as quickly as we could.

I was all in favour of this; but Aristophanes wouldn't listen. I think he had decided that it would be a glorious thing to save the lives of his fellow citizens, who had been fortunate enough to step under his shadow in their hour of trial. He was feeling decidedly cocky, as I have told you, and had come to regard this escaping-through-Sicily business as pitifully easy for a man of his intelligence and talents. He declared that he would not abandon them now, and that if they did exactly what he told them, he would bring them safely to Catana. They stared at him for a moment, then clasped him by the knees and called him their saviour; a scene which I found highly distasteful.

Of course the idiot hadn't the faintest trace of a plan of action, but he wasn't going to admit this to his worshippers. Instead, he ordered them to take off their armour and bury it, which they did most scrupulously. After all, Aristophanes explained as they were scraping over the hole, the enemy were looking for three armed men; they were not looking for five unarmed men and a mule. This appeared to strike our companions as a piece of tactical brilliance worthy of the celebrated Palamedes.

Well, a little later the sun set, and Aristophanes led out

his little army. By then he had thought of a plan, and it could have been marginally worse. Aristophanes knew that in Athens a drunken rout is given a wide berth by all sensible people. What better way out of our difficulties than for us to pretend that we were a bunch of drunken revellers, staggering home from a heavy day's drinking at some far-flung shrine? All we needed was a few props – a couple of wine-jars, a wreath or two, maybe a pinewood torch to shove under the noses of any passers-by – and these we could pick up and improvise on our way. The true brilliance of the scheme – according to Aristophanes – lay in the fact that although it is hard to speak a foreign dialect convincingly, it is not too difficult to sing it, particularly if you sing it as if you were drunk.

So there we were; five desperate fugitives singing the only Dorian song we all knew (the Hymn to Apollo by the Corinthian poet Eumelus) as we lurched through the Sicilian landscape trying to remember what it feels like to be drunk. Now I am a fair man, and will not deny credit where it is due, even if it is due to an idiot; so I must tell you that we quite obviously convinced the various travellers we met on the way. They took one look at us and bolted, some of them shouting opprobrious names at us as they ran. Perhaps I should not have been as surprised as I was at the time by the success of this ruse; it is a general rule of human nature that people will implicitly believe that you are drunk if you sing and stagger about. They want you to be drunk; it makes it possible for them to despise you on sight.

What Aristophanes hadn't bargained for (and I suppose there's no reason why he should have) was the edict recently passed by the people of Leontini, as a result of various disturbances in their city, making public drunkenness a criminal offence punishable by a substantial fine. Accordingly, when we reached the outskirts of the village, we were met by the cavalry patrol and the magistrate, who arrested us. The following dialogue took place between Aristophanes, who was riding the mule at the head of our little procession, and the magistrate.

Magistrate: I arrest you.
Aristophanes: Whaffor? We haven't done anything.
Magistrate: For being drunk in a public place.
Aristophanes: That's not a crime, is it, lads? I said, that's not a crime.
Magistrate: Where are you from?
Aristophanes: Leontini. Best little city in the world. Born an' bred in—
Magistrate: You don't sound like a Leontine to me.
Aristophanes: Oh.
Magistrate: You sound like Athenians to me.

That was enough for Aristophanes. He panicked, swiped desperately at the magistrate with his torch, and kicked the mule savagely. Considering his previous experience with the mule, he should have known better; that miserable animal immediately stopped dead in its tracks and let out a succession of roaring noises that must have woken up half of Sicily. This magistrate – a brave but foolish man – grabbed at its bridle and got the torch in his face for his pains. The cavalrymen drew their swords, and the three Athenians drew theirs and wrapped their cloaks round their arms.

Now I had deliberately chosen to stay at the back of the procession, in case sudden flight should be necessary, and I took to my heels at once. A cavalryman started to follow me, but one of the three Athenians lashed out at him and hit him just above the knee. He howled with pain and rode away, and I don't know what became of him after that. I had turned round, and I saw the cavalry-man chopping those three Athenians down, as a forester clears brushwood. I was all set to make a dash for the nearest cover when I remembered that it was my God-given duty to protect Dionysus' favourite poet. Very, very reluctantly I drew my sword and ran back.

Aristophanes, for once in his life, had done something sensible. He had fallen off the mule. He was thus out of the way of the cavalry when they were busy with the Eleusinians, and by the time I had returned to the battle he had climbed under the mule and was hiding. Now the cavalrymen had not seen me come back, and the magistrate (who was, I suppose, about sixty years old and had just been hit with a burning torch) had stepped out of harm's way and had his back to me. I grabbed him by his hair and put the sword-blade across his throat, and announced in the loudest voice I could muster that I had a hostage and was a reasonably bloodthirsty person. It was not a heroic act, I'm afraid, but then, I am not a hero.

The cavalry captain was clearly embarrassed by this. He was, I think, a local man, possibly something or other in village politics; anyway, he appeared unwilling to risk the life of the magistrate, and called his men off Aristophanes. The son of Philip scrambled out from under the mule and dashed over to where I was sheltering behind a very frightened magistrate.

'All right,' said the captain nervously, 'let him go.'

'Why?' I enquired.

'Because if you don't, I'll cut your head off, that's why,' explained the captain.

I pulled the magistrate's hair sharply, which made him squeak like a mouse. 'Be fair,' I said. 'You're going to cut my head off if I let him go. I've always wanted to kill someone in regional government, now's my chance.'

'Let him go and your lives will be spared,' said the captain. The effect of this offer was spoiled slightly by the fact that his troopers – there were ten of them – were ostentatiously waggling their swords at us, and I shook my head.

'Well, what do you want, then?' said the captain, exasperated. 'I can't say fairer than that, can I?'

'Try,' I replied.

'If you think you're going to get away with this—' said the captain. I gave the magistrate a tiny shove. He obligingly screamed.

'Go away,' I shouted. 'Quickly. Now. Save yourself the trouble of divisive local elections.'

There was a cavalryman who must have been related to the magistrate, or a friend of his, or something like that. Anyway, he pulled up his horse and rode away towards the village. The captain was furious, but he knew he was beaten. 'Let him go and we'll pull back,' he said.

'Piss off and I'll let him go,' I replied. 'Deal?'

'You won't get away with this,' said the captain.

'Oh, I don't know,' I replied. 'Did you ever read *The Telephus*?'

The captain stared at me. 'What?' he said.

'*Telephus*. Very bad play by Euripides. Perhaps it's before your time, I don't know.'

The captain looked at me, and the magistrate, and my Thracian sabre (which, as I think I mentioned before, is a very businesslike-looking implement), thought carefully, and said, 'Yes, I've read *The Telephus*. So what?'

'You will remember,' I said, 'that the hero in *The Telephus* tries this stunt and gets clear away. If some verbose idiot out of Euripides can do it, why can't I?'

I have no idea why, but this exchange seemed to help the captain make up his mind. He got off his horse, signalled to his men to do the same, and started walking backwards towards the village. I started walking backwards in the opposite direction. When I reckoned we had gone far enough, I gave the magistrate a hearty shove and sprinted off as fast as I could go.

It was quite some time before I dared stop running and look round. There was no sign of any cavalrymen; also, no sign of Aristophanes. I threw the sword on the ground and swore. Despite my ludicrous and entirely uncharacteristic bravado, I had failed to save Aristophanes. I sat down on a rock and put my sword away; I no longer cared about the enemy, or anything very much. The recollection of the episode with the magistrate and the absurd threats I had made and the inane things I had said had taken all the spirit out of me and I wanted to go to sleep. I had just made up my mind to go back to the village and give myself up when a very frightened-looking Athenian Comic dramatist came pounding down the road towards me.

'Where the hell have you been?' I shouted. 'God, I was worried about you.'

He didn't stop running; he just carried straight on past me, and I remember thinking, Oh God, the cavalry, and chased after him. Eventually he slowed down and stopped. I came up beside him.

'You lunatic,' he said. 'You nearly got me killed with all that—'

I was tired, I was scared, and I was past caring; but I was not made of stone. I kicked the son of Philip very hard. He gave me a startled look and whined, 'What did you do that for?'

The expression on his face was so comical that I couldn't help laughing. My laughter did not seem to impress Aristophanes very much; he urged me to pull myself together and reminded me that we were quite some way from Catana. That made me laugh even more; I don't imagine Aristophanes has ever had a more receptive audience. In the end he raised his eyes to heaven with a gesture of despairing incomprehension and asked what he had done to deserve all this. I forced myself to stop laughing, grabbed him by the arm and marched him off down the road. We were lost, without food or transport, going in the wrong direction, and the whole of Sicily would soon be out after our blood, but we were still alive. Not bad going, I reflected, for a pair of comedians in a world that undervalues Comedy.

CHAPTER EIGHT

We spent the night in a drainage ditch and woke up at sunrise. I suppose I had been hoping that our problems would evaporate overnight, but they were still there when I opened my eyes; and I felt extremely frightened. My trusty comrade was still asleep, curled up in a ball like a little puppy or something equally helpless, and I woke him with my foot.

'Where the hell are we?' he moaned.

'I don't know,' I replied. 'I don't think this is the road we came up yesterday.'

'How would you know?' he grumbled.

'Because we didn't see this ditch yesterday,' I replied.

'What does that prove?' replied the son of Philip.

'Besides,' I went on, 'this is a drainage ditch, right?'

'Could be,' said Aristophanes cautiously.

'Of course it is, you idiot. Now it stands to reason that it drains into something, or leads out of something. Agreed?'

Aristophanes looked at me. 'You've been seeing too much of Socrates,' he said.

'Agreed?'

'If it makes you feel good, yes.'

'Now what could that something be except the river Terias?' I said. 'And the Terias goes to the coast, just above Trotilus. Agreed?'

'You, of course, know where Trotilus is,' said Aristophanes.

'Correct. It's about a day's walk from Catana. I don't know which side the Trotileans are on, but maybe they don't either.'

'What has this to do with the fact that we have no food left?'

Now that was a good question, which I answered as best I could thus. 'Listen, you,' I snapped, 'I've had just about enough out of you to last me the rest of my life. You and nobody else got us into this mess, and I'm going to get us out of it, if I can. But if you interfere just once again, then so help me I'll cut your tongue out.'

'You've really got a way with words, son of Euchorus,' said Aristophanes. 'So what do we do now?'

'We follow this ditch to its logical conclusion.'

'Up it or down it?'

I looked up at the sun. 'This way,' I said, pointing north. 'Then we follow the river down to the sea. Then we go north along the coast to Catana. Then we go home. Simple.'

After maybe half an hour we reached the river Terias, and this cheered us both up considerably, since something had gone right at last; also we hadn't seen any Sicilians. In fact, the absence of people was quite remarkable, and I couldn't think of a reason for it. But quite suddenly it was explained.

We hadn't gone far along the river-bank when we saw a party of people coming in the opposite direction. They had seen us, and so there was no point in trying to hide. As we got closer we saw that it was a man and his whole family, dressed in their best clothes and carrying baskets decked out with wreaths.

'They're going to a Festival,' said Aristophanes brilliantly.

The family, which consisted of the man and his wife, two old women and three small children, waved to us cheerfully as we came closer to them. Aristophanes looked at me and said, 'What do we do now?'

'As little as possible,' I replied. 'Keep your mouth shut.'

They were within shouting distance now, so I shouted.

'Keep back, for pity's sake,' I shouted. 'Plague. We've got the plague.'

'What plague?' replied the man.

That threw me for a moment, but I couldn't be bothered to think of anything clever. 'Get away from us,' I yelled, as loud as I could. 'Go away or you're all dead!'

The Sicilians stared at me but didn't move. 'Where are you from?' they asked. I made a quick guess and said, 'Leontini.'

'There's a plague in Leontini?' shouted the man. 'Since when?'

'It's the Athenian plague,' I said. 'Athenians brought it there a day or so back, they were escaping from the war or something. The whole city is like a slaughterhouse. Don't go near it, whatever you do.'

'But the Festival,' said the man. 'We're going to the Festival.'

I shook my head violently. 'Keep away,' I said. 'Go home, don't let anyone near you. It's the Athenian plague.'

The man shook his head in perplexity. 'Where are you going?' he said.

'To the sea,' I replied.

'Why?'

'Why not?'

'Sorry?'

'I said, why not?'

'Oh.' The man looked at his family. One of the old women had started jabbering at him and all the children were crying. 'Well, thank you,' he shouted. 'Do you need food?'

'Yes,' I replied. 'Very much.'

'There's bread in this basket,' he said, pointing to the basket he was carrying. 'I'll leave it here for you.'

'Thank you,' I shouted – I was nearly hoarse by now. 'Please go away, before you catch it. It's very contagious.'

The man put down the basket and ran, followed by his family. When they were safely out of sight we fell upon the basket. There were five freshly baked wheat Festival loaves in it, and two honey-cakes. Good honey-cakes too, as I remember.

'I wonder whose Festival it is?' asked Aristophanes with his mouth full.

'Search me,' I replied, 'I expect it's Demeter or Athene. It wouldn't be Dionsysus at this time of year.'

'Well, whoever it is, it's a stroke of luck,' he said. 'I was starving.'

'You amaze me, were you really?' I licked the last of the honey off my fingers. 'Right, let's press on, shall we?'

Not long afterwards, we came to a farmhouse. It was completely deserted except for a sleeping dog. Everyone was away at the Festival. After making sure there was nobody about, we kicked open a door and went in.

There is a story about old Alcmaeon, the founder of the illustrious Alcmaeonid clan of Athens. The story runs that he founded the family fortunes by doing a favour for the celebrated Croesus, King of Lydia, the richest man who ever lived. His reward was that he could go into the King's treasury and take as much gold away with him as he could carry. Well, when Alcmaeon went into the treasury his eyes nearly burst in his head; there was gold everywhere – gold cups and plates, gold armour, gold rings, gold tripods, gold statues, gold everything. But as soon as he had calmed down a bit, Alcmaeon realised that the most efficient way of carrying gold was in the form of gold-dust, of which there were many full jars. So he tied up the legs and sleeves of his gown to make a sort of sack out of it, and emptied a whole jar of gold-dust down his chest; then he poured gold-dust into his hair, which was thick and curly and well-oiled; then he found two big gold jars, as heavy as he could carry, and filled those with gold-dust. Finally he took a handful of gold-dust and popped it into his mouth. Thus laden, he staggered out of the treasury to his quarters and collapsed. He nearly died from swallowing gold-dust, but his servants managed to make him throw up in time.

That was how we felt when we broke into that farm-house. There were jars of every kind of food, wine, and oil. There were fresh clothes, and newly made boots, and leather hats. Everything a man could reasonably want was there for the taking.

'It's like paradise,' Aristophanes said.

Then it occurred to me that it wasn't like paradise at all; it was like my house in Pallene, except much smaller and less affluent. Ordinary people lived here, farmers, people who worried about having enough to eat in a bad year. There we were, two rich men of the Cavalry class, who had lived our whole lives surrounded by the sort of wealth these people could never aspire to; and this ordinary house was more desirable to us now than anything we could think of.

Our first instinct was to loot the place; but we calmed down after a while and took fresh clothes and five days' food. We felt like gentlemen, for all that, in clean woollen tunics and cloaks and boots and big leather hats, with walking-sticks and a sword for Aristophanes, and linen satchels for our food. We also found a razor and a mirror and trimmed our hair and beards – you have no idea what pleasure that gave me. Needless to say, Aristophanes went one stage further and ferreted out the family's purse. There were twenty staters in it, and he refused to put any of them back.

'What we need now,' said Aristophanes, 'is a horse.'

'You're never satisfied, are you?'

'No,' he said truthfully. 'I'm an Athenian, aren't I?'

He had a point there. Nicias and Demosthenes had

failed, but here were two Athenians carrying off the wealth of Sicily. Somehow I felt a little better about plundering the house after that. A little better, but not much.

As we left, I closed the door behind me as best I could, and looked round. I saw two things: one good, and one bad. The good thing was an outhouse with its door slightly ajar, and inside it was a cart; a small two-wheeler ox-cart, just like the ones we use at home. Its storage capacity consisted of one of the big grain-jars they use on the corn-ships. A man can hide in one of those, I thought to myself, no problem at all. The family had obviously gone to the festival in the donkey-trap.

'Aristophanes,' I said, 'I've had an idea. Do you think this household keeps its ox in a pen?'

'Certainly.'

'Do you think you could find it for me?'

'All right.'

While he was away, I pulled out the cart and tested my theory. I was right. It was a bit of a squeeze, but perfectly possible. Then Aristophanes came back, leading a large white ox by a halter. We got it into the shafts after a while, and I put the harness on it.

'What's the idea?' said Aristophanes.

'Get in there,' I said, pointing to the jar.

'No fear,' replied Aristophanes.

I pointed to the bad thing I had seen, which was getting closer; a cloud of dust on the road, about a mile away. 'Do you know what that is?' I asked.

'Oh God,' said Aristophanes, 'it's those damned cavalry.'

'I should think so,' I replied. 'Now be a good fellow and get in the jar.'

He got in the jar, and I closed the lid. Then I went into the house and grabbed two large pots of green olives, and dashed back out to the cart.

'Aristophanes,' I called out.

'Yes?'

'Mind your head.' I lifted the lid of the big jar and poured in the olives. 'Sorry,' I said. Then I dumped the olive-pots, closed the farmhouse door behind me, and climbed up on to the cart.

The cavalry overtook me shortly after I had joined the main road. It was the patrol we had encountered the previous night; there was no mistaking them. I knew what a gamble I was taking. I had staked both our lives, and the future of Athenian Comedy, on a wash and a shave, a big leather hat, my ability to do regional accents, and eight medimni of green olives.

'You,' shouted my old friend the cavalry captain. 'Pull over.'

'Sure,' I replied. 'What's the trouble?'

'Is that your place back there?' asked the captain, pointing with his sword at the farm behind us.

'No,' I replied, 'it's my cousin's place, but he's over to the Festival in Leontini.' I was sweating so much that I could hardly see. I had risked a Syracusan accent instead of a Corinthian one. It was my big day for taking risks.

'Why aren't you at the Festival, then?'

'Not my Festival,' I replied. 'We had our Demeter last month in Syracuse.'

This was a desperate effort on my part. I had seen a small terracotta Demeter inside the house, newly wreathed; and I remembered someone in the camp outside Syracuse telling me how he had watched their Demeter Festival. God knows why I took the risk; but it worked. The captain nodded, and didn't look too closely at my face. 'Visiting?' he said.

'That's right,' I replied. 'First chance to get out and about since the war. Taking a few olives up the coast for my cousin. They're starting to sweat already, and he didn't want them to stand until after the Festival. What are you boys after?'

'There's a couple of dangerous Athenians loose,' said the captain.

'Athenians,' I replied. 'Well, that's a bit of news. Wouldn't have thought there were too many of them left.' And I sniggered.

'Have you seen two men, ragged-looking, on foot?'

'Tall one and a shorter one? Bald-headed, both of them?'

'That's it.'

'Couple of men answering to that were round our place this morning,' I said. 'Wanted food, offered to buy a mule. They had money, but we didn't like the look of them. Talked funny. They went back the way they came, so far as I could make out.'

'When was this?'

'Maybe an hour after sun-up, maybe later. And they were Athenians, you reckon?'

'We think so, yes.'

'And dangerous?'

'They threatened the magistrate and injured one of my men.'

'That's bad,' I said. 'That's very bad. Hope they stay clear of me, that's all. Could you spare a couple of your boys to ride me up to the coast?'

The captain shook his head. 'Sorry,' he said. 'But you've got a sword, you should be all right.'

I felt as if someone had just pulled my heart out through my ear. I didn't look down, but it was obvious that the captain could see that confounded Thracian sabre on its baldrick round my neck. Had he recognised it? I doubted very much if such swords were common in that part of Sicily. My soul cursed me for a feckless idiot, but I managed to keep my face straight.

'That's strictly for ornament,' I said. 'I'm not what you'd reckon to call a fighting man myself. I leave that to you boys.'

The captain laughed. 'Thanks for the help,' he said, and pulled his horse round.

'You make sure you catch those Athenians,' I replied.

'I don't feel so good now about leaving my cousin's place unattended if there's Athenians about. Mind,' I added, 'I wouldn't much fancy being there if they took it into their heads to break in, so perhaps I'm better off where I am.'

The cavalryman laughed again, and led his troops back the way they had come. For a moment I was afraid he would turn in to the farm – which was what I would have done in his place – but he rode straight past it and out of sight. I dropped the reins and started to shake all over. This was not my line of work, I said to my soul; and for once my soul agreed with me. But (replied my soul) you mustn't worry about it. Nothing can happen to you, today or for ever. You have been chosen to survive. You survived the plague. You survived the war. You have survived through Sicily. The old smith who could not die died. The veteran of Himera died. The Eleusinians who did not starve died. Everyone except you and the son of Philip has died and the son of Philip is protected by the God, as the old heroes were at Troy, and so he doesn't count. You are quite probably going to live for ever.

I met various other travellers that day, but none of them was any bother. By now I was firmly convinced that I was a Syracusan farmer visiting my cousins near Leontini. My name was Pelopidas son of Temenus, and I had fifteen acres mixed cereal and grazing on the slopes of Epipolae, with a few vines on the other side of the mountain. My wife, Callistrata, was a big woman with a bad temper, but we had two fine sons, Leon and Gigas, and Gigas had been taken as apprentice by a well-established potter in the City. He would do well, if he worked at it. We also had a daughter, Theodora, but she died of a cold when she was ten. During the war we lived in the City, which was uncomfortable, and I had done my bit in the fighting. I missed out on the Epipolae business, but I was in at the kill at the walled orchard, when we stomped on those Athenians once and for all. I didn't want to put in that last part, but I couldn't help it.

However much I sought to rewrite my life, I couldn't leave that out.

It was probably just as well that I wasn't called on to play this part I had composed for myself, since it was probably riddled with inaccuracies. But I must confess that I enjoyed being Pelopidas son of Temenus. He was on the winning side, for one thing, and this was his country, for another. He might not have the wealth and talents of a Eupolis, say, or even an Aristophanes, but nobody was after his blood and he didn't really care all that much if he never did get to Catana. God, I envied him.

That night, I carefully unpacked Aristophanes, who was not happy. He had a whole day's recriminations stored up for me when I finally extracted him from the jar, and he seemed to get most of them past the gate of his teeth in the first five minutes of his liberty. I took no notice of him, however; I was bored with him now, and regarded him as nothing more than a piece of inconvenient and perishable merchandise that I had to deliver to Catana. I hid him under the cart and went to sleep, and dreamed, at first, of being Pelopidas son of Temenus. But that turned into a dream about the walled orchard, the first I had had, and I woke up drenched in sweat and shivering. This convinced me that I had the fever, and worrying about that kept me awake for the rest of the night.

When Aristophanes woke up, we breakfasted on half a Festival loaf each, a cup of wine, a sausage and a handful of figs, which was the best meal we had had since we arrived in Sicily. It was a lovely morning, warm but not too hot, and there was a spectacular sunrise over the mountains behind us. We washed in the river, and then I told Aristophanes that it was time for him to get back into the jar. Much to my surprise he refused.

'Those olives stink,' he said. 'If I get back in there I'll die.'

'Please yourself,' I said. 'Only if you don't get back in there, I'm afraid I'll have to kill you.' I drew my sabre in a matter-of-fact sort of way and laid it across my knees. Aristophanes stared at me.

'I'm sorry,' I said, 'but there it is. I can't afford to let you go wandering off on your own. They'll see you're an Athenian, and then they'll come looking for me. So I'll have to kill you and bury you in . . .' I looked round quickly '. . . under that pile of rocks there. I'll give you a stater for the ferryman, but that's my best offer.'

Aristophanes opened his mouth but no words came out; and I suddenly realised what I had said. I hadn't been joking; I would have done it. That was a horrible feeling.

I stood up, and Aristophanes cowered visibly. 'So are you going to get into the jar?' I asked.

'Yes,' said the son of Philip. 'Right away.'

'Good man,' I said. 'We'd better tip the olives out first. Give me a hand with the jar, will you?'

We tipped the olives out and put the jar back in its mounting, then Aristophanes climbed in and I put the olives back on top of him. 'Can you breathe?' I asked. He assured me that he could.

'That's fine,' I said. 'Right, time to go.' I put the lid back on and backed the ox into the shafts. He was a good ox, docile and well behaved. I liked him. Then I took up the reins and we were off again.

We reached the sea just before evening, and the sight of it made me feel like a small child once more. It was huge and beautiful and friendly, and on the other side of it was Athens in Attica, and Pallene, and my house there, and my steward and his wife, and my grey horse with the black tail, and my house in the City, and my wife. I hadn't so much as thought about Phaedra since I set foot in Sicily; and now that I had remembered that she existed I couldn't for the life of me remember what she looked like. I dismissed the thought from my mind, and

went back to being Pelopidas. Only a day away from Catana. Would the olives keep fresh that far?

I had stopped for the night and was just about to let Aristophanes out when a party of men leading donkeys came up the road behind me. There were about ten of them, and I saw they were farmers taking their produce to the city. That city could only be Catana.

'Evening, friend,' said one of them, a tall man with a lot of fine grey hair. 'Going to market?'

His voice was warm and friendly, and I smiled as I replied, 'Sure. I've got olives in the jar here.'

The man wasn't so friendly now, and I realised that I was still being Pelopidas, purely from instinct. My Syracusan accent had become so good that he recognised it instantly. The trouble was, of course, that the Catanians hate the Syracusans like poison. I would have laughed if I wasn't suddenly so frightened.

That's the way it goes with fool's luck, said my soul inside me, and I could hear a horrible sort of smugness in its voice, as if it had known it would all end in tears. You muddle your way right across Sicily and manage to get out of the most horrific scrapes without really trying; then, as soon as you've got your act together enough to pass for a Syracusan, you run in with a bunch of Catanians who'll tear you limb from limb for not being an Athenian. That'll teach you to be so damned lucky.

'Just where exactly did you say you were from, boy?' said the grey-haired man. 'Maybe I didn't catch it the first time.'

'I'm from Pallene,' I replied in my normal voice – only it didn't come out normal. 'Pallene in Attica. I'm an Athenian.'

The grey-haired man scowled and said, 'Don't you try being funny with me, stranger. Are you going to tell me the truth, or do I have to beat it out of you?'

I tried to dig down into my mind for some way out of this mess; but there was nothing left. 'Oh, for crying out loud,' I said, 'I'm an Athenian, can't you see that? I'm one of Demosthenes' men. I was in the battle at the walled orchard, but I got away. I stole this cart outside Leontini because there were cavalrymen after me and I needed to fool them. I pretended to be a Syracusan just now because I didn't know I was in your country.'

The men muttered darkly to each other; they weren't convinced. I didn't know what to do.

'I don't believe you,' said the grey-haired man. 'I reckon you're a Syracusan spy, and I'm going to take you in. Get him, boys.'

'Hold it, hold it,' I shrieked. 'You're making a really silly mistake here. Look, I've got another Athenian in this jar-contraption here. He's my friend, we escaped together.'

The grey-haired man stared at me. 'In the jar?' he said.

'Yes,' I shouted, 'in the bloody jar. Get him out if you don't believe me.'

They cut the jar loose and tipped it on to the ground. There was a minor cascade of olives, and out came the son of Philip, looking extremely put out. He tried to draw his sword, but they took it away from him and tied his hands together.

'Athenians my arse,' said one of the men. 'He tried to kill me.'

'He couldn't hear you, he was in the jar,' I said. 'He thought you were the enemy.'

The grey-haired man didn't like that. 'Do we look like the Syracusans?' he said angrily.

'He couldn't see you either,' I replied frantically, 'because he was in the sodding jar. Don't you ever think?'

'Don't you talk to me like that,' said the grey-haired man. 'You're lucky we don't string you up right now.'

'Oh, do what you like,' I said miserably.

'I might just do that,' said the grey-haired man. His companions seemed to agree with this, and one of them uncoiled some rope from his donkey. Just then, I remembered something. I remembered the fat dry-fish merchant who had sat next to me during the performance of *The General*. I remembered that his name was Pericleidas son of Bellerophon and that he said he was from Catana. I could have wept with pleasure.

'Will you listen to me, just for a moment?' I said. 'I have a friend in Catana who'll vouch for me. Pericleidas son of Bellerophon, the dry-fish man. Do any of you know him?'

'Sure I know him,' said one of the men, 'I sell him tuna in the season. You know him?'

'I met him in Athens.'

'If you know him,' said the grey-haired man, 'where does he live?'

I was about to explain that I had only met him in Athens and couldn't be expected to know where he lived when suddenly I remembered that I knew exactly where he lived. The God had told me, in the walled orchard.

'Next to the shrine of Dionysus,' I replied, 'by the little gate.'

'That's true,' said the man who knew Pericleidas, 'that's just where he lives.'

'Proving nothing,' said the grey-haired man. 'Everyone knows that.'

'I didn't,' said one of his companions. But the grey-haired man ignored him.

'Take me to him,' I said. 'He'll know me.'

The grey-haired man thought for a moment. 'Who's that?' he said, pointing at Aristophanes.

'He's my friend,' I replied. 'Like I told you.'

'Does he know Pericleidas?'

'No,' I replied. 'But not many people in Athens do. Look, can we get on, please?'

The grey-haired man thought again, then nodded. 'You'd better hope Pericleidas recognises you,' he said, 'or so help me I'll string you up myself.'

They bundled me and Aristophanes on to the cart,

and we spent the rest of that day bouncing along the road to Catana. It was not the way I had intended to arrive there, and somehow it didn't feel right. My main nightmare was that Pericleidas was out, or abroad peddling his misbegotten fish. That would be just my fool's luck, and then they would string us up and make us into sausages.

A crowd gathered round us as soon as we entered the city, and we soon attracted the attention of a magistrate and some soldiers. When asked what he had got in his wagon, the grey-haired man said he didn't know; they said they were Athenians and that Pericleidas could vouch for them; but if he couldn't, they were Syracusan spies and should be hung. The magistrate thought this was eminently reasonable, and walked in front of us through the streets. As we passed, some people cheered and others threw stones; this is what is known as hedging your bets.

The cart jolted to a halt and we were hauled out. It was quite dark by now, but there were plenty of torches round us, and the whole proceeding looked like a cross between a wedding and a sacrifice. The magistrate came over and addressed us both.

'Right,' he said, 'this is Pericleidas' house. We'll see what he has to say.'

He knocked loudly on the door and called out Pericleidas' name. As I waited for what seemed like for ever while the slave came down and opened the door, I reflected bitterly on my fate, which now rested on an idiot of a dry-fish merchant I had met once in the Theatre. This could only happen to a Comic poet, I said to myself, and considered, not for the first time in my life, whether I had chosen the right profession.

'What is it?' said the slave. He was startled by the sight of so many people. 'My master is having dinner.'

'He's needed to vouch for these men,' said the magistrate. 'They say they're Athenians.'

'I'll fetch him,' said the slave. He disappeared into the

house, and there was another eternity of a wait, with the good people of Catana whispering inaudibly around me. Then Pericleidas the dry-fish man appeared, exactly as I remembered him, except that he was a trifle fatter, and his hair was quite grey. But what if he didn't remember me?

'Are you Pericleidas son of Bellerophon?' asked the magistrate.

'Sure I am,' said Pericleidas, clearly bemused. 'You know perfectly well who I am, Cleander, you had dinner here last night. Why did you bother to ask?'

This got a good laugh from the audience, and the magistrate frowned.

'Pericleidas,' he said, 'I have to ask you if you recognise these men. They say they know you.'

Pericleidas shrugged. 'What have they done?' he said.

'Never mind that now,' said the magistrate, 'just see if you can identify them for me. Can you do that?'

'I'll do my best,' he said, and turned to Aristophanes. 'I'm sorry,' he said, after an agonising moment, 'I've never seen this man before in my life.'

There was a gasp from the crowd, and muffled cheering. Then he turned to me. He looked at me, blinked, and looked again.

'Well?' said the magistrate, 'do you know this one or don't you?'

'I don't know,' said Pericleidas. 'Hell, Cleander, you know I've got a rotten memory for faces.'

That was enough for me. 'Pericleidas,' I said, before anyone could stop me, 'do you remember going to Athens and seeing a play called *The General*?'

Pericleidas blinked. 'Yes,' he said, 'I remember it well. But surely – aren't you the young fellow who was sitting next to me? Yes, I'll swear you are. You're the young fellow who wrote the play.'

'Is my name Eupolis?' I said.

'That's right,' said Pericleidas, relieved. 'You're

Eupolis, the playwright. I'm terrible at faces, but I never forget a name. Yes, this is Eupolis, I can vouch for that.'

'Are you sure?' said the magistrate. 'You said yourself—'

'No, it's him all right,' said Pericleidas. 'If I'm right, he's missing a bit of one finger.'

Now my hands were tied behind my back and he couldn't have seen them. The magistrate ordered his men to untie me. I didn't dare look down, in case my missing finger had suddenly grown back, just to spite me. 'All right,' said the magistrate, 'I guess you're who you say you are. But who's this?' He pointed to Aristophanes, and the crowd, who had been bitterly disappointed, started to hope once again. 'You don't know him, do you?'

'We never claimed he did,' I said quickly. 'But I can vouch that this is Aristophanes son of Philip, an Athenian citizen.'

'Not *the* Aristophanes!' exclaimed Pericleidas. 'Why, sir, are you Aristophanes who wrote *The Acharnians* and *The Two Jugs*?'

'Yes,' said Aristophanes. For once, there was no smugness in his voice, only relief.

'Then I can vouch for him too,' said Pericleidas.

'No, he can't,' said the grey-haired man, 'he's just said he couldn't.'

The magistrate made an angry gesture. 'The hell with it,' he said. 'Look, Pericleidas, will you be responsible for these two?'

'It would be an honour,' said Pericleidas, gazing at Aristophanes as if he had just seen a vision of a god. Not at me, you understand. Just Aristophanes.

'That's good enough for me, then,' said the magistrate. 'All right, folks, the party's over. Go home quietly, it's after dark.'

The crowd drifted away, and Pericleidas hustled us both inside.

'Stratylla,' he shouted, 'come here quick, and we'll need hot water and towels. We've got company.'

I honestly can't remember any more about that night. I think I must have fallen asleep on my feet, or something of the sort, because the next thing I remember was waking up in a bed, with light coming in through the window. For a moment I was confused; then I remembered what had happened, and that I was in Catana, safe, in a friendly house. In the bed next to me was Aristophanes son of Philip, snoring. I looked at him and realised, with a great surge of joy that nearly took off the top of my head, that I was no longer responsible for him.

CHAPTER NINE

Don't you hate it when you're listening to a story or a poem; and the hero has just got himself out of a scrape by the tips of his fingers in Argos, say, or Crete, and then the scene suddenly changes to Tempe or Phocis, and there's our hero, sitting in a nice clean tunic with his hair newly curled and his beard trimmed, having a bite to eat with the King and planning his next adventure? I do. I feel cheated. I want to hear how he got all the way from Argos to Phocis, which is probably more difficult in practical terms than duping the three-headed giant or escaping from the man-eating bull. Particularly since the three-headed ogre turned out to be incredibly gullible, or the hero was so laden down with magical hardware, pressed into his hand by some helpful god or other, that the whole Spartan army wouldn't have stood a chance against him. No, what I want to hear is how he managed to hitch a lift on a ship without any money, and what he did for food and water as he crossed the mountains, and how he got past the King's doorkeeper without a sealed pass and three chamberlains to vouch for him.

I am no Milesian cheapskate; I will not fob you off with an implied challenge to your imaginative powers. Before we return to violet-crowned Athens, I will give

you a short account of our stay in Catana and the trip home.

At first, Pericleidas was thrilled to have the celebrated Aristophanes under his roof, and for three days we were treated like princes. Everything that twenty years' accumulated proceeds of the dry-fish business could provide for our comfort and delight was showered upon us, and the only thing demanded of us in return was theatre talk. But neither of us could find very much to say to gratify our host's modest, if eccentric, requirement. It was as if we had forgotten what it was like to be Athenian literary lions. Even Aristophanes could find very little to say about his own prodigious talents and triumphs, and I was quite useless. All I seemed able to remember was the Athenian expedition to Syracuse; it was as if I had been born the day I landed in Sicily, and the things I had done before that were heroic tales of the old days, when the world was young and the Gods still appeared openly to men. Although I pretended to, I couldn't bring myself to believe in this mythical place called Athens in Attica, where they did nothing all day but grow food, write plays and talk to their friends about the weather and politics, and nobody died. The real world, I knew in my heart, was not like that at all. In the real world, terrified men marched down unknown roads and were trapped in orchards, or slept in ditches while the cavalry searched for them; and sooner or later this holiday would be over and I would have to put on my muddy old boots and cloak and go back to work.

In this mood, I freely admit, I wasn't fit company for a stage-struck tuna baron. The only thing I wanted to talk about was the War – God, how I wanted to talk about that to someone; even Aristophanes. I tried once or twice but he put his hands over his ears and yelled until I went away. Most of the time, in fact, he spent drinking himself into a coma, which seemed to work well enough for him. But when I tried it, I fell asleep and dreamed about the

War, and that was no good at all. And then Pericleidas would come bounding up, certain in his mind that at last we were ready to talk about cosy chats behind the scenes at the first rehearsal of *The Wasps*, and what Agathon said to Euripides about Sophocles.

I asked everyone I could about what had happened to the Athenians, and tried to find any other survivors who had made it to Catana. I found them, quite a few in fact; most of them hospitably locked up by the Catanian authorities, who regarded them as a public nuisance and were trying to negotiate a cheap price with a Phoenician slaver for the hire of a ship to send them back to Athens. But I heard that Nicias and Demosthenes were dead, and that most of the men who had been captured by the Syracusans had died of cold and starvation in the stone quarries. By all accounts, seven thousand men had survived the two massacres, in the orchard and the river bed, out of forty thousand who had left the camp. Of these, about four thousand lived long enough to be sold off, mostly to Phoenicians. Very few of those, I was told, were Athenians. A Corcyrean I met who had been in the quarries and had escaped said that the Athenians there had given up quite early and refused to eat, or had caught the fever and died. They had no will to live, he said, since they believed that their City was already dead. I also found out that the man who owned the farm with the walled orchard in it was called Polyzelus. He was a decent enough man, by all accounts, and when he came home and found his home knee-deep in bodies he was profoundly shocked and had to be taken away and looked after by some relatives. When he had recovered, he had to find some way of disposing of fourteen thousand dead Athenians, and for a long time he didn't know what to do. All this time the Athenians were not smelling any more wholesome, and his neighbours were starting to complain. In the end, he hired every slave and casual worker in the district and got them to dig an

enormous hole in a marshy part of his property where nothing would grow anyway, and shovelled the dead bodies into it until it was full. Then he raised a big cairn of stones over it, and set about recovering the quite phenomenal cost of this operation from the Syracusan government. By all accounts, the legal complications beggared all description, and he or his heirs are probably at it to this day.

After three days, Pericleidas came into the room where we slept and said, in a rather embarrassed manner, that he had arranged a passage home for us. We thanked him profusely. This seemed to make him feel worse. He explained that the ship we were going home on was one of his. We thanked him again. He explained further that all his ships were cargo ships laden with dried fish; they were therefore not immensely comfortable. We said that that didn't matter; going home was the important thing. Actually, said Pericleidas, wretchedly, there was only enough room on these fish-cruisers of his for a *working* crew. He hated to impose like this, but ...

So that is how, when anyone in a poem or a reading purports to give an account of what it is like to sail a ship on the open sea, I can stand up and tell him he's a liar, because I have done it myself, and it's no fun at all. You get very wet working a ship, particularly if you haven't the faintest idea what you are supposed to be doing and the rest of the crew are muttering about you being bad luck and how they ought to throw you overboard before you bring on a thunderstorm. Oh yes, we were also chased by pirates in the Straits of Rhegium. They were very enthusiastic, those pirates, and were just about to catch up with us when one of the crew had the wit to shout out that our cargo was nothing more valuable than dried fish, and to throw a jar over the side to prove it. The pirates picked up the jar, opened it, and stopped following us, which must be a very significant comment on the quality of Pericleidas' stock-in-trade.

And then, after a long and exhausting journey, we saw Cape Sunium on the horizon and heard the ship's captain saying, with evident relief, that this was where Eupolis and Aristophanes were getting off. For two pins, in fact, they would have landed us at Sunium; but we persuaded them to take us into Piraeus by giving them the remainder of our Sicilian money.

As we cruised round the Attic coast, I suddenly started to feel sick. That was not the motion of the ship – I had got over that after the first couple of days of our voyage; it was a sort of fear, that Attica would not be what it had to be, in order for me to stay sane. Attica had to be a happy ever after, a place where the story could end. I had tried to picture it in my mind while I was in Sicily, but no image would come; and I had put together a rather unconvincing reconstruction to take its place. This Attica was half an enormous theatre filled with laughing people, backing on to a maze of cosy little streets, and half a sort of pastoral idyll, jammed permanently at the end of the olive harvest, with carts creaking down narrow lanes. The reason why I chose the olive season was that I could remember what an olive cart looked like; it had two wheels, an ox between the shafts, Aristophanes in the storage-jar and cavalrymen all round it. The cavalrymen seemed a little out of place in Attica, but that couldn't be helped. Now if this phantom Attica didn't exist, what was I to do? I realised, as we sailed on from Sunium, that I really didn't want to go home; that was the very last thing I wanted to do.

Aristophanes was also very quiet. We had spoken very few words to each other since we reached Catana, and we seemed rather embarrassed to be in each other's company, as if each knew a terrible secret about the other and didn't trust him to keep his mouth shut. In my case of course, I did know quite a few things about the son of Philip that would, if made public, utterly destroy him in Athenian society, and I felt sure that he had invented a corresponding number of calumnies about me; but although we said nothing to each other about it, we seemed to have reached an agreement that when we got home, we were going to have as little to do with each other as possible.

But of course you don't want to hear all this; you are asking yourself why, if we were coming from Sicily, we passed Sunium before reaching Piraeus. Well, if you had used your head you would have realised that our captain wouldn't want to go further down the Argolid than he absolutely had to, what with the War and everything, and had thus sailed straight from Methana to Sunium across open water. He then backtracked from Sunium to Piraeus, intending to go back the way he had come after that. The result of this complex manoeuvre, besides bad temper on everyone's part, was that we didn't make Piraeus until about half an hour before dawn.

I don't know what exactly I had been expecting; whether I had assumed that the Polemarch and the Council would be there to meet us, with garlands and honey and flute-girls, or perhaps a more modest delegation led by one of the lower ranking magistrates, or perhaps just a few friends and relatives. Instead, there was nobody to be seen anywhere, not even the usual crowd who lounge about the docks waiting for someone to spill a jar so that they can dart across and steal the contents. The only living creature was a dog, whose barking brought the toll-collector out, and he was only interested in separating the captain from his harbour dues, and took no notice of us whatsoever.

When I say us, by this time I mean me. As soon as his feet touched Attic soil, Aristophanes was off like a startled polecat, without a word to me, the captain or anyone. He just muffled his face in his cloak and vanished, I think in the general direction of the City; but I couldn't say for sure. I felt it would only be polite to thank the captain for putting up with me on the voyage, so I did this. The captain made no reply, so I shrugged my shoulders at the world in general, pulled my cloak round me, and started to walk towards Athens.

Of course the old Long Walls between Athens and Piraeus are no longer there, and I suspect that many of you who are reading this will not remember them. That morning, they seemed to go on for ever, and although I had walked that way hundreds of times in my life, they seemed very foreign and unfamiliar to me as I trudged along under them. I don't know why, but I got it into my head that the City was actually empty, and that all its people were now in a hole in a marsh on the estate of Polyzelus. It was a very eerie sensation, I can tell you, and I didn't like it at all. But when I was half-way to the City I saw a man hurrying up from the opposite direction, and to my overwhelming joy I recognised him. In a way it was like seeing a ghost, but he was real enough – Cleagenes the corn-merchant, who I had done business with a few times.

'Hello, Cleagenes,' I shouted.

He peered at me (he was short-sighted) and replied, 'Hello, Eupolis. I haven't seen you about for a couple of weeks now. Have you been in the country?'

I stared at him. 'Come off it,' I said, 'I've been in Sicily with the army. I've just got back.'

Cleagenes gave me a curious look. 'Don't be funny at this hour of the morning, Eupolis, there's a good lad. The army isn't back yet.'

Back yet? 'Honestly, Cleagenes,' I said, 'that's where I've been.'

He frowned. 'Have you come back with a message for the Council or a letter from Nicias or whatever?' he asked. 'If so, you'd better—'

'Nicias?' I said. 'Nicias is dead.'

'Dead?'

'Dead.'

Cleagenes pondered this for a moment. 'That's not

very funny, Eupolis,' he said at last. 'I suppose you're just going home from a party with some of your peculiar friends. Take my advice, lad. Go home and sleep it off before you offend someone important. Some people have got sons at the War, you realise.'

Cleagenes bustled away, leaving me standing with my mouth open. But there was nothing to be gained by gawping (as my grandfather used to say), so I pressed on into the City towards my house. I saw a few people out and about once I had passed through the gate, but I didn't stop and talk to any of them. Something told me that the best move at this stage would be to keep my head down until I had managed to find out what was going on.

It was easy to rationalise, of course; obviously, the news of the disaster had not yet reached the City. This was hard to credit; surely someone in authority at Catana should have sent a letter or something. But probably someone had left it to someone else, or it was still on its way, or the ship it was on had been sunk or stopped off at Methana to do a little business.

Then it occurred to me that, if I was right, the son of Philip and I were the only people in the whole of Athens who knew about the destruction of the fleet. That was not a pleasant thought. Now it was clearly my duty (I couldn't count on Aristophanes to do anything useful) to go and tell someone about it, such as the Polemarch and the Council. But would they believe me? Of course not. Cleagenes the corn-merchant hadn't believed me, so why should the Polemarch? I would probably find myself in the prison for starting seditious rumours or something of the sort.

But I couldn't just go home, take my boots and hat off, and pretend I had never been away. Leaving to one side the fate of the City, which was now totally defenceless and at the mercy of the Spartans (who undoubtedly knew), there was my peace of mind to consider. I couldn't keep a forty-thousand-corpse secret to myself; I would burst, like the frog in the fable. Perhaps I could tell someone else who would tell the Council for me; someone they would listen to.

I was walking along thinking like this when a man touched me on the shoulder and said, 'Is that you?'

I turned and looked at him. It was Philonides the Chorus-trainer. I said nothing.

'Eupolis,' said Philonides, 'I thought you were away at the War.'

'I was,' I replied.

'When did you come back?'

'Just now.'

'This morning?'

'Yes.'

He studied me carefully; I wasn't usually this taciturn, he was thinking, perhaps I was ill. 'Have you been wounded?' he asked. 'Is that why you're back?'

'No,' I replied. 'I'm all right.'

'So what are you doing in Athens?' It was extraordinary, I thought. Here is a man I know, being friendly in a normal sort of a way, and I suddenly don't know how to talk to him. 'Glad to see you, of course. And how's the War going?'

'The War's over,' I said.

He broke into a smile. 'Already?' he said. 'I knew we could rely on Demosthenes to get it finished. He's hot stuff, Demosthenes, whatever they say down at the Baths.'

'We lost,' I said. 'Demosthenes is dead.'

'Dead?'

'Yes,' I snapped, 'dead.'

'Oh God,' said Philonides, and he seemed to sag, like a punctured wineskin. 'So Nicias is in charge of the army?'

'Nicias is dead too.'

'Nicias as well?' Philonides stared at me. 'But that's impossible.'

'No, it's not.'

'Then who's in charge of the army, for God's sake?' he said. 'Not that imbecile Menander. I couldn't bear it. Or Eurymedon, for that matter. The man's a fool.'

'There is no army.'

'I beg your pardon?'

'Watch my lips,' I said. 'There is no army. Got it? They're all dead. All except maybe two or three hundred.'

For a moment his mind rejected the statement; then he believed it. 'The whole lot?' he said.

'The whole lot.'

'So what about the fleet?' he demanded. 'Where's the fleet?'

I smiled, I can't say why. 'At the bottom of Syracuse harbour,' I replied. 'Most of it, anyway.'

He stood there for a moment, a totally empty man, a shell of a man, a man with no contents. His mouth was wide open, and I noticed how straight and white his teeth were for a man of his age. He clearly didn't have anything to say, so I reckoned it was up to me to keep the conversation going.

'I was lucky,' I said. 'I managed to get away to Catana with Aristophanes the son of Philip. He's probably at his house by now, getting drunk I shouldn't wonder. Go and ask him if you don't believe me. How did his play do, by the way; the one he left with you?'

'It came second.'

'Second?'

'Yes.'

'Oh well.'

'*All* of them?' he said. 'That whole army?'

'Yes.'

We stood there for a moment; there was no hurry about anything. Then Philonides said, 'Have you reported to the Council?'

'No,' I replied. 'I'm on my way home. I badly need a wash and a shave.'

'That can wait,' he said. 'Look, my nephew Palaeologus is a Councillor, we'd better tell him first.'

I shrugged. 'I don't mind,' I said. 'Shall we get Aristophanes to back me up?'

'Good idea,' said Philonides. He was excited, talking quickly; this self-imposed task was something he could keep between himself and what he had just heard. 'Look, my place is on the way, I'll send the boy round to Aristophanes' place – you're sure he'll be there?'

'No,' I said, 'he didn't say where he was going.'

'Oh well, never mind. We'll send the boy anyway. Then we'd better get over to Palaeologus' house.'

So that was what we did. The whole thing struck me as vaguely comical; after all, I reasoned to myself, if our army were dead now, they were likely still to be dead after I had had a wash and a shave, and probably would stay dead until I had had something to eat. But I didn't want to say anything to Philonides; I felt it might upset him.

Palaeologus the Councillor wasn't unduly pleased to see us; he had been up late the night before, he said, and he had a headache. I offered to go away and come back later, but Philonides shut me up. He said he had some terrible news. I objected that I was the one with the terrible news, and would he please stop upstaging me. He got rather upset with me at this and told me to be quiet; in fact, he was getting rather hysterical. Palaeologus the Councillor looked at me, since I appeared to be rather more in control of myself, and asked me what was going on. I told him.

'Oh God,' he said. 'Oh God in Heaven.'

'So you believe me, do you?' I asked. 'I thought I'd have difficulty convincing you.'

Palaeologus shook his head. 'We'd heard news already,' he said. 'Well, sort of. We didn't believe it.'

He explained. Two days ago, an Aeginetan scent-dealer had landed at Piraeus with a cargo of myrrh. He had sailed non-stop from Methana, and he was tired, and he wanted a shave, so he went over to a barber's shop he knew just off the Market Square. While he was being shaved he started making conversation, the way you do in a barber's shop.

'Sorry to hear about your bad luck,' he said.

'What bad luck?' said the barber.

'In Sicily,' said the Aeginetan. 'It's all over Methana. I'm sorry for you, really I am. It was a rotten thing to happen.'

'We haven't had word from Sicily for a while now,' said the barber. 'Things going badly, are they?'

'I should say,' said the Aeginetan. 'Your whole army's been wiped out.'

The barber stared at him for a second or two, then ran out into the street, still holding his razor, and started yelling at the top of his voice, 'The army's been wiped out! The army's been wiped out!' Now it happened to be just before Assembly-time, and so the magistrates and the archers were out, getting the red rope ready. They saw this lunatic running up and down, waving a razor and yelling, and arrested him.

He told them what he had heard and pointed to his shop, where the Aeginetan was sitting waiting for the rest of his shave. The magistrate marched into the shop, saw that the man was Aeginetan, and arrested him for spreading malicious rumours. He and the barber were in the prison at this very moment awaiting trial. The Council had been told, as a matter of routine, but they had ignored it. But what convinced Palaeologus was the fact that he knew (now he came to think of it) that I had been with Demosthenes' army, because he had happened to see me at the dockside when he came to wave off his brother-in-law, and someone had pointed to me and asked him who I was.

Then Aristophanes arrived, looking very irritated at being disturbed, and confirmed what I had said. So we had to go down to the Council Chamber and wait until the Council could be summoned, and then the Councillors grilled us for what seemed like hours, asking all manner of trick questions to try and catch us out. This made Aristophanes livid, and he asked if they were calling him a liar, but I realised that it was just Athenian instinct and answered their questions as best I could. Then we were shoved into a little room – me, Aristophanes and Philonides – and the door was bolted on us. We asked why we were being locked up like this, but nobody answered.

'Well,' I said, 'this is cosy. So what's been happening in the City while we've been away?'

Philonides didn't answer, and we sat there for a while staring at the walls. Then Aristophanes asked how his play had got on. Philonides told him it had come second.

'Second?' said Aristophanes, with disgust.

'That's right, second.'

'That's bloody typical, that is,' he said. 'You realise that the parabasis was a thorough condemnation of our Sicilian policy? God, we deserved to lose.'

After two or maybe three hours someone came and let us out. They told us to go straight home and stay there, and not to say anything to anybody. There would be widespread panic, the man said, and it was the Council's job to make the announcement.

We were bundled out by the back way, past the ash-heap, and escorted home by archers; hardly a hero's welcome, I thought, but then, who cares? It was nice that some things, like the Council, were still the same. I wondered how long it would last.

The archer knocked on the door for me; I imagine he thought I might try and communicate a coded message if I knocked myself. The slave opened the door and stared at me, and the archer more or less pushed me through the door.

'Hello, Thrax,' I said to the slave. 'Is your mistress here, or is she in the country?'

'She's here, asleep,' said the slave. 'We thought you were in Sicily.'

'I was,' I replied, 'but I've come home. It happens quite a lot, you know. Go and wake her, will you?'

He went scampering off, and I drew my sword and put it back over the lintel, where it belonged. It made quite an attractive ornament.

Now I assume that you are all educated people and know your *Odyssey*, and your *Thebaid* and *Little Iliad* too; so I can't describe this next scene as I would wish to, in the interests of dramatic effect, because you would object that I had stolen it from the classics. This business of not appearing to copy one's predecessors is a very real problem for a writer, and when all the most obvious approaches to a particular scene have been blocked by the previous efforts of the great masters, he often finds himself reduced to describing what actually happened. The only form of literature that seems to be immune from this difficulty is Tragedy, of course, but the Tragedians' minds are too lofty and elevated to worry about that sort of thing. At times, I feel, they live in a world of their own. But the poor, long-suffering historian has this concern as his constant companion, sitting by his elbow as he writes, and saying, 'No, no, you can't do that, it's been done before; you must have them coming *down* the hill and turning left'; or 'You must be crazy putting in a battle here; we had a battle in the last chapter that was exactly the same.' Now your historian may start off with all manner of lofty ideals, such as recording for all time the clear essence of what actually happened, but he soon gets this beaten out of him by the people he reads his work to while he is writing it. Take the celebrated Herodotus, for example. Now when he was writing his histories, he spent years traipsing all round the world asking old men what their grandfathers remembered, and writing down their answers on wax, and when he got home he sorted through these facts and eliminated the

inconsistencies and accounted for the errors in chrono-
logy arising from the fact that in some places a
generation is reckoned at thirty-three years and in other
places at forty years, and at last sat down and wrote his
history. Then he read it to his wife.

'Are you out of your mind?' said she. 'You can't expect
anyone to listen to that.'

'Why?' asked Herodotus.

'Well,' said his wife patiently, 'it all sounds so . . . well,
so *true*, if you see what I mean.'

Herodotus thought for a while; then he saw what she
was getting at. He went back to work with a vengeance.
He increased all the distances he had so carefully
measured, and doubled the numbers of Persian soldiers
which he had so painstakingly recorded; he took out the
account of how gold dust is refined in the desert by the
use of sieves and running water, and replaced it with a
ludicrous fairy-story about pygmies and giant ants; and
he invented a whole new section about Scythia, which
was the one part of the world he hadn't been to, and
claimed that he had travelled the length and breadth of
the country and seen all these fictional wonders with his
own eyes. Finally, he lodged his original draft in the
temple of Athena, in case the Council should ever need
accurate information on any of these places or subjects,
and gave readings from the revised version which were,
of course, a spectacular success.

But I see, on looking back through what I have written
up to this point, that I have given a factual and quite
personal account of what happened to me in Sicily –
written, it seems, on the assumption that my readers will
be interested in the deeds of one single man who was not
himself particularly important, which is of course a
highly doubtful assumption to make. As a result, I have
left myself no option but to describe what follows,
including my meeting with Phaedra, as truthfully as I can
after so many years, or else go back and rewrite what has

gone before, putting in nice little snippets of geography and fable and scattering about gods and miracles, just as we interplant barley in the empty ground between the rows of vines in a vineyard. I would have no objection to doing this if it were up to me; but that tiresome man Dexitheus the bookseller was nagging me for a completed manuscript this morning when I went down to the Market Square to buy fish, and so I had better press on; and if what follows seems to you to be too realistic, you must blame him, not me.

I was putting my sword back over the lintel, as I have told you, when the door to the inner room opened and there was Phaedra. I assumed it was Phaedra; but if I had been a witness in a trial and the prosecutor was asking me if I was absolutely sure I would have had to qualify my statement, because I couldn't just then remember what Phaedra was supposed to look like. What I saw was a woman of average size in her middle to late twenties, with untidy hair and the clear signs of a badly set broken jaw. As I looked at her, I could find no memories, recollections, associations in my mind about her; neither love nor hate, nothing binding me to her or repelling me from her, and I had this extraordinary feeling that it was open to me either to accept her as mine or reject her as spurious, as if she was one of the stray goats that we round up on the hills from time to time and do our best to identify. If I accepted her now – it was almost like a second wedding-day – then I would be bound to her for life. If I rejected her, I could turn my back on her and be done with her for ever.

I am and have always been indecisive. I prefer to be forced into decisions rather than to make them freely and calmly; this makes it possible for me to blame the Gods when things go wrong. So I did not take either of the two initiatives open to me then; to throw my arms around her and kiss her, or to ignore her completely. I waited for her to say something.

'Eupolis?' she said. 'Is that you?'

'Yes.'

'What are you doing here?'

'I've come home.'

Neither of us moved, and it suddenly occurred to me that I had no idea how long I had been away. Perhaps it was less than a month since we had left Athens, or perhaps it was two years. I had no idea. I had no idea what season of the year it was – ploughing, harvesting, vintage – or how long it was since we had been together last, in this room, when I still had all that expensive armour of mine which by now must have been auctioned off in some dusty square in Sicily.

'You've come home?' she said. 'What's happened? Nobody said the fleet was back . . .'

Then she ran across and put her arms around me, somewhat clumsily; rather as an enthusiastically friendly dog jumps up at you and knocks the breath out of you. 'Oh, you're back,' she said, and pulled my head down and kissed me. But contrary to my expectations, that kiss was not decisive; I still did not feel committed, one way or another.

'So what happened?' she demanded. 'Did you desert? I'll bet you did, you coward. At the first sight of the enemy, you said to yourself, "That'll do me," and you didn't stop running till you reached the ships. And now everyone'll point to me in the street and say "There goes the coward's wife." Do you want something to eat?'

'No,' I said.

'Well, I expect you're still full of Sicilian wheat. And what were the girls like there? Were they cheap? Of course you spent so much on them you haven't brought me back a present, not so much as a pair of bronze earrings. Your beard needs trimming. And what have you done with your armour? You can't have thrown it all away.'

'I have, actually,' I said.

'Eupolis,' she said, 'what's wrong?'

I wanted to tell her, but I couldn't. Now that I was home I didn't know what to do, like a seasonal worker after the vintage is over.

'There is something wrong, isn't there?' she said. 'You look just like you do when one of your stupid plays flops. And then you're hell to live with for a fortnight, and I daren't buy myself anything. What's happened? Where's everyone else? Did we win?'

'No.'

'Don't say you've abandoned the War and come home empty-handed. I knew that Demosthenes was nothing but a crook. They'll put him to death for this, you mark my words. And high time too.'

'They won't get the chance,' I said. It was as if what had happened, to the army and to me, was a sort of secret which Phaedra would have to prise out of me. If she managed it, she had won.

'I wish you'd tell me what's going on,' she said. 'Have you really deserted? Or have you been injured and sent home? Eupolis, are you hurt?'

'No,' I said, and I looked at her, dispassionately, for the first time since we met.

I remember the first time I realised what I looked like. I was playing out on the hillside at Pallene with some other boys, and there was a little stream that ran into a pool during the season, before the sun dries up all the water there. We were sitting round this pool throwing stones at the frogs, and one of the boys was telling a story he had heard from his grandmother. It was the story of Narcissus, and I couldn't understand the point of it. The prince looked into the water, they said, and saw this beautiful youth and fell in love with him. I couldn't bear not getting the point and interrupted.

'Amyntas,' I said, 'who was the beautiful youth? And how could he breathe underwater?'

Everyone laughed and called me names, but I didn't

care. 'You don't know, do you?' I jeered. 'This is a silly story and you've just made it up.'

Everyone laughed again, and Amyntas explained that if you looked at calm water, you could see your reflection.

'What's a reflection?'

'It's a picture of you.'

'My father has a picture of my mother,' I said. 'He had a vase painted with her as Penelope, though it doesn't look a bit like her. But no one's ever painted me.'

'It doesn't have to be painted,' said Amyntas. 'It just happens. Look in the pool there.'

I knew better than that, of course; this was just a trick, and they would push me in and hold me under until I started gurgling. But on my way home my curiosity got the better of me, and I stopped and looked at the water in the watering-trough in our yard. There, sure enough, was a picture. It was a horrible little boy, with a squashed-up face and big ears, and I hated him, because he frightened me. I burst into tears and ran home, and my father asked what had upset me. I told him, and he laughed.

'Well,' he said, 'there's nothing you can do about it, is there? You're stuck with that face, whether you like it or not.'

'Can't you make it better?' I asked.

'Only Zeus can do that,' he replied.

So every night I prayed to Zeus to make me look better, and every morning I went and looked in the watering-trough, and I was still the same. For a long time I couldn't understand why Zeus hadn't answered my prayers, for I had prayed very hard and even sacrificed my pet grasshopper to him. Then it came to me in a blinding flash of inspiration that he must be away visiting the Scythians or the Ethiopians and couldn't hear me, and so I would have to wait until he got back. I must have forgotten to pray to him after that, for my face stayed as it was, or perhaps got worse.

Anyway; as I looked at Phaedra then I had that same

feeling; that she was as much a part of me as my face, and that only Zeus could do anything about it.

'How's my son?' I asked, and that was honestly the first thought I had given him since I left Athens. Even now that I had remembered him, I felt no great interest in him. He was like some unsightly present that a friend has given you, and you only remember to get it out and put it on display when the friend is knocking on the door.

'He's fine,' Phaedra replied. 'He's with the nurse at the moment. Shall I send for him?'

'No, that's all right,' I said. 'So long as he's well.'

'There is something wrong, isn't there?' said Phaedra.

'Yes,' I replied.

'What?'

'Let me take my boots off first.'

'The hell with your boots,' she said irritably, and I smiled.

'But my feet are hot,' I said. 'I want to take my boots off.'

'Then take your wretched boots off, if it means so much to you,' she said. 'Only tell me what's the matter. I want to know if you're going to be arrested or not.'

I put my arms round her. She felt familiar, as if she belonged. She pushed me away.

'Not now,' she said. 'Tell me what's going on. You can be really irritating at times.'

I sat down and pulled off my boots. 'Thrax,' I called out, 'bring me my sandals, would you? And I wouldn't mind a bit of bread and some cheese, if there is any.'

'Honestly,' Phaedra said, 'I don't understand you.'

'I know,' I replied.

She scowled. 'I don't know why I put up with you, really. I mean, this is ludicrous. Tell me what's going on.'

I wished that I could; but there was no way that I could tell her now. I had handled the business very badly, but that was nothing new. Thrax brought me the bread and cheese and I ate it.

'Are you going to tell me?' said Phaedra. 'Or do I have to go to the Market Square and ask?'

I put down the plate and brushed away the crumbs. 'Phaedra,' I said, 'how would it be if . . .' I couldn't finish the sentence; it wasn't necessary, and it would sound ridiculous. I had meant to say something like '. . . if we start again from scratch', or something like that, but of course we wouldn't be doing that. Impossible.

'If what?'

'Nothing,' I said. I knew I was home, then. 'Phaedra, the army's been wiped out.'

'What did you say?'

'The army, Phaedra,' I said. 'It's been wiped out. They're all dead.'

She stared at me. 'Are you mad?' she said.

'No,' I replied, 'but I don't know why. Phaedra, it was horrible. Nicias and Demosthenes too, all dead, every one of them. There's just a handful of us left.'

'I don't understand,' she said. 'For God's sake try and talk sense.'

'The Syracusans won,' I said. 'They destroyed our army. Destroyed, killed, wiped out, massacred, put to death, eliminated, decimated, there isn't a word for it. I escaped and got away to Catana. Me and Aristophanes, son of Philip. I think there are a few hundred other survivors too. But the rest of them are all dead. I got us to Catana and we came back on a cargo ship. The others aren't coming back.'

For a moment I felt the whole weight of it pressing on me; you know how it is when you get the toothache very badly, and you think that you just can't bear the pain of it any more. It was as if having Phaedra there was thawing me out, and in a moment I would melt and fall to pieces, and everything would come out in a rush, like being sick. My soul within me was demanding that I tell her everything, now, just as it came into my mind, so that I could get rid of the poison under the abscess and be well again.

You fool, said my soul, unless you get rid of it all now, with tears and the comfort of her arms holding you, you will never be clear of it. But I held myself together for that little time, and turned back the words from the gate of my teeth; and then I was outside it all again, someone who saw it happen rather than a participant. And in that time I grabbed hold of Phaedra's hand, but I didn't do more than that, although I was tempted to bury my head in her and hide under her arms. I realised that I didn't want to get rid of this unique possession, this great secret that the God had entrusted to me. Like a miser with a pot of coins I wanted to hide it away where no one could get at it.

'Oh, Phaedra,' I said, lifting my head and looking into her eyes. 'I've seen the most extraordinary things while I've been away.'

Phaedra was marvellous, just then. She wanted passionately to make me tell her exactly what had happened – how would you have felt, in her position? But she sat there and waited while I fought it out with my soul, even though I was closing the gate on her as well as the world. If I had melted then, as I almost did, if I had lost my balance and she had caught me, our whole lives would have been different after that. It was then that I knew that she did understand me, in some undefinable way beyond communication by words or gestures.

'Is there anything you've got to do?' she asked. 'Like notifying somebody or something?'

'I've done that,' I said. 'You don't mind just keeping me company for a minute or so, do you?'

She didn't smile, or hug me or anything. 'Of course not,' she said. 'If you're sure it's me you want.'

'There isn't anyone else,' I said. 'They're all dead.'

'Callicrates?'

I nodded. She said nothing. She knew that if he was still alive I would have talked to him, told him everything. But there was no one left alive I could tell it to; not until my mind had broken it down and digested it, and made something out of it.

'Promise me you won't ask me about it,' I said. She smiled.

'All right,' she said. 'You're back safe, that's the main thing.'

'I'm glad you think so,' I replied.

'Oh, it would have been an awful nuisance if you hadn't,' she said, getting up and pushing her hair back behind her shoulders. 'Lawsuits and inheritance problems and who gets what. All your money would have been tied up for ages, and I would have had to marry your nearest male relative. Of all the laws Solon ever passed, that must be the silliest.' She paused for a moment. 'Who is your nearest male relative, by the way?'

'I don't know,' I confessed. 'I think they're all dead.'

'So long as it's not that horrible cousin of yours, Nicomedes, the one with the big hairy arms and no neck. I couldn't fancy him at all.'

'He wouldn't exactly be overjoyed,' I retorted. 'I believe he's quite fond of his wife, and he'd have to divorce her.'

'Isn't she that skinny woman with those enormous elbows?'

'Habrosyne,' I replied, dredging the name out of the silt at the bottom of my mind. 'She isn't a thing of beauty, I'll grant you. But at least she doesn't spend all her husband's money on carpets.'

Phaedra looked down quickly. 'Oh, that,' she said. 'And that's all the thanks I get for getting you the best bargain you'll ever make. Just look at the weave.'

'What was wrong with the old one, for God's sake? It had years left in it.'

'I don't know why I bother,' said Phaedra. 'I should just put rushes down on the floor, like they do in Pallene.'

'If you swept the place occasionally,' I said, 'we wouldn't have to get expensive new carpets every five minutes.'

'I bet Nicomedes isn't so petty about money,' she replied. 'Perhaps you'd better go back and get killed.'

'If you spent Nicomedes' money like you spend mine, he'd break both your arms.'

'Just shows what a low-class family I married into,' said Phaedra, triumphantly. 'You don't know how lucky you are.'

'True,' I said. 'If I hadn't a wife who makes life unbearable at home, I'd never have taken up writing plays.'

'And that's another thing wrong with you,' said Phaedra. 'You steal my jokes for your plays.'

'Rubbish. You've never made a joke in your life.'

'Are you saying I've got no sense of humour?' she said angrily. 'Just because I don't laugh at your puerile efforts at Comedy?'

'You wouldn't recognise a joke if it bit you.'

'I'm unlikely to come across one in this house.' She giggled. 'Except in there,' she said, pointing to the inner room. 'Now that's quite comical sometimes. Most of the time, in fact. And before you say anything,' she added quickly, 'that's not an invitation.'

'Good,' I said, 'I'm far too tired.'

'You usually are, thank God.'

'No,' I said, 'usually it's just an excuse. But today I mean it.'

'Are you sure?'

'Yes.'

'Please yourself.'

I leaned back in my chair and closed my eyes, stretching my feet out until I could feel the leg of the cauldron with my toes. But it was not as if I had never been away. It could never be that. Still, tomorrow I would go to Pallene, and after that to Phylae, and then I would come back to the City again, and take up some new occupation, such as composing Comedies. Something quiet and safe, where I wouldn't have to hide from the cavalry any more. I looked across at Phaedra just as she retreated into the inner room and slammed the door. She wasn't perfect, not by a long way, but she wasn't a Sicilian cavalryman, and that was the main thing.

CHAPTER TEN

'And now, Eupolis,' you are saying, 'will you please get on with the story, and stop bothering us with all this nonsense about your wife and your complicated mental state? We get enough of that sort of thing at home, thank you very much; what we want from you is entertainment. What happened next in the War?' Be patient. I've had enough of the War for the time being, and I want to put in something now that will impress my grandchildren. Yes, little ones, the silly old fool actually knew the celebrated Tragedian Euripides, whose plays you have to learn when you really want to go catching grasshoppers. The longest sustained conversation I ever had with Euripides ... Well. First I must tell you what happened when I next met the celebrated Tragedian Euripides.

The news of the disaster had broken, and the City was in a state of complete panic. Scarcely a day passed without a rumour starting that the Syracusan fleet, crammed to bursting-point with bloodthirsty Sicilians, was only one day away from Piraeus in search of vengeance, and it was the general consensus of opinion that if the City walls were still standing in a month's time, it would only be because the Spartans wanted them as a defence against the Persians. You could get any money you asked for food, particularly grain, as people started hoarding, and quite a few families sold up their land and sailed off to the Black Sea, where they reckoned they would be safe. As for me, I took no part in the general panic. I had used up all my fear for the season, and had none left to fritter away on mere rumours. It would, of course, be a suitably ironic ending to be killed by the enemy here in Athens, after flogging all the way across Sicily to get home, but I felt that it would be too great an expense of energy even for the Gods to destroy Athens completely just to round off my personal story.

When I saw how buoyant the market for grain and other foodstuffs was, I set off for Pallene to find out how much I could spare for sale, and to see to the ploughing and manuring, since it was already the beginning of October. My vintage had taken place without me, and perhaps as a result we had made a larger than average amount of wine, and the harvest had been no worse than we had all expected at the start of the season. Now I always like to start ploughing early, since that way you can plough more often, and if possible I like to get the fodder vetch in before the end of September. This year, however, there had understandably been a shortage of seasonal workers and my steward had decided to leave the vetch and start the main ploughing. That was sensible, but since I had nothing better to do I decided to get on and see to the vetch myself; for it pains me to run short of fodder and have to feed good barley to mules and donkeys. So as soon as I had taken stock of what we had in and what we would need for ourselves, and sent off the surplus to the City, I put on my short cloak, got out a rusty and broken old plough which wouldn't be needed for the main work, harnessed up a mule, and set off for the low terraces. It was pleasant to be working again, and I was making a better job than usual of keeping my rows straight, and in addition some promising verses were starting to come together in my head, so

I was annoyed to be interrupted by a pair of travellers who called out to me from the road.

'I thought it was you,' said the elder of the two. 'I had forgotten you had land out here.'

I recognised who it was: Euripides, and his cousin Cephisophon. I knew them both only slightly, and it was some time since we had last met. But these were guests worth stopping work for.

'Come down to the house,' I said, 'if you're not in a hurry. We're drinking up the year before last's vintage to make room, and we could do with some help.'

Euripides smiled and agreed. It turned out that he had been visiting relations half a day to the north and was quite tired after his journey. Of course as a Comic poet it is my duty to make nasty remarks about our leading Tragic authors, and so I had frequently insinuated that Euripides was no enemy to a cup or two of wine; but I was surprised to find out that I hadn't actually been slandering him at all. I made a mental note and asked him how he had been getting on. Was he writing something at the moment?

He shook his head. 'No,' he said, 'not just now.' He sounded rather bored with the subject, and it occurred to me that he probably didn't enjoy writing any more. I always find that hard to understand, but apparently it is an occupational hazard with Tragedians. 'Your olives are shaping up well,' he said.

'They won't get much bigger now,' I replied. 'Too dry. So you aren't planning to present anything this year?'

'No,' he said. 'I saw your people were manuring quite thickly down on the levels. That is yours down there?'

'Yes.'

'We always save the best of our manure for the higher ground,' said Euripides, 'and you're much higher up here than us. How much do you give it per acre?'

'What?'

'Manure.'

'Oh.' I thought hard. 'I can't remember offhand,' I

replied, rather ashamed of myself. Euripides looked down his nose at me. Just as I was about to die of shame, I remembered. 'At a rough estimate,' I said, 'we reckon that what we get each year from one ox will do two and a half acres or thereabouts. But we aren't very scientific about it; it's more a sort of instinct.'

'Instinct,' he said. 'I see. And do you rot it or use it neat?'

'Oh, neat, of course,' I said.

'Really?' He seemed surprised. 'So what are you getting back, per acre, in an average year?'

'What?'

'Barley.'

'Oh.' I had thought we were still on about manure. 'Fourteen medimni, fourteen and a quarter if we're lucky. Depends a lot on the rain, of course. This year we didn't get twelve.'

'Fourteen?' said Euripides, clearly shaken. 'As much as that?'

'What are you getting?' I asked.

'Eleven,' he snarled, 'and that's if we're lucky. What about your vines? What does that come to, per acre?'

'Around thirty metretes, sometimes more.'

'Olives?'

'We do quite well with olives,' I said. 'We usually make four per acre, and more if it rains.'

He stared. 'You can't be serious,' he said. 'Four metretes the acre, in this god-awful country?'

I didn't like to ask him how much he was getting. He looked quite upset. To calm him down, I said how much I had liked his last play.

'Never mind all that,' he said, 'what are you doing that I'm not? Thirty met to the acre in wine; it must be as weak as water.'

'You're drinking it,' I said, affronted, 'you tell me.'

He apologised, and I accepted his apology. 'How often do you plough?' I asked.

'Three times, maybe four if there's heavy dew,' he said. 'More than that and we'd have to take on casual workers.'

'We plough fives times, and six does no harm,' I replied, for this was my pet topic. 'It works the moisture down into the soil, you see.'

'You probably have more men than me,' he muttered. 'And like I said, I don't take on casuals.'

'Neither do I,' I replied. 'You ought to try a fifth ploughing. The fifth ploughing only takes a tenth of the time of the first, and it really does make a difference.'

'Writing anything this year?' he asked, slightly defensively I thought.

'Don't think I'll have time,' I replied, 'what with the vetch and the fenugreek to get in.'

'Fenugreek?' He stared at me as if I was mad. 'What earthly good is that stuff?'

I told him about fenugreek, and lupins too, and to give him his due he listened. But when I started up on my favourite theme of all, beans, he seemed to lose patience and said it was time he was on his way.

'Well,' I said, 'any time you're passing. And I hope you do try a fifth ploughing this year. Let me know how you get on.'

He assured me that he would, picked up his hat, collected Cephisophon (who had been helping shift my wine-surplus all this time) and started to leave.

'By the way,' I called after him. He turned. 'I thought you'd like to know, your stuff is really popular in Sicily.'

'What?' He seemed puzzled.

'Your plays,' I explained.

'Oh,' he said, 'that.'

'Yes indeed,' I assured him, and I briefly told him about the village where we had given our extempore recital. It didn't seem to please him in the least, and he was quite short with me as he left. But a year or so later he sent me a charming little bronze bowl with Triptolemus on it, as a thank-you present, and said that I had been quite right about a fifth ploughing and using less manure; he was now clearing twelve and a half medimni to the acre, and had high hopes of seeing thirteen in a couple of years' time. But I don't think he ever made a serious effort to grow beans.

While I was busy with my vetch, I started work on a new Comedy. It virtually crept up on me when I wasn't looking, for I had not intended to enter anything for a while; but before I knew where I was I had thought of a splendid entry for a chorus of sheep, and after that there was no stopping me. Of course I needed a Message, and I couldn't really think of one. The City was a very different place now, after the disaster, and the old themes no longer seemed appropriate.

It was a difficult time. As soon as the news about Sicily broke, our enemies became extremely animated and talked very loudly about finishing us off once and for all. Our so-called allies, which means our subjects, were all on the point of rebellion, and as winter came on King Agis of Sparta set out with his army. But for some reason he didn't attack the City; instead he went around trying to collect money to build a fleet. We were building a fleet of our own, of course, and we cut out all useless expenditure so as to be able to afford it. Luckily, the Festivals were spared, and I pressed on with my play. I was back in the City now, and I saw quite a lot of Philonides and his friends, since I wanted him to present the play when the time came. The Chorus of sheep had been scrapped in favour of a Chorus of shipwrights, and I had high hopes for the piece come the spring.

I was so wrapped up in this work that I didn't take any notice of what was happening in the City. Now, quite naturally, the Athenians wanted to punish someone for what had happened in Sicily, but they were unable to do this since Nicias and Demosthenes were both dead and Alcibiades was in exile. They tried and executed a taxiarch who had escaped and made his way home, on some charge of general cowardice, but that wasn't really enough to make them happy, and so they looked round for a worthier scapegoat. Such a person was difficult to find, since the fault lay with the voters in Assembly; but then some ingenious person hit on the idea of blaming the whole thing on the people who had damaged the statues, the night before the fleet sailed.

Don't laugh, it's true. The movement gathered an incredible amount of momentum, and was soon completely out of control. There was a spate of accusations, and the men who had fostered the crisis in the hope of getting rid of various political opponents began to worry in case they got caught up in the general frenzy.

Now I knew the truth behind the whole thing, of course; I had been a witness, if you remember, and had barely escaped alive. I certainly knew who at least some of the perpetrators were; Aristophanes son of Philip, for example. I had no intention whatsoever of turning informer myself, as informing is a very dangerous business and only to be resorted to if you are desperately short of money. But Aristophanes and a few others knew that I had seen them at their work that night, and this cannot have been any comfort to them. As soon as she realised what was happening, Phaedra urged me to get out of the City until things had settled down. But I was still preoccupied with my play and wanted to stay in town so as to be able to talk things over with Philonides. I had abandoned the shipwrights now; I had struck on a truly brilliant idea.

My Chorus was to be made up of all the various regions of Attica, with each region unmistakably dressed in an appropriate costume. The Chorus-leader would be my own deme of Pallene, in a costume made up of mountains and goats, and the plot would be that all the great statesmen of the past return to earth to advise us in our hour of greatest need – the whole lot of them, from Solon to Pericles. I toyed with making that Solon to

Cleon, but I rejected it, which was cowardly of me. If only I could get it right, it would be my best play by far; it would deal with not just one theme but every theme. Of course with so much meat in it, the funny bits would have to be just right, but I felt that I could deal with that, if I tried my best.

It was about this time – please don't expect me to be more precise than that – that Aristophanes son of Philip came back into my life. He was, as I have told you, horribly implicated in this business with the statues, and to be fair to him he was in danger of being put to death or exiled for something so completely trivial that it must have been hard for him to take his problems seriously. The strange thing was that, apart from the participants themselves and a few eye-witnesses like myself, nobody actually did know who had smashed up those confounded statues. As you no doubt remember, it was the night before the fleet sailed; so everyone was either asleep or drunk. We Athenians are privileged to live in a city where the sound of nocturnal breakages is so commonplace as to be unworthy of attention, and I imagine that most people took no notice. This mystery, however, added the little spark to the affair that turned it into a raging fire. The average voter took it to be the symptom of some all-embracing conspiracy; and we Athenians love a conspiracy. Of course the absence of anything remotely resembling an established fact in connection with the business allowed the creative imagination of my fellow countrymen to run away with itself; there was simply no limit to what they could convince themselves of, given time and the encouragement of like-minded people. I honestly believe that if I had had the wit to start a rumour that the frogs from the marshes did it, under orders from their paymasters, the frogs from the swamps round Syracuse, in order to prevent our ships from coming into Syracuse harbour and so getting in the way of their annual mating, then everyone would have believed it and a great deal of trouble would have been saved; except of course for the frogs in the marshes, who would have been massacred to a frog.

There were debates about it in Assembly, of course. Now one of the great things about a democracy, which anyone considering setting one up in their native city should bear in mind, is that the voters really do believe that anything is possible. If there is a food shortage, for example, it's no use explaining to them that there is no food to be had; that the Spartan fleet is blockading Byzantium and we can't get so much as a grain of wheat past them, or that the Public Treasury is so empty that you can see more floor than coins. They won't believe you. What you must do is blame somebody. You must get up on your feet and say, 'Antimachus is responsible for the corn shortage; he's done a deal with the corn factors to create an artificial shortage, and he's lining his own pockets while your wives and babies starve. I propose that Antimachus be prosecuted.' Then, when all the voters have gone rushing off like happy children to lynch Antimachus, and only a few of the old and confused are left, you propose the motions necessary to do what can be done in the circumstances, bribe the few remaining voters present to vote in favour, and then get on with the job. This is rough on Antimachus, of course, but it's a fair proposition that if he's a politician in the public eye then he's had it coming to him for a long time, so in the end the system works.

After the news of the Sicilian disaster, of course, the Athenians' belief in their own omnipotence was badly shaken. At first they were rather too preoccupied with panicking to reason the thing out, but when whole weeks had passed and still the Spartans weren't sacking the Ceramicus they stopped feeling subdued and argued thus. We ordered Sicily to be conquered (said the Athenians). It wasn't. Now anything we order done is as good as done unless some one of us deliberately sabotages it, and since we are omnipotent, only we ourselves can stop ourselves doing something. We must therefore punish the saboteurs. Now the Generals, Nicias and Demosthenes, cannot be punished, since they are dead already. But we can do anything, including punishing the guilty. It therefore stands to reason that they can't really have been to blame, especially since they died like heroes, and heroes don't go around sabotaging things and bringing about their own deaths. The only possible saboteurs were the young men who damaged the statues. They must therefore be killed. Before they are killed, it is desirable that they be found. Therefore we must find them. The fact that we cannot presently find them can only be explained by a conspiracy. Therefore we will kill the conspirators.

Which is what they proceeded to do. Their test for finding out whether someone was in on the conspiracy or not was brilliantly simple. They knew that any conspirator, when questioned, would automatically deny any knowledge of the conspiracy. So when a man was standing his trial, and the prosecutor asked him what he knew about the conspiracy and he said 'Nothing at all', they hauled him off to the prison and stood him a large hemlock. If, however, the accused was clever and said, 'As it happens, I do know who was involved in the conspiracy; it was Lysicles and Phaonides and the rest of that crowd from the Gymnasium', then they would exterminate the Gymnasium set, and the informer as well, on the grounds that if he knew about the conspiracy and hadn't told anyone before now, he was to all intents and purposes a conspirator himself.

The really odd thing about all this was that of all the people they killed, none of them actually did have anything to do with the smashing-up of the statues. Now you would have thought that, in what was effectively a random sample of the political classes, at least one of the smashers would have drawn the short straw, so to speak. But they seemed immune, and I was able to feel relatively secure. I say relatively; in context, that meant that I felt reasonably confident that if I started a bowl of porridge and ate quickly, I would probably stay alive long enough to finish it. My personal nightmare was that one of the actual smashers would be caught in some general sweep, lose his nerve and confess, giving such plausible corroborative detail that even my idiotic fellow citizens would believe him. And then of course my name would be mentioned as being someone who was actually there, and the next thing I would know about it would be an alarming feeling of numbness around the toes.

When the party was just starting to get exciting, and the juries were working flat out, in shifts, to clear the backlog of cases, a gentleman by the name of Demeas came round to see me one evening. Now Demeas was one of the masters of a trade that has now almost died out, although there are sporadic efforts to revive it; he was a professional informer. He made a reasonable living out of it – his main work was reporting contraband goods in return for a percentage of their value, and let me tell you that he had an almost supernatural ability to tell, just by looking at them, whether goods were contraband or not. I am told that he had been apprenticed in his youth to the great Nicarchus, perhaps the leading informer of all time, and that may explain where he got his instinct from. Now when this business with the statues came up, Demeas set to work with a degree of enthusiasm which should serve as an example to skilled tradesmen everywhere. He was, however, slightly hampered by a shortage of raw materials. Just as you cannot make fine pottery without glaze, you cannot bring a successful prosecution without witnesses; and since the mortality rate among witnesses in this affair was almost as high as that among defendants, most of the professional witnesses had been used up or had retired, and for once there was no rush of amateur talent to take their place. In the normal course of events, an Athenian loves being a witness, particularly in a treason trial. It gives him a chance to participate in the downfall of a leading public figure (which gives one a feeling of pride and something to tell one's grand-children), as well as the opportunity to speak in public, which no Athenian not cursed with a cleft palate can resist. But with so many witnesses being promoted from the supporting cast to the leading role, so to speak, it was getting difficult to find anyone remotely plausible, even for cash in advance. Hence Demeas' visit to me.

When a person with so much standing in the community as Demeas comes to call on you, you don't keep him hanging about on the doorstep, particularly if there are people about who might see you. Nor do you refuse to listen to whatever it is he has to say; for if you do, you risk finding out a great many things about yourself that you never knew before.

'Eupolis,' said Demeas, putting down his cup and stretching out his toes towards the fire, 'I believe you know Aristophanes the son of Philip.'

'Yes,' I said.

'You were with him in Sicily, weren't you?'

'Yes.'

'So I'd heard.' Demeas nodded approvingly. He was a short man; for some reason all the great informers are – Nicarchus was a tiny little chap, by all accounts. Demeas had broad, round shoulders, a perfectly circular head with short hair, and no trace of a neck whatsoever. He wore a signet ring with a lion on it on the first finger of his left hand, and there were wine-stains down the front of his tunic. I didn't greatly care for him, but I confess I take these irrational dislikes to people.

'Now then,' said Demeas, 'while you were in Sicily, did Aristophanes say anything at all about the dese-cration of the holy statues?'

'No,' I said truthfully, 'not that I can remember.'

Demeas put his head on one side. 'What did you talk about, then?' he asked.

'Well,' I replied, 'we discussed the War, and how to keep out of the way of the enemy, the play he was writing, that sort of thing.'

'So you were quite friendly with him?'

I smelt danger, and decided to hedge. 'I wouldn't say friendly,' I said, after a pause for what I hoped looked like considered thought. 'And I wouldn't say unfriendly, either. We just got on with the work in hand – getting to Catana and so forth.'

'But surely,' Demeas suggested, 'the two of you, in such close proximity, sharing such terrible dangers and with no one else to turn to but each other; surely you discussed other things.'

'I can't say we did, actually.'

'I see.' Demeas rested his chin on his knuckle for a moment. 'You know, I believe you, of course, but other people might not.'

'Other people?'

'Hypothetically. Reasonable men, if you like. They might think that under such circumstances if Aristophanes had, say, something on his conscience, something that was bothering him, it would be only natural for him to confess it to whoever he felt closest to at the time, or even just whoever happened to be there.'

'Would they?'

'Wouldn't you? And then you say, "No, Aristophanes told me nothing." Now they might well think, these men are friends, they've been through great trials together, it's natural – laudable, even – that the one should cover up for the other. That they should collude with each other; no, that's not the right word. It's on the tip of my tongue . . .'

'Conspire?'

'Not conspire exactly; but you get the general idea. But then these hypothetical reasonable men would start feeling confused, because they wouldn't know which of them was covering up for the other. And if they happened to be forming a jury at the time, they might execute both of you, just to be on the safe side. They would take the view that covering up for a blasphemer and a traitor is no better – morally – than committing the crime yourself.'

'That's the way they think, is it?'

'Sadly, yes.'

'And is it likely that a jury should be faced with this sort of dilemma?' I asked. 'In the near future, say?'

'Don't ask me,' Demeas confirmed. 'Where were you, the night the fleet sailed?'

'Here,' I said. 'Ask my wife.'

'Does she sleep at all, your wife? Or does she suffer from permanent insomnia?'

'She has been known to sleep, yes. Where were *you* the night the fleet sailed?'

'In Samos,' he replied smoothly, 'having dinner with the Athenian governor and his staff. I was investigating the smuggling of prohibited goods, and they were helping me.'

I remembered the trial. 'You're lucky to have such a good alibi,' I said.

'Alibi?' He shrugged his shoulders. 'You know, people are very hard on us public-spirited people. I don't care if I'm being immodest here, but I believe I make a substantial contribution to the preservation of our democracy.'

'Without men like you,' I said, 'there could be no democracy.'

'Exactly. And you know, I'm not a thin-skinned man, but I do get hurt sometimes by what people say.'

'People?'

'Just ordinary people, you'd be surprised. But not just ordinary people. There's always someone ready to point the finger.'

'Really?'

'Oh yes.' He looked sad. 'For instance, there was a play I went to a few years ago which contained a personal attack on me. I think it was meant to be a Comedy. Anyway, there was this man in a funny mask purporting to be me, doing all sorts of antisocial things on stage, and everyone was laughing. It was really quite upsetting, especially for my wife.'

That explained the interest in Aristophanes; the play had been one of his. It wasn't a particularly good scene, either.

'And that wasn't all,' continued Demeas, now sadder than ever. 'The very next year, I can't remember the name of the play or who wrote it, but there was a Chorus which suggested that I was no better than a tapeworm or some such creature, and that if ever the City found itself short of funds it should put me through a press as if I was an olive and squeeze out all the bribes and blood-money. There was also a reference to my domestic arrangements that I found singularly distasteful.'

That explained the interest in me. 'I don't know what gets into these people,' I said.

'Well,' said Demeas, now virtually in tears, 'it just goes to show. For the sake of a cheap laugh and a round of applause, some people are prepared to throw around the most damaging – I might say dangerous – accusations, and they don't give a damn if they ruin reputations or even lives. It's highly irresponsible, if you ask me. Why, men have been convicted of serious crimes just because the Theatre has poisoned the public mind against them. I think the people responsible have a lot to answer for.'

'You have a point, of course,' I said.

'You think so?'

'Indeed.'

'That's comforting to know,' said Demeas, and he got up to leave. 'Well,' he said, 'I won't take up any more of your time. If you remember anything . . .'

'I'll be sure to tell you.'

'You know where I live?'

'Yes indeed.'

'Well,' he said, 'I'll say good night.'

'Good night.'

Now I don't think they're as popular as they used to be, but at one time Athens used to be crawling with those teachers of philosophy, men like the celebrated Socrates and Gorgias the Sicilian, who used to give little lectures; it was three obols for a seat, and a drachma to take part, or something like that. They would present a moral dilemma, and then everyone would say how they would act under the circumstances, and the lecturer would prove beyond doubt that they were all as evil as Hecate, and they would go home highly delighted and tell their friends. I went to one of these entertainments once – I think someone bet me I couldn't keep awake – and the topic was whether it was justified to allow a wicked man who was charged with a crime he did not commit to be executed for it in order for a good man who had in fact committed the crime in question to go free. I don't remember what conclusion Socrates or whoever the lecturer was came to – it's an odd thing about those lectures, but nobody ever can seem to remember that – but the general impression I took home with me was that if ever I got into such a mess I should do whatever I liked, since virtually every course of action put forward had been shown to be fundamentally wrong.

As I closed the door and bolted it, I thought about that lecture and reflected that I had been cheated out of three obols, since here I was in a highly similar situation and I didn't have the faintest idea what to do. There were differences of course; Aristophanes was wicked and guilty, and I was good and innocent. Nevertheless, it was a close enough parallel for me to be tempted to go round to Socrates' house and demand a refund there and then.

'Who was that?' Phaedra asked, putting her head round the door of the inner room. 'One of your drinking pals from the Theatre? I hope he wasn't sick.'

'Sick is putting it mildly,' I said. 'My love, we are in a lot of trouble.'

'What do you mean, we?'

'We, as in I am going to be executed, and you are going to be left destitute when they confiscate all my property to pay the informer.'

'Oh God,' she said, 'what have you done?'

'I haven't done anything,' I snapped. 'That's the aggravating part of it.'

Phaedra sat down next to me. 'What are you supposed to have done?'

'Smashed up the statues.'

'That's nonsense,' she said, relieved that I had been worrying over nothing. 'I can vouch for that. You were in bed with me.'

I shook my head. 'I don't really think that'll be enough to convince a jury,' I said. 'Now if I could prove I had been in bed with the prosecutor, and the presiding magistrate, and the entire Council, I might just stand a chance. You, no.'

'But it's the truth,' Phaedra said. 'Do you think any-one would seriously believe that I would perjure myself just to protect you?'

'You'd be amazed,' I said. 'No, there's only one way out of it, and I can't do it.'

'What, for God's sake?'

'Don't ask.'

'Don't be idiotic,' said Phaedra. 'Tell me what's going on.'

'All right,' I said. 'That man just now was Demeas, the informer. You know him?'

'I've heard of him,' she said. 'He was behind that big trial of the people who were supposed to be smuggling in perfume from Corinth. And it wasn't from Corinth at all, you know. Any woman could have told you that. It was just the cheap stuff they make down on the coast and put up in those little bottles.'

'Fascinating,' I said. 'Anyway, Demeas has got it in for me and Aristophanes because we mentioned him in plays, and besides, we're still alive. He wants one or the other of us for his next production.'

'And?'

'And, of course, he wants the other one as his key witness. That was what he was here for just now; offering me the choice.'

'You've got a choice?'

'Yes.'

'I thought you said we were in trouble.'

I frowned. 'We are. You do speak Greek, I take it? Trouble. Serious danger. Material risk to life and property.'

'I don't know what you mean,' said Phaedra. 'You hate Aristophanes. I'd have thought you'd be overjoyed.'

'Inform on him, you mean?'

'Yes.'

'That's the problem,' I said, and I threw a handful of charcoal on the fire. 'Look, Phaedra,' I said, 'you know me. Normally I wouldn't hesitate. I'd inform on my own father to save my own neck, you know that. But not Aristophanes. I just can't.'

'But you hate him,' said Phaedra. 'He's your worst enemy in the entire world. He slept with your wife. He tried to sabotage your play. For God's sake,' she remembered, 'he's even guilty of the damned crime.'

'I know,' I said.

'And if you think,' she said, 'that he'd hesitate one minute before informing on you just because you saved his life in Sicily . . .'

'How did you know about that?' I asked.

'. . . then you're a bigger fool than you look. Don't you realise, you're a witness against him, and the rest of them, come to that?'

'Well,' I said, 'that's good, isn't it? It might stop them informing on me if they stop to think that I can do as much for them.'

Phaedra shook her head sadly. 'You just don't think, do you? You don't seriously imagine they'll believe you when you point to the chief prosecution witness and say, "Actually, it wasn't me, it was him"? That's the only way you could tell it to the jury and they wouldn't believe you.'

'True,' I said. 'It's not looking good, is it?'

'But you idiot,' said Phaedra, 'why can't you do what Demeas wants you to? Just go to him, now, and say you'll do it? Has Aristophanes got some sort of spell on you or something?'

'Sort of,' I said. 'I promised the God I'd look after him.'

'What was that?'

'I said I promised the God. Dionysus. Why do you think I hauled his worthless body half-way across Sicily? My duty to Comic drama?'

'Is this some sort of ridiculous male all-buddies-together oath?' she replied. 'I've heard about that sort of thing.'

'No, no,' I said, 'I actually did promise the God. In person. That's why he spared my life in Sicily; so that I could look after Aristophanes.'

'Are you drunk?' said Phaedra.

'Oh, for crying out loud,' I said. 'Listen.' And I told her about the God; how I had met him in the stable during the plague and then after *The General*, and then in the walled orchard.

'I thought so,' she said when I had finished, 'you are drunk.'

'You stupid bitch,' I said, 'I'm telling you the truth.'

'Now you listen to me,' said Phaedra, leaning forward and grabbing my tunic with both hands. 'I couldn't give a damn whether they kill you or not, but I'm not having my son grow up an oarsman, and I'm certainly not going to spend the rest of my life selling greens in the Market Square just because of some ridiculous oath you and

Aristophanes may have sworn to each other in Sicily. So pull yourself together and act like a grown-up for once.'

'Phaedra,' I said, 'just let me explain, one more time—'

'Oh, you're pathetic,' she said. 'You deserve to get killed.' She let go of me, marched furiously into the inner room, and bolted the door.

'Phaedra,' I called after her.

'Later!' she shouted back through the door. 'When you've sobered up.'

I sat down by the fire and tried to think of something. But my options were limited. I tried putting myself in Aristophanes' shoes. It was a safe bet that he would get a similar visit from Demeas if I wasn't on Demeas' front step first thing tomorrow morning clamouring to give evidence. Now, would Aristophanes be put off by the fact that I actually had been a witness, and could presumably give a more convincing account of that night's activities as a result? Probably not, for the reason that Phaedra had given. Since he had been there, he could paint an equally evocative verbal picture, and since he was the accuser and I was the accused, the Athenian public would be bound to believe him. There is a theory that we have several different laws in Athens, each one dealing with a separate offence. This is not true. Whenever a man appears in the dock, nobody bothers to listen to the charge the official reads out. They know that the accused is really charged with being guilty, and that is one charge on which they will always convict. And in Athens, the sentence for being guilty is usually death by consumption of hemlock.

Which left only one alternative: flight. It is pathetically easy for an accused person to escape from Athens. This is not sheer fecklessness but deliberate policy, since it confirms the fugitive's guilt without wasting valuable jury time which would be better employed in the more important task of convicting the innocent. It also means that the Public Confiscator can step in quickly to seize the criminal's property; there is a lamentable tendency among people nowadays to spin out their trials in order to give their relatives time to get the bulk of their fortunes safely over the border.

So I could run for it, if I chose to do so. Where would I go? I would be faced with the horrible prospect of earning a living for myself, in Megara or Boeotia or somewhere like that. It's all very well for the Alcibiadeses of this world to jump ship and escape; they can take their pick of major cities and royal palaces, all competing to provide shelter and a pension for life to a useful and well-informed traitor. When a nobody like you or me has to escape from his city, he has to take what work he can; and unless he has a valuable skill or craft, this is likely to mean something unpleasant, probably connected with the care and upkeep of pigs or the harvesting of arable produce. We Athenians are not liked in Greece as a whole; we find it hard to get work. Now my only skill is the composition of plays, and the market for what I produce is limited to one city. Beyond that, I would be lucky to get seasonal work picking olives or grapes, and that is not my idea of life. Things have changed, and I know I'm old-fashioned, but I still believe (and everybody thought so then) that a man who has to depend on another man for his living, whether you call him a servant or an employee or whatever, is in reality nothing more than a slave, taking orders and doing what he is told. A man without land is a man without freedom, and without freedom there is no point in being alive. Even when I was on the run in Sicily, I had freedom; that was all I had.

So I wasn't going to run, and if I stayed I would have to inform on Aristophanes or die. Now I called on my soul for a little good advice, but that usually eloquent spirit pretended not to hear me, and I was on my own. After a lot of thought, I saw what I had to do, and it seemed to make a sort of sense.

There had to be a reason why the God had chosen to

save me, out of all those men, in the plague and the battle. I knew what that reason was; to protect the son of Philip, for as long as I lived. Now the God had so arranged matters that I had to die in order to keep him alive; but that at least explained why I had survived the plague and the battle, and in an illogical world you tend to cling to whatever explanations you can find. Now we were talking about that clever fellow Euripides a moment ago. By and large I detest his work, which is brash and modern and clever for the sake of being clever; but there is one scene of his which I must confess I like.

It's in his *Hercules*, and it comes at the point in the play where the hero, having just wiped out his family because the Goddess Hera has driven him mad in order to spite Zeus, is being comforted by his friend Theseus. Now Theseus says that Hercules has nothing to feel guilty about; the blame lies with the Gods, who made him do it. After all, says Theseus, the Gods have no moral code; they cheat and rob each other, even bind each other in chains. Hercules is furious at this, and turns on his friend. No, he says, I don't believe that the Gods bind each other in chains, or are capable of any evil; they are pure and holy, and everything they do is for the best.

So, then; whatever Dionysus was up to with me, it was for the best. This took all the weight off my shoulders – isn't that what Gods are for? It helped me to put aside my feelings of guilt at abandoning Phaedra and my son to a life of misery, for the duty a man owes to the Gods is greater than any mortal duty, and besides, the God would now have an obligation to look after Phaedra and Eutychides, for that is how the system works. I turned this solution over in my mind, and I could find no flaw in it; my only regret was that I had discovered my talent for working out the designs of the Gods too late in life to be able to make a name for myself as a Tragic poet.

As I sat there and stared into the fire, delighted with

my own cleverness, Phaedra opened the door of the inner room.

'Feeling better now?' she asked.

'Yes,' I replied.

'So you've changed your mind?'

'No.'

'I see.' She breathed out sharply. 'Because of the God?'

'Yes.'

'You're quite mad, you realise,' she said. 'I mean, your brain has actually gone.'

'If you say so.'

She sat down beside me, and neither of us said anything for a while.

'What did happen in Sicily?' she said.

I frowned. 'Is this quite the time for reminiscences?' I asked. 'Shouldn't we be discussing how to get as much of my money out of the country as we can before they send in the Confiscator?'

'That can wait,' she said. 'What did happen in Sicily?'

So I told her. It took a long time – well, you can understand why, if you've actually read this far and aren't just skipping through looking for the speeches. I found it easy to tell her, now that I had reached my decision, and she listened carefully, not interrupting except when she couldn't follow what I was saying. Occasionally I would stop, for some reason or other, and she would give me a hug and tell me to go on. It was then that I realised that I had made the right decision in accepting her, although it seemed that that decision would not turn out to be terribly important after all. When I told her about the walled orchard and the God, perhaps she understood, I don't know. When I had finished, she sat quietly for a while, picking at the hem of her dress.

'Well?' I asked.

'Well what?'

'Does it make any difference, hearing all that stuff?'

She considered this for a moment. 'It depends what you mean,' she said.

'That's a strange answer.'

'Yes, it makes a difference,' she said. 'No, it doesn't make a difference where a difference would help. I still don't understand why you can't inform on Aristophanes.'

'Weren't you listening, then? Would you like me to go back over it?'

She shook her head. 'I don't know,' she said, 'maybe you did see the God, or maybe you thought you did; the effect would be the same. Maybe you made yourself see the God.'

'I don't follow.'

Phaedra thought for a moment and then said, 'Maybe you needed to see the God. You couldn't understand what was going on. If you didn't find an explanation for all that death and destruction you'd go mad or die. Like when you were a boy in the plague. Your soul needed some way to force you to save yourself when you'd given up and become resigned to dying; so it made you see the God. And in Sicily, it was pretty well the same thing. If you were going to survive when everyone else was dying, you had to see the God. You had to be different – special, even. There had to be a credible reason why the God should spare you and not the others. When you were a boy, that reason was that when you grew up, you knew you were going to be a great poet; that was reason enough for the God to want to save you when everyone else died. Then, in Sicily, you tried the same thing; only now you were a great poet, or as great as you were ever likely to get. It wouldn't work so well. It worked well enough to get you out of the walled orchard, but it wasn't going to sustain you across half of Sicily. And then Aristophanes turns up, and your inventive Athenian mind said yes, of course, that's it. My reason for being alive is to look after the son of Philip.'

'Clever,' I said. 'Socratic, almost. But that doesn't

explain away the other time I saw Him; in the Theatre, after my play flopped. I wasn't in any danger then.'

'Oh, you just imagined it that time,' said Phaedra. 'Over-excitement, hot sun, not much sleep the night before.'

'All right then,' I said. 'How come the God was able to predict his own reappearances? How come my soul when I was a boy was able to see that one day I'd have a play flop and end up in a walled orchard?'

Phaedra shrugged. 'Simple,' she said. 'Mental revision. You've rewritten your own memory. You've scraped off what was there before and put in something else, like the officials do when they're cheating the naval accounts.'

'You won't starve,' I said. 'You can be the first woman philosopher.'

'I thought you'd be too stupid to understand,' she said. 'Never mind, it can't be helped.'

She put her hands on my shoulders and kissed me. 'So what do you think we ought to do?' I asked. She considered this for a moment.

'I think we should go to bed,' she said. 'I don't know about you, but I'm dead to the world. Sorry, that was tactless of me. Very tired, I should have said.'

'I meant, what should we do about this Demeas business?'

'Well,' she said, 'if I were you, I'd write the funniest speech you've ever written in your life and use it as your defence at the trial. It's the only hope you've got.' Suddenly she threw her arms around me, nearly crushing my windpipe (for she was a strong woman, though you wouldn't know it to look at her). 'Eupolis, you idiot,' she said, 'I don't want you to be killed.' Then she started to cry. That nearly broke my heart, and I tried to comfort her.

'Phaedra,' I said, 'don't worry, everything will be all right. Your father will look after you and the boy, I know he will. He hasn't got a male heir, so Eutychides will be provided for. And there's plenty of time to get some of the money out; you know how long trials are taking . . .'

'Oh, you're horrible,' she sobbed. 'You're going to die, and all you think about is money. That's absolutely typical. You just don't think, do you?'

She wrenched herself out of my arms, fled into the inner room, and bolted the door again.

CHAPTER ELEVEN

The nice thing about being under sentence of death is that you stop worrying about the trivial things in life; and if, like me, you're prone to worrying, this is a great advantage.

It's all right, you haven't dropped a scroll out of the book; we haven't got to the trial yet. I was speaking figuratively. I only felt as if I was under sentence of death. Now you will say I'm exaggerating, trying to make my story more dramatic. Well, perhaps you're right. We shall see.

I went round to Aristophanes' house the next morning. I don't know what I expected to achieve, but it would have been worth trying if I had managed to see him. But the slave who answered the door said he was out of the City on business and would not be expected back for a week at the earliest. Now at first I wondered if the son of Philip had panicked and fled; this would solve everybody's problems, and I began to feel cautiously optimistic. But, to make sure, I set my slave Thrax to watch Aristophanes' house, and sure enough he reported back not long after to say that he had seen Aristophanes go out and come back half an hour later with two partridges, a sea bass and a Copaic eel. Evidently the prospect of informing on the man who had saved his life was not having a harmful effect on his appetite.

So off I went again; and again the slave told me that Aristophanes was out. He can't have remembered me from my earlier visit, since this time he told me that his master had gone off to Eleusis for a fortnight to attend the Mysteries. I asked him whether he was sure, and he said, yes, why shouldn't he be; and then I asked him if he liked sea bass. He said no. Then I gave it up as a bad job and came home.

Phaedra said I should go and see Demeas. She reckoned that I could double-cross him, by promising to give evidence on his behalf; and then, when he called me at the trial, I could swear blind that Aristophanes was as innocent as the day was long, and that Demeas had offered me money to give false evidence against him. The Athenian public love treachery but hate traitors, as the saying goes, and they might just have swallowed that and killed Demeas instead; but obviously it was too late to do that, now that Aristophanes had so clearly done a deal with Demeas, and all I could say to Phaedra was that it was a great pity she hadn't thought of that last night, when it might have done some good. Not that it would have, of course; Demeas was far too experienced at that sort of thing to be caught out so easily, and it would probably have brought about the death of both Aristophanes and me.

In spite of Phaedra's protests, I set about getting some of my money out of Athens. There were two problems. One was how to realise my assets; the other was where to send them once they were realised. There was no earthly point in sending money to any part of the Athenian Empire, since it could be recovered from there with no trouble at all by the Public Confiscator. But there was similarly no point at all in sending it into some enemy country, since then Phaedra wouldn't be able to get it back and the Spartans would probably get it and fritter it away on warships or some such nonsense. Then, when we were going through Phaedra's jewellery, we came across the pendant (gaudy but not cheap) which the Thessalian princes had given me when I went on my embassy there. We looked at each other and said, 'Well . . .' but neither of us could think of a better idea; so I sent out Thrax again to ask an acquaintance of mine who was a Councillor if Alexander and Jason were still alive and in power. The answer came back that Alexander had murdered Jason and was ruling on his own. So I sat down and wrote Alexander a letter. I reminded him of our visit and thanked him once again for the performance of my *General*, crammed in as much theatrical gossip as I could remember or invent, and added my love and best wishes. Then, as a sort of postscript, I said that I was sending with the letter a small sum of money; if he would look after it for me until either my wife or her agent came and collected it, I would be ever so obliged to him and terribly, terribly grateful. Then, in a moment of inspiration, I said that as a tiny mark of my esteem I was sending him the original manuscript of two of my plays and a copy of the collected works of Aeschylus – luckily I had one by me, quite legibly copied and sturdily boxed up. I think it must have been those two manuscripts of mine, or maybe the Aeschylus, that did the trick, because when the time came, Alexander paid up virtually in full, and added a pair of gold earrings and an iron brooch in the form of a dung-beetle, as a present.

There was still the problem of a trustworthy messenger; but Phaedra suggested my steward from Pallene. You may remember that I had used his name for the hero of my *Maricas*. He was devoted to me, I knew, but getting on in years and not up to a long and dangerous journey. But he had a son, Philochorus (named in my honour), who was young and strong and had been on trading expeditions, so I sent for him.

Now it sounds easy enough to talk of realising assets, but of course it wasn't as simple as that, not by a long way. I had sixty-eight acres of land, almost as much as Alcibiades himself, although mine was of course more widely spread, and a fair amount of it was bare rock. Still, it was a huge estate, and there was no point even trying to sell it, as a whole or in parts. Things are very different now, of course, but in my day people simply didn't sell land, unless they were destitute or didn't have enough to live on and wanted to buy a ship or something. The best I could do was mortgage it or grant long leases, and I only managed to dispose of about eight acres that way. I could only get a fraction of its value, too; not only did the people I was trying to do business with have a fairly shrewd idea of what I was about, but the market was by now well and truly flooded, what with the confiscations and so many estates being masterless after the Sicilian campaign. I was due for my fair share of that, by the way; two cousins of mine, who I had never met, were killed in the War, and I was their nearest male relative. It seemed ironic at the time; there I was about to add nearly eighteen acres to my already quite considerable fortune, and I wouldn't live to fight the lawsuit. I assigned it in writing to my son, but without any prospect of his ever coming to contest the case.

What I could dispose of was my various other interests. I had never really appreciated how valuable they were – things like shares in ships and mines and factories aren't like land; you don't cherish every little bit of them, and show them off to your son, you just leave them to the people who know about such things and go over the receipts once a year to make sure you aren't being cheated. But when it comes to raising money in a hurry, there's nothing to compare with such things. What with the War and the disturbed state of everything, of course, nobody was wildly enthusiastic to buy, but I was able to get rid of some of them by lowering my price sufficiently. Finally, of course, there was my actual reserve of coined silver; that wasn't to be sneezed at, when all was said and done. My uncle Philodemus had brought me up to keep at least a talent in ready money at all times, and I have always done this, if possible. Not for the first time, I was grateful to him. In addition to this, Callicrates' widow sent me a loan of half a talent, from the reserve Callicrates had also maintained. I really didn't want to accept it, but she insisted; it was what he would have done, she said, if he had been alive, and to please me she accepted a mortgage on some of my land in Pallene as security.

So that was that; and when Philochorus set sail from Piraeus to Thessaly he took with him a considerable sum of money; enough to make sure Phaedra would be provided for, and to enable her to bring my son up properly.

'Knowing your luck,' said Phaedra, as we saw the ship sailing away, 'he'll get robbed by pirates.'

'Or bandits,' I said. 'Thessaly is alive with bandits.'

'Not to mention your friend Alexander,' Phaedra added. 'We must be mad, entrusting that lot to a man who's not even really Greek.'

'It won't come to that,' I said. 'Bet you Philochorus will jump ship at the first stop with the whole lot.'

'I doubt it,' she replied. 'He looked stupid enough to be honest. But that won't stop the sailors murdering him and throwing his body over the side.'

We walked home together through the City, and for some reason we were both feeling remarkably cheerful. It wasn't just because we had managed to get the money out; the whole business had been rather depressing, and we were both just glad it was over. No, I really can't say what had got into us both, but soon we were laughing and pointing funny things out to each other and making silly jokes, and people stopped and stared at us as we passed them; for in those days it was rare to see a man and a woman, especially a wife and her husband, laughing together in the street. Now, of course, things are very different, and nobody laughs at you or makes faces behind your back if you happen to mention that you are quite fond of your wife. Personally, I blame the modern craze for philosophy and this so-called New Comedy we hear so much about.

But when we reached our house, there was Demeas and a small gaggle of his faithful process-servers, gathered to bear witness that I had received the summons. He went through the legal rigmarole with the sort of polished ease that makes you realise that you are in the presence of a true craftsman, looked over the outside of the house to make sure there were no obvious structural faults that would reduce its value, and waddled away.

It was a most impressive charge. Demeas was prosecuting me for blasphemy, treason, conspiracy, damage to public and private property, communicating secrets to the enemy, assault with intent to degrade, gross bribery of officials, conspiring with persons unknown to pervert the course of justice (I liked that), disorderly and offensive conduct, and attempted murder. I had no idea what the last one was for; I could only imagine that it came free with the rest of the deal, like the extra handful you get from the olive-merchants, for luck. I later found out that he always put that in, so that if the trial looked like going against him, he would fall back on the attempted murder charge, claiming that the defendant had attacked him by night in the street in an attempt to silence him; and he took a small, elderly relative about with him wherever he went to be his witness.

I heard in due course that no date had yet been fixed for a trial. I think this was an open invitation to me to run. News of my frantic efforts to get money out of Attica most certainly reached Demeas, because he put in an offer, through agents, for a share in a ship I was selling; so he must have guessed that I was getting ready to leave. This would of course be in his interests. After all, he hadn't had to name his witnesses yet, so he wasn't committed to an account of that night's events in which Aristophanes was merely an innocent witness. If I ran, he could prosecute Aristophanes too. Aristophanes would then run, and he could move on to the next candidate; in fact, I could see nothing to stop him until he was the only man left in the whole of Attica. I'm sorry if I seem slightly obsessive about this Demeas; but it's an extraordinary thing to have someone trying to kill you for the sake of your money, especially if he isn't even a relative. I suppose that's how deer and hares feel, when we kill them not out of any personal enmity or fear but for the sake of their flesh and their skins.

Enough about him for the moment. Phaedra seemed to be taking it all very badly. If she had stormed at me for being a stubborn and irrational fool, and the sole cause of my own misfortunes, which is what I had expected from her, I could have taken that in my stride. But she did nothing of the sort. She tried to be cheerful, and she made a thoroughly bad job of it. Now, I was in a very strange mood for most of the time; one moment I was full of almost childish good spirits, making funny remarks and playing practical jokes (which is a crime against good taste of which I am not usually guilty), and the next moment I would be as miserable as a failed harvest. It didn't help to have Phaedra dragging round after me like a beggar's dog, quite obviously on the point of tears and trying her very best to cheer me up. To make matters worse, we no longer even wanted to quarrel or bicker with each other. I suppose it was a bit like the Athenians and the Spartans (explain yourself, Eupolis; whatever will you come out with next?), in that we stopped hammering away at each other and turned our combined malice on the world in general and Demeas in particular, just as the Athenians and the Spartans once stopped fighting each other to resist the Persian invaders. The parallel is not intended to be exact, since the Greek alliance drove the Persians into the sea, whereas all our jokes at his expense didn't whiten a single hair on our victim's head. But the fact remained that we were growing depressingly close to each other, and I don't think anything has ever been worse timed, not even the Athenian invasion of Egypt under the celebrated Cimon. Irony again, you see; the moment our marriage was on notice to be dissolved, courtesy of my friend Demeas, we suddenly found out that we could live together after all. Together, we could put up such a barrage of comedy that our jokes blotted out the sun, as the King's arrows did at Thermopylae; and that was with both of us only giving half our minds to the job, what with Phaedra being so depressed and me so perplexed.

About a week after Demeas proclaimed the summons, I went down to the Market Square to see if I could buy a thrush and a brace of pigeons. Because of the War it wasn't easy to find such things, but I was determined to eat pigeon at least once more before I died. Men on their deathbeds have so many regrets; so many things done that should not have been done, so many things not done that should have been done. My leading regret, at that time, was that I hadn't eaten nearly enough pigeons, and I was so busy searching for some that I didn't look where I was going, and I bumped into a fellow shopper with considerable force.

The shopper turned on me angrily. 'You clumsy fool,' he said, 'you nearly made me swallow two obols ...'

It was Aristophanes the son of Philip. He fell silent and stared at me.

'Hello, Aristophanes,' I said. 'Buying poultry?'

Since he had a bundle of pigeons under his arm and

four quails in his left hand he could scarcely deny it. 'Yes,' he replied defensively. 'What's that to you?'

'Throwing a party, I see,' I said.

'No,' he said quickly.

'You're going to eat all those birds by yourself?'

'No law against it, is there?'

Just then, his slave caught up with him. The slave was carrying six partridges, another two quails, a duck and a pheasant. He looked like a fletcher's shop.

'Hungry, are you?'

'So I'm throwing a party,' said Aristophanes. 'I can throw a party if I like, it's a democracy.'

'Am I invited?'

'No.'

I sighed. 'Be like that,' I said. 'I've just got some fresh cheese and sausages from the country which I could have brought, so it's your loss. And how are things with you?'

People were starting to point at us and whisper, and Aristophanes looked extremely embarrassed. 'Same as usual,' he said. 'Why shouldn't they be?'

'Just a friendly enquiry, that's all. I haven't seen very much of you since we got back from Sicily.'

'Well, I've been busy,' said the son of Philip. 'Which reminds me, I must—'

'I was meaning to drop in and have a chat,' I said. 'I wanted to make sure you'd got over the effects of that fever.'

'Absolutely, yes.'

'You remember, don't you? When you were dying in the mountains and I got you to safety.'

'Look, it's lovely to see you again,' said Aristophanes, 'but I'm meeting this man and—'

'I was a bit concerned,' I said, 'that you might still be a bit weak, after all that time in the olive-jar. You remember the olive-jar, don't you? The one I hid you in when I got you safely past the enemy cavalry?'

'Yes. Look—'

'And there was that bump on the head, too,' I continued. 'The one you got when I saved your life on Epipolae. When you were running away. Without your shield.'

'Goodbye.' He tried to get away, but there was a substantial ring of giggling Athenians round us now, and he couldn't.

'You know,' I went on, 'a soldier looks so ridiculous running away without a shield. I remember all those jokes of yours in your plays about poor old Cleonymus, when he dropped his at that battle. Let me see—'

That was enough for Aristophanes. He started to push his way through the crowd, and the pigeons fell from under his arm. I stooped and picked them up. 'Aristophanes,' I called out after him, 'you dropped your shield – sorry, your shopping. Don't you want it?'

There was no reply; Aristophanes was hurrying away. I shrugged my shoulders, brushed the dust off the pigeons, and went home. Outside my door, the little statue of Hermes had been smashed to pieces, and on the trunk someone had scratched 'Death to the traitor'. That deflated me after my little triumph over the son of Philip, and I went in and threw the pigeons down in front of the fire.

'Oh, well done,' said Phaedra, who was sitting carding wool. 'I knew you'd be able to get some from somewhere.'

'A present from Aristophanes,' I said, and I told her about the scene in the market. She laughed.

'We won't be hearing any more shield-dropping jokes from him for a while,' she said.

'I won't,' I replied. 'Not ever. Remember?'

I reflected immediately that this wasn't a particularly cheerful thing to say. But Phaedra arranged her face so that it resembled a smile.

'Aren't you the lucky one?' she said. 'Think of it. No more Aristophanes Comedies where you're going. No more funny slaves getting hit with sausages. No more moronic puns on place names.'

'No more parabases by Phrynichus,' I added. 'Don't forget that.'

'No more Teleclides,' she went on. 'No more Choruses invoking the Gods when he can't think of anything else to put in.'

'No more houses being set on fire when he can't think of a way to end the damned thing.'

'No more automatic food scenes by Crates.'

'No more Aristomenes.'

'And never again,' said Phaedra, 'will you have to suck a pebble to stop you throwing up when Ameipsias does the scene with the old man with diarrhoea. God, you're lucky, Eupolis. I wish I were coming with you.'

I smiled. 'So do I,' I said. 'You know your Comedy, Phaedra.'

'Well I ought to,' she replied. 'I'm married to a Comic poet, remember?'

'You never used to take any interest at all.'

'I couldn't help it,' she laughed. 'God, do you remember that time when Hermippus won the prize with that thing with the whale in it? You came home with a face like mustard, hurled your stick at the wall and nearly burst into tears.'

'I call that perfectly reasonable behaviour, in the circumstances,' I said.

'I couldn't get a word out of you for a week,' she said. 'You didn't even shout, you just sat there. And then you got drunk and recited the whole of his opening Chorus in a silly voice.'

'It sounded better that way,' I remembered.

She leaned forward, putting down her wool. 'And do you remember that time when Aristophanes came third, and you held a victory party even though you hadn't even entered anything?'

'You weren't here, were you?'

'Yes I was,' she said, 'but I was sulking and wouldn't come out. And that idiot Critobulus was sick all over your new cloak.'

'God only knows what he'd been eating,' I said. 'I had to throw it away in the end.'

Phaedra was really smiling now. 'And do you remember when you won with *The Flatterers*, when you'd been expecting to be wiped out, and Aristophanes paid those men to start a fight in the audience, and you found out and paid them more? I was proud of you.'

'That was before we got back together, wasn't it?'

'I was still proud of you,' she said. 'I really wanted to be at the party, too, but of course I couldn't go. In fact, I've never been to one of your victory parties. You'd better hurry up and write another play, so I can—'

She didn't finish the sentence. I looked away.

'We've wasted each other, haven't we?' she said. 'We could have had a good time.'

'Will you get married again?' I asked.

'At my age, with a face like mine? You must be joking.'

'You'll have money,' I said, 'and besides, looks aren't everything. You could marry Hermocrates; his wife died last year and he's due for a victory soon.'

'Hermocrates?' she almost spat. 'Give me credit for a little taste.'

'Picky, aren't you?' I said. 'He's quite good-looking, if you go for that type.'

'Hermocrates,' she repeated, 'the man who presented *The Aeginetans* under the impression that it was a Comedy! I'd rather sell myrtle in the market.'

'It needn't be a Comic poet, then,' I said. 'You could marry a Tragedian. You've got the right name for a Tragedian's wife.'

'Oh no,' she said, 'a Comic poet or nothing.'

'Comic poets make very bad husbands, so they say.'

'There you are, then,' she said, 'stick to what you know. I could even try writing myself.'

'You!' I said. 'Don't make me laugh. What in God's name do women know about poetry?'

'What about Sappho, then?' she said quickly.

'Grossly overrated,' I replied, 'even for a foreigner. And half her stuff was actually written by Alcaeus. And who would you get to produce it for you?'

'Philonides,' she replied. 'I'd pretend it was one of yours.'

'You wouldn't dare.'

'There's nothing to it,' she said. 'It's a craft, like painting pots. All you have to do is study the techniques for a while and any fool could do it.'

'Rubbish.'

'We'll see.'

'No we won't. I forbid it.'

'You forbid it, do you?'

'Absolutely.'

'Well in that case,' she said, 'we'd better get these pigeons plucked.' She picked them up and called for Thrax. 'We can have some of that new cheese with them, and those sausages.'

On the very next day the date for the trial was announced; it would be in six days, at the Odeon, third case of the day. The Odeon wouldn't have been my first choice, if it had been up to me; the Archon's court has better acoustics, and the water-clock there runs notice- ably longer. However, being third was a good omen, since I had led out my Chorus on the third day when I won with *Maricas*, and also with *The Flatterers*. I was mentioning this to Phaedra and she was saying that all I needed now was a good producer, when there was a knock at the door. Thrax opened it, and in came a man whose face I recognised, though I couldn't put a name to him. But as soon as he opened his mouth to wish me good morning I remembered who he was.

His name was Python, and he was a professional

speaker. I had seen him scores of times, either in the
Market Square hanging about with Socrates and his
crowd, or at the Baths or the Gymnasium. He was one of
those people who call themselves philosophers but who
make their living teaching people how to speak, either in
the Assembly or in court. That's another trade that's
dying out, I'm delighted to say; not because it's intrins-
ically odious, like informing, but because it seems to
attract such repulsive people.

I asked him what I could do for him, and he replied
that it was more a case of what he could do for me. I
think he was delighted to be able to introduce a Figure of
Speech into the conversation so early, like a salesman
eager to display his goods. He said that, for as little as
fifty drachmas, he would undertake to prepare for me a
speech of defence that would get me acquitted by a
unanimous vote of the jury.

Of course I was very interested in this proposition,
and I asked him to sit down and have a cup of wine. He
accepted the seat but not the wine (which impressed me
tremendously; here was a man who believed in keeping a
clear head) and I asked him if he was sure he could get
me off.

'Undoubtedly,' he said. 'Failure is unthinkable,
success is guaranteed.'

I asked him if he knew what I was charged with. He
said that he had gathered that it was to do with the
statues.

'And what particular facet of the case makes you feel
so confident?' I asked. 'To tell you the truth, I haven't
much idea of what they're going to say.'

'Such knowledge would be no help but a hindrance,'
said Python. 'It would clutter the mind when it should be
clear. You should be not on the defensive but the offensive. That is what I generally recommend to clients.'

'So what sort of thing would you say in this speech?'

'A successful speech,' he said, leaning back in his seat

and putting the tips of his fingers together, 'combines clarity and elegance, persuasion and passion, subtlety and sincerity. There must be reason with emotion, but emotion within reason. A guilty man may protest his innocence; but an innocent man must concern himself with guilt. The guilt of his accuser, for example; ought we not to consider that? I have heard that Aristophanes is to testify against you. Ask yourself this. Is it the case that this is a case where the accuser should himself be the accused? Suppose we establish your antagonist's involvement in the escapade of which he indicts you; will that suffice? No; we must then proceed to paint a pretty picture of him, to gild his guilt, so to speak, in order that the jury may see with their own eyes how brazen he patently is. Thus not only will his sword be blunted but his shield turned aside; the lamb will leap upon the lion. On this reversal of roles we cannot unreservedly rely; but already we have unburdened ourselves of the burden of proof, and condemned our enemy to plough a double furrow.'

'And what about witnesses?' I asked.

'Witnesses?'

'Witnesses.'

He seemed offended. 'I will, of course, undertake to provide all the necessary witnesses.'

'Oh, I see,' I said. 'You mean professional witnesses.'

'Of course.' He frowned. 'Tell me now,' he said, leaning forward, 'if your plough broke, would you hire a potter to mend it?'

'No.'

'Or a farrier?'

'No.'

'Or an armourer, or a basket-weaver, or a wreath-maker?'

'No.'

'You would hire a carpenter, would you not?'

'Very probably, yes.'

'And if your roof leaked you would consult a builder, and if your sandals wore out you would visit the shoe-maker's shop.'

'I would indeed.'

'So you would seek the services of a professional, not an amateur?'

'I think we've established that, yes.'

'Yet whereas you would not entrust your roof to an amateur builder, or your foot to an amateur cobbler, you would entrust your life to an amateur witness?'

'Yes,' I replied. It was not the answer he expected. 'Do you know why?' I went on.

'Why?'

'Because the juries know all the professional witnesses by sight,' I said, 'and it plays merry hell with their credibility.'

He scowled at me. 'All my witnesses are credible,' he said angrily.

'Thank you,' I said, 'you're a tremendously eloquent man, really you are, but I think I can manage to get killed on my own.'

'Oh.' He looked terribly disappointed. 'You're making a great mistake, you realise.'

'Python,' I said, 'it was very kind of you to offer to help, but your stuff is strictly for civil trials – debts and minor assaults and that sort of thing. You stick to that and you'll go a long way.'

I had offended him, but that couldn't be helped. 'Well, in that case,' he said, 'I must regretfully withdraw my offer. That will be five drachmas, please.'

'Five drachmas?'

'Yes.'

'Why?'

'My dear friend,' he said, 'you don't expect me to work for nothing. You have enjoyed a lengthy conference with me, even though you have rejected my services. You don't deny that, do you?'

'I've certainly enjoyed it,' I replied, 'but not five drachmas' worth.'

'So you refuse to pay?'

'Yes.'

'You will hear more of this,' he hissed, and he stormed out of the house. Phaedra, who had been listening to all of this through the door of the inner room, came in and went on with what she had been doing.

'You weren't impressed, I take it,' she said.

'What, with that?' I laughed. 'The man's a clown.'

'Well,' said Phaedra, 'that clown has got people off worse charges than this one before now.'

'Not criminal charges he hasn't.'

'Yes,' she said, 'criminal charges. Treason. Illegal legislation. And they were guilty, too. Even the juries thought they were guilty.'

'Name one.'

She named about five; important cases, too. 'And do you know how he managed that?'

'Well it can't have been his damned professional witnesses.'

'Oh, of course not,' said Phaedra irritably. 'What gets him his results is his oratory.'

'You call that oratory?' I replied. 'That load of bath-house gibberish? I wouldn't dare put that lot in a parody; people would say I was going way over the top.'

'That's what they want these days, you fool,' said Phaedra. 'Or how come he makes a living?'

'That's a circular argument,' I pointed out cleverly.

'About the only thing that could save your life right now is a really good circular argument,' Phaedra replied. 'Look, the juries now are like the people who watch the chariot-races; they have their favourites, and that Python is one of them. They like him. They want him to win.'

'How do you know all this?' I asked. 'When did you last go to a trial?'

'Just because I'm a woman doesn't mean I'm deaf,' she replied. 'I have friends of my own, you know, and they tell me things. Look, it's beside the point how I know these things. The point is, you should get yourself a good defence speech. What have you got to lose, for God's sake?'

I took my sandals off, and lay back on the couch. 'My self-respect, for one thing,' I said. 'If you think I'm going to put my name to a lot of Socrates-talk like that, you're wrong. I'm a poet, aren't I?'

'What's that got to do with it?'

'I could write a better speech than that, in that style, and make it scan too,' I said. 'I could do it in my sleep.'

Phaedra shook her head vigorously. 'No you couldn't,' she said. 'You couldn't take it seriously.'

I lifted my head. 'What do you mean by that?'

'You'd ham it up,' said Phaedra. 'It's your instinct. You'd put in jokes, you'd make a parody of it. Which would be fine for the Theatre but no earthly use in the Odeon.'

She had a point there. 'But wait a minute,' I said. 'You're forgetting that I haven't the faintest intention of making a Python speech anyway.'

'Why not?' she said.

'Because it wouldn't work,' I replied. 'Those trials you mentioned just now. Think a minute. Weren't they all before the Sicilian thing?'

Phaedra considered this. 'All right,' she said, 'what if they were?'

'The point is,' I said, 'things aren't the same any more, not since Sicily. If they were, do you think Python would have to go hawking this stuff door to door, like a perfume merchant?'

'He'd heard about your case and wanted the job,' she said. 'I don't think that's particularly significant.'

'Don't you? Well, I still maintain that this statues business is quite unlike anything we've had before; it's gone on longer and there's more than just money and politics in it.'

'Such as what?' Phaedra asked.

'Such as for the first time since any of us can remember, we're a defeated city,' I said. Up till now, I'd been making it up as I went along, Athenian-style, for the sake of a good discussion. But now I was thinking aloud. 'That's what's different now, Phaedra; they're scared. They've been beaten, they can't understand why, and there's no one left to blame, so they're turning on each other now. For God's sake, I'm not a politician, am I? Or a general? I haven't really got that many enemies. Since when did people like me get prosecuted on political charges? And God knows I'm not the only one. Demeas is prosecuting me because I've got money, sure, but the jury's going to convict me because they want blood. And this time the initiative isn't coming from Cleon or Hyperbolus or Pericles or anyone like that, someone with an enemy he wants to get rid of; it's the juries and the voters who started this blood-bath, all by themselves, and they won't be satisfied until there's a revolution or a civil war.'

'Oh yes?' said Phaedra. 'And have you got any evidence for all this? Or have you been chatting to the prophetic Apollo again?'

'Evidence,' I said. 'Well, for a start, there's me being prosecuted, as I've just explained.'

'That's a circular argument,' said Phaedra, happily.

'Told you I could do it,' I replied. 'Ask yourself this; who's the Leader right now?'

'Leader?'

'Leader,' I said. 'You know, in Assembly. There's an unbroken line of them, from before Themistocles' time down to Cleon and Alcibiades. So who is it now?'

'Well,' she said, 'offhand ...'

'There isn't one, is there? And why? Because nobody's safe any longer. Oh, sure, Themistocles and

Pericles and the like were prosecuted from time to time, but only by idiots like my grandfather; they were never in any danger, except from their own kind. But now the voters and the jurors are so worked up they'd convict anybody; and since there aren't any big men for them to eat any more, they're feeling hungry, and so they'll eat whatever the informers give them. Like me, for instance. And the sort of clever speeches that used to make them happy in the old days, when they were well fed and knew who their master was and where their next general was coming from; that doesn't amuse them at all any more.'

'But isn't that the point of being on a jury?' said Phaedra. 'I thought the whole attraction of it was being paid for listening to clever speeches, and then voting for the one you liked best. The bloodletting was just an additional thrill.'

'I don't think so,' I said, 'not any more. These people aren't hounds hunting for someone else's sport any more, they're wolves hunting for food. I honestly don't believe a clever speech would do any good.'

Phaedra was silent for a while. 'At least you could try,' she said at last. 'There's nothing else we can do. How would it be if you tried a really good old-fashioned speech? Put in some of the stuff you've just given me, if you can remember any of it. There's nothing an Athenian audience loves more than being insulted.'

As she said that, something seemed to fit into place inside my mind. I couldn't quite identify it, but I saw a remote possibility. I don't think Phaedra noticed, and she went on, 'Just so long as you make some sort of effort. That's what really upsets me, the way you're just accepting it all.'

I smiled. 'What else can I do?'

Phaedra frowned, then called for Thrax. 'Here's eight obols,' she said, handing him a drachma and borrowing a two-obol piece from me. 'Go down to the market and get a quart of anchovies for me, will you?' Thrax nodded and set off. 'We haven't had anchovies for a week,' she said, 'and I just feel like some.'

'Why have you changed the subject?' I asked. 'Or are you agreeing with me for once?'

'I wouldn't agree with you if you were the last man on earth,' said Phaedra, smiling. 'Let's talk about something else till Thrax gets back.'

'Such as what?'

'Oh, I don't know,' she said. 'Sing me a Chorus or something.'

I looked at her. 'You're acting very strangely,' I said. 'What are you up to?'

'I'm not up to anything,' she replied. 'Why do husbands always assume their wives are up to something when they ask them to sing?'

'But you hate my singing,' I answered. 'You always say it goes right through your head, like a nail or something.'

'All right, then,' said Phaedra, 'don't sing, if you don't want to. Tell me a story.'

'What's all this in aid of, Phaedra?'

She scowled at me. 'Just tell me a story, will you?'

'What sort of story?' I asked.

'I don't know, do I?' she replied. 'You're pathetic, you are.'

So I started to tell her the story of Jason and the Argonauts; but to make it more interesting, I told it the way Alcibiades would tell it, when drunk. This made her giggle, and she stopped being cross; which was understandable, since a major part of a Comic poet's trade in those days was making fun of Alcibiades and his lisp. I was just getting nicely into the flow of it when Thrax came back from the market. Phaedra interrupted me in mid-lisp and called him over.

'Did you get the anchovies?' she said.

'Here they are,' he said, pointing to the jar he was holding. 'Oh, and you gave me too much money,' he said, and picked three obols out of his mouth and handed them to her.

'That's the price now, is it?' she said. 'Five obols a quart?'

'It's the shortage,' Thrax replied. 'They've gone up again.'

'Never mind,' she said. 'We'll have them this evening, with the rest of the beans and some soup.'

I had to laugh. 'What's so funny?' she said innocently.

'I knew you were up to something,' I said. 'Fancy you remembering what I told you.'

'What, forget my own husband's personal prophecy from the God?' she said. 'What sort of a slut do you take me for?'

'But you said I was making it all up.'

'And so you were,' she said indulgently. 'But the fact remains that you aren't allowed to die until anchovies are three drachmas a quart. It's your sacred duty.'

'He didn't say I wasn't going to die till then,' I answered. 'Only that that's when I'd see him next.'

Phaedra got up, kissed me, and went over to the fire. 'Well argued,' she said. 'We'll make a lawyer of you yet.'

That night, I couldn't sleep. Now you will say that was soup followed by anchovies, but honestly, that wasn't all. Phaedra's little trick had impressed me, for I had forgotten that inconsistent prophecy. So perhaps it was just my imagination after all, said my soul, and it tried to go to sleep. But, I replied, you'd need to have a pretty twisted imagination to think anchovies could ever be three drachmas a quart.

My soul, which has no sense of humour, made no reply and left me to my own devices. But as I lay there, half asleep and half awake, I suddenly realised what my clever idea had been; the one that was my only hope. I prodded Phaedra in the back and said, 'Wake up.'

'Not tonight,' Phaedra replied sleepily. 'I've got indigestion.'

'It was your idea to have anchovies.'

'You know perfectly well why we had anchovies. Go to sleep.'

'Phaedra,' I said, 'I've had an idea. Listen to this.'

CHAPTER TWELVE

They aren't terribly fashionable right now; but I have always had a weakness for Theban jokes. Possibly my favourite example of the genre is the one about the Theban who was riding to market on his donkey one day when he passed under a pear tree and saw a particularly ripe and luscious pear dangling only inches from his nose. He loosed the reins and reached up for it with both hands, at precisely the moment when his donkey was stung by a gadfly. The donkey started violently, sending the Theban sailing up in the air and into the branches of the tree, where his head and shoulders became so entangled in the general growth that he was left dangling there helplessly while his donkey recovered its composure and went on its way. There the Theban remained for the best part of the morning, until a traveller came along the road and saw him, inexplicably suspended like an enormous pear.

'For God's sake,' said the traveller, 'how did you manage to get up there?'

'How do you think?' replied the Theban. 'I fell off my donkey.'

And that, so to speak, was how I found myself in grave danger of losing my life on a charge of blasphemous treason. My position, like the Theban's, was decidedly uncomfortable, and there was no way I could comprehensibly explain how I had got there, even to Phaedra, who had heard my account of it all. You can understand, therefore, that all my other friends and acquaintances found it completely inexplicable; and, since they could not understand and I could not explain how I had got up there in the first place, they made no great effort to get me down. The eminent men I had cultivated for use in just such an emergency were either dead or out of town when I called to canvass support, and when I happened to meet them in the street on my way home from calling at their houses they disappeared like dreams at daybreak. As for witnesses, I couldn't think of a single person whose testimony might be useful to me, so I made no effort to find any.

For those of you with a morbid fascination with details, I suppose I must now set down what happened in all the stages in my trial. I've already told you about my summons; well, because of the pressure of business before the Courts, there was an unusually long interval between the summons and the appearance before the magistrate. Since this was a religious matter, the relevant official was the King Archon. For those of you who don't remember the democracy, there were three Archons – the King Archon, the Archon of the Year and the Polemarch – and they each had clearly defined legal jurisdictions, the precise natures of which I have either forgotten or never knew in the first place. Because the King Archon dealt with treason and political offences, he was one of the busiest men in Athens; but eventually the day arrived, and I duly presented myself, suitably awed, at his office. As I had expected, there was no loophole to be found in the indictment; Demeas was far too experienced at this sort of thing. He had applied to the proper magistrate at the right time of year in the proper form, and the action was properly based. So we each paid our drachma fee, and the indictment was neatly inscribed on a white tablet and hung up outside the Archon's office. We were then told when the second interlocutory would be held, and went home again, having wasted a whole day and nothing in particular to show for it. If you ask me, all these procedural steps make a farce of our legal system.

At the second hearing, as you know perfectly well, the plaintiff and the defendant have to set out the grounds on which they will prosecute and defend the case. Now I didn't want to show my hand, mainly because I had only a vague notion of what I was going to do, and I felt rather nervous about this hearing. I was tempted to try pleading No Case To Answer, just so as to avoid giving a proper defence, but cleverness of this sort, which we Athenians love, can often end in disaster, so I decided not to try it. The last thing I wanted to happen was for my defence to be struck out and judgement in default of defence to be entered against me.

There are five classes of evidence for this hearing – Laws, Witnesses, Witness Statements, Oaths and Tortures – and Demeas had them all. He turned up on the appointed day with three slaves laden down with documents, and a small army of witnesses. I had a rather battered old copy of the Laws of Solon which I had borrowed from a friend, and that was it; no witnesses, no statements, nothing. When it was my turn to present my evidence, I said that I had none; my defence would be one of mistaken identity, and since my wife was not competent to testify (being female) I had no one to swear an oath that I had been in bed all that night. The Archon, who was clearly bemused at this lack of preparation, gave the warning about penalties for withdrawal of prosecution and fixed a date for the trial itself. Demeas' evidence was sealed up in a huge casket, and the hearing ended. I remember the expression on Demeas' face; he was obviously puzzled too. Had I given up all hope, he wondered, or was I up to something? The answer, of course, was both, and therefore all I had to do to keep him mystified was to look inscrutable and only speak when somebody asked me a question.

Aristophanes was there, of course, and his demeanour throughout was rather amusing. He was acting the part of a public-spirited citizen who was doing his painful duty, and apart from making a formal denial of his allegations I let him get on with it. His account of what happened that night ran as follows: he had been walking home after a farewell party for a friend of his; he couldn't produce witnesses for this, since the friend and the other people at the party had conveniently died in Sicily. He had been passing my house when he saw me and a group of others whom he didn't recognise smashing up the statues with swords and calling on Hecate to confound the Sicilian Expedition. He tried to remonstrate with me, but I threatened to kill him and he fled. He had not brought this evidence forward until now since we had been in the War together and he had saved my life on a number of occasions; but Demeas had convinced him that it was his duty to the City to say what he knew.

Apart from him, I didn't recognise any of the other witnesses who swore that they had seen me that night. Since an Athenian jury loves the evidence of slaves extracted by torture (they enjoy hearing about the red-hot irons and so forth), Demeas had borrowed a job lot of broken-down old Thracians and Syrians from a friend of his who had a silver-mining concession, and these specimens were particularly eloquent for men who knew very little Greek. I think they had rather enjoyed being tortured, as a change from working in the mines; anyway, they had been so well rehearsed in their lines that they almost convinced me that they were telling the truth. And yet I am usually a very sceptical man, and find it hard to credit that a slave is more likely to give truthful evidence simply because a public official has been beating him up. A slave is like any other witness; either you believe him or you don't. But Solon (or whoever it was) has ordained that a slave can't testify unless he's been hung upside down and flogged within an inch of his life, and I suppose you can't pick and choose which of Solon's laws you're going to adopt. If you want the intelligent laws about wills and intestate succession, you have to put up with the code of evidence and hope that when it comes to your case, the slave in question will take the same reasonable view.

When I got home, Phaedra had a bowl of spiced wine and a basket of wheat bread waiting for me, and I peeled off my sandals and collapsed in front of the fire. I didn't want to talk, and so she didn't ask me what had happened; there was no point, since if there had been anything to report I would have told her as soon as I came through the door. Instead, we sat and looked at each other in silence for a while.

'Well?' Phaedra said at last. 'You're going through with it?'

'Yes,' I said. 'As far as I can see, it's the only real chance.'

She breathed in deeply and shook her head. 'It's your life,' she said. 'You know what I think about it.'

'Thank you very much,' I said irritably. 'You really know how to give a man confidence.'

'You asked me what I thought of the idea,' she replied, 'and I gave you my honest opinion. What did you want me to do, say it was brilliant and let you get on with it?'

'It's too late to change it now,' I said firmly. 'Once you start trying to amend pleadings, you might as well hang yourself and save the State the jury pay. And there was never any point in trying to make a case out of perjured witnesses and the like; that's Demeas' trade, and he's better at it than me.'

'I suppose so,' she said reluctantly. 'I mean, in theory it's a good idea. It's just putting it into practice that strikes me as dangerous. There's so many what-ifs.'

'Not nearly so many as there would have been if I'd tried to do it the other way,' I replied. 'This way, there's just one big what-if; what if they don't like it? And I've been dealing with that in the Theatre all my life.'

She shrugged. 'Anyway,' she said, 'like you said, it's too late now. Don't worry, I'm not going to go all sulky on you now.'

I leaned over and took her hand. 'That's a good girl,' I said.

'I hate that expression,' she said. 'Patronising, don't you think? As if I was about twelve years old and I'd just managed to make the soup without burning it. Tired?'

'Very.'

'Then eat your bread and get an early night. You've got work to do tomorrow.' She got up and poured me a cup of the spiced wine. 'Don't sit up all night, you won't be able to think properly.'

After she had gone to bed, I sat there in the dark and tried to get an opening line for my speech. I always believe that if you can get an opening line – for anything: chorus, speech, lyric, whatever – the rest will follow of its own accord. Now the beginning of a defence speech is crucial and very difficult to get right; in fact, the beginning is matched in complexity and importance only by the middle and the end. But try as I might, I couldn't get the form of words I wanted; it was either too colloquial or too formal, and I couldn't picture myself standing up in Court and actually saying it. Then the answer suddenly came to me. My problem was that I was trying to compose prose, which was something I had never tried before. All I had to do was compose it in verse and then say it like prose, and perhaps mess about with some of the words to stop it sounding too much like verse when I said it. As soon as I tried doing that, it started to flow like water from a spring. I had just rounded the thing off to my entire satisfaction when Phaedra came stumbling out of the inner room.

'For God's sake,' she yawned, 'it's the middle of the night. Leave it.'

'It's all right,' I said, 'I've got it. Go to bed, I'll be through in a moment.'

She blinked. 'You've got it?' she said. 'What do you mean?'

'My speech,' I replied impatiently. 'It's finished.'

'Oh.' She frowned. 'Just like that?'

'Yes.'

'Is it any good?'

'Do you want to hear it?'

'No.' She yawned again. 'I mean, if it's good now, it'll still be good in the morning.'

I had expected a little more enthusiasm, but I could see she was tired. 'All right then,' I said, 'I'm coming.'

'Good,' she replied.

I know it's a classic; but I don't like the *Odyssey*. In particular, I don't like the opening. Now I know it's all very clever, the way Homer keeps back the first appearance of Odysseus until the poem is well under way; this is designed to create suspense and intrigue the reader. But I can't be doing with suspense. My attention lapses. I start thinking of something else. Then, when I rejoin the poem or the play or whatever it is, I find I've missed an important bit and can't get back into it. So I won't try and build up the tension any more, although it would be easy enough to do; instead, we'll go forward to the day of the trial itself.

We left the house just before dawn and walked slowly down towards the Court. On the way, I bumped into a friend of mine called Leagoras, a neighbour at Pallene. He asked where I was going, and I told him that I was on my way to stand my trial. He asked what the charge was, and when I told him he was most surprised, and said that, since he had no business in the City that day that could not wait, he would come with me, and take a message back to Pallene when he went home should that be necessary. I thanked him, and we went on together to the Odeon.

The first case of the day was just starting, and we sat down on the benches outside to wait. It had turned out a sunny, drowsy sort of a day, the kind of day I love to spend in the country, when there is not much that needs doing. It was hard to make my mind work properly, and both Phaedra and Leagoras were no help at all; Phaedra didn't want to talk, and Leagoras was full of the news from Pallene – whose vines were doing well, who was suing who for trespass and moving boundary-stones, who had got whose daughter pregnant and so on; and although as a general rule I like listening to this sort of gossip, at least when I'm in the City, I couldn't give it the attention it needed if I was to take an interest in it. To tell you the truth, my mind was as nearly blank as it ever can be (for I am a restless man by nature) and I felt a great wave of lassitude creeping up from my feet and infiltrating every part of me. Very soon, I knew, I would fall asleep; and falling asleep in the sun does me no good at all. I wake up with a sore neck and a headache, which I generally don't lose until nightfall. This of course was the worst possible thing that could happen to a man who is about to stand his trial, with the exception of toothache or diarrhoea, and I was on the point of getting up and going for a walk to wake myself up when I saw a familiar figure walking up the street towards me.

It was no surprise to see Socrates the son of Sophroniscus hanging about the Law Courts; although he fervently denies it, he can generally be found some-where in the neighbourhood of a good, juicy trial. He is not, strictly speaking, one of the speech-writers, like Python; but he makes a lot of money from what he calls his thinking lessons, which are little more than pre-paratory courses for litigants, and is always on the lookout for new clients. Since the disgrace and exile of his most prestigious pupil, the celebrated Alcibiades, business had been rather slack, and I hadn't heard his name quite so often in the Market Square or the Baths.

Phaedra and Leagoras obviously wanted to avoid him, for they tried to snuggle down inside their clothes and disappear; but I regarded Socrates' arrival as an omen from the Gods, like an eagle or an owl flying over my head. So I called out and waved to him; and sure enough he came bounding over, like a hungry dog who hears the sound of a plate on the kitchen floor.

'Good morning, Eupolis,' he said through one of those enormous grins of his. 'You're rather out of your way here, aren't you? Shouldn't you be down in the Market Square, nosing out some bits of gossip for a play?'

I smiled in such a way as to communicate lack of amusement. 'And shouldn't you be at the Lyceum?' I replied. 'You don't want to lose your pitch if there are gullible young men about, with money in their pockets.'

Socrates laughed, displaying his fine collection of yellow teeth. He never cleans them, even when he eats onions and garlic, since he purports to regard such practices as effete and not worthy of an ascetic. For an ascetic though, he's merciless on stuffed quails. 'You know better than that, son of Euchorus,' he said. 'You'll get me into trouble, saying things like that. You've been watching too many of your own plays.'

'Are you busy?' I asked, making room for him on the bench. 'I have an hour or so to kill, waiting for my case to come on, and I know you're always ready for a chat.'

'I certainly am,' he replied. 'Free of charge, seeing it's you. Only you must promise not to pirate any of my material in your lawsuit. Are you prosecuting or defending?'

'Defending,' I replied.

He nodded. 'A serious charge?'

'Fairly serious,' I replied. 'They say I was one of the men who damaged the statues.'

Socrates raised his eyebrows. 'Is that so?' he said, and sat down next to me. 'And did you?'

'No,' I said. 'I was in bed at the time with my wife here. But of course she can't give evidence, being a woman, and I can produce no one else who saw me. And that's a point that intrigues me, Socrates. Perhaps you and I could clarify it between us, if you have nothing better to do. Why is it that a woman should be forbidden to give evidence in a court of law, when men and even slaves, if tortured, are acceptable as witnesses?' I scratched my nose, then continued. 'After all, they have the same five senses as we do, and minds just like men. We listen to the evidence of men with doubtful characters, don't we, and trust ourselves to be able to assess its weight. Why can't we accept the evidence of women?'

Socrates leaned back in his seat, with his hands clasped around his left knee. 'So you are saying that there is no difference between men and women?'

'Certainly there is a difference,' I replied, 'just as there's a difference between Greeks and foreigners, and Athenians and other Greeks. But this difference doesn't make such a great difference that we should refuse to accept anything they say as the truth. I mean, when you ask your wife what's for dinner and she says dried fish, you believe her, don't you?'

'Yes,' said Socrates, settling himself more comfortably in his seat. 'Invariably.'

'And when you ask her what she did while you were out and she says she mended the hole in your tunic, you take her word, don't you? In the absence of contrary evidence, such as the smell of wine on her breath, or the bedclothes being ruffled up?'

'Indeed I do, Eupolis.'

'And yet,' I said, 'Xanthippe isn't an unnaturally

truthful woman, is she? She's not under some curse, like that woman in the old story who cheated Apollo and was cursed with the inability to lie?'

'She's the same as other women in that respect,' said Socrates, plainly wondering where all this was leading. 'I couldn't say for sure.'

'But if there was a prosecution and she was a witness, she couldn't give evidence,' I said. 'Tell me why that is, I'd like to know. Then I might be able to persuade the Court to let Phaedra testify, and perhaps I wouldn't have to die after all.'

Socrates furrowed his brow for a moment. 'What is the difference, would you say,' he said, 'between women and men? The main difference, I mean, not just the obvious anatomical differences. We can take those for granted.'

It was my turn to frown. 'I suppose,' I said, 'it's that women stay in the house all day while men go out to work in the fields.'

'Exactly,' said Socrates, and he let go of his knee and sat upright. 'Now, have you ever seen a rabbit?'

'Often, Socrates, often.'

'And aren't rabbits hard to see, because of their grey fur?'

'Well,' I said, 'it's not easy to see them, unless you know what to look for.'

'And the first time you saw a rabbit,' Socrates continued, 'did you identify it for yourself, or did someone point it out to you?'

'I'm not sure,' I replied, thinking hard for a moment. 'I believe someone said, "Look, there's a rabbit" and I said, "Where?" and he pointed, and I saw it.'

'So he saw the rabbit first, and showed you what to look for?'

'As far as I can remember, yes.'

'And you had been looking in that direction,' said Socrates, 'and saw the same things as he did, but because you didn't know how to pick out a rabbit against a background of grey rocks, you hadn't identified it as a rabbit?'

'That's pretty much what happened,' I said, folding my arms in front of me, 'so far as I can recall. It was a long time ago, you understand.'

'Oh, of course,' said Socrates. 'Now, supposing you had never had a friend who knew what a rabbit looked like, do you suppose it's possible that you could have gone through life looking at stone outcrops and never known that there were rabbits all around you?'

'Perfectly possible,' I said, and scratched my ear.

'Or take speedwell,' Socrates went on. 'You know what speedwell looks like, of course.'

'I should say I do, Socrates,' I replied. 'I was brought up in the mountains, you know. It has a long, thin stalk and blue flowers.'

'But if no one had ever told you what it was,' said Socrates, looking me straight in the eye, 'if you had been abandoned on the hillside at birth and brought up by wolves, like the child in the story, you wouldn't know that the blue flower was speedwell, would you?'

'Come to think of it,' I replied, 'I don't suppose I would.'

'Now let us suppose you are walking in the hills and you look up at the sky and see black clouds. What would you expect?'

I knew the answer to that. 'Rain,' I replied.

'And why precisely would you expect rain? Because someone had told you that it rains from black clouds?'

'Yes indeed.'

'Or perhaps you found it out for yourself, by experience,' said Socrates, leaning his chin thoughtfully on the back of his hand. 'You worked out that every storm of rain you could remember was preceded by black clouds, and your mind, being rational, rejected the explanation that this was a mere coincidence.'

I nodded profoundly. 'That's what a rational mind would do,' I agreed.

'Well then,' said Socrates brightly, 'now that we've established these preliminary points, we can return to your original enquiry, about women and the Courts. Suppose there was a lawsuit, and it was vital to the evidence whether there had been a rabbit, or a sprig of speedwell, in a particular place. Would a person who couldn't identify a rabbit at sight or tell speedwell from soldanella be able to give good evidence?'

'I suppose not.'

'Exactly,' said Socrates, grinning. 'There might well have been a rabbit or a speedwell plant there, but this person would have looked straight at it and not recognised it, and would in all honesty tell the jury that he hadn't seen a rabbit or a speedwell plant. And then the jury would think that the defendant, who had just claimed there was a rabbit or a speedwell in the place in question, was a liar and not to be believed on any matter, and vote to have him put to death. Whereas if the ignorant witness had not been allowed to testify, admittedly the defendant's evidence would not be corroborated, but at least his own credit as a witness would be unimpaired. Am I right?'

'Yes indeed.'

'Now let us suppose you were in court and your defence turned on there having been a storm of rain. And imagine that, although you could find no one who had been out in the rain and thus was able to give evidence that he had got wet through, you knew that your neighbour had walked home an hour before and must have seen the dark clouds. Couldn't you expect him to testify that it had been about to rain an hour before you said it would rain, which would give at least some weight to your account of events?'

'Most certainly.'

'But supposing that your neighbour had spent all his

life in one of those hot countries south of the Ethiopians where it never rains, and so had not made the mental connection between dark clouds and rain. Would his evidence be any use to you? Or would it be potentially dangerous, like the evidence of the man who couldn't recognise rabbits or speedwell?'

'Potentially dangerous, of course.'

'So we are agreed that a misleading witness is worse than no witness at all?'

'Indeed we are.'

'And that a witness who has no knowledge or experience of a thing is likely to be a misleading witness, even if he is inclined to tell the truth?'

'Absolutely.'

'And didn't we say,' said Socrates, leaning back again, 'at the very outset of our discussion, that the main difference between men and women was that men go out in the world and women stay at home; and that therefore men have knowledge and experience of the world that women inevitably lack? And isn't it true that the sort of thing that generally crops up in lawsuits as needing to be proved by evidence is exactly the sort of thing that happens out in the world, where men meet and do business and have contact with one another? The sort of thing, necessarily, that women have no knowledge or experience of, and therefore should not testify about?'

'Naturally,' I replied.

'So you agree that only men are qualified to give evidence in lawsuits, and women should be debarred?'

'I do.'

'You do realise,' said Socrates, 'that everything I've been saying up till now has been a load of old rubbish?'

'Yes, Socrates.'

'And yet you found yourself forced to agree with it?'

'Yes, Socrates.'

'Because I was talking so fast, and so fluently, and

with such an air of intelligence and authority and being about to make some intelligent point, that you didn't care to interrupt me? And by the time you had worked out that I was talking nonsense it was too late to contradict me without seeming petty or just plain stupid?'

'Exactly so.'

'Well, Eupolis my friend,' said the son of Sophroniscus, rising to his feet and brushing the dust pointedly off his backside, 'that's the one and only way to win lawsuits in this City. If you can charm them with words and bewilder them with plausible ideas, you'll be all right. If not, you'll have to accept that in the absence of divine intervention you're probably going to die, and it serves you right for not consulting a competent expert, like myself. Only I wouldn't have helped you if you'd offered me all the wealth of King Gyges, after what you said about me in those so-called Comedies of yours; and neither, I expect, would any of my fellow philosophers. Good luck, Eupolis, you need it.'

'And the same to you,' I said. 'See you around.'

'I doubt it,' said Socrates over his shoulder, and he walked happily away down the street.

'What an unpleasant man,' said Phaedra. 'He'll come to a bad end one of these days.'

'I hope so,' I said. 'But at least he kept me from falling asleep, which is more than you could do.'

'I don't see what you're complaining about,' interrupted Leagoras, who had listened to our discussion with rapt attention. 'It all seemed to make perfect sense to me.'

Phaedra and I both looked at him, and he seemed rather offended. 'Don't worry about it,' I reassured him, 'it's not your fault.'

'It certainly is not,' Phaedra agreed. 'Isn't that Aristophanes over there?'

We all looked round, and saw the son of Philip,

dressed in an unusually sombre gown and carrying a plain olive-wood walking-stick, following Demeas and his crowd of witnesses, slaves and other attendant Furies. A friend of my uncle's once told me of the mighty carvings his grandfather had seen in Sardis, when he went there as a young man; vast reliefs, stretching as far as the eye could see, showing the Great King of the Persians marching to war with all the nations of the earth in the van, and his hawks and his hounds and his gigantic royal umbrella. I suppose the Great King of Persia looked every bit as menacing to his subjects as Demeas did to me then, on his carvings at least. But Demeas achieved his effect without hawks and hounds and umbrellas. He had presence.

He seemed to look straight through me as he passed, as if I was already a hungry ghost twittering hopelessly on the wrong side of the river. But Aristophanes accidentally caught my eye, and gave me such a look of repressed hatred that I was quite startled. For a moment I wondered what was upsetting him so much; then it occurred to me that he blamed me for putting him in a position where he would have to make a public exhibition of himself, giving evidence against a Comic poet at a political trial. I could see his point; there is, even in Athens, a certain stigma attached to participating in one of these affairs, and there are still a few right-minded people in the City who disapprove. But even so, I took it rather hard that I should be blamed; it was Demeas' fault, after all. Perhaps I'm too sensitive. Anyway, I looked away until the procession had taken itself off to another part of the porch.

'Nervous?' whispered Phaedra in my ear.

'No,' I said truthfully, 'or at least not in the way you think. I feel like I'm about to send out a Chorus.'

'Oh, you,' she said. 'You're just vain, that's your trouble.'

I hadn't thought of that. 'Perhaps you're right,' I said.

'Or perhaps I just can't take this sort of thing seriously. There's Socrates back again, look; I expect he's going to listen to the trial.'

'You ought to charge him a drachma,' said Phaedra. 'He would, in your position.'

'Where I'm going,' I replied, 'I'll only need two coins, on my eyes.'

'That's the spirit,' said Phaedra, 'think positive. How are you feeling? Sick? Dizzy? Splitting headache?'

'That comes later,' I said, 'just before it's my turn to speak.'

Leagoras leaned across and said, 'Best of luck, Eupolis. If you don't make it, can I have your plough with the bronze handles?'

'If you can beat the bailiffs to it,' I replied, 'certainly you can. Tell them I borrowed it from you and forgot to give it back. Though they won't believe you. It's not in your nature to forget about a thing like that.'

Leagoras seemed offended again, and sat back in his seat. A moment or so after that, the herald came out and summoned Demeas and me into the Court. I kissed Phaedra on the cheek, quickly, and avoided her eyes; then I stood up, shook myself like a dog waking up at dinner-time, and walked towards the gate. I remember thinking that this is how my actors must feel, when the herald calls them on for the first scene.

The first thing I did when I got inside the Court was to examine the jury. I was looking for at least one familiar face – out of five hundred and one men, I must know at least one of them. But at first their faces were a sort of brown and black porridge, and they looked like a great legendary monster such as Hercules might have faced in one of his less probable adventures. Then I caught sight of a man I recognised; I couldn't think of his name, but I had seen him recently, in the Market Square or the country. He was biting a chunk off a thick black crust of barley-bread, and he had his little wine-flask, shaped like a donkey, in his left hand, ready to soak the pap in his mouth to make it soft and malleable for his few remaining teeth. I have rarely seen a less prepossessing creature. Next to him was a tiny little man, seventy if he was a day, with a few scruffy wisps of white hair on a pointed brown skull, and he was talking very rapidly to nobody at all. I knew him for one of Cleon's Dogs, the old hard-core jurymen of the Brotherhood of the Three Obols. Many of them had recently died of old age (or, some said, of grief at the death of their master) but there were still a few to be seen, walking in along the country roads before dawn to get to the Court in time to be at the head of the jury queue when their tribe was on duty. And wasn't that one of Little Zeus' brothers, huddled up under the wall in a very old cloak? I hoped it was; surely he would be for me. Then I remembered hearing that they were all dead; there had been a little resurgence of the plague in their village in the mountains, which had wiped out the entire population except for an old man and a baby. One thing at least reassured me; they looked remarkably like all the theatre audiences I have ever inspected, with that same air of relief that the Tragedies are over mixed with impatience for the Comedy to start.

Then the indictment was read out.

'Prosecution by Demeas son of Polemarchus of Cydathene against Eupolis son of Euchorus of Pallene, on the grounds of blasphemy. Penalty proposed: death. Demeas will now speak.'

The water-clock was filled up and started to run. No one who has ever heard it from the dock will forget the sound that thing makes; someone, I can't remember who, said it reminded him of a dwarf pissing into a tin bucket. I swear they designed it on purpose to put off defendants; you sit there listening to it gurgling and plinking away, and you forget all about the case that is being carefully built up around you like a wall round a besieged city. Then when your turn comes to speak you're still listening out for it, and you lose your way in the middle of your best sentence, like Theseus in the Labyrinth. I still have nightmares about it, and I wake up sweating, only to find that it's the rain trickling down off the roof, or one of the slaves skimming the milk.

Demeas started with a blistering attack. I can't remember who or what he was attacking – I don't think it was me particularly – but I could see the faces of the jurors getting grimmer and grimmer as he reminded them of this terrible injury that had been done to them. There was, I remember, a short account of the sufferings of our men in Sicily; and for someone who hadn't been there, Demeas did it very well. First the fever in the camp by the marshes; then the horror of the night on Epipolae, and the dreadful confusion and the screams of the dying; then the desperation of the battle in the harbour, and the slow misery of the march to the walled orchard. 'And of these thousands,' I remember him saying, 'so few returned to the City of the Violet Crown; what irony, men of Athens, what terrible irony that one of those apparently chosen by the God should be the sole author of all this misfortune! But I say that this was Zeus' work; he did not give this man the chance of a hero's death, but preserved him to stand his trial before you today. Witness the ease of his escape – was this not some God, my friends, leading him like a sacrifice to the altar of Justice?'

I thought of the smithy, and the cart with the olive-jar, and giggled. Unfortunately, Demeas saw this and pointed. 'Our friend thinks it's amusing, does he?' he thundered. 'Just as he thought it amusing to smash the statues of the Gods. Does the thought of our Heavenly patrons always produce this show of levity, I wonder? Does he snigger his way through the Lady's procession, or deliberately sneeze at the moment of the sacrifice?'

I wanted to know how a man could sneeze deliberately; but that would have to wait until after the trial.

Anyway, Demeas rounded off his introductory remarks with a graphic description of the night of the mutilation of the statues, and started calling witnesses. I kept expecting Aristophanes to be called, but every time I saw the son of Philip prepare to get up from his place, Demeas called on another slave or hanger-on, and Aristophanes would settle back and fold his arms. At last, when I was beginning to think that Aristophanes wouldn't be used at all, Demeas called him and put him on the stand. There was a faint murmur of satisfaction from the jury, and most of them stopped eating or cutting their toenails. Someone woke up the little old man, and he leaned forward on his stick to be able to hear what was said. When Aristophanes had settled himself, Demeas cleared his throat and began. He asked his questions in the usual tone of voice, and Aristophanes answered loudly and clearly, with his chin up.

Demeas: Were you outside Eupolis' house on the night in question?
Aristophanes: I was.
Demeas: Were you just returning from a party in honour of some friends going to the War?
Aristophanes: I was.
Demeas: Did you see Eupolis smashing up statues with a Thracian sabre?
Aristophanes: I did.
Demeas: Was he alone or with others?
Aristophanes: With about ten others, whom I didn't recognise.
Demeas: Was Eupolis actively smashing statues, or simply watching the others?
Aristophanes: He was actively smashing the statues.
Demeas: Did you report this at the time?
Aristophanes: No.
Demeas: Were you afraid of what Eupolis would do to you if you reported it?

Aristophanes: I was.

Demeas: And were you subsequently in Sicily with Demosthenes and the army?

Aristophanes: I was.

Demeas: Did you and Eupolis escape through Sicily to Catana after the defeat, and did you repeatedly save Eupolis' life during that time?

Aristophanes: Yes.

Demeas: During the escape, did Eupolis freely confess that he had taken part in the desecration of the statues?

Aristophanes: Twice.

Demeas: Why are you now giving evidence against a man whose life you saved?

Aristophanes: Because I feel it is my duty as a citizen.

Now you can tell for yourselves, from this unusually long and detailed cross-examination, which lasted for at least a pint of Demeas' time, that he expected it to be his most telling evidence; normally, Demeas would have given a précis of this himself and just called Aristophanes to affirm it, but in this case he wanted to drag it out for as long as possible, to get the maximum value out of it. He was right to do so, for the jury simply lapped it up. I have never seen such attention to a cross-examination in my life. Dramatically speaking, it was shrewdly done. I speak as a professional; if you can get away with doing something in a new and shocking way, it makes a much greater impression; and in something like a trial, if you can lodge something in the jury's mind they are likely to believe it, even if you offer nothing in support.

The rest of his evidence Demeas called in the usual way, by depositions, and then he had the law read and set about winding up his case. I shall always remember what he said.

'Men of Athens,' he started off, 'ask yourselves this. What is a citizen? What does it mean to be a citizen of this City, to walk in our streets, vote in our Assembly, worship in our temples, serve in our army? What is our part in this great enterprise we call Athens? It is a man's duty to work for his city, and not to work against it. Look around this City of ours. Look at the Long Walls, which Themistocles built to protect our corn supply in time of war, to link us for ever with the sea. Look at the Council House which Solon built, to house our democracy. Look at the Nine Fountains which Pisistratus and his heirs built, to bring water into the City and defeat drought and pestilence. Look at the Walls, which our forefathers built to keep out the Persians. Look at the Acropolis, which Pericles built to be our crown and our citadel. Look at all these things, which will stand for ever, and think of the men who caused them to be. They will be remembered; yet they did no more than their duty, which is, as I have said, to work for their City. And now look at the empty streets that used to bustle with young men, and the empty houses where so many citizens lived who are now dead, buried in unmarked graves on the island of Sicily. Think who caused this desolation, and remember him; the man who brought about the destruction of our army and our fleet by his terrible blasphemy. That is a man who did not do his duty, a man who did the very opposite of his duty, by working against his City. And now prepare to do your duty, men of Athens, by voting for his condemnation and execution.'

Now that was meant to be the end of Demeas' speech; and it would have made a good finale, and perhaps cost me my life. But as it happened, Demeas had been speaking rather quickly, and so he had come to the end of his prepared material rather earlier than he had anticipated. As soon as he stopped speaking, the water-clock made one of its characteristic noises, rather like a gurgling belch, as if to tell the jury that this particular speaker was giving them short measure, and Demeas realised that he was faced with a slight problem. You see, in those days it was regarded as the mark of a good speaker that he could exactly fill up his allotted time, uttering his last syllable precisely when the last drop of water hit the bowl; and conversely, a man who finished early was regarded as being no good and therefore a liar. After all his experience of the Courts, Demeas knew just by the sound of the water-clock how much was left in it, and so started improvising a little coda to fill in the excess time. Now when I say that he improvised, I am exaggerating slightly; all practised orators are familiar with the problem, and have little timed pieces, relevant to any theme, which will last a pint or a pint and a half, or whatever the time is that they have to fill in. They have to keep changing them, of course, for fear that the jury will recognise something they've heard before and start throwing olive-stones, but generally speaking these codas are traditional in form and substance; and an orator is often judged, by the *cognoscenti*, on the quality of these set pieces. It is argued that you can't properly judge an orator's talent by his actual speech, since he may have a really awful case to present (which hinders him) or an absolutely marvellous one (which gives him an unfair advantage). But the coda is more or less standard, and is marked partly on its content and presentation, and partly on the skill with which the orator makes it relevant to the prosecution in progress.

Demeas, then, hesitated for a split second and then launched into his coda. This went as follows:

'Only one thing remains to be said, men of Athens; and, at the risk of telling you what you already know well enough, I will remind you of just why this crime is so terrible, and, more particularly, why punishing it is so important. This crime is a crime against the City, and any crime against the City, as opposed to a crime against an individual citizen, is of course an attack on democracy itself. Democracy is a joining-together of people; rather like a marriage except that in a democracy all the partici-pants are equal. In a democracy, no individual has authority over another, because the State has authority over all. In a democracy, every man has liberty because he deliberately subordinates himself to the good of the whole, which we call the State. Now when one citizen separates himself from the whole, either actively by committing a crime against the State, or even passively, merely by being in some way different, he loses his identity as a member of that State. He loses his purpose, his function, his reason for existing. It is as if he is already dead. That is why exile is such a terrible punishment – some say greater than actual execution. Such a person is like a hand cut off from the body; the blood of communal existence no longer flows through the severed organ, and it becomes little more than a piece of meat for the dogs to chew on. We as Athenians, living in the world's only true democracy, are in truth ten thousand bodies with one common soul.

'So when one of us separates himself from the whole, not only does that person damage himself irreparably, but he offends against us and so deserves the most severe punishment. He has offended against our unity; he has, so to speak, removed a stone from the walls of Athens, and the removal of one stone can cause the collapse of the whole wall. When a man ceases to be in all respects an Athenian, he cannot be permitted to live in Athens, or indeed to live at all. If a man starts to grow in the wrong direction, he must be pruned off before he starts to warp and misdirect those around him. This is because in a democracy there must be consensus.

'Now in the case of this despicable man, who has done his best to bring about the maximum possible harm to his city, it is an easy matter to see where the best interests of the City lie. But that is not the point I am addressing myself to. I am concerned that, because this man is a Comic poet – and a good one, let me add – and has given many of you much pleasure with his witty words and spectacular Choruses, some of you may say to yourselves,

"Eupolis has done wrong, and will be punished; my fellow jurors will see to that. But after all, this is a secret ballot; nobody will ever know which urn I myself put my pebble into. I think I'll vote for his acquittal; after all, he did write *Maricas*." Now that seems like an innocent whimsy, and no doubt a few of you were considering doing just that. Think again. In a democracy, not only those who do wrong and those who conspire with them or aid and comfort them are guilty and must be punished; but also those who spare them for private or individual reasons. Because this is a democracy, built on consensus and fortified with unity, we cannot allow ourselves the luxury of personal motives. If I was on your jury and my own father was in the dock and was guilty of a crime against Athens, I would have to vote against him, though all the Furies in Hell haunted me for the rest of my life. That is the great burden of living in a democracy; we must all fit the mould, or be cast aside as useless and dangerous. I say again: anyone who votes for acquittal will be as guilty as if he had done the crime himself. So vote, as I know you will, for conviction and death; only by doing so can we, as a city, lift from our shoulders the miasma of this man's blasphemy.'

As soon as he stopped speaking, the water-clock gurgled for the last time, and the Court was absolutely silent. I wish I could capture for you the look of pleasure on the faces of those jurors. This was good, old-fashioned stuff, but spiced with those little touches of novelty that excite the palate. Each man turned to his neighbour and nodded, and I almost expected them to stand up as a Chorus and start singing the anapaests. But if I had prayed to Zeus and Dionysus and Pan, god of shepherds and confusion, and my prayers had been answered, I could not have asked for a more helpful speech. It fitted exactly what I had prepared, and only a few minor adjustments would be necessary to the speech I was carrying, like an eight-months-pregnant woman, in my mind. As the herald called out my name and told me to state my case, I felt the weight of fear slipping off my shoulders, as if I was a man who couldn't afford a mule laying down a heavy basket of olives I had carried into town from the country. I stood up, waited for the clock to be refilled, and started to speak.

CHAPTER THIRTEEN

'In all my years of attending debates,' I said, 'I don't know when I've enjoyed a speech more than the one Demeas has just made. It had the lot, didn't it? It had structure, pace, style and diversity; the only trick he missed was having a couple of slaves walking up and down handing out free hazelnuts. As soon as he had exhausted one theme, he switched straight to the next; but you didn't notice that he'd changed tack, so skilfully did he make the transition. It just seemed to flow, like the streams in the mountains when the ice melts in spring. In fact, I admire his speech so much that I can't bring myself to answer it; that would be a worse desecration of the beautiful and holy than the one I stand accused of. So I won't even try. Not a word about Demeas' speech.

'But I don't want to cheat you of your entertainment. Three obols isn't much for sitting on those cold, hard benches all day, especially for you older men, and you have a right to be diverted by some fancy speaking. So I'll make my defence quickly, and then fill up the rest of my time with some jokes or a song or something.

'Now we're all grown men here, and we know the score. I'm not talking to a party of colonials just off a wheat-ship, who think the Propylaea is a ship, or the Council Chamber is a wine shop. You know and I know that Demeas is prosecuting me because he needs the money, and Aristophanes has given evidence against me partly because he's an ungrateful arsehole and partly because he's scared shitless of Demeas, and all the other witnesses are hired by the day for a drachma down and two bushels of figs later. We also know that you're going to convict me because you want blood after Sicily, and because Demosthenes and Nicias got themselves killed before you could impeach them. Everyone here today, with the possible exception of the red-haired man in the second row from the back who hasn't got the common decency to stop eating while I'm talking for my life, also knows that my only hope of getting out of this in one piece is to give you one hell of a good speech, so that you'll let me go to show everyone how cultured and intelligent you are. And then you'll pick on some other poor sod who can't make jokes or think up fancy phrases, and glut your blood-lust on him. That's what we call a democracy, men of Athens.

'A democracy is a pack of wolves without a permanent leader. When there are plenty of sheep about, everything's well, and they congratulate themselves on how beautifully the wolf-democracy works, and maybe vote themselves all an extra hour's sleep at the new moon. But when they've eaten all the sheep, and the shepherds have banded together to hunt them out of their nests with dogs and nets, they start turning on each other and eating the fattest and the weakest. Then they find out that the wolf-democracy isn't quite what they thought it was; there's still this mystical Whole that Demeas has told us about, but the Whole consists of those wolves who haven't yet had their number called. The hunger continues, of course, and so does the democratic process. You can have a democratic process right up to the point when there are only three wolves left, and two of them can outvote the third and eat him. Then you only have two, and that's an oligarchy.

'Now this would all be perfectly laudable, if only you got something out of the democratic process, beyond satisfying your perverted craving for human blood. But you see, where the wolf image breaks down is that you don't actually get to eat your victims; you don't derive any benefit from killing them. The only people who gain are men like Demeas here, who get the informer's share of the proceeds of sale. Now you will say to me, "Eupolis, you're wrong, as usual. All your considerable wealth will be confiscated and the proceeds will go to the public purse. We've fattened you up, and now we're going to kill you." Mathematically speaking, yes, you're right. The cost of this trial is – let me see now, five hundred and one jurors at three obols a day comes to a touch under two hundred and fifty-one drachmas. The public purse will get far more out of my carcase than that, even when Demeas has had his share. As a method of raising revenue for the public purse, judicial murder beats harbour dues into a three-legged stool.

'But what makes you think that any of that money will be used to benefit you? If my wealth were divided up, so many drachmas a man, that would, I concede, be fair and equitable. But it won't be; it'll all be frittered away on the War, or public buildings, or ambassadors' wages, or hiring mercenaries, or any one of the hundreds of ways in which a community of people such as yourselves can dissipate money which they no longer regard as their own. And what benefit will you derive from that, may I ask? Don't bother thinking, I'll tell you. None. You won't get it, Athens will get it. And what's this thing we call Athens? I'll tell you. It's an enormous misunderstanding, self-perpetuating and carried on with in the hope that one day it'll sort itself out.

'It started like this. Once upon a time, long, long ago, when the world was young and people had to earn an honest living, before the Law Courts were invented, three shepherds met together in what is now the Market

Square. There was a fig tree growing there, and they sheltered under its branches from the sun. But one day the fig tree died, and so the shepherds, who had grown used to meeting in that place, piled up a few rocks and bits of wood to create an artificial shade for themselves and their flocks.

'After a while, other shepherds in the area started dropping by to take shelter under this pile of rocks, and soon there was no room for all of them. So the pile was made bigger; and the bigger it got, the more people came to take advantage of it. The pile of rocks became a recognised place to meet people, trade, and discuss the season's prospects. The next thing that happened was that the pile of rocks had become a market, and a man (I can't remember his name offhand; you'd better ask Herodotus) built a house there so that he could be near the market when it opened in the morning. The next thing anybody knew, there was a little village, and the village became a town, and the town became a city. The trouble was that so many people lived in the area that there was no longer any grass for their sheep to eat, and soon all the people were looking as thin as Peison the painter. So they stopped herding sheep and started growing barley. But you can't grow barley unless you know which bit of land is yours and which bit belongs to someone else, so they had to invent property; and once you've got property you have to have laws, so laws came next. Of course, this brought them into conflict with all the people who didn't live in the City, whose land they started taking in (because there wasn't enough to go round) and therefore it became necessary to invent war.

'And so, one by one, all these things like war and law and property started appearing out of nowhere, like long-lost relatives when a will is being challenged; and soon there were dockyards and archons and taxes and prosecutions for illegal legislation and informers and politicians and street-fights and ostracism and philosophers and plague and mortgages on redemption and oratory and boundary-stones and policemen and hectemorage and hemlock and dried fish and Solon and the oligarchic tendency and the empire and silver money and figures of speech and civil war and jury-pay and the market commissioners and the Theatre and ambassadors and red ropes for Assembly and all those wonderful ingredients which go to make the boiled stew we call the Athenian democracy. And nobody could remember where they had all come from or what in hell they were there for, and nobody wanted them or knew how to cope with them; and so a commission of wise men was set up, under the chairmanship of the King Archon, to decide what to do next.

'Well, they sat and talked and argued and took votes and prosecuted one another, but in the end they had to admit to each other that they were no nearer the truth of it all than they had been when they started. The more they thought about it, the more difficult the problem became, and soon there was talk of packing the whole thing in and emigrating *en bloc* to Sardinia.

'But, just as the Commission was on the point of coming to blows yet again, someone came up with a wonderful idea. Again, I can't remember his name, but I'm sure you know who I mean. Anyway, this gifted individual realised that all the Commission had to do to avoid being impeached and condemned to death for failing to execute its task was to claim that there was a huge conspiracy going on, prosecute a few unpopular people, and simultaneously declare war on Sparta.

'Of course it worked like a charm, and we've been following the same recipe, with subtle variations, ever since. This conspiracy about the statues, men of Athens, is nothing new; it's the same conspiracy they were wetting themselves about when my grandfather's grandfather was herding goats on Parnes. The conspirators change, sure, but the conspiracy goes on. It's aimed at the overthrow of true democracy in Attica and it's such a huge conspiracy that every single one of you is involved in it. It's a conspiracy by the people to enslave the people, and we call it Athens.

'Please don't think I'm advocating any other system of government. It's inhuman to expect a man to obey the orders of another man, be that man a king or a dictator or an oligarch or an aristocrat or a rich man or a soldier. Just imagine what it would be like if Athens was ruled by a dictator, as it was in Pisistratus' time, when they built the Nine Fountains and opened the silver mines and planted out the waste land with olives. There would be taxes, and restrictions on freedom of speech, and endless wars, and trumped-up political prosecutions, and all that sort of thing. Admittedly, we have all those already under our democratic system, but at least we know that they're democratically instituted. Like the Theban soldiers that time, when they were fighting a night-battle, and one lot of Thebans started shooting arrows at random and hitting their own men. And the men on the receiving end of the arrows were greatly distressed and didn't know what to do, until one perceptive man pulled the arrow out of his friend's belly and looked at the feathers in the flight and smiled with relief and said, "Don't worry, mate, it's one of ours."

'There is, after all, a sort of horrible Socratic logic about what you – I mean we – are doing to each other, or do I mean ourselves? The facts: the Athenians have got themselves into a terrible mess. The necessary course of action: someone must be punished. Therefore Athenians must be punished. Therefore we must punish some Athenians. I can do that sort of thing for ever. You know what I mean: if you have not lost something, you must still have it. You have not lost horns. Therefore you still have horns. There is a horse: you do not own it. There is a horse you do not own. Therefore you do not own a horse. If a man is in Megara he is not in Athens. There is a man in Megara. Therefore there is not a man in Athens.

Somebody must be punished. Eupolis is somebody. Therefore Eupolis must be punished. Water will travel uphill, if you put it in a jar and carry it.

'Stick to the point, son of Euchorus, and don't try to be clever with us. But men of Athens, what do you want from me? Why have you put me here, who never did anything but write you plays, bite your enemies and fight the Sicilians for you? Don't be a fool, Eupolis, you know what we want from you. We want blood and Comedy, and not necessarily in that order.

'So how would it be if I told you what a democracy is, and then you tell me whether a man who seeks to over-throw it, as Demeas says I do, deserves to die or to be honoured with a statue, like we honour Harmodius and Aristogeiton, who killed the Dictator? Is that a suitable way to pass the time until that contraption over there finally runs dry and it's pebbles-down-the-slot time? Well, I think it is and I'm the one on trial, so if you don't like it you know what you can do.

'Democracy is a system whereby you cut off the feet of tall men so that they're the same height as everyone else, and then say that everyone is equal. Democracy is a way of saying things so that people believe what you deny and don't believe what you assert. It's a state of mind in which you'll credit any slander about a man, however incredible, but you won't believe anything good about him, even if you see him doing it with your own eyes. A democracy is a place where the reward for doing good is death by hem-lock, and the punishment for doing wrong is a pension and a statue in the square. Democracy is a system of counting where the highest common denominator is also the lowest common factor, and where two and two always make five – four, plus one extra to bribe the relevant official. A democracy is a city where the only qualification for holding power is wanting it, and the only people prepared to hold power are those who should at all costs be prevented from doing so. Democracy is where everyone can read but no one can understand; where nobody is guaranteed a square meal when he's hungry, but he can rely on a public funeral if he's killed in battle. Democracy is where everybody contributes, but nobody gets anything back. It's where a clever word at the right time can do more harm than King Xerxes' army, but where a good idea is the shortest way to prison. A democracy is a city where a Monday can be made into a Thursday by a majority vote of the citizens, and where black is white if enough people want it to be. A democracy is a way of ordering your life whereby you can't say where your next meal is coming from, but you can have the Generals executed if you're starving. Democracy is a cannibals' harvest festival, where everyone does their best to feed the hand that bites them. A democracy is a theory of logic by which everything clever is true, everything that tastes nice is good for you, everything that's somebody else's is yours, everything that's yours is liable to be confiscated. In a democracy, the impotent old men have a right to sleep with the pretty girls before the handsome young men do, and everyone has a right to pay taxes. In a democracy – only in a democracy – a man can be had up on a capital charge of which he's entirely innocent, but can, if he's really clever, get off by yelling abuse at the jury.

'At least one child has been born in Athens today. He's going to grow up a citizen of the greatest democracy the world has ever seen. If he doesn't get killed in the War or by the juries, he'll live to see the end of democracy in this city – there'll be an end to it, although it'll cost a lot of people their lives, and probably be replaced by something worse. But while it lasts, the democracy will carry on the way it's always carried on. Now you all know about the mythical monsters, with the heads of lions, the bodies of goats, the backsides of gryphons and the feet of camels, who got killed by heroes in the old days. The man who overthrows democracy in Athens will kill a monster made up as follows:

'First, it has a hundred ears, all on the left side of its head. This enables it to overhear what it's not supposed to hear, and that's what it believes. It can't hear what people tell it, but then, it wouldn't do that if it could hear it. It's got ten thousand mouths, which all speak at once and which must all be fed three times a day. They often speak with their mouths full, for example when they vote for free corn distributions, which the City can't afford but which win votes. In these mouths are many long, sharp teeth, which are like the teeth of an adder; very good for biting and killing people, but useless for digesting food and chewing over the facts. The head has no eyes but a very keen sense of smell; as a result, the monster can't see where it's going or where it's being led, can't recognise its friends or avoid its enemies; but it can smell a conspiracy at a thousand yards, when the wind is in the opposite direction.

'This remarkable head is perched on the end of an enormous neck, which is permanently bent backwards at an angle. This makes it possible for the monster to see what everyone else is doing, and to stop them doing it, but it means that the monster can't see what it's doing itself. The neck ends in a pair of broad shoulders, on to which a lot of unscrupulous individuals have tied some very heavy baskets full of their own interests. These baskets are full of warships, arrows and suits of armour, and the weight of these baskets is slowly distorting the monster's spine, so that it can no longer breathe properly, and will eventually break its neck.

'Next to the shoulders is the monster's enormous belly. All the produce of the world goes into that belly; but it has no digestive organs, so all the good things that go in through the ten thousand mouths go straight out again through the vast arse, and do nobody any good at all. Because of this, the monster has permanent indigestion, which sours its temper. Next to the belly is the most enormous arse you've ever seen, which ends in a long, straggly tail. The monster spends a lot of time standing on this tail, which means that however much energy it expends in trying to go forward, it usually stays exactly where it is.

'The immense weight of this monster is supported by two spindly little legs called the Long Walls, with razor-sharp claws on the end of them. These claws are called the Assembly and the Law Courts, and the monster uses them to catch its prey. However, because of the problems the monster has in moving about, it can never move fast enough to catch anything, and so it has only two sources of food. One is a large, rancid stew, left over from the time when a man called Cimon hunted a herd of Persians across Asia Minor, let them get away, and started catching Greeks instead. He put all the Greeks he caught into the stew, and the monster has been eating them ever since. But this stew isn't enough to keep the monster going, so to supplement its diet it carves off lumps of its own flesh and eats them. For this purpose it sometimes uses the claw called Assembly, and sometimes the claw called Law Courts. The wounds which it makes by doing this don't usually heal.

'This monster is in the middle of a long and compli-cated food-chain, which depends on it for its continued existence. For example, the monster is crawling with parasites; informers, politicians, mercenary soldiers, foreign governments and a good many fleas. There are also many scavengers who follow the monster about, picking out the undigested goodies from its shit. Among these we may number the Spartans, the Persians and most of the other Greek states – those of them who weren't put into the stew by the celebrated Cimon.

'Because of its peculiar biology – I can't say life-cycle, because this thing doesn't breed, it eats all its own children – this creature has a harmful effect on its environ-ment. For example, it poisons, tramples and lays waste good agricultural land all over the world, but particularly in Attica. It also pollutes the sea by discharging into it many hundreds of warships, which sail up and down burning cities, discouraging merchant trade, and then getting sunk by hostile nations. The smell of unburied bodies, rotting food, unjust accusations and fermenting rumours that hangs around the monster is so offensive that it reaches the noses of the Gods themselves, and from time to time they send a plague to try and kill it off, or sink its fleet, or wipe out its army. But the monster is very hard to kill by these methods, and until it eats up the last scraps of Cimon's stew or gets gangrene from its self-inflicted wounds it won't starve or die of disease. The greatest threat to its own survival is therefore itself, for the time being; but if a man were to be born who didn't believe all the terrifying stories about the monster's invincibility – a Sicilian, for example – he could kill it quite easily by feeding it a great fat cheese poisoned with lies, or by sailing up its arse with all the ships he'd captured from it during the war. And although the monster is very good at damaging things in general, it has no defensive armour except two long walls that serve it as legs and link it to the sea. Once those are broken down, the monster will no longer be able to stand up and will die of starvation, neglect and despair. Its fat will rot away, and when all the flesh has been stripped off its bones by the flocks of Peloponnesian and Asiatic crows which always circle over it, it's possible that a few hardworking Attic farmers may creep under the shade of its ribcage to build nests and try and grow some barley. But whether they'll succeed or not I couldn't say; because although nobody's worked the land around for years it may be poisoned by all the blood, silver and shit that's been soaking out of the monster's pores these last hundred years or so, and so be quite incapable of producing anything.

'There is, of course, another way of dealing with this thing. We, the men of Attica, could sacrifice the monster

to whichever of the Gods is sufficiently demoralised to
accept such an offering, cut up its carcase and divide it
up among the demes, so much fat to each one. We could
then live on this fat until our vines and olives are productive again. This system could work; it worked once
before, in Pisistratus' time. But then it took a dictator to
overcome the monster; and although he thought he'd
killed it, and could hand on the carcase to his sons to
dismember in peace, the beast wasn't actually dead at all;
it lifted its head and snapped up the dictator's sons in two
sharp little mouths called Harmodius and Aristogeiton,
and a man called Cleisthenes sewed all the bits back
together again. Besides, the dictator kept back most of
the meat for himself and his cronies. If you, men of
Athens, were to slaughter the beast and take away its
flesh to your villages in the country, that would be an end
of it, and we could all live happily ever after.

'But of course you won't do anything of the sort, will
you? No, you'll vote guilty, as you always do; then you'll
go home and sleep soundly and dream untroubled
dreams, as you always do; then you'll wake up next day
and go to Assembly, as you always do; and you'll listen to
some speech proposing that you send a fleet to conquer
the moon, as you always do; and that fleet will be
destroyed, and thirty thousand men with it, as it always
is; and then you'll execute some innocent little man
because he coughed during the Sacred Hymn, as you
always do; and then you'll wonder why the Gods hate
you worse than Styx, as you always do; and you'll execute
somebody else for making the Gods angry, as you always
do and always will, until the King of Sparta or the Great
King of Persia comes and takes all your dangerous toys
away from you. And then, when you're old and crippled,
you'll tell your grandchildren that once there was a
democracy in Athens, and in those days honey flowed
down the middle of the streets in a great sticky torrent,
and all you had to do was grab a chunk of bread and go

out and mop it up. You'll have forgotten about the informers, and the riots, and the war, and the plague, and the trials of innocent men, and the inordinate quantity of blood you could buy for three obols. Then the poets and the writers of history will say that in the Golden Age of Athens there was a democracy the like of which men shall never see again, when all men were equal and worked together selflessly for the good of the State. And what will happen then, do you suppose? Why, for ever and ever there will be fools who wish they could have a democracy as perfect as the democracy they once had in Athens in Attica, and they'll fight civil wars and kill each other and paint the walls of their cities black with their blood in the name of democracy, and liberty, and the inalienable rights of man. As they always do, men of Athens, as they always will, unless someone stands up and stops the nonsense, once and for ever.

'Once upon a time there was a dictator in Athens, and his name was Pisistratus. He seized power in a coup, and abolished democracy. He levied a tax, and with the money he paid for Attica to be planted out with vines and olives, so that in future the Athenian people would have crops to sell and would be able to buy the flour they couldn't grow for themselves. And for a while everyone was happy, and the Dictator died. And his sons succeeded him, and they tried to carry on his work; but the people of Athens had food now, and they wanted entertainment. So they grew tired of the sons of Pisistratus and wanted to get rid of them; but they were too cowardly to take up arms. And one of the Dictator's sons fancied a pretty boy called Aristogeiton; but Aristogeiton had a boyfriend called Harmodius, who was pathologically jealous. So together Harmodius and Aristogeiton murdered the Dictator's son, in a particularly cowardly way: they waited until the Festival, and hid swords in their laurel-wreaths, and when the Dictator's son went by they killed him. Then, when the dangerous work had been done for them, love of liberty burnt in the blood of the Athenian people, and they shook off the yoke of tyranny. The first thing they did was set up a statue to the celebrated Harmodius and the celebrated Aristogeiton, whom we honour today as the Tyrannicides. That is how we honour men who set us free by accident, prompted by an unworthy motive. How should we honour men whose sole purpose is to set us free?

'Well, well, the water-clock just burped at me and told me to get stuck into my closing remarks, and I haven't even begun my defence yet. So I think the only thing I can do in the time available to me is to change my plea to guilty. Yes, men of Athens, I confess. I did smash the statues, just as Demeas and Aristophanes the son of Philip say I did (although between you and me, it's pure coincidence). I smashed the statues, and I did it in a cold-blooded and calculated attempt to overthrow the democracy, because I want to be remembered as the true Harmodius, the man who set Athens free and gave her laws that are equal for all men. Because, like Harmodius, I will never wholly die, but live for ever in the Islands of the Blessed. Isn't that what the song says, men of Athens, the one song that every Athenian knows? I want you to convict me, I beg you to convict me; please, please vote guilty, so that I can become a martyr and have a statue in the Market Square and a drinking-song all of my very own. Please, please send me to the prison, where I can drink the hemlock that better men than I have drunk in far worse causes. I implore you, men of Athens, not for my sake only but for the sake of my wife and my little son, vote guilty and condemn me to death, because if you do you'll be condemning not only yourselves and your children but all the democrats in Attica, and then I will need no avenging Furies with torches and fancy cos-tumes, like an Aeschylean chorus. So cast your votes, men of Athens; vote guilty, just like Demeas said. And remember: any one of you who votes innocent is no true

Athenian but an enemy of our democracy and everything that it stands for.'

And that was my speech.

When I finished speaking, there was dead silence, and the only sound was the gurgling of the water-clock. Then everyone started muttering and shaking their heads, as if something very peculiar had just happened and nobody could decide whether it was a miracle or an abomination. The herald, who was looking very puzzled indeed, rose slowly to his feet and instructed the jury to cast their votes.

Now usually there's a stampede to get to the urns, with everyone pushing and shoving, and toes being trodden on and pebbles being dropped; but this time it seemed as if nobody wanted to be the first to vote; everyone was waiting for somebody else, and the herald lost patience and repeated the announcement. Then the old man I told you about earlier hoisted himself up on his walking-stick and hobbled over to the urns. There was a trickling sound and a faint plonk, as his pebble went down, and in his case at least there was no difficulty about knowing what his vote had been. The sound of a pebble going down a spout seemed to break the spell, and the jurors started casting their votes, until the Court was filled with the sound of falling pebbles, like rain on a flat roof.

For some reason, I wasn't a bit nervous. Don't imagine that I was in any way confident about the result; I had no clue whether my gamble had paid off or not. I had put my faith in the Comic dramatist's oldest gag, violent abuse of the audience; but I had seen that gag fall flat often enough to know that it's about as safe as a country bridge. Yet I was feeling perfectly calm, and the only way I can explain it is by saying that I didn't care, one way or the other. But it wasn't that carelessness I had felt in Sicily, or during the plague; that feeling that I was going to live for ever. I believe that at that moment I had lost that feeling at last. No, it was rather a feeling that I had done what I had set out to do; I had made the Big Joke, and I was satisfied with it and knew it was good, and it didn't actually matter all that much whether anyone laughed or not. Inside me, I was laughing, being a man who rarely laughs at jokes and never at his own jokes. This moment was, so to speak, the punch-line of my life, and I had delivered it to the best of my ability. If the audience failed to get the point, that was their fault for being stupid.

The votes were all cast now, and the counters were hard at work. They counted; and then they counted again; and then they conferred with the Archon, who told them to count a third time. And now I began to laugh out loud, because the immortal Gods were obviously joining in on my joke and adding a little touch of their own, to make it superlatively funny. Finally, the Archon was satisfied, and nodded to the herald, who cleared his throat and stood up.

'The votes cast,' he said, 'are as follows. For Guilty, two hundred and fifty votes; for Not Guilty, two hundred and fifty-one votes. The prisoner is therefore discharged.'

Stunned silence; then a gabble such as you only hear when there's been a serious accident, or someone has murdered somebody in the street. For my part, I nodded to the jury, said 'Thank you very much', and started to walk out of the Court, feeling rather subdued. But when I was nearly at the gate, a familiar figure stood up and barred my way. For a moment I panicked and looked round for a way to escape, but my soul told me not to be stupid, and I turned and faced the man. It was the lawyer Python, the one who had offered to write me a speech.

'Eupolis son of Euchorus,' he said in a loud voice, 'I hereby summon you in the presence of witnesses to answer at your trial for the sum of five drachmas, plus two obols interest at the usual rate, being the price of professional services rendered to you, and which you have failed on reasonable notice to pay. If you do not pay this just debt plus the interest aforesaid within five days of this day, I summon you to stand your trial at the Court of Debts at the old and new moon. I name Strephocles son of Xenocles and Pythias son of Conon, both of the deme of Cholleidae, as my witnesses that this summons was truly served.'

I borrowed five drachmas and two obols from someone and paid him; then I started laughing hysterically and had to be taken home.

CHAPTER FOURTEEN

If you can remember back that far, you may recall that this was supposed to be the history of my times, written so that the deeds of great men might not be wholly forgotten, or some such brilliant idea. Perhaps I'm just unendurably self-centred, because it seems to me that what I've written is the history of my life, with particular reference to me. Now you've probably read more of this sort of thing than I have, and so you'll know better than I do where a History is supposed to stop; or perhaps you've read this far in the ever-diminishing hope that sooner or later I'd break down and start recording all the speeches and battles and votes that took place during the period I've been covering – if so, I'd better tell you now that I'm not going to, and you can take the book back to my friend Dexitheus and explain that there's been a misunderstanding, and I expect he'll give you your drachma back, so long as you haven't spilt milk all over it or torn any of the rolls. But if this is going to be the history of my life, then it stands to reason that I can't possibly finish it until my life is over and I know what happened to me in the end; and then, of course, I won't be able to write about it, because I'll be dead. I know that sounds a bit Socratic, but there's a serious point in there somewhere. For all I know the great tragic events of my life, the truly worthy subjects for dramatic treatment, all lie ahead of me, so that everything I've covered so far – my part in the War, my trial and my acquittal – will all be notes in the margin, put in by the copier to explain references in the main text. But I want to believe that the Gods don't need me as a witness to any more remarkable events. For my part, I'm sick of writing this book; it's made me remember things I wish I had forgotten completely, and reminded me that I was just as much a fool in my youth as I am now.

So I was tempted when I started work this morning to make the moment of my acquittal the last scene in this drama, taking it as a good cue for the final chorus, a little dance by a soloist, and then straight off to the party. Certainly it seemed like one at the time, particularly to a man like myself who has an innate sense of dramatic structure. It seemed to me as I walked home that day that everything appeared to fit into place; all the actors had had the right amount to say, all their exits and entrances and changes of costume and mask had worked out all right in the end, every theme introduced could be justified in terms of the play's overall effect. Quite often, when I've written a play, I'm sitting there feeling complacent when the herald calls on my chorus and I suddenly think of the perfect joke or the perfect line of dialogue that would round off a scene or thatch over a gap; and then, of course, there's nothing I can do about it, and the poor thing is doomed to be incomplete for ever. But I had no such feeling that evening, when I peeled my sandals off my unusually damp feet and fell on to the couch in my own familiar house. The funny story about Eupolis of Pallene seemed to be over, and its protagonist appeared to be free to go.

But of course it didn't work out like that; it never does, and that's where your great poets go wrong. One day, I want to write a great big long epic poem about what happened to all the heroes of Troy after they finally got home, regained their thrones, hung up their shields in the rafters and settled down to do a little farming. I want to make all those tired old men jump through a few more hoops, just when they thought they could change into their old clothes and have a rest. I want to make Odysseus come out of retirement to deal with a catastrophic outbreak of sheep-blight in Ithaca, or to try and get the island's council to find the money to get the harbour properly repaired and the roads put in order. I want Menelaus to have to get up off his backside and do something about the shortage of seasonal labour in the Spartan olive-growing industry; though it may just be an excuse on his part to get out of the house and away from Helen, who has got very fat since she returned from Troy, and is always on at him to redecorate the inner room. I want Neoptolemus to wake up one morning to find that some bastard has stolen his best plough and left the gate of the sheep-fold open.

After my trial, the first thing I did, apart from getting a good night's sleep and eating far too much breakfast, was make an attempt to straighten out my affairs, which were in a dreadful state. The bulk of my movable fortune was up in Thessaly, and for all I knew had been spent by the delightful Alexander on chariot-races for the local chieftains. I had a number of disastrous mortgages and leases to try and wriggle out of somehow, and in addition quite a few inheritances to dispute – several distant relatives of mine had died in Sicily leaving no heirs, and my claim to their property was as good as anyone else's. In fact, when at last everything was sorted out and the best part of the money I had sent to Thessaly had quite remarkably been returned to me, I found I was better off than before, because of these inheritances. It only goes to show that the best way to get rich in a city like Athens is to live longer than anyone else.

But it all took time, and I couldn't count on any help or co-operation from anyone. The nature of my escape from Demeas made me an object of great suspicion in Athens for a while, and when I think about it, it was a miracle that I wasn't had up all over again on any one of a vast number of charges. After all, I had quite clearly recommended the overthrow of democracy in a public speech, and men have died just for hinting at less. But I reckon that saying it all in such an outspoken manner was such a grotesque and incredible thing to do that nobody could really believe that I had done it. And that's something I've noticed about communities such as ours; if you have courage, or what looks like courage, people don't like tangling with you. If you let them see you're afraid of them they'll have you; but if you make yourself look bigger than you are, they'll leave you in peace and pick on someone else. Nevertheless, it was obvious that I shouldn't push my luck. The best thing so far as I was concerned would be if the name Eupolis was completely forgotten, at least for a while.

Of course, this meant that anything so conspicuous as presenting a play was out of the question. Whatever I put in the anapaests, however innocuous, would be regarded as an incitement to civil war, and Demeas or someone like him would be after me like a dog after a lame hare. But this self-imposed exile from the Theatre turned out to be less of a hardship for me than I had anticipated, at least to begin with. I found that there was very little I wanted to say, and the urge to write Comedy had left me. At first I was surprised; I couldn't imagine being Eupolis and not wanting to compose verses. But it left a larger gap in my life than I had ever dreamed it would.

For example, as a general rule, when I can't get to sleep I don't count sheep or make lists of the names of cities beginning with each letter of the alphabet, as other men do; I compose speeches and choruses. When I'm working out of doors, I keep from getting bored by thrashing out anapaests. Even when I'm walking down the street, I tend to walk to an iambic rhythm, with a loud clop of the right foot for a spondee and a little pause to mark the caesura. Again, I find it hard to pattern my days if I haven't got a play in progress. Under normal conditions, you see, life is a battle to carve out a few uninterrupted hours for serious work from the rocky wastes of meaningless chores that surround me on all sides; without the excuse of a play to fiddle with, I have no excuse for not taking part in all those hundreds of pointless activities which all the other members of my species seem to regard as necessary and I abhor. I suppose politicians have the same trouble when they're in exile, or blacksmiths or pirates when they get too old to work.

But, for a while at least, I was happy not writing; in fact, I was happy doing nothing, which anyone who knows me would regard as a contradiction in terms. I am the sort of man who is capable of doing any amount of work, just so long as it doesn't feel like work. Anything that I've got to do makes me feel like I'm wearing lead boots. But after my acquittal, I did nothing at all, until Phaedra got quite sick of the sight of me in a chair and told me to go away and write something. But there was nothing for me to write, and I can no more write when I don't feel like it than I can be sick when I don't feel ill. I came to the conclusion that Athens was not the place for me to be, and so, four months after the trial, Phaedra and I set off for Pallene. There is, I told her, always something for a man who still has the use of his arms and legs to do in the country, and once I was in Pallene I would soon snap out of it.

I was wrong. Instead, there proved to be far more nothing for me to do. If I tried working in the fields, I would end up leaning on my mattock gazing at the hillside, until my steward politely asked me to go away because I was setting the slaves a bad example. If I went out with the goats it was even worse, and someone would have to be sent out after me to stop them straying and getting taken in and rebranded by an unscrupulous neighbour. There was one dreadful occasion, I remember, when I was entrusted with a load of figs and told to go and sell them in the market. I got the cart most of the way down the mountain; but then the axle broke, and the whole load went everywhere, with a tremendous smashing of jars and cascading of figs; and instead of swearing terribly and jumping down to see to it, I just sat there on the box of the broken cart thinking how funny it was, until someone else came up behind me and yelled at me to unblock the road so that he could get his cart through. In the end I got everything sorted out; but by then it was too late to go to market so I went back home again, and everyone was extremely surprised to see me.

One thing I did do that was constructive and useful was to spend a little more time with my son. This in itself was frowned on – it's not a father's place to go interfering with his child's upbringing before the child has reached an age where a father's influence is valuable. But those around me reckoned that, given the state I was in, I could do less damage to the efficient running of the household if I took the child up on to the hill and sat watching him crawl about. I say it was constructive and useful; I'm not meaning to imply it was constructive and useful to the boy, who probably didn't recognise me. But I enjoyed it. I'd never greatly cared for children before then – anyone you can't discuss Comic poetry with, I had always thought, is largely a waste of time. But there's nothing like spending some time with a prattling child for putting your life in perspective. To a child, you see, everything is so terribly immediate; present discomforts are insufferable, present wants and ambitions are all-important, and the most distant future imaginable is sunset. Now I was in the middle of trying to work out what I really wanted out of my life – though I didn't realise it at the time – and this new way of looking at time was a useful comparison. The way you measure time depends on what you do and who you are. A child, as I have just said, measures time by the day. A farmer thinks in three-year blocks; one year's produce in the field and two years' supplies laid up in the barn. Landless casual workers and Comic poets measure time by the year; either where this year's work is going to be, or what he's going to show at this year's Festivals. This annual approach is marginally better than the child's, but it doesn't make for stability. The other way of looking at things, which I couldn't help doing, was the way a man uses time when he's unexpectedly alive after resigning himself to dying, and that's by the minute, or the second.

But the main factor in the great rearrangement of my life was Phaedra. Almost incidentally, in the tremendous disturbances that Demeas brought into my life, I had discovered that Phaedra and I could, if we were careful, not only endure but enjoy living together. I wanted to make use of this discovery and put it to the test. For her part, Phaedra seemed mainly to want to get on with sorting out the store-cupboard or making a coverlet for the bed, and regarded all my attempts at sitting down and talking things through as irritating interruptions in her daily routine. But I persevered; and although we never had the grand debate about the nature of married life that one of those semi-philosophical writers would have inserted into the story at this point, we seemed to come to a sort of unspoken settlement; we both agreed to accept the change in our attitudes towards each other, so long as neither of us ever mentioned it out loud.

It was about this time, when I was in Pallene getting under everyone's feet, that the political situation began to change, subtly but in such a way that even I began to feel distinctly nervous. Now the last thing in the world that I want to suggest is that my speech had anything to do with it; but perhaps my acquittal was a symptom that something was changing. At any rate, the first thing that I couldn't help but notice was the institution of a wholly new arm of the legislature: a Council of Ten, set up to 'advise' the main Council. These ten men were elected, as democratically as possible, but it stands to reason that when you put a certain number of men, be it ten or a thousand, in a position of authority for any length of time, they will soon have little in common with their original mandate. One thing that amused me about the business was the fact that one of the Ten was the celebrated Sophocles, the playwright. He was well into his eighties by now, virtually blind and completely senile. He knew what he was doing, of course; he wasn't legally incapable, as he proved at a trial about this time, when his family wanted to get control of his property and he made his defence by reading out the play he had just been writing and demanding to know whether a senile man could have written that. But he no longer lived in, or even appreciably near, the real world, and he had got it into his mind that Athens was in the grip of some great tragic cycle, such as he might write a trilogy about; and that since nothing could be done to save the old place, the kindest thing would be to hasten it towards its inevitable destruction, and so precipitate its rebirth. The other nine Councillors dealt with more mundane things, such as public order and the water supply.

It was about this time, too, that the revolt in Chios began to be taken seriously, and a large force was sent to deal with it. Now I can't remember how long all this took; and in my desire to get to the end of this story, perhaps I'm rushing forward by months or even years. To tell you the truth, I have only the vaguest recollection of the sequence of events after my trial, since I was out of them, more or less, and took little notice of what people told me. But I do remember that the institution of the Ten and the rebellion in Chios – or was it the other one, in Samos? – had a lot to do with the rise of that extraordinary fellow Pisander. I always get Pisander muddled up with Phrynichus (not Phrynichus the Comic poet, Phrynichus the General), but to be honest with you, the main characters don't matter all that much. What mattered was the change in the way people thought, and that was quite startling.

For years there had been rumours of an oligarchical tendency in Athens; young, rich men with lots of time on their hands who wanted to overthrow the democracy and seize power. This had started as a conspiracy rumour, and nobody took any notice of it unless they needed it for an impeachment or a Comic play. Now I don't know which came first, the rumour or the actual tendency, but by this time the dream was starting to take shape, and a very unpleasant shape it was, too. Up till now, oligarchs had been like giants or centaurs – you believed in them up to a point, and you knew someone whose uncle had seen one, but you never expected to meet one yourself. But now, you began to suspect that the peculiar people whose names you heard so much about, if you were the sort of person who listened to that sort of talk, might indeed be oligarchs, and you began to worry about the greatest single issue of the day, the return of the lost leader, Alcibiades.

I have deliberately not said much about Alcibiades; partly because I didn't know him well enough to talk about him, and partly because I think his importance has been vastly exaggerated. To hear some people talk, you would think the fellow was a one-man city, with fleets and armies and money of his own. Not a bit of it; he was a rather glamorous individual who spent his exile from Athens amusing himself with peripheral intrigues at the courts of Sparta and the Persian governor Tissaphernes. He may have made a great many suggestions to influential men among our enemies; but I doubt whether he put a single new idea into their heads. We Athenians, believing with absolute sincerity that only Athenians can achieve things in this world, need an Athenian to be the cause of what happened next; and since Alcibiades was in the area at the time, we naturally assume that the

Spartan–Persian pact, which finally did for us in the War, was something to do with some grand design or policy of the celebrated Alcibiades.

But if Alcibiades himself was of little importance, his name was another thing altogether. Wherever two or three Athenians met together to talk, his name would inevitably be mentioned; and out of that three, one would be pro-Alcibiades. Probably just to be perverse; now that it was permissible to think and talk about such things, those Athenians who loved to debate and argue (which means all Athenians) were starting to talk about and debate a change of constitution. Would an oligarchy actually be a good idea, they asked themselves? What could be said in favour of it, and what against? Now once Athenians start to talk about something, you can be sure that sooner or later they'll try doing it, particularly if it's something that hasn't been done before. In fact the greatest thing in favour of the idea of oligarchy was its novelty, coupled with a certain air of secrecy, wickedness and danger. Add to this the continued feeling of doom and despair because of Sicily, and a degree of revulsion from the excesses of the first reaction to the disaster, and you have a fine hot stew on which to feed and make yourself thoroughly ill.

Of course my name was linked with the nebulous conspiracy right from the start, because of what I had said at the trial, and as a result of this I was probably right to keep as much out of sight as I did (although, as I have explained, this was hardly policy on my part). But I'm sure the Tendency looked upon me as One of Us, and the democrats whispered about me as being One of Them. Everything in Athens is either One of Us or One of Them, and the only things that change are the definitions of Us and Them. These change regularly and out of all recognition, but nobody ever seems to notice this. Sometimes I wonder what it would have been like to have lived out my life in some more normal city, like one of those orderly little places you hear about in Crete or Euboea, where things never change and nobody takes any interest in what their city is doing because their city never does anything beyond a little unobtrusive road-mending. In a way, it would be heavenly, but I expect I should have gone mad within ten years, unless I had been born there and known no other way of life.

As it was, even in my self-imposed retirement in Pallene, I started to feel that tingling sensation that an Athenian gets when something is about to happen in politics. In my case, this sensation manifests itself most strongly in those parts of the body and the soul concerned with the composition of anapaests. Now I've never wanted to change the way people think; but I do like writing anapaests. It makes you feel involved. And you will remember that just before my trial I had thought up that marvellous idea for a play, with all the various Demes of Attica coming on as a Chorus, and all the great Leaders of the past coming back from the Other World to give advice. I think what sparked it off was that scene Aristophanes and I put together in the smithy in Syracuse, where we brought Aeschylus back to life to debate poetry with Euripides. In any case, I started thinking more and more about it when my mind was empty, and the thing seemed to gather a momentum of its own. I had made a deliberate decision *not* to write anything more for a long time, but the play was taking shape in my mind, like an unmarried girl's pregnancy, and there was nothing I could do about it. If Athens was in a crisis, I would have to write something, and that something would have to be relevant.

It was Phaedra who made me break my vow. One evening we were sitting together in my house in Pallene. She was sewing away at something, and I was staring at the hearth with my mouth open, an occupation which was rapidly becoming my profession and career. It certainly irritated my wife who tried not to look at me when I was doing it. On this particular evening, however, she seemed to lose patience with me altogether.

'What's got into you?' she said. 'If you don't close your mouth soon, a spider will come and weave a web over it.'

'Stop moaning,' I replied. 'There's nothing needs doing, is there?'

Phaedra looked at me for a moment. 'There's something the matter with you,' she said. 'I don't know what it is, but the sooner you get rid of it the better. You're beginning to make me feel uncomfortable.'

'I don't know what you mean,' I said, and I put my feet up on the couch and pretended to go to sleep.

'I know what you remind me of,' she said after a while. 'Do you remember that man who used to live near the fountain, the one who had the two white dogs?'

'Vaguely,' I said. 'Was his name Euthycritus?'

'I couldn't say,' Phaedra replied, 'and anyway, that's beside the point. You remember that he had a stroke?'

'That's right,' I said, 'so he did.'

'And you remember,' Phaedra went on, 'how he couldn't move or talk, but his eyes were just the same as they had been. And his wife used to get the slaves to carry him in his chair to the front door and park him there so that he could watch the people going up and down.'

'And everyone used to look the other way,' I said, 'because they couldn't look him in the eyes without cringing. I remember. Wasn't he once an athlete or something like that?'

'Possibly,' Phaedra said, biting through her cotton and putting her work down. 'Anyway, that's who you've been reminding me of these last few weeks.'

I didn't think that was funny at all. 'You do say the most ill-omened things,' I said to her. 'Fancy comparing me to a cripple.'

'Well, it's true,' she said. 'I think you'd be perfectly happy sitting in a doorway watching the shoppers.'

This startled me, because it was quite probably true.

'Have I been as bad as that?' I said.

'Yes,' replied my wife, 'or worse. You'd sit there even if there weren't any shoppers. What do you think about, for God's sake? Are you working out geometrical theories or just counting birds?'

'I'm not thinking about anything,' I said, 'except occasionally how glad I am to be alive.'

'That's odd,' she said. 'You're behaving just like a corpse. And a docile corpse, at that.'

'Aren't wives supposed to pray for inactive husbands?' I said. 'You never used to like it when I was always dashing about doing things.'

'And all that nonsense you've been talking lately,' she went on, 'about our relationship and so on. What sort of talk is that for a husband and his wife? You sound like a philosopher talking to his boyfriend.'

I frowned. 'I just wanted to get things straight,' I said.

'Things are naturally straight,' she said, 'unless you fiddle with them. You should just get on with life instead of thinking about it.'

'That's a very solemn remark,' I said, smiling mockingly at her. She frowned disapprovingly.

'You know what I mean,' she said. 'Don't start being all Chorus-like and commenting on everything I do as if I were Clytemnestra or somebody. You do a lot of that, I've noticed.'

'A lot of what?'

'Observing,' she said. 'You look at people, and listen to them, as if you were a judge at a fair. Nobody wants your assessment, thank you very much.'

'I know,' I said, 'but I can't help it, I do it naturally.'

'What you need to do,' Phaedra said, standing up and collecting her sewing things, 'is to find something to do. Otherwise you'll turn into a god or a lump of rock or something.'

'Explain,' I said.

'Well,' she said, sitting down again, 'you're just like

that sometimes; a god on a mountain, or a boulder, or a tree. You just stand or sit there and watch, as if the world was a play put on for your benefit. Now when you used to write plays, this was more or less justifiable, because you made some sort of use of it all. You needed to catch how people speak and act, and make some sort of judgement for your anapaests. But now you just seem to do it for your own entertainment, and it's not natural. Either snap out of it or start writing again.'

'You're odd, too,' I said. 'I never really know whether you approve of me writing or not. You never seem to take any interest while I'm composing something. You always give the impression of being a patient wife allowing her husband to pursue his childish hobby, as if I collected seashells or carved miniature ships on scraps of ivory.'

Phaedra shrugged. 'I don't know,' she said. 'I don't think you're particularly clever, if that's what you mean, just because you can compose lines that scan. And I'm not a Comedy enthusiast, like some people are; I prefer Tragedy, personally, and I'm not a very literary person when you come right down to it. Most women aren't, actually. But I suppose you do it as well as anybody,' she said fairly, 'and probably better than most. And you've got to do something, so you might as well do this.'

I sat up and put my hands round my knees. 'So you think I ought to write a play, do you?' I said.

'Yes,' she said. 'For my sake if not for yours. Then people won't point to me in the street and say, "There goes that woman who's married to a corpse." I really can't stand much more of this godlike stuff, you know. It was different after you got back from the War, when the trial was on; you had a purpose in life then all right, and I rather liked you. But now ...'

'All right,' I said, 'I get the message. You can't stand the sight of me just sitting here peacefully. You want me to be busy.'

'Only because it's your nature to be busy,' she replied.

'At the moment you don't really seem to exist, and that's unnerving for a girl. I never know when you're going to start walking through walls or slowly disappearing, like a dream in a poem.'

So the next day, I took the plough out over the fallow, and instead of getting to the end of the furrow and then stopping, as I had done the last time I tried it, I went straight on and did a day's work, without knowing it. When I got home, I had an opening speech fully fledged in my mind, and it was the best I had ever composed. Now one thing that always worries me is whether what I'm doing now is as good as what I've done before. This is quite an obsession with me, and I end up hating things I've written because I can't seem to do as well any more. This time, though, I knew it was good. The lines seemed to have a crispness and a crackle about them, and instead of ending a line off with a conventional jingle, I had tried my best to find something new and startling, the way you do when you're just starting out in the Theatre and every word is important to you.

Shall I tell you all about the play? I've been very good so far, and not bored you with little synopses of my various brilliant dramas, so I think I'll allow myself the indulgence, just this once. The story was as follows. The Athenian State is in a crisis, because it hasn't been able to think of anything new to do since it sent a fleet to conquer the moon. So worrying is this mental sterility that our hero takes it upon himself to go down to the underworld, like Odysseus, to ask the opinions of the glorious dead.

Once he has made the journey, the first person he meets is the celebrated Myronides, the general who led Athens to victory at Tanagra, the battle I told you about which ended the previous war with Sparta in my grandfather's time. I picked on him because he seems to represent, to my generation at least, the last honest citizen and competent general of the old school. In fact he was just as much of a rogue as all those who came before and after him, but I was not concerned with absolute historical truth. No Athenian is, or we wouldn't celebrate Marathon as a victory. Anyway, Myronides acts as our hero's guide and takes him to see all the great statesmen of our history, from the immortal Solon to Pericles, and each of these gives his considered opinion about what should be done. To put each of these towering figures in his place, I made my Chorus up of the demes of Attica, with Pallene as Chorus-leader; because, when all is said and done, it is the demes and not the city which make up Athens.

I had set out to write a play, and as good a play as I possibly could; but the more I wrote, the more serious this Comedy of mine became. As you can see from what I've told you, it was a very political play; and I don't suppose I would ever have written such a work at any other time. I had set out with no clear message in my mind; but as the play progressed and I tried to think what advice Solon might actually give us in our present situation, I found a strong theme emerging and did my best to do it justice. It wasn't at all what I thought myself; but that's not really a poet's job. Aristophanes, for example, has consistently attacked the War and demanded an end to it from the moment he started to write; but he has nothing personal against the War, and at least until he went to Sicily thought very little about it. But his characters are mainly heavy-infantry farmers, and such people naturally disapprove of the War; so in order to write what he wants to write and make the sort of jokes he likes, Aristophanes must present himself as a peace-lover and a countryman, which could hardly be further from the truth. Similarly, in my case, having appointed myself the spokesman of our great political leaders, I was virtually forced to make an impassioned plea on behalf of the democracy. But, to be fair to myself, I argued for the good parts of our constitution, the parts that Solon envisaged and Themistocles and Pericles didn't manage to spoil between them. I argued that what Athens needed now was the sort of democracy where everyone was entitled to be heard so long as he spoke sense; where the majority should not oppress the minority in the way that the Few had oppressed the Many in Solon's time. Obviously (I said) you can't create that sort of system by legislation or the creation of new institutions. A democracy is the most vulnerable system of all. Furthermore, a democracy more than any other form of government tends naturally to incline towards repression, intolerance and violence, because it is the form that imposes the least restraint upon human nature. But a democracy where men restrain themselves, thereby doing to themselves what nobody else either can or should do to them, is potentially the best of all forms of government, so long as it is based on mutual tolerance and consideration and a general intention to do what is best for all, and above everything, what is possible in the circumstances.

Well, that's what I said in the play. As you know, I don't believe a word of it. I don't believe that any state the size of Athens can govern itself, whatever form of government it chooses, without causing immeasurable damage to the people who live in it. But I honestly believe that in my play I gave the City the best advice that I could, and I am proud of what I wrote then. It came out of my own experience in the way that no Comedy has ever come out of experience before, because instead of attacking and making fun of what was being done, it suggested what should be done; and instead of being hurtful to a few for the sake of pleasing many, it was designed to say what the author thought – or at least what the composite creature representing the author would have thought had such a person ever existed. And in one respect it did reflect my own personal opinion; that the demes, the villages and regions of Attica are what matter, and that the great men and their political factions and movements are the servants of the demes and should never forget it.

'There now,' you are saying, 'that was very clever of you, Eupolis, but what happened next?' Well, I wrote the play, completing it fairly quickly by my standards, and sent it to be copied. It had occupied my attention fully all the time I had been composing it, and apart from political gossip I had taken no notice of anything else. But, as any playwright will tell you, writing the thing is the easy, relaxing part. The hard work would be getting it accepted and produced.

CHAPTER FIFTEEN

Obviously, the first thing I had to do was go and see Philonides. Now he hadn't had anything to do with the Theatre or the training of Choruses since the Sicilian disaster –I don't know if there was any deep meaning behind that, or whether it was just coincidence – and when I told him that I had a new play which I wanted to put on at the Festivals he didn't seem to want to know. He argued that he was getting old (which was true enough) and that he wasn't interested in that sort of thing any more; but I bullied him and wheedled away at him, and finally, more to get rid of me than for any other reason, he agreed to hear the play and look at a copy of the written version.

I was so confident about the play that I never had any doubts that once he saw it he would be won over completely, and as it happens I was right. As soon as he heard the entry of the Chorus, he was hooked; for unlike so many of the people who have tried to emulate him, he knew that he was first and foremost what his title said he was, a trainer of Choruses. To him, as to me, the Chorus was the heart of a play, and its costumes, movements, singing, verse-speaking and general effect were his primary concern and greatest love. He excelled at marshalling and controlling men *en bloc* and in Sparta they would have made him a general. It was because he was so good with Choruses that he was able to control and manipulate individual actors; as he himself used to say, if you can reduce a whole Chorus to tears with a single tirade, you should never have any problem imposing your will on just one man. Now Philonides could see that my Chorus of demes, if properly handled and appropriately costumed, could be the most spectacular and effective Chorus he had ever seen led out, and the temptation was too strong for him. He put up a good fight, right up to the last minute, but in the end he gave way and agreed to train this as his last and best Chorus.

The next thing was to go and see the Archon to apply for a Chorus for the Dionysia, and I must confess that I was not at all sure that I would be able to get past this obstacle. I'm convinced that I wouldn't have succeeded without Philonides' backing; as it was, I had a terrible time before I finally won through.

To start with, there was the problem of the play having been written by me. As I said just now, I was pretty thoroughly identified in the public mind with the oligarchs, because of my defence speech, and so it was natural enough for the Archon to feel that choosing a play by Eupolis was tantamount to declaring himself an oligarchic sympathiser. On the other hand, the play itself was patently for the democracy, and it was a brave man in that climate who identified himself in any way with such an outspoken statement in support of either side. There was a general feeling in the City that the mysterious leaders of the planned oligarchic coup – nobody knew who they were supposed to be, but everyone was convinced that they existed – were going around and preparing lists of diehard democrats who would have to be liquidated come the Glorious Day, and nobody wanted to be on those lists, for understandable reasons. So it was asking a lot of the Archon to demand that he choose a play that denounced oligarchy. I can only suppose that he came to the conclusion that my supposed oligarchic sympathies and my outspoken democratic views in the play cancelled each other out, and that by endorsing the play he was hedging his bets.

But those two factors weren't the only things against me. For one thing, it was a while since I had asked for a Chorus, and unless he submits work very regularly, like Aristophanes always has, it doesn't take very long for a poet, however strong his reputation has been in the past, to be forgotten about or supplanted by some up-and-coming young pretender. Just then, there were several men who were being talked about as the New Generation of Comic poets, and there had been many applications for Choruses. Suffice to say that I was forced, for the first time, to submit to the indignity of a series of postponed decisions, and to be chosen last out of the three competitors. In fact it was a very close thing at the end, since the Archon very nearly gave the Chorus to a young man who has never been heard of since, who had put together an entirely innocuous, if not particularly good, piece of nonsense about Hercules and a cauldron of lentil soup.

But in the end I got the Chorus, and the next difficulty was putting together a cast. Now since I had been given my Chorus last, and only after a long delay, all the good actors had been snapped up by the other poets and I was left with the no-hopers and the young apprentices, who had to be trained virtually from scratch. To make matters worse, Philonides, who was getting more and more enthusiastic about the project every day, had thought up some of the most fiendishly intricate and difficult dance routines and bits of business ever seen on the Attic stage, and with not enough time to rehearse and an inexperienced and generally feckless cast, I was all for watering these masterpieces down to make sure we had at least something to show the audience come the day. But Philonides would have none of it; instead, he set out to train every actor and Chorus-member as if he had never been anywhere near the Theatre in his life. This used up huge quantities of time, money and patience, all three of which were soon in short supply, and Philonides took to venting his fury and frustration on me, which I found rather unfair. But in the end he won through, as I knew he would. There is nothing Philonides can't make a Chorus or a cast of actors do, if he's determined that they'll do it. I believe that if the Council had given Philonides a Chorus and told him to use it to sack Sparta, he'd have pulled it off, and ahead of schedule.

As I said just now, money was a considerable problem. It was just my luck to have appointed as my producer a certain Promachus, notoriously the meanest and most humourless man in Athens. For a start, he hated the very idea of being made to finance a Comic play, since he disapproved of Comedy on principle and my play in particular. It would have been difficult enough if it had been an ordinary sort of play; but with Philonides calling for the best of everything for his Chorus, and new and expensive machinery for special effects, Promachus soon declared that he was going to deposit twelve hundred drachmas with me, and that was all that could be expected from him. So in the end I found myself paying for most of the expensive things, and I didn't enjoy that particular experience at all. Of course, when the time came, Promachus took all the credit, as a producer would be entitled to do under normal circumstances, and set up a magnificent votive statue recording how much had been spent on the production (two thousand drachmas). He didn't say how much of that money had been provided by me, of course; in fact, I don't think he mentioned my name at all.

What with him, and Philonides' regular outbursts, I didn't have much time to worry about anything else, such as whether the play was really as good as I believed it was. Still, I managed to spare a few hours' anxiety for the activities of my old comrade-in-arms the son of Philip. I hadn't actually set eyes on him since the trial, but as soon as I emerged from my slumbers and started work again, I started to hear rumours that he was furiously angry with me for having been acquitted after he had given evidence against me, with all the damage to his reputation that inevitably ensued, and that he had sworn to have his revenge on me, come what may. I heard from a fairly reliable source that he had done his best to persuade the Archon to reject the play, and also that he had tried to dissuade Philonides from taking it on. I confess that I found this behaviour rather excessive, coming from a man whom I had no great cause to respect, but I didn't dare try any form of retaliation in case it made things worse. I know a man is supposed to help his friends and harm his enemies, but I couldn't be bothered just then.

I also heard that Aristophanes had got mixed up very deeply with the oligarchs, and although you could find some such rumour about anyone you cared to name at that time, I was inclined to believe it in this instance. The gist of the rumour was that he was terribly friendly with the celebrated Phrynichus, the General, and this is actually borne out by various things he says in some of his plays, for what that's worth. He was also supposed to be doing his best to ingratiate himself with Pisander, the other main ringleader; but apparently Pisander couldn't take him at any price and refused to have anything to do with him. That I can well believe, for whatever his faults Pisander wasn't without a measure of common sense, and the son of Philip would be a definite hindrance to any cause to which he attached himself. But it seems, if the rumour had anything to it, that Aristophanes was quite serious about the oligarchic cause, and wasn't just in it for the fun and the mischief. He saw himself as part of the ruling faction, up there with the best of them, and presumably once there in a position to settle some old scores, such as me. Now I can honestly say that that particular prospect didn't lose me any sleep; but I was rather concerned in case he should try anything nasty against my play. Good-natured sabotage, as I'm sure you remember, is all part of the fun of being a poet, but the whole climate in Athens at the time was such as to make you wonder what a vindictive person might not try and do. Everything seemed just that tiny bit more dangerous than ever before; it was as if the Athenian Game had got rather out of hand, and people were taking things a touch further than they would have before. This was true in everything, not just the Theatre; I don't really know how to describe it to you. You know how a game of catch can sometimes turn nasty, with the players deliberately throwing the ball at each other when they lost their tempers; well, I suppose it was like that, in a way.

Of course, violence and other forms of extreme behaviour were nothing new; but all the light-heartedness seemed to have gone out of politics and the other forms of public life in Athens, and I think this was because, as a City, we had rather lost our nerve after Sicily. Before, we were all that bit more prepared to take risks, and accept the consequences if we failed – I suppose because we were certain in our hearts that we couldn't fail, and so there would be no consequences to take. But now, Athens seemed to have become old and sour instead of young and exciting, and the endless search for novelty wasn't so much a quest for new sensations and fresh objectives as a sort of desperation, because nothing seemed to be going right any more. All the old energy was still there of course, but it was the furious energy of someone who knows he's losing, rather than the vigour of ambition. For example: we built a new fleet in next to no time, and won a few quick victories with it, which made us all feel elated and safe for a while. But we could do nothing about the revolts in our subject cities, and still less about the Spartan fortress at Deceleia on our borders, which was very slowly grinding us down. The fortress made me think back to the old days my grandfather used to talk about, before the Persians came, when the Athenians could not rest easy at nights for the thought of Aegina being still unconquered, and Themistocles urging them every day to wipe out the 'eyesore of the Piraeus'. The thought of a Spartan fortress on Attic soil would have been intolerable to the Athenians of his time, but we seemed to be able to put it to the back of our minds and get on with something else. In the meantime, to divert our attention, we thought more and more about domestic matters, including the constitution; and this sort of brooding was definitely bad for us. Hence this sourness that I've been describing. All the old, typically Athenian characteristics were still there, of course: the energy, the love of words and novelty, the random cruelty. But they were like those warships of ours which had been captured by the Syracusans; they were ours, but they were being used against us, to do us harm.

I guess it wasn't the best time to be putting on such a very political play; but I had written the thing, and it was topical, and I wanted to see it staged. But there was more to it than that; I suppose because, since my speech in my defence, I too had been thinking rather more than usual about that sort of thing. Now do you see what I mean? At the time when this story starts, your average Athenian would no more have been rethinking the democracy than he would have been rethinking the sky; the democracy was just there, and it was impossible for it to change. I may not have liked the democracy very much, ever since I was old enough to consider these things, but it simply wasn't one of the things that a man could expect to do anything about; just as, if he doesn't get on well with his family, he can't expect to be able to resign from it and join another. You can't deliberately divorce yourself from your City; your City can banish you, but even that is a most extreme measure, in many ways as drastic or more so than putting you to death. No, if something big was happening to the political system of Athens, even I couldn't stop myself from having my say.

Rehearsals became more and more frantic as Festival time drew closer, what with Philonides shouting and the actors not yet knowing their words and the fullers accidentally dyeing a whole batch of costumes purple instead of red; and the fury in the Theatre seemed to be matched by the frenzied activity outside it so that, after so many years, I can no longer separate them in my mind. I say 'activity' deliberately; nothing substantial appeared to be happening, but a great amount of energy was being expended by a great many people; and when so much heat is produced in such a small space, something, sooner or later, is likely to be broken or at least melted down. The situation in the War was no less exciting, but that seemed like a peripheral issue to us in the City, and we regarded it as little more than a source of new and rich debating-points – how would the oligarchs react to such and such, or what would the Old Guard make of the developments in Persia? This was very short-sighted of us, because we were in grave danger of losing control of our most productive subject-states. The Spartans were starting to think like sensible, rational human beings at last, instead of Homeric heroes, and they were getting ever closer to making a treaty against us with the greatest of all enemies, the King of Persia. If I hadn't been so wrapped up in the preparations for the play, I'm sure I could record a great many matters of interest to generations yet unborn about those truly fascinating few months before the Dionysia in March; as it was, I had only a vague idea of what was going on outside the City and in the War, and if I were to give you a detailed account it would be mostly hearsay, and Athenian hearsay at that. But I can tell you a little about that year's Dionysia, if that will do instead.

The main – or only – talking-point was the

extraordinary set of plays that Euripides was supposed to be presenting. He was keeping very quiet about them himself, and this only fuelled the furious speculation. For at least one of them was (apparently) going to revolutionise our entire approach to Tragic drama, the Gods, and pretty well everything else. We knew that one of these plays was going to be about Helen, and that Euripides had taken his old hobby-horse, the story in Stesichorus that Helen never went to Troy but was spirited away to Egypt while Paris was left with a replica made of cloud, and used it to create some vast metaphysical question to which there was no immediately obvious answer. Then another play was going to be about Andromeda, dealing with the story in a roughly similar way; and both plays were to have happy endings and be closer in many respects to Comedy than Tragedy. Now I belong to the school of thought that many of Euripides' plays are unintentionally Comic, and so I couldn't wait to see what would happen if Euripides tried to be deliberately funny; I expected the entire audience to be in floods of tears before the entry of the Chorus. Several of the Comic poets, Aristophanes included, were desperately trying to get advance copies of these plays, by bribing the Archon's slaves or getting the actors drunk, so as to be able to include snippets of parody in their next Comedies; and even I felt a vague irritation, because Euripides hadn't had the decency to put on these grotesque farces of his in time for me to use them in my masterpiece. I had been reduced to having another go at the *Telephus*, which was the one weakness that I could think of in the whole play.

Of course, you will be thoroughly familiar with those two boils on Tragedy's backside, Euripides' *Helen* and *Andromeda*, and you'll be wondering what all this fuss was about. But there were some very curious things in those plays, particularly in the *Helen*, when you think of what I've been telling you about the situation at the time. For example, in the *Helen*, there's no end of praise for

Sparta, mostly dragged in without any perceptible justification from the plot or the characters. If Euripides' intention was to shock the audience he certainly succeeded, and there were quite a few normally intelligent people who were very impressed. Then there was that extraordinary line about how even the most widely travelled men can't tell the difference between true gods and false ones and things which are half-divine and half-mortal. Now when a man has a reputation for obscure profundity, such as Euripides has, he can get away with saying anything at all, and people will do their very best to read something wonderful into it; and there was no shortage of idiots who took this to be a highly intelligent comment about the statues that were smashed and the expedition to Sicily. In fact I remember having the whole thing explained to me, in detail, by a barber while he was trimming my beard about a week after the Festival, and I was unable to argue with him for fear of moving my chin too much and getting my throat cut. At the time I was thoroughly convinced by what he said, as it happens; but I'm afraid I can't remember a word of it after all this time.

What with the Euripides scandal and politics and the War, therefore, nobody seemed particularly anxious to find out in advance what Eupolis was going to put on that year; in fact, the general opinion as I heard it was that Eupolis was well over the hill, hadn't written anything worth bothering with since *Maricas*, and should retire gracefully and let one of the newcomers have a chance. This sort of talk just made me all the more determined to show them all that I still had something to say, and I started making rather a nuisance of myself at rehearsals, just when Philonides and the cast had reached an uneasy truce. As a result of my interference, which consisted mainly of wholly unreasonable demands that the Chorus-numbers be made even more spectacular and that the actors learn whole new speeches with less than a week before the Festivals began, we very nearly didn't have a play to put on at all. But Philonides triumphed over adversity, and just when I was ready to give up, we had a last rehearsal at which virtually everything worked. I remember walking home after that final run-through and going straight past my house because I was saying Solon's speech over to myself in my head, and I hadn't finished it by the time I reached the door.

At last the time came for the official preview, two days before the start of the Festival proper. In those days we did it slightly differently; the poets, producers, Choruses and actors went down to the Odeon (you can imagine my feelings on revisiting the place) with costumes but without masks, and the poet had to get up on a platform and announce the title of his play, with a brief summary of the plot. Naturally, nobody ever said what the play was actually about – that would have been a disastrous mistake; instead, we would put together a sort of Delphic riddle to inflame interest. I had never enjoyed this stage in the proceedings before, since I used to have no great confidence in my ability to project my voice. But, after my trial in that very building, I knew all about the acoustics in the Odeon, and it was a positive pleasure to stand up on the platform where I had made my defence and announce my Comedy. It was really a sort of declaration of defiance on my part, and to mark the occasion I had written rather a good little piece. I was well into this, and getting a very healthy reception from the audience, when a couple of men at the back of the hall started shouting and throwing olives at me. I recognised them as some of Aristophanes' regular hangers-on, who he paid to clap and shout 'Encore!' during his plays (some of them had been with him for fifteen years, and were as well known in Athens as the actors themselves). This, I reckoned, was a bit hard. It's not uncommon for a poet to organise little riots during the play itself, as I seem to remember telling you before somewhere; and I recall with great pleasure the time Cratinus got his supporters to start making a noise during one of Euripides' early efforts – he had heard that Euripides had included a speech in praise of money, and he got his people to object to this on moral grounds, with the result that the poet jumped out of his seat, ran down on to the stage and begged them to hear the rest of the play and see what a bad end the money-loving character came to. But to organise a disturbance at the preview was something entirely new; and what made it worse was that Aristophanes had somehow found out what the plot and best scenes of my play were going to be, and had told his men to shout this secret information out at the tops of their voices. But Philonides had apparently suspected something of the sort (although he hadn't seen fit to share his suspicions with me) and had hired a mob of his own. These men jumped up and started yelling that Aristophanes was part of the oligarchic conspiracy and ought to be taken to the top of the old tower in the Potters' Quarter and thrown off. So in the end Aristophanes' trick backfired on him, because Philonides' riot got far more laughs and the son of Philip was so frightened that he ran home and hid under the bed for the rest of the day.

The lots were drawn: I was to come on the second day, following Euripides' Tragedies. I was in two minds about this. On the one hand, you could be sure that the Theatre would be packed as tight as whitebait in a jar; on the other hand, the audience might be so worked up about the Tragedies that my Comedy would be virtually ignored. I'd seen that happen many times; the audience are still talking about the Tragedy, usually at the tops of their voices, when the Comic Chorus makes its entrance. Nobody has heard the opening speech, and so they haven't the faintest idea of what's going on. On balance, I decided, it would be a good thing. Nobody, not even a foreigner, would be able to ignore the opening scene of my play, with Athena coming down from Olympus on the machine.

On the first day of the Festival, I was awake long before dawn; and Phaedra and I were among the first people in the streets waiting for the procession to go by. Now not even the strange atmosphere in the city could spoil the opening day of the Dionysia. It's all different now; but in those days there was nothing like it in the world. Bear with me while I describe it; for my own satisfaction, if you like. It was very much the best side of Athens' character, and after all the terrible things I've been saying about her, I reckon it's only fair that I should give her a chance to be seen in a better light.

Shortly after dawn all the prisoners in the gaol, except for the dangerous ones, were brought out under guard to watch the procession, and the girls who had been chosen as basket-bearers were scurrying about showing off their new outfits while there was still time, before they had to take their places. The procession was always late starting; but when it came out everyone always declared, every year without fail, that it was the best one yet. The statue of the God would go by, and the basket-bearers, and then the young men chosen to sing the satirical songs and shout vulgar abuse at anyone famous they recognised in the crowd – because now the God was in charge of the City, and mere mortals, however important, had to be made to recognise that fact. Then one of the sacrificial animals – usually a large and savage bull – would always manage to escape and gore someone or other in the crowd, and there were fights and robberies and people fainting and getting trampled, and all the other ingredients of a good day out.

Then came the solemn, rather boring part, with the singing of the dithyrambs by massed choirs and everybody trying to look serious and devout and doing their level best not to cough in the wrong places. I don't know why it is, but even the most brilliant poet, when called upon to compose a dithyramb, inevitably turns out twenty minutes' worth of the most turgid rubbish you ever heard in your life, the sort of stuff that would be hissed off the stage without a moment's hesitation if it was put in a play. But, because it's the dithyramb and somehow sacred and privileged, the entire audience pretends it's the most marvellous poetry since Hesiod, and nobody says a word or throws so much as a pine-cone. But everybody is very relieved when it's over at last, and the real fun can begin.

First, there's the sticking of the pig, with all the blood and squeals, which the children always like; then the libations are poured, while most of the audience queue up in front of the sausage-sellers and chatter away to each other about the harvest. But they're all back in their seats for the procession, when the young men carry the jars of silver left over from the tribute after the City's expenses had all been paid – this was often a bit of a joke, of course; about this time the City was virtually bank-rupt, but the procession went ahead all the same – and after that came the presentation of suits of armour to the sons of the men who had been killed in battle that year. Now as you can imagine, this part of the proceedings could be actively embarrassing. At the Dionysia after Sicily, for instance, there simply wasn't enough armour to go round, and they had to get the young recipients to run round the back and pass on the armour they had just been so movingly presented with to the next candidate. In the end, I believe, they all got their armour, for it's a serious matter and not even the politicians would dream of cheating; but some of them had to wait several years, and even then there were complaints that a few of the suits of armour didn't fit, or were second-hand stuff bought from the people who go around stripping the bodies of the dead after battles.

Finally, the names of the judges for the plays are drawn out of the sealed cauldrons brought down from the Acropolis during the procession, and you can picture for yourself all the producers of the plays sitting there in rapt attention as the names were announced, hoping that they had bribed the right people.

Then there would be an interval, and everyone would get up and rush out to buy more sausages, or wine, or apples, or things to throw. There would be queues outside as the foreigners who had come late tried to buy tickets, while the citizens who had only just arrived from the more remote parts of Attica strolled in past them and made sarcastic remarks. When the noise of fifteen thousand chattering and munching human beings had reached its unendurable height, the trumpet would sound and there would be the most frantic rush for seats, like an infantry line collapsing under cavalry attacks in flank and rear. Then you would see the unedifying spectacle of virtually the whole citizen body of our great democracy accusing his neighbour of stealing his seat or his cushion, or sitting on his hat, or blocking his view of the stage. In the middle of this confusion, there would be a blast on the flutes and everybody would break off in mid-recrimination as the first actor of the Festival came on to speak his prologue. This silence generally lasted only long enough for the actor to identify himself and say where the play was set; as soon as everyone realised that it was going to be yet another Orestes' Return, they would resume their arguments with their neighbours where they had left them. I imagine this is why Tragedies have prologues; I can see no other justification for them.

That was what the opening day of the Great Dionysia was like in my day. Now you will say it's just the same now, and that I've been wasting your time telling you about it, and isn't that just like a senile old man? But I must ask you to think again. Isn't it all the more subdued and deliberately literary these days? Remember, we were seeing these great Tragedies, which you respect as much as Homer because you were told they were good when you were a boy, all for the first time, and we didn't know they were going to be good when we took our places in the Theatre; and bear in mind also that most of them weren't – the ones you read are the good ones. And besides, nowadays a lot of people don't even bother to go to the Festivals, whereas then it was really the only time when everyone in Attica who could possibly manage to spare three or four days was sure to be together in one place, absolutely confident that he was perfectly capable of understanding everything that was said, and that his judgement was as good as the next man's, because Athens was a democracy. That has most certainly changed, and now you have people who understand the drama, and people who know what they like, and a lot of people who say they don't like plays at all and think they're boring.

I know what you're thinking, and you're right; I am starting to sound like an old man. I think it's writing this book that's doing it. Before I started on this fool's errand, I hadn't given the old days much thought – I'm not the sort of man who likes to dwell on the past – and to a certain extent I've been thinking aloud for a lot of the time, as things occur to me that I never realised before. But we Athenians aren't terribly good at noticing the passage of time. For example; Aristophanes continued putting on the stage Choruses supposedly representing men who had fought at Marathon long after all but the last few veterans of the battle were dead and buried, but nobody in the Theatre seemed to find this strange. They still imagined that there were plenty of Marathon men still alive, and so nobody ever got around to seeking out survivors of the battle and actually asking them what happened and writing down what they said so that it would never be forgotten. Then along came men like the celebrated Herodotus, and they wrote their books and gave their recitals, and there was nobody left to say whether they had got it right or not. Which is why I started writing this, I suppose – that and the money Dexitheus offered me, of course, and the prospect of something to do over the winter. Dear God, I really am starting to ramble now, aren't I? I'd better get on with the story, before I completely lose touch with reality.

Now I've told you that I was listed to send on my Chorus after Euripides' Tragedies on the second day, and that I was in two minds whether this was good or bad. Well, I sat through the opening day like a small child who's waiting to be taken to see the market for the first time, and I hardly noticed the Tragedies. The Comedy was absolutely dire; it was one of the first of these miserable domestic farces that are so popular nowadays, all about a young man who wants to marry the girl next door but can't, for some improbable reason, and there were hardly any jokes about the politicians or the War, while the Chorus-songs had nothing to do with the plot and seemed to have been bolted on as an afterthought. I hated it, and it was very depressing to hear the audience applauding it. I take it as a personal insult when people applaud a bad Comedy, unless, of course, it's one of mine. When this travesty finally ground to a halt I went straight home instead of hanging about as I usually do, talking to people I haven't seen since last year and generally enjoying being involved. Philonides came round later on, to go over a few last-minute points; but more out of politeness than for any other reason. He had everything firmly under control, rather like a good Persian governor, and needed no help from me. I asked him if he'd heard whether Aristophanes was planning any more tricks, and he looked at me very strangely and said that I was becoming obsessed with Aristophanes, so I dropped the subject. I had an early meal and went to bed, but of course I couldn't sleep. I wanted this play to win more than any other I had ever written, and I think it was at that point that I knew that if it did win, it would be my last, and I would be through with the Theatre after that.

I didn't know why. I still don't.

At last it was morning, and I went over to Philonides' house at least two hours before dawn, to find that he was still in bed and not particularly pleased to see me. He was feeling generally depressed – naturally enough, considering that it was his fifty-seventh birthday – but after a cup of hot wine with honey and cheese and a mouthful of bread, he was soon rushing about like an eighteen-year-old, and then the Chorus-leaders and the actors arrived.

I shall remember that morning till I die. The Chorus-leaders were the first to arrive, and they were full of energy and enthusiasm. Then the two supporting actors came in, and they had hangovers but were otherwise intact. The protagonist, however, was nowhere to be seen. Now the man in question, one Philocharmus, was notorious for being late for everything, and so at first we didn't worry. But when there was only an hour to go until the first Tragedy and he still hadn't turned up, Philonides started sending messengers out to find him, and we sat and stared at each other, wondering what on earth was going on. Philonides was thoroughly worked up by now, and passed the time by saying what he would do to Philocharmus when he got his hands on him. But in the back of my mind I already knew what had happened to him, and so when one of Philonides' men came bursting in and blurted out what had happened, I wasn't in the least surprised.

Philocharmus (said the messenger) was in the Market Square. He was completely and hopelessly drunk, having been fed wine doctored with poppy-essence, and there was no earthly chance of sobering him up by this afternoon. The messenger said that he had met a couple of men who had seen our leading actor having a drink with a red-headed man and a tall man with freckles the previous evening, and that was all we needed to hear. Those two were the leaders of Aristophanes' claque – the same men who had made the scene at the preview. God only knows why Philocharmus hadn't recognised them. In fact, I believe he did, and that a fair amount of coined silver changed hands.

So that seemed to be that; we had no leading actor, and so no play. At least half the lines in the play were spoken by the protagonist, which was the usual thing in Comedy in my day. Philonides nearly had a stroke, mainly because it should have been his job to make sure something like this didn't happen. But I can't blame him; the people you usually have to watch are your rival Comic poets in that year's Festival, not someone who isn't even competing, and I'm sure he had taken all possible precautions against sabotage by my two immediate rivals. It hadn't entered his head that Aristophanes would carry his personal grudge against me this far.

With about half an hour to go before the start of the first Tragedy, we still hadn't thought of a plan; and I was all for going to the Archon and telling him, so that he could arrange for something to fill in the time. But Philonides would have none of it. He simply looked at me and said, 'I'm not having my best work thrown away like this. One of us will have to do it.'

I stared at him. 'You're crazy,' I said. 'I don't know the first thing about acting.'

'I know,' he said. 'And your voice is all wrong, and you move like an ox-cart with a missing wheel. And you're too short. No, you certainly can't do it. Not in a thousand years.'

We looked at each other. We had known each other for many years. Philonides had been the first man I had spoken to that day I got back from Sicily. If I had a single friend in the whole of Athens, it was Philonides. He was also perfectly capable of out-acting Thespis himself; he had a marvellous voice, a magnificent sense of timing, and the sort of authority that would make an audience sit up and take notice. But there was one drawback. He was terrified of speaking in public.

He once told me about the only time he had spoken to a large audience. It was a lawsuit, something trivial about a small debt a neighbour of his owed him, and after a lot of worrying and putting it off, he finally took it to Court. He wrote a brilliant speech for himself to deliver and learned it perfectly by heart. He rehearsed himself in it for a fortnight, doing nothing else from dawn to dusk. He went along to the Court to get used to the atmosphere of the place, took advice from seasoned litigants, and even read a couple of books on the subject. But when the day came, and the water-clock started running, he dried up completely. For all his titanic efforts, he couldn't bring himself to say a word, and the case went against him by default. Yet this was the man who could bawl out the most recalcitrant of Choruses, reduce professional actors to tears, and persuade authors to rewrite their best speeches, all by sheer force of personality. And now I was asking him to get up on the stage in the Theatre of Dionysus, for the first time, at the Great Dionysia itself, in front of perhaps eighteen thousand people, and play the leading role in a Comedy.

We sat there in silence, glaring at each other like two stray dogs in the market competing for a scrap of offal, with the terrible thought that one or other of us was going to play the leading role in a Comedy that afternoon.

'You know,' said Philonides after a very long time, 'if you held yourself a bit straighter and spoke very slowly, you could probably get away with it.'

I smiled frigidly. 'They say acting is totally different from speaking in Court,' I replied. 'For one thing, the audience is on your side. You'll probably enjoy it once you get over the early nerves.'

He ignored me as if I hadn't made a sound; it was a gift he had, and he used it to great effect when dealing with actors. 'After all,' he said, 'it's not that many years since the author regularly used to play the lead. Before the War, it was very much the done thing. Aeschylus did it all the time.'

'It was Aeschylus who put a stop to it,' I pointed out, 'when he introduced the second actor. I remember hearing someone say once that Aeschylus used to come out in a horrible rash all over his face every time he had to go on stage. He had to have a specially padded mask.'

Philonides tried a different approach. 'It must be really aggravating for you writers,' he said sweetly, 'when the audience come out after the play and all they talk about is how good so-and-so was as the hero and never even mention the poet, like the actor just made it up as he went along. And they'll never know it was you with the mask on; they'll think it was Philocharmus. So if you make a botch of it he'll get the blame, and if you're a real smash you can raise your mask at the end so that everyone can see it was you.'

'No fear,' I said vehemently. 'This is a good play, and I'm not having some idiot like me make a mess of it. Face facts, I couldn't get through the opening scene without dropping something or falling off the edge of the stage. And there's that bit where the Chorus dance in front of me; I'm so short the audience wouldn't even see me, even in the boots.'

'You're just chicken,' Philonides said desperately. He was streaming with sweat, even the backs of his hands, and his eyes had become very big.

'Yes,' I agreed. 'So are you. So which of us is going to make a fool of himself in public?'

'I've got my reputation to consider.'

'You said yourself,' I reminded him, 'they'd never recognise you under the mask.'

'Someone would be bound to recognise my voice,' he said hysterically. 'All those people I've shouted at over the years.'

'My voice is far more distinctive than yours,' I said. 'And it's not nearly so good,' I added quickly. 'You're always saying how no actor can speak lines properly. Now's your chance to show them how to do it.'

'I've retired, remember?'

'So, you've got nothing to lose, have you?'

But he shook his head vigorously, until I was convinced it was about to fly off his shoulders. 'No,' he said, 'I'm not going to do it, and that's final. It's your play; if you want it salvaged, you'll have to do it yourself.'

'Listen,' I said, 'it won't be salvaging it, it'll be ruining it. No, it's obvious, there's only one thing I can do, if you won't play that part. I'll have to go to the Archon and tell him that because of your negligence and carelessness there won't be a play this afternoon. Then I'll fiddle with it a bit and put it on another year, maybe under a different name. Of course, your reputation in the Theatre will be dead meat; *you'll* never be able to work again after the news gets out; but then, that won't matter to you because you've retired, like you said.'

I stood up to go; and I had actually picked up my stick and got as far as the door before Philonides called me back. 'If you say anything like that to the Archon,' he said, 'I'll kill you, I promise. It's your precious enemy that's got us into this mess.'

'I don't seem to have much choice,' I replied. 'And look at it this way. If I go out pretending to be an actor you've trained, and I make a hash of it, as I undoubtedly will, who are they going to blame? Not me, the poet. They're going to blame the Chorus-trainer, "He's really lost his grip this time," they'll say. "Over the hill," they'll say, "just like I was telling you, he should've retired years ago." But if you do it, at least you'll only have yourself to blame. Come on, man; if some of those losers who call themselves actors can do it, you can do it, no trouble at all.'

I reckon it was that last bit that did the trick, for Philonides basically despised all actors. He sat there for what seemed like for ever, not saying a word; then quite suddenly he made a noise like a splitting wineskin and started calling me all the names under the sun. Blackmailer was one of them, I remember, and there were several variants on the theme of cowardice. I took this to mean that he would do it.

'But on one condition,' he said. 'We're going to spend the rest of the day going over this thing inch by inch with a full cast, costumes, everything, until I could do it with my eyes shut; because that's probably how I will have to do it, all right?'

'All right.'

'And when it's over,' he went on, 'I want you to promise that you'll hold Aristophanes' arms for me while I break every bone in his body. Agreed?'

'It'll be a pleasure.'

He stood up, looking as if some unkind person had strapped a marble block to his back. 'A really lovely birthday this turned out to be,' he groaned. 'Right, we'll get the Chorus together and then we'll make a start.'

So I never got to see those notorious experimental plays by Euripides that have since become so famous; while they were shocking a largely unprepared audience, I was hearing Philonides through his big speech for the fifth or sixth time in the big courtyard behind a friendly corn-chandler's warehouse near the Pnyx, while a thoroughly disgusted Chorus tramped miserably backwards and forwards and calculated how much they could get away with charging me for overtime and missing the Tragedies. I'll say this for Philonides, however; although he kept breaking off every six or seven lines to call me some new name he'd just thought up, he never once suggested cutting a word of the play to make life easier for himself; nor did he make one alteration to the moves and routines he had planned with such reckless enthusiasm. And whenever he'd finished his speech and could turn to look at the Chorus, if any of them was so much as a hair's breadth out of position he would tear into him like a lion devouring a goat. If he was going to have to make an idiot of himself at his age, he said, the least everyone else could do was try and get it right for once, and anyone who cocked it up that afternoon was going to get the same as Aristophanes, or maybe even worse. Finally, after going through the play six times at top speed, he declared that he was as ready as he would ever be, and that all he needed now was a very stiff drink.

I was completely opposed to this idea, but Philonides ignored me and sent a slave off to the wine-shop to bring him a jar of the strongest, roughest Attic wine he could find. The slave dashed away like a frightened hare, and came back with a jar covered in cobwebs and marked with the double chalk cross that usually means 'Not for sale': so I imagine he had gone somewhere where Philonides' reputation as a hard man with a bottle was properly respected. He then went off to get some water to mix with it, but he was wasting his time. Philonides just put his thumb through the wax, lifted the jar to his face, and poured. Wine went sploshing down all over his tunic, but a fair quantity of it ended up in his mouth, and he kept on gulping until I thought he must surely burst. Then he put the jar down, wiped his lips with the back of his hand, and smiled broadly. 'Right,' he said. 'Lead me to it. Someone bring that jar, I may need it again.'

We packed up the costumes, counted the Chorus to make sure everyone was there, and set off for the Theatre. When we arrived, we found we were only just in time; the Chorus of the *Helen* was just going off, to rather patchy applause, and the audience was starting to talk about what it had just seen, very loudly. I hurried over to the seat reserved for me as a competitor (the Theatre was more full than I had ever seen it before, because of the Euripides plays), evicted the foreigner and his three small children who had occupied it in my absence, and sat down to catch my breath. Just down the row from me,

I could see Aristophanes son of Philip, who was staring at me as if I had at least two extra heads. I waved at him and smiled, and offered up a little prayer to Dionysus. If he got me out of this mess in one piece, I said, I would most certainly give up the Theatre for ever and never try his patience again. Then, as if the God had answered me, I felt something under my foot; it was a broken wine-flask, and it gave me a happy idea. I stooped down, picked up one of the sherds, and took the brooch out of my cloak. With the point of it I scratched a few words on the bit of broken flask and asked my neighbour to pass it down to Aristophanes. I can't remember exactly what I wrote, but it had its effect; because as soon as he read it he dropped the apple he'd been eating, gave me a look of pure hatred, and hastily left the Theatre. Now I come to think of it, I believe what I wrote was something to the effect that just before leaving home I had sent a few slaves and friends over to his house to set fire to it, and if he hurried he might be in time to stop them. The foreigner and his children took Aristophanes' seat, and since it wasn't reserved he couldn't get back into it when he returned from his fool's errand, which meant he had to watch the little of my play he eventually got to see standing at the back among the slaves and the drunks.

Philonides didn't come on until well into the first scene; so if he had still got that jar with him he had plenty of time even now to get hopelessly drunk. Although I was desperately proud of my opening dialogue I couldn't bear to watch, and if the audience laughed at all I didn't hear them. And yet there is no sensation as sweet to me as the sound of people laughing at my lines in the Theatre, so that when I hear it I can think of nothing else; so you can judge for yourself how nervous I was. But I heard Philonides' cue loud and clear, and I opened my eyes and stared at the entrance he was due to come through. For about the time it takes for an olive to fall from a tree he didn't appear; and in that brief instant I formed two mental pictures of him; one of him lying on the floor with an empty jar beside him burbling like an idiot, and another of him cowering down behind the backdrop and refusing to budge, while the slaves kicked him and called him names. Then he strode on to the stage, looking like King Theseus himself, and the audience suddenly fell silent. He seemed to hesitate for a fraction of a second, and then he launched himself into his opening speech, which is one of the best things I have ever written. His voice welled up from the stage like a spring from a split rock, making him seem twice as tall as he was, and for a while the audience were too overawed to laugh. Then the first big joke came crashing through, like a wave of the sea when there's a great storm, and the sound of laughter made the earth shake. For me it was like the first lungful of air to a suffocating man. I sucked that laughter in through every pore in my skin, and held it inside me. It seemed to do something to Philonides, too. Just for a moment he seemed frightened, as if he had been suddenly made aware that he was not alone in the Theatre. Then it was as if he had swallowed all that enormous volume of sound and digested it, all in the time it takes to move a finger, for he thundered out the rest of the speech as if he were a god delivering a prophecy. I have never seen an audience take to an actor as they took to Philonides, and I've never ever seen an actor respond so well to a good audience. They clapped and cheered and whistled and shouted, and he got better and better. It was a long speech, that first speech of his, but time seemed to stop running while he was delivering it.

In other words, the play was a success. When the Chorus came on, there was a moment when you could have heard a coin drop, while the audience all looked twice to see if their eyes were playing tricks on them. Then they seemed to go mad, and there was such a stamping of feet that the Spartans at Deceleia must have thought that a huge army was coming to get them. But it wasn't the noise that impressed me so much as the silence when the big speeches were being delivered. Usually there's at least one idiot or drunk who talks or sings during the speeches; not this time. Except for sporadic waves of laughter or cheering, there was total quiet, and you could hear the heels of the actors' boots grinding on the floor of the stage. I have heard louder applause for a play in my time and louder laughter for a joke, but I've never heard such attentive silence in all my life. For they weren't just laughing, they were also listening, and that was what made me feel happier than I had ever felt in my entire life.

I don't remember anything about what happened after the play, or during the rest of the Festival; let alone at the Victory party after I was awarded first prize by a unanimous vote of the twelve judges. I've heard that Philonides and I got completely drunk and went all round the City reciting the speeches from the play, and wherever we went people came out of their houses and cheered us, and that we were finally carried home on the shoulders of complete strangers, fast asleep. All I remember is waking up afterwards with a murderous hangover and vowing never to get in such a state again as long as I lived. I've kept that vow, and I've also kept my vow to Dionysus never to write another play. After the *Demes*, there seemed to be no point, for I could never have another triumph as great as that one. I did start to write a play about three years later, but the words just wouldn't flow and I gave up after the first few speeches. The desire to write Comedy had left me, and it has never come back. Shortly afterwards, of course, things were so different in Athens that I wouldn't have written anything even if I could; so, all in all, it was just as well that I wrote my last play when I did, and that Philonides overcame his nerves enough to play the leading part.

Shortly before he died, not many years later, I asked Philonides how he managed to go on, considering how unwilling he had been to do it. Had he drunk the rest of the wine, I asked him, or was it his soul telling him to be strong? He said it was neither of those things. In fact, just before the time for his cue he got such a bad attack of panic that he started taking off his mask and boots. But then (he said) he thought he saw a large man with a black beard standing behind him, looking at him with such utter contempt that he was shamed into putting the mask back on. When he looked round again, the man had disappeared and Philonides swore blind that there was nowhere he could have got to; he must just have vanished into thin air. Now at the time Philonides was suffering very badly from the fever that finally carried him off, so this may just have been his mind wandering at the end. Or perhaps it was a hallucination he'd had at the time, caused by fear and residual alcohol. But it's perfectly true that there are very few places a person can disappear into at the back of the Theatre of Dionysus, so perhaps he was telling the truth after all.

CHAPTER SIXTEEN

Towards the end of April next year, the democracy was overthrown. It was a relatively peaceful way for the world to end; four hundred leading oligarchs held a meeting outside the City at Colonus and then marched in, threw the Council out of the Council Chamber with the help of a gang of young bloods (who probably mistook the whole thing for a drinking-party), and declared that there had been a return to something they called the Ancestral Constitution. This meant, in theory, that the franchise was limited to five thousand citizens who had the necessary property qualification, but since these five thousand good and honest citizens were never actually named and nobody had the faintest idea who they were, this clearly didn't mean very much. The essence of the situation as it emerged over the next few days was that four hundred men now controlled Athens absolutely, drawing their mandate from a couple of gangs of large, taciturn men with clubs and swords. The leaders of the coup were Pisander, Phrynichus, the politician Theramenes, and Antiphon, a man who wrote speeches for the Courts (rather like my old friend Python). Apart from a few routine murders of generally unpopular people, they did very little that any reasonable man could object to, at least to start with; but that was not the point.

At the time the main Athenian army was in Samos. When they heard what was going on, they were all for sailing straight home and killing the oligarchs there and then. But before they were ready to leave, who should turn up but the celebrated Alcibiades, who had been roughing it at the court of the Persian governor, Tissaphernes the Magnificent, waiting for an opportunity to make his comeback in suitable style. He sailed in on a handsomely decorated Persian yacht, made a speech or two, persuaded the army to stay put, and sent a blood-curdling letter to the oligarchs demanding that they publish the names of the mysterious five thousand good and honest citizens who were to be the twin anchor of the ship of state. As it happens, no list was ever received by the army at Samos, but the messenger service was notoriously slow at that time of year, what with the winds and the great oar-blade shortage, and after a while the soldiers forgot all about the list and concentrated their energies on pampering their newly restored Lost Leader.

Meanwhile, the oligarchs were working flat out to cobble up some sort of end to the War, so that they could get the backing of the Spartans and the Persians for their new régime. In order to demonstrate that this was not in fact what they were doing, they set about fortifying the entrance to the Piraeus. This fooled nobody, of course; even the most innocent of us could see that their real intention was to make it possible for them to cut off the City from its grain supplies. But there was nothing we could do about it, so we let it happen. There was a wonderful feeling of helplessness in the City, something that none of us had ever known before. Things were happening and we were totally unable to interfere, we could only be passive and wait to see what would happen; and meanwhile, it was nothing to do with us, not our problem. It was a sort of euphoria, I suppose, and as such obviously impermanent. But I reckon most of us hadn't realised what was really happening – we thought it was just a weird sort of holiday, and that soon it would all be over and we could go back to being democrats again.

Sure enough, the rule of the Four Hundred ended as quickly and as effortlessly as it had started. Phrynichus was stabbed to death in the Market Square on his way to buy fish one morning, the men who were fortifying the Piraeus took this as a signal for a general holiday-cum-riot, and the oligarchs called out their supporters, in arms, into the streets. But before any serious fighting could be done, the Spartan fleet appeared off the Piraeus, apparently intending to come in and storm the City. This was obviously no coincidence; the oligarchs must have sensed a week or so before that they couldn't hold power without outside help, and sent for them. As soon as the news of the Spartan attack reached the City, the oligarchs' armed supporters manned the walls and launched our fleet, the Spartans retreated, and we chased after them. Our fleet was seriously mangled off Euboea, as it happens, but that was Foreign News, and nobody seemed to care. They were far more interested in the situation at home, which was becoming decidedly lively. For after the Spartans had gone away, a good old-fashioned (and thus illegal) Assembly was held on the Pnyx, the Four Hundred were formally deposed, and the clever lawyer Antiphon was condemned to death. And that, apparently, was that. Business as usual. We apologise for any inconvenience caused.

Wrong. The Assembly didn't vote for the restoration of the democracy; they voted for Alcibiades. In a sense, this was a wise move, since Alcibiades had our army in the palm of his hand over on Samos, and nobody, not even the most dedicated seekers after new experiences, wanted a real full-scale civil war, with Alcibiades storming the City and anointing himself King Alcibiades the First. So what they voted for was his immediate return to Athens and the establishment of – believe it or not – the rule of the five thousand good and honest citizens, which was what Alcibiades had called for when he went over to the army on Samos.

Alcibiades was understandably confused, and he stayed abroad with his army and his fleet (they were decidedly his, not ours, by this stage) while we, apparently sincerely believing that what his lordship wanted was the rule of the Good and Honest, set about making it possible. We actually appointed a Five Thousand (who in the end came to about six thousand five hundred or so, but that's Athens for you) and waited patiently for instructions. And that, not the great and mysterious *coup d'état*, was the end of democracy in Athens. People at the time blamed the odious Theramenes, who wriggled out of his involvement in the *coup* with a speed and dexterity that won him universal admiration, and set himself up as Alcibiades' vicar on earth; but I don't think his part in it was particularly significant. I honestly believe that the Athenians unconsciously realised that they didn't want the democracy any more. Since they didn't know what they did want, they made Alcibiades a god and left the whole mess up to him to solve. Alcibiades obligingly responded in a truly godlike fashion by not turning up when invoked and turning a deaf ear to their prayers, and everybody was, for the moment at least, happy. They turned their attention away from politics and started interesting themselves in the War again, to find that it had got wholly out of hand and that we were losing.

So ended the greatest and most perfect democracy the world has ever known, the ideal which generations yet unborn will strive in vain to emulate. Actually, there's more to it than that; the democracy was restored briefly, before the end of the War, amid the most horrible blood-letting that Athens has ever seen, until the Spartans disposed of it when they finally took over the City. But the monster that Cleophon and his fellow butchers created then had nothing really in common with the old democracy as it had been; it bore as much relation to the complicated organism originally spawned by Solon as my parodies do to the plays of Euripides. And I don't want to think about what happened then, because it makes me sick just to think of it. My story ends here.

So I'll just tie up a few loose ends, and then we'll call it a day. For instance; did Philonides and I ever get round to killing Aristophanes for getting our leading actor drunk, or was it just another empty promise? Well, by the time we had slept off our hangovers and regained the use of all our limbs after the Victory party, we found that our grudge against the son of Philip had faded rather. After all, not only had I won the prize for Comic drama but Philonides had won the prize for best actor – there had been a little trouble about that, since Philonides hadn't formally been entered, but it was smoothed over and he got the prize in the end – and all this good fortune was due, in a roundabout sort of way, to Aristophanes. So we let him off his beating for the time being, and decided to think up a more subtle punishment at our leisure. Then, what with one thing and another, we never got around to it, and so I suppose the matter lapsed, like an old mortgage. Later, during all the unpleasantness of the following year, when there was actual physical danger attached to any show of resistance to the new régime, Aristophanes did a couple of truly noble and courageous things, and we nearly forgave him.

Shortly before the actual *coup*, when the atmosphere in Athens was becoming very unpleasant and several outspoken people had been murdered in the street, there was talk of cancelling the Comic plays, since political comment was out of the question. But Aristophanes went marching into the Archon's office (there was still an archon, though he bore about as much relation to a proper archon as I do to Zeus the Thunderer) and demanded that he be given Choruses for both the Lenaea and the Great Dionysia. Since he still had a degree of standing in oligarchic circles, and it would have been a nuisance to have such a relatively prominent person killed, the archon agreed, and so there was a Lenaea and a Dionysia after all. And the plays that Aristophanes wrote that year were decidedly clever, too, though I wouldn't go so far as to say they were good.

He recognised that any sort of overt criticism would be impossible, so he put his mind to it and came up with a rather neat answer. There was a common joke throughout Athens at that time that the oligarchic experiment was so extreme that, when it failed, the only logical progression would be to turn the government of the State over to the women, as being marginally more bizarre even than the rule of Antiphon. Aristophanes took up this joke and based his two plays around it; but he disguised them thinly, one as literary criticism, the other as a general plea for peace. But in both plays the women take over part of the function of the State, and the way they act is remarkably close to the way the oligarchs were conducting themselves. In one play they even capture the Acropolis, as the celebrated Cylon had done several hundred years ago, when he tried to set up a dictatorship; and there are all sorts of veiled references – to citizens being arbitrarily arrested by the police, to secret conspiracies and negotiations with the enemy to end the war at any price, to puppet magistrates and to the previous *coup* by the Whitefeet, who seized Leipsydrion. This was pretty outspoken stuff in the circumstances, but the oligarchs either wouldn't or couldn't be bothered to do anything about it. They pretended to take both plays at their face value, and let Aristophanes have his brief moment of glory. Since the *coup* went ahead as planned, I don't think many people actually did get the point of those two plays; or if they did, they ignored it.

Nevertheless the son of Philip did make a gesture, which only goes to show that deep down there is some good in all of us. But if you're hoping that Aristophanes will turn out to be all right in the end, I'm afraid you're going to be disappointed. Shortly after the *coup* he patched up his tiff with the oligarchy and was heart-broken when the Four Hundred were deposed. He soon came to terms with the men behind the Five Thousand, however, and as soon as they had got their version of the Rule of the Few sorted out, he ingratiated himself with the right people and became quite a big man for a short while. During this brief period he made several attempts to get me into trouble; for example, he tried to get me removed from the citizens' roll on the grounds that my great-great-great grandmother had been born in a small village on the wrong side of Troezen at a time when the village wasn't strictly speaking part of Attica; he managed to get me lumbered with the cost of fitting out a trireme and producing a play, both in the same year, by making out that I had volunteered; he spread rumours that I was a friend of Theramenes when Theramenes was out of favour, and that I made nasty jokes about Theramenes' wife when Theramenes was back in favour; and he pirated large chunks of a play of mine which I had composed about seven years before but scrapped, having first bribed my houseboy to steal the only surviving copy from the big cedarwood chest in my inner room.

When the Five Thousand were put down by Cleophon's rabble, Aristophanes barely escaped with his life and for a while had to go into hiding. Various friends of his put up with him for a while, but not many people can take more than a week of his company, and besides, the reward for his capture was very tempting; I guess it was running at just under four drachmas a pound for a while, until the men in power lost interest. It was then that Aristophanes found that he had nowhere to go. So he came to me, at a time when a thousand drachmas would have done me no harm at all.

I remember that it was the middle of the night, and I had just ridden down from the country because Phaedra was ill. I was desperately tired and I had fallen fast asleep in front of the hearth, still wearing my riding boots. Phaedra was asleep in the inner room; she had a bad dose of fever, and hadn't been able to sleep for two days. Then there was this diabolical hammering on the door, and I woke up as sharply as if someone had stuck a skewer through the seat of the chair.

I was terrified, as you can imagine; when you heard knocking on your door in the middle of the night in those days, you expected something horrible. But the last thing I wanted was for Phaedra to be woken up, so I hauled myself on to my feet and opened the door a tiny crack.

At first I didn't recognise the son of Philip – he had dyed his beard and brushed his hair forward over his bald forehead; but when he put his not inconsiderable weight behind the door and pushed it open, I knew who it was, and I was not at all pleased. I was about to say something or other, but I never got the chance. He thrust himself into the house and slammed the door behind him.

'For God's sake,' he said, 'what do you mean by keeping me hanging about on the doorstep for half an hour? Can't you see I'm in danger?'

I was still half asleep, and I couldn't understand. 'Danger?' I mumbled, through the mouthful of greasy wool I appeared to have woken up with. 'What are you talking about?'

'They're on to me, that's what,' he said, helping himself to a long swig of wine straight from the ladle. 'That bastard Euxenus has sold me down the river. I got away just in time.'

'You mean someone's trying to kill you?' I said.

'Got it in one,' said the son of Philip. 'Now, where's the best place for me to hide? They may have seen me come in here, since you took so long answering the door.'

'You mean this house is likely to be searched?' I said, horrified. 'My wife is sick in there, she can't be disturbed.'

'Too late to worry about that now,' said the son of

Philip. 'You should have thought about that when you were contemplating opening the damned door.'

I thought quickly, but all that came into my mind was those deceived-husband stories, where the wife hides her lover under something or in something when her husband returns unexpectedly. As it happens, Aristophanes had filled in a gap in one of his recent plays with a handful of these old chestnuts, and my semi-conscious mind couldn't think farther than that.

'For God's sake,' said Aristophanes angrily, while I was trying to think, 'make up your mind or we'll both be dead. Do you want them to catch me or something?'

It hadn't occurred to me before then, I swear to you, that here was a chance to get even with the son of Philip for a lifetime of malice and slander, and that nobody could ever blame me for it. After all, it wouldn't be my fault if Cleophon's thugs chose to kill a poet; and Aristophanes hadn't followed the correct formula for putting himself under my protection, namely clasping my knees with his hands and proclaiming himself a suppliant. He had no claim on me whatsoever, and it is a good man's duty to hurt his enemies, as the philosophers are always telling us. But once again I remembered that Aristophanes had been put under my care by the God himself; and so, rather wearily, I told him that there was a space just large enough for a man to hide in next to the kitchen boiler. It was a big open jar where we put the rubbish and the emptyings of the chamber-pots until the cart came to take them away, and since the cart hadn't been for a week there was quite a healthy build-up of material for him to hide under. He objected furiously, of course, and I was tempted to remind him of the olive-jar in Sicily; but I didn't, and eventually he crawled down into this jar, while I laid a nice thick layer of ordure over the top of him. I imagine it was quite nice and snug under there by the time I had finished, once you got used to the smell.

About ten minutes later, there was another loud knocking at the door, and I went to answer it. This time I wasn't quick enough to stop Phaedra being woken up, and she came to the door of the inner room, asking sleepily what was going on.

'Don't ask me,' I said as I slid back the bolt. 'Go back to bed, there's a good girl.'

There were five or six men at the door, with drawn swords in their hands, and they were not in the best of moods. I didn't recognise any of them; I think they were foreigners. Anyway, they demanded to know where Aristophanes son of Philip was. I told them I didn't know.

'Don't be funny with us,' said their leader, a big, grey-haired man. 'He was seen coming in here not half an hour since. Where have you got him?'

Phaedra burst out laughing, and they asked her what was so funny.

'You idiot,' she said, 'don't you know whose house this is? Eupolis is Aristophanes' worst enemy in the whole world. You don't imagine for one moment that he'd shelter that bastard, after everything he's done to this family?'

The leader of the men scowled at her. 'Shut up, you,' he said. 'We're going to search this house from top to bottom, and if we find him here you're both of you going to die. Is that clear?'

'Search away,' said Phaedra. 'I can promise you that you won't find him.'

So they searched. They tore the inner room apart, slit open the mattress, emptied the chests out all over the floor, and pulled everything down from the rafters. They sacked the rest of the house so efficiently that you would think they were Italian pirates. They went all over the courtyard and the stable, and nearly cut open the horse to see if Aristophanes was hiding inside its skin, like Odysseus in the Cyclops' cave. But for some reason they didn't empty out the trash-jar, contenting themselves with sticking my spear into it a couple of times. When they had finished, Phaedra said, 'Satisfied?'

'All right,' said the grey-haired man, 'you win. Just think yourselves lucky, that's all. And remember, we're going to keep an eye on you from now on. One step out of line, and you're dead. Got it?'

I waited for an hour after they had gone before pulling Aristophanes out from under the rubbish. One of the spear-thrusts had gone through his cloak, missing his chest by about half an inch, and he was profoundly unhappy. Not nearly as unhappy as Phaedra was, though. She stared at me as if I was mad.

'You imbecile,' she said, 'what in God's name did you want to go doing a thing like that for? You very nearly got us all killed.'

'I'm sorry,' I mumbled. 'It seemed rather clever at the time.'

Phaedra shook her head several times in utter contempt, and swept off back to bed, leaving me with a foul-smelling Comic poet to dispose of somehow. The best thing to do with him at that moment seemed to be to feed him, because he wouldn't be able to complain so effectively with his mouth full. While he was eating, I put my finger under my nose to keep out at least some of the smell, and tried to strike at least a little spark from my brains.

The best I could come up with was this. Obviously they would be keeping an eye on the house for a day or so, and it would be impossible for Aristophanes just to walk out of the front door and go quietly away. So I had to get him out in something or under something; the problem was, what? The my eye fell on the big Bactrian carpet hanging on the wall, and I had an idea. First thing in the morning, after an extremely restless night, I put the horse in the shafts of the cart and led him round to the front of the house. My slaves then carried out the carpet, tightly rolled up and tied with rush cord. We manhandled this carpet up on to the cart, trying not to show that it was heavier than it should have been, and I took the reins and set off slowly for the country. In retrospect it was a stupid idea; had anyone been watching the house, they would immediately have started wondering why the urge to move furniture had suddenly come on me, and taken a good look inside that carpet. As it was, I had a nicely uneventful journey to Pallene; the Sicilian cavalry I was expecting to materialise from round each bend of the road never actually turned up. We unloaded the carpet into my house, cut the cords, and rolled out the son of Philip, who was fast asleep. From Pallene, I believe, he went up into the mountains and spent a month or so pretending to be a shepherd on Parnes. I wish I could have seen Aristophanes being a shepherd. It would have made up for all the trouble he had put me to.

When I got back to the City I found that Phaedra's fever had got much worse, and I knew then that she was going to die. She took a long time about it, though, and I think those were the worst few weeks of my life. I suddenly realised that I had let her slip through my hands like a precious opportunity. You know how it is; there's something you're always meaning to do, such as go up to see the wild flowers in the mountains around Phyle and take a picnic with you, but you keep putting it off, and by the time you get there everything has faded and withered, and you eat your food in silence and then go home feeling miserable. I had never found time to get to know my wife properly, and when I was forced to make a start it was too late. She was delirious with the fever half the time, and said a lot of things I hope she didn't mean; and when she came out of it, she would say exactly the opposite, telling me over and over again that I had been a good husband in the circumstances, and that she had had a better life than she had any right to expect.

After a while I couldn't bear it any longer, and in my heart I wanted her to die and make an end of it. But the thought that the next day or perhaps the day after she wouldn't be there any more was completely intolerable to me, and I kept pestering her with doctors and miracle cures when all she wanted was to be left in peace. Finally she begged me not to bother her any more, and I gave up and tried to accept the situation. I stayed with her all the time, however, because both of us were terrified that if I went away for a moment she would be dead when I came back. And even then I failed her. She had just come out of a dreadful bout of delirium and appeared to be sleeping peacefully, and I was so tired that I fell asleep in my chair. I can't have slept for more than ten minutes, but as soon as I woke up I knew she had died on me. I didn't look for a while, and then when I opened my eyes I thought for a moment that she was just asleep, and that I had been imagining it. But she was dead all right, and as soon as I had made sure, I started sobbing and wailing like one of those dreadful old women who make a living as professional mourners in the City, until one of the slaves gave me a cup of wine laced with poppy essence, like the potion that Aristophanes' men gave to my leading actor Philocharmus. After that, they tell me, I went off my head for a day or so – the idiot had put too much of the poppy stuff in it, and nearly killed me too – but I don't remember any of that. All I remember was waking up with a dreadful headache and knowing that she was dead.

I buried her at Pallene, next to my father's grave, where I will be buried myself; and I had the best stone-mason in Athens set up one of those carved slabs, with a verse on it. Now being a poet I should have produced a really fine epitaph; and I thought I had. But when I saw it, it just seemed silly, so I had it chiselled off and replaced with a simple inscription recording her name and her father's name and her deme. I miss her more and more as I get older, which is strange considering that when I am honest with myself I have to admit that I didn't know her all that well. Perhaps that explains it, I don't know. I think that sometimes I forget what she was really like, and get her confused with the legendary heroines like Penelope or Laodameia, the archetypal perfect wives. She wasn't perfect, by any stretch of the imagination, but I would willingly have traded all my prizes in the Festivals, even the prize for the *Demes*, just to have known her a little better.

So now I have outlived all the good or interesting characters in this book, and you are left with me. If you do not share my undying fascination with myself, I suggest that you leave out the next bit and carry on down to the top of the last roll.

I have never been to Delphi or any of the great oracles, and so I have never been given any insights into my future, other than those the God Dionysus gave me, as I have described above. But when I went down to the Market Square this morning to buy some fish, they tried to charge me one and a half drachmas a quart for anchovies; and when I said that the price was outrageous, the fishmonger said that anchovies were on their way up, because of the War, and that he confidently expected to be charging two drachmas a quart by the end of next month. Didn't I mention we are at war again? Indeed we are, and with Sparta too, but it's nothing like the Great Peloponnesian War; it's like a fight between two extremely old men, more funny than violent.

Two drachmas a quart; what a price to pay for anchovies. When I look back over my life, I feel rather like the three men from a tiny city somewhere on the edge of the Black Sea, who had always wanted to see Athens. They were stone-masons by trade, and from every building and statue and tombstone they made, they set aside a few obols towards the cost of a trip to the City of the Violet Crown. After twenty years or so of saving in this manner they had enough put by, and so they booked a passage on a wheatship. All the way, as they sailed past Byzantium and along the Thracian Chersonese, they talked about what they were going to see – the temples, the Theatre, the Nine Fountains, the great civil buildings, the Propylaea, the Erechtheum. Eventually they landed at Piraeus and walked up under the Long Walls – this must all have been before the end of the War, when the Long Walls were pulled down by Lysander, the Spartan general – and into the City itself. The trouble was that they didn't know what the great monuments they had travelled so far to see actually looked like. So when they passed one marble structure, one of them would turn to the other two and say, 'That must be the Erechtheum.' And the other two would nod excitedly, and they would stand for a moment and drink in the full splendour of it. Then they would pass on and come to another magnificent pile; and another of them would say, 'No, that must be the Erechtheum.' Then they would think back over everything they had heard about Athens, and they would agree that the building in front of them was indeed the Erechtheum, and the one they had seen before must have been Solon's Council Chamber. And then they would find themselves standing in front of a still more imposing edifice (I shall run out of words meaning building in a moment, and then this story will grind to a halt) and they would all be forced to agree that *this* must be the Erechtheum. When they had been all round the City and seen everything larger and more impressive than a water-tank, they looked at each other in silence for a while. Then the eldest one said, 'Anyway, we've seen the Erechtheum. Let's go and have something to eat.'

You take my point. Everything I've seen and done has seemed to me at the time to be the crucial point of my life; and then something else has happened to me that makes me reconsider. This has made writing a coherent history of my times rather difficult. So if I have any advice for you, ground out like flour between the stones of the turning years, it is to go and have something to eat immediately, and leave the sightseeing until later. In other words, don't be what I have always been, an observer; or you will find, as I did when Phaedra died, that you've been looking in the wrong direction all your life. That was the one regret of my life, and the one thing I didn't find any Comedy in. Everything else I have laughed at, in one way or another.

One last joke, while I remember. The celebrated Socrates was put to death, along with a lot of better men, after the end of the War. He was brought to trial on a palpably trumped-up charge, his real crime being that he used to give Alcibiades lessons in clever speaking; and at his trial he remembered me and tried making a Comic defence-speech, as I had done. But this time it didn't work, and much to his surprise he was condemned to death and executed. I remember going to see him in prison while he was awaiting execution, and the poor fool still believed that he would be reprieved, right down to the last moment, when they handed him the cup of poison. He has become very fashionable since his death, and people have started writing down those great long one-sided conversations he used to have with people who couldn't get away in time. In fact, there is a strange wave of nostalgia for the War and all the celebrated men of the time. No sooner had Euripides died, up in Macedon where he went to escape from Cleophon's men, than they started reviving his plays in the Theatre. They don't revive any of my work, of course, but then, I'm still alive.

My son has been, generally speaking, an unmitigated disappointment to me, for he has taken to writing epic poetry, and nothing good will come of that. On the other hand, he married a nice girl and has two sons, and when I die he will inherit a large and well-cared-for estate, which I think he will look after. He has the makings of a good farmer, if the Muses don't get to him first. He hasn't inherited wit from either me or his mother, which is probably a blessing. He has her looks, though, and a little of my skill with words. When he was young he wanted to be a soldier. I made sure that I got to know him well enough, for fear of making the same mistake twice, but by and large I wasted my time. I have known hundreds of men like him, and they don't interest me much.

And Athens is still standing, more or less, and will probably still be there in ten thousand years' time; but it is an unimportant place now, the market town for that mountainous, unfertile district of Greece called Attica. The most important place in the world these days is probably Thebes, where the eels and the idiots come from; and if that isn't irony, I don't know what is. That is a good joke, and this is a good time to die.

PAINT YOUR DRAGON

Tom Holt

The cosmic battle between Good and Evil . . . But suppose
Evil threw the fight? And suppose Good cheated?

Sculptress Bianca Wilson is a living legend. St George is also
a legend, but not quite so living.

However, when Bianca's sculpture of the patron saint and
his scaly chum gets a bit *too* 'life-like', it opens up a whole
new can of wyrms . . .

The Dragon knows that Evil got a raw deal and is looking
to set the record straight. And George (who cheated) thinks
the record's just fine as it is.

Luckily for George, there's a coach-load of demons on an
expenses-paid holiday from Hell who are only too happy to
help him. Because a holiday from hell is exactly what
they're about to get.

Paint Your Dragon is a fire-breathing extravaganza of
imagination-boggling mayhem from the athor of
Ye Gods! and *My Hero*.

<u>MY HERO</u>

Tom Holt

Writing novels? Piece of cake, surely . . . or so Jane thinks.

Until hers start writing back.

At which point, she really should stop. Better still, change her name and flee the country.

The one thing she should not do is go into the book herself.

After all, that's what heroes are for. Unfortunately, the world of fiction is a far more complicated place than she ever imagined. And she's about to land her hero right in it.

My Hero is Tom Holt at his dazzling, innovative best. And Fiction may never be the same again . . .

'Wildly imaginative' *New Scientist*

'*My Hero* . . . deep down, it's smart' *Maxim*

OPEN SESAME

Tom Holt

Something was wrong! Just as the boiling water was about to be poured on his head and the man with the red book appeared and his life flashed before his eyes, Akram the Terrible, the most feared thief in Baghdad, knew that this had happened before. Many times. And he was damned if he was going to let it happen again. Just because he was a character in a story didn't mean that it always had to end this way.

Meanwhile, back in Southampton, it's a bit of a shock for Michelle when she puts on her Aunt Fatima's ring and the computer and the telephone start to bitch at her. But that's nothing compared to the story that the kitchen appliances have to tell her . . .

Once again, Tom Holt, the funniest and most original of all comic fantasy writers, is taking the myth.

'Tom Holt stands out on his own . . . If you haven't read any Tom Holt, go out and buy one now. At least one. But don't blame me for any laughter-induced injuries'
Vector

THE CONQUEST

Elizabeth Chadwick

When a comet appears in the sky over England in the spring of 1066, it heralds a time of momentous change for Ailith, a young Saxon wife. Newly pregnant, she has developed a friendship with her neighbour, Felice, a Norman wine-merchant's wife who is also with child. But when Felice's countrymen come not as friends but as conquerors, they take all that Ailith holds dear.

Rescued from suicidal grief by Rolf, a handsome Norman horse-breeder, Ailith is persuaded to become a nurse to Felice's son, Benedict, but it soon develops into a situation fraught with tension. Ailith leaves Felice's household for Rolf's English lands and becomes his mistress, bearing him a daughter, Julitta. But the Battle of Hastings has left a savage legacy which is to have bitter repercussions, not only for Rolf and Ailith, but for the next generation, Benedict and Julitta.

From bustling London streets to the windswept Yorkshire Dales, from green Norman farmland to the rugged mountains of the Pyrenees and the Spain of El Cid, this is an epic saga of love and loss, compassion and brutality, filled with characters you will never forget.

THE ALIENIST

Caleb Carr

New York City, 1896. Hypocrisy in high places is rife, police corruption commonplace, and a brutal killer is terrorising young male prostitutes.

Unfortunately for Police Commissioner Theodore Roosevelt, the psychological profiling of murderers is a practice still in its infancy, struggling to make headway against the prejudices of those who prefer the mentally ill – and the 'alienists' who treat them – to be out of sight as well as out of mind.

But as the body count rises, Roosevelt swallows his doubts and turns to the eminent alienist Dr Laszlo Kreizler to put a stop to the bloody murders – giving Kreizler a chance to take him further into the dark heart of criminality, and one step closer to death.

'*The Alienist* isn't only an ingenious thriller. Carr brings enormous gusto to his portrait of old New York . . . the city seems to rise off the page.'
Anthony Quinn

THE ITALIAN HOUSE

Teresa Crane

Secretly treasured memories of her grandmother's Italian
house, perched high upon a mountainside in Tuscany, are
very special for Carrie Stowe; for not only do they recall
and preserve the happy childhood summers of the golden
years before the devastation of the Great War, they are her
only escape from the mundane and suffocating routine of
her life with Arthur, her repressive and parsimonious
husband.

When she discovers that she has unexpectedly inherited the
house Carrie sets her heart upon going to Tuscany alone to
dispose of the effects of Beatrice Swann, her eccentric and
much-loved grandmother.

Arriving late at night and in the teeth of a violent storm she
discovers that she is not the only person to be interested in
the Villa Castellini and its family connections. A young
man, an enigmatic figure from the past, is there before her;
and as the enchantment of the house exerts itself once
more, Carrie finds herself irresistibly drawn to him . . .

Other best selling Warner titles available by mail:

☐	Paint Your Dragon	Tom Holt	£5.99
☐	My Hero	Tom Holt	£5.99
☐	Djinn Rummy	Tom Holt	£5.99
☐	Odds and Gods	Tom Holt	£5.99
☐	Faust Among Equals	Tom Holt	£5.99
☐	Grailblazers	Tom Holt	£5.99
☐	Here Comes the Sun	Tom Holt	£5.99
☐	The Conquest	Elizabeth Chadwick	£5.99
☐	The Italian House	Teresa Crane	£5.99
☐	The Alienist	Caleb Carr	£5.99

The prices shown above are correct at time of going to press, however the publishers, reserve the right to increase prices on covers from those previously advertised, without further notice.

WARNER BOOKS
Cash Sales Department, P.O. Box 11, Falmouth, Cornwall, TR10 9EN
Tel: +44(0) 1326 372400. Fax +44 (0) 1326 374888
Email: books@barni.avel.co.uk

POST and PACKAGING:
Payments can be made as follows: cheque, postal order (payable to Warner Books) or by credit cards. Do not send cash or currency.

U.K. Orders	FREE OF CHARGE
E.E.C. & Overseas	25% of order value

Name (Block Letters) _____

Address _____

_____

Post/zip code: _____

☐ Please keep me in touch with future Warner publications

☐ I enclose my remittance £ _____

☐ I wish to pay by Visa/Access/Mastercard/Eurocard

Card Expiry Date

_____